THE BURNING CROWN

THE WILD ROAD

MICHELLE WEST

THE BURNING CROWN

THE WILD ROAD

MICHELLE WEST

This is for Thomas, who shows us daily what quiet kindness and responsibility mean, and for Daniel and Ross, who have learned how to be their father's sons.

If they had been luckier, they could have had a better mother, but they wouldn't have found a better father anywhere.

Dramatis Personae

Breodanir

Maubreche

Stephen of Maubreche
Nenyane of Maubreche, his huntbrother
Cynthia, Lady Maubreche, mother of Stephen and Robart, wife to Corwin
Corwin, Lord Maubreche
Arlin, his huntbrother
Robart, son of Cynthia and Corwin
Mark, his huntbrother

The Dogs

Steel
Patches
Sanfel
Brylle
Pearl
Corran
Senshal
Marrel

Elseth

Alexander (Alex) of Elseth
Maxwell (Max) of Elseth
Gilliam, Lord Elseth, father of Alex, Max, William, Justine and Ingrid, husband of
    Espere
Espere, wife of Gilliam, mother to Alex, Max, William, Justine and Ingrid
Elsabet, Lady Elseth, mother of Gilliam
William of Elseth, Gilliam's heir
Lucas, his huntbrother
Stephen of Elseth, Gilliam's huntbrother; namesake of Stephen of Maubreche; dead 17
    years

Bowgren

Lord Ansel, heir to Bowgren
Heiden, his huntbrother
Allise, Lady Bowgren
Anton, Lord Bowgren
Barrett, huntbrother to Anton; died in the Sacred Hunt of 429

THE KING'S PALACE

Breodan, Lord of the Covenant; the Hunter God
Iverssen, chief priest of Breodan
The King of Breodanir; also known as the Master of the Chamber
The Queen
Lord Declan, Keeper of the King's Keys; Huntsman of the Chamber
Lord Grayton, Huntsman of the Chamber
Weslin, huntbrother to Lord Grayton

ANNAGARIANS

Gervanno di'Sarrado, a caravan guard
Leial, Gervanno's dog
Devarro di'Sarrado, Gervanno's father
Evaro di'Pierro, husband of Sylvia, caravan leader, deceased
Sylvia di'Pierro, caravan cook, wife of Evaro, deceased
Silvo, a caravan guardman, now deceased
Yollana of the Havallah Voyani

THE FREE TOWNS

Adala, a young woman of Hansleigh
Trevor, a young man of Hansleigh
Eva Juwal, the leader of a merchant caravan

THE CIRCUS

The circus master
Carrick, a circus member
Katie, a circus member
Iyan and Mercy, twins and circus performers
Lysan, a member of the circus
Chenni, a member of the circus
Ulrich and Eric, twins and circus performers

ESSALIEYANS (AVERALAAN)

Jewel ATerafin, the Sen of Averalaan, Lord of the East
Avandar, Jewel's domicis
Ararath
Shadow, Snow, and Night, Jewel's cats
Haval
Celleriant

Torvan, captain of the Chosen
Jarven ATerafin
Lucille, secretary to Finch and Jarven
Kallandras of Senniel College, Master Bard
Meralonne APhaniel, member of the Order of Knowledge
Sigurne Mellifas, Guildmaster of the Order of Knowledge
Master Levec, of the Houses of Healing
Moorelas, also called Morel of Aston
Amarais ATerafin, previous Terafin

JEWEL'S DEN

Finch ATerafin
Teller ATerafin
Adam of Arkosa, a Southern healer
Joker
Angel
Carver
Arann
Calliastra

KOVASCHAII

Valerio
Arsenio
Arkady
Constanso

THE SHINING COURT

Allasakar, Lord of the Hells, Lord of the Frozen Wastes
Cortano di'Alexes, Annagarian exile, former Sword's Edge
Ishavriel, member of the Lord's Fist
Isladar
Anya a'Cooper, human mage
Rymark ATerafin, Essalieyan exile, mage
Memonryenne
Endarone
Lordanel
Mordanevalle
Darranatos

ARIANNI

The White Lady
Illaraphaniel, last of the firstborn princes
Caralonne
Narianatalle, firstborn prince, Sleeper
Fanniallarant, firstborn prince, Sleeper
Taressarian, firstborn prince, Sleeper
Shandallarian (Shianne)
Sarrantil
Andarion

Evayne a'Nolan

Fox, known as the Eldest

PROLOGUE

I.

9TH DAY OF WITTAN, 429 A.A. AVERALAAN, EMPIRE OF ESSALIEYAN

He would never tire of Averalaan's trees.

The Three—as they had, in the span of a short year, come to be called—towered over the city. There was no place in which one had a view of the hundred holdings that did not include those trees. At a distance, the whole of their height could be more easily seen, but Adam preferred to stand in the long shadows they cast. Those shadows did not change in length, regardless of the sun's height.

The tree of ice glittered in the mid-day sun; it never melted. When rain fell, drops of water froze against trunk and branches. Those frozen drops did not melt either, but the new ice did not change the shape of the tree, or add weight to its branches. The tree of ice shed no leaves— nor did the tree of fire, which had been a minor concern at first. In the shadow cast by that tree, it was warm; beneath the branches, it was hot, and the heat did not diminish. Both trees seemed above the weather of a simple, mundane season.

The third tree seemed almost normal in comparison; were it not for the shadow it cast and the tree's magnificent height, it would have been unremarkable. But the buds on the branches had never opened, never blossomed. Adam had been informed that bookmakers—which still existed in the city Averalaan had become—were collecting money against their eventual blooming. He had never placed a bet, but knew that Jester and Carver had. The third tree was simply called The Tree. Ice tree, fire tree, The Tree.

It was far easier to reach the Common than it had been when he had first arrived in the city; of The Ten, the Terafin manse was the sole manse now situated within the hundred holdings; it stood to one side of where the statue of Moorelas had been.

His early days in the city had been under the auspices of a dour and cantankerous Levec in the Houses of Healing.

Finch had come to that place, and she had offered him a different home. He had accepted because she spoke his mother tongue and he was far from home, and in desperate need of anything that resembled the life he had known.

He was not that boy now, although perhaps others could not clearly see the differences. That boy had never seen these trees. That boy had never seen their planting, their growth; had never stood beneath their branches and in their shadows.

He stood beneath the tree of ice, watching the gathered crowds. People had come, as they had always come, for the market. If those people noted the presence of the three trees, he could not see it; to those who worked here, to those who came to buy the necessities of daily living, the trees were now simply geographic landmarks.

Adam wondered if he would ever feel the same. They invoked both awe and memory. Standing beside the Matriarch as she had stood at the height of the walls—walls that had not existed when he had first been brought to the city—he had seen the unfolding wonders of the ancient world. And he had seen the damage and the death.

The Matriarch had repaired the damage done to the city; she had changed the shape of buildings across the whole of the hundred hold-ings; she had extended her walls—although that had come later—so they might better encompass the farmers whose wares fed the citizens. But she could not call the dead back, and many had died on the day the city had truly awakened.

He closed his eyes, lowering his head in respect for the fallen and the dead; some had fought, and some had not. War had taken both, regardless.

His dreams had been restless of late, his sleep poor.

It helped, to stand beneath these trees. It helped to hold the memory of that battle: it meant that he had purpose. He had been useful to the Matriarch—perhaps even necessary. It was his hand that had returned to her the Terafin signet; it was that signet that had been the final weight placed on the scales of her choice.

He did not envy it.

She was sometimes called the Lady, and sometimes a god. She was no longer considered human, mortal; she was no longer considered of this world.

It was the one thing Adam would change, if that change had been in his hands. It was the one thing he wanted to shout from the figurative rooftops. The Matriarch was human. Still.

How could she be anything else, who had surrendered almost all of her life in order to preserve the things she loved? How could she be inhuman, who felt such sorrow and such regret, such guilt? The den she had loved, the den she had sworn to defend and protect, were lost to her for all but a scant hour or two in a day—and on some days, she did not emerge from her chambers at all.

It was not safe for the den.

No, he thought, as he left the long shadow of the tree of ice. It was safe for the den; she would never harm or alter them. It was not safe for the rest of the city. She was no longer what she had been—or rather, what she had once been was no longer all of what she was now. She clung to it as she could, held a space for herself that was the shape of Jewel Markess ATerafin. But she could not occupy it for long.

She was Sen. She was the mother of the city. In as much as she could, she had left the city of her childhood alone. Even so, it was a markedly changed place.

She was the ruler of the wilderness that wrapped itself around the city. He knew. He could hear her name in the rustle of branches above his head; could feel it beneath his feet when he walked along the remade streets; could even hear it on the few occasions he ventured toward the harbor, to watch the sea.

The birds there did not screech her name; the people who worked at the port did not whisper it unless they were drunk. He did not travel often to the port; the sea wall provided a view of the bay.

Today, he continued his trek toward the last of the trees in the Common. They were smaller than The Three and, in shape and color, similar to the *Ellariannatte*, although they did not grow as tall. These trees—the Thirty-Six—marked the boundary of the new Common, its outer edge. Sometimes he placed hand against trunk as he offered a nod of respect and gratitude. Sometimes, he did not. These trees were tended, watered; their leaves—as those of the trees of ice and fire—did not fall.

It was the Thirty-Six that haunted Jewel. The seeds of the trees of ice and fire had come from conflict and aggression; she had taken the power of the attack and transformed it, making it her own. The third tree had been planted from the feathers of the cats that often prowled the skies, complaining.

But the Thirty-Six had been planted in a different way; she had asked no permission, and the people who had become these trees had, in the end, had no say, no choice. Had they attacked her, had they attempted to kill or harm her or her den, she would have felt nothing for their fate; they had not.

Thirty-six of the citizens of Averalaan had fallen asleep, victims of the Lords of Dream and Nightmare. With Adam's help—with Jewel's —they had awoken. But not completely. They would never wake completely. Their essence was human. What remained of their bodies was not, and would never be again.

"YOU SPEND TOO MUCH TIME HERE."

Adam, accustomed to the brusque, low voice, nodded without turning to see the speaker; he knew who spoke.

"You know," a second voice said, high and sweet and sharp, "if you weren't so *rude*, you'd make more friends." She did not wait for acknowledgement of any kind—she never did. She bounded toward Adam, joining him; her hand reached for his, and he accepted it, smiling down at her.

"I don't think Colm wants more friends."

She returned his smile. "*Some* of us are happy to see you."

"Your mother will worry," he told her, as if the words were a ritual greeting. They almost were.

Stacy snorted. "She's *always* worried. I told her nothing bad will happen to me. I told her I'll live forever."

"And it doesn't make her worry less."

Stacy shook her head, her mother's worries dismissed as irrelevant or irrational. Her mother's worries were not what occupied the youngest of the Thirty-Six. Stacia A'Scavonne was the daughter of a wealthy man of middling power. Before she had fallen asleep, she had been a normal, if somewhat reckless, child. Now she was one of the guardians of the city.

Adam thought it oddly appropriate that the guardian to whom he was most drawn was a child. Children were the future.

Stacy would see that future. But Stacy would also see her parents age and eventually die. And she would see it unchanged, an eternal child. Adam understood her mother's growing concern well.

"She's worried," Stacy said, her voice softening, her eyes becoming wide and blank as she stared into a distance that Adam could not easily perceive. He knew that she wasn't speaking of her mother, whose worries seemed ridiculous. She was speaking of Jewel, the Sen of the city.

Adam nodded again. "But she, like your mother, always worries."

The man who had first spoken exhaled and marched—there was no other word for the movement—to Stacy's side. Colm Sanders had been a retired soldier, and looked it: he had the scars, the physical build, the observational skills and, sadly, the temperament. But his bearing and his tone reminded Adam of his Ono in the distant South. Or perhaps Levec.

It was a familiar gruffness. Perhaps, had Adam not seen Colm with Stacy, he would have found the man more intimidating.

"Why are you here?" Colm demanded. He was looking ahead, so the demand could have been meant for either Stacy or Adam himself; Colm viewed them both as children. Adam thought, a century from now, he would still view Stacy as a child—because that's all she would ever be.

"I'm here because Adam's here," Stacy snapped. Her lips turned down at the corners as she glared at the old soldier. "Why are *you* here?"

"I'm here because you are," he replied.

"Well, I don't need you here!"

Colm Sanders shook his head. "I made a promise to your mother. I won't be an oathbreaker."

"Then go spend time with my mother!" She almost stomped away, her hands in fists by her sides. She had never attempted to hit Colm Sanders, perhaps viewing that action as the line not to be crossed.

Adam silently disagreed. She could hit him, kick him, and even attempt to bite him, and Colm would endure; although she had a father, it was clear to Adam that she was a treasured child to the older man, who had none. Her mother, however, would have been both shocked and furious.

But she paused, her hands slowly uncurling as she reined her momentary temper in. "She's worried," she said again. This time, eyes narrowed, she looked up at Colm Sanders. "You tell him."

"I think he believes you," the man replied, his expression shifting, just as Stacy's had done. "And he's more likely to listen to you."

"If you weren't so rude, he'd listen to you instead—most people do." This was more sullen.

"It's because I'm rude that most people listen."

"It's because you're big and people think you're scary."

"That's what I said."

She shrieked in frustration, but it was wordless. The soldier placed a staying hand on the top of her head, which increased frustration, but lessened rage. Children, Adam thought, were always difficult. But precious.

"Tell me," Adam said quietly.

"But why did you come?" Stacy demanded.

He hesitated, but had learned with time and practice that honesty put off simply increased a child's future pain. "I'm not certain how much longer I'll be able to remain in Averalaan."

Stacy fell silent.

Colm simply nodded. "If I had to guess," the soldier surprised Adam by saying, "you've overstayed your welcome. You're not a young child anymore, and you have responsibilities elsewhere. You've kin who will need you."

Adam nodded. "I wanted to spend as much time as I could in the Common. I wanted to see the trees and, hopefully, see you, Stacy."

"But—where are you going?" Stacy asked, rage at old soldier and stupid worries forgotten.

"Home. I was born in the South. I was born in a traveling wagon; I lived with my sister and my mother."

"Not your father?"

Adam shook his head. "My mother passed away, and my sister is alone. Alone in a city that was once like this one."

"Have you written to her?"

"No one would deliver the letters, even if I had. The city she lives in has no trade—that I know of—with any of the normal cities in the Dominion. I wanted to stay while the Matriarch—ah, sorry, The Terafin—needed me. I owe her a great debt."

"You did," Colm agreed. "But you have far more than repaid it." As if Adam were a child, Colm placed a gentle hand on his shoulder. "You miss your homeland."

Adam was silent.

"Sometimes, when you come to us, I can see the desert sands, the desert night, and the roads that wind through the Terreans. They are not pleasant memories, but you gentle them."

"She's worried," Stacy said, "because you need to go home. It's only here that you're safe. She can't go with you. She can't leave."

Adam nodded.

"But she wants to speak with you now."

"Now?" He frowned. It was far too early in the day. The Matriarch met her den—which included Adam—in the evening, sometimes for dinner and sometimes after. She came to the kitchen, because that was where all den meetings of import had always been held.

"Now." She paused, frowned, and then brightened. "She says I can come with you, if you want."

"And Colm?"

"She says he can come too. But you know, he has to be nicer."

Adam doubted Jewel had said the last part, but Stacy was a child seeking advantage, almost innocently, where advantage could be gained. Colm knew it as well, but Colm was not a child. He glanced at Adam.

Adam nodded, but hesitated as he turned toward the new Terafin manse. Above the spire, birds gathered.

"Stacy, could you do me a favor?"

"Maybe?"

"I want you to go find Finch and tell her that we've been summoned."

"But she only asked for you."

"I know."

"Promise to wait until I get back?"

"I promise."

FINCH UNDERSTOOD the nature of the Thirty-Six. Intellectually. She was somewhat discomfited to have one of them show up in her office without opening the door or, apparently, touching the floor across which enchanted carpeting had been laid. The carpets weren't necessary in the fashion they had once been. No doubt it was part of the reason that Jarven avoided the office. She had seen him only twice in the past half year.

She remembered the girl's name; Adam had introduced them.

"Adam asked me to come," Stacy said, as Finch rose from her chair. "Wow, you have a *lot* of work here."

It was true. If Jay had remade the city and its buildings, the paperwork had only partially recovered; new contracts were being negotiated to replace those that had been lost. In some cases, the contracts existed in the hands of those who had made the original deals, but in some, not. Finch suspected that, in the latter case, some of the other parties had not been entirely truthful.

"I do, as you can see. It's very tiring. What can I do for you?"

"Adam said — no, wait. Jewel summoned Adam."

"Summoned? For when?" The child's expression was guileless. Finch's was neutral, but neutral was the mask she donned when she was worried.

"For now."

Finch capped her inkwell. She did not think she had time to properly clean a quill. "Tell Adam that I'll meet him in the foyer."

"What if he gets there first?"

"Tell him to walk slowly." She reached for a paperweight, half buried beneath two stacks of paper. Touching it with her left hand, she drew a sign, den-sign, against its opaque surface.

It connected immediately to Teller. "Finch?"

"Adam is coming to the manse. Can you leave your office?"

"Now?"

"Now."

"I'll meet him when he arrives." Teller didn't ask why. He didn't demand explanations. He trusted Finch. She trusted him, in turn; she made no attempt to offer what was not required.

ADAM'S PATH to the manse was shorter than Finch's, but he walked it slowly, talking with Stacy. Or listening, for the most part; the child was a wellspring of words, her babble a stream of mostly connected thoughts. She was careful with those words, when not desperate; today, a hint of desperation colored them. She didn't want Adam to leave.

Adam treated her as if she were a normal child. She wasn't, and they both knew it, but the difference was irrelevant to Adam. He could feel it when their hands were connected, but he understood that he himself wasn't entirely normal.

They both had been, once.

Adam was grateful for his gift now. But it wasn't considered a gift among his own people. Or rather, it was far too precious, far too dangerous; it invited men of far greater power to acts of conquest, kidnapping, enslavement. Had that not been known to him, Levec in the Houses of Healing would have made it quite clear: if there were no slaves in the Empire, people were nonetheless enslaved. Or murdered, to level the playing field—a phrase Levec had used that had not made sense to Adam.

He was certain that this was the heart of the Matriarch's fear. Adam was young, and helpless; his power was not a destructive or defensive power. When it became known—and power always did—he would be a target. If he remained within Averalaan—within the borders of the Matriarch's city—nothing could harm him. Not physically.

He reached the wide steps, Stacy's hand tight around his, and climbed them. He knew Jewel would never harm anyone she considered den, but he felt a growing uneasiness with each step.

THE STEWARD WAS absent as the doors rolled open to reveal the large desk that occupied the back half of the foyer. Standing almost directly in the middle of its dark, gleaming length was a very familiar man.

"Teller."

Teller looked up from whatever it was he'd been reading. He lifted his hands in den-sign. Adam stumbled. After a pause, he signed, *I sent for Finch.*

Teller nodded.

"Where are we meeting?" Adam asked, aware now that the kitchen would not be the right place.

"I can show you!" Stacy said. "Should we wait for Finch?"

It was Teller, the right-kin, who said, "Yes."

ADAM EXAMINED THE FOYER, Stacy in hand. He lived in this building, and perhaps that was one of the reasons he left it for excursions into the rest of the city. Here, in the heart of the seat of her power, the Matriarch could not help but effect small changes. Although the desk was as he had last seen it, and the walls were of similar height and width, the ceiling had changed; it was far higher, and while its arches rose and the rough shape of the ceiling had been retained, there were now images painted—or tiled, at this distance it was hard to determine —across its width.

The central image was of the Matriarch herself, the walls of the city beneath her feet; growing up at the base of the walls were the buildings that housed the survivors of that terrible, chaotic day. People in working clothes formed the edge of the fresco, the market stalls small but exact. Surrounding the Matriarch were the crowns of The Three.

He frowned.

Depicted beside her—but at a distance—stood a single man, and not a man Adam knew well, although he did recognize him: he had come with the Matriarch from her foray into the wilderness. He did not fight by her side, but remained there after the battle was done. Adam would have expected to see her den there and, if not her den, her domicis, the prickly, terrifying Avandar. He, too, was absent.

The uneasiness that had plagued Adam's steps as he approached the manse grew weight and texture as he entered it, as if it were a binding wrapped around his feet, his ankles. Each step he took beneath the high, stone ceilings deepened it.

The doors behind them rolled open. Finch stood framed by them, breathing shallowly and quickly, a sign of her exertion. Her face was red with effort; given her expression, it might otherwise have been pale.

"We're here!" Stacy shouted, although it would have been hard to miss them, given where Adam stood. "Sorry I didn't wait—I didn't want Adam to leave without me." She looked down at her feet, a child who understood the pain of being left behind, but who nonetheless felt the need to inflict it.

Finch shook her head. She knew that Stacy—that any of the Thirty-Six—could travel quickly and invisibly between any part of the city that would be their only home. Most of the Thirty-Six didn't avail themselves of this power; they wished to live the lives they had lived before gods and wild magic had altered them forever.

Stacy's desire to be accepted warred with her desire to explore, and often lost. Adam wondered if that would change. Was the wisdom she had accrued until now the only wisdom she would ever have? Would experience change nothing?

He shook his head to clear it. These thoughts, he could have later—when Stacy was absent.

"Do you know what the purpose of this summons is?" Finch asked the child.

Stacy's face lost light and excitement as she glanced at Colm Sanders, who had accompanied them so silently he might not have been there at all. "She's The Terafin," that man replied. "She'll let you know."

Finch's hands moved in swift den-sign; behind his back, Adam was certain Teller responded. He was far faster than he had once been with den-sign, but when movements were subtle or quick, he could still miss words in the silent language the den had developed since childhood.

Since, he thought ruefully, they had been roughly the age he was now.

Stacy, unaware of the meaning of the gestures—or unwilling to grant them significance—tugged Adam's hand. "Can we leave now?"

"Yes, yes, yesssss. Why are you all so *slow*?"

Finch's expression was familiar to Adam, and it vanished almost the moment it crossed her face. She was frustrated and resigned. Anyone who lived in the manse was subject to the unwanted company of the three winged cats.

The grey cat—the cat who disliked Adam, and always had—strode into the foyer, each step heavy, claws striking the marble surface as if they were percussion instruments. He was always cantankerous, so it was difficult to separate bad mood from normal, but Adam felt the cat was genuinely annoyed.

The cats were one thing he would not miss when he finally left this city.

"We're mortal," Finch replied, as if the cat's complaining had been an actual question.

"Not *all* of you."

She ignored that, but her lips thinned.

Stacy, however, shrugged. Colm failed to hear the cat in almost the exact same way he failed to hear Stacy at her most petulant.

Shadow hissed, turning his glare on Adam, who had said nothing. There was nothing to be gained by defending himself from the cat's annoyance, and Adam was good at silence. Shadow glared at him; Adam averted his gaze. There was also nothing to be gained by descending into a staring contest with these cats. Or any cat, if it came to that.

High above, a hissing laughter could be heard. Snow was circling in the air above their heads, and he was soon joined by the third brother, Night.

Stacy glanced up, tightening her grip on Adam's hand. She liked the cats, and they tolerated her; she would often ride them when they condescended to land. But she understood that they were attempting to rob her of an important duty. "*I'm* escorting Adam—I know the way!" Her higher voice echoed in the rounded ceiling above.

"You are *too slow* and she is *waiting*," Shadow said.

Stacy began to drag Adam, by the hand, out of the foyer. She didn't approach the forbidding stairs but, instead, went to the hall that opened up beyond the long, single desk. Finch joined her immediately, and Teller trailed behind. It was to Teller that Shadow went, but he didn't go silently; he had much to say about stupid, slow, useless people. Only Stacy was irritated; everyone else was so accustomed to this behavior that Shadow might have been simply breathing. In the end, he started cursing his brothers, and they responded in kind, coming down from the heights that had contained them to land on Shadow.

They adroitly avoided landing on Teller, aware that there were some transgressions Jewel would never accept.

Adam knew the shape of the halls through which Stacy led them; they had not markedly changed. Jewel had taken care to leave the physical shape of the building alone, in as much as she had that control. But her control was not perfect; Barston had removed paintings and other works of art from most of the offices occupied by the right-kin, whom he still served. He did not want to lose them if The Terafin had a particularly difficult dream; things changed with little warning, and some of the most precious works in the right-kin's office had been replaced, the originals lost.

The halls could not be bare of art; younger artists had been gratified to receive new commissions for works that graced these halls of power, where they might be seen by the wealthy, the powerful. They were aware that these halls did change, having lived in the city, and were warned that the commissions would be bought outright and no guarantees about the safety of the work could be offered. But very few refused to work under those conditions.

Today, the artists were out of luck. As Stacy strode—anxiety and pride blending, as they often did at her age—down the halls, he could see that the stone alcoves had been replaced by trees; the ceilings, which had been far higher, were now conjoined branches of those trees. He recognized them by their leaves: *Ellariannatte* all.

The discomfort that he had felt faded, although he could not say why. Stacy had failed to notice, regardless.

The boughs above them, entwined to form ceiling, flowered suddenly over their heads and Adam revised his opinion of the species of the trees. He wondered if *species* had any meaning in the wilderness, where so much could be altered so easily; they felt familiar to him, regardless.

This forest also felt familiar. The whispers caused by the rustle of leaves spoke Jewel's name, but he could almost hear the faint trace of his own. They were not blood kin, but kin regardless, and Jewel did not abandon her kin. Not here.

The halls did not follow the shape of the galleries through which the public could walk; the corners of those halls had been softened into a natural, tree-lined bend, such as might be found outside of this manse, this city. He did not require Stacy's assistance; there was only one way to go, and that, forward. But he held her hand as she walked

—or bounced—by his side. He glanced once at Colm Sanders and then away; something about this path had caused the dour soldier to fall into a particular silence that Adam recognized: memory. Memory and loss.

"Shadows, boy," Colm said, voice rough. "Shadows of war."

Adam could not see what Colm saw, but Stacy clearly could; she grabbed the old soldier by the hand, and her fingers were white-knuckled with the tightness of her grip.

"She's just afraid," Stacy whispered, her voice so low Adam could barely catch the words.

"War should scare her," Colm replied, voice neutral. "You saw the battle in the city. That's war, Stacy. It'll kill soldiers. It'll kill anyone who's fool enough to stand in its way if they have a choice." He exhaled. "If we have a choice. There are some battles you fight—it's not for glory or fame or honor." He spit to the side at the last word. Stacy frowned at him.

"It's for survival."

"Will there be another war in this city?"

Colm shook his head. "Not in the city itself. But the Empire is larger than the city. She knows. It's why she's worried."

"Will you fight?"

"I'm like you now—I'm safe in the city, and I can't leave it. Now stop talking. We're almost there."

"She doesn't care if I talk."

"...No. No, she doesn't."

"You told me I had to learn to be practical."

"This *is* practical. You talking takes time and some of us don't have much of it left." He glanced at Adam as he spoke.

"He could just stay with us," Stacy murmured.

Colm said nothing. He didn't tell the child that the Matriarch would not have summoned Adam in person had she not felt it necessary that he leave. Stacy had never been a stupid child, if one did not count recklessness as stupidity; she knew.

THE PATH beneath their feet led not to a door, but a clearing. In it stood a single tree. In height, it was not as impressive as The Three, but in shape its shorter crown was far wider; branches stretched toward either side of the clearing as if those branches kept the rest of the forest growth at bay. This was the heart of the Matriarch's territory; Adam felt the tree was familiar, although he could not immediately say why.

Beneath the boughs of that tree stood the Matriarch. He struggled to call her by name, or had; he wasn't certain when he had given up on even the attempt. Here, in the heart of the wilderness, respect was measured. Adam offered her a perfect Southern bow.

Margret, his sister, had always disliked them. They were not a greeting between Voyani and their elders; they were, in their entirety, meant to appease the suspicious, hostile clansmen in the Terreans' cities. Adam had disagreed. He had learned because he understood his position in the hierarchy of power. At the mercy of the greater power, the best hope of survival lay in offering the powerful the gestures of respect they felt were their due.

The Matriarch was not the person to whom he bowed; it was the tree.

To Jewel's left stood a white cat; to her right, a black cat. Snow and Night. They stared at Adam, unblinking.

Adam retrieved his hand from Stacy—or tried. She clung to it stubbornly. Glancing down at her, he saw her lips were compressed in a tight, disapproving frown; she was glaring at the cats. The cats ignored her.

Adam was grateful that Shadow was absent, if surprised. All three of the cats had been in the foyer, complaining about boredom. The city had become far more *boring* after the battle, and he was certain every citizen of Averalaan, high or low, knew this in great, endless detail; the cats were loud, and their voices carried farther than they once had.

The branches above the Matriarch's head began to sway; leaves of green and gold rustled against each other. It was deliberate.

You may approach.

This sounded like permission; it was not. Adam recognized a command when he heard it. Jewel had not spoken; her expression shifted only when she gazed at Stacy. He approached the tree and knelt.

"No," Jewel said. "You never have to kneel to me."

It wasn't to Jewel that he knelt, and the tree knew; its leaves once again produced a whisper of sound. He rose. The tree was the Matriarch's servant, one of the elders; it owed fealty, loyalty, to her. What she did not demand, it could not demand—but it accepted Adam's gesture of respect, freely offered, regardless. The air in the clearing warmed.

She wore not her usual clothing—and, by usual, he meant the clothing appropriate for the den, not the meetings of The Ten—but a dress of pure white; she, who hated crowns, wore a circlet across her brow. Two rings adorned her hands, but he recognized only one clearly: the signet of Terafin. The symbol of her office.

He understood. She had summoned him here, rather than meeting in the kitchen, because this was not a decision taken as Jewel, as den-kin. She was Matriarch here.

He wondered if Margret would ever be or become Matriarch in the way Jewel was, but knew, even as the idle thought passed, that she would not. Margret was not Sen. She was the Matriarch of Arkosa, with all the terrible weight of responsibility that implied, but she was human, mortal.

Jewel was not. He knew. He had never told the den, but they had never asked. Not of him. Not of each other.

"I want to keep you here," she said, fully meeting and holding his gaze.

He nodded. As a child, he might not have understood, but he had learned early, observing his mother and her treatment of both her own self and Margret, that one could want entirely opposing things, and both of those desires were true. The role of the rulers was to make the terrible choices that people like Adam would never be tasked with making.

It was to become heartless when that cold-blooded clarity was necessary.

And to cling to the heart when it was not.

As he had for his mother, Adam wished that the Matriarch might simply abandon her heart. It had seemed to him that such warmth caused nothing but pain, guilt, and even resentment. Absent that heart, the decisions wouldn't change; all that would change was the pain.

He could see that in her, now. Pain. Guilt. Fear. And beneath those things, resignation. Before she could speak, he spoke.

"I wish to return to Arkosa."

She closed her mouth.

"My sister is in Arkosa and, if reports are true, the home of Arkosa has risen from its long slumber in the Sea of Sorrows. She is alone, and she is Matriarch." But she was not Matriarch as Jewel was; not Matriarch as his mother, Evallen, who had walked to her death, had been. Margret should never have become Matriarch. Had his mother any other choice, any other daughter, perhaps she would have been spared.

His sister was not cold enough, not harsh enough.

Adam would never have to be cold or harsh; he was a son. As a son, he was almost pampered. He was certainly indulged. Sons could not become Matriarch. The burden of responsibility, the terrible weight of it, would never rest on Adam's shoulders—which made Adam safe to love, to coddle.

He regretted only that Margret had not been treated the same way; desperation was neither warm nor comforting, especially not when blended with familial love.

None of the words he had spoken were lies. But truths existed in multiples. In truth, he wanted to stay in the city, to remain with the den. He wanted to visit the Common, to see the trees, and to spend time with Stacy, who was a lonely child. Lonely and reckless.

But he asked for permission to leave because he knew she must send him away, and he had no desire to burden her with the guilt his reluctance would cause; she carried enough guilt.

"She will need you," Jewel said, her voice somber. "I cannot travel with you. I cannot guide you on the roads you must travel. But I cannot keep you here; you are needed in the South. The paths from the desert of the Northern Wastes to the heart of the Dominion are strong; stronger than the paths to any other kingdom."

Adam said, quietly, "You need not fear for me, Matriarch."

The word made her flinch.

"Unless my head is instantly removed from my body, I will not die."

"And if it is not your death I fear?"

He smiled. It was genuine, but lacked joy. "Fear is fear. I am no longer a child by the reckoning of my kin; I am adult, and tasked with the responsibilities of an adult."

"She is not what you are. Margret, your sister."

Adam nodded.

"I cannot send any of the den with you. They are needed, or will be needed." Ah, the shadow that crossed her face. It was not Adam's loss that she feared. No, that was unfair. It was not only Adam's loss that she feared. He felt her fear as if it was his own—and it was. He was not as close to all of the den as Jewel herself, but he loved them like kin.

She wouldn't send Finch to danger. She wouldn't send Teller. Not
unless the world's survival depended on it—and even then, he thought
she might let the world burn.

But Adam was neither Finch nor Teller. Adam had traveled
through the wilderness by her side. He had awakened the ancient,
slumbering half-gods, the sisters of the Summer Queen. He was, like
the Matriarch, *of* the wilderness. He accepted that, as he stood in front
of the ancient tree and the Sen of Averalaan, although until this
moment, he had never thought of himself that way.

Yes, he was healer-born, but Levec's House of Healing had many
healer-born students, and they were not what Adam now was. His
sojourn in Averalaan, his travels with the Matriarch—who would
never again leave her city—had changed his understanding of the
power to which he had been born, and of which he had remained in
ignorance for most of his life.

Margret was Matriarch. What would she think of him, now? How
would she welcome him when he returned, at last, to Arkosa? What
did Jewel think he would, or must, do?

Adam wanted to ask but waited, aware of the great tree's presence,
aware of its judgment should he be, in the elder's opinion, disrespectful.

"I do not wish to send you into the wilderness alone. The roads are
well-traveled, but they are broken in places, and it is far too easy to get
lost." She gestured.

Snow, spitting words from the corners of an otherwise closed
mouth stepped forward. He was ill-pleased. The cats seldom cared
about respectful behavior; they felt it was their due, but not their
responsibility. He padded across the short distance between Jewel and
Adam, and spit something, with resentful disdain, in front of Adam's
feet.

The branches above the Matriarch's head rustled, the sound wordless, as if a strong wind had shaken the tree's many boughs. The Matriarch lifted a hand and touched the tree's trunk, and the shaking stilled.
"He is what he is," she said, voice soft. "The wilderness has always
accepted his nature, and I do not seek to change it."

Adam knelt to retrieve whatever it was Snow had spit at his feet; it
was wet with cat saliva, and it gleamed in the sun's light, although the
sun did not pierce the boughs above.

It was a ring. A simple ring, adorned with four embedded gems,
spread evenly across an otherwise flat band. He did not ask what it

was or what purpose it was to serve; he simply waited. Long years of
practice were put to use, here.

"I cannot leave Averalaan—not and be certain to return. While the
war approaches, I will not take that risk. Nor will I require a healer,
but, in your absence, Daine serves in the Terafin healerie." She turned
to Snow. "Will you not travel with Adam?"

Snow growled.

"You are more knowledgeable, more powerful, than Adam."

"Of *course* I am. *Anyone* is."

"If you will not consent to be his guard in my stead, I will not
command it," she continued. Her cadence, her tone, drove all thoughts
of kitchen from his mind: she was at home in this place, in that dress.
Only her worry, the concern born of loyalty and affection, bound her
to the woman she had once been.

Snow hissed as she returned her attention to Adam. "You will have
companions on the road you must travel, although they travel a
different road, and must reach a different destination."

Adam bowed. "When must I leave?"

"Prepare, Adam. Gather the things that have meaning for you here,
but understand that you will spend much of your time on foot. The ring
is a gift, from me to you; it will not weigh you down." She frowned.
"Nor will it draw unwanted attention; don it, and you will understand."

He wiped the ring dry as Snow hissed laughter, and then looked at
his hands; he did not wear rings, and would never have worn so fine a
piece on his fingers, where it could be seen, envied, and targeted by
thieves. He slid it, at last, across his middle finger; it glowed as it
touched his skin, each gem brightening as it did.

He watched it, as she had instructed; to his eyes, the gems radiated
light, and they reminded him of wind, of water, of fire, and leaf.

"Yes," she said, as if he had spoken. "There will be places you reach
where light is essential, and there will be light if you lift your hand." As
she spoke, the gems began to fade. "If there is no need, there will be no
light—and no ring." The band became transparent, almost invisible; it
vanished from sight.

He could still feel its peculiar warmth, its weight.

"I have other gifts—I've been told they're necessary for a proper
leave-taking. But those gifts, ah. No. I *will have* proper gifts; they have
not yet arrived. But neither have your companions." She glanced at
Snow. "Watch the roads."

"Why *me*?"

"Your brothers are also watching. If you feel the need for the safety and protection of my lands, you may of course stay; there is a high possibility of combat on the mortal road."

Snow shrieked in outrage.

Adam kept his lips from twitching as the cursing, outraged cat immediately took to the air, knocking branches with his wings in his displeasure.

"I'm grateful that you asked if he would accompany me," Adam said.

"But grateful at his answer?"

"The cats will obey you."

For the first time since he had entered the clearing, he saw a familiar expression cross her face; she snorted. "If I command them, they'll obey—but I'll pay for the loss of their dignity. I wouldn't have asked, but the road will be dark, Adam, and dangerous, and I have walked it for days—or longer—seeking endings that do not involve death.

"Snow is one such companion, but that is not guaranteed."

"The cats have never liked me."

"They do," Stacy said. "They never complain about anyone they don't like—they just try to murder them."

"Shadow tried to kill me," Adam replied.

Stacy's eyes rounded.

"He was not entirely himself at the time," Adam added, to be fair. "But they do not trust me."

"Oh. Then they're stupid."

Jewel's expression shifted again; Stacy had amused her. "Don't say that where they can hear you." She exhaled. "Snow is the safest of the three—but all of the cats are reckless." Her expression once again grew grave. "War comes to the Dominion; it is there that the armies of enemy will strike first, although they gather as we speak in the Northern Wastes."

She walked toward Adam, the train of her dress passing over leaves and grass. "I don't want to send you."

He nodded. "But I have to go. If the enemy's attacks are anything like the destruction Averalaan faced—" He could not finish.

"Be prepared to leave. The roads are watched, in as much as they can be watched beyond the boundaries of my lands—but the roads in the wilderness are more easily traversed if one wishes to avoid detection for a time. None of those roads," she added softly, "are mine." Then: "Stacy."

Stacy nodded.

"Let go of Adam; he has work to do. If you want, keep me company."

"Will you come with me if I go swimming?"

"Swimming?"

"There's a lake."

Jewel looked down at her dress. "Yes, I think I'd like that — but I have to change."

Adam bowed to the Matriarch — or tried. But she crossed the last of the distance between them and enfolded him in her arms. As if she were sister or Ona. "You will always have a home here," she whispered, briefly tightening her hold.

"I know."

II.

She first met him in the orchard, the stretch of wilderness within the domain Jewel ruled that was rumored to be almost mortal in form, in use. It was not a meeting she had planned or arranged; she had come to the orchard because it was so seldom occupied. The trees here did not speak, even at whisper; the fruits here were not considered useful or powerful. These trees might have grown in mortal lands; they might have come from them, transplanted here at the whim of the lord who ruled both.

She did not know, and had not asked; she accepted their sudden presence. These lands were not hers; no more the lord. The lord demanded no oath of fealty for those granted permission to remain within her boundaries; had she, Shianne would not be here. She had never sworn such an oath to any lord, from the moment she woke, whole, conscious, to now. Oaths had not been considered necessary in the dawn of that ancient world. Why would they be?

She had one Lord, and only one; she served that lord while she lived.

Now, that service was measured in decades; once, it had been eternity. She had made her choice in a dawn long past, and had not thought to regret it, bitter though it was.

Perhaps, with the frailty of this mortal body, regret came nonetheless, visiting her as grief did: at unexpected moments. The White Lady's host was comprised now of her sisters, those born first to Ariane. They guarded her, and when she chose to ride, they rode at her side, silvered horns adorning their hips.

She had power to rival—to surpass—ancient mortal magi; that power had not deserted her when she had made her slow, painful transformation. But her body was not what it had been. Of the White Lady's court, she was the only mortal; she and the Summer King, her child.

The White Lady's commands, she had never broken. The White Lady's will, she had never betrayed. Had she, she would not now be alive, and perhaps that would have been for the best. She knew mortals died in childbirth, and mortal childbirth had been a painful, terrible revelation.

She had listened to the White Lady's song in the long dusk of her captivity, her pregnancy extended by that captivity until the moment the Sen of these lands had found the sisters in the ancient halls the White Lady no longer visited. Only when she had been freed by the hands of the mortal child, Adam, had that pregnancy, so bitterly paid for, taken its course.

In truth, she thought that child would be in the orchard. But he had been absent these past few days, troubled in the fashion of mortals by things he could not change and daunted by things he might, were he bold enough. She had kept the boy by her side before her child—the child that would herald Summer—had been born, for if the child died in birth, her sacrifice and loss would amount to nothing.

He had been companion for such a short period of time, she could barely countenance an attachment; he was a mortal child. Some of her kin had kept mortals as beloved pets, but she had not been among them. And now? Now she was mortal, lesser in every way than she had been; she would again never rise to the heights she had once occupied with such disdainful ease.

She missed Adam.

Perhaps because he was weak, weaker than she had become; perhaps she could momentarily feel powerful and significant when she offered him protection. Or perhaps because his quiet, still presence was calming in some fashion. Calm, she had never before desired. She felt no envy, no jealousy, and no regret when she walked by his side. It was through no fault of her sisters and her lord that she felt these things, these blemishes that had never once marred her previous devotion.

Perhaps mortals could not be devoted in the fashion of the White Lady's kin; perhaps some innate frailty prevented it.

She had never expected that.

She would lay down her life for the White Lady or any of her sisters; she would avenge their deaths, their injuries, while she still breathed. But she was aware, now, that she was no longer *of* them, even if they were not. The White Lady's love was given her; the White Lady's attention, care, protection enveloped her.

Had the White Lady exiled her for her choice, she would have accepted exile in both pain and resignation; that had been the risk when she had chosen to become what she now was.

She had not been exiled; indeed, the White Lady and her sisters oft hovered around her, as if desperately aware that time was now of the essence; they must spend it while she remained for the scant handful of years given mortals. Thus, she felt her mortality more keenly in their presence. She was not worthy of their company, and she could not help but know it. This, too, was new and unexpected.

In Adam's company, she felt her age as it had once been: scion of the children of gods, beloved sister; she could shape mountains, forests, lakes; she could change the face of the wilderness—even the wilderness she did not rule herself—at whim, and with effort.

She thought she might still do these things but to what end? Ah, her thoughts were scattered and unwelcome, and she had come, at last, to this quiet almost-mortal place to be alone with them.

But she was not alone.

A man worked—*worked*—in the orchard, cutting leaves and branches with slow deliberation, as if he intended to subtly change the shape of the trees in their tidy, regimented rows. He did not possess mortal implements; his cuts were made by the magic of their kin—and he was, or once would have been, kin. She had not seen him before, but felt she knew him, and she was drawn to him because of that sense of familiarity.

He turned to her as she approached; he offered her a bow just short of obeisance, as if she were still the White Lady's sister, the firstborn of their kin.

"Do not," she whispered, the words almost a plea. Frowning, she put more force into the words as she repeated them, and he rose, as if by command.

Her frown shifted and deepened as she studied the stranger's face; he was kin—ah, no. In the distant past, he would have been kin, but there was something about him that was unusual. He seemed both young to her senses and yet, at the same time, old. He did not wear the armor of the Arianni, but here, in the domain of the Sen, armor was unnecessary.

So, too, what he now did: gardening.

Had he put his effort into the living, talking trees—or the ephemeral flowers with their striking colors, their inimitable beauty— she would have passed him by without thought for anything but the work itself. But here, he was tending mortal trees, silent except for their slow growth; trees that had never been wakened, had never grown in the lee of the elders who had gained voice when the Firstborn had passed beneath their boughs.

Of what value were these trees? What import did they hold to the Arianni?

"They have no value to the White Lady," he answered, as if she had asked the question aloud.

"Have they value to the Sen, then?"

The hint of smile that had graced his lips deepened. "I have not been told as much. But they will have far more value to the Sen than they would to the White Lady. The Sen's people are mortals, and fragile; they require food, and some joy in the eating of it."

"Did she tell you to plant this orchard?"

"Ah, no. It was here, in a far less pristine state; I discovered it when I searched the forest."

She did not ask for what. His voice was familiar. His bearing. Even the deliberate grace of his movements as he tended these trees. She was certain she had not seen him before, but certain that she had, that her memory had somehow betrayed her—as if her memory was also a function of her transformation. Her hands became fists.

She accepted the inevitable; she could not change it, could not fight against it. But she could not lose the bands of regret at the loss of what she had once been. If even her memories were to become mortal, they would fade and wither, just as she herself would, one day. What, then, would be left of her?

"You are mortal?" he asked, as he continued to inspect the branches, the blooms that would become fruit.

"I am." The words were low.

"You must be Shianne."

She nodded.

"The trees speak your name in a hush of reverence when I walk in this forest."

"And my former kin?"

"They are afraid to speak your name at all, lest the White Lady hear it."

"And is my name such a bitter sound to our Lord's ear?"

"It is the herald of loss and pain, of grief that will persist for eternity." His expression was oddly sympathetic—odd because it was an unusual expression to grace the face of an Arianni. "They do not speak my name either, if you draw any comfort from that, and for entirely different reasons. I am an exile. My lord, once exiled, chose to remain at a distance until he could fully redeem himself.

"My passing will cause no grief, no sense of loss; I will be forgotten by the wilderness.

"There are mortals who might remember me, although not by name; I will become part of their written history, archived in their mortal libraries, while their lines persist. But the truth of me? The truth of my solitary existence? No one will remember."

"Our kin will remember, if we cannot," she said, voice soft, bitterness replaced by curiosity.

He shook his head. "To them, I am not a person; I am a shadow of a person, cast by the last of the firstborn princes. There is no place for me when I am at last summoned home; I was herald to Illaraphaniel and, for our failure, we were separated. When we meet again, I will become what I once was: part of him. What I was—what I have been during this long exile—will vanish.

"He will attain his full power."

"And you?"

"Am I even real, Shianne? I will become his strength, as I once was before the White Lady chose to separate me from him, to breathe life into me, to grant me a name."

"But you do not go to his side now, when our ancient enemy once again threatens war in these lessened lands?"

"By his command," the man replied.

"What is your name?"

"I am called the Master Gardener by mortals. And while I wait, I will garden; it is the sole gift I have that is, in its entirety, what it once was when I was an unconscious part of him. I have sword, I have armor, and I do not believe I can be killed, not while he lives. And he lives, or I would also vanish like mortal dust."

"If he called you, would you join him?"

"Instantly, lady. It has been the whole of my desire: to see him, to serve him, as I was created to do. But such was her anger at our ancient failure that when we encounter each other again, I will have a glimpse of him, no more, before I am unmade." In a lower voice, he said, "Never anger the White Lady."

She nodded. "May I rest here while you work?"

"If it pleases you. These gardens are not my gardens, but perhaps, if you have time, you might see what I made of the mortal landscape; for it, too, will be lost. It is the nature of mortality: what lives, changes."

CHAPTER ONE

9TH DAY OF WITTAN, 429 A.A. DEMESNE OF BOWGREN,
BREODANIR

Allise, Lady Bowgren, stood a moment in front of the mirror. Her personal maid, when such services were required, hovered to the side, hands fluttering in silence. Dawn had only just broken, the brightening of the sky visible through windows whose curtains had been drawn; below, the sounds of dogs and the men who handled them could be heard in the courtyard.

She gazed at her clothing, her hair, the anxious set of her eyes and mouth. The latter, she banished, acknowledging her fear but allowing it no more purchase in her expression. This, she had been taught since childhood. Where the ruler was frightened, fear spread, as if a contagion; where the ruler could contain that fear, those who must obey her orders remained calm.

Today, however, there was little over which she must be lord. Adjudications had been postponed for a week, to celebrate Lord Ansel's return. Heiden had already reached out to some of the village elders, who had been almost tearfully overjoyed to see him again. It was Heiden's responsibility as huntbrother, but he had come to it far too early.

Barrett.

She closed her eyes, inhaled, and opened them again, donning the mask she habitually wore; it came so naturally it had become her natural expression.

"Andrea," she said, "I'm ready."

The maid fussed, but Allise was correct; this was not a grand occasion. A year ago, she would not have been nervous at all; she might not have attended her husband and her sons. But that had been before Barrett's death fractured everything. One day, she would have time to mourn properly.

Perhaps today would be the start of it. "Come. If we don't leave now, we'll miss them. They won't wait."

———

ALLISE FELT, as she reached the courtyard, that she had stepped back in time. The scene that greeted her as she reached the doors to the courtyard was the same scene that had greeted her on the day Ansel had been granted his title and had proudly gone alone on his first hunt with his dogs and Heiden. Then, as now, the servants had taken the time to come to the courtyard, or stand nearest the doors and windows to see the young lords who would be their future masters—if they survived the Sacred Hunt.

The reality of that possible loss had haunted them for months.

Barrett's death had broken so many things. Allise had feared they were damaged beyond repair, but she had held on to bitter, bitter hope: that her son would recant his refusal to join the Sacred Hunt, and risk the same loss, the same death, that Anton had faced.

She must be cold-hearted, cold-blooded; else how could she willingly send her sons to face the Hunter's Death, year after year? How could she proudly send them off without cowering at the terrible, deep fear of their loss?

Ah, because she was Bowgren. She was Lady Bowgren.

She took a steadying breath. Ansel and Heiden were coupling the leading dogs as the dogs almost keened with their desire to reach Anton. If the dogs were aware of Barrett's absence, it didn't show; perhaps that was why even his dogs had presented little comfort to her grieving husband.

But Anton was there, kitted up for the hunt, and his sons were with him. Ansel had attempted to fulfill Bowgren's responsibilities when

Anton had faltered. She had been afraid that the hunt itself would return her husband to the state of grief he had only barely left, but Heiden and Ansel insisted: Bowgren needed to see Lord Bowgren as he was now, not as he had become upon Barrett's death.

Still, she hesitated, but the keykeeper enjoined his quiet approval of the hunt to their louder voices, and she had relented. Bowgren did, indeed, need to see Anton as the Hunter he had once been, and all of the servants in the manor were of Bowgren; all felt the loss of Barrett. All knew that sometimes the Hunter did not recover from that loss.

She understood. Heiden was looking at and to her, and she offered him a nod of silent approval.

Anton's expression was bleak, but as Ansel asked a question that required some thought—a hunting question—Anton's eyes brightened, his lips curving briefly in a genuine smile. His emotions had never been so carefully hidden or husbanded as Lady Bowgren's, but that was accepted from Hunter Lords.

"If you don't leave soon, all of your prey will go to ground," she said, surprised at her words, and her tone.

Anton reached out, gripped her hand in his, and held it tightly for a fraction of a second too long. She did not pull back; she whispered his name.

"Yes. Yes, Allise." He released her gently and turned to his sons. "I've heard you've developed quite the attitude. Do you think you'll fare better than your father?"

Ansel laughed. "I'll fare at least as well."

"Bold words. Let's put them to the test." He unleashed the dogs; they began to run circles around him, like ill-behaved puppies, so great was their excitement.

She watched them leave. She listened for the sound of their laughter until they could no longer be heard, as if laughter were water and she were desert.

And then she turned to the servants, as caught in hope and its fear as she, and frowned.

They went back to work, as she herself must do.

GERVANNO WOKE to the sound of Leial's barking, which was far closer to his ears than it should have been; the mutt had jumped up on the bed and was alternately licking the cerdan's face and ears and barking, his pitch high and urgent. Gervanno tumbled out of bed, grabbing the sword that was tilted against the bed's wooden frame.

The fact that the dog's tail was almost a blur of motion made clear that there was no immediate danger. His grip on the hilt loosened, but it would be a while before he was able to sleep again. "It's too early for you to be hungry," he told his dog, as he began to dress for the day.

Leial barked.

"Hungry and food are not the same word."

He was not entirely displeased to be jarred out of sleep; his dreams had been troubled.

The sands of the Sea of Sorrows had all but enveloped him, the pitch of keening wind a voice—the voice—of the dead, lost to life and caught in the grip of the Lord of the Sun. The wind carried grains of sand; his eyes were narrowed, his lips pressed tight; he sought shelter, had been seeking shelter. Dreams had their own logic, separate from the rationality of the waking world: he knew he had been searching for something; that it had been urgent, even natural, to search for it in this empty, arid wasteland.

But the storm would destroy him. He knew it. He had to seek cover.

The logic of dreams prevailed here; there was cover, if he could but reach it. His steps were slowed, his visibility poor, but the certainty that shelter existed, that he could reach it if he persisted, reigned. He found a gathering of abandoned buildings, their shape obscured by the drifts of the sand that had piled up against their walls; here and here, rooftops existed, and the walls themselves remained functional.

He found such a wall, a break against the wind, and lowered his face covering enough that he could breathe the dry, dusty air. He gathered himself, then another howl joined the storm in a broken descant. A different voice: the voice of the dead.

He frowned, moving; he reached for a sword. His hands remained empty, the absence of sword a terror in its own right. He could not fight. Whatever approached, he had to use the storm to avoid. He must have lost his sword, dropped it—a shame in itself that was akin to death—and he began to navigate walls as he searched with increasing desperation through drifts of sand.

Perhaps one of these empty, abandoned buildings might have something he could use as a weapon. Not furniture—although there was furniture. Something he could carry. Something he could wield, if it came to that. Not even cooking knives could be seen. There were no bodies immediately visible in any of the buildings.

But he paused as he came to a mirror. Mirrors in his childhood had been rare and mostly very small, carried by hand and passed down in the family. This house boasted a standing mirror, as tall as Gervanno, and twice as wide as Gervanno's chest. The mirror had been cracked, but not broken. If worse came to worst, he could break it and arm himself with the shards; he was reluctant to do it, as if the absent people might return to reclaim the homes through which he traveled as he attempted to avoid sand-laden wind and any other hunter that had joined the storm.

But the mirror was useless; it reflected neither room nor Gervanno.

He broke it, cracking it carefully; shattered, it would not help him. Armed, he began to move again; whatever hunted him was drawing closer, although the wind would not carry his scent cleanly.

He navigated storm, moving between buildings when the storm drew figurative breath, finding walls, finding places that formed buttresses against the wind. As he walked, his steps slowed, his legs aching; he gained a rough sense of the size of the ruins, of the placement of walls and buildings.

It was only when he reached one such empty building that he realized where he was. He hadn't recognized the village, empty and covered with sand; how could he, who had defined it by its inhabitants in his early life? But this one he instinctively knew: it was the home of his childhood. His father's domis.

The sand-laden winds of the desert had covered the streets so thoroughly, it had taken him time to realize that the placement of empty buildings fit the shape of his childhood home. His village was a buried ruin, all of his childhood friends, companions, and rivals gone.

The barking woke him as his hand reached for sword — for the sword that was solid, real, and close at hand.

His village was in the far South, in the Dominion of Annagar; the forests of the Kingdom of Breodanir were not the howling, ageless desert, the Sea of Sorrows. He had left his home after a heated argument with the father he had loved and respected. His father had been both proud of his action during the battle in the Averdan valleys, and grateful that his son had survived where so many had not. He was shocked, appalled, and enraged when his son professed the desire to avoid any further battles in the war against demons.

Ironic, then, that he had faced demons—and more—in his attempted avoidance. He had come face-to-face with a cowardice he would have said was not in him. He had disgraced himself in a fashion so complete that, were he in the Dominion, the Lord would have struck him dead—and it would be a death he deserved.

He lived, now, on borrowed time. He lived by the Lady's grace, offered a chance to redeem that complete loss of all honor.

His hand shook; he clenched it to stop the tremors. Turning to the corner of the room, he saw young Silvo's sword. He had the duty of returning that blade—unstained by cowardice or betrayal—to Silvo's family.

It was an honor he did not deserve. He could not speak of his own disgrace. Could not speak of the instantaneous, helpless nature of Silvo's death. To return the blade to the family was the only comfort he could offer them, who would never see the body; it had been consumed in fire, taken as ash by the winds.

"I'M AWAKE. I'll take you to the kennels if you'll let me get dressed. No, Leial, I can't put my legs into pants while you jump up on them."

Leial barked, that familiar yapping burst of sound, and headed to the closed bedroom door. Gervanno had never loved the enclosed, almost box-like nature of Northern rooms, Northern inns. He found them almost suffocating at times, the walls so thick in comparison to the screens of his youth. On the other hand, the residents of his wing of the Bowgren manor would be far less likely to be disturbed by the sounds of his dog.

Perhaps the thickness of walls was part of the reason the Northerners could be so boisterous, so loud; they were not raised to be continuously mindful of the small noises that crossed the thin barrier of screens, and they had not developed the skills to husband noise, to move silently so as not to disturb one's family.

Perhaps not. The servants here were not invisible, and they often chattered and gossiped loudly enough that the lords might hear them. It was unthinkable that such servants—or serafs—would have dared to do the same in the South.

So much was different in this place, at least on the surface. Power was not absolute, and in Breodanir, power came with a responsibility that could end in death. He had seen the truth of that in Ansel, and in Bowgren itself.

It was not so with the Tors of the South. There were, of course, laws in both Breodanir and Annagar, but power was the arbiter. For minor infractions, should the Tor be unreasonable, men such as Gervanno would die. For failures to Tyrs, that death was almost an absolute.

Nenyane's existence as the prickly but loved daughter of Maubreche made clear that Northern standards of failure were different. She lived. Nor did she live because she was the best sword master Gervanno had ever met. Her skill might have stayed the hand of Southern lords—but not, in Gervanno's opinion, for long. She could move silently, but apparently it took more effort than she cared to exert.

Leial was scratching at the door and barking joyfully when Nenyane opened it without the customary Northern knock. "Are you going to sleep all day?"

He forgot about the differences between their two countries the moment she stood glowering in the door's frame. He forgot about his disgrace, his lack of power. Nenyane of Maubreche, younger and slighter than Gervanno, made him feel both old and young. Old, because he did not have the same speed or endurance he had had in his youth; and young, because the fire of her brilliance kindled the dreams that had almost become ash. The dreams of becoming a sword master, of finding a master whose skill was legendary, and who might see—in Gervanno—some seed of future greatness.

He had far more dignity than Leial; he offered Nenyane of Maubreche a perfect bow. She snorted at it; bows, as most manners, were a waste of time to the Maubreche huntbrother.

"We've got the yard for the next two hours," she snapped, turning.

He made haste to follow her.

"HOW LONG WILL they keep at it?" Alex asked. He'd come to the yard after Nenyane and Gervanno had begun to spar.

"Until Gervanno tires." Stephen had some sympathy for the Southerner, but it was scant; he'd already sparred with his huntbrother, and was recovering.

The Elseth Hunter winced on the cerdan's behalf. "Nenyane doesn't, does she?"

Stephen shook his head. "Gervanno looks forward to this."

Alex nodded.

"Nenyane insisted that training be kept up while we're in Bowgren." He glanced at Alex, saw the Elseth Hunter's expression, and turned to face him. "What's happened?"

"Lady Bowgren informed us—well, me, as Max is out with your dogs—that she's received word from the King."

"The King? Not the Queen?"

"The King." Given Alex's expression, it wasn't what they'd hoped for.

"He wants us back at the Redoubt." Stephen's voice was flat.

"He commended us on our successes in Bowgren first, if that helps."

It didn't.

"And it's not *us*. It's Max and me."

"But not Nenyane and me?"

"Unless you receive a separate message, no. Lady Bowgren was sympathetic, given the debt she now feels she owes Elseth and Maubreche, but she's a ruler. He's the King. But...she does want to speak with you when it's convenient."

In Lady speak, that meant *now*.

"Do you want to wait in the yard? I'll go speak with Lady Bowgren."

"Max wants me to tell you that if you're not going back to the King's City, we're not going back either."

Stephen winced. "Did you hear from Lady Elseth?"

"No. We sent a message the normal way. If she feels it important, she'll expedite a response—but I'm not sure it will arrive before we have to leave. Lady Bowgren is willing to allow us time to recuperate from our battles, but she *did* send Ansel and Heiden to the King's City. She's going to expect us to vacate obediently within a reasonable time."

Stephen nodded; it was true.

THE LAYOUT of the Bowgren manse was not entirely familiar to Stephen; he had to stop to ask for directions. He was informed, stiffly and formally, that Lady Bowgren was in her private office, and that office—as it was in Maubreche—was tucked away somewhere on the second floor. A page was summoned to lead Stephen to that office.

There, the page knocked on the door, and when he was given permission, opened it. Lady Bowgren's desk was cluttered with paper, ink, and a quill; books the width of his arm occupied the leftmost edge of the desk. She was seated, but rose as Stephen entered; the page bowed and left, closing the door gently behind him.

"Alex told me you wished to speak with me."

"A message was sent from the King." Without resuming her seat, she opened a drawer and removed a scroll case. "It bears your name. Given Alex's reaction, the news he received was not good. Before you ask, I did not read the letter meant for the Elseth brothers; I did, however, receive instructions meant for me that have some bearing on the messages sent to you.

"We expect Anton, Ansel, and Heiden to return within two days, possibly three. You will no doubt wish to see them upon their return." Her expression was gentle, if neutral. "You have until then to make ready for travel; I have put the keykeeper at your disposal. Anything that we can give, we will grant you immediately. Anything that is not immediately available, we will attempt to arrange.

"Bowgren owes you a great debt, but we are Hunters, and we serve at the whim of the Master of the Game."

Stephen nodded. Lady Bowgren handed him a letter opener, and he used it to break the seal.

He read what was written with a growing sense of dismay, and then offered Lady Bowgren a perfect bow—or as perfect a bow as the yard clothing he wore for sparring allowed—and left the office.

ALEX MET him before he made it back to the yard. "They're done for the day."

"That's early."

"Nenyane was in a foul mood. I assume it's because you read your letter."

Stephen winced, but nodded.

"She said we should head up to your room—that's where she'll be. Max is just finishing up with the dogs; he'll meet us there as well."

———

ALEX WAS, of course, correct; Nenyane was in a foul mood. The glare she turned on Stephen was sharp, swift, and uncompromising. He was very glad that this discussion would take place behind closed doors. Nenyane was huntbrother—no one who had met her could deny that—but she had never considered herself beholden to Breodani customs. Or fealty. She understood the hierarchical order of power, but treated it as if it were irrelevant. Only to avoid their mother's ire would she force herself to behave well, but she couldn't maintain that for more than fifteen minutes at a stretch.

Cursing the stupidity of the King, in loud and certain terms, was no noble's idea of good manners.

"I'd hoped that," Alex said quietly, "as you weren't mentioned, you wouldn't be forced to go back."

"You know that's not the way these missives work. Your message was sent to representatives of Elseth; ours was sent to representatives of Maubreche. What will you do?"

"You already know. Where you go, we're going. If we returned to the King's City without you, our father would disown us. We told you—he sent us for a reason."

"He never made that reason clear, did he?"

Alex shook his head. "He doesn't talk about loss. He doesn't talk about grief. The closest he comes is rage, when he remembers. You're all that's left of his huntbrother."

"He's not. He's Bredan and Cynthia's son." Nenyane's expression was murderous. Only to snap would she join conversation.

"And Corwin's," Stephen said, voice as soft as Alex's. "It doesn't matter. If Mother had not seen Stephen of Elseth in the Between, I might not exist at all. She gave me his name, or as much of his name as she could, given Maubreche."

"We're going to have to set out as if we intend to go back," Alex said. "I think Lady Bowgren knows."

"Heiden's probably guessed." What Heiden knew, he would share only if he felt it helpful to Maubreche and Elseth. "Both of her sons have graduated. The Bowgren hunters have not been called back."

"If they were, they would go. Lady Bowgren would make certain of it. She sent them the first time, and Ansel was enraged." Nenyane's voice was not soft. "Ansel is the only son. The only heir. They don't even have a daughter they'd could marry to a second son to preserve the demesne." She was restless. Had been restless since they'd returned to Bowgren in triumph. The demons they had faced in the wilderness reminded her of the dangers she could not dredge up from her shattered memories; demons had always had that effect.

"Did you tell Gervanno we're leaving?"

His huntbrother nodded, eyes narrowed. "We're taking him with us."

"If he's willing to continue, given what we're likely to face."

"He has to go South."

Ah.

"We have to go South. We have to find the Green Deepings before the tangle moves." She glanced at Alex, and away. Max, leaning by the wall closest to the window, also glanced at Alex. Neither Elseth brother spoke for a long beat.

"So, you intend to go South?"

Nenyane nodded. "I wanted to leave Stephen behind; it's safer for him here."

"Given what we've already faced?"

"Given that, yes. I'm not saying it's safe, it's just safer."

"I never took you for a hypocrite."

Nenyane shrugged. She liked the Elseth brothers, but not so much that she cared what they thought of her.

Alex exhaled. "We're pretty much ready to go. We're going to have to pay lip service to the King's command."

"Lady Bowgren isn't a fool."

"No, of course not. She'll suspect that we won't be returning to Hunter's Redoubt any time soon. But if we lie, she won't be in the uncomfortable position of knowing we intend to break the law."

Nenyane hated lying, but this was a lie of omission, which she could—barely—stomach. She nodded. "We'll leave in two days."

"Two?"

"We need to discuss where we're going and how we'll get there. Gervanno came up from the South taking the common caravan routes. We can probably head south using the same roads."

THERE WERE ONLY two moons over Amberg, but the moonlight that shone on the tree that had grown just west of the village was brighter, sharper; the moon's face seemed larger, as if the tree itself coaxed the moon to approach more closely.

Meralonne APhaniel, robed as a member of the Order of Knowledge, approached the tree, lifting a hand to lightly touch its bark. During the daylight hours, when the sun, not the moon, reigned, the tree was ringed by village children, and the elders—too old to farm and till—who minded them. If respect was a coin demanded by the powerful in the wilderness, it was not a coin well understood by the mortal Breodani.

Born of the wilderness, born to its greatest scion, Meralonne understood that the tree took no offense; that children clambering up its roots—and falling off them—incurred no wrath. Children of this age could not show respect; they could offer, instead, the fear that was often at the heart of respect in the wilderness. To expect such fear from children was a sign of weakness; the powerful had no need of it.

The elders were respectful; they understood the full weight of the debt owed this silent tree. The children? They merely understood that the tree was safe. Thus bolstered by this minimal understanding, they included the roots—and even the trunk—in their childish games. It was an odd chorus: the laughter and tears of the young, and the sheltering silence of the tree itself. The tree would not bespeak the Breodani; they did not have the gift to hear its voice.

But the tree was aware of theirs.

Aware of Meralonne, as he stood in the silence left by dinner and bedtime.

"Does it not offend you?" the mage asked.

The tree's branches trembled a moment, as if at the wind that accompanied the mage. But Meralonne had once been a power in the wilderness, high or low; the tree answered, its voice thin and reedy. Had the barriers not been cracked, it would have no voice at all; this was a test of the encroachment of the ancient and the wild upon the lands of the mortals.

"It does not offend me, Illaraphaniel. Perhaps once, when the world was new, it might have. But in my isolation, the songs and stories of these fragile, fragile creatures became a boon, else I would not have taken care to protect them, for we both had little power.

"I find it oddly joyful to see them. Yes, they lack respect; they clamber up my roots—they cannot reach my branches unless I choose to bend them—with their dirty feet and hands; they shriek and proclaim themselves kings while they teeter.

"The eldest of the villagers know gratitude, and it will last the length of their lives—but those that come after? No. And these children? They have passed from gratitude to this: I am a special tree, which means I am subject to their hands, feet, and voices. It is odd, to one who has listened to the songs of the White Lady and her sisters at the dawn of time, to find such peace and clarity in their tiny shouts.

"They are people without passion, without dedication, without the loyalty that defined both those who ruled and those who served. Their lives, like the lives of the forest creatures, are focused on banalities. And yet, for no reason I can say, I find them precious. And you, Illaraphaniel? You who lived your long exile in mortal lands, on mortal soil, and whose life must be comprised of nothing but mortality—do you not feel the same?"

"I am not as they are," was the cool reply. "I serve the White Lady —and I understand the depth of demand loyalty makes upon those who do. To me, mortals are fireflies; the White Lady is the sun regnant. I barely notice mortals at all."

"Perhaps it is because you were not rooted in anything but that loyalty," the tree replied, a hint of regret in its whispering voice. "I find some small joy in their noise and their activity, and perhaps some gratification as well. Were it not for a whim, they would not now be here; it is evidence that, even trapped as I was, I was not without power."

"Had you power, Eldest, you would not have seen them at all."

"That is unfair, Illaraphaniel," a new voice said.

He recognized it, and turned to face the eyes of the golden fox, the second most powerful of Jewel's wild denizens. "Eldest."

"Indeed. I am pleased to find you resident within these mortal lands, for I have been tasked with delivery of a message. But perhaps I was tardy; I, too, find these odd mortal sprouts almost endearing. Perhaps the persistent, faint presence of my Lord affects me, even now. It is strange; Jarven is mortal, if somewhat altered, and he finds them merely annoying."

There was only one being who could task the fox with delivery of a message. "What would your lord have of me?"

The fox sat, his eyes brightening, his ears still. "You are aware that she houses one of the ancient healers in her lands."

Meralonne frowned. "Adam."

"Indeed, Adam, born of Arkosa—a City of Man. He must return to that ancient city, newly risen from what we presumed was its grave— or it will fall. Our enemies have far more traction in the South than they have in the Empire. Her lands are not yet in danger. In some futures, they will be; in some, they will not. In some, everything for which she cares will perish."

"I fail to see what that has to do with us, unless she ordered Adam to seek us in Breodanir."

The fox's eyes narrowed. "Do not disrespect my Lord, Illara-phaniel. You are a considerable power, but you are without shield and the forces in the wilderness grow strong."

"You were always worthy of respect, Eldest, and I mean no disre-spect to your lord; I labored at her borders before she had fully claimed the power of the Sen."

The fox nodded gravely. "She wishes you to travel to Averalaan; she does not expect you will remain there. But, as your party must venture South, she wishes to send Adam of Arkosa with you. He, at least, understands the respect the elder forces require."

"It will not save him," Meralonne replied. "You understand what he is; as the wilderness wakes, as the walls fall, it will become clear how much of a threat he is."

"There *is* a reason my Lord makes this request."

"Request?" Meralonne's smile was slender.

"Of course it is a request; she is not your lord. She would not accept any oath of service you cared to offer; she would know it to be a lie. She cannot command you."

"No more can you, respect and long acquaintance aside."

"No. No, indeed; nor would I presume to do so. But I have an interest in one of your company."

"Perhaps you should tend to your cub. The mortal you profess such an interest in is bound to the child; he will not leave her side until and unless she commands it. Mortal loyalty is fraught, muddy, easily changing—but his is not."

"Perhaps that is why he interests me."

"You prefer to watch things that will never be yours?"

The fox chuckled, but his eyes were cold as he looked up at the scion of the Firstborn. "You speak thus to *me*? You, who have diligently served a mortal mage? Ah, but her time is coming to an end. What, then, will you do, Illaraphaniel?"

"What I have always done. I will see the final battle, and I will face the god we do not name, be it over a sea of blood or no. I have found Nenyane, and Nenyane has found her master."

"You are not the equal of the three princes who perished."

"No, not alone. But will it or no, Eldest, this battle cannot be fought alone by any of us. If I am not all that I once was, our enemy is not what he was."

"Not yet. Can you not see it coming?"

Meralonne was silent. He wished for his pipe, which surprised him.

"My Lord bids me tell you one other thing. She has spent her days walking the timeways, looking into the heart of the Oracle's territory, but from its edges; her power rests uneasily in her mortal frame. When Adam of Arkosa leaves her lands, he will have a companion of significance to you as his own.

"She saw his best chance of survival in your companions: in some cases, you followed; in some, you could not."

"Could not?"

"In those possible pathways, your squire chose to join Adam, and you chose to remain distant to preserve him. It is folly, in my opinion, for which you have not asked."

"He is not the significant presence of whom you speak."

"No, although he currently tends a garden in my Lord's domain — with her blessing. Shianne will accompany Adam if he is to walk the path that leads to his ancient home."

Silence.

"Is there a future in which she does not?"

"No. There are futures in which she does not survive, and futures in which Adam does not survive. She will follow him when he leaves."

"When will he set out?"

"If my Lord knows your company will travel to Averalaan, he will not leave until they arrive. If she does not, he will leave in a few days."

When Meralonne failed to answer—or to move at all—the fox continued, voice softening as if to placate the rage he could feel emanating from the prince.

"My Lord believed you would not approve; she has spoken with Shianne. But Shianne does not serve my Lord. As you must know, Jewel does not demand obedience; it is against her nature. There is nothing she can do, short of confinement or imprisonment, that will prevent Shianne from leaving her forests.

"Nor has she sent word to the White Lady, the Summer Queen — for the Summer Queen might indeed command where Jewel could not."

"Why has she not done this?"

"Because Shianne's will *is* important. Shianne is no longer sister to the White Lady. Where her sisters ride, she cannot ride for long, and on the few occasions she has joined them, she has been protected as an object of veneration and terrible pity."

"That would not be to her liking."

"No. I believe she values young Adam; she is close to him. But, in part, her decision will take her away from the White Lady and the shadow of the loss Shianne's ancient choice has inevitably engendered. She chose; she accepts the consequences. But they wound her nonetheless — the fate of survivors in such circumstances.

"I am uncertain that your presence will be of aid in this regard. But the road is dangerous now, and your guidance and protection are required if Adam is to have the companions that will become his — and their — best chance for survival."

"Why is she sending the child away?"

The fox did not reply. "I cannot command you. My Lord cannot command you. But you must leave, and soon, if you are to grant her request. What will you do?"

"Return to your lord," Meralonne replied. "Tell her that you have delivered her request. The rest is not in your hands."

THE FOX WAS NOT the only stranger to visit the mage as he stood in the shadows of the great tree as evening fell. The last visitor was the bard.

He offered the mage a perfect bow and rose. "It seems that you have had a visitor this eve, APhaniel."

Meralonne nodded, his gaze distant; what he could see was clear neither to bard nor himself. "You have had one of your own?"

Kallandras nodded. "The time will come when all such visits cease. But I will accompany the Hunters to the heart of Essalieyan."

"Do you believe that is where they will go?"

"Yes. For some little while, my path and theirs must coincide."

"Will the bardmaster agree?"

"If I ask it, yes, if reluctantly. Across the Empire, events such as the turnings in Breodanir have taken—and are taking—place, even as we speak. Our journey to the South is a web that crosses many futures, but there is one person we must reach."

He knew then who the bard's visitor had been. Resentment flared, but it was embers; the bonfire was Shianne. Shianne and Adam. "The child of the Lord of the Hells."

"Even so. Until we have reached the heart of Arkosa, I will travel with Adam. But so, too, the Maubreche and Elseth Hunters, and the lone cerdan."

"That is not Nenyane's destination."

Kallandras said nothing.

"And you ask me to accompany you."

"No. I merely seek to inform you of what must occur."

"And the Hunters?"

"They have reached their own decision; I believe they intend to travel to the South by the road Gervanno di'Sarrado knows. It is the merchant road the Southerners travel, which would take them very close to Jewel's city."

"They will not be safer, were they to travel with Adam as their guide. In the lands of his birth, he was unremarkable to most of his companions; in the wilderness, he is a threat, an ancient threat."

"He is the most powerful healer Levec has ever seen."

"It is irrelevant. His power does not affect mortals in the same fashion it might affect the scions of the wilderness. If Jewel wishes his safety, he should remain within her city."

Kallandras did not reply, perhaps understanding how little his words would matter. He bowed to the mage. "I believe the Hunters intend to depart on the morning of the 12th."

Meralonne did not move.

12TH DAY OF WITTAN, 429 A.A. DEMESNE OF BOWGREN,
BREODANIR

Nenyane was up before dawn had altered the color of the sky.

To Stephen's surprise, the dogs were assembled; only Pearl proved restive and difficult, but by this point Nenyane and Max expected that. Max, of course, had gone to the kennels, but Nenyane had joined him, preferring to let Stephen perform the well-mannered, socially appropriate thanks and leave-taking usually expected from huntbrothers.

Lady Bowgren had offered them formal breakfast; Nenyane had declined. The compromise was food that could be eaten on the road. Had Lady Maubreche been present to witness this, she would have been highly displeased; Nenyane had been curt to the point of rudeness.

Ansel and Heiden had both winced, and Heiden had immediately interjected, adding the words he was *certain* Nenyane would have spoken were she less anxious to perform her duties. It was a fluid defense, one that no one believed. Ansel, being Hunter Lord, was less fussed about Nenyane's manners, and Lord Bowgren likewise unconcerned. Lady Bowgren's lips set in a narrow line, but she accepted Nenyane's impatience and ill-humor with as much grace as any Lady could; she was aware of the debt owed Maubreche and Elseth for their part in the salvation of Amberg.

She did not ask where they intended to travel. She made no effort to confirm that they intended to obey the King. Stephen considered confirming it for her — a lie, of course — but Nenyane shook her head.

"She's doing this for us, to lessen her debt. Let her. She doesn't want to make liars of us; the blow to our reputation when we fail to obey will be large enough."

Stephen swallowed, aware that Lady Bowgren was shouldering a burden that wasn't, or shouldn't have been, hers to carry. But Ansel and Heiden accepted it — even approved of it.

"We'll miss you," Heiden said, stepping away from Ansel to speak quietly. "If you need us, call."

Stephen shook his head. "Bowgren needs you. Lord Bowgren needs you both."

"I won't ask where you intend to go. But you'll always be welcome in Bowgren."

Stephen smiled. He couldn't promise the inverse; he wasn't certain that he would be returning to Maubreche any time soon. He knew, however, that his absence would make Maubreche safer for his family.

"Are you going to talk all morning?" Nenyane asked, her voice far louder than Heiden's.

Alex winced, but Max was clearly almost as impatient to be gone as Nenyane. Gervanno, who had joined them, was silent and reserved; he stood apart from the gathering of Hunters, as if he were a simple, anonymous guard.

He would never be that again, in Stephen's opinion. Leial, his dog, sniffed around the feet of everyone, as if searching for miraculously discarded food. This much, people expected from dogs; no one was offended. Gervanno understood that they would not be, or he might have moved.

Kallandras of Senniel College was likewise ready to leave, but of all of the people present, he was the most gracious in his words and gestures of departure. Lady Bowgren smiled—genuinely, in Stephen's opinion. He could understand why bards might be considered of great political use in the Empire that Kallandras called home.

Nenyane said nothing, but he couldn't help but be aware of her irritation. She had forgiven the bard his existence, and she offered him a grudging trust, but made clear she could claw it back at any moment.

Kallandras accepted this with grace. Or, in Nenyane's opinion, condescension. She hadn't decided which. Stephen, however, assumed grace. Kallandras seemed to accept the things he could not change; he could effortlessly match Breodani customs and manners, but could just as easily fall into behavior that Gervanno, as a Southerner, better understood.

The bard turned to Stephen. "Meralonne will join us on the road. He does not have much patience with leave-taking."

Neither did Nenyane; she wished she could have joined them on the road as well, but she couldn't as huntbrother.

Horses were brought from the stables at Lady Bowgren's command. "We will return Lady Margen's horses to her. Please accept these as replacements for the time being."

To GERVANNO, horses were far, far more significant than dogs. Of the six horses Lady Bowgren had brought from the Bowgren stables, one had been meant for him. He was accustomed to walking the merchant road, but he knew he could not keep up with the Hunters on foot if they were horsed.

He opened his mouth, but closed it again; it was a gift not given to cerdan in the South, except by the lord they served—and even then, it was rare. Still, these were Northern horses, bred more for endurance than speed. For just a moment, the horses' reins brought back the memories of the small stables that had nonetheless been his father's pride, and he remembered his dream.

He did not imagine that his village had been buried by sand and war in the Sea of Sorrows, but understood that there was no home for him there. He had one mission in the South: to visit Silvo's family and return the boy's sword. Until that moment, he would serve the Maubreche Hunters as the most loyal of cerdan.

The road lay before them, literally and figuratively, as they took their leave of Bowgren.

Gervanno thought he would miss the courtyard and the training. On the road, they might practice in the yard of an inn—if the inn had a yard. Many did not. He was uneasily aware that his sword might once again see real use as they traveled. But he had taken the time, before sun's rise, to offer the Lady ablutions here, in the North, where the Lady did not reign.

He had felt her watchful eye, regardless; here, and in what Nenyane of Maubreche called the wilderness. Or perhaps he conjured the familiar when so much was unfamiliar.

It was his duty to guide the Hunters along the merchant roads he knew. He had argued with Nenyane about this; it was on merchant roads that his entire caravan—and much of his honor—had been destroyed.

"We don't have alternatives," she told him. "We would need a solid pathfinder to navigate around the Free Towns—if the Free Towns still exist in any recognizable form. Breodanir has some protection against the turnings; I'm not certain if the Free Towns do."

"There is some protection there," Kallandras told them. "But even with protection, Breodanir has suffered. We are still following the roads in Breodanir; it is when we leave its borders that we will discover how much the world has changed. Do you wish to stop in Maubreche before we leave the kingdom?"

Nenyane opened her mouth but snapped it shut.

It was Stephen who was left to answer. "I would love to visit Maubreche, but then I would leave my mother with the burden of knowing her oldest son intends to disobey the King. It is better for her —and the rest of my family—that she not be involved. If I return, she will know that I have no intention of remaining within Hunter's Redoubt. She will know that nothing she can say—or do—will change that outcome.

"And I'd like to avoid getting into a fistfight with Robart."

"You could take him," Nenyane said.

"I think that's beside the point," Alex told her. "Robart's always been a bit sensitive about Stephen's position. Some younger sons want to be heir to their demesnes; Robart doesn't. He's angry at Stephen because he feels Stephen is better than him in every way, and Stephen won't become Lord Maubreche."

"That's not exactly Stephen's fault," Max said.

"Robart's young. He'll be a good Lord Maubreche. An angry, good Lord Maubreche. But Corwin should be Lord for decades yet. By the time Robart inherits, he'll understand."

Nenyane snorted, clearly in disagreement. She liked Robart to a point, but she considered his resentment of Stephen ridiculous. Nothing she had said—and no fist she had thrown—had altered Robart's view.

It was Max who said, "What about the dogs? You're in possession of four of the King's dogs. You may be charged with theft if you leave the country with them."

It was Stephen's only regret. He missed Corwin's dogs, missed the rest of the pack that was technically his, legally his father's. The King's dogs were, as expected of the royal kennels, almost flawless—but he had not raised them or trained them himself.

You don't need to train dogs. They just do what you tell them.

They still need to be raised.

Nenyane thought he was being ridiculous. Of course, she did. She tolerated the dogs, and helped him tend them—but to her, they were living tools. They were his armor, his shield. Armor required mainte-nance; she accepted that the dogs required maintenance and care as well.

But she felt no sentimental attachment to them. She felt no attach-ment to horses; felt very little attachment to Maubreche, although she had respect for, and affection for, Lady Maubreche and Lord

Maubreche. The only person her affection — and it was sharp, hard affection — was turned to was, and had always been, Stephen. He glanced at the Elseth Hunters; she liked them, and always had.

Was it their mother's blood? Was it because they had a quarter of Bredan's blood flowing in their veins?

No. It's because they're Gilliam's sons. It's because they're yours. Where you go, they'll go.

And Gervanno di'Sarrado?

She was silent for a while. *He's yours as well.*

He's not. He's yours.

Yes. But you are the master I've chosen; he will protect you with his life because he understands that I value your life more highly than I value my own.

I don't want that!

Nenyane did not answer. She didn't speak again until they came to their first rest stop, and when she did, it was to Gervanno. He had led them to caravan camping grounds that existed to one side of the King's Road.

The caravan grounds had been cleared; they were kept cleared — or so Gervanno told them — by the King's order. It was not clear in the way the grounds at Maubreche were clear, but there was a wide area in which weeds, not trees, stood; Stephen could see indents that had been formed by wagons in rainy weather in some of the exposed ground.

———

"ARE they going to do this the entire way to wherever it is we're going?" Alex asked. He was seated beside Stephen, knees bent, as he watched Gervanno and Nenyane spar.

"Wherever there's space and time, yes." Stephen watched his hunt-brother's expression; ferocious focus, and beneath that something that approached joy. Gervanno, more pressed, nonetheless responded in kind, as if they were two rivals with a deep and abiding respect for the skills of their opponent.

"I think he's getting better."

"He was always better than I am. He'll never be better than Nenyane."

Alex nodded and fell silent for a bit. But he had always been more talkative than Max when it came to non-hunting-related things. "I don't know Nenyane as well as you do, obviously—but this is the first time I've seen her take any interest in anyone who wasn't you."

"Gervanno's hard not to like. Nenyane says he's far better with a sword than he thinks he is."

"Better than you."

Stephen nodded. "I'm better than most Hunters she's seen wield a sword, but it's like Gervanno has spent his entire life honing his craft. No, it's more than that. He looks at Nenyane, at her sword work, and he's almost awestruck." Pearl sauntered over and dropped her head on Stephen's shoulder.

"I think Pearl's telling us it's time to go."

Alex rose, dusted off his pants, and silently called Max, who was exercising the dogs.

Nenyane put up her blade; Gervanno froze, blade mid-arc, as he responded. It was Kallandras who said, "These two could be sword dancers, if they ever desired to exhibit their skills."

"Sword dancers?" Alex asked.

"Yes. It is an art form seldom seen in the North; some of the dancers from the Dominion venture to Averalaan during the Kings' Challenge. It is a dance of blades, a movement of steps, that shows both practice and trust in one's partner. Very, very few are those who master the art; it cannot be mastered alone."

"I'm not sure Nenyane would care enough to do anything like this in crowded city streets." Stephen rose as well.

Kallandras nodded, gazing into a distance that was composed of more than trees. "But the dancers are not aware of the crowd when they dance. They are aware of each other."

NENYANE HAD BURNED enough energy sparring that the restlessness that almost defined her was quiet. She still refused to ride, choosing instead to travel—as she usually did—on foot. Stephen had never questioned it, even as a child; he had accepted it as a simple part of his huntbrother. He was not the only one, but everyone else had taken time. Adults assumed she would flag with exhaustion and repent her decision.

Stephen knew better. Nenyane made no rash claims; if she said she could do something, she could do it. She'd said she could teach him

how to wield a sword. She was half the age of the weaponsmaster — or
less — but Stephen had believed her. Getting other people to share that
confidence had taken time.

But Corwin believed her, now. His mother tended to worry;
Nenyane was as much her daughter as Stephen was her son. Robart
was sometimes hostile; if it weren't for Nenyane, Stephen would be a
normal Hunter, in his opinion. Any attempt to explain that this was not
the case had met with resentment and anger. Nenyane had never
seemed to care, which further exacerbated Robart's hostility.

MERALONNE DID NOT JOIN their party until they had crossed the
Bowgren border. He stepped lightly between the trees that girded the
road, his pipe in hand, the scent of tobacco caught briefly in strands of
his hair. In the midday sun he seemed out of place, a hint of moonlight
and evening. He lifted chin in greeting, but offered no words.

Gervanno offered a nod, no more, but Alex broke the Northern
widan's silence. Meralonne carefully emptied his pipe's bowl, and
walked beside the Elseth hunter. Alex was adept at navigating the
mage's company, but perhaps it was the presence of the pipe that made
him seem approachable.

Gervanno had seen the mage fight. He knew the mage was not
human. In Meralonne's presence, the shadows of all of the battles yet
fought had lengthened and darkened enough that the light that cast
those shadows revealed the truth of his essence.

The manners of his distant youth served Gervanno well; they had
always been dependent on the relative power of the individuals
involved. Gervanno offered Meralonne a nod because it conformed to
the mage's desire. It was not, could never be, a nod that passed
between equals.

NENYANE CALLED a halt before they had fully passed through Margen
but had she not, Meralonne would have. The area surrounding the
road had turned. It was the first such turning they had encountered
since leaving Bowgren. Nenyane was frustrated, but she was aware

that they as a group couldn't just walk through such a turning as if it were weather.

Meralonne approached the subtle dividing line between Breodani land and the wilderness, and bent to examine the weeds and grass on either side of that line. "These are not the lands once ruled by the lord we defeated; they are not lands ruled by the lord who reclaimed his territory." He frowned.

Nenyane frowned as well, but it was harder to separate that frown from the expression she'd worn all day. Only when she sparred with Gervanno had she lost that pinched look.

"Is it something we can circumvent if we follow the forest?" she asked.

Meralonne glanced at the bard; the bard closed his eyes, lashes resembling a skirt of gold, they were so long. Stephen hadn't noticed that before; he wondered why he noticed it now—but there was something striking about the bard's face in this moment, as he listened intently for the sounds of the wilderness, the sounds of Breodani wildlife, separating them until he once again opened his eyes.

"No. I hear no lord's name in the breeze on the other side. I do not feel its cadence in the plants moved by that breeze. The trees are silent as well, as if waiting, or yearning. Their reach is simply that—but the land will spread before we are clear of it. Lord Margen can deal with this turning."

No Hunter in this party wished to encounter Margen's lord. Were they headed back to the King's City, it would have mattered little; they were not.

Nenyane said, "If the turning isn't inimical, I think we risk the forest. We can cut a wide swathe around it—but we can't afford to just wait by the roadside for rescue like helpless children." She folded her arms as she spoke.

The mage and the bard exchanged another glance, this longer.

"You will not be under suspicion of anything but common sense should we choose to wait," the mage said.

"They'll just invite us back to the Margen estate. We don't have time for that."

"No, we do not. I had intended to accompany you through the Free Towns; if we are to encounter danger, it will be there. There are dells and havens in which the Free Towns were rooted in the past, else they would not have survived. They are considered city states in their own right, but they are not large enough to grace that name with truth.

"There is no way to reach Averalaan but through the Free Towns, and the time in which the roads can reliably be said to lead to the sanctuary Averalaan has become is diminishing." To Stephen's surprise, given the gravity of the mage's tone, Meralonne produced a pipe from the folds of his robes.

"Can we bypass Averalaan?" Nenyane asked, her tone one of demand, not curiosity.

"Not with ease, unless you believe crossing mountains is easier than following the road. Beyond the population and the wealth centered in Averalaan, there are reasons the caravans from the South choose to route through that city. Gervanno's former caravan is no exception, and it is the road he knows."

"And you?" Nenyane's hands found her hips as she glared at the mage.

"I can, of course, arrive in Breodanir or the Free Towns without the tedium of normal travel. I cannot, however, take more than one or two of you with me; the cost of attempting to move you all would be ruinous. While demons are active, it is not the time to risk mage fevers."

Nenyane snorted. "You want us to go to Averalaan."

Meralonne was silent.

"Why?"

Kallandras drew Stephen away from the brewing argument; Nenyane was fearless. She was also suspicious and annoyed.

"She's not in danger," Stephen said, voice soft.

"No. No more is Meralonne. But their disagreement is something best left to them." He nudged Stephen toward Alex; Max was further afield with the dogs, although he was careful to keep them away from the strange lands the road now led to. Stephen glanced at Gervanno, and was almost amused to see the cerdan a full step back from Nenyane, but ready to interfere should she require it.

When they were far enough to the side of the road, Stephen turned to Kallandras. "You know why he wants us there."

Kallandras's smile was slight, but it lingered. "I do. But he, as I, am beholden to masters who dwell within Averalaan; if we have a home, it is there. I require permission to travel where you will travel — but I will request that permission. We are at peace with the Dominion of Anna-

gar, but there are rumblings in the distance that imply peace might not
hold.

"It is to find out the truth of those unsettling rumors that I am likely
to be sent and, as you intend to travel South, I hoped for your companionship for some part of the journey."

Stephen frowned. Alex, beside him, frowned as well. Neither
accused the bard of lying; neither felt he was being truthful. The bard
was pleasant, tactful, and diplomatic. No one expected frank truth
from a diplomat.

"That isn't the only reason," Stephen said quietly. Alex became
watchful. Max brought Steel and Patches forward to join his brother.

Kallandras smiled, the movement of lips a brief slash of expression.
"No, it is not. You have traveled, briefly, at the side of Meralonne
APhaniel. You have taken his measure—but you have not seen his full
power. No more have I, and I have seen him fight.

"Word was carried to us from distant Averalaan. He did not lie; he
has been summoned to the city. I did not lie; I, too, have been
summoned. But for complicated reasons, you are considered of grave
import. We do not wish you to traverse the wilderness without
adequate protection—if that is even possible.

"You will better understand when you reach Averalaan. It is a new
city, a city remade at the behest of the Sen, and it is her guidance and
protection that we seek in the war to come. And she has seen you,
Stephen of Maubreche. She has seen the two Elseth Hunters. She has
seen Nenyane of Maubreche. No mention was made of Gervanno
di'Sarrado.

"She desires your presence, who are not a citizen of the Empire.
You are free to refuse; she cannot command you. But she holds sway
where Meralonne is concerned, and similar sway with my bardmaster."

"Why did Meralonne not speak of this?"

"I do not know. And I should not speak of him at all. It is never
wise to interfere with the powers of the ancient world."

Alex stepped forward. "We will need to confer. It is not us you
must convince but Nenyane of Maubreche; it is her will to go South."

"It is ours, as well; I did not lie. Rumors of war are spreading on
the winds. I ask only that you consider visiting Averalaan before you
make that journey."

"And if we choose not to do so?"

"The choice, of course, is yours. But Meralonne can pass around the Free Towns, and I am uncertain that it would be such a simple journey without his presence."

"You cannot?" Alex's tone was skeptical, his expression politely neutral. He really was Lady Elseth's grandson.

"I cannot with such ease, no. The paths that exist in the wilderness —and they exist, although they are not as easily traversed or even discovered as the King's Road in Breodanir—are now Summer roads, not the Winter roads upon which I trained."

"Summer isn't safer than Winter?"

"In the wilderness, you will find a great and terrible beauty; you will witness landscapes that rob you of even the simplicity of breath for moments at a time. You will find denizens there whose home has only finally begun to bud and bloom at the passing of Winter. But you will not find safety. Winter or Summer. People fear the cold because it can kill.

"Fear the Summer, Hunters. Fear the wilderness. That is the only coin that will pass as respect should you find yourself on those roads." He frowned, glancing toward where Meralonne and Nenyane stood.

Around them, leaves rose like a barrier, carried by a sudden gale of wind.

Chapter Two

Stephen immediately turned in the direction of the violent, localized storm; Nenyane's feet were no longer on the ground—and her sword was no longer in its sheath. But Gervanno had not yet drawn his; he had stepped back from the edge of the storm's circumference, and he watched.

Kallandras placed a gentle but staying hand on Stephen's shoulder. "This is an argument they must resolve; should we enter the wilderness for any reason, we will be far too marked if they converse thus."

"This isn't what most of us call a conversation," Alex said, looking to Stephen for guidance.

The bard, not Stephen, answered. "No, indeed. But they are not as we are."

"We?"

"We are mortal. We are human. Neither she nor the man you call Meralonne are." He frowned, glancing at Alex. "Surely you understood this? You bear the blood of Bredan, although you are not god-born in the fashion Stephen is. You must have sensed at least this much."

"Did you?" Alex countered.

To Stephen's surprise, Kallandras chuckled, his eyes implying genuine amusement and grudging approval. "I would not have noted it immediately, no. I told you—I am human."

"Humans don't generally give commands to the wind."

"Perhaps the wind followed Meralonne's orders."

"As well, yes."

Kallandras lifted a hand. "Tell me, scion of Elseth, what do you see?"

Alex frowned, thinking the question odd. "You mean the ring?"

"I do, indeed. What can you tell me of it?"

"Diamond, maybe platinum band. It looks plain; it was probably expensive."

"More than you can yet imagine. Stephen?"

Stephen shrugged. "I see the same ring."

"Might you call Gervanno di'Sarrado over?"

Stephen's frown was deeper, but Gervanno clearly had no intention of interfering in the discussion between mage and sword master. Not until the sword master had drawn her sword. Even then, he left his sheathed as he watched, hand on hilt. Nenyane was a better swordsman than the Northern Widan—but not by much. Rage did not weaken her skills or her observation, but even raging as she was, Gervanno felt that she did not intend to kill her opponent.

Stephen gestured. Gervanno, always aware of his surroundings, caught the movement. If he was Nenyane's, as she claimed, he was guard to Maubreche; he obeyed.

"My apologies for interrupting you as you carry out your duties, Ser Gervanno." Kallandras offered Gervanno a bow Stephen now recognized as Southern. "I have a simple question. Your answer would aid us in our discussion."

Gervanno nodded. He did not glance at Stephen for guidance. Stephen had gestured him over; Stephen, therefore, intended his guard to cooperate.

"Tell me, Ser Gervanno, what do you see on my hand?"

Gervanno frowned. "I don't understand."

"We have been discussing ancient things of power, but indirectly, as one must. I wished to ascertain something. Tell me, what can you see, if anything?"

Gervanno frowned; his eyes narrowed, the sweep of thick lashes almost closing as they did. "My apologies, Master Bard, but I cannot quite see anything on your fingers."

"Nothing at all?"

"There is a blur when I attempt to look at your hand—perhaps due to the angle of the sun." Gervanno spoke, as he often did, seriously. It was the first time Stephen thought the Southern man was lying, and it surprised him.

Kallandras thanked him as he lowered the hand and turned back to Stephen and Alex. "You do not understand, do you?"

"I think we do," Alex replied, when Stephen failed to find words. "You're willing to take us South because if we encounter patches of wilderness—or worse—you expect us to be able to see all of it."

"It is not a matter of willingness," the bard replied. "I am willing to have Gervanno accompany us. I am surprised that he could sense anything; many mortals cannot. But he, too, has encountered the elders of the wilderness, and such encounters oft leave their mark. None of us are guaranteed to survive."

"Stephen will survive," Nenyane said, her voice stretching past the barrier of wind, leaves, and small branches, the words a snarl. Stephen felt it as a vow. An oath.

He had to fight every instinct he had not to sanctify it, to bless it, to *accept* it. He understood why she offered it; how could he not? He was assaulted by the flood of visceral emotion that she barely kept contained. What she feared was not her own death—never, ever that. She feared his. She feared being left alone, again, in the ruins of everything she had once loved.

Even if she could not remember it. What was left her was the sense of a loss so complete it had shattered her.

"Stephen will survive." The repetition was not Nenyane's; it was not a vow. Not a plea. The wind that had torn at Nenyane's words lifted and exalted the mage's. "Nenyane, I swear to you that I will not abandon him in this life. I will not abandon you. What you cannot remember yet, I will remember for you. The battle you must fight is the only battle, in the end; all else is skirmish and distraction."

"You won't even *be here*!" Her voice rose with effort.

Meralonne did not disagree. "I will accompany you to Averalaan. There is safety there; it is a newly born City of Man. But I cannot see what shape the company will take beyond that point; there is a man there I must not meet until the final battle, should we make it that far. It is a tricky negotiation, but he understands it well; his existence, his continued existence, depends upon it."

The wind released Nenyane without warning; had she been Stephen, she would have fallen in a heap. She was Nenyane; she landed on her feet, bending slightly into her knees. Had they been in

Maubreche, she would have stormed off, and not returned until after dinner—no matter the time of day she had chosen to rage at a distance safe for the rest of the family.

She didn't have that option on the road; she didn't have that option off of it, either, as there was no guarantee she could make her way back to the rest of her company unless they failed to move. Meralonne clearly intended the trek to continue.

"I had hoped to remain horsed until we reached the border. Guiding the horses through forest will be onerous and may well slow us down."

"We'll take that risk," Stephen told the mage. "Unless we cannot find the road again, we'll lose less time overall."

BY SILENT CONSENSUS, the Hunters followed Meralonne's lead; Nenyane chafed at it, and often scouted ahead. The first time she left, Max glanced at Stephen; he shook his head.

"She can find her way back to me; she's not going far."

Meralonne preferred Nenyane as scout, over the dogs; Pearl found this offensive. If the walk was relatively quiet, it wasn't entirely peaceful. The horses, however, had no problems following the Hunters; the Breodani proceeded with care and a mind to them. It became clear that Meralonne's preference had been to abandon the horses by the roadside, assuming that the Margen lord would retrieve them near the turning and eventually return them to Bowgren.

But they made slower progress than they would have had the road been passable, and they did not return to the King's Road until the sun had begun its descent. "How far are we from the inn?" It was Alex who asked.

"We can make it before dark if we push the horses."

Nenyane refused to ride. She had excellent night vision; the sun's fall was not of great concern to her. Gervanno was the stickler here; while he was willing to push the horses in an emergency, he was always reluctant. As there was no immediate emergency, he voted—verbally, which surprised everyone but Nenyane—to camp in the merchant hollow.

"How do you know about this one? You didn't make it this far." Nenyane, subtle as ever, demanded.

If the reference to his previous masters caused pain, none of it showed on his face. "Evaro had a map. He intended to make his way to certain demesnes before he came to a stop in the King's City."

"And you looked at the map?"

"There was very little else to do; the guards might drink on the road if the road is safe, but I did not think that advisable on duty. I merely wished to know what the land would be like on the off chance there were bandits. We can feed and water the horses at the inn nearby for a small charge, and we can resupply in the village."

"We don't need to resupply yet."

"We resupply where we can. It doesn't matter if it's a day or two's worth of food—if we take a wrong turn and end up in completely unnatural lands, it might save our lives."

Gervanno had been in the Southern army; his bearing today made that clear. Stephen found it quietly amusing, possibly because Nenyane accepted it and even approved of it. Gervanno as a guard had always been almost invisible. Invisibility was clearly not his choice, having committed to serve.

Nenyane had never minded camping. Stephen preferred an inn, with an actual bed, decently cooked food, and a bath. If Gervanno felt supplies were necessary, shouldn't sleep be necessary as well? His huntbrother snorted in derision at his train of thought, but allowed him to maintain some dignity.

———

GUARDING the small camp was done in shifts; Max and Gervanno took the first shift, with Steel, Patches and Brylle; Stephen and Alex, with the rest of the dogs, took the next shift; Kallandras and Meralonne, the last. Nenyane did not sleep at all. If she was not officially assigned to guard duty, it mattered little to her. She had never required much sleep.

This had been a concern of Lady Maubreche for as far back as Stephen could remember, and Nenyane had learned to stay in her room during hours in which children were expected to sleep—although she sometimes left by the window and returned before the bells announced dawn, and their permission to shed the pretense of sleep.

Stephen tried, once, to get her to rest; he knew sleep was beyond her. He failed. They almost argued, but he had conceded before it could get to that stage. Nenyane was on guard duty, everyone else's schedules be damned.

Stephen was grateful for Gervanno's guidance; while it wasn't impossible to camp in Breodani forests, setting up in the clearing made a difference. He did not fear Breodanir; he did not fear bandits, should they be encountered. Bandits tended to be more numerous in times of drought, which they were not facing.

It wasn't Nenyane who awakened him during the final shift of the night—it was the horses. They had been quiet and docile during the forest trek, and restless when the group had finally returned to passable road. They were none of that, now.

He was up, weapon in hand, as he mentally reached for his dogs. The dogs were awake and bristling; the horses were almost wild with panic. Pearl and Patches could scent blood; one of the horses had been injured.

The mage and the bard had been on watch; neither had yet drawn blades. The wind, however, was no longer a simple element of nature.

Nenyane was armed with blade as Stephen burst out of his tent; Gervanno, Alex, and Max were also emerging from theirs. Gervanno's gaze immediately found the horses; the Southerner did not draw sword, but went straight to them.

Three of the six horses appeared to be missing. Stephen assumed they'd fled, given the panicked behavior of the remaining animals. He left care of the three horses to the one person present who valued them so highly, and turned instead to his dogs.

Steel was at Max's side; Brylle joined the grey alaunt. Pearl was closest to Gervanno, crouching slightly as she growled. None of the dogs could sense anything that might have spooked the horses— certainly nothing that could have injured them. One of the three horses left behind, however, was bleeding heavily from the belly.

I knew we should have left the horses. The fact that Nenyane spoke through the Hunter's bond, instead of out loud, made clear she wanted caution.

"APhaniel," Stephen said.

The mage shook his head. "We are in Breodani territory; nothing has changed around us. I sense no intruders now."

Kallandras said, "Nor do I, but I can almost hear them; the wind carries their voices, but their voices are faint."

If we lose only one horse, we'll be fine, Nenyane said. *I have no intention of riding.* It came to Stephen then that she wasn't speaking this way for safety's sake; she was speaking this way because Gervanno would be unhappy. Horses meant far more than dogs in the Dominion.

Gervanno calmed the horses, quieting them with his presence alone, absent weapon or panic. Even the injured horse stayed still as Gervanno assessed the severity of its belly wound. He did not utter a word until he retreated—and he retreated only for supplies, cursing his lack of things he deemed necessary for treatment.

Meralonne then came to examine the hurt animal. He was not Gervanno; he did not stoop to comforting words—or any words at all. He gestured briefly and the horse lowered muzzle. "The rest of you, eat if absolutely necessary, and pack up. We will need to move." He exhaled. "It is best at this point to leave the horses at the inn. We can ask the innkeeper to hold them for Bowgren, and send word that they are there."

"You intend to walk all the way to the Empire?" Alex asked.

"If we make it that far, yes."

"What caused this? Why are there no further traces?"

"Something is hunting," Meralonne replied. "If I had to guess, they did not expect to encounter so many of us."

Nenyane snorted. "Meaning they didn't expect to see you on guard duty."

"Meaning that, yes. Their numbers, therefore, are not high or their leader is not present. We had best move now."

"But—what do you think is hunting us?" Alex was busy disassembling the tent, but asked the question on everyone's mind.

"Not bandits," Meralonne replied. "The barriers have indeed thinned in the past year. If the lands can be repelled, the invaders who managed to evade detection cannot so easily be whispered back into the wilderness."

"Who would dare to hunt you?" Nenyane asked. "None of your own kin, and they are the greatest hunters feared across the breadth of the wilderness, high or low."

"Not my own kin, no. But Nenyane, if the Wild Hunt crossed all lands in pursuit of their prey, they were not the only hunters. If you mean to ask was the horse's injury caused by the dead, the answer is almost certainly no. But the dead are not the only creatures mortals must fear." He closed his eyes briefly. "We were far too late in our leave-taking."

GERVANNO CEDED command to the mage, although in both cases the
right of command was not theirs. He asked for Kallandras's aid in
keeping the horses in the camp soothed, and Stephen's in finding those
that had fled. Stephen commanded his lymers to follow their scent, and
the horses, some hours later, were recovered.

Nenyane was almost as impatient with Gervanno's concern for the
horses as she was with Stephen's concern for dogs—even when they
weren't his own.

Yes, Stephen told his huntbrother. *But it's the fact that he is, and can be,
concerned that makes him who he is.*

He'd be the same if he didn't care.

Stephen shrugged. He was unwilling to have an argument with
Nenyane in the midst of so much uncertainty. Pearl and Patches
scouted ahead; he had to focus on them, not on an argument he'd had
so many times he knew it by heart.

The dogs, however, were not nervous, except by extension; they
mirrored their Hunter's ill ease. He exhaled and forced his thoughts to
calm. These were not Maubreche lands, but they were Breodani
forests; the dogs accepted them as their natural hunting grounds as
long as their Hunter was calm and focused.

Breodani dogs were not, at heart, good scouts. They searched for
the scent of familiar prey; prey on which they'd been trained from the
moment they could run. When properly trained, they could separate
the scents they expected in the environment from those for whom they
must hunt, if the scents were new enough.

There was the faint trace of something different. Something
strange.

Stephen froze for one long moment, and then he called them back.
Ordered them back, much to Pearl's outrage. "How dangerous are
these creatures to normal people?" he asked the mage.

"Normal is a very subjective word," Meralonne replied, eyes
narrowing. "You found their scent."

Stephen nodded. "Are they like Biluude?"

"They are nothing like Biluude. In the wilderness, they would not
be considered a credible threat by anyone of power."

"Do they look human?"

"No. They could not pass as one of your people, even if their existence could be considered very similar in other ways. There is a reason they retreated; I believe they intended to cripple the horse—they could eat it later—and kill its rider. They are thieves at heart; they value their own safety highly. They are not foes that humans cannot handle. If you mean to hunt them, you will waste time we do not have."

Stephen hesitated.

"If you are concerned, pass word on to the inn. Strange creatures that move in small groups and use tools are committing acts of banditry on the merchant roads."

He's right. If you feel the need to fix everything, we won't be prepared for the real war. Nenyane's impatience was almost a physical force.

Stephen glanced at Gervanno, who nodded and said, "If these are creatures people can counter, they are very like bandits." Bandits were the reason Gervanno had been hired to guard a merchant caravan. Bandits, not demons or the growing expansion of the other world into this one. "Will you let them go?" he asked.

"Yes," Meralonne said, before Stephen—to whom Gervanno's question had been directed—could answer. "We will leave the horses at the inn, we will pass on a warning, and we will make haste on foot down the King's Road until it reaches the Breodanir border. Unless you wish to risk the horses. We will almost certainly have to abandon them at some point; I had hoped they would take us to the Free Towns."

Since horses were more practical on the roads, Meralonne must have a reason for believing they must be abandoned. He almost asked—but he had seen the turning on the Margen leg of the King's Road. He had encountered such a turning as they traveled to Bowgren. In Breodanir, the turnings were considered under control. Beyond the borders, the Hunters had inferred, they were not.

"If we are lost in the wilderness," Alex said, speaking for every Hunter present except Nenyane, "will we be able to return to mortal lands?"

"Perhaps. Perhaps not. It is the reason I now travel with you. Where you might find the wilderness geographically confusing, I will not—and I might serve as pathfinder between the wilderness we enter and the wilderness ruled by Jewel. But fools and traitors contest her borders; it is reaching the lands she has claimed that will be the challenge."

They had traveled in the wilderness; they had faced the lord who ruled it. They understood.

"It is not my first choice," the mage continued, eyes gazing ahead. "I would prefer that the roads hold, and that we travel by them. But I can hear the winds in the distance, and they have voice. Come. We have light. Let us make our way to the inn."

17TH DAY OF WITTAN, 429 A.A. THE KING'S ROAD, BREODANIR

The road for four days had been clear, if one didn't include merchants, wagons, and horsed messengers. By this point, Lord Declan—and the King himself—must be aware that the Maubreche and Elseth Hunters were delinquent. It was possible that other turnings served as traveling roadblocks, but, by this day, the Hunters could otherwise be expected to arrive in the King's City. Hunter's Redoubt would remain empty.

In both Maubreche and Elseth's case, the family rule of land was not in question; heirs existed who could take up the family name and duties. But there would be political anger and pressure that would fall squarely on the shoulders of both Lady Elseth and Lady Maubreche as their children's absence stretched out.

Nenyane, predictably, wasn't concerned. Neither was Max. Alex and Stephen were fretful but determined.

"I don't know why you're bothering to worry. Either you're going back to the palace, or you're not. And we're not." This was Nenyane's philosophy in life, and it generally governed her mood to positive effect.

Today wasn't one of those days. "Father will understand."

"So will Cynthia, eventually. Look, we're either doing the right thing, or we're not. I wish you'd stop moping."

Max winced. "It's natural to care about the consequences family will suffer for our decisions," he pointed out. "Even I do."

"Fine. I'm not your huntbrother, and I can't hear you doing it. Stephen's been doing nothing but."

Meralonne seemed to find her irritation amusing. Kallandras did not appear to hear any of it. Although the King's Road was still passable, the bard often scouted ahead. Stephen had tried to send Nenyane ahead to give everyone else a break from her irritation, but she had declined. She was restless and she was worried.

"I'm worried about the turnings. I'm worried about demons. I'm worried about things we're likely to have to face—I'm not worried about Mother or Lady Elseth. Only a fool would attempt to pressure either of them, and the Queen isn't, by all reports, a fool."

"She is not," Kallandras agreed. He opened his mouth, his expression pleasant, agreeable; it froze before transforming into one that Stephen had never seen on the bard's face.

***

KALLANDRAS LIFTED HIS CHIN, his eyes narrowing; strands of his hair began to fly in the grip of a breeze that touching no one else. He lifted his hands; into his palms, in silence, came two weapons.

Meralonne glanced at the bard. "If you wish aid, ask; I understand well that there are conflicts between kin that should allow for no outsiders. But even I could not stand for long against two of my brothers."

"Could you kill them?" the bard asked, his whisper clear above the growing wind.

Meralonne did not reply.

"It has been long since I have faced them on this particular field. They have no permission to hunt me now." He glanced at Stephen.

Nenyane's expression shifted, her eyes narrowing.

The mage turned to Stephen. "Send your dogs with the Elseth Hunters; keep them out of range."

Stephen turned back to Alex, who winced. Max looked mutinous, but maintained silence. "The mage fears that assassins are coming—very like the one Nenyane killed in the Queen's gallery. I would not have survived had Nenyane not been present."

"You didn't have your dogs."

"No—but the dogs would have died." He was certain of that. The dogs responded to Stephen's commands, and he had had no time to make them. "The mage feels that this is not our fight."

Nenyane cursed the mage. "It's our fight if you're their target."

Alex grinned. "When he says not our fight, he never means you." To Stephen he added, "Max isn't happy about it."

"Does he want to lose the dogs?"

"Oh, he'll listen—he's just not happy. No one likes to be useless."

"Tell him to try being me. I'm useless *and* I'm the reason this is happening at all."

"He says you win."

Stephen nodded. "But before we reach the border, we need to talk about the dogs."

"Why?"

"Because Max needs dogs. I know you don't, not in the same way."

Alex's black-humored grin faded. He nodded and turned back down the road, to where Max was waiting.

NENYANE'S SWORD was in her hand; Gervanno's was unsheathed a heartbeat later, if that. She turned to face the road at their back; Gervanno faced the road to Stephen's right. Meralonne came to stand by Stephen's left when Alex and Max fell back. Kallandras stood before Stephen, armed. The only person who was not was Meralonne.

"The dead are not here," Nenyane observed.

Kallandras nodded. "I will ask that you fight if you must; Stephen is your responsibility. But where he is not in danger, do not interfere."

Nenyane's eyes narrowed. "They're coming. They're like...you."

"You do not hear my former brethren. You heard the echoes of the Dark Lady's command," the bard whispered. "Our Lady. My brothers no longer hunt me; they would never attempt to kill Illaraphaniel."

"They're here for Stephen." Nenyane's words were flat, soft.

Since this was obvious, Kallandras did not reply. He turned face into the wind—his or Meralonne's, it was hard to differentiate. He then lifted head, exposing throat.

He spoke words into a terrible silence. Stephen was grateful for the silence; what he saw as he looked to the older man who stood in the folds of air felt so private the mouthed words should never be heard by any except the person for whom it was meant—and perhaps not even then.

Nenyane had never trusted Kallandras, but she had come to grudgingly accept him as an ally, a man who was willing to fight—and die—on the road they must travel.

Watch, she said. *Watch and understand*. Her blade caught light, reflecting it as something struck its flat and bounced.

Stephen did not move. Instead, he sought the eyes of his dogs. There was no scent on the air, no sudden obvious movement that caught their attention until Nenyane deflected a weapon no one present had seen. Magic?

No. She fell into a familiar silence as her sword moved again. Light glinted off blade, the sound of metal striking edge unmistakable.

The third time she deflected a projectile, she leapt forward.

Nenyane — wait!

She ignored him.

The bard asked us to refrain from combat unless we were in immediate danger.

They aimed that at you. That's pretty immediate.

They had no chance of hitting me — not while you were watching.

And he's going to know that?

Of course *he's going to know.* Stephen tried to keep frustration from his tone.

Fine. But if you're injured, it's him I'll kill.

BARD-BORN HAD meaning in the kingdoms; it had meaning in the Empire.

Kallandras had been born in neither, but all things had meaning, even in the Dominion of Annagar, where the Tors and Tyrs ruled. In the Dominion, his talent was not considered a gift; it was not considered a power. It was considered a curse, a threat.

Men made curses of such things, as if to prove their own beliefs true. He lost his family to the fear of his power, and nearly lost his life. It was no longer a life he valued, but survival had been bought at such a high price he could not simply throw it away. He had been far enough away from home, and returned from an errand, when he had heard his family's raised voices, their screams of pain, their terrible silence.

The men who had killed them had come searching for him: the demon-spawn. The cursed child. That they had not found him had been luck — but whether good or bad, he could not, at that time, say.

Those men had not found him. But another, eventually, had.

He had been picked up on the streets of the Tor Leonne, where the poor and destitute could gather in greater numbers, the city was so large. He was not branded seraf, but the pride of a free man in the Dominion did not long survive the lack of food, of family, of reliable shelter. He did not sing. He did not speak.

He could remember the despair of the child he had been, although that orphaned youth was far enough in the past despair did not cling; it was a pale, grey ghost, acclimating with the passage of time. He could no longer recall the faces of his lost family.

But he remembered the day the world had changed. He remembered the man who had found him, sitting with a bowl in his lap, gaze turned inward as if to deny the existence of the world. The old man had offered him a home—a home that struck fear in those who knew what it presaged. To Kallandras, almost starving, fear had been distant; the desire for safety, for family, for a place to belong, had been far, far stronger.

And the home he had found had been everything he had ever wanted. It had become everything. He had learned to use his weapons; he had learned to fight in the dark; he had learned the rudiments of the talent to which he'd been born. He had learned how to observe, how to listen.

He had learned the names of the men who formed the brotherhood; the men who served the Lady's shadowed face. He heard their names. He heard their voices. He heard—with an Empire standing between them—when new brothers joined the *Kovaschaii*. Those names lingered. He was certain that they, too, heard his.

It was Evayne a'Nolan who had destroyed that life. Cold, young, she had told him what their fate must be in the long war to come. He was destined to lose them. He was destined to lose everything. If he could not abandon the brotherhood, if he could not leave his brothers, they had no hope of survival.

He had surrendered almost everything in order to prevent their deaths. He had survived the shattering betrayal. Years, those he loved had hunted him at their Lady's behest. They did not hunt him now. That had been the Lady's mercy; the *Kovaschaii* did not kill except at her command.

But if they did not hunt him, they were here today. Two of the *Kovaschaii*, both younger than he. He had heard their names a handful of years ago. He had not trained with them; had not sheltered with them; had not broken bread by their sides.

And yet, even in that absence, he knew them. *Arsenio. Valerio.*

They did not hunt him; they hunted Stephen of Maubreche. Stephen's name, Stephen's image, was as clear as their own. Could he bespeak the Lady, he would have told her that Stephen's survival was vital for any hope of victory in the battles, the wars, to come.

But he understood, now, what she feared.

The *Kovaschaii* were bound to their Lady by blood oaths and unshakeable loyalty, just as Biluude had been bound to the lord she had not chosen, and would never willingly choose, to serve.

Somehow, Stephen of Maubreche had broken that binding—and not just Biluude's. He had freed all of the denizens of that land from their lord's compulsion. He might free Kallandras from his; might, likewise, free his brothers.

Stephen would not be thanked for that freedom. Kallandras, torn by it, nonetheless had no desire to abandon it: it was proof that he had once lived among his brothers. He knew he was the discordant note; he was the stain that had permanently tarnished the unity of the *Kovaschaii*. He was proof that the brotherhood was not absent betrayal or abandonment.

He would never ask for freedom from the Maubreche Hunter; he would never accept it, were it offered. He could not divorce his current pain and loss from the elements that made it so deep, so endless: he whispered names, one in particular, as he felt the air change.

Arkady.

He would never hear Arkady's voice again. Arkady would never hear his. Death was the only release from service the *Kovaschaii* knew. It was the only release Kallandras would know, foresworn and lost. He did not expect that he would pass the bridge to the Beyond for his crime; the Lady's anger was great.

But his brothers would survive; Kallandras's death would free them, at last, from the shadow of betrayal. His name would not be spoken; his presence would not be missed. But they would live. They would live.

How much had decades of his life worn away at that determination? How much had his life attenuated the longing, the love, the visceral desire to return to a place that would never be his again?

He had killed his brothers. He had danced for them, in the pattern of the five-pointed star; he had returned them to the side of the Lady they loved and served. The first time, he had been almost shattered. Now?

He could almost see the end of the road. He could almost see the path he had struggled to find and follow in his youth. It was to preserve their lives that he had started, so bitterly, so angrily, to walk it. He had known, if Evayne had not—and how could she not—that some of those brothers would die by his hand. He had survived that.

He would survive it today.

He did not speak; they did.

Valerio did. Kallandras felt his entire body stiffen at the command inherent in the younger man's words. The surprise almost killed him; it would have killed Stephen, for Valerio moved quickly, silently. It was not Kallandras he had been sent to kill, although Kallandras felt both rage and desire in the single word Valerio had uttered.

Nenyane moved before Kallandras could free himself from compulsion; Valerio's voice was powerful. The Hunters, Gervanno—all were frozen. Kallandras laid his own vocal compulsion across Valerio's, shattering it. Slow, too slow; he felt a moment of wonder, a moment of recognition, as if Valerio was a distant mirror brought suddenly close; a window into a past not taken, a past in which two terrible choices had not been offered, a past in which he had remained in his truest home.

Valerio was who he might have been, had he remained. Had he chosen to take the time remaining him with his truest companions, his brothers of the heart.

He called the wind; he called his weapons; he turned.

Valerio had not survived, would not survive, the injury Nenyane inflicted, for his younger brother's voice did not move her, did not force her into unnatural stillness; it did not reach her at all.

Kallandras's wind did not touch her; the earth did not touch her. For a moment, as she leapt, she was a singular entity, shorn of all context except one: Stephen of Mabreche, frozen by the command of Valerio before Kallandras could break it.

Nenyane could not be stopped, could not be denied, could not be killed. The Lady could not target her, could not consecrate requests for her death; he knew it. He had known it since the first time they had clashed in the Queen of Breodanir's throne room. This death, the Lady could not bless, could not consecrate; this death would be personal, should any achieve it. Something in Nenyane's nature was different, Other.

But she was Stephen's huntbrother, and he knew well the meaning and intensity of that bond. Stephen of Maubreche could be consecrated; Stephen's death could be offered to the Lady.

Valerio had not been sent to kill Nenyane; she had not been his target. But his failure to understand the Breodani bond was costly; he paid with his life. Nenyane's was the hand that ended him; in her cold fury she granted Valerio a clean death.

He knew that death must be the only outcome, but felt it as a blow, as the severing of a limb. He who had been trained to continue the fight regardless of injury could not entirely disregard the shock of the pain. The loss.

Valerio. Brother.

The Maubreche huntbrother had once aimed her sword at the bard. No hand had stayed her; not even the outrage of the Queen had had that effect. Nenyane was almost kin to the wind; she could not be commanded except at great cost. She could be cajoled — but no words, no sentiment would turn her blade if Stephen was threatened.

He freed himself from too many compulsions, too many emotions, as he turned toward the remaining brother, Arsenio. *Leave. Leave, Arsenio; it is not only me that you face.*

He did not speak the words aloud; he let the wind carry him to Arsenio, knowing that the younger man would be shattered by Valerio's death. Shattered and determined, the weight of the Lady's command now carried on his shoulders alone.

Arsenio was not interested in Kallandras or Nenyane, except as obstacles. He was aware of them because he had to survive for long enough to kill his target, to dedicate his kill to the Lady. That was now his only duty; not vengeance, not survival, but the Lady's command.

How proud Constanso would have been; how proud he must be now.

And how broken by yet another loss, yet another death, of the brothers he had so carefully gathered and trained, lost to him again.

I will dance for them, Constanso. It is the only thing left that I can offer.

He met the young man's blades with his own — the shape of the weapons among the many he had learned under the tutelage of his older brothers in the hidden labyrinth, substance of the weapons something the *Kovaschaii* had never encountered. Nenyane did not strike Arsenio; she made no attempt to insert herself into the fight.

Arsenio struggled to control his rage, control his sense of loss, but he was young. Young enough that Kallandras's presence grew weight,

substance, demanded *something* from him and of him. Had it been
Kallandras who had ended Valerio, Arsenio would have lost focus and
control.

He held it now.

Kallandras struggled in a different way, but he did not tell this
youngest of brothers to flee, to preserve his own life; here, at the end of
it, he did not wish to insult the young man.

Did not wish to kill him. Had he not surrendered the whole of his
life to preserve his brothers? Had he not abandoned all paths but the
one that led, at last, to the final war?

But some would survive. Some, if they won. Evayne a'Nolan, a
woman he had hated with what he assumed was an undying passion
and determination when he was younger than Arsenio, had used her
talent and her birthright to thread a shaking needle. It led to the end.
To death. To freedom, at last, from the terrible longing and guilt.

Before that moment, he could not allow himself to die; could not
open his arms to embrace the brother whose blades would be his death;
could not offer apologies and the broken remnants of the strongest love
to touch his life.

He could offer only death. If his talent was song, his skill was
death: his enemy's death.

The wind took the ashes of his memories of youth, of the roots of
love, of home. He had no home, no youth, and the weight of his love
was isolation and solitude.

And death, always death. He should have killed Arsenio quickly; he
had that in him. If youth honed and sharpened Arsenio's reflexes, experience sharpened Kallandras's. Kallandras, born with the gift of the
voice, Kallandras, armed with sentient weapons, Kallandras, who wore
the diamond ring crafted in a bygone age by an Artisan without
compare.

It was not hope he gave Arsenio. Arsenio would die here. But for
himself, he wanted just a moment, just two, just three, of the complicated dance between two people who had mastered their weapons, who
had been trained by the same people, in the same dark place, and who
had emerged from that darkness into a light that would guide them
while they drew breath.

He had never been gifted hatred; could not, facing the death
Arsenio desired for him, find the hatred with which Arsenio
enwrapped himself. This was what was left him: these moments of

dance that must end, the only safe expression of the desire to return to his chosen home, the pain of its loss renewed, sharpened, as if the blade that ended Arsenio's life would take some part of his, measure for measure.

He did not call wind. He did not use his bardic voice. Neither were necessary.

Arsenio stumbled, breaking the flow of the dance; Kallandras moved away, constantly in motion, as Arsenio righted himself. Once, twice, a third time.

Arsenio's rage banked; he lost sight of Stephen of Maubreche. His first mistake, but how could Kallandras judge him for it? He had wanted that; he had wanted this brother with whom he had not trained, had not broken bread, to look at him, to see him.

To see him as a lost brother.

Just that moment, that subtle shift of expression; more than that, he could never have. He wore no mask now. He wanted, as life fled, to be seen. To be truly seen.

He heard the wind howl its rage, its jealousy—for the elements had always been possessive. He was reckless; he ignored its rising voice. Ignored all the other voices that rose within him, and within Arsenio, both. His brothers. His masters. His chosen family.

His blades found Arsenio's heart. He would not let them feed. The wind almost lifted Arsenio from the earth, his knees and lower legs braced there as if to prevent his inevitable fall. He would not allow it. It was dangerous to command the wind; he would pay.

But no price the elemental air could exact could be worse than the price he had chosen, again and again, to pay. He meant to exert his will, but the wind stilled before he could. Stilled, quieted, and left Arsenio to collapse.

To collapse, the earth becoming not brace but bed. He was not foolish enough to catch Arsenio as he fell. Could not. The road he must walk could not safely be traveled were he to be injured. While life remained, Arsenio was deadly.

But he did kneel when all but a slender thread of Arsenio's life remained; it was twined around Valerio's. "**Illaraphaniel**," he said.

"Nenyane, gather the rest of the Hunters and the dogs. Gervanno, bring your dog and follow. We will continue our journey; Kallandras will meet us when he is done here." When he failed to hear the sound of motion, the mage said, "There is nothing that will threaten Kallandras here; there is nothing that could. But he requires a moment, and we will *give it to him.*"

"You are not my master," Nenyane snapped. Kallandras did not want to hear what he heard in her voice; he could not simply fail to hear it.

"Nenyane," Stephen said. Raising voice, he passed word to Alex and Max; the dogs he could command silently, and did.

Kallandras remained on his knees until all of the others, dogs or man, began to move. Only then did he allow his shoulders to slump, his arms to fall.

———

MERALONNE DID NOT SPEAK as he took the lead. Gervanno joined Meralonne; the King's Road was clear, and if the cerdan had not traveled it for long within the borders of Breodanir, he had studied Evaro's maps, and had received much counsel about his duties as a guard on that road.

That left the Hunters and their dogs, who followed at a reasonable pace, keeping steady distance from the mage. Meralonne had become uncharacteristically grim. Stephen did not care for pipe smoke, but Meralonne with pipe was far less threatening. The pipe as a symbol of the mage's mood was sorely missed.

Nenyane found this annoying, but she managed to keep that annoyance to herself. The appearance of assassins — the existence of assassins — had pushed her into dangerously quiet focus.

Stephen's thoughts annoyed her even more.

Stephen understood her respect for Meralonne, then. She did not snap at him, did not sully the mage's silence with words. Words of irritation were too petty.

The bard's choice to kill — and grieve — the fallen had evoked something in the mage, some bitter reminder of loss. Such losses were understood, and feared, by the Breodani Hunters.

Pearl, however, didn't care. Stephen had difficulty curbing her desire to scout ahead and, in the end, he allowed her to follow Gervanno; she was willing to compromise that much. She obeyed when Stephen's mood indicated genuine danger, but was sensitive enough to the shift in his mood that she knew complete obedience was not required here.

She was also the best of the scenthounds with whom he had ever worked. Some dogs were at their best with a rigid hierarchy; Pearl was almost like a cat. Her hierarchy involved Stephen and Pearl. She had no need for any other structure.

AT THE END of the fourth day, they reached the final—or first—inn near the Breodanir border. They encountered no further difficulty. Gervanno had traveled this stretch of road before, and the swordsman grew increasingly silent during their trek. This road was familiar to him; it shadowed his expression.

The inn stood perhaps a mile from the border. It had a large yard, to better accommodate merchant caravans and wagons; Evaro had chosen to stay there, grumbling about the cost, as he grumbled about all expenses. Gervanno remembered little of the inn, but the innkeeper had recognized Evaro and Sylvia—or perhaps just Sylvia, who tended to be garrulous when given any opportunity.

They had removed themselves, as a group, from the road, but not by much; the discussion involved their quarters for the evening. It was clear Meralonne wished to continue onward.

Gervanno was not in favor of it; they had perhaps an hour of walking left them, but they'd be pitching tents at the edge of sundown in forests that were not as safe as they had once been. Nenyane wished to continue. Stephen agreed with Gervanno.

Kallandras was silent, listening as the group discussed their immediate future.

Beyond the border, the road continued, less well maintained. It was the road the caravan had traveled.

What the Breodani called *turnings* should have been as frequent in the unclaimed lands that led to the Free Towns as they had become in Breodanir; many merchants would have avoided the road between the Empire and the Western Kingdoms, of which Breodanir was a small part, were it not for economic constraints. Yes, dead people could not barter or trade—but without money, they could not eat. This had made sense to Gervanno at the time, but had Evaro chosen caution, the caravan master would be alive.

He had not: *Men need to eat.*

They appear to need to eat a lot, Sylvia had snapped back. Her worry was a large flag she carried with pride. Or it had been.

"You took the merchant roads to the King's Road," Meralonne said, the statement rising slightly at the end, as if he asked a question.

"We did."

"Did you follow the road through the Free Towns?"

Gervanno nodded again. "Evaro knew there'd been trouble on the merchant roads. We traveled more slowly than he would have liked because of it. But he—as we—believed the trouble would be in line with bandits. None of us expected to face demons on that road." Or to cower in terror, desperately praying to be overlooked.

"Did you encounter difficulties on the road through the Free Towns?"

Gervanno shook his head. "Other caravans lost guards—or merchants—on those roads, but the roads themselves did not suddenly lead to different lands. Those who were lost had left the road in search of something they had seen while on the road. Evaro's guards were more disciplined."

"As was Evaro, I presume?"

Gervanno shook his head. "His wife, Sylvia."

"That is good news for us, then. But the road between the last of the Free Towns and the Essalieyan border might prove more difficult. We have magi in the Free Towns; they were sent, as I was sent to Breodanir, to evaluate the road, and the progress the wilderness made into these lands. The road leaving the Free Towns towards the Empire is not safely traveled at this time."

"We traveled it."

Meralonne nodded. "But you understand how terrain—and its ownership—can change with very little warning to those who live within its shifting borders. It is for that reason that I have urged speed. Where incidents may have occurred on your travels to Breodanir, the wilderness might have consumed large stretches of road, by now."

"What aren't you telling us?" Nenyane asked, her voice blunt enough in tone it sounded like a command.

"We will not face—or should not face—a creature the equal of the lord who attempted to break through to Bowgren, but there are many lords in the wilderness. Some lords have no desire to interact with humans in any fashion; some desire—as the lord we defeated—to hunt them.

"Old lords fall; new lords rise. Any compact between lords and land will shift, and in the most extreme of cases, those lands will not be recognizable at all."

"Which we already know." Nenyane was now almost waspish.

"Very well. The Free Towns have protection similar to, but very different from, the protections that are laid into the earth of Breodanir. I would expect those protections to afford some safety to the inhabitants of those towns. But the towns themselves are otherwise entirely mortal.

"It is through those towns that the barriers that separate the wilderness, high and low, from mortal lands, have been historically thinnest, but it is because of that weakness that the Free Towns have remained markedly unchanged."

"You think that's not going to last."

"I am of the opinion that there is genuine danger now, yes—but I am uncertain. Magics of a type unknown to almost all, even the greatest of sages, were woven into the townships. More than that, I will not say. It is not the road between the Free Towns that I fear; it is the road leading to them."

"The one we walk when we leave Breodanir?" Alex asked.

Meralonne nodded. He was never the most good-humored of men, but whatever trace of humor—bitter and somewhat black—he possessed had not returned.

Alex turned to the bard. He had recovered well from the assassin attack; Stephen would not have known anything untoward had happened, if judging only by the bard.

"I concur with Meralonne," Kallandras said. "Speed is of the essence. I do not hear the voices of the wilderness, but the wind does, and the voice it hears is fell. But Gervanno has the right of it; we do not know when we will have a chance to rest and resupply." He turned to the mage. "Let us take to the inn; we will see to our supplies before we bed down, and at dawn's light, we will cross the border."

THE CUSTOMERS in the inn's dining room were subdued. This close to the border, information and gossip traveled from beyond Breodanir and fear of the unknown, the unknowable, set people on edge. Although bandits could cause loss and death in tougher years, they were hated, not feared; guards could be hired, and Hunter Lords called for aid, when evidence of bandits could not be denied.

Bandit encounters were a despised, but rational experience. Not so the stories of the forests that had grown strange—and grew stranger—as the days passed. Whispers of Breodan's displeasure circled the dining room. Kallandras therefore set about bringing ease to the room. He ate quickly—and incredibly neatly—and then armed himself with the bard's premier weapon: his lute.

Meralonne was as quiet as the uneasy denizens of the dining hall, but he wore the robes of the Order of Knowledge, and men such as he were not casually or comfortably approached. Alex and Max were quiet, but their shifting facial expressions made clear they were having a discussion, the contents of which bred disagreement.

Nenyane, never much for being social—or eating, if it came to that—excused herself early, and after perhaps ten minutes, Gervanno rose to follow her. The sun was almost entirely gone; there would be little time for sparring in the yard, and if Nenyane was willing, the Southern cerdan did not wish to lose a minute.

"I admit," the mage said as he drew his pipe from his robes, "the addition of Gervanno has been a surprise."

"He has business that carries him South, and—because of your advice—so does Nenyane," Stephen said.

"You do not."

Stephen's smile was slender. "I do. She's going. I'll go with her."

Leaves were placed in the bowl of the pipe then lit by mage fire, small and carefully controlled. "Do you understand what she is?"

It was not the question Stephen had expected. It drew the attention of both Elseth Hunters; Alex was curious, and Max defensive. Beyond them, the strains of gentle music could be heard as the bard began to work his way through the room.

"She's my huntbrother," Stephen replied, leaning toward the Max end of the spectrum. "I don't need to more than that."

"You are not a fool, or not an obvious one," the mage countered. He paused to inhale smoke and exhale almost desultory rings with a quirk of lips and deliberate breath. "You are Stephen of Maubreche. But you are Bredan's son. I understood that you were necessary in future plans of war—but I admit that even I was surprised at the skills your birth has given you. It worked to our advantage in the battle against the lord who conspired with the dead.

"What you are is of import. You are not Ansel or Heiden; you are not Maxwell or Alex. And you are not Nenyane. Yes, she is yours. She is your huntbrother. She will not forsake you, no matter how dire the situation. I asked you the question I asked because if *huntbrother* is the title that defines her choices in life, it is not the whole of what she is." Another ring of smoke, steady enough it almost seemed solid, rose through the ring that was dispersing.

Stephen said nothing.

"You know that she must go to the South; you do not understand why. But the why will be critical."

"She wants to recover her memories," he said, grudging the words, but grudging silence more. It was petty, he knew it, but he did not want this man to think he knew Nenyane better than Stephen did.

"Yes. But recovery of memories is not a simple thing for one such as Nenyane. She must walk the tangle, Stephen. It is not a place for people such as you. Gervanno would, I am certain, follow anywhere she allowed him to follow—but the tangle will almost certainly kill him. It will, in my opinion, kill you should you attempt it."

"And not Nenyane."

"No. Not Nenyane." He placed pipe stem in mouth, corners folding around the stem as he thought. "You do not understand what the tangle is, what it was, what it might become."

"And you do. Would you walk it?"

"No, not given any other choice. It is inimical to the living, Stephen. Those who enter it in their folly seldom emerge; those that do are oft changed beyond recognition."

Alex cleared his throat. "I don't think this is a conversation for a public dining room."

"Yes, yes," the mage replied, with some irritation. "The public dining room believes we are discussing the merchant road and our concerns."

Max frowned.

"I do not wish to invite you all to my room in this place, and if I am mage-born, there is no pressing reason to do so. People cannot eavesdrop here, or rather, they can—but they will not hear what we actually say. Does that satisfy your concern?" he asked Alex.

Alex nodded, interested in the magic that had achieved this privacy. "What *is* the tangle? It's not something I've heard of before, not even in children's stories."

"And he read a *lot* of children's stories," Max added.

"That is an unfortunate question."

"Why?"

"Because the wisest and most learned man here cannot answer it," the mage replied. "The wise do not know, and the gods who might once have understood it are beyond easy reach. They do not speak of the tangle, when questioned—and those who have the ability to summon them to the Between do not ask twice.

"However, even in my youth it existed. We did not call it the tangle, then; we called it the graveyard of the gods."

"You—you want Nenyane to go to a graveyard? How is that supposed to help her?"

Meralonne considered this question better than the previous one. "How do you think gods die?"

Alex frowned. "Lack of belief?"

"So you believe that Breodan would perish if the Breodani ceased to believe in him?"

"That wouldn't happen."

"The lack of belief?"

"We saw what refusing to honor our vows as his Hunters did to Breodanir as a whole. He *is* real, and the effects of his gifts and his obligations, equally real."

"Then it is not lack of belief, but lack of adherence, that would kill your god?"

Alex shook his head. "We'd die, or most of us would, in the end. I don't think it would kill Breodan."

"Indeed. Let me ask again: how do gods die?"

Alex shrugged. "I don't know."

The mage smiled. "For the most part, they killed each other in a time before humanity's rise. Gods are wild creatures; wild, and bound to their very nature. They sought supremacy, as powers do; they claimed lands in the high wilderness, and some in the quiet of the low, but they were ever restless, ever seeking greater power, greater dominion.

"You would not recognize the whole of their many wars; would not see them as you might see the clashing of mortal armies if you are unlucky. They raised and lowered mountains, sank continents, created pockets of reality in which they might be safe from reality. They created cities of unimaginable splendor—and destroyed them in like fashion. They were larger than you can conceive, and what they touched they changed or destroyed.

"The powerful killed; the less powerful died."

"And the dead were somehow interred?"

"Another excellent question. The gods are not mortals; they are not mortal in custom. But they are living creatures, just as we, and they know rage and pain and grief; they know loss and the eternity of emptiness loss presages. No, they did not deliberately inter their dead. Let me continue with a second question: you know, or must have observed, that I can, should I desire it, summon the wild air. It is not the only such element I can bespeak, but the air is fractious in the presence of any other element.

"Fire and air clash, and if the will of their summoner is not strong, or if they too are distracted in combat with their mortal enemies, the struggle between the elements will cause far more damage to the landscape than a simple sword fight could."

Having seen Meralonne fight, the word *simple* seemed contrived.

"Tell me: how do the elements die?"

"Pardon?"

"You might, should you wish to invoke the ire of the kitchen staff, douse their cooking fires. Do you believe you have killed the fire? No, of course not. You might enter a building in a storm, one that serves as a windbreak, and wait out the storm — but do you believe the storm has died? Again, no.

"Gods are like, and unlike, the elements. The early gods — or so we were told — were much more like the elementals; primal, wild. They did not reason as we reason, if they reasoned at all, and their instinctive hatred of all others drove them to destroy what could not be destroyed, just as air and fire, water and earth, will clash when summoned.

"All of these elements exist in your world now, but not as we summon them. They are not truly alive, and they cannot, therefore, die. The wild gods were like them, but their offspring were different. Those children are what we called gods in my youth; they were fractious, and they warred, but they warred in a fashion we could recognize. Warred, hated, loved; their children, called the Firstborn by the ancient world, were like them.

"Those gods could, and did die, in a fashion. What they had learned, what they had become, was lost to the world — to the many worlds — the gods were said to occupy. But at the heart of their essence was something akin to the elements. They could not live as they had once lived; they could not die as your kin—and mine—know death.

"The gods that survived came to understand this, and in an effort to preserve their creations, they came together in an attempt to destroy those elemental remnants. It could not be done.

"What could be done, however, was to contain them, to confine them, in a fashion. They created the graveyard of the gods, and it is to that graveyard that the dead inevitably traveled. Do you understand?"

Stephen wasn't certain he did. "How could they guarantee that the remnants of the dead would travel there?"

"You will have to ask the gods," Meralonne replied, his smile slender but genuine. "It is, nonetheless, what it is. It is called the tangle, now, perhaps a gesture of respect to the dead. It moves, but moves slowly and unpredictably. I could tell your huntbrother where it might be approached from your lands; I cannot guarantee that will be true in the future. She understands this.

"She understands, as well, that this is where she must go, if she is to remember all that she was."

"I don't care if she remembers it." As Stephen spoke, he swallowed. He remembered her weeping, Nenyane who never cried, and barely acknowledged physical pain. She didn't remember anything but the terrible, profound sense of loss; how much worse would it become when she did?

"If she cannot remember who she was, or why she was, she will not be able to fulfill the purpose for which she was born. She knows, Stephen. I would counsel you against the tangle for all the reasons I have stated, but for Nenyane the tangle is safe. In the end, if you command otherwise, she will not go.

"Can you do that?"

CHAPTER THREE

"What did Meralonne talk to you guys about?" Nenyane stood by the side of Stephen's bed, hands in fists. Her own bed, perfectly made, implied the story of her sleepless, restless night. She could not sit or stand still. Were she any other person, Stephen might have been concerned for her, as they were to start their trek into an unpredictable stretch of forest that was not claimed — and therefore not protected — by Breodanir's covenants with Breodan and the ancient earth.

She was Nenyane. In their childhood, Stephen had oft wondered if Nenyane slept at all. Lack of sleep did not affect her. He'd been fool enough to try to keep up with her once, as a matter of pride: she was an unfortunate orphan who had almost lost her life, and he was the son of a Hunter Lord. Of course he could do what she did. He would prove it to her.

That had not gone well. He had thereafter accepted the truth of her claim: she did not require much sleep. Their mother had been far less accepting, and Nenyane, not prone to care about irrelevant concerns, could be far more oppositional, but she was quietly so.

Nenyane could argue with Corwin, come to blows with Robart and

Mark in their later years, and shout at the dogs in frustration. She almost never raised voice to their mother.

The room was dark; the sun had not yet risen, and no light showed through the small gaps in the room's curtain.

Stephen could, with effort, protect his thoughts and emotions from his huntbrother. It was more difficult when he was newly woken and groggy with sleep, but he made the effort. She knew. Of course she did. But he had not yet answered the mage's question.

If you command otherwise, she will not go. Can you do that?

If the mage went unanswered, it was little concern of Stephen's. No, the person to whom the question must be asked, and of whom it must be answered, was Stephen himself. Nenyane had always been possessive; it was considered normal for new huntbrothers, who had everything to lose.

Stephen had waited, with as much patience as a child could, for the edges of that desperate possessiveness to blunt. Time, familial safety, food, shelter—all of these things contributed to softening the fear from which desperation arose. It was the Hunter's duty, usually imperfectly handled, to make the huntbrother understand that when they joined the family, they became an inextricable part of it. In Nenyane's case, that was Maubreche.

But she had always been unusual; just how unusual wasn't made clear to Stephen until Robart's huntbrother was introduced to Maubreche. Although he knew his parents and Arlin considered Nenyane very strange, it hadn't mattered to Stephen.

From the moment he set eyes on his huntbrother, he knew that she was the only one for him. His huntbrother would be Nenyane, or he would have no huntbrother. Her sullen silences, her awkwardness when speaking with any person who was not Stephen, her sleeplessness, her lack of hunger—none of it mattered. He had been protective, but that was expected of a Hunter.

You're mine. I'm yours. Nothing else matters. Nenyane had said that within the first week of her tenure in Maubreche. Stephen had accepted it. If she needed to say it to believe it, to feel at home, it was fine.

It was to Stephen she had looked; it was to Stephen she always looked. Yes, they'd fought—and no doubt would argue again. They weren't perfect. But he trusted her; he had always trusted her. He had accepted her nagging, her anger, her disagreement and even her sulking. They were rooted in the place she stood: huntbrother to Stephen of Maubreche.

Ah, no. Accepted? That implied reluctance. He had been waiting for Nenyane for the whole of his life. He had been waiting for the person who would complete him, who would give him direction and meaning. He had accepted her declaration not because it was the right thing to do, but because the words were his own. They were, unuttered and silent, his truth as well.

He had been the center of her world, but that was easy for children; it was simple. What other responsibilities, what other duties, did they have? She was no longer a child; no more was he. Truthfully, he did not want Nenyane to go to the tangle. He did not want her to search for her memories. He did not want her to find the cause for her shattering grief; it had nothing to do with him. It had nothing to do with their lives.

Was he that petty, in the end? Was his half of the bond so feeble, so timid, that he wished to believe he was the only important person in her life?

That was part of his reluctance. He accepted it and despised it. Was he once again a child, with a child's longing and demands?

He knew instinctively that Meralonne was right. If he commanded Nenyane, she would obey. If he demanded she forsake the attempt to find the memories she lost—and with them, the necessary understanding of her power, her knowledge, possibly her *self*, she would obey. She would be safe from the tangle and from anything she discovered in it.

That wasn't the question the mage had asked.

It wasn't the question Stephen was attempting to answer. *Do you want her to go?* No. No, he did not. He knew nothing of either Dominion or Empire, except the dry, book-learned history of their wars. To do what she intended, she would have to cross into Imperial terrain, and from there, into the Dominion, with its different customs, its different beliefs. If he followed her—no, *when* he followed her—his golden eyes would become a stigma, a curse. In the South the golden-eyed were not suffered to live.

His dogs would be suspect. The kennels that existed for dogs such as Stephen's were not found easily in the Empire—if at all. He had money, but he wasn't certain how far it would stretch, or for how long; while Maubreche would make good on promissory notes and debt within Breodanir itself, no such courtesy or respect could be expected outside of the kingdom.

He shook his head. Even if he commanded Nenyane to abandon the tangle, he would still have to face difficulties in foreign nations. Fear of difficulty was natural, but it was — as his mother often said — a trial to be overcome. Fear could not be master of a Hunter Lord. Which Stephen was not.

If he commanded Nenyane to abandon the South, he would be commanding her to abandon herself.

No. No, he could not do it.

"Stephen? I asked you a question."

"Meralonne chose to tell us about the nature of the tangle."

Silence, beneath which lay Nenyane's sudden anger.

"There's no reason to be angry with him. The more information we have, the better our chance of survival will be."

"What, exactly, did he say?"

Stephen wished to avoid a repeat of the argument between his huntbrother and the mage. "He said that the tangle was once called the graveyard of the gods. He believes you will be safe there; he believes the rest of us will not."

"He's right," she said, her tone implying the opposite.

"I won't ask you not to go. I understand how important it is to you. Do me the grace of not demanding that I stay behind."

"The tangle isn't meant for someone like you!"

"No. Nor is it meant for Alex or Max. Perhaps, in the end, you must face what you face alone — but there's a long, long road between then and now. Or did you expect us to turn tail and go back to Maubreche and Elseth?"

"I expect you to do what you need to do to survive!"

"And I will. I am. Accept it: either we both go, or we both stay."

"You can't follow me there." Her voice was low, almost guttural.

"I can't decide what you'll do. I can only decide what I'll do." He exhaled. "We can revisit the wisdom of my choice — or yours — when we reach your destination. According to Gervanno, that'll be a long way away. We head to the Empire, now. Gervanno says we can skirt the capital, but he doesn't recommend it."

"Why? Meralonne and the bard have to go. We don't."

"Because the roads are strange leading there, and they're likely to become more dangerous when we leave. All merchants who travel from the South stop in Averalaan; it's there that Gervanno thinks he can find relevant, current information about his homeland. It's in his homeland that the tangle currently resides."

If she could have turned and walked South immediately, she would have done it, she was so restless. She couldn't. He felt her struggle to think pragmatically, waited for the grudging nod that was sure to follow. A knock interrupted them before they could descend into genuine argument.

Meralonne stood at the door; Alex and Max were behind him. Behind them was Kallandras. Only Gervanno was absent.

She glared at Meralonne, who seemed impervious to her humor, before nodding.

"How wild will the roads become?" She chose to ask the mage a question he could not pretend not to hear.

"We are about to find out. This is the border. In the wilderness, lands have lords; in the mortal world, they have rulers who are distant from, separate from, the land itself; ownership is a matter of paper, treaty, and the threat of armed conflict, but the rulers often have very little experience with or of the land itself." When Nenyane failed to acknowledge his reply, he glanced at her. "I told you speed was of the essence. Where the wilderness is unaware of the boundaries—or accepting of them—that were drawn so long ago, the roads will see little change; where the lords are more aggressive or resentful, the lands might be so different we will lose the road entirely.

"If that happens, I will guide you; if I am unable to be your guide, follow Kallandras."

Nenyane's eyes narrowed. "He's mortal."

"Yes, what of it?" Meralonne almost snorted, which surprised Stephen. "The Sen were born mortal. Mortality does not guarantee incompetence or ignorance." His tone implied that was generally the expected outcome. "He walked roads that few mortals have walked before the barriers began to crumble; he is sensitive to the shift in land because he is beloved of the wild air and he chooses to listen to what it carries in its folds.

"You do not trust him; that is fair. Lack of trust is no excuse for deliberate ignorance."

Alex cringed; Stephen froze. Max rolled his eyes. It was as if Meralonne *wanted* Nenyane to storm off in furious rage.

Pearl turned to the mage and lowered her head, which would have been fine had she not bent her forelegs; she was bristling.

Max's jaw dropped as Stephen stepped forward; he had called Pearl back, and she had failed to obey. He came to stand by her side and this time, when he said her name—loudly, clearly, and with obvious displeasure—she left off her growling to look at him. She was still prepared to leap.

"Dogs don't normally like Nenyane," Alex said.

"Pearl is not a normal dog. *Pearl.*" The dog rose, her growl banking; if looks could kill, Meralonne would be bleeding out on the spot. Stephen made no attempt to likewise restrain his huntbrother, but Pearl's almost open threat had calmed Nenyane.

Nor did he tell Alex that Pearl wasn't responding to Nenyane's anger, although she was certainly aware of it; she was responding to Stephen's.

"Illaraphaniel," Kallandras said. "Do not take offense on my behalf, who takes none. She is aware of who I am; she is aware that I am an ally. It is my nature that precludes trust."

"Perhaps. But she trusts me, and I, as you, have sworn my loyalty, pledged my obedience, to one being, and one alone. Should the White Lady command me, I would abandon her Hunter to his death; should she command me to kill him, I would kill. We are not so different."

Kallandras did not reply.

"There are things you must do. Things Stephen must do. Stephen will do what is necessary, if he but understands it. It is you who are my gravest worry."

Nenyane did what she always did when her frustration had reached dangerous levels. She went off to the yard to spar. Gervanno was no doubt waiting for her.

BY THE TIME Gervanno and Nenyane had called a halt to training, the Southerner was sweating with what had become obvious effort. Nenyane was not. They had gathered observers: the Hunters, the mage, the bard. None had attempted to interfere or otherwise join the two. Nor had Nenyane called Stephen to join her, giving Gervanno time to recover.

Gervanno had sparred with Nenyane for perhaps the last time until

they reached the townships and he knew her state of mind; she had
never troubled herself to hide it. She was the best swordsman
Gervanno had ever encountered—and young enough that she was not
yet at her zenith. Young enough, as well, to have failed to master
anything but the sword. She could not curb her impulse, her irritation,
or her worry.

It was Nenyane for whom he most feared in the Dominion.
Stephen, Alex, and even Max could be themselves, and were—but
within the confines of manners and etiquette. Nenyane breached the
boundaries of those manners. She had been raised in Maubreche, but
her adherence to the will of her lord—Lady Maubreche—was one
born of familial affection.

He knew it was Stephen's acceptance, Stephen's intervention,
Stephen's making of gentle or subtle excuse, that had created the well-
worn space she occupied. Nenyane felt that she was absolutely necessary to Stephen's survival; given the assassins, Gervanno concurred.

What she failed to see, in the older man's opinion, was how much
Stephen was necessary to hers. She considered danger to be physical
and immediate—and in that she was correct. But she could not see the
paths she had taken that would lead to that immediate mortal threat.
Perhaps Gervanno was overly sensitive; the mores and manners of the
South were not the manners of the North or the West. But it was to the
South she intended to go.

Could she cross forested lands on her own to reach the Dominion,
he thought she would have little difficulty; she could not. She would
have to take the mountain pass from the Empire, and as she crossed
over into the Dominion, she was certain to attract attention.

He had thoughts about how to best protect her from that unwanted
attention, but was almost certain she would not accept it. The next best
option was also one that would ruffle feathers, and he set it aside; he
found it difficult to be aspirant student to a brilliant master at the same
time as being a would-be guardian or teacher.

He turned to Stephen.

Stephen nodded, and Gervanno faced the road that had brought
him to Breodanir the first time. All that remained of the caravan were a
sword and a handful of gems that had not been melted by the breath of
flying creatures. Silvo's sword. A young Southerner from a poor but
free family, who had looked up to Gervanno, because Gervanno had
taken part in the war in Averda—and survived it.

He had sparred with the boy who was barely man; had instructed Silvo in a far more rudimentary fashion than Nenyane instructed him. *I could not save you.* Gervanno thought it, and accepted it, for perhaps the first time. *But I will see you home.*

Leial padded toward him and stopped on his foot, literally. "Are you ready?" he asked his dog.

Leial barked, as if he understood—and he probably did. Gervanno had tried to find a home for Leial at the inn. Leial, suspicious, was snappish and fretful, his barking higher and whiny. In the end, Gervanno had not tried his hardest. He had met Leial on the edge of the wilderness, and the dog had followed him into its heart. He did not know where the road would now lead them, but he did not truly wish to entrust the dog to strangers, who might take his coin and discard the animal once Gervanno was gone.

He might have asked Heiden to take care of Leial, but Heiden and Ansel were Hunters, and the Bowgren kennels meant for hunting dogs; Leial was two-thirds of the size of the smallest of the Bowgren alaunts, and could not be used as a working dog, which the Breodani valued.

Stephen's dogs accepted Leial, but not as part of their pack. Still, Leial avoided them where possible, and they avoided Leial. Perhaps that would change as they traveled, perhaps not.

"Come on, Leial." He began to walk down the road, taking the lead while, at his back, hostility and resentment had a chance to cool.

The stone of the King's Road gave way almost immediately to the packed dirt more common in the Dominion, but the ground was dry, and easily passible for foot traffic. Flattened weeds and wild grass implied the passage of wagons or caravans in the recent past, but the foliage seemed normal for the region.

He was not surprised when he was joined by Kallandras, the Northern bard who had, in Gervanno's opinion, deep roots in the South. Kallandras could be a man of many, many words, but words were his tools. Left alone, he seldom used them. Nor did Gervanno attempt to start conversation until the wind changed, the breeze shifting direction.

He looked in the direction from which the breeze now blew.

"Yes," the bard said. "The wind has changed." The bard continued forward. Gervanno's gaze swept the roadside. The composition of the trees had not changed; if this was a turning, the shift had taken place beyond the road. He assumed something had changed beyond their immediate vision; the air felt warmer. Kallandras increased their pace. If there had been a change in the landscape beyond the road, it was best to avoid it; it was the turnings on the roads that presented the greatest difficulty for those who traveled.

What would take three days' travel by caravan should need only two solid days, as they were without wagons and the horses that pulled them, but the dogs would need to be fed, just as the horses in Evaro's caravan had. The Hunters had also acquired a mule as a pack animal at the inn, after much discussion; while the Hunters could carry their own food and supplies, they were also responsible for eight dogs. Gervanno could carry Leial's necessities, but Leial required less than half the food the larger dogs did. Leial believed he required far more, but that seemed part of the natural state of being for dogs.

Gervanno thought they could reach Hansleigh, the first of the Free Towns as they traveled east, by the end of the second day, unless the roads turned strange around their passage. Two normal days of caravan travel separated the townships, but the Southern cerdan doubted that normal travel—or planned travel times—would be reliable. The roads between the towns had been safe, when he had traveled toward Breodanir. It had been the roads between the Empire and the first of the towns which had added days to the caravan's route.

MERALONNE ELECTED to push for the two-day arrival time. Gervanno's opinion was asked and offered: he wished to take three. Given the unpredictability of a landscape that could transform without warning, he saw risk in pushing to near exhaustion.

"I have lost one group of friends," he said to the mage when the mage remained unmoved. Gervanno could not unclench his jaw; his words were forced through it. "We have already encountered demons in our travels; we must assume that, as we approach the Empire, we will encounter more. We cannot afford to be in rough condition should they attack again." It was a risk; he knew it. Stephen's was the voice of command here, and Stephen had not asked him to do more than share his opinion; he had certainly not asked him to argue with the mage.

"Your friends were, no doubt, worthy people, but they were not accompanied by me," the mage replied, eyes narrowed. "You have seen

me fight. You have seen me battle the demons you fear. Think you that
something so trivial could kill when *I* am by your side?"

Gervanno did not back down. He would remember that later—that
and Leial, who had come to stand by his side, head lowered, lips raised
above his teeth as he faced the Northern Widan. "We are not what you
are. We will never be what you are. And you are a single man; you
cannot be in all places at all times. What is trivial to you is death to us."

"Follow my orders, and you will be safe."

"Illaraphaniel."

Both men turned to the speaker: Nenyane of Maubreche. Neither
spoke. She didn't make space for any words but her own. "I told you.
Gervanno is mine. It is not your orders he must obey, but mine."

"Stephen's, surely?"

"When it comes to combat, I speak for Stephen. We are one."

Meralonne then turned to Stephen. "What, then, is your will? I
would not press you, but we have no time, Stephen; can you not feel it?
Did Bredan not make this clear?"

Stephen did not answer; Nenyane did, her voice a snap of sound,
sharp as blade. "We will take three days. Gervanno has walked this
road before; he is mortal, and his understanding of mortal limits is far,
far greater than your own. Stephen is mortal; Alex and Max, mortal as
well."

The mage turned then to the bard. "Your opinion?"

"It is to guard Stephen of Maubreche that I—that we are all—here.
I will accede to whatever he deems wise in this case. But Meralonne, I
hear it, too. The wind whispers its warning. We cannot exhaust the
Hunters enough that their instincts are dulled. Gervanno is correct: in
such a circumstance, everything we are trying to build could be lost to
us in a moment."

Nenyane met the mage's gaze; both narrowed their eyes, but they
no longer had need of words.

19TH DAY OF WITTAN, 429 A.A. THE MERCHANT ROAD

Stephen found the dogs more difficult to handle at the end of the
second day on the road. Travel itself had not been an issue; finding a
place where they might camp in relative safety or comfort was. On the

first day of their trek, the campsite at which Gervanno's caravan had stopped was nowhere in evidence. Gervanno was competent at reading and understanding the maps used by merchants to navigate the stretches of forested land; no one doubted that his memory of the camping grounds was true. Everyone accepted that it was no longer relevant.

Meralonne had spoken little for the two days they had traveled; he was irritable, but he had never been the most social of men. Kallandras became more social as Meralonne became less so, as if sociability between these two men — who were not related in any fashion Stephen could see — must always be at a certain level.

But the bard often played his lute in the lulls between travel.

Meralonne found the first camping site; Meralonne found the second. The path chosen deviated from Evaro's travel route; no one thought it wise to attempt to pitch their small camp in the same geographical location that the Southern caravan had. If the cleared grounds Evaro had used on the road were no longer present, no one thought it wise to trust what had grown up in their place.

Meralonne had found smaller clearings that might accommodate them. Stephen suspected the mage had cleared them himself.

"He did. These are not Breodani lands; our own sense of what is, and is not, foreign is of little use here. But he is adept at finding quiet dells, places in which he does not hear the name of anyone spoken by earth or wind. I think you could do it," Nenyane added, voice uncharacteristically soft, "but not as quickly, and not without danger."

"Danger?"

"If you listen for the wilderness, the wilderness will listen for you. If you are heard, they will come."

"They?" It was Alex who asked.

Nenyane shook her head. "I don't know. Demons have hunted Stephen before, but the wilderness doesn't easily accept their passage; the lord of the lands that harbor them must agree to do so. The lord we defeated in Bowgren wasn't demonic. She wasn't dead. But she would have killed Stephen eventually; she would have killed all of Bowgren.

"Demons have been the enemies that figure largest in our stories, our warnings — but that wasn't always the case. Almost any denizen of the wilderness of any note could destroy whole towns and villages without pause for breath. Wanton destruction wasn't rare; many of those who remained in the wilderness were the scions of gods, and gods could refashion whole countries in their wars for primacy.

"Follow the mage, make sure the dogs stay within the perimeters Meralonne has marked. Tomorrow we should see Hansleigh, if Gervanno's estimates were right." She had no doubt they were.

IT WAS STEPHEN WHO HESITATED; Alex, Max, Kallandras, and even Nenyane entered the small clearing Meralonne had either found or created without pause. Gervanno was highly alert, but had been so since they'd crossed the Breodanir border; his watchful manner had become so normal, it was barely noticed.

But, as Stephen stopped moving, Leial turned to Gervanno. Gervanno instantly turned back; Nenyane, in the process of setting her pack down, turned as well.

"What is it?" she asked.

Alex and Max turned at the sound of her voice.

"Illaraphaniel," Nenyane said.

"There is no safe place here," the mage replied. "I have been forced to claim this patch of ground. The wilderness has not taken the road, for reasons I do not fully understand, but everything around that road is beginning to revert." There was a hint of accusation in his tone.

"You've been forced to claim land?" Nenyane looked shocked or outraged; with Stephen's huntbrother, it was often difficult to separate the two.

The mage nodded. "It is a tiny area, and unlikely to be noticed by any who do not cross it; the wilderness here is otherwise unclaimed, or I would not have taken the risk. We will be safer here than we would in any other place, and I count Hansleigh among them." He then turned to Stephen. "Does it seem unsafe, to you?"

It did. Stephen couldn't explain why, and didn't try.

Kallandras said, "It is Meralonne's name the wind carries, but he is beloved of the wild air; I would not have noticed the difference."

Nenyane said, "It's not just the wind. The earth also whispers his name, but it's dreaming; it isn't fully wakened." She exhaled and turned to Stephen. "He's right," she said, the two words grudging. "We can stay here in safety for the evening. Tomorrow we should reach Hansleigh."

Stephen exhaled. Nenyane felt no fear, no hesitation. She trusted the mage, and respected him enough to argue with him. He stepped foot into the clearing, understanding now why it felt so strange. He was willing to accept what Nenyane accepted. When it came to the turnings and the creatures that sometimes arose from them, he had always trusted her instincts, privileging them over his own.

MERALONNE TOOK GUARD DUTY; Gervanno had begun to arrange a guard roster, but the mage declared it unnecessary. "I do not require sleep." His tone was curt. "You do. Sleep now; I will keep watch. No other guard is necessary." Or welcome, his tone implied.

This time, Gervanno did not choose to argue, although he glanced at Stephen. When Stephen nodded, he shrugged and accepted the mage's recommendation. The dogs were fed, Pearl was brushed, and the Hunters camped down before the sun had fully set.

As Stephen closed his eyes, he realized that the sun had still not set; he could see its colors through the inexpertly tied flaps of his small tent. He wondered, as he drifted, if the sun would set at all, or if the mage would decide against it. The small clearing—made at his command—was Meralonne's, in the fashion that the golden field that had belonged to the large, friendly man who lived in a small cabin belonged to him. That field had been entirely surrounded by the lands of Bowgren's enemy, but had never fallen to her. There, the sun reigned; beyond the field it was endless night, the two natural moons joined by a third.

He was in Meralonne's hands in this small tent; should the mage decide, on a whim, to kill them all, he could.

He could do it anyway, Nenyane snapped, annoyed.

He would have to kill you first, Stephen snapped back.

She had no answer to that. He felt her ambivalence; she wasn't certain Meralonne could kill her, but she wasn't certain she could kill him either. She considered them almost evenly matched.

Only if he wields sword, Stephen pointed out.

If he doesn't, he can't kill me. There was a casual certainty in her words; she believed them, but felt they were irrelevant. *And this is pointless. Go to sleep.* When Stephen failed to instantly start snoring, she added, *He will not harm you. You, of all people present, he needs.*

That was part of the problem. *To do what? What does he need me for?*

She didn't answer; she didn't know. He knew he shouldn't have asked, but he was on edge himself. Perhaps he had been at home in Breodanir because the earth was Breodanir's, the echo of its voice so faint, he had not heard it before he had reached for it in battle. Such subtle certainty did not exist here. It had not existed in the territory claimed by Bowgren's enemy.

Oh.

That was the problem. That was what was wrong. To Stephen, the *land* felt wrong; it felt very much like the land in the wilderness that had struggled to break into Bowgren. It was not his land, was not land that the Hunters had protected since the dawn of Breodanir. It was other; it felt strange.

Yes, Nenyane said, irritation leaching out of her voice. *Meralonne has never claimed land, to my knowledge. That he does so now is significant.*

It's dangerous.

It is, if his enemies are looking for him. But the demons won't and can't be; the dead won't dare to touch what he has claimed. She exhaled. *What's done is done. Let's take advantage of it to get what rest we can. We don't know that Hansleigh will be safe; we don't even know if it will still be there when we arrive. Gervanno is sleeping, now. So is Max. Alex is fretting.*

How do you know?

Their breathing, she replied. Her own was now calm. "Sleep, Stephen." She then said a word she almost never used. "Please."

Unfair, he told her, his internal voice a grumble.

I know. But you need to stop worrying and sleep.

He tried. It was hard to let go of his worry, because he couldn't explain his reticence; he couldn't explain his discomfort. How could he, when he didn't understand it himself?

IN THE BLESSED silence of the sleeping and the almost asleep, Meralonne drew his pipe from the folds of his robe. He would have to replenish his tobacco supply; he had not thought, when he left Averalaan, that he would have much need for it. Quiet moments such as these were unexpected. Wind tugged his hair, playfully, a demand inherent in that play; he whispered a benison, laced with affection and admiration both.

He had not thought to claim so much as a yard of territory in the wilderness, but he had sensed what Nenyane did not sense.

No, that was inaccurate; he understood what he sensed. Nenyane did not. She did not, and could not, hold her memories—not of herself, and not of her past. The ancient world was waking, slowly but certainly; those memories could not lie fallow if she were to do what must be done.

She intended to find the tangle; she intended to traverse it. He had advised her to leave Stephen behind—but he had never expected she would acquiesce, because Stephen would not. The boy's measure, he felt he understood. He could not say what would transpire in the tangle, but she had chosen Stephen; Stephen must, in the end, be present.

He lined the bowl of his pipe as he considered their immediate future. Hansleigh would be in reach by tomorrow evening; perhaps by late afternoon, depending on the shifting terrain.

"It has been many years since I have seen your pipe," a familiar voice said. He stiffened; he had felt her presence only when she broke the silence with words.

He turned to her, pipe unlit. "Evayne."

"Meralonne. Illaraphaniel." She was not young, tonight; nor was she at the zenith of her power. "I have come to offer warning, if you will accept it."

"Of course you have. Does it involve our enemy in the North?"

"No, not yet. I wish to inform you that Caralonne shelters within the heart of the Sen's domain; by his side is Shianne."

He considered setting his pipe aside, but settled on leaving it unlit.

"It is they, not you, who must travel to the South. Bring the Breodani to the edge of the Sen's lands; she will send a guide to lead them to the city itself."

"We had not intended to approach her lands in the wilderness."

"No. But a poison is seeping into the Free Towns, and you may find it necessary to leave the mortal road. You are aware—I am told—that the Free Towns have never been entirely cut off from the wilderness; they are not Cities of Man, but they will persist for some time. Passage between the towns will continue—but passage beyond them, in either direction, will come to a close. Do not take the road out of Evanston; it will not be safe."

"Is it safe now?"

"Yes. But you will not reach Evanston in one day." She glanced at her hands. "Kallandras will travel with the Hunters for some time. If the bardmaster attempts to send him north, he must refuse."

"And you did not wish to tell him this yourself."

"He is unsettled by my presence; there is much he does not forgive." She was younger this eve than Meralonne had first assumed.

"I will tell him."

She nodded, and then lifted her chin. "Do not interfere with the Hunter and his huntbrother."

He stiffened, his eyes narrowing; the wind was displeased with the visitor, echoing his response. He reined it in with difficulty.

"We face the same war." Her voice was cool; her robes rustled and moved at her feet, and the shadows they cast were not cast by the sun's light. "The same enemy. Our goal, until the moment he falls, is the same. You understand what Nenyane can be, but you do not understand how very broken she is. Leave them be, if you can find it in yourself to do so."

"If I do not?"

"It will cause damage. The Oracle was not specific about the possible consequences. She bid me offer two warnings. That is the first."

"And the second?"

"Nenyane's brother will seek her."

Only by force of will did the mage not crush his pipe. He made no reply. Aware of his mood, his former student offered him a nod. She was not comfortable in his presence; when she was older, discomfort had become irrelevant. She took one step forward and vanished.

He glared at the pipe, torn between wasting the leaves and tossing it aside. He compromised; he set it aside, asking the wind to hold it until he was done his work. Were it not for the presence of mortals, he would never have cast the spells he now cast: Summer magic at its height seeped into the ground.

He would have preferred to destroy the *Kialli* by his own hand; there was little risk for him in that. But the mortals were fragile, and this was not yet their time to stand and fight.

Only when the Summer sanctification of the ground was complete did he lift his pipe from the miraculously gentled folds of breeze.

HE DID NOT ASSUME that all of the Breodani would survive. This was not their war. On a field comprised of gods, the Firstborn, and the most powerful denizens of the wilderness, what place was there for mortals? What could they contribute to a war that echoed the past so strongly?

With the exception of Stephen of Maubreche, there was no place for them on that battlefield, that echo of power and fury from which Meralonne APhaniel had been born, and to which his beloved kin had surrendered their lives. No, they had not died—not then. But they had disgraced the White Lady, and in the end, had returned to her, as all dead must.

No place for mortals? He inhaled, and exhaled rings in quick succession. No place?

Jewel ATerafin existed.

She was mortal. She was Sen. In her city, he almost felt young again, infused with awe and wonder. With something like hope that redemption would not remain forever beyond his grasp. It was for that sliver of hope that he had traveled.

He understood that Stephen of Maubreche was an oathbinder. Even in the time when men flourished only in their cities, oathbinders were exceedingly rare, but necessary—how else were alliances between the powerful to be sanctified, and therefore trusted? Binding oaths did not care about the relative levels of power between the two who swore them; did not care that one might be god and one merely mortal, a bare step above an animal in lifespan and impulse.

In this war against the Lord of the Hells, powers would meet, powers would clash; it was the oathbinding that would settle their conflict and prove their determination, forcing them to divulge truth of purpose and commitment.

An oathbinder would make the gathering of martial forces and allies much cleaner, much more transparent. Therefore, Stephen of Maubreche was necessary. Meralonne's sources, some greatly resented, had made this clear. Mortals had lived without oathbinders for so long they no longer remembered them. Meralonne did.

He had come to Breodanir to secure Stephen of Maubreche. To preserve his life. No other oathbinders had survived their childhoods, and if a few existed, they were far too young to be of use.

What he had not expected was Nenyane.

Nenyane's presence as Stephen's huntbrother changed everything.

Almost, he had not recognized her. How could he? She was in no way what she had once been. Yet if he had not immediately recognized her, something in her very essence had drawn, and held, the entirety of his attention. Some hint of her essential self could be found in the silver of her eyes, especially when they narrowed.

He had seldom wondered what had happened to her at the end of a battle in which he and his brothers had nominally survived, and Moorelas had perished. His thoughts had not been turned in her direction; he had assumed that the White Lady would take her, and guard her, until the moment a second opportunity for her use presented itself.

She had not. Clearly, she had not. Nenyane of Maubreche was no part of the White Lady's court. And Meralonne, exiled from that moment, had had no way of investigating, no way of confirming. No way of asking the White Lady what had become of Nenyane.

He had understood what Stephen was to Nenyane in that moment of realization, and as all plans must in the face of unforeseen information, his became far more flexible. It was not, now, as oathbinder that Stephen of Maubreche had value, or not only because of his divine parent. Stephen had made clear that he would not consecrate binding oaths.

Divine parents drove their children in subtle, indirect ways. Stephen would not break any vow he chose to make; broken vows would anger him. But he would make no effort to ensure the consequences of broken vows.

Nenyane accepted this; of course she did. She would launch herself —with sword—at any who attempted to use Stephen's birthright, at any who attempted to coerce him to use it. No warning had been given Meralonne.

But perhaps Evayne, or the version of Evayne that had visited him, had been too young; perhaps Nenyane had not yet come to her in need of salvation and succor.

He wanted to know what Stephen saw in his huntbrother. He wanted to know what Nenyane saw in her Hunter. He wanted to assess the way they worked together.

He had no doubt now that Nenyane had made her choice.

He had grave doubts that that choice was correct. Stephen was not Morel of Aston; there was almost nothing, to Meralonne's eye, that overlapped with the hero of so many bardic lays and stories. He was not at all certain that Stephen could take up the burden that he *must* be able to carry in the end.

And he knew Nenyane did not understand the whole of it. She was broken, shattered, her memory no longer under her own control. She could not be trusted to make a choice in her current state—and yet, she had. He had hoped that the bond between Hunter and huntbrother was the normal Breodani bond. Surely such bonds could be broken?

The Breodani had been much studied over the years within a small branch of the Order of Knowledge; their god had not been considered a true god, but the gifts bestowed on the Hunter Lords were genuine.

He now understood that he did not understand that bond.

His service to the White Lady had been absolute.

His interactions with his lost brothers had not. There was, in the Hunter and huntbrother interaction, the attachment he had felt to the three brothers that had been lost forever on the day they had defied the White Lady's command. But there were differences he had not clearly recognized, perhaps because all thought of those brothers was a torment to which he did not often choose to return.

He had loved them because they were his brothers—but they were the scions of the White Lady, her chosen princes. As he had been. They were not the same men, but the differences were minute, and not easily discerned by mortals or other creatures birthed in the wilderness at the height of the age of gods. And yet, the three had chosen disobedience; only he had not.

He could not and did not judge them, even now. He could not, even if they had earned the ire and the eternal disdain and disappointment of the White Lady. They had come late to the terrible understanding of what the White Lady would lose in the completion of that war, and they *could not* be the instrument of that terrible damage.

The loss had occurred, regardless.

Yet the attachment between Morel and what the gods had, in concert, created had been stronger, tighter, and far more intimate than the bond between Meralonne and the White Lady. And if that sword had had a name, it was not a name Meralonne or the princes of the White Lady's court knew.

It was certainly not Nenyane.

To Alex and Max, the relationship that existed between Stephen and Nenyane seemed normal, natural; even predictable. It was an echo of their own bond. No, he thought, it wasn't an echo. They were different mortals but they lived within the confines of the same truth, the same state of being.

This was truth, and it was wrong; what was needed now was not the everyday interaction of Breodani children. He accorded Stephen respect because the Maubreche Hunter was the child of Bredan, Lord of Covenants, upon whose power the safety of their dim mortal world had depended. But the god-born were mortal, their lives shortened, not lengthened, by the burning blood of one of their parents.

Had he any say at all in Nenyane's choice, he would not have chosen Stephen of Maubreche.

But he would never have chosen Morel, either.

Ah, he remembered.

BENEATH THE CHILL, pale sky of enduring Winter, the White Lady stood above a cradle of molten earth and stone. A wild forge. She had waited decades to approach it; there had been little choice. The grave-yard of gods had paused here in its unpredictable passage through the wilderness, lingering for decades and denying access to those who had need of the forge's elemental power.

It had finally moved on. The forge had been damaged by its passage, but not destroyed.

The forge will fire, and it will temper. But it cannot be used in the same fashion again, for the tangle will return to it and essential elements of its nature will finally be absorbed, returning at last to the graveyard, which contains what remains of its creator. You will accomplish your task when the tangle moves, or you will never accomplish it at all.

So had the Oracle spoken to the White Lady and the Artisan; so had the Oracle spoken to the remaining gods.

And perhaps that was fitting, for the god who had birthed this forge had perished at the hands of other gods, who feared the power of what was tempered and blessed there. They feared with reason. Perhaps the remnants of that ancient smithy could do the necessary work because it bore animus towards the gods themselves; he had not asked.

The White Lady had waited. The wait was done.

The gods then came, a concert of power, suffocating in the multitude of their gathered presences, even to Illaraphaniel.

Mist rose from the graven earth; the ground retained heat. Here, it would; he sensed that. But he did not hear it; the wild earth in this place had fallen silent. He heard, instead, the song of stone and the whisper of flame. He saw the delicate white blossoms of flowers that he had never before seen, for the graveyard often left some hint of its passage in its moving wake, some echo of a power that had once had form and volition when contained within the shape of a living god.

The air was cold in the forest beyond this place, and snow, a blanket over the living and dead. But above the forge, the breath of spring was in the air, the hint and promise of newness, of life.

The gods worked; the Artisan touched every part of the power they offered him, focused now on carefully fusing it to create what would become his greatest work. They did not disturb him, did not question him; mortal Artisans were prized because their greatest work came from a place that rationality did not entirely touch.

He labored for hours, asking for items he needed without apparently being aware that the Firstborn and the gods were not meant to fetch and carry. As if the respect due power was absent in this small space, the gods did as bid. It was perhaps the most shocking element of this experience.

He could remember their faces; their names were multiple and seldom used. Many of the gods were absent, and in the intervening years, many more would join them in death. They were not his gods. She was.

The whole of her endless anger, her perfect concentration, her determination, rested in the hands of an Artisan. It was almost an act of folly. But she was the White Lady, and where she led, he would follow. The hours passed; the day passed; a second day passed. The mortal did not stop; it seemed to Illaraphaniel, watching him, that he *could not* stop, driven by the weight of a talent gifted only, inexplicably, to mortals.

A third day passed as he worked in a frenzy, his hands steady, his breath ragged, all other breath held; only the sounds of his muttering, for he spoke as he worked, could be heard. Even the air was still. At the end of that day, he was done; he collapsed, and the White Lady's people gently removed him from the environs, carrying him as if he were a beloved servant of their lord.

He immediately became irrelevant; in his absence, he no longer had a use. His work was done. All could see the proof of that; could feel it, as if were lightning waiting for the perfect moment to strike.

"IT IS DONE," the White Lady said to her kin, for the gods had returned to their own lands, their own conflicts.

No one dared to break the flow of her words, for they desired much the sound of her voice, the movement of her lips, the slight change in the shape of eyes bright and shining silver, the Winter metal. It had been long since those who might interrupt or question had graced her presence; he remembered them, then.

"What the gods have given has been long in the gathering; it encompasses all of the seasons of the wilderness. All of their anger, their despair, their love and their hope were offered. And ours, the Firstborn, as well. What we crafted, what we forged, is here.

"It is a weapon that can kill a god, and it will be raised against the god I will not grant the respect of a name. His hand alone, of the living gods, has been absent in the whole of this endeavor.

"And now, we will wait. Word will pass to the peoples of the nations that have survived the war that the unnamed god has carried across the whole of the world, open and hidden. They will come. They will come," she said, moving at last, her feet tracing steps of light in the air, "and they will see."

They would see what her people now saw: a sword.

IN THE WINTER of that ancient world, gods died. He could not recall how many, because in that world gods were plentiful, and even he had not encountered all of them. He heard their names in the wilderness when they passed; the wilderness mourned. He himself did not. The possibilities inherent in the wilderness were boundless, and the miracles and wonder without number.

He had seen swords before.

No sword he had ever seen was like this one; he knew it instantly, although nothing about its physical shape or appearance was remarkable. It stood, unsheathed, point to blackened earth, a blade of steel beneath a simple, unadorned hilt. But he could hear it; it seemed to hum as it stood.

"Do not touch it," the White Lady said. "Do not approach it until and unless approach is desired."

"Will you choose who among us might be worthy of wielding this blade?" It was Narianatalle who spoke; few else would have dared, although the question occupied them all.

Her smile was Winter. "If worth was the sole defining trait required, think you that I would not wield it myself?" Her voice was bright and sharp, like the blade; it cut them all, swept across them, forcing each and every man standing to his knees.

"No, then." They could not hear her smile. But they could feel it, the hint of warmth at the heart of ice.

"What power does such a blade lend its wielder?"

"I know not. I know only that this blade can kill gods. It is not a god." Gods could kill gods; gods and the scions of gods—the Firstborn. But even the offspring of the Firstborn—the Arianni—could not. "Some choice was given it; it will choose its wielder. We will accept that choice, no matter how wrong it might seem, how weak, to us. That was the agreement reached before the blade was forged.

"We will not see its like again. The gods rest now. We will guard the blade until the moment its wielder is found."

They did not ask how long that might be, although they did wonder.

And perhaps they resented the sword itself, for if the sword had choice, there was only one wielder worthy of a blade forged by the gods—by all the remaining gods—and she would not touch it or wield it because the sword had not somehow consented.

THE FIRST DEATH came a decade later, perhaps two.

The first hand that attempted to take the sword by the hilt was Arianni; not a prince of the Hidden Court, but a hunter come new to the hunt. What drew him to the blade, they did not know and could not later say; perhaps a moment of greed, a moment of desire—for if his hand could wield that blade, he might be considered instantly worthy, instantly special to the White Lady.

He did not survive.

He could not release what his hand had gripped—although he greatly desired to do so almost the moment his palm curled, his fingers closing around the hilt.

It took him three days to die. On the first, the young Sarrantil attempted to cut off his arm, but the White Lady forbade it. She watched, dry eyed; she listened to the cries and the pleas of the man who had disobeyed her. No other eyes were dry, when the end mercifully arrived.

Death was the only mercy offered.

TWO DECADES PASSED, the seasons turned, before one of the hunters was foolish enough to try again.

The results did not change.

Nor did the sword. It stood, as it had stood when the White Lady had first revealed it; nothing moved it, not even death.

AT THE END of the third decade, the third death. But this death was not the death of the callow and youthful. Andarion, of the court, beloved by all, caught one of the younger Arianni, brash with youth and its optimism, in an attempt. "I will have no brothers if this continues," he said. "And I have loved you all—just as the White Lady has loved you. How could I not? We are made of the same fabric, we are willed into being by the same intent.

"She has given her commands. I have followed them faithfully. Have I not?"

Silence; it was the silence of assent, but beneath it, a growing unease.

"Andarion," Illaraphaniel had been moved to say, "Do not do this."

"If not me, then who? Understand," he said, to the Arianni, "that I do not do this from a desire to wield the blade itself. The blade is not for me. It is not for us. If the White Lady herself will not touch it, who among us could imagine that we would be better suited to it?

"She was there at its forging. What she gave, I do not know—but we have seen it. We have all seen it. And perhaps it is because she gave of herself so freely, in the name of this war we *must* win, that we are drawn to the blade.

"But it will not accept us. Need you proof? I will provide it."

"Andarion."

Andarion shook his head, and the wind caught his hair in ferocious denial. Illaraphaniel had not summoned the wind, had not spoken any of its names, but it came to him, pulled at Andarion, tried to lift his feet from the earth on which he stood.

And on that day, the earth came—but it did not come in hatred or enmity, and this was almost unheard of it. Where the wind sought to lift Andarion, the earth sought to anchor him, to encase his feet in stone braces that would prevent him from moving.

They knew.

How could they not? The forest that had begun to reassert itself in the past four decades was crying and weeping and pleading. Andarion heard them all. He heard them, as he heard his brothers.

"This is the last gift I can offer you, whom I have loved all my life — or all of yours. I cannot stand and watch as you try, again and again, in what must end in painful death. Think you that you have greater worth than me?"

The wind howled. The earth rumbled.

The Arianni bowed heads; there was not one among them, save perhaps Narianatalle, who could answer that question with anything but *no*. And no was said, no was shouted, no was whispered.

"Then let me be the last test. Let me show you what you must, and should already, have known."

And the White Lady did not come. Her word, and hers alone, would have prevented what followed. She must have known. Perhaps she did know. But she could not give what Andarion now gave, for if she perished here, the Arianni would perish in the wake of her passing.

He turned, fighting wind and earth, and they could not approach him, did not dare, for he was Andarion. *Andarion.* The equal of Darranatos, whose name was not and could not be spoken.

Andarion took the sword. Andarion *moved* the sword.

"I ask this of you, in return for this gift: do not attempt to take or wield what is forbidden us. Do not spend your lives in anything but the defense of the White Lady. By my death, I seal the oath that you must offer."

Three days.

Three days of endless pain and loss.

And on the last day, silence, blessed and terrible. Andarion was gone.

Only at the end of that day did she come. Before his terrible existence shuddered to a pitiful end, she reached his side. She wrapped her arms around him; she kissed his brow; she whispered words that none of the Arianni could hear, although they could see her lips move. But she did not save him.

Could not save him.

And when she rose, her silver eyes were glittering. "I will kill any of my kin who approach this sword. I will kill you in Andarion's name, and in gratitude for the sacrifice he has chosen to make. I will not exile you, in respect for Andarion, but you will die as if you were, and have never been, my kin."

None of her people ever attempted to touch the blade again.

IF THE BLADE was not meant for the people of the White Lady, the knowledge of its existence spread, but spread slowly. The sword could not be moved, and the White Lady did not venture far from it; there was no need.

The *Allasiani* came.

What the living could not do, the dead could not do—but it was tried, and tried again. As if they had never deserted the White Lady, they too lingered for three long days. Their pain should not have affected the Arianni, but it did, for these had, until their betrayal, been brothers-in-arms.

Kin.

Some died in their attempt to reach the sword; it was a more merciful death. But they could not take what had been wrought.

IN THE NEXT FOUR DECADES, others came. Winged predators. Beings of fire and light. The spirits of the great trees, the first to wake.

None could take the sword. And the god whose destruction was the reason for the sword's existence continued to gain land and power as he walked the wilderness.

From a remove of centuries, in the wake of loss, Meralonne could almost see his brothers. They stood as one: Illaraphaniel, Narianatalle, Fanniallarant, Taressarian. What the White Lady wanted, they did not question. Not then. They understood her rage, the deep chasm of her growing hatred; the *Allasiani* had once been hers. They were *of* her, as the Arianni were of her, and yet they had abandoned her. No one of the Arianni could understand why.

But it was clear to him then, clear now: Allasakar, the god whose name they did not speak, could not create the Arianni. He could not come close. His work, flawed, did not long survive or endure—only the death he caused did. His children were not wholly and entirely his own.

Calliastra, the tragic and broken primal daughter, had been given form and shape not by that god but by the other parent—to her great despair. Her life was pain and loss and hope and pain and loss, an endless cycle.

Yet Allasakar desired the Arianni. He desired the White Lady.

She would not surrender her kin—would *never* surrender her kin. But they were not slaves; they were not owned in the way one could own a sword. In the face of that god, even the Firstborn Princes had perceived the depth of a beauty, a power, they could not touch and could not equal.

Was it envy? Was it lust? What could take them, what could take even Darranatos from the side of his brothers, from the side of the White Lady? He could not see it, could not understand it. Even now, incomprehension was the emotion that remained.

Ah, no. Incomprehension and a deep, abiding fury.

The Arianni had been considered a cold people, a distant people. But they knew all-consuming love. And they knew all-consuming hatred. There was nothing they would not surrender in their pursuit of the destruction of Allasakar.

Nothing except the White Lady herself.

HIS LIPS MOVED SOUNDLESSLY over the syllables he could not speak aloud.

He felt, as he tried, immeasurably ancient. Immeasurably weary. At this moment, in this Summer patch of land—called and created at mortal need, not his own—he wished for only one thing: an ending.

CHAPTER FOUR

I*llaraphaniel.*
　　She heard his name. She heard his name, spoken in a voice that was so familiar, she startled from sleep. From what passed for sleep. She felt the warmth of earth beneath layers of cloth. She habitually slept facing Stephen, and this did not change when camping; not for Nenyane the restless movements during the hours set aside for sleep.

If she began to move, to rearrange her position, to struggle restlessly to find comfort or ease, she would rise. In the very early days, this woke Stephen, but Stephen did need sleep and he adjusted quickly. He slept now.

She almost wanted to wake him; she wanted to hear him speak the mage's name in a voice she knew. A voice she could remember in all its iterations. She wanted the familiarity of certainty.

What she had now was certainty without familiarity.

Illaraphaniel.

A memory. A memory fragment. A voice that felt so *right*, it shook her. Could she go to the speaker—could she travel to where he must be —she would travel immediately and without question, the pull felt so strong. She needed to shake herself free of it. If she could put name, put face, to the voice, if she *knew*...

But she didn't. She made her way out of the small tent and into the sunlight; sun would reign in this space while Meralonne ruled it. Sunlight. Summer. Both inimical to the *Kialli*. Beyond the land's periphery, she saw moonlight, starlight, the faded colors of lesser lights across the small horizon.

Gervanno slept. Alex and Max slept. Even Kallandras, a man she *could not* trust, now slept. He was like Gervanno in that way: where the opportunity for actual sleep was presented, he availed himself of it, as if sleep or rest had never been guaranteed. They were soldiers, both, lessons of battle ingrained so deeply they had become almost comfortable habit.

Illaraphaniel would not sleep. She found him leaning against a tree, smoking a pipe he would never have touched in the distant past; when he exhaled, he exhaled rings and, as the rings extended and dispersed, blew smaller rings through them. This man, this Meralonne APhaniel, was familiar in a conscious way—but he felt unfamiliar and subtly wrong on an instinctive level.

Or perhaps in visceral, untouchable memory.

But when his lips moved, silent, between these rings of smoke, she felt a glimmer of recognition, although she could hear nothing; she had seen these motions of mouth and tongue before, but they had never been shorn of sound.

He did not turn to her, did not look at her; she felt, for a moment, his endless loss and the anger that it invoked. Nenyane had never been good with emotion; she was not a person who had ever had the ability to offer comfort. People were either comfortable around her or not on their own recognizance, although it was true she'd never much cared.

She felt, in this moment, that she might once have cared; that this was, along with her memories, lost to her. She had no words to offer him. Words were Stephen's strength, not hers. Her strength was measured in her sword arm. In her skill. In her ability to keep him safe. To protect him.

She had nothing else to offer, now.

STEPHEN WAS NOT ASLEEP. He could not sleep with any comfort here; he understood what had happened, and why. He accepted it as a practical necessity. But the sense of discomfort did not lessen; it grew. He didn't understand why; he had walked through the wilderness to which the Bowgren village of Amberg had been lost. Those lands had been ruled by a lord who wished to be free to hunt mortals in lands she would claim as her own. Perhaps his heightened sense of her enmity made the very idea of comfort—or trust—ridiculous. Perhaps the natural base state was that of a constant emergency, and here, without that enemy against which to throw the whole of his focus, he noticed the differences he had not felt as clearly there.

Or perhaps it was the sunlight, seen through tent flaps and even the cloth of the tent itself; it was daylight here, and daylight hours demanded both action and wakefulness.

Patches nosed her way into the tent; she was followed by Sanfel and Brylle. Steel was nestled between Max and Alex; he lifted head, but did not rise to join the other dogs who sought Stephen in the tent he shared with Nenyane.

Pearl, oddly enough, was asleep—as if daylight sleep suited her contrary nature. Corran, Senshal, and Marrel had fallen asleep outside of his tent. In inclement weather, they set up tents for the dogs, but during hunts the dogs were accustomed to sleeping outdoors; it was the only time they did.

Patches shoved her nose into his cheek, a pointed demand for attention. He offered it, finding grounding comfort in her need. But he could see, through Corran's eyes, that his huntbrother and the mage were standing watch. He could sense Nenyane's confusion and internal strife; his touch was very light. She had always needed more privacy than most huntbrothers were reputed to require; Stephen had no way to test the veracity of that claim.

Tomorrow, they would enter Hansleigh, if the wilderness did not interfere in a fashion that lengthened their travel.

What had Meralonne said? That Hansleigh, the first of the Free Towns when approached from the west, the last if approached from the east, had never been entirely free of the wilderness?

Nothing he had heard of the Free Towns implied the strangeness and the danger of the lands that had almost swallowed Bowgren. True, his tales were from merchants and their various guards; the turnings that affected Breodanir had certainly impacted merchants as well. But Gervanno had had little to say about the strangeness of the towns; Breodanir had seemed far more dangerous, in the end, to the Southerner's eyes.

Demons. Demons and lords of the wild. The Free Towns had had none of those, according to Gervanno. He trusted the Southerner; Gervanno had become a comrade at arms and, better, Nenyane trusted him completely. There was almost no other person of whom Stephen could say that. She might trust *intent*: in that sense, she trusted Max and Alex; she trusted Lord and Lady Maubreche; she trusted Arlin.

With Gervanno, her trust of intent was wedded to her trust in his competence. Was he her equal? No, of course not, not even in her own eyes. But he was close enough in an emergency that he could protect Stephen should it be required.

He shook his head, patted his dogs, and tried to go back to what passed for sleep when he was fighting his instincts. The dogs' presence helped. They piled to either side of him, falling neatly into the space Nenyane would have occupied on a normal hunt.

Normal was gone. It would not return.

THE SECOND TIME HE WOKE, it was to the sound of clashing blades; it was an oddly comforting sound. He knew Gervanno and Nenyane were sparring; somehow, she'd found time for that. There was no scent of breakfast; the rations they had did not require cooking. As he left his tent, he could see Max and Alex seated on the ground, knees bent, as they watched the two swordsmen.

Kallandras watched as well but stood instead, eyes slightly narrowed as if intense concentration was necessary to catch the details of the bladework. It was.

Only when Stephen joined them did Nenyane call a halt. Gervanno stopped immediately, attuned to the sudden stillness, where a moment before Nenyane had been in a frenzy of motion. She turned to the Southerner, voice low. "You've improved. You've really improved."

Gervanno bowed to her, and held that bow. Stephen wondered if it was because he could not quite hide the pleasure—the joy—that transformed his expression.

"Eat," Nenyane told him. "We leave when you're done."

Meralonne, leaning against a tree, arms folded and eyes closed, merely nodded.

20TH DAY OF WITTAN, 429 A.A. THE MERCHANT ROAD

The road remained—to the Hunters—almost shockingly stable. In Breodanir, the roads turned strange without warning; it was rare not to encounter any such disturbances during a full day's march. But the road beyond the border—packed dirt for the most part, although some stretches of the road had been reinforced to either side—did not change. There had been no rain, so mud wasn't an issue; to Stephen's eye, the road and its environs seemed a little too dry.

This was not what he had been expecting; it wasn't what Nenyane had been expecting, either. Gervanno's lack of surprise could be expected; this was the road he'd traveled to reach Breodanir.

They made Hansleigh in good time; the sun had begun its ascent toward the height of sky. The town—if such a large place could be called a town, not a city—was gated, but the gates were intended as a checkpoint, not a genuine defense against outsiders. They answered questions about their destination—the Empire—and their business in Hansleigh before they were waved through.

The roads on the interior of the town were not packed dirt, but worked patches of stone between which weeds grew, to be crushed by pedestrians and wagons; Gervanno's doomed caravan had clearly not been the only one to travel through in spite of the turnings

"No, we weren't," Gervanno said, "and Evaro did good business in the townships. We gathered information from merchants coming from the Western Kingdoms; we offered similar information to those who were traveling the roads that brought us here. I intend to visit the inn we stayed at while here. There are other inns; I don't suggest we stay in the merchant inn Evaro frequented. Things may be too chaotic, and I don't believe they have kennels for your dogs."

"Is there an inn the Breodani frequent?"

Gervanno looked to Kallandras, who nodded. "It is where we discussed staying, the Silver Shield. If we leave in the morning, we should make Callenton in two days. I would suggest resupplying in Hansleigh. If we're forced to forage for food, we'll lose time."

"If foraging is necessary," Meralonne said, "it is safest to do so while we're within the townships and their environs."

"The environs in which you claimed land so that we could camp safely?"

"Indeed."

GERVANNO DEPARTED, Leial at his feet, once rooms had been secured at the Silver Shield. The Hunters went to settle their dogs and inspect the kennels; the mule was put out to feed in a heavily guarded pasture. The town had working dogs, although they weren't trained as hunters.

Stephen had never stepped beyond the borders of Breodanir. He had the advantage of not wearing Hunter colors, here, but his dogs marked him immediately as a foreigner. Breodani silver and gold were considered good coin in the Free Towns; Meralonne said they could exchange it for foreign money when they reached Averalaan. Kallandras agreed. The Breodani favored silver coins in different denominations, although gold was also used. In the Empire and the Dominion, gold was in favor.

Alex and the bard headed to the market district nearest the Silver Shield. They had arrived in good enough time that they wouldn't have to lose any travel hours the next morning by shopping, and Alex, of the four, was excited to be outside of Breodanir.

Max tended the dogs; if Alex was excited, Max was content to experience the foreign and strange through his brother's eyes, at a distance.

Stephen and Nenyane sparred. She treated their sparring sessions very differently from her sessions with Gervanno, but Stephen knew he wasn't Gervanno's equal.

"You'll get there," she told him. "Gervanno is naturally talented, and he's had a lot of experience with his blade."

"And I'm not."

"Not the way he is, no. But the greatest of your heroes wasn't a genius either. I've told you this before: it's practice and work that are necessary. Talent just means you get more out of the effort, but without the practice and work, talent is meaningless. You're not untalented. Mark? Mark is untalented. I've never seen a person take up sword so poorly—the first time I watched him, it made my teeth ache."

Because she'd been grinding them. He remembered.

"Now, he's competent—but only barely. If hunting required swords, I'd've suggested Corwin find Robart a different huntbrother." Which would have gone over so poorly that Robart might never have spoken to Nenyane again. "You're way better than Mark, and better than Robart.

"But you're not better than Gervanno. I hope you'll be as good as he is in the future."

Stephen was afraid that would never happen.

"It will." She spoke with confidence and certainty. Then again, she almost always did. She frowned as Max entered the yard they used for training. Steel was beside the Elseth Hunter, not in the kennel. "Max?"

"I think we might have trouble," he told her. "I'm heading into town."

"What's happened to Alex?" It was Stephen who asked. Max had Nenyane's temperament; he tended toward blunt anger when annoyed. Very little could make him uneasy other than his oldest sibling, his grandmother, and any difficulty Alex—who was far less obvious in his anger—faced.

"There seems to be a problem in the market he and the bard are visiting. They're there now."

"Trouble?" Nenyane tensed instantly.

Max frowned. "I'm not certain what it is—but Kallandras is now uneasy, and Alex has picked up on it. No one is attacking them." His expression made clear he wasn't certain this peace would continue.

"You're heading out?"

Max nodded. "Kallandras is with Alex; Meralonne isn't."

"Do we have time to get changed?"

Max said nothing; the answer was clearly *no*.

THE THREE HUNTERS headed toward the market. The streets were unfamiliar, but Max navigated them as if the buildings that lined them were large, inconveniently placed trees; he knew where Alex was.

A moment later, so did Stephen and Nenyane; or, rather, they knew where the bard was. They could see a sudden storm of localized wind; it carried hats, paper, pebbles from the road, and dust into the air above the town. A handful of fruit, visible by their color, also moved quickly in the folds of the wind.

Nenyane's eyes narrowed. "What is that idiot doing? You two— wait here." She began an instant, all-out sprint.

Max and Stephen couldn't match her speed, but they took off in her wake. Max had been leading; Stephen, knowing the connection between the two Elseth brothers, had been content to follow. They had walked briskly but otherwise normally before, so as not to draw undue attention.

The windstorm had drawn attention; normal was now irrelevant.

"I don't understand what's happening!" Max shouted. Steel kept pace with Max, attempting to position himself between the two; had they been on an empty road, this might have been possible. People, however, had stopped to stare, to gape, to point; the two Hunters were forced to thread around them as they ran.

But when they reached the intersection and turned a corner, they slowed. It was impossible to run through the tightly gathered crowd in front of them. It was above the heart of this crowd that the wind raged, but Stephen could now see that it raged above heads, not at the crowd's center.

Nenyane was no longer in sight, but she hadn't bothered to navigate the people in the street; she'd leapt above them all to land at their center, which formed a thick, uneven ring around four people, of whom Alex and Kallandras were two.

She had landed beside Alex; when her feet touched ground, she had dropped hand to sword hilt, but did not draw blade. Neither the bard nor Alex were armed.

A couple stood in front of Alex and the bard; they were brightly dressed, brightly colored; their make-up would have been beyond gaudy in a different context. Here, they carried what Nenyane had first assumed were clubs and knives—but they weren't wielding them, and they carried six of each between them.

Nenyane, I think they're performers.

If they were regular performers, the bard would bring out his lute, not the wild air. But she was confused. *There's something off about them.*

Stephen stopped attempting to see the strangers through his hunt-brother's eyes. She wasn't in immediate danger. Neither was Alex.

"I think—I think they're performers," Stephen told Max. Both he and Max continued to push through the crowd, earning the annoyance of the people they jostled in their attempt to reach Alex, Kallandras, and Nenyane.

Stephen was elbowed twice and cursed at various volumes as they did; people parted only because he told them Nenyane was his sister.

"Sister? The one who jumped?" An older woman asked, brows furrowed, as they tried to move past. "You're with the circus?"

"Circus? No...she's just...very athletic."

"She's good enough to join the circus," the woman replied. She did not say the word *circus* the way Stephen—or any of his acquaintances in Maubreche—would have; there was a hint of awe, of reverence in the word. And a hint of envy: Nenyane could join the circus. She was good enough.

What is going on here? Stephen asked his huntbrother.

I don't know. I can hear the wind; the wind is angry. But I can't see any reason for it. The only time the wind responds like this is in the immediate presence of other wild elements. I don't think Kallandras was expecting that here; I think he's struggling to keep the wind from destroying things in an attempt to get to whatever is enraging it.

Stephen reached Nenyane's side and turned to face the man and woman in bright raiment, to see them through his own eyes, Nenyane's vision being peculiar in many ways. They were younger than they appeared to Nenyane; the woman was perhaps a few years older than Nenyane, the man of the same age. They both had hair of pale spun gold, with hints of sunset in it. They were both of a height, that height not inconsiderable, but there was nothing—besides the gaudy clothing and make-up—that should have caused Nenyane instant suspicion.

Nothing that should have made them appear older, Other.

What had Meralonne said? The wilderness had not completely vanished from the Free Towns.

To Nenyane, the two did not look young; their appearance in Stephen's normal vision and their appearance in hers clashed. They looked human to her eyes, but oddly liminal; something was different about their presence.

I think they're part of the circus.

Circus?

Someone thought you were trying to prove that you were worthy of joining the circus. People here seem to consider the circus the most desirable of places.

If she could have dragged her eyes from the gaudy strangers, her expression would have been a blend of disgust and annoyance. Becoming an entertainer of any sort was not high on her list of worthy or necessary endeavors.

But the two performers smiled, and Stephen thought the old woman wrong; if Nenyane had the necessary physical talent, her ability to light a fire in the heart of an audience was sorely lacking. She considered unwarranted smiles suspicious by nature, as it usually meant someone wanted something from her—something that she was not inclined to give.

The wind finally banked.

Nenyane frowned and turned to the bard. "Your hand," she said, the words inflected with a concern she had no desire to feel. The bard's hand was bleeding, the red emphasizing the diamond ring he wore on his thumb.

Kallandras failed to note what Nenyane had pointed out, his gaze rising. Hovering in air that had been a localized, angry storm was Meralonne APhaniel. The air did not immediately drop everything in folds; it set it down, fruit and debris coming to rest on the ground before or between people's feet.

Nenyane nodded. Meralonne had taken command of the air; it carried him as he slowly descended to stand between Kallandras and the two entertainers.

Their eyes widened as they gazed at Meralonne APhaniel, the friendly, compelling smiles momentarily absent, as if surprise had robbed them, briefly, of control of their facial expressions. Stephen noted that their eyes did not reflect the mage; what they saw seemed to shed too much light, given the color of the reflection.

The two waited until Meralonne had alighted upon the ground. It was the young woman who bowed first, although the young man was not far behind. Of the two, he seemed the more dazed.

"You honor us with your presence," the young woman said, rising slowly as if the unspoken permission to do so might be revoked at any moment. "We did not expect you; you did not join us when last you passed our way."

Meralonne inclined his head, his eyes narrowed. "You are known in the townships," the mage replied, surprising Stephen.

"Yes, and much active of late; it is odd that our paths have never crossed. I see you are acquainted with the newest members of our audience." She glanced at Kallandras; if she noted his bleeding hand, she failed to comment on it, but perhaps that was because her gaze came to rest on Nenyane, as if Nenyane was the center of gravity that drew, and held, attention.

"They are my traveling companions," the mage replied. "These four, the bard, and one other."

"You've chosen a difficult time to travel," the young woman replied. "But you might travel in any lands and be welcome; perhaps the shifting of the roads and the paths was not a necessary consideration for you." As she spoke, she tore her gaze away from Nenyane to fully face the mage.

Her companion did the same, but it seemed to Stephen that he deliberately avoided staring at Nenyane for long.

"It is a necessary consideration if I am to travel with companions," the mage replied, voice cool. "But I consider the roads through the townships safe at this time."

"Do you? How odd." The young woman looked at the ground; the fruits had disappeared, but the stray debris had not. "I should think you would have informed your chosen companions of the possible dangers inherent in their passage through Hansleigh, Callenton, and Evanston—but perhaps not. Who would expect such a small, fierce storm in a crowd such as this?"

"Enough."

She bent instantly again. "My apologies. It has been long indeed since I have spoken with those who do not live for the entertainment we offer. Remember, if you think back on this, that there is power in joy and delight—and such power, slight though it might be, has deep roots in places such as this." She rose fluidly, her gaze moving past Meralonne toward the crowd of onlookers. Lifting voice, she said, "I apologize for the interruption! Let us now make it up to you all!" Grinning, she bowed to the crowd. She did not rise from that bow, but bent into it, rolling suddenly forward toward the crowd's edge. When she rose, there were daggers in her hands.

People held breath, but the knives weren't being used as weapons; no one felt threatened.

She then leaned back, pushing herself off the ground and somersaulting in mid-air, knives glinting in the afternoon light; her partner caught her feet with the flat of raised palms.

Meralonne watched, glancing once at Kallandras, whose gaze now followed the movements of the entertainers. "Have you encountered them before?"

The bard shook his head. "The townships were not considered a danger to the Kings and the bardmaster."

"I would not consider the townships a threat," the mage replied. "They are like a small, almost invisible kingdom, although each town has its own rules. They have never attempted to enlarge their rule over each other. Hansleigh and Evanston have, over the years, expanded their borders—but never at the expense of other settlements.

"Those small settlements are gone, saving only those that joined the townships themselves."

To Stephen's eyes, Meralonne looked worried.

There's something he's not telling us, Nenyane said, in agreement. She was more annoyed, though.

I don't think he considers the entertainers a threat.

I think he thinks they could be; if he didn't, he wouldn't have made clear that we travel with him, and not the other way around.

Alex and Max chose to continue shopping at the market. They had the same difficulty navigating the gathered crowd, now watching the two performers, as Max had had attempting to break through it from the other direction. Both brothers were unsettled, but they had work to do if they were to leave Hansleigh in the early morning. That leave-taking had become more desirable in the past fifteen minutes.

———

THE HUNTERS RETURNED to the Silver Shield to find Gervanno waiting for them.

"What news?" Kallandras asked.

Gervanno's frown deepened. "The roads between Evanston and Hansleigh have seen very little change; some of the guards that travel with the merchant caravans have disappeared, usually pursuing something off the road. Advice offered to strangers is to not leave the road for any reason."

"Sound advice."

"And common," Gervanno replied. "But for the most part, most of the talk was about the circus."

"The circus." Nenyane folded her arms.

"The circus. Apparently, there will be a large performance tomorrow in the heart of Hansleigh, involving most of the acts; one is reputed to be a Southern sword dance."

Nenyane showed an immediate—and immediately begrudged—interest.

"The performance is offered for free to those who wish to watch, but any funds or proceeds will go to housing those whose homes, on

the outer borders of Hansleigh, were lost to the turnings. They therefore encourage generosity."

"Tomorrow when?" Nenyane asked.

"I believe the show begins after lunch."

"We'll be gone by then."

Gervanno hesitated.

"Don't tell me you want to waste a day just to watch entertainers?"

"One of the merchants advised us to wait and watch," he finally
said. "A merchant, not her guards. She hails from the Empire, and she
hasn't lost a guard to the turnings, although she's had trouble in the
past with bandits."

"You recognized her?"

"We've shared caravan grounds before. Evaro respected her."

"Did she say *why* she thought it was a smart idea to watch?"

Gervanno exhaled. "Travel at this time makes us all a bit superstitious. But she said the circus had been very, very active of late—and
that was either a good sign or a bad one."

"Did she happen to explain this at all?" Nenyane's impatience was
on full display; she hadn't liked the two performers. Their skills at
juggling and acrobatics were not going to change that dislike; if
anything, it deepened it.

"No. Not in so many words. But she believed that there was safety
to be found in the circus, should safety or shelter be required. They've
been far more active in the past year, year and a half, than they were
before things started to go strange." What she'd actually said was *before
things headed south*. Given his homeland was in the South, Gervanno
elected not to repeat this. "She believes the circus becomes active in
times of trouble, to the benefit of those who are also caught up in the
chaos; if the circus is here to offer a full show, the wise merchant
knows when to surrender a day or two."

"Does she believe they protect people from trouble, or cause it?"

"She has lost exactly two guards to the circus in all of her travels
here—but they did not seem to be coerced or forced to join, and she
made them pay for breaking her contract. No, she doesn't believe the
circus entirely predatory. And even if it were, she's a merchant; she is
not above making deals entirely advantageous to herself."

"May I ask the merchant's name, if you know it?" the bard asked.

"Eva," Gervanno replied. "She never introduced herself to the
rest of us; I know only her given name because Evaro used it." He

had been a simple guard; the business of his master was not his to know.

Kallandras's frown was one of recognition. "Was she an older woman? Iron hair, visible facial scars?"

Gervanno nodded. "You've met her before."

"She takes great pride in leading caravans through difficult terrain; she has never lost one. During the merchant wars, she did lose guards. I'm not sure she's forgiven the various Houses for those losses—she is not aligned with an Imperial House. Is she staying at the Silver Shield?"

Gervanno shook his head. "She's staying at the Traveler's Hearth— it's on the eastern side of town. It has the largest compounds for the caravans that pass through. Most merchants choose to stay there when in Hansleigh."

"And this Eva suggested that we remain to watch the circus?"

Gervanno nodded. She had asked after Evaro and Sylvia; he had told her, quietly, that the entire caravan, with a single exception, had been destroyed by demons.

Her expression was a brief grimace, but she spared him overt sympathy. It was not her mode of interaction. She had also offered him a job with her caravan, should he be in need. *Evaro spoke highly of you.*

If the dead could speak, he would not speak so highly now; of this, Gervanno was certain.

"She felt that the circus performance implied the roads were in danger of becoming less stable between the towns, and no, she did not explain why." Gervanno, on the other hand, had not demanded an explanation. While he had been introduced to Eva, he had struggled to find his footing in the brave new world outside of the Dominion's borders. He had found Eva intimidating enough that he had avoided her company.

He regretted that, now. Had his view of women like Eva not altered with experience and time, he might never have found Nenyane, might never have recognized her value, her worth. Women did not wield swords in the Dominion; Nenyane would never have been taught, trained, or valued; she would have been derided, judged, or, depending on her family, worse. What a terrible loss that would have been, what a monumental and complete betrayal of talent.

He thought Nenyane would like, even approve of, Eva—if she cared at all. At the moment, however, she was irritated. It was clear that she had no desire to avail herself of the advice of a total stranger. This was not surprising; she seldom desired to avail herself of the advice of even her closest friends.

Kallandras turned to Meralonne, lifting a brow.

Meralonne's expression made clear he disliked the choice set before them. "The circus will perform tomorrow?"

Gervanno nodded.

"I know the merchant in question, or know of her; Sigurne admired her—from a safe distance. Ah, excuse my lack of respect. Sigurne Mellifas is the current guildmaster of the Order of Knowledge. In as much as I obey anyone there, it is she." He reached for his pipe, held it a long moment without retrieving leaf with which to line the bowl, and turned away. "I dislike the loss of time. I do not regret our work in Bowgren, but it is now eminently clear we could ill afford it."

EVA JUWAL HAD INTENDED to retire for at least a decade. Everyone who worked with her, in any location she visited, had heard her say this; the first time, they might have even taken her seriously. But Eva was not a woman given to easy trust; she could form alliances of necessity, but found them cumbersome absent that necessity.

She found the road very trying. But she had survived the demonic attack at the heart of the merchant's guild in Averalaan, and that attack made clear to her that the dangers of the road were far more mundane than the dangers she might encounter within the city itself. Or they had been.

But, if she were truthful, the stunning transformation of the city she had called home for much of her adult life was equally discomfiting to her. Many merchants—those who had spent very wisely and saved accordingly—had chosen to abandon the road for the time being. Eva had enough money set aside—barely—that she could have chosen to do the same.

But people needed to eat, people needed to work. And Eva was confident in her ability to survive and shepherd both the goods she had taken on and the people she had hired to aid in their delivery.

She had not spent the whole of her life in Averalaan. She had been born to the towns, or the Free Towns, as they called themselves. She had desired to see the wider world, as the young often do, and had both survived and excelled in her chosen profession. If she retired at all, she might return to the towns. Many people did.

But to do so, she would have to pass the caravan on to other hands. She had tried this once; she had become successful enough, known enough, that she could organize and send out more than one set of wagons. That had not gone well, in no small part because of the conflicts that arose between herself and the people she had chosen to fulfill her role with the second van. She had her way of doing things, and clearly they thought to improve on them. Had they *actually* improved on them, she might have accepted it.

As it was, they had not. In the end, they accused Eva of being overly controlling and hugely condescending, and had left to join one of The Ten as House merchants. Good riddance.

She stared into the surface of her almost untouched ale, while around her voices rose and fell, mostly in laughter, some in anger. The anger, she paid attention to, because anger might require her intervention. Laughter seldom did, although not never; ugly laughter was a type of fire that needed to be instantly doused.

When a shadow crossed her drink, she frowned, lifting her chin.

A familiar man stood beside her table. Brave or foolish, that. People left Eva on her own when she was drinking; they never interrupted her more than once unless something was almost literally on fire.

There was no fire that could harm this man, no fire that could cause him to panic.

"Might I join you?" he asked.

She shrugged. Kallandras of Senniel College was a well-known bard; had he come for information, he might have found it just as easily by plying the prettier parts of his trade. But he was known to be fastidious in his interactions; she did not entirely dislike him.

Kallandras correctly interpreted her shrug, and took a seat opposite her. She noted that he did not bring ale of his own, but didn't feel a need to waste her own coin offering to buy him a drink. He would accept it, take a few anemic sips, and be done.

"I see things are grim, if they've sent you," Eva said, lifting her glass. Yes, Master Bard Kallandras of Senniel was well-known. He was sent into war zones — or zones that were almost ready to become battle-fields — because he always survived.

Those around him weren't always so lucky. Eva liked bards in general, and knew she was being unfair — but life was unfair, wasn't it?

"I was not sent by the bardmaster. Nor was I sent by the Twin Kings."

"So you're just traveling to take the pulse of the land? You'll pardon my skepticism."

"Of course," he replied, with an easy smile.

"Why did you come to me?"

"I travel with Gervanno di'Sarrado; at the moment, he is hired as guard to the Maubreche family of the Kingdom of Breodanir, and we share a mutual goal."

This surprised Eva. "You're traveling with Gervanno?"

"I am. Our paths run together at least until Averalaan."

"So he sent you."

"No, he did not. It is a curious thing about cerdan: they serve the master they agree to serve, and they make every effort possible not to know that master's business. Only when that business crosses the lines of duty will they endeavor to learn more."

"He doesn't know what you want."

"He does; as I said, our goals are mutual."

"A pity. I'd've taken him, if he were willing."

"I doubt Stephen of Maubreche would cede his contract to you." Again, the bard smiled. Eva was an old hand; she thought this smile almost genuine, and was surprised by it.

"I've come to inquire about the advice you gave him."

Aye, of course he had. She should have kept her mouth shut. But Gervanno was shadowed by loss, by the guilt of that loss; he was a guard, and the only man to have survived a demonic attack. He was exactly the type of person who could become reckless with guilt and a sense of failure. She'd seen it before. The walking dead; the men and women who felt that death had accidentally passed them by, and meant to make certain they'd never be overlooked again.

She'd liked him. She'd liked his fussiness, his overly perfect manners, the genuine respect he showed Evaro and, notably, to Sylvia, Evaro's wife. He'd treated Eva with the same care, but he'd been far more reserved. She knew why. He wasn't the first Southern guard she'd seen take to the road. Eva Juwal was not considered an anomaly in the Empire; she would have been considered an abomination in the Dominion.

And had been.

Gervanno knew to favor position over gender; not all of the cerdan she'd encountered were as observant. And more: she'd seen the young puppy who'd followed him around, drinking in every word, every gesture, as if Gervanno were a living hero. Gervanno had tolerated the regard with affection, but with a clear eye; the boy's near worship had not affected his own view of either himself or his duties.

"What exactly did you want to know about the circus?"

"You suggested to Ser Gervanno that he remain in town to watch their presentation."

Eva shrugged, uneasy now. This was the price of interference in the life of a man who was almost a stranger. Still, she tried to live a life in which regret wasn't left on every path she walked. "The circus has been at home in the Free Towns for the entirety of my life."

"I have passed through the Free Towns before; the circus was never mentioned."

"There's your answer, then. You've never lived in the Free Towns — you've passed through them. They're transit points to you. The circus performs rarely; if any of your travels had brought you to one of the towns in which they'd set up their tents, you'd've heard of them — it would be impossible not to."

"And the circus is significant?"

This was the second reason Kallandras had always been difficult. He was bard-born. Eva had had a lifetime to develop necessary skills of prevarication and bluffing; she was a merchant, and a successful one. But the bard-born talent could easily separate fact from fiction if she spoke. "As you suspect, or you wouldn't have come here." She lifted her mug again.

"You dislike speaking of the circus." Not a question.

"I do. You can find anyone in the streets who'll talk your ear off, because they perform here tomorrow."

"We had planned to be on the road at the break of dawn."

"Aye, so Gervanno informed me."

"And you believe this decision will lead us into danger."

"How could I assess what's dangerous to a man like you?"

His eyes narrowed. Clearly Eva had had enough to drink, and his presence ruined the relaxation that came with ale at the end of a day.

"You've survived every war zone you've been sent to. If we know you're coming down the road, we take a different road, or we turn back. You're like a weathervane." Definitely too much to drink. "The circus performing on such short notice could be considered the same type of warning, but the conclusions we draw are the inverse. When the circus performs, you watch if humanly possible. You don't risk the roads. You don't shelter in your home.

"The circus *is* performing on short notice. Those who've lived in the Free Towns know to enter their big tents, to become their audience. I grew up in the Free Towns. Losing a day's travel is difficult, but losing a caravan would be far, far worse. And my people are pleased to have the day off."

Kallandras nodded. "You do not consider the circus harbingers of disaster?"

She shook her head. "We considered them a shield against disaster. They weren't regular performers, but in our history, their big tent performances—not the little ones on the streets—were usually held on Scarran. The circus master said it was a way of providing the light of joy on the darkest of days—I remember that. I first saw the circus as a child."

"And we are all in need of joy," the bard replied. "You don't believe that was its sole purpose."

"I did, when I was a child—but we were taught to fear Scarran in the Free Towns. Scarran was the night when all manner of things could go wrong, when hunting creatures from the darkness could step foot—with will, effort, and great power—into the Towns themselves. As a young adult, I laughed at the superstitions I'd believed as a child; I thought this to be monster-under-the-bed material. A way of scaring children into compliance.

"But given the changes on the road and in the kingdoms to the West, given the rumored difficulties of the Empire at its borders, and given, finally, the demonic attempt to destroy the merchant guild, I've decided that childhood contains kernels of wisdom, after all.

"If the circus is staying to perform—on a day that isn't Scarran— I'll stay in the big tent. I can't give you a better reason, and I'm not generally considered superstitious, but it is what it is."

"You've never been part of the circus."

"Me?" Eva laughed. "No, I haven't. If you came seeking information, I've given you all I can."

"The circus seems to be almost revered in Hansleigh."

"You'll find similar attitudes throughout Callenton and Evanston as well. I used to wonder, as a young woman new to the Empire's borders, how it was that the Free Towns had survived. They hadn't been amalgamated into the Empire."

"Or the Kingdoms?"

"Breodanir is the kingdom closest to the Free Town's borders, and they're an odd bunch—but you'd know that, traveling with them. They've never tried to expand their borders, and they defend them with their god's wrath, or so I'm told. It's the Empire that should have been the bigger threat. But it never has been. The Free Towns have always held their own."

"And you believe that the circus has played a larger role in their survival as independent entities."

Eva nodded, her glare daring the bard to mock her for her superstition.

Kallandras failed to accommodate that expectation. To Eva's surprise, he looked both thoughtful and concerned. She probably should have expected that—bards were famed for their ability to socialize "naturally" with anyone. "Thank you for your time. I will advise the Breodani to wait for the circus. Understand that I am not master here; I serve in a limited role, and my position with regards to those Hunters is very similar to the position Ser Gervanno occupies. The advice is theirs to accept or reject."

"You're a bard," Eva replied, emptying the last of her ale. "Persuasion is what you do."

His smile deepened. "You have not yet met the Breodani in question; one is immune to all persuasion, and she is very, very protective of her Hunter."

"She?"

"Yes. She. It is apparently very unusual to have a young woman as huntbrother, but that is her role."

"You're certain the wool isn't being pulled over your eyes?"

"I am absolutely certain. But perhaps, if you intend to attend tomorrow's performance, you will have a chance to judge her for yourself."

NENYANE DID NOT WISH to stay. She left the decision in Stephen's hands; she had at least that much self-control. But her demeanor made her reluctance clear to everyone who knew her—even Gervanno, who

hadn't the years of familiarity the Elseth brothers did—and stalked off
to the yard to practice. Stephen both accepted and dreaded this; it was
through her sparring that she spoke most viscerally. Perhaps because
he had known her for so short a time, Gervanno had no such dread.
Stephen was grateful for the Southerner's company. He blunted some
of Nenyane's edge—and her edge was on full display here.

The circus made Nenyane uncomfortable. It made the bard uncomfortable. But the bard appeared to believe the merchant's warning had
merit. He knew Nenyane would be against it, but offered his opinion
regardless.

Meralonne, pipe in hand, listened to Kallandras's information. "I
dislike both of the choices we are offered," he said at last. "You must
know that the unfortunate storm that occurred in your presence was
due to the presence of the circus performers. No, I do not think that
was their intent; they were careless with their performance because
mortals do not, and cannot, command the elements.

"I do not believe they will make that mistake again."

"Were they not mortal?" Stephen asked.

"What did you see?"

"A young man and a young woman, both excellent acrobats and
jugglers," Stephen replied. He hesitated before asking the mage, "Is
that not what you saw?"

"It's what I saw," Alex added.

"And I," Kallandras concurred.

Max felt no need to add his experience, and so remained silent. All
eyes turned to the mage. "I saw a man and woman; I would not
consider them young by mortal standards. Nor would I necessarily
consider them enemies. But what they saw in me, you do not generally
see either. They have a perception at odds with their appearance." He
lit his pipe again; aromatic smoke began to climb into the air as he
turned to Stephen. "If it will not cause conflict between you and your
huntbrother, I would suggest we remain to see the performance."

STEPHEN TOLD himself he wasn't irritated when Nenyane reversed her
opinion because of the mage's words. He mostly believed it. She was
restless, and when she was restless in this particular way, she was
almost itching for a fight. Stephen was seldom considered a viable

target, and, given the presence of the circus, he was much farther down the list than usual.

She wasn't happy with Meralonne, and Meralonne rose from the table at which they'd been eating, indicating with a wave of his pipe that Nenyane—and Gervanno—should join him. Only when the three were well away did Max speak.

"Where does she know the mage from?"

Alex gave his brother a sharp look; clearly this wasn't a question he thought should be asked out loud.

Stephen shook his head. "I don't know. But he recognized something in her, and she recognized something in him. She feels that she knows him, that she can almost trust him."

Max whistled. "Nenyane? Trust a stranger? She took years to accept us."

Stephen shook his head again. "She trusted your intent from the beginning. She's a harsh judge of character, but she has good instincts. It isn't that she didn't trust you."

"She just didn't trust us with you." Alex's voice was softer. "She trusts the Southerner."

"In a pinch, yes. But she considers his sword work excellent."

Alex nodded. "We'd noticed that. I think he's the first person she's ever treated with respect in that regard."

"He is. And he almost reveres her. If she gave him permission, I think he'd follow her to the ends of the earth."

"He's hired on as a Maubreche guard?"

"He was—until we reached the King's City."

"And now?"

"I've promised, in the name of Maubreche, to cover his wages. He intends to return to his homeland, and we're traveling that way as well. Nenyane thinks having a local guide would be helpful."

Alex was almost shocked.

"She *can* be practical when it's necessary." Stephen frowned.

"Are they arguing?" Alex asked; he recognized the look on Stephen's face.

"She's committed to stay to watch the circus. At this point, she really doesn't expect to enjoy it. The mage has given her very little practical information with which to work, but it's clear that the performers have been drawing on the powers of one of the wild elements. Which should be impossible. Meralonne concurs, but says that element isn't fire. He is intrigued, but he isn't worried, which implies that he knows more about the circus than he's willing to put into words."

Alex now winced. He knew Nenyane well enough to know how happy she'd be about that.

Stephen rose. "They're going to be arguing for a bit—but neither of them needs much sleep. We should grab what we can."

"Are you expecting trouble tomorrow?"

Was he? He couldn't answer, and the silence was answer enough.

CHAPTER FIVE

Gervanno was surprised to see Stephen's full hunting pack following Stephen and Max from the kennels. Leial remained with Gervanno; no one minded the small mutt, and many people ignored Leial because Leial didn't seem to be much of a threat. No one could ignore the Breodani dogs. They weren't coupled for hunting, but they were watchful in a way that implied Stephen himself was on high alert.

Nenyane wasn't as fond of the dogs as the other three, although in Max's case Gervanno considered that impossible, but she said nothing as the dogs, and her Hunter, joined them. Meralonne glanced at the dogs, lips slightly pursed. He, too, did not demur.

This acceptance on the part of both Nenyane and the mage put Gervanno on alert.

He had not seen a Northern circus, but had seen his share of traveling entertainers in his childhood. Were the situation not so fraught, he might have anticipated the performance with something approaching pleasure.

The bard joined them late and last, having spent some time in the dining room earning the coin that would carry him on the road. The crowd was not thin, although all of the patrons talked about the circus. Most were happy, even relieved.

Some were not.

Gervanno noted that those who bore more shadowed expressions were all natives—the innkeeper, the barmaids, the men who worked in the stables. They were appreciative of the circus, but something in that appreciation spoke of possible disaster. Although he could speak to them in a language they understood, they were reticent. This did not surprise him; he and his party were foreigners. Only Kallandras seemed immune to the natural suspicion outsiders engendered.

Had Gervanno never seen the bard fight, he would have assumed that this geniality, this approachability, this use of natural charisma was, like skill with sword, something one had to work to master. All skills required work, dedication, intention.

But he had seen him fight. The bard was not the equal of Nenyane; not even the silver-haired Widan was. But he would have been considered master of his unusual weapons in Gervanno's homeland.

Gervanno exhaled. He was curious about the circus, but any anticipation of happy discovery had been tempered by the subtle atmosphere amongst Hansleigh's residents—and, if he were honest, Nenyane's desire to avoid the performance entirely. She would not do so; Stephen intended to attend, and in this unknown land she would not leave his side. But she was restless, had been on edge since the night before they arrived in Hansleigh.

She clearly trusted the Northern Widan, but this trust was ambivalent. Nenyane was not a person given to ambivalence, in Gervanno's limited experience.

Gervanno, less of a master than Nenyane of Maubreche, was accustomed to ambivalence. It was clear to the cerdan that Meralonne APhaniel was invested in Stephen's survival; clear as well that the Northern bard was committed to it.

Alex and Max were family, kin. Gervanno expected their loyalty, although he was well aware that in the South—which seemed so distant, at the moment, that any homecoming must be chimerical—kin vied against kin for seats of power. Blood, however, was thicker than water in the Dominion. He was uneasily aware that that was not the case for the most powerful of the Imperial families, who all but eschewed blood ties.

Leial whined.

"You've already been fed," Gervanno told him. He had attempted to convince the dog—as if the dog could actually understand his words —that begging implied an unacceptable lack of personal dignity or honor. Leial's tail had been a blur of motion throughout the lecture. He had intended to leave the dog in the inn; Leial, in comparison to the Breodani dogs, seemed much more like a pet.

"You value the dog?" the innkeeper asked.

Gervanno frowned. "I do. He's been with me on battlefields."

"Then you don't want to leave him here." Again, a flicker of discomfort crossed the innkeeper's face, a ripple of expression, here and almost gone in the same instant. Gervanno, sensitive to the difficulties that being an outsider might cause, deliberately chose not to notice the discomfort. He was—had always been—polite, almost diffident; that did not change.

"I don't much hold with foreigners," the innkeeper continued, to Gervanno's surprise. "Strange, eh? My livelihood depends on them. Some of the guards around these parts are little better than bandits in the bad season."

Gervanno nodded.

"But you've been polite. You've caused my staff no trouble. You've interfered before trouble could start—seems like you've had your own experiences keeping the unruly in line. Tell your friends, especially your bard, to stay on the circus grounds. And take your dog."

At this, Gervanno winced. "I found him on the road, but he's not as well-trained as I'd like. I'll do my best." He hesitated, but decided against asking for more information.

The innkeeper paused, as if expecting questions; when none came, he smiled. "You ever want to settle down, Hansleigh's a good place. Especially now. You know how to handle merchant guards—I'd hire you on tomorrow. Remember—stay on the circus grounds."

"You'll be there?" Gervanno asked.

"Me and all the staff, yes." But his expression flickered again. Worry.

Gervanno nodded, grateful for the intent behind the innkeeper's words. Nor did he attempt to explain that, as a guard, it was his duty to follow the orders of his master; if Stephen chose to abandon those grounds, Gervanno had little choice but to follow.

This was his second chance at a life lived with honor, a death earned honorably. He could not forsake it.

He turned toward the door, aware that Stephen and Nenyane had already departed and he should have been with them.

He didn't make it through the door before another man ran through it. He was older than Gervanno, but not by much; heavyset, sweaty, and a little too wide-eyed. Gervanno stepped between the man and the innkeeper, but the man didn't appear to even notice the cerdan.

"Where is your daughter?" the man demanded, approaching the counter that generally kept the innkeeper separated from his guests.

The innkeeper closed his eyes. When he opened them, he moved from the safety of the counter, and headed directly toward the wild-eyed man. "Devon," he said, placing one hand on the larger man's shoulder. "They're not fools. They know. Your son cares for my daughter—he won't put her at risk."

Ah. The source of the discomfort was family. Nothing, in the end, could cause so much worry.

"He cares for her, aye—I'm not saying it's my son who will put them at risk. You know she's got him wrapped around her little finger!"

The innkeeper stiffened but did not disagree. "Maybe they wanted to find a private place from which to watch the circus," he began.

Devon snorted. "You know that's not what's happened." His voice was low, a growl of sound; his hands were fists. Gervanno hesitated; he did not wish to abandon the innkeeper in the face of danger.

But friends were a different kind of danger, a different kind of enemy—and in non-lethal conflicts between friends, a stranger had no business interfering.

"Enough. I've set Jeffers out looking for Adala. If he finds Adala, he's certain to find Trevor; he'll bring 'em both back."

Devon wasn't mollified. "They won't come. Adala told Trevor she'd received the word: she's been called. If Trevor had been chosen as well, they'd be at the circus now, bristling with excitement. He wasn't. And you know there's no marriage allowed between circus and the rest of us.

"I've tried to talk sense into Trevor but sense has leaked out of his ears."

"She received word?" The innkeeper had paled.

"She didn't tell you?"

"You know we're not supposed to know beforehand."

"Well, she didn't include Trevor in that."

"And Trevor told you."

"He was wrecked, Ian. He was totally wrecked. Of course his mother got it out of him." The man had calmed, in a fashion; there was no threat of violence between the two fathers. "She didn't tell you because she had no intention of letting you know."

The innkeeper closed his eyes, and the larger man now placed a steadying hand on his shoulder. "Jeffers will find them," the blacksmith said.

"...you don't believe that."

Devon abandoned his shaky attempt at comfort. "How can I? That damnable daughter of yours could hide from bloodhounds if she put her mind to it — it's not a small wonder she got the call. But if the circus has laid claim to her, let's trust the circus to find and protect their own. If they find her, they'll also save my idiot son."

"She's not part of the circus yet," the innkeeper whispered.

To that, Devon had nothing to say.

———

"WHAT HAPPENED?" Nenyane demanded, when Gervanno joined them; Nenyane had, clearly, decided to wait. She was on high alert; she wanted everyone to be in the same place.

Alex glanced at Gervanno, and then to the bard. The bard's eyes were on Gervanno, and had not moved since he joined them.

"Where is APhaniel?" Gervanno asked.

"He will join us when the performance begins." It was Nenyane who answered, as if the mage were barely relevant. "What happened? Why were you delayed?"

It was private business, family business; Gervanno hesitated. But Nenyane was on edge because of the circus, and clearly the difficulty involved that very circus. "The innkeeper's daughter has gone missing."

"I thought everyone in town would be attending the performance." It was Alex who made the observation.

Nenyane's eyes narrowed. "The innkeeper is worried because she might not be there."

Gervanno nodded. Nenyane marked the silence. "Tell us the rest."

"His daughter, Adala, is involved with Trevor, the son of one of the smiths in town. Both of the young people have gone absent without leave."

This annoyed Nenyane. "And this is our problem how?"

"It isn't."

"Do I look like a font of patience?" Nenyane snapped. Behind her back, Max rolled his eyes.

"You did not appreciate being told that you might be good enough to join the circus," Gervanno said. "Were you offered a position, you would refuse it. I did not speak directly to the innkeeper; he has made clear that we are, inasmuch as it is possible, to attend the performance. I only heard about his daughter because the innkeeper stopped me when he realized I'd left Leial in my room."

"He stopped you because of your dog?"

"Yes. He wanted to warn me to bring my dog with me, and he did. But his friend came into the inn before I could leave, and I overheard their discussion. I inferred from it that Adala and Trevor are young, in love, and somewhat reckless because of it. And that Adala was invited to join the circus, where Trevor was not."

Nenyane's frown spread across the whole of her face. "And you don't think she can just refuse."

"Again, I was in no position to interrogate the innkeeper. But yes, that is what I inferred. Someone was sent to try to find his daughter, but his friend scoffed; if Adala doesn't want to be found, it is unlikely that she will be found."

"What the hell is this circus?" Nenyane demanded—of the bard.

"I know no more than you. But yes, there is an element of the circus that seems to verge on the unnatural. I believe the circus— unnamed and unknown—is the reason Meralonne chose to camp outside of Hansleigh before our arrival; he senses something on the road and in the town itself. He does not consider it a threat to us, and that is the whole of his focus."

"If he considered it entirely irrelevant, he would be here," Nenyane replied. She turned to Gervanno. "We've already made the choice to allow other people to deal with threats that can be dealt with. Is this one of those?"

It was Gervanno's turn to close his eyes, to center himself, to listen to instincts that had always served him well—if survival was his only concern. "It is not my place," he began.

"Don't waste more of my time," Nenyane snapped.

Gervanno annoyed Nenyane further; he turned to Stephen of

Maubreche, technically his master. This clearly surprised Stephen, which also deepened his huntbrother's irritation.

"Please answer the question," Stephen told the cerdan.

"No, it is not a situation I believe the townspeople can deal with. There is something off about it. Not the young lovers—I believe they exist in any country, any kingdom, any empire. If the circus were a religion, the situation would be similar if the two were from families of strongly held, different beliefs—but it is not that, or not only that. I believe it is a matter of safety to be where the circus gathers, because Eva Juwal believes it—and that woman believes in nothing that is not beneficial to her."

"I would not say that is true," the bard said quietly.

"You are acquainted with her?"

"I travel many roads. I have traveled with her caravan before." He turned to Stephen. "Ser Gervanno is correct. Eva feels it essential. No guard that wishes to maintain their place in her employ will be absent today." To Nenyane he added, "Can you not feel it in the breeze? Can you not sense it, in the wind? There is a reason Meralonne chose to camp outside the boundaries of this land.

"I would not trust it beneath the night sky. But it is day, and we are promised entertainment. If this is a cunning, dangerous plan, Eva would not attend."

"What do you fear?" Nenyane asked of the bard.

The bard's smile was slender; it was all the answer he offered.

THE STREETS beyond the inn were crowded; had Stephen wondered where the circus event was to take place, the crowds themselves formed a human map, a living, moving sign, a river that flowed toward its end. No one questioned the presence of his dogs; no one questioned the presence of Leial. Stephen was not surprised to see cats held in arms; had Gervanno not been on duty, he was certain the cerdan would have scooped up his dog in a similar fashion.

They were close to the inn, and the composition of the crowd nearest the Breodani reflected that; men and women who were not residents of the large town mingled with people who clearly were. The impatience on their faces made clear that they, as the Breodani, had never attended a circus performance before; he was almost certain that they would have declined the opportunity had they not been told it was free.

Nenyane had never cared for crowds. It was in crowds that assassins—and demons—could be hidden, both cloaking their natures and their goals. As Stephen had made clear many times, she could not just cut through the crowd should she feel it necessary; she felt hampered, as collateral damage was unacceptable. It was very difficult, in a crowd such as this, to draw sword; almost impossible to wield it if people did not move out of the way.

Nenyane could wield long knives, and, in a pinch, daggers—but she hated them. Forced to their use, she considered herself unarmed.

She chose not to complain about this out loud, and not for the reasons that would have prevented Gervanno from speaking. She did not want to give warning to possible enemies.

Silence suited the Southerner. It didn't suit his dog, who clearly found the crowds just as uncomfortable as Nenyane. Stephen's dogs, however, created a space around themselves simply by being large. Stephen kept them under perfect control, but could not make them smaller or meeker in appearance; they were alert, now, influenced by their master's unvoiced discomfort.

That discomfort was eased somewhat by the presence of children, some too young to pay heed to their parents. The crowds prevented them from freely running wild, but they seemed to approach the legs of strangers if they were obstacles designed for play. He knew, having had his leg grabbed by at least two before the children were caught, reprimanded, and brought back in line.

Some adults, clearly not related by blood, aided parents in the gathering of their two-legged strays; they were good-natured and lacking in judgment as they did. They offered sympathy to frazzled parents of the very young; the older children, impatient, nonetheless waited in line. That sympathy was the one time people spoke to each other.

That was why the crowd struck him as wrong: the silence that enveloped it. That silence contained unvoiced anticipation, but also fear. He could not ask people what they feared; touching unvoiced fear was always dangerous, especially when such disturbance came from outsiders, foreigners.

Nenyane was silent, but her silence, like that of the crowd, was the wrong kind. She was watchful, as she always was, but tense, uncomfortable—as if something in the air itself touched the memories she could not consciously recall.

"Yes," the bard said. "There is something in the air. Something beneath our feet." He turned to Stephen and added, "A river runs through this town, to the west; I can hear the water's voice."

Nenyane's eyes narrowed as she turned to the bard. "You hear them all?"

"Fire is silent," he replied.

Why are you worried?

If he can hear the voices of the three elements, he speaks of living wind, living earth, living water. And that should be impossible.

Stephen did not doubt the bard's hearing.

Neither did Nenyane, but she was frustrated. *You saw what happened when wind met earth near the street performers. The elements, when conscious, won't co-exist peacefully. Only when they are in the command of someone truly powerful can this happen. And if he's right, it means someone powerful is present in Hansleigh.*

Meralonne is close.

Meralonne is not that power. He can cajole the wind; he can command it. So, too, the earth and the water. But he cannot summon them and command them if he intends to do anything but command and control. Even should he, the risk is too great. He will survive. I will. Unsaid were the names of the rest of her party, the only people for whom Nenyane cared.

Are you worried about the circus grounds themselves?

Am I breathing?

I don't think, given the townspeople's presence, that we're in danger.

She frowned, but nodded. *There has to be a reason that the circus is performing now—and that every person present in the town will attend.*

Stephen glanced at Gervanno. Not every person. He would have asked what she feared would happen beyond the confines of the circus, but conversation—even of a private nature—was halted by the booming voice that filled the street.

"WELCOME. WELCOME ALL!" The words were measured, soft; the greeting was spoken by at least a dozen people in careful unison, none of whom could immediately be seen from the vantage of the crowded street. Pearl lifted her head a fraction of a second before the rest of the dogs did. The pack came to bracket Stephen; they were now ill at ease, but were not yet aggressive. If there was an enemy here, there was no prey. Not yet. Stephen's horn remained at his side, an ornament in this place; this was not Breodanir.

He turned to his huntbrother, arrested by her sudden silence. It wasn't just lack of words; Nenyane seldom spoke. It was her stillness. Even breath, for one long moment, seemed an afterthought, a social conceit.

Nenyane?

There was no answer. There were no thoughts. Just that stillness. Everything about it felt wrong, unfamiliar. Stephen reached out and grabbed Nenyane's shoulder, the motion instinctive—as if, by touching her, he could somehow bind her to this reality, this shared life. If she felt his restraining hand at all, she gave no indication.

Her eyes were wide. He wanted to know what she saw, but couldn't bring himself to slide behind her eyes and share her vision. At this moment, given her utter stillness, it felt wrong. He could not push back against the feeling; he barely tried. In this moment, Nenyane was foreign, huntbrother or no. The bond remained, but he was no longer certain to whom it was attached.

He might have asked, but there was something about the hush surrounding her that silenced Stephen. He finally recognized it: it was awe. The hush, the stillness of awe, an awe that could not be transcribed or captured in simple words.

She was, at first glance, staring at something; he looked in the direction of her gaze. He saw nothing but Hansleigh's crowded streets; the line—several people wide—seemed to go on forever. But the crowd had stilled, just as Nenyane had. Max, Alex, and Stephen were the only people whose gazes darted from person to person, street to building. Gervanno's did not; his gaze was fixed to Nenyane's profile. He was alert, concerned, and almost motionless.

The bard, however, was not. He was silent, but he was not still; Stephen felt the wind in his hair, and saw it lift strands of Nenyane's. No attempt to cut her hair had ever lasted. It *could* be cut, but it returned to its natural length within hours.

It was morning, although the sun had fully crested horizon; sunlight through those strands of moving hair made her hair look like new steel, like a sharp, glinting blade's edge.

It does, doesn't it?

He looked up, his eyes tracking Kallandras's rise, although he knew the speaker was not the bard. Something about the voice—something about the hint of echoes in the words—was familiar. He had heard it before, or heard its like before—but never here. Never while his feet were firmly planted on the soil of lands in which mortals lived.

But the wind moves it, and it does not retain the quality that makes it so resemble blade's edge; it wavers too much, even now. You have bold companions, child. Too bold.

Beneath Stephen's feet, the earth began to rumble, tremors passing beneath the soles of his boots and spreading in all directions.

Far too bold.

In an instant, the clear, blue sky darkened, clouds moving in so quickly it seemed as if the curtain of night had been unceremoniously dropped across the town, as if the town were a large stage, a detailed prop through which actors might move.

The crowd turned slowly, almost as one person, which was disturbing; they looked up and up again, to where Kallandras of Senniel College stood on point in the folds of the wild air.

"**How dare you?**" the voice that had spoken said, a crack of thunder in the coming storm. "**How dare you show such disrespect in the wilderness? You bear the taint of the ancient and the dead, and I have not invited you into my lands.**"

No echoes followed the clash of syllables; all voices spoke at once, trembling with rage.

Yet the speaker did not appear.

No. In the place of the speaker came a second familiar figure—bright and shining, girded in chain that glittered in the light, just as pale, platinum hair did. Meralonne APhaniel's eyes were flashes of silver—no, that was wrong; they were nothing as soft as silver. Even the cape the mage wore was silver—a drape that caught light and reflected it inward, as if to illuminate its wearer.

"The wind," the mage said, "is mine."

Silence eddied through the crowd as the mage gestured; the bard returned slowly to the ground.

"**And the bard?**"

"Mine as well, for the nonce."

"**You are lying, little prince. He is not yours, and cannot be, unless you intend to kill gods.**"

"Ah, but I do." The words were delivered with the coldest smile

Stephen had ever seen grace the mage's face. "And you must be aware, you who linger nameless here, that it is the whole of my intent even now.

"I should have known your hand was in this; I hear broken syllables, a tapestry of sound that fails to fully cohere into any name, any word, known to even the ancients whose words are long lost in the dust of history.

"But you will not harm the bard, and you will not touch those who travel with me."

"You are bold indeed to demand that from us; we have not given you permission to even tread across the boundary of our lands."

"You have not." Meralonne gestured and the crowd nearest to where he chose to land dispersed. "But the children of man have ever been free to cross your boundaries, and the bard is mortal. If you will it, I shall depart."

"You will not take them with you, not yet, not now."

"Think you that I cannot protect a handful of mortals? Have you lived so long in this place that you have forgotten who I am?"

Silence, and then, from all directions, high and low, came the booming sound of laughter. No one who had witnessed this exchange would have dared to laugh; none would have even considered laughter a possibility.

"And that is a question I intended to ask of you, bold prince. Illaraphaniel, I bid you welcome to my small lands. You will find them unchanged—one of the few lands of which that can be said in this, or any, age. Come. Come, the circus is waiting. I would not have you outperform these talented younglings, nor put to shame their years and decades of training.

"Come. I will overlook the lack of respect shown by your companion in this place, for I, too, have been waiting." The speaker clapped, hands invisible, the meeting of palms the roaring applause of a crowd.

As that thunderous applause spread, the clouds fell away from the sky. In their place, the answer to the question of where an event that housed the whole of Hansleigh—town in name, but small city in any practical sense—appeared, and Stephen understood, then, that Nenyane had seen it all along.

Around the town and through the streets, buildings grew and spread, each much taller, and much, much finer, than the homes of the townspeople. The residents cried out in delighted recognition, in welcome, in excitement; it was clear that these buildings were familiar to the people who made Hansleigh home. They were colorful: walls of blue, red, and green rose toward the sky; some were slender, and some as wide as the King's palace; all were almost dizzying in height.

Toddlers and younger children were beside themselves with the excitement that infected the older townspeople, the feverish sense of wonder, of discovery colliding. Awe of the type that had rooted Nenyane to the spot was beyond them in their youthfulness, and they raced through the streets, often colliding with each other, as if they must reach the nearest building or perish. Parents caught them before they could vanish.

Buildings such as these did not exist in Breodanir.

They had not existed in Hansleigh until this moment.

But the homes, the shops, the inns, began to fade from view, as if their mundanity, their normalcy, was the illusion, the phantasm.

"Welcome, old friends and new; welcome family—welcome to the circus!"

Music filled these new, strange streets; the cobblestones beneath Stephen's feet were the only element of the original town that remained. Even the shape of the streets had shifted and changed, to accommodate this new city. Stephen did not look for the inn at which they'd been staying; he knew he would not find it. Instead, he looked to Alex, Max, and Gervanno, and from them to Kallandras. The bard carried a lute in his hands; he stood, eyes closed, fingers resting against the lute's neck and strings.

It was difficult to look at Meralonne for long. There was something in him, some unnatural radiance, that forced a squint—at best. Stephen felt as if Meralonne was a natural part of these new streets, this new city; that he, not they, belonged in this place.

He doesn't, his huntbrother said. *But he's been given permission to remain.* She now sounded irritable; the grip of stillness and awe had loosened, and she appeared to resent its prior existence. *It's not that,* she snapped. *He knew. There was a reason he chose to make a claim in the wilderness outside of Hansleigh. He knew.*

And he hadn't informed them. Stephen frowned. *Do you recognize these lands? Do you recognize their lord?* It was always tricky to ask Nenyane such a question.

I don't remember them, no—but they feel familiar to me for other reasons. One day, if you pass through the Deepings, you'll understand.

"Were we in any other lord's land," Meralonne said, his voice soft although every word carried, "I would warn you to mind your manners. Given Nenyane is one of our company, I imagine that my warning would be beyond you. But the lord of these lands will take less offense than any other lord, and with reason: he understands mortals. He has tended them, in his fashion, for all of my existence.

"There is very little left in this world—your mundane, grey world— that reminds me of my youth. I would explore for a moment, if you will pardon me. In this land, unless you offend its lord, you will not be in danger."

He strode away; the crowd parted in silence, and Stephen noted that that silence was kin to awe. Or fear.

"He was many things, in his youth," Nenyane said, voice soft. "Firstborn prince of the White Lady's ancient court, and a warrior that even the gods might fear. His youth was war, and the gladness of it; do not think that this land invokes softer sentiment in him." Her eyes were on the mage's armored back, and they remained fastened there until the mage was lost to sight.

GERVANNO UNDERSTOOD why the innkeeper had suggested he bring his dog if he valued the dog at all. He had no idea what would become of the town that had vanished. But the circus, if not regular, was a known entity to the townsfolk; they had been more afraid of missing it than of attending.

It was the fear itself that was odd.

Gervanno watched the city emerge. Its bright colors, its tall build-ings, and even the flowers and trees that girded the streets, reminded him of what Nenyane called the wilderness; the landscape had changed between one sentence and the next. The vibrancy of color reminded him of newly dyed silk—things unworn, untouched, things waiting their intended ceremonial purpose. But such ceremonies were as old as the Dominion itself; the newness of one implied the ancient, invoked a past that could not be touched in any other way.

This, then, was the circus in Gervanno's view: new and old, the present and the distant past, entwined.

It is, indeed.

Gervanno frowned. The voice was a stranger's voice, but some of its tone and texture reminded him of the fox. He turned in the direction of the spoken words, aware of the subtle currents of power in the wilderness and aware, as well, of power as claimed by mortals.

You are far from your homeland, the voice continued.

Gervanno could not see the speaker, but nodded, for the speaker could clearly see him and he had much to be cautious about when dealing with a being who could create a city such as this in a moment. Or perhaps reveal it. Perhaps it was always present, in the way the wilderness was, and the circus master had simply opened the door that allowed people in.

I am certain you have a tale to tell. I am aware of many such tales, after all. The towns of Hansleigh, Evanston, and Callenton have taken in many of your countrymen, scarred and broken by the battlefield. They have made their homes here, and have found wives and families. Or husbands and families.

But you are not yet ready to retire, I see.

"I have a duty to perform in honor of a fallen comrade; until that duty is discharged, I cannot remain." He hesitated, and then said, unbidden, "If I have any skill at all, any skill of value to anyone, it resides in my sword. I have offered that sword to my master, and that duty also leads me, in the end, to my homeland."

Indeed. The tone of the voice shifted between one word and the next. *It is easy to lose track of mortal time, even when that mortal time marks us all; I did not expect to see you here, at this moment.*

Nenyane had turned to Gervanno; his spoken words had clearly been heard by more than his intended audience. He fell silent, not in embarrassment, but in worry. This voice, this person who must be the master of the circus, had somehow expected to see Gervanno in this place, this Free Town.

He cleared his throat. "It is not the first time I have passed through this town. I have traveled through it before; I have stayed in one of Hansleigh's inns."

It is the first time, Ser Gervanno, that you have come as visitor to my circus. I offer you advice—and as all unasked-for advice, it is perhaps unpleasant—but you, at least, will humor me. Do not leave the circus grounds. Wait until the circus grounds leave Hansleigh.

Nenyane stepped in to Gervanno's side. To the cerdan's alarm, she had drawn sword—in utter silence. No sound of metal against metal had been heard, although perhaps it had been muffled by the cries—joyful and resentful, both—of children. Nenyane's northern sword was raised; raised and pointed.

Gervanno heard the voice as if the speaker was moving—swiftly—in a circle of which Gervanno di'Sarrado was the center. Nenyane clearly did not hear it in like fashion.

The Northern Widan snapped a warning—her name, no more. Gervanno could not see the mage, just as he could not see the speaker; the mage had vanished into the circus. But clearly, he maintained some invisible connection to the Maubreche Hunters. To Nenyane of Maubreche in particular.

Gervanno was not surprised when she failed to hear it, failed to heed it. Nor was he surprised when Stephen of Maubreche joined his huntbrother, although Stephen did not draw obvious weapon. Swords were not required to arm the Breodani Hunters, as Gervanno now understood; Stephen's dogs changed their formation.

Just beyond them, so did Alex and Max, as if they were part of Stephen's pack. They were not blood kin, but they were kin, and they had shown themselves devoted to Stephen of Maubreche.

"I have offered advice; I have given no commands. Nor have I offered him a place in my circus. Set your blade aside, child of all. Set it down, or you will invoke my wrath—for you are not mortal, and my expectations of you reflect that. You were once his comrade; pay heed, now, to Illaraphaniel."

Nenyane was rigid.

Gervanno's hand rose to sword hilt, and froze halfway there at the sharp, shallow flick of Nenyane's free hand. To his surprise, she spoke; he wondered, given the intensity of her glare, if her eyes could see what his could not.

"Gervanno is mine. For what reason do you seek to offer unasked-for advice?"

"The advice was freely offered," the lord—for Gervanno was certain it was the lord who spoke—replied. "There is no cost to it; no price he will be demanded to pay. Ser Gervanno has clearly met elders in the wilderness for whom that has not been the case, but while he remains within the circus grounds, he will be safe." A voice that had seemed familiar, even avuncular when its words had been directed at the cerdan, was now sharp and chilly.

"That does not answer my question."

"You, however, must pay a price should you wish me to give you the answers you desire; as I said, you are not mortal, and you have not therefore been granted what grace I *choose* to offer. You are Stephen of Maubreche's huntbrother, or I might have refused you entry at all; **do not test my patience.**"

Meralonne appeared, shimmering into existence within the range of Nenyane's sword. He looked down at her—his feet did not touch the ground—but if he spoke at all, the words were inaudible to Gervanno's ears.

Nenyane sheathed her blade, but the flashing silver of her eyes took longer to quiet.

"You will understand her, in time," the voice said. This time, Gervanno failed to speak. Had he not replied aloud the first time, Nenyane would not have taken note—and she would not have risked offending the power in this place.

As if the thoughts were words, the voice continued. "But perhaps you have no inkling of why she asked her question—a question she had no right to ask. Perhaps, had she asked permission, it might have been granted, but perhaps not; she is brittle, broken, and arrogant, and the arrogance of the boundless wilderness has ever been displeasing to us.

"Understand that the circus is as you see it, or as you *will* see it. You have a choice to make, Ser Gervanno."

What choice? What choice was given a cerdan, a foreigner at that, in the wilderness?

The speaker laughed. "Mortals are endlessly fascinating, so alike in the brevity of their lives and their circumstances, and yet so very, very different. Even those who are planted in the same soil often grow to their fullness as different plants, different flowers, even different trees. There is a newness in your youth, in your childhood, and even in the way you face—or run from—death, as if each life is unique, each life a mystery and a tale.

"I never tire of it. But please, avail yourself of the festivities. I would suggest a venue to visit first, but the firsts are yours."

"WHAT DID THEY SAY TO YOU?" Nenyane demanded. "Don't jump like that—they're gone. For now."

"They are not immediately present," Meralonne agreed, the tone of his voice an argument beneath the surface of his words. "I understand that you do not have immediate control of your memories, but you know far, *far* better than this. You might survive the wrath of the lord, but you cannot say the same of your companions."

"I can."

"We are given leave to attend because of those companions. Do not disrespect the lord of these lands."

"I don't want him to compel Gervanno to join this bloody circus!"

Gervanno's brows rose. "That is not what he asked of me," he said.

She wheeled. "Do not trust the lords of the wilderness! I thought you understood that!"

"We left Bowgren in the lee of such a lord." It was Alex who spoke, not Gervanno. But he spoke the words that might have left Gervanno had he been raised in the North.

Nenyane snarled, almost wordless. She was on alert in this place, but felt almost helpless; Gervanno sympathized, but could not lessen that burden.

"Had he offered, I would have declined—and he would have accepted it." But even as he spoke the words, he felt far less certain of their truth. The innkeeper's daughter had run away, had she not? Because she had been chosen, and the boy she loved had not. Had she the right of refusal, would she not have simply stayed?

"The lords of the wilderness do not simply *accept* a refusal with any grace," Nenyane snapped. Perhaps this was all Gervanno could offer her: a stone against which to blunt the edge of her temper.

"I had no reason to offer one."

"Then what did the lord *want*?"

To that, Gervanno had no ready answer. "The lord said I had a choice to make."

"And didn't tell you what it was?"

"No. Perhaps he thought I suffered from some internal conflict. I do not. I serve Maubreche until I have seen you reach your destination in the Dominion."

That was enough for Stephen. To Gervanno's surprise, it was not enough for Nenyane in her current mood. "And after that? Given what we might face, do you have no intention of continuing your service?"

Meralonne chuckled; as he did, the armor he wore dimmed, its light hidden by the sudden appearance of a worn robe. It had once been the color of clear midnight, when the moons were both at their fullest, or so it seemed to Gervanno. "If someone has demanded Ser Gervanno make a choice, it does not seem to be the lord of these lands." He glanced at Nenyane, one brow slightly raised; she failed to hear him.

The mage drew a pipe from the folds of his robes. "It is not the way of this lord to command or demand, save at need. Choices are made, yes, and often the lord makes clear what those choices are; he did not do so today. If there is a choice to be made, it is Ser Gervanno's choice in its entirety.

"But the consequences of that choice will be his to bear; that was also the way of this land's lord." He turned, pipe in hand, to the Southerner.

Gervanno was silent for a long, stretched moment. "Those who are invited to join the circus have as much say as those who are commanded to join the armies of Tors. Those who disobey become fugitives—if they survive."

"I did not say the choices were good. Those choices and commands, however, are entirely in the hands of mortals and mortal hierarchy. But tell me, why do you believe that those who join this circus are conscripted?"

It was not his business. He, who had been raised in the distant South understood better than the free Northerners that such separation, such distinction, was a necessary part of life, of interaction; it had never been wise to know too much. But the daughter of an innkeeper was not the son of a Tor; the daughter's lover was not the commander of an army. They were, to his eyes, children—young enough to make foolish mistakes.

Old enough to die, should the consequences of those mistakes be too costly.

Nenyane glared at the mage, and then transferred that glare to Gervanno. "Answer his question. The townspeople considered an invitation to join the circus an honor—possibly an exaltation."

Gervanno exhaled. "The innkeeper stopped me as I left the inn; he was concerned for Leial, and advised me that, should I care for the dog, I should bring him to the circus. I have attended performances in the Dominion—I assumed the circus here would be a local variant of those performances." He glanced down the street, toward the towering buildings that seemed both too solid to be dream, and too dream-like to be real. "Before I could leave the inn, one of the locals came rushing in. I overheard their conversation."

"Go on," Nenyane said, eyes narrowing, grey glinting as if it were silver.

"The innkeeper's daughter and his friend's son ran away before the start of the entertainment. They ran together—because the daughter has been called up to join the circus and the son has not. I believe them to be in love."

Nenyane had never been patient with simple, emotional concerns, although perhaps Gervanno had not had enough experience with her to make this judgment fairly. Her snort, however, deepened this impression. Love of this nature, at this time, was at best trivial.

"I thought little of it; they are not my kin, and their difficulties are personal and private. I did not speak of it; they had not intended to share the information with me. Were it not for their fear, they might have waited to discuss the emergency until I had departed. And I would have departed, had the friend not been blocking the exit.

"But, had the call to join been entirely voluntary, I believe the daughter could have simply rejected it. That her rejection involved flight implies that such an invitation is more command than offer—for it is clear to me, in these streets, that the circus is far more than simple street entertainment; that the innkeeper's fear for the safety of Leial was rooted in experience and knowledge, both of which we, as foreigners, lack.

"The Free Town roads have been safe for merchant caravans and travel. Safer than Imperial roads at the border, and safer than the Breodani roads. I assume the kingdoms to the west of Breodanir also suffer from the turnings and incursions of the wilderness. The Free Town route doesn't, until one reaches the borders of the Western Kingdoms.

"And now, perhaps, I understand why." Once again, he looked around. The streets had begun to empty as the citizens of Hansleigh sought one building or another; even the sound of children grew distant as parents or grandparents scooped up the youngest and entered various buildings with them.

"Yes," Meralonne said. It sounded like *no*. "Do not meddle in the affairs of this circus." He spoke to Nenyane, but the words could be applied to Gervanno. "Come. It is unlikely that you will see the wonders of this circus again; let us dispense with wasteful irritability." Those words were almost a command. Gervanno could have told the

mage that commands would have little positive effect when it came to
the sword master; he did not. Stephen's grimace was enough.

Meralonne then turned to Gervanno. "If it will put your mind at
ease, your pet will be safe."

Leial barked; Gervanno set him down. He was not surprised when
the dog walked off toward one of the buildings; he *was* surprised to see
that his mutt appeared to be tracking the scent of something.

He had been told that caution was not necessary in this place, but
his instincts had been honed on battlefields, sharpened with time and
experience; he scanned the landscape, caught by the strangeness of it,
but aware on some visceral level that any place could become a battlefield. Like any person, Gervanno could be moved by beauty, could be
caught in the currents of wonder—or awe—when he encountered it.
Nenyane's swordwork was perhaps the most beautiful thing he had
ever witnessed.

But beauty did not imply an absence of malice. There was no safety
in it, and many a young fool had courted death and disgrace because
they were drawn to beauty, as moths were to flame.

That is a lack of self-control, his father had said. *Self-control is the
defining characteristic of an adult. It is the underpinnings of duty and honor.
Hone it, boy. Uphold it. It is a necessary tool for survival.*

Men of power did not require such rigid self-control.

*No. But that is the Lord's will. Those who were born to power far greater than
ours but who cannot bow in the face of even greater meet the same foolish end as
people like us. It is not a sign of weakness to bow to greater power. It is a sign of
necessary respect.*

The words of his father—his angry, disappointed father—had
proven true, time and again.

*But understand something, boy. Respect is offered. Do not bow or bend knee
in abject fear. Understand the difference between the two, or you will live on your
knees—and die there.*

He had wondered what one offered the Lord of the Sun, should
that mythic Lord ever grace the Dominion with his cleansing flame.

*Awe is not fear. Offer fear and you have proven yourself unworthy of being
graced by His light.*

As a child, Gervanno had not understood the difference. He was no
child now, but in this strange, wild place, he felt almost as if he were:
young with wonder, young with awe. Young with anxiety, with the
seeds of fear. He had long accepted that what he felt did not matter—it

was what he expressed that did. It was control of the things he could control: his voice, his expression, the rigidity of his posture.

But not, apparently, his dog.

Nenyane trailed after Gervanno; her mood remained sour. Almost, he wanted to spar with her in these open streets; they were not sword dancers, but they were both good enough with their chosen weapons to draw—and hold—attention.

And did he want attention? No. But he knew she would be at ease if she could but draw sword, and knew as well that she was just self-controlled enough she would not.

Was she worried for him? Did she follow the path Leial had chosen because of that worry? He could not say. But Stephen remained with his huntbrother and Max and Alex followed Stephen. Only the bard chose a different route, for the Northern Widan followed as well, his concern the behavior of Nenyane of Maubreche.

Nenyane's behavior was cause for concern, but it would have been disastrous had she been born and raised in the South. Gervanno felt a twinge of sympathy for the mage, but no more. Had she been raised in the South, she would never have gained mastery over blade. She might have picked one up in the privacy of the women's courtyard, but would never have progressed beyond that.

You are wrong, the now familiar invisible voice said. *You are wrong in every possible way. You think of her in the context of your own small life—the life you lived in the South before you chose to come North seeking peace, in a fashion. But that is not the life you will live, Gervanno di'Sarrado. Not now. You bear the taint of the wilderness about you; you bear the scent of one of the eldest.*

He will not find you here. He will not cross the borders of my lands; we are not friendly. But we are reluctant allies, nonetheless. Nenyane would have been Nenyane no matter where she was raised. Understand that she is not of Breodanir, as her master is. She might have lived in a field; she might have toiled on the sea; she might have been taken as seraf; she might have a Tor's daughter. Nothing could change her essential nature.

One-sided conversations were difficult, but they were not unknown when the difference in power was great.

I am feeling almost nostalgic, Ser Gervanno. Because I am, and it is a distant but almost warm feeling, I will answer the question you would not dare to ask. No. Those who dwell within my lands, those who were born to them and of them, do not have the right of refusal. You understand the Breodani in a fashion. You understand that they have the right of refusal. They lose their authority over

the lands they call home should they fail to live up to their obligations and respon-
sibilities.

The Free Towns are not Breodanir, but there are similar duties, similar oblig-
ations, and similar ancient—to your kind—agreements. It is considered an
honor to be invited to join the circus, for only the strongest, the brightest, can
perform on this stage. Children in my streets daydream about one day joining the
circus—just as children in the streets in which you grew up daydreamed of being
heroes, warriors without parallel in the face of whom demons would perish.

But we have no such agreement with the mortals who cross our paths seeking
either West or East, and even if we were to make an exception, you would have a
choice that those born in my protection might lack. It is coming, he added,
voice softer. *But not yet. Not quite yet. Your dog is enterprising.*

Gervanno said nothing about his dog. Nothing about the circus.
Nothing that would draw the attention—and ire—of Nenyane of
Maubreche.

Those born within the Free Towns are our children. They are precious to us —
and necessary. Do you think it harsh? Even in the home of your childhood, chil-
dren were born, bred, and offered to the engines of war, there to die in the honor
they pursued; serafs were forced to oil that machinery, raised from birth without
the freedom you enjoyed. I will ask you a question. What does freedom mean to
Ser Gervanno, long from that childhood?

"I am not a soldier, now," Gervanno replied, aware that Nenyane
would hear those words.

No? And yet you are far more embroiled in the war you hoped to flee than you
would have been had you remained in your homeland. Or did you merely mean to
leave what you assumed was the battlefield? As you have discovered, the battlefield
is not so strictly defined; there are some lords, however, who can prevent war from
encroaching upon their borders. If I am not mistaken, it is to one such land that
you intend to travel, should you survive.

Gervanno frowned.

Averalaan, the newly born City of Man. Your angry companion aside, I was
greatly tempted to offer you what she has denied you, but I perceive it is not an
offer you could accept. Disgrace comes in many forms, Ser Gervanno. Mortals
have oft believed the entirety of the value of their lives can be decided in a single
moment.

But even that is a choice; you might see many things but dismiss them all
under the weight of that choice.

Gervanno did not speak; it was difficult to maintain silence. As
cerdan he was meant to be invisible; to be the arm and the shield of his

chosen master. Weapons did not speak. They could be wielded, oft in silence, but they did not raise voice of their own. And he had not. But here, it was different; he chose silence because Nenyane was unsettled; almost she reminded him of the angry youths he trained. She was looking for a fight, her temper frayed enough that any fight, no matter how inadvisable, would do.

But the lord was the true power here, and silence was not his desire.

It is not, that lord agreed. *But perhaps I understand better why you bear the scent of the eldest. Do not serve him,* the lord added, his voice both chillier and far, far deeper. *Do not serve. He is fickle; he does not understand duty as you understand it. But he is drawn—as we have always been drawn—to elements of the things we do not ourselves possess. He can see the beauty in it, and the tragedy will never be his problem.*

Gervanno nodded. The words of this invisible lord meshed with his own instincts. But even had they not, he was bound to Stephen of Maubreche.

LEIAL LED them to a building the color of the bright sky, when the sun was ascendant and no clouds marred its brilliance. He had assumed the walls to be smooth wood, and painted, but this was wrong. No sign of brush strokes marred the surface, and no hint of paint existed around the frames of enormous windows. The windows were curtained on the interior, but the curtains were so fine that he could see movement beyond the glass—for the windows here were glassed, just as they so often were in the North. The curtains seemed gossamer, the stuff of night stories, the hint of the Lady's delicate grace. A hint of her mercy in the blazing light of day—a whisper that not all power was defined by victory in combat.

It was a hint that no man should search for, and no man require.

But he had already proven that he was not a man in any way that mattered to the Lord. Even his determination to fight the lord of the wilderness that had been intent on conquering Bowgren had been made at the height of moons—three moons—during the endless night that was the Lady's time.

Leial barked. Gervanno blinked; Pearl reached out and batted the

much smaller mutt with her left forepaw. Leial went rolling through an
open arch into the blue building.

"Sorry," Stephen murmured.

Gervanno shrugged. The dogs could express their annoyance in
very physical ways—with each other, and when no hunt was in
progress. Stephen probably wouldn't have noticed Pearl's annoyance
because there was no killing intent behind it. But the cerdan moved
ahead quickly to retrieve his dog; he intended to carry Leial for the
time being.

If Pearl was willing to hit Leial, the lymer would not make the same
mistake with Gervanno himself.

Leial, however, was not so easily retrieved. He was not particularly
upset with Pearl, either—but he was clearly entranced by the scent of
cooking. Leial could eat his body weight in food and remain hungry.
The dog righted himself on the other side of the arch that served as a
public entrance and headed further in.

Gervanno followed, as if he were one of the parents or grandparents keeping an eye out for excited, inattentive children. The rest of his
companions followed.

"WELCOME, weary travelers. Come and sample foods from far-away
places. Take your ease in the music and instruments of lands you might
never walk on your own feet. There is wine for the daring, and the
sweetest of water for the tired, and there are cards, spheres, and leaves
of tea grown in the special gardens of the Oracle.

"Will you face your future? Or will you support others who are
more daring than you might consider wise? Come one, come all—we
implore you. No matter how dark the day without, there is only light
and warmth in the circus." A young woman in an odd, gaudy dress, the
lower half of her face powdered in pale jade, her lips the blue of sky,
spoke. Her eyes were muted by a short veil; he could not see their
color.

At her side, in silence, stood a much taller, much beefier companion. Gervanno was surprised that the man carried no sword; he was
not surprised to see the handle of an axe peering out from behind his
back. His face was ruddy with sun, a white map of faded scars across

his right cheek and jaw; his eyes were the brown of the South, and his hair the same black, although it was very strangely styled.

He could not imagine the guard a necessity in this place. No townsperson would dare to lay hands upon the circus performers—and it was clear to Gervanno that this slender woman, with her oddly colored face, was exactly that.

If the presence of the lord of this circus was so pervasive, what need a guard?

Humans are surprisingly fragile, just as they are surprisingly strong, that lord said. *But they all bear attachment to their families, and some families are more possessive than others. Elodia is new; she has been here a handful of years. Her parents and her siblings are still among the living.*

"Surely she is allowed to converse with her family?" He made no attempt to bite back the words.

Nenyane turned instantly. *"Enough,"* she snarled. "Show yourself!"

"At your *request*, little hunter."

CHAPTER SIX

T he light in the building dimmed; for a moment, Gervanno was
    caught by an overwhelming sense of night, of darkness so abso-
lute it implied the loss of moonlight, of silver. His hand was upon his
sword hilt, but he did not draw blade. If the tone of the lord implied
anger, the presence of the circus—if it remained—implied a desire for
joy. The night did not extinguish that.

"No. All mortal days are ended with night's curtain; all mortal
nights, with dawn. You are sensible and sensitive. Both are admirable
traits, but they seldom twine so completely and in such a balanced
braid. Tell me, why do you tolerate her? If you intend silence as a
protection against her ire, it will not serve you well."

"It is not her ire I fear, lord," Gervanno replied, bowing in the darkness. "Nor even her disapproval. But she defines protectiveness, and
once she has claimed a person as one of her own, she will be sensitive
to those who she feels might encroach."

The man laughed, his voice rippling out to surround Gervanno
until all that existed in the space was the warmth of that laughter. It
was not unkind; it held—and conveyed—genuine amusement. "And
you are willing to be so claimed."

"She is the best swordsman I have ever seen, in all of my years in
training and battle. There are none who could face her blade and

triumph; at best, they might survive, and only if they surrender—or flee. Demons are not proof against her sword."

"No. Nothing is, as was intended. You are willing to serve her."

"It is the only way I might learn. I am no youthful fool, and she is so far above me, I feel only awe, not the bitter sting of a young man's envy."

"It is not only the youthful who are burned and scarred by envy."

"Perhaps, if I felt I could become as she is, I might take the reins of that envy and allow myself to ride it to improve. But I cannot. I knew it, the first time I saw her wield blade; I knew it the last time I saw her fight. But I can learn. I can improve. And it is my small pride, the remnants of the man I once believed myself to be, that when she chooses to spar, I am her partner."

"And that is worth the road you have chosen—and are, even now, choosing—to walk?"

Gervanno nodded.

"I perceive much in your answer that you are, perhaps, unaware of. Very well. She is known to me, although she is much diminished; that will have to change if you are to survive the road she must walk. But follow her you will; I see that clearly now.

"Tell me, Ser Gervanno, is the leader not influenced by the people at his disposal?" It was a rhetorical question, to Gervanno's ear. "Do not be greatly upset, no matter what you might hear or see in my lands—I mean you no harm, and I mean your master no harm. Remember that."

Gervanno nodded again, and the darkness began to dwindle, condensing and narrowing until the gaily colored building and its many occupants could once again be seen—and heard. The night did not vanish entirely; instead, it took on the tidy shape and form of a man, dressed oddly in a style that Gervanno had yet to encounter in either the South or the North, although if pressed, he would have said the clothing Northern.

Northern, in that it was composed of jacket and pants—but the jacket itself was slightly the wrong shape; very stiff at the shoulders, and very long at the back. The cloth was unadorned by gold thread or beading. The pants were of a color with the jacket—a black as dark as the brief darkness by which the circus had been eclipsed. The shirt beneath the jacket was white and collared. Gervanno disliked Northern collars.

The man himself was of an age with Gervanno, or perhaps a touch older; his hair was the color of his suit, and his eyes, the color of his hair. His jaw was strong, almost square, but his brow, high; his hair gleamed with oil, pulled entirely back from his forehead.

A hush traveled across the crowd nearest Gervanno, although voices could be heard at a remove — the voices of those who had not yet noticed the appearance of the man who ruled the circus.

The young woman in her half veil fell instantly to the ground, kneeling in a posture of subservience better suited to serafs than free men. The physically imposing guard by her side surprised Gervanno; he fell into the same posture. Around, as if they were dominoes, the others who occupied the vast hall did the same.

But the visitors did not, although even the whispering voices in the distance fell silent as silence made itself felt. This hush did not extend to the youngest of children, one of whom began to wail, to the embarrassment of their mother.

It was the reason children did not exit the harems in families of note until they were old enough to behave; such cries, expected and even predicted, could be disastrous for the families of the infants. Here, it was clear they would not be. In Gervanno's village, children such as these were a fact of life. Only the powerful could take offense at the cries of the young — but the consequences they inflicted could destroy whole family lines.

Gervanno, as the other visitors, did not immediately drop to one knee, although he stood closest to the circus master. Or perhaps Nenyane did. Nenyane's legs would have probably broken had she been forced to bend them.

Stephen and Alex, however, dropped into the most formal of their Breodani bows, with Max following seconds later. Gervanno's bow was Southern.

Leial, however, wandered in a circle around the lord of these lands; Gervanno almost stopped breathing when his dog lifted a leg as if to *mark* the man.

"Leial, come here."

The dog looked up at the sound of his name.

"I am the circus master," the man said, glancing at Leial. His glance did what Gervanno's words could not. Leial headed straight for Gervanno, and took up a standing position behind the cerdan's knees. "And as you have rightly guessed, I do not choose to take offense at the disrespect shown by those who do not even understand the concept of respect." His smile was warm. His voice was warm. "But I believe I have interrupted you. The circumstances are as you see them. The circus extends both hospitality and safe haven to those who have chosen to visit. Even to you, Nenyane of Maubreche although in theory, you *do* understand respect in its many forms, and you have chosen to withhold it."

Nenyane shrugged. Gervanno almost reconsidered his decision to join her when she traveled to the South, the shock engendered by her carelessness was so immediate.

"Do I need to show respect to every god I encounter?" Nenyane's voice was low; she was tensed, standing as if her blade was already in her hands.

"Perhaps not. But you are not immune to injury or damage, as you must be well aware, child."

STEPHEN FROZE for one brief second. He then reached out to do what Gervanno would never have dared: he put a staying hand on his hunt-brother's shoulder.

Nenyane had just implied that the circus master—an oddly dressed but very tidy man—was a *god*. Stephen had some experience with gods, for he was god-born. But he spoke with his father in the misty, cloudy Between. He knew of only one god who was said to walk their world in the flesh—and that god, unnamed, was enemy to all.

Nenyane—

"You don't understand what's happening here."

He was almost certain she didn't either, but she was rigid with antagonism—her own. Nothing in the presentation or tone of the circus master implied aggression or danger to Stephen.

What do you think gods are??

One of them is my parent.

And do you think of him in any way *the way you think of Corwin?*

He was not grateful for the question, but was grateful that she had once again fallen silent. *No. And you know that.*

Children of gods are created for a purpose. *Do you think that purpose is to be coddled and cherished like that wailing infant??*

But the infant's sobs had quieted; one glance across this odd bazaar made clear the child had finally fallen asleep.

The purpose of Hunter sons, he said, turned away from the sleeping child, *is the continuity of the family line and the retention of the family lands. We weren't born to be loved, either. We were born to become Hunters or the Ladies who govern their lands, to fulfill the duties of lords to the people whose lands we rule. We were not born to be* coddled *or* cherished.

"But they loved you anyway."

Yes. He thought of Robart, resentful and sullen. *But if you believe love is only pleasant, positive things, you haven't been paying attention.*

"Do you think your father loves you?"

Silence.

"Don't expect love or mercy from gods. Even in fragments of stories that speak of the love between gods, their love could scour whole continents of all lives save one." She had not once looked away from the circus master.

A god.

"She is not wrong. Gods do not love as mortals love; they love as gods do. Mortals have oft misunderstood the nature of that love because they wish to view gods as benevolent—as loving parents, protective parents. Why do you think this is, Stephen?"

Stephen met the circus master's gaze and held it. Nenyane had called this man a god, if indirectly. Had she always been so hostile to gods? She had often resented Breodan, but she had never been so openly hostile. He exhaled. If his huntbrother was right, there was now pressure to answer the question asked.

Oddly enough, he had an answer, for it was a question he had asked himself from the age of five or six, when the world had collapsed; when his ability to believe he had two fathers, both of whom loved him in different ways, shattered. Had he known then, had he *always* known what he'd learned then, with so much guilt and pain, how would he have lived those early, childhood years?

God-born, not a god. No wisdom came from his mixed blood, and he had been told that even the hint of divinity would shorten his life span—what mortal could carry the power and blood of a deity for long?

He had been a child. As a child, he had believed in the wisdom—the near omnipotence—of his parents. He believed that they wanted what was best for him; he believed that what was best for Stephen was best for Maubreche. The two were inseparable in the mind of the boy he had once been.

What the god wanted had been almost irrelevant. It had remained irrelevant while he grew; while he learned to walk, and then to run; while he spent time with his father's dogs. Irrelevant while he played with Robart, disappointed by the frailty of infants and Robart's lack of ability to speak and move as Stephen himself did. Age had been a barrier that existed as a permanent schism between Stephen and his parents, but Robart's birth impressed upon him the truth: time passed. People aged. Age meant independence and the power of a true adult.

He knew the stories of Breodan—every citizen of Breodanir did. He knew that the god had given, to his Hunter Lords, the abilities they possessed. And he understood why huntbrothers existed, what their role was: it was to remind the Hunters, always, that high rank and high birth did not grace all citizens; that the Hunters must value—and trust —those other children, taken from orphanages and city slums; that they must learn to understand what life outside of the manor and its duties meant.

Again, this was as he'd been taught. But he knew, now, that the first of the huntbrothers had not been children; that they were men whose physical infirmities had meant they could not participate in the very necessary duties of feeding a population on the brink of starvation in a strange, new land. They were essential to feed the god, because if they did not, the lords who *could* hunt and protect would be taken in their stead.

Breodan was revered and respected in Breodanir. Because of his interference, the land grew fecund, and the fields produced wheat and corn. Because of Breodan, people were not literally dying of hunger, and while lords served Breodan's will, they would not starve.

But to those early sacrifices, what did Breodan mean? Were they volunteers? Were they set aside as useless in a time of desperation?

"I see you have asked that question of yourself, and have yet to come to a conclusion. It is good to think; it is not good to become so embroiled in thoughts that you cannot move. Your huntbrother has not —yet—offended me, although she is dangerously close. Take her with you, and proceed through the pavilions. But understand I will have your answer before you leave this place."

He then turned to the kneeling young woman who had greeted their party. "Attend me; we will leave our visitors to their own devices."

She rose. "Master."

The circus master glanced, again, at Stephen. "Do not fear for my servants, but do not despise them. They are not what you are."

To Stephen's surprise, it was Gervanno who replied—Gervanno, who was silence personified when on duty. "Perhaps, perhaps not. But they were once what we are."

"They are my performers now, and they are bound to the duty they have undertaken. If they have left the towns of their birth, they have never strayed far, and it is the power of their choice that has protected the towns, even on the worst of Scarran nights."

"How many do you conscript?"

"Enough, Ser Gervanno. I have guided these towns for longer than Bredan his Hunters, and I **will not be questioned further.**"

Gervanno bowed immediately in surrender or apology; it was difficult to discern from the brief glimpse of his expression before it was lost to the movement of a bow.

But Stephen noted that the young woman in her odd raiment and her half veil followed her master's unspoken command as he proceeded through the hall in which she'd been standing. It was for the best. Nenyane was now worried about Gervanno. Ah, no. She'd been worried before, but that worry was familiar to Stephen: it was possessive. Almost jealous. Hints of that remained, but she had been genuinely shocked by the Southerner's question.

Only when the master had dwindled in the distance enough that he could not be seen did she turn to Gervanno. "*Never* do that again."

He nodded.

Alex glanced at Nenyane. He knew her well enough that he made no argument and asked no questions—not of her. But he did speak to Gervanno. "Hunters are not conscripted in the sense that soldiers are. We are born to Hunter Lords and their wives; we are taught the necessary skills to handle the dogs and the hunting weapons; we are shown how to skin, how to cure meat, how to handle the wagons that will deliver our kills to the villages.

"We take vows, but Breodan can't command a random number of people to take those same vows. Our birth defines our service. It seems to me that something similar is happening in Hansleigh. But understand that it was not so long ago that Breodan hunted *us*. Barrett of Bowgren perished in the Sacred Hunt." Gervanno nodded; he could not fail to know that, given their journey into the wilderness surrounding Bowgren. "But his death was peaceful, in as much as death can be. They did not have to find the scattered parts of his body; did not have to accept that some would never be found.

"We understand the toll on Breodanir should we fail to respond to the call of the Master of the Game once a year. Do you believe that Hansleigh's residents are under the same compulsion? Do you fear that they must die, as we must die?"

Gervanno did not answer, not directly. "I asked the question because I understand the building of armies, large and small. I have more in common with Imperial soldiers than I have with those of my people who have never wielded sword against them. Sometimes, when war has passed, old soldiers from either side of the conflict can speak of the shared experience."

Nenyane's eyes narrowed. "You thought you could just talk to an... old soldier?"

"Perhaps. We have never faced each other—these performers and I —across the field of battle. But I believe our enemies are now the same."

"Why would you care?"

"It is information," Gervanno replied. "And information about a battlefield can be crucial to survival."

Alex exhaled. "They won't talk to you now."

"No. I believe the young woman might have chosen to do so, but so did the circus master; it is why he chose to have her accompany him. She is new to the circus—or seemed new, to me—and awkward with the insecurity that plagues the young." He exhaled again, a longer sound. "It is possible—it is probable—that her family is here, in a different building. If the children are chosen and are not given a choice, seeing them may cause difficulties.

"At least for us—for those of us who survived—home was waiting. It was to protect that home and return to it, that we joined the war in the first blush of arrogant youth."

"And in the second?"

"We fought for each other. We defended the men within arm's reach, and they defended us. They became our family as the war continued. Closer than kin in a very visceral way. What I've inferred is that those who join the circus persist; age does not touch them in the same way it touches the families they leave behind.

"Were it simply a job, they could return to their families when the season is over."

"The season," Nenyane said, voice so soft it was almost lost to the returning sound of a happy crowd, "is never over. Summer or Winter, it is all war. But that is still not an answer."

"Soldiers have some commonalities that those who have not fought in war do not share. If the performers here are soldiers, I might learn something from them, should I be willing to expose my own experiences in like battles."

"Their battles are like yours?" Her derision was muted by genuine curiosity. It surprised Stephen.

"Some of them, yes. The circus master believes that the Free Towns have survived—absent walls and armies—because of the circus itself. If the circus people are similar to the Breodani, then the war they have been fighting recently might well resemble the war we fought against the wilderness beyond Bowgren."

Nenyane did not argue further.

"We came back," Stephen said, when his huntbrother failed to speak.

ALEX HAD ALWAYS HAD an interest in history. His interest, however, was not satisfied by the rote learning of dates and numbers and dry, dry facts; he considered those facts to be the surface of a globe, and he looked for cracks in that surface, for ways to look beyond the surface into the substance beneath it.

But he had now lived—briefly—in the world that existed beyond that surface, and it had not quenched his curiosity; it had lit a fire beneath it. A cautious fire, to be sure; he had long understood that the fire itself must remain tightly controlled, or it would escape him. He had accepted his father's decision to send both he and Max to the King's City in nominal disgrace.

Disgrace had not concerned him, excepting only the effect it had on his very strict but much beloved grandmother, Lady Elseth. She was tired, now; she had ruled Elseth for her son, when Alex's mother should have taken up those duties. But Lady Elseth had understood how much of a disaster that would have been for Elseth itself, and his father had been—as Hunters so often were—unconcerned with such disasters. They had never been his responsibility.

It frustrated Alex.

It did not frustrate Max. No brothers could be as close as Alex and Max, but they were different people. Were it up to Max, they would never have crossed the borders of Breodanir. He loved his home, his father's dogs, and the hunt itself. So, too, Alex. But Alex had hungered for more.

Neither Max nor Alex would desert Stephen, and they had therefore left Breodanir. Max did not complain—not out loud—but he found the foreign streets, the lack of real dogs, confusing; he had become far more silent as a result. Alex spoke more, because for Alex, the duties which they'd undertaken offered him glimpses into the wider world. He wanted the adventure. He wanted the knowledge.

When in the company of Hunters, Alex let Max do most of the talking, where speech was required; in the presence of their Ladies, Max hung behind Alex, content to let Alex speak. Alex now realized that the world beyond Breodanir's borders was, to Max, very much like the salons and gatherings of the Hunter Ladies; foreign terrain and almost not worth the effort to learn to navigate.

Now, there were eddies of regret. Max did not so much ignore as observe. He had never considered the meetings of the governing women to be a battleground; he could sense hostility and political movement but, to Max, those movements were petty, irrelevant. No lives would be lost in pretty words.

Words have power, Alex had said. *Words start wars. Wars end lives. Far more lives than hunting ends.*

Max accepted Alex's words as truth, but it was an acceptance of a truth that was, to Max, as superficial as dry dates and names. There, but like moonlight, starlight—some natural, constant occurrence that could illuminate, but only at a distance.

Would you travel without me? Max asked, the tone curious. Neither brother could remember a time when they could not speak through the huntbrother bond. They had been physically separated before—especially in the King's City, where Alex made the rounds with Lady Elseth and Max chose to avoid them.

No. But if we have to travel anyway...

Max nodded in return, satisfied. *Hungry?*

Alex snorted. *That noise wasn't made by* my *stomach.*

THE CIRCUS MASTER had invited guests to partake of the hospitality
offered. Beneath the ceiling of this building—a ceiling that appeared to
made of cloth—were aisles and rows of stalls, manned by people in
colorful garb.

The food in the stalls the Hunters now walked between was neither
out of reach nor ethereal. It was real enough to start more stomachs
than Max's grumbling with hunger. The scents certainly piqued the
interest of the eight dogs that traveled with them in a hunting pack,
and at least one of those dogs was unlikely to take *no* for an answer,
unless Stephen commanded otherwise.

Given Pearl's unique—and difficult—personality, he'd probably
pay for it if he did.

The first strange thing about these food stalls was that no coin was
demanded in exchange for the offered wares. No coin was accepted.
The men and woman who labored in the stalls narrowed their eyes at
the coins Alex held out before shaking their heads.

"It's not that it's we don't trust the quality of your coin, but it's not
useful here."

Behind Alex, Nenyane stiffened, which should have been impossible given her current mood. "Nothing is free," she snapped; she didn't
curse, but her tone implied the words that she managed not to say.

"While the circus is performing in town, food and shelter are free."

"And if we choose not to accept this gift?" Nenyane's hands found
her hips. She was irritable, but she was not—yet—offended enough to
draw sword. "Nothing is free in the wilderness. Everything has its
price."

The man's eyes widened; the woman beside him placed a staying
hand on his arm. It was she who spoke. "The price has been paid; it is
not your burden to carry. There is food here, and shelter, while the
circus performs."

"And when does that performance start? We don't have time to
spend waiting for pretty entertainments."

The man now paled; the woman, however, did not, although her
brows drew together before she spoke again. "The standard for the
behavior of guests seems to be much lower than one would expect;
perhaps Breodanir does not understand the concept of hospitality as
we in the Free Towns offer it."

Nenyane's jaw dropped. Her eyes narrowed.

Alex leapt in immediately, groaning. Stephen was not his brother, but at times like this, he wished the bond he and Max shared could be expanded by one. "Forgive us. We have spent time in domains other than the lands we rule, and it has been fractious and all but deadly. Our companion is therefore concerned, and she is sensitive to what she perceives as charity. If you have served the circus for a length of time, you might better understand her concern than even we.

"Free shelter, free food, is the responsibility—in our lands—of the ruling lords. We serve those lords; it is seldom that such charity is offered us. But is shelter required?"

"You're certainly better with words than your friend, boy."

Boy. Something in the woman's voice made her seem, for the length of the sentence, almost immeasurably old. There was warning in the tone and delivery of words that might otherwise seem mild. She waited for Alex to interrupt; he did not. When it became clear he wouldn't, she nodded in approval. "The whole of the circus *is* shelter. You don't live in the Free Towns, so you won't understand the significance of the circus."

"Food might be appreciated, but we won't require shelter."

Her smile was faintly condescending, but still better than her frown.

"We were informed that the performance would be this afternoon?"

"That is often the intent—but it may well extend for a few days, given the inclement weather. If everything that must be said and shown is somehow finished within the few hours of an afternoon, we will close our stalls and return to our own lands."

"Inclement weather?" Alex asked. They were inside a building, although the ceiling was high and the color of the external walls; it could, were it not for the walls and the windows, be mistaken for sky if one did not look carefully. Alex had.

The man smiled, his expression far more amused than the question should have warranted in other circumstances. There was a hint of something other in it, something possibly bitter; it was gone before Alex could examine it more carefully.

"Inclement weather," the man repeated. "It happens, even in the circus."

NENYANE DID NOT WANT anyone to eat the vast array of foods offered in this pavilion. She kept the words to herself; only Stephen was aware of her visceral reaction. He considered it as they strolled. Had she felt the food truly dangerous, she would have spoken. No, she would have done worse.

I'm not an idiot, she snapped.

Leial, Gervanno's dog, had set about barking, and the barking could not be diminished by anything but food. Pearl, annoyed, swatted Leial on the head, the gesture almost maternal. There were hierarchies Leial was falling foul of—clearly, if anyone was to be fed first, it was Pearl.

Gervanno took little offense at Pearl, but did procure human food for his dog. The Maubreche hounds were not fed from the table; they were not given food meant for people. They were, however, dogs, and as most dogs, had had to be trained not to beg or whine; at their size, at their strength, they might otherwise be terrifying to people who did not hunt. Villagers did not fear the hunting dogs because the hunting dogs symbolized the strength of the Hunter Lords, and that strength meant food in the winters.

But young children did and could find that fear; they had not yet fully absorbed the nature of hierarchy, and they understood, on an instinctive level, that the dogs could easily kill them.

It was Stephen who asked about food for the dogs. Until the man at the stall had mentioned the possibility that the circus event could continue for days, he had not considered the feeding of the dogs to be an immediate necessity.

Nenyane's impatience found a target. "They can eat what we eat here. There's no difference. It won't be harmful for them if it's not harmful for us."

"It's not about harmful, and that's not always true. Dogs—like any hunting beast—have to know what food they're meant to eat, and when. If food meant for people is served to dogs, it causes confusion in that training. Our dogs aren't like Leial. They're hunting dogs. They're trained because they can bring down prey—it's why they must be controlled well. People food will blur that dividing line."

The vendor had clearly been listening. "I see. I don't remember the last time the circus had visitors from Breodanir—although such visitors have passed through on the way to the Empire. None of those visitors brought dogs such as these. I will confer with the master, but I believe

food can be provided for your dogs. I apologize for the lack of preparation on our part."

"No apologies are necessary," Stephen began.

The man lifted his hand. "Hospitality and its rules govern our part
of the circus. To have such fine dogs as guests, and to have no fare for
them, is a breach of those rules." He spoke gravely.

"It is not yet the time at which they would normally be fed,"
Stephen replied, choosing his words with more care. "No rules have
been broken. But perhaps if you might set aside a small area in which
the feeding could be done, it would be a blessing."

This time, when the man smiled, it seemed genuine to Stephen. "I
will return—but perhaps, while I attend the necessary preparations,
you might avail yourselves of any food offered here."

The woman looked at the gathered group, although her eyes rested
last, and longest, on Stephen. Lips pursed, she said, "You'll do. You're
not one of us, and you won't be, but you show some glimmer of understanding that'll hold you in good stead.

"Rules of hospitality govern the circus—but they also govern
expectations of the guests. There are some lines that are *never* crossed
when it comes to those who serve the circus. I don't think you'll need
the warning, but I'll give it. We've had some caravan guards who get a
bit boisterous. Be good guests, and the circus will pass like the best
dream you've ever had. Be bad guests..." she shrugged.

Nenyane didn't even find the warning annoying. She was never one
to appreciate warnings offered her—most were condescending or
dismissive. She was not an imposing figure if one paid very little attention. But the woman's warning had been offered in a different way—
grudging, perhaps, but it had been a gesture of respect.

You offered them a way out of a possible mistake—and she knew it. They
both did. Her grimace was a ripple of expression, here and gone;
Stephen felt it.

As if in thanks for receiving it, she took a plate from the stall's
table. She was the first of their number—if one didn't count Leial—
to eat.

GERVANNO WAS the only guard in their group, but took no offense at
the woman's warning. In truth, it surprised him; guards were, in the

eyes of the powerful, servants with swords. They were mean to be invisible, to be like shadows: they moved as their lord moved; as their lord commanded. Service, fervent service, could be a detriment to a lord, and he had seen that, as well; in his youth, he had lost a friend to that overzealousness.

But perhaps he also took little offense because the woman had glanced past him in the same fashion she had the dogs and the Elseth Hunters. Her gaze had lingered longest on Stephen, but Stephen was golden-eyed. His eyes drew attention no matter where he walked; they would draw that attention in the South.

Gervanno glanced at the food the Maubreche Hunters accepted, but it was not that food that drew his attention, so long from his homeland. He could tease out a familiar scent, wafting in a very gentle breeze. Such breezes were not unknown to him; in the South, homes were far more open, rooms far less segregated, than they were in the North, and gentle breezes often made their way through arches and open doors.

Here, the scent of spice grew stronger; he lifted his begging, whining dog once again and followed the path the scent laid out. He did not fear for Stephen here; Stephen had Nenyane, and Nenyane had chosen, grudgingly, to accept the hospitality of food. A clearer sign of safety could not be had.

He could not recall entering this building in search of food, but food appeared; he wondered if all buildings had such offerings, for food was the clearest sign of hospitality in almost any place his travels had taken him. What had they offered beyond food? Fortune? Fate? Glimpses into either? Thus did the Voyani eke out a meagre living in the villages, comprised mostly of serafs, through which they traveled: glimpses of a pleasant or yearned for future.

He, too, had been a child once; he had known better than to show any excitement or desire for Voyani stories. His father had considered them petty frauds, but while his mother never disagreed with her husband in public, it had become clear to Gervanno that she did not share her husband's opinion. Voyani carried not just stories of pretty futures and love—although the older girls often sought advice of that nature—but spices and cloth and adornments as well.

And the whispered words of fraudulent fortune?

He recalled his mother's soft voice. *Is there a price on hope, Na'Gerri?*

Hope, his father had said, annoyed, *is a scourge. It breaks, it shatters, and when it does, it takes good men with it.*

His mother had nodded, her expression at odds with the gesture. He thought so often of his father while he traveled in the North, but seldom of his mother. But he could see, in the lines of her face, that unspoken disagreement. Life without any hope would be too bitter.

His father could see it, too. *It's not hope they offer. It's stories. They make the hopeful part of a story about themselves. It's fine, when it's just a glimmer, boy. But if the story takes over their life, they can no longer see their life. They believe in things that aren't real.*

Can't we make them real?

Maybe. Maybe not. But if you believe in the story too strongly, you can't see the reality, and it's reality that will kill you.

Gervanno had not accompanied his mother into the Voyani caravan then, or any of its wagons, afraid of being judged harshly by his father; afraid of being seen as weak. Women could not bear swords. Women could not be soldiers. Women required the hope that men—strong men —abjured.

And yet, here he stood, in this land that his father would have dismissed instantly as a fever dream, walking in the company of Nenyane of Maubreche, the only sword master he had ever met to whom he might have devoted his life. She reminded him of many things, for she, too, disdained weakness; had she met his father, had she demonstrated her skills, he was certain his father would have grudgingly approved. But silently, always silently. To support such a sword master went against everything he had both taught and been taught.

He glanced back over his shoulder; Nenyane, grim-faced, was chewing food as if it was a personal enemy. Max ate as if food were a necessity, like air, but otherwise of little interest. Alex and Stephen, however, seemed to genuinely enjoy what they'd been offered.

He could not see the mage, and he could not see the bard—but he heard the soft song of the lute as it slowly traversed this enclosed pavilion. Kallandras had done the same in the inns they had traveled, and his music had brought ease, if not joy.

Gervanno then considered his own food, for he found himself hungry. Like Max, food was a necessity, not a luxury or a source of delight. Given his time in the army, it couldn't be. But if food had not been a source of unfettered joy in his impatient childhood, it had been a source of comfort and familiarity. It had been many years since he had sat at his mother's table and eaten his mother's cooking, but on the rare occasions he had done so after coming of age, he had felt it far more keenly.

Now, he was drawn by a familiar scent, a scent that reminded him of the home he had all but abandoned, or perhaps of a childhood left behind. He could return to the South, and would, but childhood's gate was locked and barred, never to open again.

Hints and echoes of it returned in just such a fashion: in scents of childhood food and the memories of the family with whom he had shared meals. He made his way to a stall. There, food had been ladled into wooden bowls, wide and carved with low sides; the work was good, but plain. There were no symbols engraved on the sides; perhaps they had been worked into the bottom of the bowl, but if so, they were buried beneath spiced meat and vegetables.

There were no forks and knives, although there were hand cloths and bowls of warm water. Instead, there was a wide array of flat breads, because this food wasn't meant to be eaten with Northern utensils. The bread was all that was required; it was soft, and warm like the stew, but it was weighty enough to be filling.

To his surprise, and slight embarrassment, he had begun to eat in front of the stall, as if all layers of hunger had ensnared him at once. He only noticed because others had formed a line to one side of where he stood, impeding their access. He meant to retrieve his bowl, but the woman on the other side of the stall caught his wrist before he could step away, and his awkwardness at the realization he had momentarily lost his manners allowed her to grab it.

"That bowl is empty, Ser. Please, take another. It is seldom that circus guests visit this stall. But not never, as you can see." She looked past him. The sun had not been kind to her; lines were etched in her brow, and the corners of her lips and eyes. But there was, in that, a familiarity, almost a comfort. "It is not always comfortable to stand while eating; there are tables to the south of this stall should you choose to sit at them, but there are also cushions, should that be more comfortable.

"Of course a soldier such as yourself might be accustomed to eating in any circumstance, but if you would take your ease, take it. Sweet water is on the table, as well."

Sweet water.

"I—maybe this question is inappropriate. I know you are part of the circus—but were you once, did you once live in the Dominion?" He spoke his own tongue.

Her eyes were bright, but the smile dimmed. "I did. It was long ago. Certainly before your time. I was a simple seraf, and if you were a man sent to retrieve me, you would not leave the circus alive. But I perceive that you, too, have reasons to leave your homeland—and not so dire as mine. Regardless, you are welcome here."

"Were you living in the town of Hansleigh before you joined the circus?"

"No—I had made a small home for myself as an herbalist in Evanston. But you will find citizens of all of the Free Towns within the circus itself. And you will find that the Free Towns are home to citizens from many different places; some, like yourself, were soldiers who sought a peaceful retirement within the townships. Some had sustained injuries that kept them from their only chosen profession, and some had simply tired of war and loss.

"You know that winning a war does not prevent loss or death. Victory is supposed to justify those losses, those bitter sacrifices—but for some, it doesn't. You will find perhaps one or two of your countrymen in the circus, but they are circus now, not Southern, and the circus takes care of its own." She exhaled. "I've said more than I should, and more than you asked for, but even I remember the lands of my birth. It is odd to have two homes, or in my case, three—but in the circus it is not unheard of."

"Will I find food like this for every day the circus is in town?"

Her smile was far more natural. "You will. In any pavilion, food is provided; strong drink is provided in a few, and this isn't one of them. The point of this pavilion is fate and fortune, and yes, there are mysteries contained herein that you may have heard whispers about when the Voyani came to visit your towns and villages."

"And the other pavilions?"

"There will be one very large building in the center of the town; it is closed, for the moment, in preparation for the performance. But there are pavilions that house wild beasts, creatures of all sizes and appearances; there are pavilions that house arts and crafts, for those who wish to adorn themselves before the performance begins. There is one pavilion that houses our instruments and our weapons—ah, I see that word has caught your attention.

"But you're not far from your battlefield, are you?"

Gervanno nodded, fresh bowl in hand; he had to hold it away from Leial, who occupied his other arm. "No, as you perceive—but Serra, neither are you."

Her face froze as she met his eyes, hers the dark of the Southerners, just as his. "Women don't go to the battlefield," she replied. There was no friendliness in her voice or her expression, but as yet, no hostility.

Gervanno smiled. "That is a very Southern thing to say, Serra. But my battlefield has been in the North, and there are none so bold, so fearless and so skilled as the sword master with whom I train." His eyes sought some glimpse of her in the crowd.

"You've set yourself quite the task, Ser Gervanno. *Quite* the task. I don't envy you, but I won't resent you, either. She is a wild force all on her own; if you follow her, you will be lost to the shadow she inevitably casts."

"I am sworn to the service of her household. I have seen the shadows she casts—but I have seen the shadows cast by demons, and it is only in her shadow that the light is not red flame and ash. It is the light of the sun. It is the Lord's light."

The woman then smiled; her expression reminded Gervanno of his aunts, come from the fields to make dinner and feed their families. "You remind me of my nephew. Stubborn, foolish, and clinging to honor. I was not born a seraf; nor was he. You have appreciated my cooking as more than just an exotic marvel. It is enjoyable to offer people a glimpse into another land, another culture—but it is not, in the end, quite the same.

"I will give you a ticket, Ser Gervanno. Use it as you see fit." She handed him a gold coin. It was, to his surprise, a solari, the coin of the wealthy in the Dominion of Annagar.

"This is a ticket?"

"Yes. Our tickets take many forms and shapes, but this one is mine. We are allowed to offer tickets to the circus to those who we favor in some fashion, and I have chosen, this time, to offer mine to you. It will not save your life; it is not so great a charm as that."

"What is its intended use?"

"It grants entrance to the circus." She laughed at his expression, and the laughter was genuine, to his ear. "Yes, such a ticket hardly seems valuable at the moment. But you stand in the pavilion of fortune and fate, and I perceive the hints of a path in which it might be precious to you. If it is not, preserve it as a memory of this fabled place."

GERVANNO FOUND the tables the woman had mentioned, more for the water than the need to sit while he ate. He set Leial down on the ground, bribing him with food from his second helping. If Breodani dogs did not require leashes, Leial did, but Gervanno had none; he wondered if a leash could be obtained somewhere in this place. He had the sense that if Leial ran off in the circus, he might be lost forever.

But Leial, for the moment, was content to beg for scraps; food, as it so often did, held far more appeal than exploration. The dog was small enough to be carried otherwise, and arms would serve as a leash until a more practical one could be found.

To his surprise, the Hunters found him at his table, bearing food of their own; they joined him and availed themselves of the water. Stephen's dogs, as expected, were far better trained than Gervanno's — or perhaps they cared enough about their dignity that they could not allow themselves to be seen publicly whining and begging for scraps.

Nenyane's mood had not improved. Stephen's, however, was better.

"It took forever to find something edible," Max said, as he sat. Clearly Max was not adventurous when it came to food. He and Alex were eating distinctly different things.

"Nenyane's on edge," Alex, not Stephen, said. "I swear she expected the food to come to life and assassinate us all."

The Maubreche huntbrother's expression soured further.

"She ate," Stephen pointed out.

"Yes — as if she was putting a permanent end to one such assassin." There was a teasing note in Alex's voice; Gervanno would not have dared. But the Elseth Hunter seemed to know Nenyane well enough that he was certain to survive it. Or perhaps he hoped to lighten the mood.

"We haven't found out much about the circus," Alex continued. "In particular, we haven't found out where they're sourcing their food. I doubt it's Hansleigh. There are at least four languages spoken in this pavilion — but I wouldn't be surprised to find more in the others. I'm not sure when the actual event starts."

"It's started," Nenyane said, voice glum. "This is all part of it."

Alex did not ask her how she knew; he knew her well enough to avoid that particular trap. Even Gervanno, who had known her for weeks, was aware of the danger.

"Have you found anything that catches your eye here?" Alex, surrendering the idea of conversation with the rest of his companions, turned to Gervanno.

"Food. Food that would have been familiar to me when I was a child in the Dominion."

"Leial seems to like it."

"Leial likes anything edible. The woman at the stall said all of the pavilions offer food, but alcohol is more sparingly served."

Max grimaced.

"But she said, as well, that this is the pavilion of fate and fortune. I did not assume fortune was a reference to gambling—but perhaps I was wrong. Games of chance were often offered in our festivals."

"Fate and fortune, then?"

"Fate, perhaps. There are no doubt those who offer a glimpse into the unknown future—those were common as well, in my childhood."

"Shall we look?" Alex asked.

Gervanno nodded, and finished eating. He caught Leial in one arm and headed further into the pavilion along with Alex, past the tables and water and food stalls.

MAX TRAILED BEHIND THEM; they all expected Stephen and Nenyane to follow. Nenyane was slow to rise. Stephen did not believe she would become comfortable anywhere within the lands now called *circus*; the best he could hope for was grudging acceptance.

What are you worried about?

"Everything. The lands of the wilderness conform to the whims of their lord. If the power is not absolute, it's strong enough—you saw that when we fought outside of Bowgren. Dawn never came; night never ended. The creatures in the wilderness were bound to their lord's service. That was an advantage to us, in the end; servitude of that nature requires power. The lord's power.

"Are these people bound in the same way?"

Stephen frowned. It wasn't a question he'd thought to ask, because everyone they'd seen so far was human and went about their jobs just as the innkeeper's barmaids had done. The stray thought annoyed Nenyane, but Stephen was resigned; he expected everything to annoy his huntbrother until they were quit of this place.

"I don't know," he said. "I couldn't see the bindings until the end. And even then, only because of you. I could see what you saw."

"I couldn't see them on my own," Nenyane replied. She held out her hand.

Stephen took it, understanding the demand in the gesture. He closed his eyes. Without the battle that had raged around him in the wilderness prior to this, he found the effort to see through his huntbrother's eyes less fraught with discomfort; it was still difficult. He wondered if it would ever be natural.

Wondered why she saw things so differently. And wondered, last, why she couldn't see what he could see through her own eyes unless he and she were physically connected. She had no answer to offer, but the question didn't offend her.

He could not see the binding vows that existed between Max and Alex because neither would swear or accept the huntbrother's oath. Ansel and Heiden had; Aelle and Brandon had. But the bindings between lord and slave had not been golden; they had been dark strands, with glimmers of light spread through them, like an extended web viewed at sunset.

Townsfolk wandered the pavilion; those who offered food or directions usually stood behind tables. They appeared normal to his huntbrother's eyes, although the pavilion itself did not. It seemed blurred, almost out of phase; he could see one stall as if many stalls had been placed, in the exact same location, but slightly misaligned.

Yes, Nenyane said, her gaze narrowing.

But the stall itself was bright, brightly colored; everything, in Nenyane's view, was. Stephen nudged her forward; he found it hard to see people clearly in the mess of blazing color. Nenyane did not, but was willing to move, attached to Stephen by hand as if they were still young children.

"I've never been that young," she snapped. She might have said more, but a wave seemed to move through the landscape; given the lack of response in the crowd, Stephen guessed it was only visible through his huntbrother's eyes. Her hand tightened around Stephen's, almost crushing his; she took the lead, and Stephen opened his eyes, retreating from behind hers.

He had seen no sign of the binding between lord and slave, but Nenyane was no longer concerned about the existence of such a compulsion; she strode—quickly—through the crowd. He made stuttering apologies to the people who hadn't moved quickly enough out of her way. Nenyane hadn't noticed them at all. She strode down the aisle, moving quickly enough that Stephen had to retrieve his hand before she pulled him off his feet.

Where the entrance to the pavilion had been bright and cheerful in color and decoration, the back of the pavilion was darker; the walls were a muted, coal grey. Color, where it existed, was in the signage for the stalls and the clothing of the people who occupied them; torches, lamps, and candles provided illumination as they walked.

Nenyane was focused on a single destination. If she noticed the stalls and their bold claims at all, she gave no sign of it.

"Gervanno!" she shouted, the single word bouncing off walls that seemed almost created to gather and echo sound.

Silence followed the command. It was an absolute silence; even breathing could not be heard. His own. His huntbrother's.

Down the aisle, at what appeared to be its end, was a stall much wider than those that ran up either side of the wide hall. Unlike the stalls that seemed to lead up to it, this one bore no sign, no painted words. The signs above other various stalls seemed to shift letter forms until every person making the attempt to read them, could. This one lacked a sign.

It did not lack a table; it did not lack light. The light, however, seemed centered in a crystal ball the size of two cupped palms. It rested between two hands, in fact.

Standing before it was Gervanno di'Sarrado. Alex was to his right, Max to his left; the light illuminated their profiles, making harsher the lines of their noses and jawlines.

Gervanno turned at the sound of his name. He carried his dog in one arm, and therefore did not immediately reach for a weapon, but he had clearly recognized Nenyane's voice; the urgency in it implied emergency, but there was no obvious enemy in sight.

"Come here. Whatever it is you're being offered, don't accept it."

"It has not been offered to you, Nenyane of Maubreche; it has been offered to your companion." The woman who sat on the table opposte Gervanno spoke softly. Her voice carried. The lower half of her face could be seen; the upper half was obscured by the folds of a dark hood.

"Alex? Max?"

They understood what Nenyane meant by the terse use of their names. Alex, as usual, spoke for both of them. "We followed Gervanno. He approached the fortune-teller. She offered—as I imagine all of the people here are—a glimpse of the future."

"Don't imagine that this fortune-teller is anything like any of the others here. Gervanno?"

Gervanno di'Sarrado was silent.

Nenyane stormed forward until the Southern guard was within arm's reach. She proved this by grabbing his shoulder and literally yanking him away from the stall; she moved into the position he had occupied.

The person on the other side of the table lifted the small, glowing orb she held in both hands. "There is no compulsion in what I offer," she said. "And you must know that. Well met. Well met, Nenyane. And to you, Stephen of Maubreche, Stephen of Bredan, oathbinder and oathbreaker, both, I say: well met."

The glowing orb, she enclosed fully in her hands; light bled between her closed fingers as she drew it to her chest. Stephen could now see the dark, midnight outlines of robe in both the loose, almost training sleeves and the hood that obscured the top half of her face, her eyes. He did not immediately recognize her face, but he recognized the robes themselves. How could he not? He had seen them before, on the most significant day of his life. Then, they had been midnight graced by strong breeze, and when those robes moved fully for the first time, fabric drawn back by sun-aged but certain hands, he had seen his fate.

Nenyane of Maubreche, huntbrother.

His godfather's reaction to this stranger had been similar to Nenyane's now—but worse. It was clear Gilliam of Elseth both knew the stranger and considered her an enemy. But it was clear to Stephen that she had not kidnapped a random girl to bring to the Maubreche estates. The girl had been rail thin, pale, silent; to his eye it seemed like she was a survivor of the famine that could be caused by war.

She was not Breodani by birth. Had he not seen her eyes, had he not met her gaze, he would have thought her fragile. But her silence was not the silence of anxiety—a silence he had known extremely well in his childhood. Her eyes were flat, grey, and the expression on her face implied childhood had ended so long ago it was phantasm, daydream.

When that steely gaze met his, he knew who she would—who she must—become. Light glinted in those eyes; they were silver to his gold. Or platinum to his gold.

And the woman who had guided her and protected her wore the robes of the fortune-teller who now sat before Gervanno, a table between them.

"Evayne a'Nolan, I greet you."

CHAPTER SEVEN

"That is not the name by which I am known here," she replied. She rose; wind took the folds of her robe, pulling it back from her legs and arms as if the robe itself desired to extract her from this reading. "But yes, I am Evayne."

Nenyane planted herself in front of Evayne. Or rather, between Evayne and Gervanno; she intended to be shield wall to a threat that no one else perceived.

But the movement of midnight cloth had dislodged the hood, pulling it back to reveal face and hair; her eyes seemed almost grey, but a tinge of purple shifted the color into something unique. And cold.

This woman was not the woman Stephen had met in a childhood that seemed increasingly distant, but perhaps that child's memory played false; here, she seemed younger, harsher, the contours of chin and cheekbones implying privation, they seemed so sharp. Yet it did not seem to Stephen, in this suddenly wild place, that there could be another Evayne; her eyes carried the same cold light. He moved to stand by his huntbrother's side. Evayne's gaze tracked him slowly, but when it moved to Nenyane, it stopped there, Gervanno all but forgotten.

"I am Stephen of Maubreche," he said, for he felt it was somehow necessary. "And this, my huntbrother, Nenyane of Maubreche. We travel with Ser Gervanno di'Sarrado, and Alex and Max of Elseth."

"...Elseth." For the first time, her expression shifted. She seemed to falter.

It was Alex, standing back and observing, who now moved forward to speak. Max was uncomfortable in the presence of this stranger, and he would not stray far from his brother. Both of the Elseth sons had heard of Evayne a'Nolan in their childhood; their father resented her, but respected her in a chilly fashion.

They knew he blamed her for his own huntbrother's death—in a foreign land, a foreign city. They understood the cost of that loss; although neither had taken the first of the Hunter's Oaths, they knew. They had seen the consequences in Bowgren, but had not been surprised. They could imagine—in the darkest of their twinned thoughts—what the loss of their brother would mean to them.

"You are Espere's children, then."

Alex nodded. If he was surprised by the question, it didn't show. Max's, on the other hand, did.

"My apologies; I met your father in his youth, and your mother as well." She then moved her gaze to Stephen. "Son of Bredan." Her expression once again shifted, but the ice did not return to her eyes. "What year is it, in your lands?"

It was Alex who answered. Stephen, aware of Nenyane's tension, remained silent. "Four hundred and twenty-nine, by the Imperial calendar. The 21st day of Wittan. And in these lands?"

"Time does not move at the whim of the Imperial calendar in the confines of the circus—but I am certain you are aware of that."

Alex nodded. "But it doesn't *feel* like wilderness, to me. Not here." Max glared at Alex's profile.

Evayne's smile was tinged with shadow. "It would not. The lord of this wilderness has always valued humans and found delight in their tasks, large and small. The circus is designed for humans; it is husbanded by those who dwell in the Free Towns, when their time comes." She did not sit again, but her eyes met Nenyane's narrowed—and very suspicious—gaze.

And you aren't? Nenyane demanded.

Suspicious?

Yes.

He wasn't, and Nenyane knew it, which annoyed her.

Does she look like the Evayne who brought you to Maubreche to your eyes? She's the same person.

She's too young. Or she looks too young.

That could be artifact, illusion. Something.

Stephen shook his head. *She looks the same to you?*

Nenyane had glared, but hadn't studied; she had always been quick to judge in any social circumstance where judgment would not be—in her mind—deadly. He could feel the way her regard sharpened; could feel her slough off irritation, anger, and the bitter sense of shame at the *idea* that she owed her survival to anyone.

Ah. He shouldn't have asked.

But he was curious. Nenyane's response to the people she met was entirely rooted in who she was and how she saw the world. It was not Stephen's response; it was not Alex's. She recognized people familiar to her, but her memory was often sharper, harsher, and clearer than Stephen's.

She had known, at a glance, that Kallandras was dangerous. Deadly. No one who had met the bard while Stephen was witness found him intimidating; some found him also embarrassingly attractive. She had called him *assassin.*

Until they had entered the wilderness from the Margen demesne, Stephen had not seen Kallandras kill. But he accepted Nenyane's instinctive, visceral reaction, because on the day she had attacked him in the Queen's audience chamber, Kallandras had not died. Had not come close. He had made no attempt to injure Nenyane; all of his moves were defensive in nature.

But he survived.

What she had seen in him, Stephen had not—and did not—see until the battle against the lord of the wilderness that menaced Bowgren. And he almost couldn't hold it in mind; when he thought of Kallandras, he heard a song, carried by the bard's voice, in a language that was almost irrelevant.

Now, however, she looked at Evayne. Stephen hesitated; he had not recovered from the headache of viewing the circus through his hunt-brother's eyes. She knew, and narrowed her field of view as he attempted to see through her eyes, but it didn't help.

How can you look at her at all?

It's not like I enjoy it, but it's not hard. Evayne no longer looked like a person in Nenyane's eyes.

She does.

She no longer looked like a person to Stephen when viewed through Nenyane's eyes. *Better?*

Evayne was the very heart of white fire, a light so bright it obliterated all other colors or shades. He could make out the outline of limbs —arms, legs—and above and around the pure, painful light, a shadow that stood ready to eclipse it.

It's her robe, his huntbrother said.

He knew he would suffer for it later, but opened his own eyes; for a moment, he could see Evayne a'Nolan clearly, superimposed on the brilliance Nenyane saw. *Did she always look like this to you?*

Almost always.

He didn't ask for the exception. Instead, he withdrew from Nenyane's viewpoint as a wave of nausea threatened his ability to stand on his own two feet.

"Are you part of the circus?" Alex asked, drawing Stephen's attention.

Evayne's brow furrowed, adding lines to her forehead that eased when her expression once again became neutral. This time, she studied Alex. "Not as the others you will meet here are, no. But the circus is a place I can traverse at will—one of the very, very few." She had already abandoned her chair, and the crystal ball she had cupped in her hands was absent, but her gaze left Alex to settle on Gervanno.

It was her interest in Gervanno that had unsettled Nenyane, and it was clear to all present that that interest remained.

"I had not expected to see Gilliam's sons here," Evayne said. "Nor had I expected to meet Stephen of Maubreche." She did not mention Nenyane.

She doesn't remember me. She hasn't met me yet.

It came to Stephen that Evayne's age had meaning, here. The Evayne who had brought Nenyane to Maubreche had been older, more certain of her power. That certainty was absent from this younger version.

"Will you stay until the circus performance is done?" Alex asked.

"I am not yet certain. The circus is not my home, and I may be called away with little warning. I came only to offer a warning to Ser Gervanno di'Sarrado."

Nenyane's eyes narrowed to slits; Evayne could not have chosen worse words, but Stephen had no sense that she'd chosen them to deliberately anger his huntbrother.

"What warning?" Nenyane demanded, stepping forward; she had already chosen to stand between Evayne and Gervanno, and her step brought her into arm's range of Evayne.

"If he chooses to share what he has seen, I cannot prevent it." Evayne stepped to the side, circumnavigating the now empty table. "But if he so chooses, I will take no offense. Your time is short, Ser Gervanno, should you desire to intervene. Not all do."

Nenyane turned to Gervanno. "What did you see? What does she mean?"

Gervanno bowed head — to Evayne. It was, for the moment, all of his answer.

Evayne opened her mouth to say more, but closed it again before audible words escaped. Her expression rippled, and something that was not quite a smile crossed her lips before vanishing. "I see yours is not the only attention I've drawn."

Stephen turned to look back down the aisle. At its entrance stood Kallandras of Senniel.

"WELL MET, KALLANDRAS," Evayne said to the bard, who did not move.

"Well met, Evayne."

"I told you there were things of which I could not speak; you are standing in one of them now."

"Why have you come?"

"Why indeed? You need not fear me here — or anywhere, now. In truth I did not expect to encounter you again ere the end."

"And this is not the end."

"No — but it is much, much closer, and there is still far too much that must be done if we are to survive."

"Will you walk with me, then? For we are bound to the circus lands until their performance is finished."

"Are you? You may leave the grounds at any time, for that is the nature of the lord of these lands." The words were softly spoken, but so bitter Stephen felt he must look away.

The bard held out an arm, and Evayne approached him. She hesitated for one long breath before placing her hand on the crook of his arm. "Yes," she said. "Yes, I will walk. Here, the path cannot move beneath my feet."

Nenyane waited until the two had progressed beyond Stephen's normal vision, and then turned to Gervanno, eyes flashing silver. "In future, never accept Evayne's offer. Never."

Gervanno nodded.

"She doesn't help people unless they can serve her ends. Understand that she will sacrifice you—and everything around you—should she feel it necessary. What she reveals to those who choose to look is not a kindness."

Gervanno nodded a second time. It was clear to Stephen that he did not wish to speak of what he had briefly glimpsed in the crystal before Nenyane had interrupted them.

It was therefore clear to Nenyane, but as usual, she didn't care. "What did she show you?"

Gervanno exhaled. "A stranger. A stranger's face."

Nenyane frowned. It was impossible for her eyes to narrow further without closing. "A stranger."

Alex and Max both looked in Stephen's direction. Neither of the Elseth Hunters had asked—or would ask—Gervanno for information he clearly had no desire to share. But Stephen couldn't stop Nenyane if Nenyane was determined, and they knew that. Alex was, no doubt, curious.

"The innkeeper's daughter," Gervanno finally said. "And the young man she loves. They are not in the confines of the circus."

"The ones you told us about."

The Southerner nodded.

"Were they dead?"

"I did not see a single image," he replied, "but many, as if I had been dropped in a river composed of nothing but possible futures of those two people, each rushing by almost too quickly to grasp."

"Were they dead in all of them?"

Gervanno's exhale was long and slow. "No. Not in all."

"She wants you to save them." Nenyane's voice was flat, but anger seeped out between the syllables.

"She did not speak. She offered me glimpses of the possible future —and she made clear that these were possible, not definite."

Nenyane's frown shifted, her brow folding slightly. "Who else?" she finally asked. "Who else was dead?"

Gervanno did not answer immediately. When he did, his tone was neutral. "As a child, the Voyani offered glimpses into our futures during festival seasons—especially harvest, were they there for it. It was a game, a way of earning coins that did not involve obvious theft. But there was one Voyani woman no one but the desperate sought, and if she were the one offering such glimpses, we closed our eyes and turned away. She was terrifying.

"Evayne was terrifying in the same way, but I did not recognize it in time. Had I, I would never have approached."

"Who? Who was the woman who terrified you?"

Gervanno shook his head. "She was Havallan, the matriarch of that line. And she terrified because her glimpses of the future were not the gossamer and glow of daydream. She offered, instead, to draw the curtains back from the truth, and those who were cursed or blessed by what she shared could not understand what they saw until it was far too late.

"I am not the child I was, when the Voyani seemed both free and almost magical. I do not believe in kind future and kind fate; I have seen too much death."

"The possible futures she reveals aren't entirely random. What you saw when you looked was the answer to a question you haven't asked yet."

Gervanno bowed head this time. "Yes," he said, when he lifted it. "I was thinking about the circus, and about Breodanir and the Hunter's Oath, or Hunters' oaths. And I was thinking, as well, about conscription and sacrifice. The young woman, Adala, is the innkeeper's daughter, and this, I think, was meant to be her first circus. She did not choose to join—but I am not certain that the choice is entirely hers. Evayne said that all people within this lord's lands have choice."

Nenyane's nod was slower to come, and far more measured.

"But you must be aware that sometimes the choices we are offered are between two different disasters, two different losses."

"Why do you care about the innkeeper's daughter?" she demanded.

"The innkeeper saved Leial. Had I left Leial in the inn, I believe he would not have survived what is to come."

"And what's to come?"

"While we remain within the circus grounds? A performance, sword master." Gervanno bowed. "But I think it time to visit other pavilions before we're called to attend the grand performance." He rose. He did not turn away; he merely stopped speaking, and adopted the visible invisibility of a Southern guard.

Had they been at the inn, Nenyane would have demanded a sparring session. They were not. But she had added apprehension to her anger and resentment, and if it was narrow, it was deep; a sword's perfect thrust, instead of a sweeping strike.

GERVANNO DID NOT SPEAK of the brief—and interrupted—shards of future he had seen. He understood that Nenyane considered the fortune-teller a very significant threat, but not in the immediate way bandits were. He did not understand why—but why, for a guard, was irrelevant unless it directly affected the physical safety of his master.

What he did not say—what he could not bring himself to say—was that he had not finished. He wanted to return to that stall, that table, and that very odd crystal; he wanted *time* to draw as many images, as many possibilities as he could, from its shifting clouds.

He was certain he would not be offered a second chance.

But he was also certain that Alex had seen something, for both of the Elseth Hunters had framed him; standing on the right and the left of Gervanno, both had looked at the crystal. Neither had spoken, but it seemed to Gervanno that Max had seen nothing. It was Alex's silence that implied he, too, had seen something unsettling.

In some of those brief futures, Gervanno had seen the circus and elements of its performers. In some, the circus was gone—or he was no longer within its boundaries. And in some, the Hunters were outside of the circus as well.

In two, Alex was injured; to Gervanno's eye, mortally. He therefore did not speak of what he saw. If there was something that should or must be done, he wished to do so without the company of the Elseth Hunters. Had he seen Nenyane? Stephen?

Yes.

But it was only in those images—the last of the ones revealed—that he had seen the circus itself crumbling, falling—falling to flame, falling to storm and the breaking of earth. In the moving wall of fire, he could see the dim outlines of things that were human—and things that were not.

The crystal ball was interesting; he had studied it with his eyes, but he could feel the heat of flame, could inhale the smoky dense air that came with fire's destruction. He could hear raised voices; the tone, the terror, was clear but the words too indistinct, as if he must move closer —quickly—to hear the words conveyed. For a moment, this had been his reality.

And then Nenyane came and the clouds at the heart of the crystal once again veiled everything. Too soon. Too soon for Gervanno to return to reality.

If he had, as a child, dreamed of bright hints of the future, he had also dreamed of acts of pure heroism, untarnished by the truth—the many truths—he had discovered, about both war and himself. Dream gave way, step-by-step, day by day, to reality, the brightness of hope and idealism tarnished until he could no longer see those early dreams as anything but folly, ignorance. Or perhaps they had been too heavy, too costly, to carry; he had simply not been, had never been, strong enough to fully bear their weight.

Now, he had no desire for daydreams. Had he, his encounter with the fortune-teller, Evayne, would have been deeply disappointing. What he had was the desire for information; information could turn a rout into a retreat. He did not demand victory, perhaps because he no longer believed victory was permanent.

His side had won the battle in the Averdan valleys, at great cost— but demons had continued their war on different fronts, different battlefields. The deaths of his comrades had been the blood price paid to stave off demonic victory, no more.

It was bitter.

He had feared the demonic, as a child fears monsters that lurk in the darkest corners of the domis, waiting for parents to slumber so that children might be carried off and devoured. But encountering demons on the field of battle had been akin to encountering gods; they were so far above his abilities, so far beyond his feeble strength, that the best he could do was avoid their immediate detection until he had the opportunity to strike—to cut off feet, ankles, cut through hamstrings.

But by that point he had given up on beautiful dreams of heroic stands; he focused on survival. His. His men's. The people beyond the valleys who would die at the hands of demons should they lose this necessary battle. Would they care if he did not stand his ground, sword in hands, staring into the eyes of his enemy?

No. They might make stories or songs of heroic battles; they might offer them as comfort to terrified children, those who had already lost people in the lee of war as supplies and food were commandeered by the armies. He shook off memory and turned to follow Stephen, his titular master, in silence.

If childhood dreams were dead, why had he chosen to walk through this hall at all? Why had he chosen a fortune-teller who offered a glimpse of the future? No present desire, no adult desire, had driven him here. Somewhere, in the ashes of those childish yearnings, embers clearly still burned.

ALEX FOLLOWED STEPHEN AND NENYANE, but some of the bright curiosity had left his gaze. Everyone noticed. No one asked questions. No one but Max.

Max had never understood Alex's love of history and lore; he had never really understood why his brother was fascinated and eager to try untasted foods with ridiculous sauces and spices, or his attention to details—cloth, lace, the *way lace was made*. It was the same attention he paid to the rituals of the hunt, and the rigors of the hunt itself.

But Max focused on those because they were practical. Alex *could* be practical; he usually was. But this place, this circus that made Nenyane so irritable, might have been created to appeal to Alex of Elseth alone.

As a child, Max had resented anything that differentiated his brother and he, for he felt they were the same, and meant to be the same. Differentiation was akin to abandonment. Max had never felt he needed anyone but Alex.

They had come early to the huntbrother's bond, had come to it naturally; no oath had had to be offered, no oath accepted. They had learned to speak to each other almost before they could speak with their parents or anyone else. It was that bond that had saved them. It was the sensitivity that came with the silent communication; words did not come first, just awareness. Max had been aware of Alex. He knew where Alex was at any given time; could find him easily when he was lost in exploration, in a way that servants or the rest of the family couldn't.

Alex's words—to Max—came first. Max's followed, as if he couldn't bear to fall behind his brother. But what the bond conveyed was Alex's delight. His joy in discovery. His certainty that this was something he could share with only one person: Max. Max found no joy in musty history tomes or, even worse, made-up stories. But he found joy in Alex's joy. Or perhaps in the fact that Alex conveyed that joy to him so naturally, so easily. No one else felt it as Max did. If Max could not, firsthand, feel as Alex did, he could nonetheless feel what Alex felt. He could notice what delighted Alex. He could even—with effort—offer Alex some of the things that were likely to invoke that happiness.

It was the only way he could share it.

It was an effort he made because it was Alex. He would not have made the attempt for any other reason, to his grandmother's frustration and dismay. Perhaps that had been unwise on his part: Lady Elseth now knew he *could*, and that he chose not to. But really, the effort was great enough he was only willing to make it for one person.

Alex, in turn, understood Max, and in the same fashion, but Max was not given to joy the way Alex was and had always been. His happiness, such as it was, was found in the hunt, in the Elseth forests, in the particular silence that came in what he had once called the wilderness. Max was born to be a Hunter, in a very visceral way.

It was why their argument about the huntbrother's oath had been so bitter. Alex wished to swear that oath, and argued—with many, many more words than his brother—why that role should be his. Max argued with far fewer: no.

Their mother didn't care. Their father had reservations, but understood exactly why his two sons each refused to accept a huntbrother. Lady Elseth had been the most dour in her disapproval, although most of that fell on Alex, because Alex was likely to care.

Alex told him not to mind it; Alex's relationship with their grandmother was not Max's. Mostly because Max avoided having any. He found her rules and her manners and her etiquette both intimidating and irrelevant to the life he chose to live.

You accept me. I accept you. That's all there is to it. I don't want you to be me. I don't need you to be like me. I just need you to accept me. I'm your brother.

I'm your huntbrother—and you're mine, before you lose your temper again. You can't bear her disappointment for me—it's not yours to bear.

But I need to do something.

No, you don't. Lady Elseth is Lady Elseth. She is harsh because she rules; she is harsh because she worries. But she loves, is capable of loving; this is just her way of expressing it.

I don't want it.

No. But Max? I still do.

Max gave up on the need to understand. But he would never give up on Alex. When Alex fell silent, it had always been uncomfortable for Max; Max's silence didn't seem to bother his brother in the same way. But Max's silences were not like Alex's. Emotions didn't bubble up out of them. Silence was not a way of protecting others; it was not a way of gaining privacy. It was just what it was.

Alex's silences were different.

The silence now held the faintest hint of fear. It was tightly contained, tightly controlled—which simply meant Alex was deliberately thinking about anything else. But while the circus had been a source of excitement, that excitement had dimmed greatly. Now, in the shadows of its buildings and awnings, Alex felt the wilderness, and the wilderness of the ancient world was not their home. It was not the forests of their demesne, beloved and well-known—and even those forests could offer death as a consequence to the foolhardy.

No, it was more than that.

Gervanno had looked into the crystal heart of the seer. To Alex's eyes, to Max's, she had never been a simple fortune-teller, a simple performer; there had been, about her, a dark crackling aura, confined and released through what appeared to be a cloak. Her voice, low, was pleasant, but it hummed, as if a third person were speaking as she spoke, their words exactly and perfectly timed to match her own.

Max had not looked beyond the clouds in the orb; they had resisted him, a blur in his vision; he made no attempt to focus. Whatever tricks were being played there, he wanted no part in them. If she wished to impress, let her do the work.

But Alex, being Alex, did look. Alex had seen *something*, and that something had doused all excitement, all curiosity, except one. Had Max looked through Alex's eyes, he would know what Alex had seen, and he would know what Alex now feared.

Alex watched Gervanno; he was now far more aware of the Southerner than he was of the surrounding circus.

Max wanted to speak with the seer. His hands became fists as he
scanned the circus crowds; she was easy to spot because of her robes.
She had walked away with the bard, her gaze oddly apprehensive. The
bard was easy to miss unless he wished for attention, and clearly he
had no desire for it now.

Let it go, Alex told him. Max had never bothered to hide his
emotions from his brother. He'd never learned how. Alex had. *If you
want to know what I saw, you could—I don't know—just ask me.*

Max exhaled. *Fine. What did you see?*

Alex, predictably, did not respond immediately. He looked around
the circus grounds as if searching for some place that lacked people.
Stephen stopped and glanced back at the brothers.

Nenyane cursed. Her words—or her tone—drew attention in the
sparse crowd. Had people been standing closer, they would have moved
away. His huntbrother didn't appear to notice. She moved to Alex's
side, caught his right arm, and shook her head. "Don't. Just don't."

"Don't what?" Max asked, the words just shy of demand. He
seldom interfered with Nenyane, but Nenyane was seldom attached—
by white-knuckled hand—to Alex.

"She didn't offer to show you your future. You shouldn't have seen
anything at all. Don't act on it. Don't use it."

Alex frowned. "Why?"

"Because she never does anything helpful for free, and sometimes
the cost of her help is worse than whatever fate you managed to avoid."

Alex's voice was soft. "I doubt that."

Nenyane tensed.

"Why do you distrust her?" Stephen asked, choosing to speak
aloud because Max and Alex were involved. "She saved your life. She
brought you to Maubreche."

In a low voice, Nenyane replied, "I don't know."

It was Alex who risked continuing the conversation. Stephen
understood that *I don't know* was a wall—a spiky, dangerous wall. "You
remember your arrival in Maubreche?"

Nenyane nodded.

"Do you remember what happened before that? You arrived with
Evayne. You were injured, and you had no accessible memories. But

when did the lack of memory occur? Do you remember her intervention at all?" His tone was urgent.

Nenyane closed her eyes. "Not well. It's scattered. I couldn't see my
enemies—not as I see you. But I saw Evayne. I remember that clearly.
She was white lightning, blue lightning, dark fire—all at once—as if
she were standing at the nexus point of overlapping lands. And her
voice..."

"But she came to rescue you."

Nenyane was silent; her eyelids flickered, her lashes trembling at
the movement. "Yes. Maybe. But not because she had any interest in
me. It was because she considered me *necessary*."

Alex said nothing.

"Can't you see it in her? Can't you hear it in her voice? There is
nothing she would not do if it served her goals. Nothing she wouldn't
sacrifice."

Max turned to Alex in silence. *Do you think she's right?*

Alex was silent this time as well, but Max could sense the uneasiness in his brother take firm root and begin to grow. Alex didn't think
Nenyane was right; he feared she was right.

It was Max, therefore, who turned to Nenyane. "Does she choose
what she reveals?"

"I don't know. I've never looked into her crystal."

Max had seldom been frustrated with Nenyane's lack of memory. It
was a fact, a part of Nenyane of Maubreche, like the color of her hair.
It was also Stephen's problem, not his. "She didn't offer Alex a glimpse
of the future."

Nenyane nodded.

"So maybe what Alex saw wasn't what she meant to reveal."

"Look—I know next to nothing about seers. I don't think it works
that way. But...you two are a bit different, because of your mother."

"Because she's god-born."

"Because she's god-born, but not the way human children are."

Max shrugged. Alex almost glared.

"Don't start," Nenyane told Alex. "You know just as well as we do
that when your mother joins Gilliam on a hunt, she takes on an animal
form. She does it sometimes when she sleeps at home as well."

Max had always found that comfortable. So had Alex and their
brother and sisters. Lady Elseth, however, had not, nor had the Elseth
keykeeper. Their mother learned to maintain a human form while in

the Elseth manor, unless she was exhausted. But they were her children. Max thought it natural that they were better hunters than any of
the other lords' children, given their mother.

According to Alex, Lady Elseth agreed—but not with any
happiness.

She was worried that we would be more like our mother than our father.

She was worried we'd never be like her, Max snapped.

Does it matter?

You tried. She made you try.

Alex pinched the bridge of his nose, his uneasiness fading as he
faced Max's familiar annoyance. *I tried because I love her, even if she's
difficult.*

Our sisters help her now.

Alex nodded. *It's why I didn't fight coming to the King's City. I was the
runt—we both know that. Mother didn't expect me to survive. Grandmother did.*
He spoke, as always, without resentment. *Reading was important to her.*

She thought it should be important to everyone.

Max could feel his brother's smile, although none of it moved his
lips.

*She did. Still does. I always had questions about anything I read, but she
liked my questions. She just...liked it when I had questions. And I had so many.*

Max hadn't.

She never demanded I look at the world the same way she did. She didn't, he
added, at Max's snort. *She asked that we all* behave *in the same way when
dealing with strangers—but she never told me what I should see when I first meet
them, or what I should look for. She didn't demand that I find them interesting,
even if she did.*

She did.

*She didn't, Max. You assumed it. You assumed that she wanted the world
ordered in exactly the way she did it—but you're wrong. Maybe if I had been
William, it would have been different. Maybe if there was only one Elseth son, not
three, she would have been harsher. But I look at the circus, and I think of her. I
think she would have loved it.*

Max's grandmother had never loved *anything*, in Max's memory.

*But she can't see it. She can't leave Elseth unless and until William's future
wife becomes Lady Elseth. She can't travel as we travel.*

Because she can't hunt.

Do you think we'll be hunting here?

Max was silent for a beat. *Don't you?*

His brother exhaled. *No. Not here. Not in the circus. Come on. Let's look over there.*

Alex, what did you see?

Alex shook his head.

AS IF THE silent conversation had caught the attention of the lord of the circus, the pavilion Alex chose to explore next—with walls a lily-yellow and awnings of pale cream cloth that were heavily embroidered in gold and silver—was a bazaar. How a bazaar existed in a venue which refused to accept coins in exchange for goods, Max didn't know. Alex was curious as well, but it was normal curiosity.

It's not that Alex shared everything with Max—but questions had always led him forward, sometimes cautiously and sometimes reck-lessly. He realized that was the thing that was wrong: Alex wasn't asking questions. Alex had seen something from the side of the crystal, and he was trying, desperately, not to think about it at all.

It wasn't like him.

Almost, it seemed as if he wanted to forget anything he'd seen. Max exhaled. He knew Alex well; Alex wouldn't be able to forget for long. Let him try. The circus itself was an entirely new experience, and one he was unlikely to be able to repeat.

Nenyane had no desire to visit another pavilion. Loudly. But Alex entered the pavilion, and her hunter followed. The dogs were skittish, which split Stephen's attention between circus, alaunts and annoyed huntbrother. Without thought, Max reached down to place a staying hand on Steel's head. Steel, who always accompanied Max, but who belonged to Stephen. Max missed the Elseth dogs. The one regret he had about the various Hunter's oaths was this: he would never have dogs of his own. Not while he remained in Elseth.

Stephen's case was unusual. All dogs, should Stephen desire it— and sometimes when he did not—were Stephen's on a fundamental level. Legal ownership meant very little to dogs. Had Stephen been a different person, Max would have likely resented him. Or worse.

But Stephen was, to their father, a beloved nephew. Alex had taken some time to puzzle this out. Max hadn't bothered. The legality, the actual words that described their relationship, was irrelevant. To Gilliam, Stephen of Maubreche was part of Elseth in a very visceral way. Precious because he was a Stephen, his dead huntbrother's child.

How didn't matter. The fact that his golden eyes made clear his father was not the former Stephen of Elseth didn't matter. Not to Gilliam of Elseth.

It was for Stephen's sake that the Elseth Hunters had been sent to the King's City. It was Stephen they were meant to protect. His father had tried to protect *his* Stephen, Stephen of Elseth, and had failed. The ghost of that failure, the regret and the rage, had always been part of their life.

As long as it didn't cost him Alex, Max was willing to do anything necessary to return to Breodanir with Stephen of Maubreche at his side. He glanced at Stephen; Stephen stood beside Alex, the two slightly bent over the table at which Alex had paused.

Books.

The merchant had books on offer. Alex, of course, had been drawn there because Alex could smell a book a mile away. Stephen was never far behind. Nenyane had, reluctantly, joined her Hunter, but stood back from the table, arms folded, eyes narrowed. And the Southerner stood back as well, although there was no sign of displeasure on his face.

Were it not for Gervanno, Alex would not be so unsettled. Alex would not have had something he wished to keep secret, even from Max.

"Sometimes, one asks the question," an unfamiliar voice said. Max glanced in the direction of the speaker. He expected to see the circus master, the man in tidy but very unusual black. He was surprised to see that the speaker was an elderly woman, voice rough with age, and low with it as well.

"And does he get answers?"

"Often questions beget more questions," the old woman replied. She looked as if she had come from tending the field at the end of a long harvest day; sunset was reflected in her eyes. She wore a sorting apron, and bits of debris clung to its edges; her hair was grey, but not yet white, and her eyes were, sunset aside, a dark brown. She did not stand by a table.

"Not yet. I have been waiting for my guest." The woman smiled briefly, lips forming etched lines at the corners of her mouth. "And I believe that must be you. Do you not read?"

"I can."

She chuckled. "Come, then. I have not been part of the bazaar for many, many years; I have not been asked to man a table, there to wait." Her smile slid from her face, and with it, the wrinkles and the touch of sun. "But it appears that this circus will be long, and we must all contribute as we can."

"I'm not a member of the circus."

"You would not survive it."

"They're not finished yet," Max replied, trying not to bristle.

"I have nothing for the others. But the decision is yours. If you wish to wait, wait. The bazaar will close when the circus performance begins, and if you've not found your way to my table before then, anything that might have been meant for you will vanish. Remember, boy: choice is yours, in this place.

"And consequences of those choices, yours to bear as well. There is no true choice in the absence of consequences."

Max glanced at Nenyane. Nenyane's gaze was on Stephen; it hadn't faltered at all.

"No, as you suspect, she did not hear me." The old woman lifted a hand towards him; the hand was unblemished, while her clothing implied labor that had not been etched into the skin.

Max glanced at Alex's back; Alex had picked up a book, and his head was bent in the particular way it did when something had caught his attention and had planted a seed that might blossom into delight or urgency. Stephen had yet to find something that caught his eye, but he continued to browse, much to the impatience of his huntbrother.

Max understood the offer—and demand—in the old woman's gesture, he had seen so many village elders in his life. He placed his hand across hers, and as their palms made contact, the rest of the pavilion fell utterly silent.

Only then did Alex look up, look around; Max could still see clearly. He just couldn't hear. Steel's posture beneath his other hand shifted. Perhaps he growled. Perhaps the sound caught Nenyane's attention. Perhaps not.

But Max allowed the old woman to lead him past the many stalls. Each had visitors in front of it; one had something of a line. He glanced at what was offered there: ribbons in so many different hues it was a wonder that they could all find room for them all on what was other-wise a modestly sized table. He would not have noticed had the lineup to reach that table not crossed his path; people moved slowly out of his way.

Or out of hers.

"Why can't I hear anything?"

"You can't?"

"Just you. And myself."

"Well, the latter shouldn't be much of a surprise, given your personality," she replied. "But that *is* unusual."

"What would normally happen?"

"In a place like the circus, there is no normal. But what I would *expect* is slightly different. No part of your perception should have been altered; you should be able to hear the sounds other visitors make, just as you did before."

"I can't."

"So you've said. I will have to think on it, but later. This is my stall."

The stall, as she'd implied earlier, was absent visitors—all but Max. She released Max's hand and took her place on the other side of a table that was otherwise empty. A tablecloth covered its surface, the fabric cream and gold-edged, as if she'd taken the awning outside down for her personal use. She bent to retrieve something from beneath the table. When she unbent, she carried a battered box in her arms, its wooden sides scored and scratched by what appeared to be daily use. She set it on the table, and took a seat on a chair that Max hadn't seen until she sat.

"Just wait a moment. It's been a long time, for me."

"Where do you normally work, if not here?"

"That is a question I cannot answer to anyone foolish enough to ask," the woman replied, a hint of a smile transforming her expression. "But accept that we all serve the circus, while the circus remains." Her voice had softened as she spoke. "In my youth, I performed. But there is little value in my performance, now. If an emergency occurs, all of those who did perform will be called to the stage, but our presence there would buy time, all of it scant." Her tone made clear that she assumed none would survive such an emergency.

"And for us?"

"We would buy the time necessary to give our guests some chance to escape. Tell me, child, what do you think the circus is?"

He had seen his share of performances in his life. Performers often came to the Elseth manor, invited—and no doubt paid for—by Lady Elseth. The circus grounds here were far larger, far more elaborate, than any such grounds in the lands of his childhood. But that made sense to Max; they had been invited to come to the circus; the circus had not come to them.

He understood that this circus, for all its human workers, was a wild space, a land ruled by a lord whose will was law. But the battered box and the bare table, along with the older woman who sat behind that box, altered his concept of wilderness. Where before it had been alien forests and the creatures who inhabited them, it was now... stranger. As if the familiar elements underlined the difference, rather than muting it.

"Well?" the old woman snapped. "We don't have much time. Are you just going to stand there?"

Max blinked.

"The *box*, boy. You can examine anything in it, and you can claim what you like. Think of it as a lost and found."

"And no one else has claim to the contents?"

"Not anymore, no. You'll discover this in good time: the dead don't need things meant for the living to use."

Max hesitated.

"The world is changing, even ours—and the circus has survived, unchanging, since the time the gods walked the world in which you live. But everything that knows a beginning knows an end. Even the circus will one day shut its doors, and those who serve the circus will, at last, be free to return to the homes of their childhood."

Max, now slightly bent over the box, could see her expression: one of unutterable weariness. Had Alex been here, he would have had questions, but none of those questions were in Max to ask.

"You'll waste your time," she said, as if she could hear his thoughts. "And you don't have much to waste."

"Has the circus ever been invaded?"

"Aye, although that was before my time. Well before yours."

"But it survived."

"Demonstrably."

The box had no lid, and the sides were made of rough planking; had Max's hands not been so callused, he'd have been picking out splinters. But he was almost appalled that the items in this box had been shoved into such a humble container so haphazardly.

The first thing he drew from the box was a sword. He laid it on the table, his brows folding. The sword was too long to fit the box, but it clearly had. Alex would have had *so* many questions.

Where are you? His brother asked.

Down on the other side of the bazaar, toward the end, just past the table with the ribbons. Did you find anything?

His brother nodded. *What are you looking at?*

You can find me and ask yourself. He could sense Alex already trying. To the old woman, he said, "Will the others find me?"

"If they're meant to, they'll find you." Sounded a lot like *no*. But the old woman had probably never met hunting Breodani before.

Max continued to pull things from the box, laying them across the table with care. There was an axe, another sword — a shorter one — and a long sword with a curve, which reminded him of Gervanno's weapon. There were two daggers, one whose hilt and sheath were so ostentatious in design he almost threw it back into the box.

There was, to his surprise, a badly folded knapsack, and beneath it, now that he had cleared out the heavier items, he found things that were much smaller: cuff links, earrings, a pendant on a silver chain. A worn wooden figurine. A tarnished horn. A ring of stone, unadorned by gems; a ring of gold, and one of silver. And marbles. There were marbles that covered the bottom of the box itself, or so it appeared to Max. Those, he chose to leave in the box, although one caught his eye; it appeared to be made of pale gold, and it caught light in a way the rest of the marbles didn't.

He almost left it in the container, but the light was distracting. Still, if he could only choose one thing, it wasn't going to be a marble.

Of the three swords, Max immediately discarded the long curved blade — putting it back into a box in which it shouldn't fit. He knew Nenyane considered both him and Alex functionally competent with a sword, but no better. He'd even resented it, as a child, until he'd seen Nenyane wield one. After that, the sword was her weapon, and no one else's, although she trained Stephen mercilessly.

Functional, given their possible enemies, was still better than nothing. Max's current sword had been good enough for the sparse use it had seen when their home had been Elseth. It had been less acceptable when they'd faced demons in the streets of the King's City.

Steel sat as Max drew the long straight sword, the shape and length of which were familiar. Max was no blacksmith, but he could see that the sword had seen use in the past. Whoever had owned it previously had taken good care of the blade; it had no obvious signs of rust, no visible notches. The hilt was solid, but the leather that enwrapped it was slightly worn; he could almost feel the shape of the hand that had last held it as he lifted it to the light.

He sheathed it again, moving it to the other side of the box. The axe was a small axe, clearly meant for practical use, not battle. It was simpler than the sword in construction. Given their overland travels, it might be useful—as long as it wasn't taken to the wrong tree. If they were lucky, the axe would see more use than the sword.

He set that on the other side of the box as well.

The jeweled dagger he almost tossed back.

"You might want to take a look at the blade before you judge it," the old woman said.

He really didn't.

"What, you'd be too embarrassed to be seen with it, is that it? Some men would carry it visibly with pride at what it implies."

"Pride in what?"

"Wealth, boy. You've never gone hungry, have you?"

Max shook his head. "I can feed myself if necessary."

"Bold claim, but I'll not deny it."

Max lifted the dagger he had managed—barely—to leave out of the box. He found the ornate jeweling of both the hilt and sheath almost offensive. Had it only been the sheath, he would have been annoyed— but the hilt was also gemmed. As if the dagger was entirely an orna- ment, a setting for a random collection of gems.

He pulled the blade from its ostentatious sheath; if the blade was good, and he chose to keep it, he'd ditch the sheath. And maybe, just maybe, there was a practical use for the dagger: he could sell it. Funds on the road would be tight. In Breodanir, Hunter Lords were accorded respect and necessary lodging, and costs were paid by their demesne.

He doubted that such an arrangement existed outside of Breodanir.

The woman laughed. "I knew there was a reason I liked you. Being practical wins wars, boy. Don't forget it." She actually had to wipe her eyes, she'd laughed so hard. "Yes, you could sell it."

Max hadn't spoken the words out loud. He should have been more upset that she knew what he'd been thinking, but Alex had always said Max was an open book.

Having freed the dagger from its sheath, Max looked at the blade.

Or tried to look at the blade. If he had seen the dagger in passing, he would have assumed there wasn't one.

"Is this made of *glass*?"

"Look again."

He hadn't looked away. But he held the dagger up to the light—to the daylight that seemed to emanate from the physical ceiling—and saw that the blade existed, and that it wasn't made of glass. Glass reflected light; the blade—and its edge—did not.

"What *is* this?"

"That's a good question. I don't know."

"But you've seen it before."

"Of course I have. It's my stall."

He sheathed the blade again, but this time set it to the left of the box, thinking of Alex. The second dagger, far more quotidian in nature, was also examined, but this one he put back into the box. He had a decent dagger, a decent utility knife.

The short sword was also examined with care; Max hadn't used a shorter sword since he'd aged out of childhood. But attacks on Stephen had occurred indoors as well, and a shorter sword could be useful in cramped halls. The hilt and blade of the short sword were clean and solid; the blade seemed sharp enough, but the steel was dark. Not rusted, and not the type of steel that retained edge at the expense of brittleness.

He wouldn't have many opportunities to buy new equipment, even should it become necessary. He set the short sword to the left of the box.

That left very few things of interest to Max. The jewelry, while it looked pretty enough, was an expensive trifle, ostentatious in the way the dagger was, and just as practical.

"It could be practical in an emergency," Alex said.

His brother had found him.

"I see," the old woman said, turning her gaze to Alex. "You are twins; that might explain much."

Alex offered the woman an incredibly formal bow, as if she were a lady of power and renown. "I am Alexander of Elseth," he said, as he rose. "And this is my brother Maxwell. We hail from Breodanir, and we are not twins."

"You have that look about you, though."

"We have an older brother and two older sisters, and we five were born within an hour of each other. Because we are youngest, we have no necessary duties to Elseth; it is why we were permitted to travel abroad."

Max stared at his brother's profile.

"Well. As you have found me, I offer you what I have offered your brother: a choice of the wares it has been my duty to husband. I see you have already visited other stalls in the bazaar." She nodded to the book Alex had tucked under his arm.

Where's Stephen?

He's with Nenyane. I didn't mean to lose him.

I don't think you losing him had anything to do with your choice. This place —it's just wrong.

Do you think he'll be in danger?

Did he? Max shook his head. *We might be. There's something off about this woman.*

Yes. But that could be because she's part of the circus. There's something unusual about every person we've met here, save one—the first woman who welcomed us to the building of fortune and fate.

She was new.

She was, and is. Alex exhaled. Exhaling, he approached the table.

"These are the items I'm considering," Max said, gesturing at the swords, the axe and the ornate dagger. "And these are the items I'm examining."

Alex immediately picked up the pack. In his hands, its dimensions shifted, as if the pack were somehow alive and intended to hide itself. When its faint shuddering came to a stop, it was no longer something to be carried by shoulder straps; it was to be worn across the hips. It was modest, and in this shape, looked well-worn; not so old that it would fall apart with use, but old enough that it had clearly seen that use in a different person's hands.

Max gestured to the left of the box, and Alex nodded. Before he could add it to Max's growing pile of possible items, the old woman rose.

"No," she said. "Do not put that there. For better or worse, it has chosen."

"Chosen?" Alex asked.

"Your ears must be better than mine, at my age, and I hate repeating myself. It's yours."

"I don't need it," Alex began, his tone apologetic. She might have been an angry village elder.

"Doesn't matter. You," she added to Max, "don't stand here all day. We've all got places to be, and I need to get to mine." To Alex, she added, "Try not to touch too much else."

But Alex didn't appear to hear her. Max, knowing Alex, knew this wasn't pretense. Small pouch—and it *was* small now—in hand, his brother bent over the odds and ends of jewelry that Max had intended to scoop up and dump, unceremoniously, back into the box of odds and ends.

He picked up the marble. Of course he did. Alex had always liked marbles. Max winced, but was not surprised, when the odd glow that suffused what was otherwise a small glass ball suddenly sharpened and brightened, spreading as if the marble intended to become a miniature sun.

Max would have dropped the marble. Alex did not. Maybe more could be said about their fundamental differences, but to Max, this moment underlined them perfectly.

"Can I keep this?" Alex asked the old woman; he didn't offer to pay, but he knew that money was not the coin of this realm.

The woman exhaled. "I wouldn't have chosen that if the choice had been mine."

"For me?"

"At all. And now, I don't think you have a choice." Her expression was no longer one of irritation; she looked at Alex with something akin to pity. It made Max bristle. Alex, however, accepted it without comment—or reaction. None of the pity lasted as she turned to Max. "Are you going to stand here all day? Your brother's barely arrived and he already has two items."

"I'm trying to decide," Max said. He couldn't keep defensiveness out of his tone and didn't bother to try. He had always been slower than Alex. In everything. Once, he might have resented it—but he'd made peace with it over the years.

"Take them all, for all I care. It'll make the box lighter, and I'm old enough to notice the weight."

"But—"

"I never said you could only choose one."

Max felt it had been implied, but acknowledged that she was right. He therefore took the two swords, the ugly dagger, and the axe. The

only other item he might have examined was the pack, but Alex now
had that, and at a size that made it seem less useful.

"Max," his brother said, speaking out loud.

Max, juggling the three largest items in the box, immediately
turned to his brother.

"Look at these."

These, as Alex called them, were rings. Max had less than no
interest in rings. He hated the way they felt on his fingers, and as he
wasn't heir, there was no practical reason for them. "They're rings," he
said, his tone reminding his brother of his history with jewelry of any
kind.

"Yes. But *look at them*." In his hand, he held two.

Max did. They looked like rings. Their bands were both larger than
usual—which made them worse than most rings—and an odd color, a
blend of turquoise and silver. Each had a gem set into it, a rectangular
cut of a startling green, like an emerald that emitted light. They were,
to his eye, identical. "They're rings," he repeated.

Alex didn't need to be told more than once that there wasn't a limit
to the items they could choose. He took both rings. Max grimaced; he
knew where Alex meant to leave one of them: on Max's hand.

But Alex hadn't finished. Max had.

The old woman's lips were a thin line, and her eyes had narrowed,
which wasn't usually a good sign. Alex, however, could weather such
storms with more grace and ease than Max, who often took other
people's anger as a sign that they wanted to fight. He could feel his
brother's growing excitement; it wasn't pure delight. Something about
the scattered gems had caught his attention, some strand of detail that
he wanted to catch and pull out before it vanished.

And because Alex was going to be minutes yet—as many minutes
as the old woman was willing to tolerate—Max picked up the last of
the items: the tarnished, but oddly shaped, horn. He was a Breodanir
Hunter; he had a horn, although without the dogs it seemed superflu-
ous. But Alex's experience at this table made clear that things weren't
what they seemed, and maybe the horn would have use on the road
they meant to travel.

If it worked.

He lifted it to lips, and blew; discovered that its mouthpiece and its
odd shape strangled the notes he'd intended to sound.

Alex laughed, remembering the first notes either of them had tried to blow. It was a similar sound, some forgotten childhood humiliation that had grown, with time, to become nostalgic.

Max frowned, adjusting his lips as he lifted the horn again. He paused because Alex had set the book that he'd carried under arm down on the table, its cover—dark blue cloth at base with an intricate silver pattern on its cover, and no words to make title or content clear—now visible. Max grimaced as the silver pattern began, as the marble had, to glow; its light was moon to sun.

It wasn't just the book's cover that glowed. On the table, partly obscured by other pieces of jewelry, one pendant began to glow as well. It was a large pendant, but delicate in construction—or seemed to be, to Max's eye. Small vines of silver were entwined around four diagonal lines, framing a smaller shape at its heart. Layers of threaded silver led to a central gem, a sapphire, or what he assumed was a sapphire. He had never been good at telling precious gems from semi-precious; they were all the same to him.

The pendant's glow was less bright, less harsh, than the marble's glow had been, but the design of the pendant and the emblem on the book's cover shone with the same faint light.

The old woman looked at Alex, her eyes moving in a triangle that included Max's brother, the book's cover, and the pendant itself. "You have a choice, gentlemen. The circus offers choice. It's never promised to offer informed choice. Were it not for your brother, you would never have found my stall. And had you not, you would not now consider the pendant.

"I am uncertain that it will be of use to you in any fashion you will appreciate." Her expression was now flat—it gave nothing away. But her tone had shifted. Even Max noticed.

"Is it dangerous?" he asked.

The woman pulled her gaze from Alex. "There is very little on the road you now walk that is not a danger. Were I either of you, I would not take it. But were I either of you, I would not walk the road you have chosen."

"But you have," Alex said, voice much softer than Max's. "You have walked it for far longer than either of us."

Her brows rose briefly, before settling once again into inscrutability. "I have not. I have remained in the circus, and if the circus occupies a stretch of the wild road, it sits above it. What price I am asked to pay, I have paid; the circus cannot take more from me than I have already chosen to give.

"It is not the case with you and your twin." They'd already corrected her, but the correction had been ignored. She waited.

Max didn't. He felt a curious sense of pressure—a change in the air, a subtle shift in the temperature. Alex assessed what the woman had implied, considering the cover of this book—which had no obvious title Max could see—and the pendant.

Max shook his head, reached out, and took the pendant.

What are you doing?

You're going to take it eventually. I'm just saving time. He held the pendant out to his brother, who accepted it hesitantly. Ah, no, not hesitantly; Alex was afraid to damage it. *Grab the book. We have to go.*

Even as he spoke, the old woman began to gather the rest of her items, returning them to the worn crate just as carelessly as Max would have. She froze briefly at the touch of a chilly breeze, her expression shifting into one of worry.

Alex said, "A question, before we leave."

"Ask it. We're here to help." Sarcasm laced her words.

"If someone is invited to join the circus—"

"Invited?" The word was sharp.

"Summoned? Commanded? If someone is commanded to join the circus when the circus presents itself, and they choose to run away, what happens to them?"

The woman's face paled. It was clear she could don a neutral mask, but clear as well that that mask did not come naturally to her. "Why do you ask that question?"

"One of our companions mentioned it. An innkeeper's daughter was called to join the circus—something that's supposed to be an honor. She's not here. She didn't accept."

"Now? Now of all times?" The woman's hands trembled. "If she has been called and she refuses the call, she will die."

"Will the circus kill her?"

"No. But the circus doesn't come to town if the shadow of death doesn't lie across the Free Towns—and it is dark and bitter, now."

It was Max, not Alex, who heard fear in the old woman's voice. She was not afraid for the girl whose death she spoke of; she was afraid, now, for the circus. He was as certain of it as if she had spoken that fear aloud.

"What will her refusal mean to the circus?"

The woman continued to pack her things. She did not answer.

CHAPTER EIGHT

Stephen's perusal of the books was less exact, less thorough, than Alex's, but not by much. Where Alex was interested in everything, Stephen found very little that spoke to him enough that he was willing to add weight to the traveling packs they would be carrying for a journey of indeterminate length.

He chose a compact, thick book, because its pages were blank. The book's cover was ornate; all of the books here had similarly decorative covers. Very few had titles — or titles he could read.

Nenyane had never cared for reading, although she could be pressured into doing so. She had never minded listening if Stephen chose to read aloud. It was not a surprise that she kept her distance from the stall. Gervanno failed to join Stephen and Alex as well, having retreated into the posture and presentation of a guard. Guards focused on duty, not acquisition.

The Southerner understood that his duties as a guard weren't necessary in this place. But whatever Evayne had shown Gervanno had unsettled him, and as many people did when unsettled, he had retreated into the known, the comfortable. Stephen wanted to know what he had seen, but Nenyane had no desire to have it discussed, as if discussion alone could somehow indebt those who hadn't looked into the seer's crystal.

"Are you finished?" Nenyane asked.

Stephen nodded.

"Alex left."

"When?"

"Maybe ten minutes ago. I think he must have gone to join Max." She looked over her shoulder at the pavilion's entrance, frowning before she turned away from it. "Let's go."

A wind rose in the pavilion. It touched nothing but Nenyane. Hair, more silver than grey, flew away from her face, as if the air itself wished to gently nudge her toward the open doorway.

"Can you see Max?"

"Steel can. Max is at one of the stalls—he's not in danger."

"I think we should go get him."

"What is it? What's wrong?"

"Nothing yet, but the air is changing—while we're surrounded by four walls and a roof."

———

BY THE TIME they found Max and Alex, Stephen could feel the wind. It was a winter breeze, although the skies above this circus had been summer skies when they had first been granted entry.

The movement of air was gentle, subtle; it was not the wind that now moved Nenyane's hair. Pearl was the first to notice; she lifted her head, her nose. Patches was a very close second. Neither of the dogs were panicked; the rest of the pack followed Stephen quietly. None of the dogs liked crowds; all of them had been trained to accept them.

Hunter dogs were not small dogs; they were not pets. Ill-trained, they could threaten the very people they were meant to help feed. In a crowd, Hunters kept tight control of their pack. Stephen's control was effortless, but it was present.

"Is it the circus master?" Stephen asked, speaking aloud for Gervanno's benefit.

Nenyane frowned, but shook her head. "It's getting colder."

Stephen nodded. "It feels like early or late winter, to me."

"It does. It's not a good sign. Winter in the wilderness isn't like winter in Breodanir. It shouldn't be winter here."

"And the lord of these lands can't choose the season the way the lord we defeated did?"

"It was Summer in her lands," Nenyane replied. "It was endlessly night, but it was Summer."

Stephen had stood in that lord's blizzard.

"Winter is not about snow," Nenyane snapped. "It is nothing so simple. But Winter magics and Summer magics differ greatly, and it is in the Winter that the *Kialli* are at their strongest."

Kialli.

"There's no way the circus master would have granted entry to the dead. No way."

"Is it Winter, now?"

She shook her head, and began to jog ahead.

Stephen sped up to keep pace, and to subtly steer her in Steel's direction. She could, with effort, sense the presence of Stephen's dogs, but seldom tried. She trusted that Stephen could get the relevant and necessary information from them without necessitating that effort.

Normally, he could. But there was an odd blur, an odd fuzziness, in their connection. Steel knew where he was. Steel knew where Stephen was. But almost by instinct, Stephen was moving around the area in which Steel—and therefore Max and Alex—stood, rather than directly to it.

Nenyane was annoyed—not at Stephen, but at the circus itself. At Evayne. At the circus master. At the air that moved her hair. "Enough of this," she snapped. "*Enough*." She took the lead, catching Stephen by the hand before she did. She wasn't looking for Steel. Stephen had been, and Stephen knew the way—he just had difficulty following it.

Nenyane didn't. Between the two of them, the odd blurriness dissipated instantly, as if it had been cut. Nenyane began to run, her hand still entwined with Stephen's. The row of stalls seemed to elongate as she did; at the speed she'd chosen, they should have traversed the building's entire floor in less than a minute.

The stalls they passed were manned; people behind tables lifted their heads as they caught sight of Nenyane and Stephen. The crowd was thin here, although one stall had a long enough line that Nenyane barely avoided a collision.

Stephen stopped entirely; the stall offered what appeared to be ribbons. Cloth, presumably dyed, but in so many shades, so many colors, he couldn't begin to imagine the necessary components to create those dyes.

Now is not the time for this, Nenyane told him; she had made her way past the line. Stephen and Gervanno had not.

Stephen agreed, but said, *I think we need to stop here before we leave. Once we have Alex and Max.*

Why?

He had no answer. Nenyane wanted one, which was ironic, given her inability to answer similar questions. *Instinct.*

Max and Alex first.

THEY HAD Alex and Max in sight—finally—when Nenyane froze and Stephen collided with her. He managed not to knock her over, or fall himself. Gervanno had kept enough of a distance that he avoided both, but Gervanno's steps never seemed to carry his momentum; he could stop instantly.

Over Nenyane's shoulder, he could see the Elseth brothers clearly. Nenyane did not move toward them. Stephen stepped to the side to bypass her, but she lifted an arm to block his passage. She did not speak at all.

Gervanno, however, she allowed to walk past her, to where both Max and Alex stood.

The woman in the stall looked up as Gervanno approached; if she saw Nenyane or Stephen at all, she gave no sign. Perhaps she did not, for her brows rose as Gervanno approached the Elseth brothers, before they settled back into a lower position.

"You came for these two?" she asked, voice gruff, as her expression smoothed into neutrality. Neutrality could often be mistaken for animosity because it lacked warmth. Her tone, however, did not.

Gervanno offered her a half bow. When he rose, he said, "We are far from our respective homes, and it is easy to become lost, even within a single pavilion." His tone was apologetic.

"The boys weren't lost," she replied, and this time her voice carried the hint of chill.

"Indeed. I see they are both safe, although perhaps somewhat more encumbered." Gervanno's posture shifted as he spoke. It was subtle, a minute tensing of shoulders, a very slight widening of stance. He did not draw weapon.

Nenyane, let me join them.

She did not lower her arm.

Stephen therefore moved around her lifted arm—or tried. To his surprise, to his dismay, he found it very, very difficult to lift a foot.

"Aye, they are. Only one of 'em should have found me, but we don't put too much stock in *shoulds* here. You found me, and you had no business here." She glanced at Alex, her frown deepening, then back to Gervanno. "I'd welcome you to the circus were I in any other stall."

"I have already received more welcome than is perhaps my due," Gervanno replied. "My first choice of pavilion was that of fortune and fate."

"Ah. You saw the child, then."

"I saw a young woman in robes better suited to Widan or magi; she was not, in my eyes, a child, although I confess I did not study her for long."

"It's what we call her, when we mention her at all—and we try not to mention her. When I first met her, she wasn't part of the circus. She was audience." The woman's expression cracked a bit, shifting into something that might have been pity. "But I understand why you're here, even if I had no warning and no time to prepare. Come, then. Join the twins. Find an item that suits your purpose."

"My purpose," Gervanno replied, "is to serve as personal guard. The jewelry seems, to my eye, very fine—but it will not aid that purpose on the road."

"Not all battles are fought with swords, as you are well aware. Some are fought simply with nerves and appearance. But I perceive that your version of a guard implies invisibility in a social sense."

Gervanno nodded, but he was drawn to the table regardless; he stood between Max and Alex. Neither of the Elseth brothers had moved. At all.

Stephen, watching, wondered if they, too, were trapped, somehow aware but unable to move or turn. He did not believe Nenyane was trapped in the same fashion. She did not want to approach the older woman; she did not want Stephen anywhere near her either. But usually she'd talk through their bond.

"You are here for a reason. But even this one," the older woman added, indicating Alex with a movement of chin, "was unexpected. Come, then. If you feel disdain for my wares, there is nonetheless something that might aid you in future."

"Or burden me?"

"You're no longer a boy; you understand how aid and burden can come hand in hand."

GERVANNO APPROACHED the table as if dragged there by the weight of her words, her voice. Perhaps it was because she spoke Torra—but all here seemed to do so when they spoke to him. He was uneasily certain that everyone heard their mother tongue in the circus grounds.

So spoke demons: anyone who could hear their words heard them in their mother tongue.

He did not expect to be drawn to any item spread across the table, but he could see the pendant Alex held because it was shining. Alex did not spare Gervanno a glance; nor did Max. "They can't move, can they?"

"They can, but slowly; you might appear as a blur to their eyes." The woman's smile was sharp and brief. "I mean no harm to any of you; you are all human. All but one, and that one cannot be harmed by one such as I; I doubt they can be harmed by anything in the circus at all."

"What would you suggest, among your many wares? I have no eye for gems, and Max seems to have taken what weapons you had to offer."

"You wouldn't have touched the weapons he chose; there is a sword that is more in your style. I would suggest you at least examine it. Your blade is solid and sharp; you take good care of it. You have wielded it against our common enemy, and you have done damage; most weapons crafted by mortals cannot. She travels with you, and she is nature's sword against the foes you face; her influence travels and touches those she has chosen.

"But you will find that, separated from her, that your sword will be far less effective; it was forged for wars of man, not wars against the forces we do not name."

"You did not bring that sword for me; you did not, as you said, know that I would arrive here at all."

She smiled, although it added lines to her face. Lifting a hand, she pointed up, and he could see a sign—a cloth sign, words embroidered in his mother tongue.

Lost and Found.

He read the words three times before once again turning to the woman, who had waited to gain his attention before she continued to speak. "How much of the future do you know? How much could you have predicted? We do our best to be prepared when the circus opens, but if we are not flexible, we will not be good hosts. I am given my crate, and my table; I am offered instruction where it might be necessary.

"I was surprised to see a Southern sword in the mix, but not surprised to see an axe; nor was I surprised to see jewelry. The marbles were unusual. There are odds and ends that remain—but examine the sword Max left behind, and examine the contents of the crate as you will. The performance will start somewhat soon, but I have seen to it that you've time. Use it wisely."

In his childhood home, Gervanno would have—politely—disdained *any* weapon that came out of a worn, wooden crate. Should the person offering the weapon insist, he might have accepted it with outward grace and gratitude, and later set it aside in a neglected corner of his family's domis.

But this was the circus, and he stood in unfamiliar, wild territory—a territory created to mimic mortal fairs and performances while rising above them in all ways. He had already given in to the embers of childhood daydream. He had vowed he would never do so again. But no childhood daydream had involved finding a worthy sword in a wooden box on foreign fairgrounds.

He therefore looked into the box. He could see the sword, and could see, as well, that the box was far deeper than it had initially appeared. The shape of the sheath was the right shape; the sword was long, not short. His hands trembled as he reached for the weapon. It was light, almost weightless; no sword of any worth could weigh so little.

A small pang of disappointment hit him, and he realized, again, that the embers of childhood had never been entirely extinguished. But he drew the sword from its plain, unadorned sheath. Weight returned instantly to the weapon; something about the sheath lightened its natural weight.

For a moment Elseth and Maubreche were forgotten.

This blade had seen use; it was not newly tempered, newly forged. Some other hand had wielded it in a different war. He wanted to ask the woman if she knew its age, or its history.

"I know very little about it," she said, as if he had. "And no, we want none of your coin. If there is a price to be paid, I believe you're beginning to weigh it, even now. You're certain nothing is free."

Gervanno nodded; he was. Max and Alex did not appear to have that belief, given what they now carried.

"You've met the seer. She seldom visits the circus, but on the rare occasions she does, there are always threats to the circus' existence. She has a freedom we do not; but she carries a burden we *could not*. You have questions; ask them of the master. We are not allowed to answer them, and the master's anger is long indeed; his forgiveness, such as it is, is far more pragmatic in nature."

"What would you advise, Ona?"

Her brows rose at the use of *Ona*. In the North, the related term — aunt, or auntie — was not used when addressing women who were not related to one by blood. In the South, it was a sign of respect.

"There's a burden to advice, even when it's wanted," she replied. "And a weight of worry, of guilt — was it the wrong advice? Was it genuine? Was it offered in bad faith, as an act of manipulation?"

He nodded. "Would it be offered in bad faith?"

"This is my country, child." It was the first time she had called him a child. "You are a guest. I have the duty of hosts, and that duty does not involve sending you out the back door immediately to retrieve something inadvertently left behind in the driving rain."

Gervanno understood, then. "Tell me, how important is it to the circus that we find the child left in the storm?"

"The seer is here," was the grim reply. "And she shows the future as it might happen. Nothing she shows you is writ in stone, but she shows you what must become should you decide against any attempt at intervention. If she showed you such a future, and you, a guest, it means she knew you might intervene in some fashion. No, do not tell me what you saw. I can guess.

"The circus comes to town in the lee of the great shadow and its many servants. In no other way would the Free Towns survive. We are not great cities, or even moderate ones; we do not have the many cathedrals of the gods and the magi who grace the various orders, although some have made their home in the Free Towns. Nor do we have a standing, trained army of any note.

"You must have wondered how the Free Towns have remained free over the decades and centuries."

"The circus."

"The master of the circus, yes. These two boys might understand, better than you, how sacrifice can preserve a people, for they are of the Breodani, and their blood is offered to their god. Here, it is the same — but we face no inevitable death, no one's blood must be spilled on some hidden circus altar."

"Not blood," Gervanno said, voice soft. "How do I speak with the circus master?"

"Ask. Ask anywhere, and he will hear your request. If he does not appear, it means he has no desire to grant you an audience. We do not call him — but you must be aware that rules are different for guests than for family."

Gervanno nodded. "I will take the sword."

"Take anything else you fancy." Her smile was genuine. "If you're not like the boy I was meant to meet, you'll understand that practical uses might come from what appears as vain frippery on the surface."

But he already knew. He examined the various rings, bracelets, and necklaces on the table; some had fallen beneath Alex's unmoving shadow. His perusal was a show. From the moment he had arrived at this table, he had seen two rings, their gems — rubies — emblazoned in memory. He had seen the hands that had worn them, neither of those hands his.

The discussions had with the innkeeper — his own, accepting unasked-for advice; and the blacksmith's — had caused a deep unease. That unease had found a small purchase. Had he already attended the performance, he was certain it would have been uprooted; the performance's beginning and end heralded the end of confinement in the circus.

But he had wandered — following Leial — into the pavilion of fate and fortune, and he had chosen to seek his fate in the shadowed hall in which people sat with cards, tea, or crystal balls before them on their clothed tables.

He had heard two names while waiting for the blacksmith to leave him enough room that he could gracefully — and quickly — abandon the inn. *Adala. Trevor.* The rings, as he picked them up, felt almost unnaturally warm. He pocketed them, and then cast a glance at the crate, rather than its spilled contents.

Marbles. Marbles such as he'd envied as a child, when glass was expensive, and only the domis of the rich and the powerful might boast any. What was childhood, that it led him to these pointless memories? He had long ago accepted his place in this life. He had never tried to rise above it. There were things he was meant to have, and things he was not; duties he was meant to carry, and duties that belonged in the hands of the powerful.

He had never felt powerful, and a glimmer of understanding peered out between the growing clouds of certainty. He would never feel powerful, even were he to gain power that could only be dreamed of in his childhood. Power was relative. Even the Tyr'agar was not guaranteed to survive the attacks of the demons.

The whole of the Terrean of Gervanno's birth would have fallen to the creature Gervanno had faced in the wilderness, shadowing the demesne of Bowgren. It was not armies that had won that battle — or not armies of cerdan, led by powerful men.

In the wilderness, power was not defined in the way it had been defined for the whole of Gervanno's life. Tyr, Tor — all were meaningless to the lords of the wilderness.

"Will you release them now, Ona?" he asked the old woman, in the softest of voices.

"Of course. They were not trapped by anything but a hint of passing time, and I perceive that we are done." She glanced, smile deepening, at Gervanno's fist; in it was a handful of marbles. These, too, he pocketed; he wasn't certain he had kept the flush of embarrassment from his face.

"Then go as you must. I'll pack up here — I'm expected to make certain people take their seats in an orderly fashion. It is also my duty to round up those who may be so immersed in their browsing that they miss the rather audible call when it comes."

"I was about to ask that."

"It is all but impossible to miss the announcement while you are on the circus grounds."

She began to put away the unclaimed items, her box much lighter than it had been. "I do not know what the outcome of this event will be; I fear it, and I anticipate it. To those who visit, the circus is a wonder, a mystery, and a place of complete safety." She did not speak of those who lived in the circus, and it was not of her that Gervanno had to ask the questions to which he now knew he needed answers.

He offered her a perfect bow, as one respected equal to another,

and when he rose, Alex had moved, the hand holding the pendant
drawing it toward his chest. The book, he tucked back under his arm.

Alex was examining a small pouch—new, to Gervanno's eye—with
wary caution.

And Nenyane and Stephen joined them.

Nenyane looked murderous, but her expression did not change the
old woman's countenance at all. "People are beginning to pack up,"
Nenyane told the Elseth brothers. "And Stephen wants to look at
ribbons."

The old woman nodded. "You'd best be on your way, then—that's
always one of the most crowded of our many booths, and the performance should begin soon."

———

STEPHEN'S BROWS rose when Gervanno met his gaze, but lowered
almost immediately. There was an unspoken question in the shift of
expression; Gervanno nodded, but did not speak. Instead, he waited
until the Hunters were once again moving together, and he followed
Stephen and Nenyane. To properly examine the sword, he had had to
set Leial down. Leial seemed content to walk at heel for now.

"Why ribbons?" Max demanded. He wanted time to find a place
for his new weapons, and his axe. The dagger he had chosen was
almost blinding, and Gervanno felt he could be forgiven for immediately assuming it was decorative in nature. Max, however, must have
felt the same, as he didn't slide it anywhere visible.

The other three items, he carried in two arms.

"Don't ask me—ask him." Nenyane glared.

"I was," Max replied.

"They have a lot of colors. I thought it would be useful to have
those colors as armbands or hilt decorations—they're a silent way of
knowing who is, and who is not, part of our group," Stephen said.

Max's annoyance vanished, although his frown remained. He
nodded.

Alex had less difficulty with his newfound wealth than Max, but
he'd chosen a necklace, a marble, and a book. Gervanno could see
nothing else. Alex handed the book to Stephen, and then looped the
necklace over his head; the chain was long enough that he could. He
retrieved the book immediately before turning to Max. "Give me the

axe. We can figure out what to do with your old sword after the ribbon hunt is finished."

"No, wait a minute. I want to try something." Max fiddled with the worn pouch at his brother's waist. It had clearly seen use, but Gervanno did not recall it being among Alex's possessions prior to the circus. That invoked a smile. Surrounded by finery, the Hunters adhered to the practical.

Practical, however, was not the first word that came to mind when Max attempted to put his sword into a pouch that could not contain it. Given the environs, Gervanno was only slightly surprised when the sword vanished, as if the pouch were slowly swallowing it.

Max held out his hand; Alex returned the axe to it. The axe fit in the pouch. The short sword also fit the pouch. The new sword, Max chose to wear. He did, however, make sure he was able to retrieve the short sword and the axe; the pouch would be less than useless if he couldn't. Last, he put the ostentatious dagger into the pouch.

"Do you want to wear it?" Alex asked his brother, possibly for the benefit of witnesses.

"No. She said it chose you. You wear it. It's not heavy, is it?"

Alex shook his head. "It's the weight of my normal pouch. Maybe a touch lighter."

Max whistled. "We should try putting the contents of our packs into it—but later."

Gervanno slid rings and marbles into his own pouch as they approached the stall of which Stephen spoke.

Ribbons in many, many hues were laid across the table's surface, and, unlike other stalls, this particular table did not seem in danger of running out of freely given gifts. Women walked away with ribbons in their hair; men, with ribbons in their pockets. Children wore ribbons as bracelets; there were three people behind the larger table, and one woman was an expert at tying those ribbons into elaborate bows.

It was not for adornment that Stephen wanted ribbons; Gervanno understood. A brightly colored swatch of cloth could serve as a uniform in a pinch to people who otherwise had none. Meralonne APhaniel could never be mistaken for anyone else, and often dispensed with gravity. The same could be said of the bard. But the five bound to ground and less blessed with obvious, visible differences might find it useful.

Discussions, however, arose almost immediately. The natural color for a ribbon worn by Hunters was green. There were multiple shades of green, but Gervanno felt the colors to which the Hunters were naturally inclined were too dark to serve their stated purpose; at best, they would blend in with the colors of their normal clothing. Nenyane agreed with Gervanno—for he dared to make that reservation known.

White was the color of Imperial mourning; no one desired white. They intended to reach the Empire, after all. A pale yellow was considered, and a pale turquoise. Nenyane, however, chose silver. "It's reflective," she pointed out. "Look." She touched a silver ribbon and, as she raised it, the fabric caught and reflected the light in this place.

Gervanno frowned and lifted a silver ribbon. He had expected that somehow it was embroidered with fine silver thread—in itself not impossible, but costly and difficult. It was not. The entire fabric seemed to be that thread; he wondered at it, and wondered why the town's many children had not chosen the glittering fabric. Gervanno, as a child, would have—although he might have chosen gold, instead, for golden, reflective ribbons also existed.

Had he been informed, at any point in his tenure as a soldier, that he would be standing in front of a stall that sold—or gave away— ribbons, engaging in a discussion about their color, he would have made his disgust known. Truly, the future was unpredictable.

"Well?" Nenyane asked him.

"Silver," he replied. Silver was moonlight; gold was sun.

"Silver is Winter, gold is Summer," she countered.

Silver, to Gervanno, was the color of mercy, the color of private warmth; the sun was merciless. But her tone made clear that this was not the case in her mind; she had not grown up in the Dominion.

Max, much like Gervanno in his own youth, did not join the discussion. He had steeled himself to accept the practical use of such strips of cloth, but could not bring himself to have a preference.

Stephen looked between his huntbrother and his guard, and then turned to the stall's master. "We would like gold ribbons for each of us. And nine for our dogs."

"Would you have them tied, or will you carry them and tie them yourself when the circus shuts its doors?"

"We'll take them with us."

She did not count out ribbons; she lifted a stack and handed them to Stephen.

Gervanno, however, said, "I would like two more of the gold, and three of the silver." If the ribbons persisted, and if he had the courage to return to his home, he thought the silver ribbons might make modest gifts for his mother and her sister.

But the gold ribbons might see different use.

LEIAL DIDN'T CARE for the ribbon Stephen had acquired. Max didn't care for his either. Alex ignored this. He tied the ribbons around both of them. Leial's became a slender collar; Max's, a headband. Alex then handed a ribbon to Max, who tied it across his brother's brow.

"Can't we wait until after the performance is done?" Nenyane demanded, clearly as annoyed as Max.

Alex shook his head, and glanced at Gervanno. Alex had also looked into the crystal ball, albeit from the side. Gervanno accepted a golden tie as well, but attached to the hilt of his sword. He understood Nenyane's impatience. Had he been in mortal lands, he would have felt exactly as she felt, although he might have chosen to express it in silence, if at all.

Max and Alex helped Stephen tie gold ribbons to the collars of the Breodani dogs; Nenyane accepted a ribbon around the hilt of her sword. Stephen, however, wore the gold as the Maubreche brothers did.

GERVANNO ALLOWED the Hunters to walk ahead, and when the distance between them was large enough, he called for the master of the circus. He did not shout; he did not make demands. He spoke softly—softly enough that only the sharp-eared Nenyane might hear—and with the humility necessary between the powerful and the powerless.

But as the old woman—whose name he had never asked—had said, the lord of these lands could hear his name even at a whisper.

"Gervanno di'Sarrado," the circus master said. He remained an oddly dressed man, neither too large nor too small; his eyes seemed to shift color so often it was difficult to identify a color at all.

Gervanno bowed. He bowed low. He did not fall to the ground, did not assume the posture of utter obeisance uncommon even in the Dominion. "Lord."

"You have called me, and I have chosen for reasons of my own, to answer your call. This does not imply that I will answer your many, many questions."

Gervanno nodded. His throat was dry, of a sudden. But he did have questions, who should never have thought to ask them of this lord, in this place.

"I have traveled to the west of the Free Towns, as you must know. I met demons on the road—the mundane road, the human road—and lost myself there. I had two duties after my disgrace: to warn the magi of the demonic attack, and to deliver the sword of a comrade to his family in the distant South."

The circus master nodded.

"But Breodanir was not—quite—the mundane kingdom I expected. There are ancient oaths that bind its people, and lives lived—and lost —that are tied to those oaths. I was told that if those oaths are broken, it is the land itself that suffers; there is drought and there is famine."

"Many are told, but few listen. I see you have listened."

"Their lands are not my lands; their vows, not my vows. But even an outsider can see the truth of those vows and that way of life."

"And that brings you to me."

"And that brings me to you, in a fashion. You are not Breodan."

The circus master laughed. The sound was arresting: warm, loud, and very, very full. Gervanno thought he might listen to that laughter for the rest of his life and feel almost blessed; it was like a perfect song.

"No. No, Ser Gervanno, I am not Bredan, or Breodan as he is called in the kingdom. My name is not known to you, nor should it be. But I perceive you mention Breodanir for a reason."

"It is a land in which the rituals of the ruling class preserve the kingdom itself, in as much as that is possible; power devolves to those who are most tightly entwined with that ritual, as does the responsibility of ruling."

"Yes."

Gervanno inhaled slowly. "This circus has its rituals. It is tied—in some fashion I cannot fully perceive—to Hansleigh, Evanston, and Callenton. The Free Towns."

All hint of the warmth of amusement left the circus master's face. He nodded, but did not speak.

"The townspeople seemed to feel that it was a great honor to be invited to join the circus. One of my companions was told that she was 'good enough' to join."

"That would not have amused her."

"No," was Gervanno's grave reply. "But she did not understand at the time what the circus is."

"She knows now, and I believe it would pass from unamusing to grave insult were she to be offered a place here. Nor would I do so; the circus is not her home. It will never be her home, even should she desire it."

"When I left the inn this morning, the innkeeper stopped me. He gave me advice: should I value my dog, I should make certain my dog accompanied me. But shortly after, one of the town's blacksmiths arrived."

"Devon."

Gervanno nodded, unsurprised that the circus master knew the blacksmith's name. He thought, should the circus master desire it, he might name every living being in the town of Hansleigh.

"And every person who has ever lived in it, yes. Your memory is kinder than the memory of my kin. There is only one way we might forget, but even then the memories linger where we do not. But I perceive it is not my memory that you have called me to discuss, nor is my memory the reason I have chosen to accept your request."

Gervanno nodded, gazing at the backs of the Maubreche Hunters as they moved ahead through the crowds.

"The innkeeper's daughter apparently received an invitation to join the circus as one of its members."

"It was not, as you now suspect, an invitation."

"She is not here."

"No."

"I know, from the Hunters, what happens if the Hunter Lords fail in their duty to their god."

The circus master's nod was grave, but silent.

"What, then, happens to the circus should the townspeople of the Free Towns fail in like fashion?"

A smile grew on the circus master's almost graven face. For a moment, his eyes flickered red in the dim light. The smile was one of approval, but no words adorned it.

"The circus performs at times of danger for the townships. I do not

know if the residents of all three towns will be in the audience, or if it is
only the people of Hansleigh and those visiting there. But there is
clearly a reason that the circus has been open."

"Indeed."

"I have met the demons you call the dead on the road in Breodanir;
it is the demons I fear. But not, now, only the demons."

"Yes. I sense a hint of Winter; it clings to you, even in Summer. But
it clings, as well, to the corners of the wilderness, where those whose
power is strongest in Winter rule. Adala did not accept the summons.
She is not within the boundaries of the circus.

"And as you suspect, the circus draws its power from those who
serve it. But we are not the Breodani: our summons come only at times
of danger to the Free Towns. Adala has a gift. But she is mortal, and
young. Trevor is not one of ours. You travel with one man who was
once considered a power in the ancient world. It is possible his presence—and the presence of the Maubreche Hunters—will make up for
the weakness her flight has caused.

"But yes, Gervanno di'Sarrado, Adala's absence means that there
are no longer any guarantees. Think of the boundary of my lands as an
unbreachable wall. The stonework of that wall needs tending and
repairing. She is stone, and she has not come to take her place.

"The walls will hold, but they will be imperfect, and in that imper-
fection, elements might encroach who would never be accepted as
guests."

"If she could be found, if she could be convinced to accept her
responsibility, would the circus then be safe?"

"Yes, as you must suspect. But the time is short, for beyond my
walls, the dead gather, the dead mourn. Mourning, to your kin, is
seldom filled with such rage and such bitter envy; it is seldom a thing of
hunger and death. That is not so with the *Kialli*."

Gervanno exhaled, then. "And if I find your lost circus member?"

"You must make that decision on your own. I am not your lord. I
am not your master. I am neither lord nor master to any but those who
join the circus. Even then, choice is offered. Adala has made her
choice. If you would have her unmake it, you must bespeak her, you
who are not lord, not master, not family. She must choose."

Gervanno was silent, waiting.

"But if you choose to search for her, in the realm of the mortals, you
will find that the lands themselves are not the lands you know. The

Free Towns are not Breodanir. The covenants that exist within that
kingdom exist within the ancient earth and the promise of a distant
god, but the lands *are* mortal lands. It is not quite so with the Free
Towns. They have survived because they are a strand, a patchwork, of
my lands.

"Perhaps that is the better analogy. The Free Towns are a tapestry,
and a tapestry is composed of many strands. The edges have frayed,
and the tapestry is unraveling — but the thread needed to repair it is no
longer at hand. If the thread is found — in time — the tapestry will be
repaired. If it is not, people will die. Not all of them, and not all at
once; this is not the first time in the history of the Free Towns that such
denial has happened.

"But it is the first time it has happened when a god is intent upon
their destruction. You, however, are likely to survive."

Gervanno knelt, falling to one knee as was the Northern custom.
He bowed head in the presence of the circus master, aware, as he did,
that the sword — the new sword — had come to his hand for a reason.

"I will grant you a boon, should you undertake the finding of
Adala," the circus master said, as if he were a multitude and not a
single man. "But you are not what the circus itself needs; if you intend
to offer yourself in Adala's stead, I can appreciate the sentiment, but
cannot accept a pointless sacrifice. Your role is not in the Free Towns,
and your duty is larger than you know. Nor can any of the young men
remain in her place; there is one that might do, were the circumstances
different.

"But Nenyane is now aware of our conversation. She is unhappy,
and I have no wish to face the fullness of her wrath in my own lands; it
would demand a response from me, as master here, that we would both
have cause to deeply regret."

"Can you offer any guidance? Can you tell me where you believe
she might be found?"

"All the guidance that can be offered has been offered in the
pavilion of fortune and fate." Even as he spoke, he began to fade from
view, shimmering, the black cloth of his clothing reflecting a multitude
of different colors before he was lost to sight.

Gervanno rose only when he could no longer see the circus master.

Nenyane of Maubreche had cleared all distance that he had
managed to put between them and had landed — sword drawn — in
front of where Gervanno knelt. She was bristling; he could see that in

her posture, in the lines of her shoulder, her back. Stephen had not yet joined her.

"Nenyane," Gervanno said, "he is not our enemy."

"He is not our friend," she replied. She did not sheath sword. Not until Stephen—flanked by his dogs—arrived. "Gods don't have friends. They have allies, while their interests align. I've made clear that he is not to interfere with any of mine."

It was absurd to feel any pleasure at Nenyane's claim of ownership, but Gervanno was clearly absurd. He did.

"What did he want?"

"It was not he who initiated that encounter. It was me."

"Why?" Her sword finally returned to its sheath as Stephen touched her shoulder. No one else would have dared.

"I wished to ask him what the consequences to the circus—and therefore its visitors—would be should someone summoned to join the circus fail to heed that summons."

"And?"

"He answered."

Nenyane cursed—at least by tone. He did not recognize the words. "What did you see when you looked into the seer's heart?"

"Demons," he said. "Demons and Hansleigh, and a hint of circus pavilion and tent. Forests unlike the forests through which we traveled to reach Hansleigh; the wilderness, struggling in fury against the dead it so despises."

Nenyane was not content to let that answer stand, although it was more than he had said to this point. She waited, grim-faced, arms crossed as if only in this posture could she leave her sword sheathed.

"I saw a young woman—your age—and a young man. They were fleeing. It was not a single continuous vision. It was as if I was wandering down an endless hall of windows, all curtained. As I passed, some of those curtains were drawn, and I could see through the exposed window—but I could not linger long, and I could not return to previous windows. I did not see one thing, but many.

"In some such windows, they were dying. In all, they were in danger. In some they had already died. But in one or two, I arrived in time."

"What killed them?"

"Demons and their allies—or at least that was my assumption. But the shadow of their deaths—or the shadow of Adala's—encompassed the circus. The circus had vanished; the Free Town of Hansleigh remained. But its streets were littered with the dead and the dying." He closed his eyes. It had mostly been the dying, and the deaths were horrific. The detritus of circus wares lay in the streets.

"The circus was destroyed?"

Gervanno frowned. "I am uncertain. Were I to guess, I would say the circus retreated, leaving its audience in the Free Town."

"And this happened when she died—or after she died?"

"Understand that I was not fully in control of what I saw. What I was shown was not the answer to any question I asked. But it seemed—and seems—to me that it is her death that weakened the circus. It was the demons that attempted to use that weakness. Were the lord of the circus lands powerful enough, he might have kept the people of Hansleigh—and the outsiders—within the circus grounds until the danger had passed. In the vision I was shown, he did not."

Nenyane's expression lost both frustration and anger as she considered Gervanno's words. "You said she survived in some of these fragmented visions?"

Gervanno nodded. "Where she survived—and returned—Hansleigh was untouched."

"What else are you not telling us?"

Gervanno was silent. Nenyane turned and bellowed: "Alex!"

Alex winced. He had not gone far, and had no doubt noticed the moment Nenyane had turned back to retrieve Gervanno. "I'm here." He met Gervanno's gaze, held it for a long moment, and shook his head.

"You saw something in the seer's crystal," she said, transferring the intensity of her interrogation to the Elseth Hunter.

Alex nodded.

"Gervanno saw a girl named Adala. And the end of the circus in the worst possible way. What did you see?"

Alex turned to Gervanno. "What did she look like?"

"Brown hair too long for the battlefield, sun-dark skin; she was taller than Nenyane, but not quite your height. Coltish in build, but not delicate; her feet were large. She wore a frayed traveling cloak, dark pants, a worn pack."

Alex exhaled. "I saw her as well."

Nenyane's eyes were so narrowed they seemed closed. "What are the two of you hiding?" Her hands were now loosely bunched fists as she glared.

Alex opened his mouth as if to speak, but words failed to emerge. Gervanno understood. There some things one wanted to avoid speaking of at all, lest that speech make the vision a reality, a truth.

Alex would have been considered adult in the Dominion, as he was in Breodanir, but he was newly come to adulthood, and he had not been trained as a soldier. He had come on this road for the sake of family and friendship. What he owed was personal.

Gervanno was no longer cerdan in the armies of the Tyr, but his experience on the fields of battle, large, small and terrifying, was the greater experience. He had learned to consider death objectively, pragmatically; only by acknowledging the possibility—real, visceral—could he find a way to avoid it in future.

"I saw Stephen," Gervanno said, voice low.

Nenyane's posture shifted, but she did not draw sword. Stephen's hand on her shoulder tightened.

"I saw Alex and Max."

"And me?"

Gervanno shook his head. "Nor did I see the man you call Illaraphaniel. I did catch a glimpse of Kallandras."

"Where was I?"

"Nenyane—he just said he didn't see you. I don't think you can ask that question and receive any useful answer."

"I saw Nenyane," Alex said, his voice a tremor that carried syllables.

"Was she alive?"

"Yes."

"Was Stephen?"

Alex was silent.

Gervanno filled the silence. He understood Alex's hesitation; it was kin to his own. "Stephen was not dead in any of the visions I was shown. He was fighting, as were Alex and Max. Two of the dogs were dead or dying."

Stephen flinched, but asked no questions.

Nenyane did. "Were we fighting on the circus grounds?"

"No. We were not in the circus. We were fighting demons," he added, as if that were necessary. "In the visions in which none of us were dead, the bard was present; the mage was not."

"Then we'd be safe if we don't leave the circus."

Gervanno's exhalation was long. "I believe the circus itself was in danger. My apologies for speaking with the circus master in your absence. I wished to confirm the importance of Adala to the safety of the circus—and Hansleigh."

"Did the circus survive in any of your visions?"

"The circus did not figure prominently in anything I was shown."

"Alex?"

"I didn't see the circus either. But I didn't see as much as Gervanno, and Adala was not as prominent."

"The demons?"

"We fought them. But something else was there, something else was a danger—and no, I don't know what it was. It was more felt than seen." He swallowed. "If Gervanno saw a hall of curtained windows, I didn't."

"What did you see?"

Alex's silence now was one of deliberation. "It was as if I had stepped into a small stream. I could see a much larger river in the distance, and I knew that if I followed the stream, it would widen—but the stream branched, and branched again. I had to choose which branch to follow. I could retrace my steps and choose again—but I had to do it quickly. I had the sense that if I failed to find the right approach, I'd never reach the river."

"And the river in this analogy was safety?"

Alex shook his head. "There was no safety. But the river was as close as I could get. The branches that I saw or experienced—I didn't see them at a distance. I felt them; they were all true. Only one small branch of the stream lead to a place where I could see no deaths—but we all know that safety and survival-for-now aren't the same thing." He was pale as he spoke, but steady now. Max had arrived.

"And did you believe that this Adala was somehow necessary?"

"Nothing I saw made her essential—but everything I saw implied that she was. I *felt* that our survival depended on hers, a stranger I had never seen before."

Nenyane was not happy. "Was she absent in any of your visions?"

Alex shook his head.

"Then the visions that both you and Gervanno saw were wrapped around this stranger. What if we just avoid her entirely?"

"Hansleigh will not survive," Gervanno replied. "And we are in

Hansleigh now, or will be. If what you mean to ask is whether or not it is safe to ignore Adala, the answer is no. We will fight, regardless, but the chance that all of our company survives then is low."

"You want to find her." The words were almost accusatory. "You wanted to find her the moment you first heard her name and her circumstances. That's the reason you saw what you saw."

Gervanno did not deny them.

"The seer showed you this because she meant you to find her."

Alex, however, shook his head. "I'd never heard of her. I didn't know her name. But what I saw involved her."

"And what did you want, when you caught a glimpse of a crystal vision you weren't deliberately shown?"

"What I've wanted since we met in the King's City. I want us all to survive. Our survival, in some fashion, depended on her survival."

"Some of the deaths you saw—or felt—were *because* we were trying to save her."

Alex wanted to disagree, but couldn't.

Gervanno could. "Some of the visions I saw through those open windows did not involve her. We—Maubreche, Elseth, the bard— were central to what I was shown. On those occasions where she was not present, the danger was far higher, the consequences worse. I believe the seer did, and does, intend that we find Adala and Trevor."

"Was Trevor the person with Adala?"

Gervanno nodded. "It is a path into conflict if we do not move quickly—but it is also the safest of the many unsafe choices we might make." He exhaled. His training in the Dominion, his life of military service to date—a life he had fled—held him for a long moment. But Nenyane was the master his heart desired: sword master, genius with the weapon around which Gervanno had built his life, and with which he had proved his worth.

"I did not have time to examine every option. It's possible that if we left now—if we fled immediately—we would not face the dangers the seer showed to me. But I did not feel that those dangers were lies. I felt them all, saw them all, as truths formed by the contexts of the choices we *can* consciously make.

"On the road, we chose to allow the nearby village to deal with the non-demonic creatures that had managed to straggle into our lands from the wilderness. We accepted this because we felt the creatures were not worse than bandits, something all towns deal with from time to time. It was not better, it was not worse.

"But this is not the same. Should we attempt to flee, everyone here will likely die, and almost no death will be clean. This is not something the people of Hansleigh encounter regularly, not something for which plans have been made and prior experience can become a guide. To leave a town equipped to deal with bandits is one thing. To leave a town to perish by demons—when we have greater experience and some chance of saving that town—quite another."

"We don't have to flee. We just have to stay here."

It was Alex who shook his head. "Gervanno's been worried about this since we arrived. I don't think the circus will remain safe if we remain—we'll be part of the carnage in Hansleigh."

Gervanno was surprised, but should not have been. Alex was far more talkative than Max, and far more curious than any of his traveling companions, but he noticed small undercurrents in the silences of his companions. "That is my fear," he hesitated, and then added, "I did not intend for anyone else to leave the circus—but I think, given the seer's crystal, that I am meant to find Adala."

Alex shook his head. "You saw us. We were there."

"You were not present in all of the glimpsed visions."

"We were present in the ones that mattered. Or am I wrong?"

Gervanno exhaled. "No. But I did not have time to continue exploring." He failed to look at Nenyane; he meant no criticism. He thought he might have wandered through possibilities for days, lost in the desperate attempt to find and memorize only the right ones. But he knew he—and they—did not have the time for that, if time moved in the circus the same way it had moved in Hansleigh.

Nenyane accepted the criticism without a change in expression. He had told them that they were present—all save Nenyane. Gervanno had feared her absence for perfectly good reasons. Nenyane did not. But Alex had seen Nenyane.

Alex had, no doubt, seen death, as Gervanno had. Gervanno had not seen his own death; he had seen the deaths of Alex, Max, the dogs. Stephen had survived, but bore wounds. Even Kallandras had been injured. He had wandered the seer's odd hall of visions looking for a future that did not include the deaths of Adala or any of the Hunters.

Nenyane met his gaze, held it, and then transferred her silent interrogation to Alex. She had known Alex for far longer than Gervanno; it made sense that Alex's equally steady gaze would carry more weight. He was not a child, nor a youth, to feel the sting of the difference in her regard.

But perhaps there was much in this place that invoked childhood's desire and worry. He looked to Stephen, surprised to find that the weight of Stephen's gaze was upon him. Surprised further to see that Stephen's lips were curved in a subtle smile.

"The performance hasn't started yet," Stephen said. "And if Adala's presence is necessary for the safety of Hansleigh, we'd best start now."

Nenyane's nod was grim but instant. She made no further attempt to dissuade them.

To start what was to be a hunt was easier said than done.

"Adala understands Hansleigh and the circus," Gervanno said, moving quickly to exit the pavilion. "What she doesn't understand is Breodani Hunters. They have hunting dogs in Hansleigh, or so I've been told—but their dogs are not equal to Breodanir's."

No one disagreed.

"If we can find the innkeeper in this crowd, we might be able to pick up Adala's scent; she lived in the inn. I'm certain her father isn't carrying her items with him."

"The scent would be too muddied if he'd handled it or carried it for long," Max replied. "But if we know which room she occupied, we'll have a better shot at finding her. I doubt we'd be able to track her path through Hansleigh—but we would have better luck at finding her trail outside of the town. Did either of you notice which direction she chose as her exit?"

"She wasn't trying to avoid the dogs, or she'd've followed the road. She was trying to avoid being seen. I think she left well before the circus opened its doors."

"She would have had to," Nenyane said, voice flat. If she offered no argument against the search, she was *deeply* unhappy to be enmeshed in the circus's troubles. Or Hansleigh's.

This was normal, for Nenyane. Even Gervanno recognized it.

"The circus master is likely to know which route she took to leave the town. I don't think she'd take the risk of heading east—she'd have

two towns to travel through or around if she did, and the Free Towns
are all beholden to the circus."

No one asked her how she knew; Alex at least had to struggle. He
did. "You think she headed toward the Western Kingdoms?"

"It's what I would have done in her shoes. And the first of the kingdoms would be Breodanir."

"She won't make it that far." Gervanno scanned the crowd. It was
sparse; most people had chosen to explore the various pavilions, and
were no longer in the streets. When the performance started they
would emerge, but it would be harder to find a single man when
they did.

It was luck, then, that of the few people who stood in the streets,
the innkeeper was one. He was pale, his skin damp with sweat and
heat, although the streets themselves were cool. He appeared to be
waiting for someone. His daughter, no doubt, who would not arrive
without intervention.

Gervanno approached him immediately; the blacksmith, Devon,
was absent. But Devon's son had not been called to the circus; he had
risked his own death. Gervanno knew that love made fools of men, he
had seen it so often.

The innkeeper caught sight of Gervanno. Face pale, he lifted a
trembling hand in greeting, and Gervanno realized that it was not
Adala for whom the innkeeper waited; it was Gervanno.

"I'm to take your dog," the innkeeper said. "If he'll stay with me."

"He'll stay. For now, he'll stay. But if you lose sight of him during
the performance itself, no blame or failure will accrue to you. I met
Leial on the road, full grown; I have not had a hand in the whole of his
training, which was poor."

Leial whined, as if he understood Gervanno's words, but allowed
himself to be handed to the innkeeper.

"And I have this for you—I was told you would need it." The
innkeeper handed Gervanno a key. "I'm sure your dog is better trained
than my daughter."

"We teach children, we don't train them," Gervanno replied. "Who
told you to wait for us?"

"I saw it in the pavilion of fate and fortune. The seer was there."
The word *seer* was inflected with dread and awe. No one present felt
any need to ask who the seer was; they knew. "I went there because

Adala didn't arrive. I wanted some hint, some word, some hope that she would." His voice was low, shaky. "You were the only hope offered.

"We're strangers to you, I know it. And I know she's not a child. But she is wild with love. I was once, too. But the consequence of my love and my youth wasn't..."

Gervanno placed a firm hand on the innkeeper's shoulder. He took the key in the other hand. "This is to her room?"

The man nodded. He didn't fear theft, or perhaps he didn't care. If his daughter could be found, what did petty theft matter?

"How do we leave the circus?" It was Nenyane who asked.

"Follow the road, either east or west, to its end. There's a fancy gate on either side, but it's not attached to a fence or guard house. If you ask to leave, the gates will open outward." He hesitated, and then added, "If there are enemies at the border, the gates won't open at all."

"Which exit will take us closest to the inn?"

The innkeeper blinked. "I believe both exits will take you to the town center. From there, Gervanno knows how to find the inn." He swallowed. Opened his mouth. Closed it again. "Find her," he said, on this third attempt to speak. "Find her and I'll owe you whatever I can offer. It's not much—but it's not nothing, either."

"We will do our best." But it came to Gervanno, gazing at the innkeeper, that he had also seen some of what Gervanno had seen, focused not on the Southerner's companions, but on his own child. Death. Many deaths. And only a slender possibility of survival.

Gervanno turned to the west, widening his stride as the Hunters fell in line.

CHAPTER NINE

As the innkeeper had said, a free-standing gate—closed—stood before them. It seemed to be made of metal—but new metal, an oddly bright silver. The bars of the gate were widely spaced. Had Gervanno desired to do so, he could have fit arm and shoulder easily through any of the openings.

Beyond the gate, the road seemed to continue, uninterrupted by anything so mundane as buildings. There were trees in the distance, but they lined the road neatly, as if planted solely to do so.

Nenyane disliked the gate on principle; it was attached to nothing. There seemed to be no reason for its existence; if people wanted to leave, they could just walk around it.

Alex was far less certain, but Nenyane's impatience won; it was the Maubreche huntbrother who practically stormed the closed gate.

No one present had expected the gate to speak: "Please return to the circus grounds. The performance is about to begin." The words rang out as if they were chimes; as if the bars had been physically struck.

Nenyane was unimpressed. Stephen's hand once again paused on her shoulder; she shrugged it off, clearly annoyed. "We wish to leave the circus grounds."

"There is no guarantee that you will be permitted to return for this performance," the gate replied.

"I'd be totally fine with that." Nenyane's words were distinct and rapid. "We need to leave. Now. While I'm asking nicely."

Gervanno felt his jaw drop and quickly closed his mouth; no words would have escaped, regardless. He knew Nenyane could be reckless, but felt that she was crossing an invisible line. Before any of the Hunters could intervene, he did; he lifted hand to touch the bars of the gate. When he spoke, he spoke in Torra.

"We are aware of the great honor that we have been offered; we desired to be part of the audience, for the circus in these parts is almost mythical in nature, and to see the performance rather than hear whispers of it was our desire."

Ringing again, this time absent words—a tinkle of sound as if the bars were not fixed in place, but hung like wind chimes near a domis's entrance.

"But one of the members of the circus has yet to arrive, and we have been tasked with her finding. She is not on the circus grounds, nor has she approached them, according to the circus master. We are visitors, not residents, and our loss will not affect the circus. Her loss will. We regret the lost opportunity, but in return for the hospitality we have been offered, we wish to find the missing member."

"We're doing *them* a favor!" Nenyane was outraged. Clearly, Nenyane could understand Torra—or had borrowed her Hunter's understanding. "We don't need to *grovel* while we're doing it!"

"And is the presence of your impulsive companion necessary?" the gate asked.

"She is the strongest of our company. You know what lurks without."

"A price must be paid to open these gates."

Gervanno was unsurprised, but grimaced regardless. Nenyane's impatience and irritation would soon boil over.

"I will pay the price," a familiar voice said.

"And I have been given freedom of your lands," a second voice added.

Gervanno could see the warped reflection of two men in the sheen of the bars.

Kallandras of Senniel and Meralonne APhaniel had arrived. The wind did not carry them; they stood on the same road as the Hunters and their dogs. Gervanno had expected the bard; he had not expected a man who might put lie to his claim that Nenyane, of their company, was the strongest.

Honor dictated that he not lie, but even had it not, it seemed important that he not lie in this place.

"Very well. But pay it quickly. There has been some small delay in the performance; perhaps, should you find what you seek, you will still have the chance to join the audience."

The bard stepped up to the gates; the Hunters—and Gervanno—moved to the right and left to allow him to touch the gate itself. Kallandras did—but before he did, he cut the mound of his palm just enough that blood beaded there. He then gripped the bar in his hand—the left—and bowed head. "We wish safe passage to the place where the lord's lands are entwined with the mortal realm." Speaking thus, he released the bars.

The gate did not so much roll open as fade from view. As it did, the streets of Hansleigh appeared: not in front of them, as Gervanno had expected, given the existence of the gate itself, but around them. The road, however, remained the same circus road—clean, well laid, untroubled by weeds and the cracks of much traffic.

"I see your propensity for stepping off figurative cliffs has not deserted you," Meralonne said. His robes were once again the dark blue of his order, but the hood had been pulled up, and the silver strands of his hair could not be immediately seen.

Gervanno nodded. "But say, rather, that the land drops away beneath our feet without warning. There are paths we would not take had they not seemed solid and reliable."

"I would, but it would be a lie, and I believe you disdain those."

Gervanno nodded and turned immediately toward the Silver Shield. He had always had a good memory for geography, which had served him well in the heat of battle and in the planning that led to it, however imperfect those plans proved to be.

The inn was not locked, although all of its customers and employees had abandoned it for the circus; in any other circumstance, doors would not open so easily. But the buildings themselves were safe to abandon when the circus came to town. It was, therefore, a simple matter to enter.

He withdrew the key that he had been handed by a terrified father; it was warm in his palm. Stephen's dogs followed Gervanno, which was unusual; they did not linger with their master or Max. Pearl, in particular, shoved her way to the front of the pack, which caused some hostility on the part of Patches.

Pearl moved out of the way reluctantly as Gervanno found the room: it was not numbered the way guest rooms were and it was at the height of the inn, not on the ground floor where he had assumed it would be found.

The door was locked, but the key unlocked it easily.

He made a silent apology to the young woman before he entered a space that would never otherwise be open to him. It was not a single room, but a small suite; he had opened the door not into a bedroom but into a room that might have served as a small office, given the desk and the untidy appearance of shelves. Books lined two, which was surprising; in his travels in the North, books were not common, and seemed the province of the wealthy.

But he glanced at Alex. Perhaps some books made their way to Hansleigh through the circus, where gold was not the coin for which they must be paid. But while he himself could speak and read enough of the merchant tongue that he could manage simple tasks; he could not read these books without effort, and did not try.

Instead, he moved from this room, with its tidy desk, to the next: a bedroom. He expected to find closet, armoire, or drawers, and was not disappointed. Pearl, however, trotted toward a large, partially filled basket. Ah, yes. Dirty laundry better suited the purpose of the Hunters than clean.

The white scenthound began to nose her way through that laundry as Stephen entered the bedroom. It was not large enough to fit their entire party, and the dogs were Stephen's, but Gervanno was not surprised to see Max follow.

"Will this do?" the cerdan asked of Stephen.

Stephen frowned but nodded. "There's more than one scent on the clothing — or more than one that's strong."

"It is not just Adala we need to find; she fled the circus in the company of a young man."

Meralonne joined them in the now crowded bedroom. He glanced at the laundry, frowned, and proceeded to the bedside table. On it was a small box — a chest. The mage attempted to open it, and discovered it to be locked. He frowned and spoke a single, sharp syllable.

The wood cracked with the force of it.

Stephen's eyes widened briefly. Max's did not. The mage then opened the box, having destroyed the simple lock. It was empty. If it had previously contained jewelry, Adala had taken it with her in her flight. It was the first practical thing she had done, in Gervanno's opinion.

But perhaps that was unfair. She, like Gervanno himself, had her goals. None of them included joining the circus. Was she aware of what the cost to the circus—and to all of Hansleigh—might be? Would it have stopped him, in his distant youth?

"What did you hope to find?" Stephen asked the mage.

"Some item of sentimental value, perhaps. You have seen Nenyane at work. Her skill is not mine but it is possible she might have been able to find this Adala, just as she found the Margen Hunters."

"Could she do that outside of the wilderness?"

"Ah, no. But there is a reason I chose to camp well outside of the town. The Free Towns are not what Breodanir is. The fabric of the township is woven both of wilderness and mortal land, never wholly one or the other. The Free Towns have bandit difficulties, things that one might expect of a normal town or village. Should mortal armies attempt to move through the Towns to conquer them, they will encounter unexpected difficulties. The weave is subtle, but it is there.

"Only when the enemies are the dead does this change. The missing young woman intended to flee—and did—but how and where will depend on her knowledge of this fact. If she understands, she will not flee to the east, for all three of the Free Towns are connected. The circus may appear in any of them."

"Then we move, as previously decided, to the west—toward Breodanir."

Stephen moved from laundry hamper to the bed, or rather, the small table beside it, a tidy wooden square that contained one drawer. He opened it, and retrieved a book. A notebook, similar in style to the one he had chosen for himself at one of the circus stalls. "This, maybe."

Meralonne frowned.

Stephen opened it, read a few lines of handwriting. "I think it's a diary."

Meralonne held out a hand; Stephen waited for Patches, held out the book for her olfactory inspection, and then passed the book to the magi.

STEPHEN HANDLED the smallest piece of dirty laundry with care; he had chosen a knit scarf in a shade of faded red. He wasn't certain that Adala would follow the road if flight was her intent. He would have, using the roads as a solid river, a way to blend his scent with so many others that lymers might lose it in the crowd. But Adala was unlikely to fear hunting dogs.

Until he had entered the circus, Stephen hadn't questioned the existence of the Free Towns in any meaningful way. Meralonne's insistence that they set up camp well outside of Hansleigh, which could offer the comfort of an inn—or several—had not prepared him for the circus, but perhaps it should have. The Hunters had intended to follow the road through the townships, toward the heart of the Empire of Essalieyan.

Were he Adala, he would have made the Empire his goal: not because it was inherently better than Breodanir, the first of the kingdoms to the West, but because the information he would have about that Empire would be far more complete. Merchants traveled to Breodanir, and from—but very few of the Breodani left their borders.

Adala had left town before the circus opened its gates. He was uncertain by how much. If she wished to avoid or escape the circus, she would have planned her flight as early as possible.

Nenyane, who had waited in the hall, nodded. The impatience, the discomfort, that had characterized her stay on the circus grounds had become much less marked; she was prickly, but in the usual way. She had been reluctant to accept this hunt, but understood that Stephen intended to find the missing young woman.

She even understood, on a visceral level, why.

"It's the wind," she said, as they retreated from the room. "There are dried meats and fruits in the second pantry—we should fill up on those. We might need them."

Gervanno stiffened but did not argue against what was clearly theft.

Stephen, however, shook his head. "We'll take the rest of our gear with us."

"It'll slow us down."

"If everything of value remains in the inn and we fail, we won't be returning."

Alex and Max blinked, glanced at each other, and then glanced at

Nenyane. Meralonne nodded. Kallandras, however, had clearly already retrieved his pack, his supplies. The Hunters split up to do the same.

The wind. Stephen had not felt it as clearly as his huntbrother. He felt it when they left the inn and entered the empty streets. Gervanno had spoken of his glimpse of Hansleigh if the circus fell: the streets in that vision were not empty.

"The circus can prevent demons from reaching the towns." Stephen's tone trailed up, as if it were a question.

Meralonne nodded. "It depends on the power of demons involved. If all are unwelcome to the untamed wilderness, they are capable of walking those lands, regardless. But it is seldom that three mortal towns prove of interest to their unnamed lord. Yes, the towns are protected in a fashion. Even absent the heart of the circus, these lands are claimed. But they can be easily reached by ancient paths carved into the wilderness in wars long past, if one knows the geography.

"The White Lady did not venture here often—but she was welcome, and all of her kin." He looked as if he would say more, but fell silent instead.

Nenyane, however, did not. She turned to Gervanno. "We should just leave. If what you saw was the future that would occur absent this Adala, we should leave the Free Towns."

Alex turned to the Maubreche huntbrother. "Why?"

"There are some *Kialli* even I'm not guaranteed to survive. If what Illaraphaniel says is true, one such lord is likely to be close by. If we fail to find this stranger—and if we fail to convince her to return— that's what we'll be facing. She's a stranger. The townspeople are strangers. They're not Breodani. They're not our responsibility."

"And if the demons destroy the towns, where do you think they'll head next?" The Elseth brothers were quietly appalled, and this time, it was Max who spoke, not Alex.

Nenyane considered his words as if there was nothing emotional in them. She exhaled and nodded. She turned to the west; the Silver Shield was on the main street that passed through the town.

"I am not a hunting dog," Kallandras said. "But I will scout ahead on the road. Call me if you find the girl's trail."

MERALONNE DID NOT ACCOMPANY the bard. As Stephen moved to follow Kallandras, the mage retrieved Adala's diary. Stephen had made no attempt to stop him from taking it, but felt uncomfortable with the invasion of privacy. This, predictably, annoyed Nenyane.

I understand why it might be necessary. I'm just not comfortable with it.

I know that. Your discomfort is yours. My annoyance is mine, as well. You didn't say anything. I didn't say anything.

The mage had opened the book from the back, which was blank; he flipped pages until he reached one that contained writing.

Stephen gathered his dogs, paused, and knelt before Steel. "Max."

Max nodded. Stephen had sent Steel with Max so often he was accustomed to the hound. Max felt the lack of Elseth's hunting dogs keenly. Alex missed them as well, but not in the visceral way Max did. Neither of the Elseth Hunters complained.

"What are you doing?" Nenyane demanded.

Stephen ignored her. He spoke to Steel, but not with words. Steel had become Max's guard, Max's follower, since the Hunters had left the King's City. Steel was Stephen's. It would make more sense to attempt to hand over the reins of the new dogs, the dogs that had come from the King's personal kennel. But those dogs weren't his, and in the future, should they all survive, he was honor bound to return them to the kennels and master from whom they'd come.

He wanted Steel to bond with Max, not in the half-hearted fashion he had done to this point, but completely. He wanted Steel to *be* Max's dog. But he couldn't simply cut Steel loose, couldn't just command him —not in a matter of such import. He had no intention of abandoning Steel; had no intention of simply leaving him behind.

"Max, come here."

This time, Max frowned.

"I know it's not a full pack, or even half a pack. But...Steel is willing to become your dog. Yours, not mine."

Max froze.

Alex glanced at his brother, before turning his gaze to Stephen, who held it. Stephen nodded, the nod an answer to the question Alex felt no need to put into words. Max was tense.

The Elseth Hunter opened his mouth. Closed it. Opened it again.

"You've always worked better on a hunt with dogs than without," Stephen said, replying to the question Max hadn't asked. "One dog might not be the same as a pack, or the four I brought with me, and Steel's an alaunt, not a lymer, but…" he shrugged.

Max wanted Steel. Max knew Steel was *technically* a Maubreche dog. The answer should be *no*. Or a variant of *no* that included gratitude, gravity. But he couldn't make himself say it. The words wouldn't leave his open mouth.

Alex finally exhaled in mild disgust. He shoved his brother—harder than strictly necessary, which implied they'd been arguing—toward Stephen. Max stumbled but didn't even glare at Alex, because he'd stumbled toward Stephen. Or rather, toward Steel.

Stephen could talk to any dog; any dog would gravitate to him. From birth, the alaunts had loved him in the obsequious way of well-trained dogs. Steel understood what Stephen wanted, and why. Stephen could have asked Steel to leap headfirst off a cliff, and the dog would have obeyed without question.

But the trust of the dogs had never been broken. Stephen could not simply send Steel to Max. He could not cut him out of the heart of the pack without Steel's consent, Steel's desire. Grudging acceptance would give way to a feeling of abandonment—and that, Stephen would not do.

Steel, however, understood what he would lose and what he would gain. If he joined Max, he would be Max's first—and only—dog. He would be the start of Max's hunting pack and, in future, the pack would be Steel's. He was not abandoning Stephen, because Max would not abandon Stephen. And he liked Max.

Stephen very carefully extricated Steel from his dogs.

If Max didn't argue, no one else would. Not even Nenyane.

I don't care if you give them all to Max.

The King would.

The King is never getting those dogs back. He gave them to you.

Steel's bark prevented an argument.

Dogs were both bought and sold, but not often, and almost never at Steel's age. Some were retired, if injuries sustained in a hunt were too severe. Steel was not a puppy; he was a Maubreche dog. But if Stephen's effect on dogs, well noted over the course of his life, was unrivaled, the Elseth children's—the sons of Espere of Elseth—were close.

Steel licked Stephen's face and then turned, tail beginning to blur, toward Max.

Max did not kneel. He simply waited in silence, because words were not necessary. The grey alaunt walked toward Max, head lifted, tail moving. Only when he reached Max did he stop. Max bent, dropping his hand to the top of Steel's head, where it had often rested. No words left his mouth, but no words were necessary. Max already had a strong bond to Steel. Stephen had chosen Steel for a reason.

When Max lifted his head again, his eyes were red, but he did not weep. Instead, he offered Stephen a nod.

Stephen felt the connection between Steel and the rest of his pack thin. He rose, waiting for the moment it snapped. Remembering Steel as a puppy. Remembering Steel on the hunt. He wondered if this is how parents felt when they sent their daughters to be married. Steel would be happy to hunt with Max. And eventually, with other dogs.

Max won't have other dogs for a long time, if ever. There was a reason he was sent to the King's City. He won't take the oath. He won't accept it.

Stephen shook his head. *I won't accept it, either—but I have dogs.*

"Can we start moving?" Nenyane asked, the words an impatient demand.

"Kallandras hasn't returned." It was Alex who pointed this out. His eyes, however, were on his brother.

"If you wish something to do while we wait," Meralonne said, "peruse this diary. She may have written about her escape plans there." He handed the diary to Alex.

Stephen thought this mildly unfair, as Alex hadn't been the one complaining, but Alex accepted the book with only minor signs of discomfort. As if he, too, understood just how important Adala was.

"While you are reading, I, too, will prepare."

THE DIARY WAS WRITTEN in the Weston language, although *scrawled* would have been a more accurate description; Adala's handwriting was messy and uneven, the words slanting to the right. Alex had been taught to use a ruler as guide; Adala had not. She abbreviated longer words, but not consistently; she often dropped words, as if the diary itself had been written in a rush at the end of a long day. In two places, candle wax attested to that truth.

This had been in a beside drawer no doubt accompanied by whatever small items Adala had valued; she had not taken it with her.

Perhaps she assumed—correctly—that there would be no danger of its discovery. Everyone in the inn, family included, had gone to the circus.

But some people had returned.

Alex had seen Adala—or a woman he assumed was Adala—in the seer's crystal. It was not that woman that had been his concern; she was a stranger. Max and Gervanno were not. Nor were Stephen and Nenyane, but only Stephen had been gravely injured. Stephen and his dogs.

Nenyane had been armed, but her sword had been the one sharp light he had seen in his vision, as if it were a container, a containment, for the sun and its merciless heat.

But Alex had seen demons; he knew what she fought. Nenyane might have slaughtered dozens, but no blood would cling to her sword. He had had a brief glimpse of the bard, but none of the mage.

He understood, as he opened the book from the back, that he was violating a young woman's privacy. But her privacy was of far less import than the lives of his companions.

The last few pages were almost illegible, the scrawl itself ferocious.

19th Wittan: We're leaving. We're leaving before the circus opens its gates.

He moved back through the pages, toward the front of the book, as if crossing time. He was, of the four Hunters, the fastest reader—but most of what he read was not written in this fashion. Breodani letters were cleaner and clearer. It was more difficult to search for key words or relevant words when the writing itself was so messy.

Alex exhaled and began to look for numbers instead. Dates.

None of Adala's entries were long, and almost none were detailed. But he paused his backward search when he found the 6th of Wittan. The first of the month. The Hunters had passed that time in Breodanir, in Bowgren.

Adala had been here.

6TH WITTAN: It's happened. I've received the summons. A scroll arrived at the front desk. I hoped it wasn't for me. I prayed it wasn't for me. What's the point of praying to the circus master?

7th Wittan: I left the scroll. I went to speak with Aunt Tallia. She's seen the circus perform more than any of us, but she's not part of it. Both her younger brother and her own aunt received the summons. Summons only arrive when the circus intends to perform. T said they didn't join the line to enter. They accepted the summons and the gates opened—for them—early. I asked her if they ever came home. If they ever came to visit. She said no.

She saw them again, but only in the circus. And in the circus, they barely aged. I didn't tell her that I'd been summoned.

I talked to Trevor. I told him I'd been summoned. I love him, but sometimes he's thick as a plank. He was excited *for me. He was happy. He said I'd always had the talent to join the circus. So I told him: I join, and we're separated forever.*

8ᵗʰ Wittan: I won't join the circus. I won't leave Trevor.

12th Wittan: Father and Mother found out about the summons. I tried to look happy. Father kept on about honor and family and home. About work and duty and the greater good. He knows how much I hate it. He knows why.

13th Wittan: We can't travel to the east. We can't stay on the road between the towns. We'll be found. I've some money saved. We'll buy perishable supplies on the 19th, and anything else we might need before that. Trevor can shop. I can't; my father's been watching. My mother's been bragging—and she's not supposed to do that. Her "this has to remain between us" has been said so often the whole town must know. Her daughter is going to join the circus.

I won't.

ALEX LOOKED UP. "She didn't take the road."

"Where did she go?"

"Haven't got that far yet. I'm not sure she'll write her plans in the diary. I wouldn't have."

"You don't keep one," Max pointed out. He fell silent as Alex continued to read.

15TH WITTAN: Everything we need, we have. Trevor's kept the bulky things; his father's been busy, and Trevor wasn't summoned, so he's not being so careful.

17th Wittan: I saw them. I saw the gates. I saw people walking past them, and people walking through *them, as if they didn't exist. I couldn't walk through them. They were real, for me. I came back home—I had to work, so no one was suspicious. Except my father. He knows. He knows I should be gone.*

18th Wittan: The gates opened. I met him. I met the circus master. I meant to ignore him, but I couldn't. I don't think anyone could ignore him. He told me he was waiting. He told me that the safety of all of Hansleigh—of all the Free Towns—depends on the circus. Like I was a stupid child. Like I didn't already know. I thought it was all over, but he said: You have a choice. Everything I have built in this place was built on choice: mine. Yours.

But what choice? If he summons, I have to go to him. If he commands, I have to join the circus. I'll lose Trevor. He'll lose me. How is that a choice? *But he didn't force me through the gates. He didn't have me dragged off. He just told me that if I reject the summons, I had best be far from the towns.*

"SHE DIDN'T WRITE her plans here," Alex said, closing the book. Had they a few days, he might have read it all, looking for hints about the circus and the circus performers. He didn't. "Except for one thing: she knew to avoid the roads and the other Free Towns. She didn't say whether or not she intended to head west or east, kingdoms or Empire. But she met the circus master before we did. She was expected to join the circus before it was open to the public.

"But he knew she had no desire to join. He didn't force her to enter. He said she had a choice." The words were bitter.

"Choice?"

Alex nodded. "Just like we have a choice when it comes to the Hunter's Oath."

Silence, then. Each of the four Hunters present had made their choice. Had the cost been theirs alone to bear, the consequences would not have weighed so heavily on them. But Elseth and Maubreche also bore the weight of their decision.

Hansleigh would bear the weight of Adala's.

Alex had been a child, as had Max, when they had jointly refused to accept a huntbrother; they had been children when they had demanded the right to *be* huntbrother to the other. As children could, they fought—Alex wanted to swear the huntbrother's oath, and Max wanted to swear it.

"Did he tell her what would happen if she chose not to join?"

"If he did, she didn't write about it. She's not big on long entries. She did prepare. Trevor prepared. But she didn't argue with her parents, and she didn't tell them she had no intention of joining. I'm not sure they would have accepted the refusal. She knows she has to be as far from Hansleigh as she can get—but she probably couldn't give herself much time before the circus opened. She didn't write an intended destination. I think destination didn't matter. Trevor did."

"Did she write about the circus at all? I mean, in relation to the Free Towns?"

"She might have—but it would have been earlier." And it might take an hour or two to find such a mention. "But it's clear she knew the invitation to join was mandatory. She knew she'd leave Hansleigh. And she knew Trevor couldn't follow her into the circus. I'm not sure she thought much beyond that at the end."

That impulse, that kind of love, was something Alex had never experienced. He'd read about it, heard about it—but it was almost like hearing about exotic foods and weather. He tried to fit it over his own experiences, tried to find similarities that might help him understand her intent.

Maybe he was making it harder. He had rejected a huntbrother. He had Max. He had no desire to have someone else take Max's place in his life, and no intention of letting someone take his place in Max's. Was it as simple as that?

But Elseth would not fall or rise by that choice. It had been a choice Alex had made for himself. Had there been no other sons, he would have *wanted* to make that choice, but it would have been harder. If Elseth's fate was destruction in the face of his choice, he would have likely made a different one.

I wouldn't, Max said.

Only one of us would have had to accept a stranger, Alex replied.

THE FASTEST WAY out of the Free Towns was west. That might not have been the terminal destination, but if distance was a necessity, it would be fastest to take the road. Stephen had sent Patches and Pearl ahead, searching for any trace of Adala.

The bard had not returned by the time Alex closed Adala's diary.

Meralonne had remained silent as Alex read, and silent as Alex closed the book and added it, with characteristic care, to his pack. He intended to return it to Adala—no doubt with apologies—when she was found. If she was found in time.

He closed his eyes, falling behind Patches' gaze.

Nenyane was silent. It was the silence of the mage. But the mage's expression was neutral; Nenyane's wore open disgust.

What is it? Stephen asked.

The town. It's quiet enough now that I can hear the name of the lord. Meralonne told you that the Free Towns are not entirely mortal lands. At Stephen's nod, she continued. *They're not. I don't understand how, but the influence of the lord exists and persists in what appears to be mundane land. With the daily noise the townspeople make, the lord's name is inaudible. It's not inaudible now.*

Stephen could not hear it.

Alex, however, frowned. "I think we need to leave Hansleigh," he said.

Nenyane snorted, but turned to the mage.

"I will not ask for aid in this endeavor," the mage replied. "The petty obligations of the mortal are not the obligations incurred when one receives a favor in the wilderness. Should the lord choose to bestow favor, accept it where it is not onerous; if the lord does not offer, do not ask."

Gervanno surprised them all. He spoke. "I will accept that burden."

"You have already accepted the burden of finding Adala," the mage replied. He did not otherwise argue. "If any might survive such a favor unscathed and otherwise unburdened, it would be you.

"There is a reason that Evayne a'Nolan came to you."

Gervanno had sought Evayne—and fate, and fortune—at his own desire. They knew it. No one, however, attempted to correct the mage.

"We are no longer on the circus grounds. How likely is it that the circus master will hear me in the streets of Hansleigh?"

"He will hear you in the streets of any of the Free Towns, but he may not choose to interact or appear while the circus is open. The circus is entirely of his making, and entirely within his power; it is the very heart of these lands. Seldom is it that the lords in the wilderness choose to open up their hidden courts to any and all who might pass by.

"But ask what you would ask."

Nenyane said, "No."

Given Stephen's expression, he had an opinion, but chose to share it privately, as Hunters could.

"I don't care. Gervanno doesn't understand the burden of a debt owed a god. I do."

"Debts owed by the powerful," Gervanno said quietly, "are to be avoided where at all possible. Debts owed by the powerful to the powerless can often be discharged by simply removing the powerless. If we find Adala, the...god...will be in our debt. If we find her because we have asked for his help, that debt will be lessened. Lessening the debt is desirable."

"Nenyane," the mage said, the word almost cold. "He is correct. But I fear the circus master will not be able to offer much aid. Can you not hear it? The wind is ill-pleased."

"Gervanno doesn't belong to the circus master."

"Nor does he belong to you."

Stephen winced, but it was clear Gervanno was not offended by Nenyane's possessive streak. Their eyes met. Stephen nodded; Gervanno nodded in return. The Southerner then bowed head, as if in prayer.

If the lord of these lands heard Gervanno, there was no immediate response.

Do not tangle with gods, Stephen. You must know—especially you—how little they understand or care about the hearts of your people. Your survival, maybe. But not all survival is a boon or a blessing. Nenyane's frown rippled, although it remained attached to her mouth, eyes and brow.

Stephen heard, clearly, the barking of a dog. It was a familiar sound, but belonged to none of his hounds, or Steel.

Ah. Leial came running down the street, barking at high pitch, tail almost a blur, as he ran straight for Gervanno.

GERVANNO'S POSTURE IMPLIED PRAYER; he did not pray. No Southerner prayed during daylight hours. During the Lady's time, prayers might be uttered in privacy and shadow; the Lord disdained those who pled and begged. Or so Gervanno had been taught so often the knowledge had become part of him, just as breath was.

But he knew that Nenyane had been right. The lord of these lands had heard his request. To find his wayward daughter, his wayward servant, he had sent aid, in a fashion. The dog that Gervanno had left in the safety of the circus now bounded down the road.

Stephen's dogs had dignity. Leial had none. He leapt up, almost dancing on two legs, as he reached Gervanno, tongue hanging out of his open jaws.

"I think," he said, speaking to the Maubreche Hunters, "Leial might offer us some hint of where Adala's trail can be found."

LEIAL BARKED LOUDLY before dropping down to four paws; he circled Gervanno in what appeared to be a frenzy of delight. Gervanno did not pick the dog up. Instead, he knelt. Leial's tongue was wet, warm, and not entirely pleasant. "Show us," the cerdan said.

Leial barked again and turned and ran off.

Adala had taken the road to the west. This, everyone expected.

What they had not expected was Leial's sudden and immediate deviation from that road as it left the town, or the town's buildings, behind. Pearl was unamused. It was beneath her dignity to follow Leial, a creature she barely considered a dog, but she was smart enough to know that Leial was tracking Adala, if not by scent.

The deviation off the road made no sense. If distance was necessary, following the road was the most certain way to gain it. Adala had not, to their knowledge, taken horse or pack animal; she had packed what she could in secret. If she had valuables to sell or barter, she required people who might have interest in them.

Perhaps she didn't trust the circus master's words; perhaps the choice he had offered was subtle threat. That would be fair; they were seeking her now, with eight Breodani dogs, a talent-born bard, a mage, a swordsman of exceptional skill, and four Hunters.

Do you know anything about these lands at all? Stephen asked his hunt-brother.

No more than you do. Not as much as Adala does.

Do you think the invitation itself offers information?

Why would it? If she hasn't accepted the offer—or the command—she's an outsider. And the insiders clearly don't share.

The circus master mentioned choice. It's almost a theme. How much of a choice can be made in ignorance?

Hunters make the earliest of their vows in ignorance—or they did. How much does a child understand of the choice that will guide, and possibly end, their life? Gods aren't people, Stephen. You know that. Don't forget it.

Why do you keep calling him a god?

The question made no sense to Nenyane. *Because he is.*

But the gods aren't supposed to be here. They can't survive it properly. If they could, there would have been no need for the Sacred Hunt, no need for the deaths of Hunters and huntbrothers.

This god is a little bit different, Nenyane replied, the undercurrent of her response tinged now with familiar frustration and self-loathing. Stephen knew she would spiral into anger if he continued to press her; he was saved by his dogs.

Pearl had found the scent whose absence had pricked her pride. Patches was by her side, but the dogs had not been coupled in the usual fashion. Nor had anyone but Nenyane considered it. If this was, in some fashion, a hunt, Adala was human. Finding her did not involve her death; she was not food to offer villagers to sustain them through the winter.

Leial stumbled when Pearl shouldered him out of the way. Gervanno immediately moved to lift the small dog; it would not be first time the Southerner carried Leial in one arm.

Steel had already passed word to Max, not that it was necessary; Max and Alex were Hunters. They knew the behavior of lymers on the scent.

"Will the bard find us?" Alex asked.

"Almost certainly." It was the mage who replied. "Unless and until the bard explicitly asks for your aid or your concern, spare none for him. These roads were new to him when he was the age you are now, but he has walked them for decades. In Averalaan, he is almost mythical to those who know parts of his story. It is said the bard can walk into conflagration and war and be certain to walk out again."

"How much of that conflagration does he cause?"

Meralonne chuckled. Stephen noted that that was the whole of his response.

"Can you tell us when we've left the lands the circus lord has claimed?" Stephen asked.

Meralonne nodded. "We have not escaped them yet."

"They've had hours," Alex pointed out. "And every reason to move in haste."

"They have—but it is not the circus alone that they must fear. Think: when is the circus open to the townsfolk?"

Gervanno said, "We have not forgotten. But speed is now of the essence if we are to arrive in time. They are young, they are deter-

mined, they have incentive; if they cannot escape, they will be separated. The young oft feel that death is the better alternative."

"Why only the young?"

"Because they have seldom seen enough death," Gervanno replied.
"Time heals much; it is a truth that the young have not fully absorbed
because they have not fully experienced the meaning of it." He began
to jog ahead.

THEY HAD NOT YET FOUND Adala and Trevor when Meralonne shed
the robes of the magi. He did not set them aside; they shimmered in
place and slowly vanished, as if the threads themselves were so weak,
so faint, they could not sustain their shape. In their place was the chain
mail with which the Hunters were now somewhat familiar. He lacked
cloak; his hair fell down his back as if determined to make up for that
lack.

Nenyane was aware of the mage's transformation long before it was
complete. "I don't sense them," she told the mage.

She was not speaking of Adala now.

"No more do I, but there is the faintest trace of familiar magic in
the air, and the ground beneath our feet trembles in unbanked rage."

"We're still on circus lands."

Meralonne nodded. "When we leave them—and it will be soon—
we will be in immediate danger. Stephen, leash your dogs, or run them
with extreme care."

Stephen nodded. He might have slowed, but Gervanno's expression
was one that traced the edge of anxiety. Whatever deaths he had seen
in the seer's crystal involved demons. Had he forgotten what the
cerdan had said? Perhaps, in the focus on the hunt that was not a hunt.

Nenyane said, "I'll scout ahead."

"No, you will not," the mage replied. "Here, so close to the dead,
Stephen cannot afford to be without you. I will scout, as you call it.
But listen, now, for the wind and the wind's cadence; I am not bard-
born, to offer verbal warnings in the heat of combat."

If there was combat, if it required Meralonne's full power, they
would hear traces of it long before the subtle, wordless breeze might
reach them.

Or perhaps not. Stephen remembered the Silences. When they

were present, he could not even bespeak his huntbrother in a fashion she could hear.

"Stephen," Gervanno said, voice a bark of sound. "We are headed in the right direction."

Stephen looked to the Southerner. In Gervanno's hand, taken from the low-hanging end of forest branch, was a ribbon. It had not been tied there in warning; it had clearly been caught and left behind. Gervanno cut it free; he did not feel he had the time to untangle it.

Clearly, neither had Adala.

One more item to offer the lymers, should the need arise. One more item of possible value to a young woman lost in a moment. Echoes of loss. Both the Maubreche and the Elseth Hunters had rejected utterly the earliest of the Hunter vows, and in so doing, had absented themselves from the governance and the laws of the Hunter Lords.

Was Adala's choice, in the end, so different from their own?

Yes, Nenyane snapped. *Her choice leads to the destruction of Hansleigh. Her choice all but guarantees the death of the people she loves. Your choice—which was stupid—was the inverse. You would not allow me to make a vow that could end in my death. Alex and Max are the same. Both were willing to be the ones who promised to die; they weren't willing to allow their brother to accept that fate.*

Stephen understood why Nenyane felt it was different. He could not be so certain himself. But Meralonne's shift into armor, the appearance of his sword, had unsettled him in ways he did not express.

Against demons, Hunter weapons were far less effective.

The forests of the Free Towns were not the forests of Breodanir. Stephen had seldom hunted outside of the Maubreche demesne, but not never. Bowgren's forests had been geographically unfamiliar but, on some instinctive level, felt like home. The forests of the Free Towns did not. The trees here were familiar—they were not that far outside of Breodanir—but the ground beneath his feet felt subtly wrong.

To Nenyane, the difference was distinct, sharp; there was no subtlety in it. *They cannot act freely in these lands; the lord is present. But be ready, Stephen—the boundaries of the wilderness are distinct, and complete change often follows between one step and the next.*

We won't be in the wilderness when we leave these forests. We'll be in our own lands.

No. Your lands are Breodanir, and there has always been a tenuous connection between the land and the Hunter Lord who rules it. It is not the same.

Meralonne leapt. It was an effortless motion that ended not in earth, but in air. The wind moved the cloak of hair, but gently. He did not land. Instead, he flew like a human arrow in the direction the dogs had taken. Nenyane wanted to join him, but his warning made clear that the risk of such decision would be Stephen's to bear.

Stephen was less certain. Nenyane had arrived in Maubreche injured, half-starved; the damage had been done by demons. She was not invulnerable. She was, however, now irritated.

Something bothered Stephen as they picked up the pace. It had not bothered him until this moment. *How could Meralonne become lord of a land, however tiny that land was, if the land outside of the Free Towns was our land? Mortal lands aren't part of the wilderness.*

Now you ask?

Why had he not thought to ask earlier? What, exactly, was Meralonne APhaniel that he could claim that absolute ownership of what should be normal earth?

Nenyane didn't answer. She remained annoyed, but the annoyance had shifted. Stephen's worries about his huntbrother had almost always offended her; his worries about most other things had not.

He felt a twinge of anxiety. It was Nenyane's. She had no answer to the question because she had not thought to ask it herself. Now that Stephen had, she did.

Worry about that later, she said.

GERVANNO ALLOWED Stephen's dogs to take the lead. He could walk at speed for hours, his stride wide, his steps brisk, but could not sprint in the same fashion. He had chosen to bear the sword given him by the circus.

Lost and found.

His desire to escape the threat demons posed had led him to the merchant caravans and their routes. That choice had not led him away from the demonic. He understood—had understood in Bowgren—that offering his services to Maubreche meant there would be no escape in the future. If he chose to guard and protect, he would face demons time and time again. He would not be a soldier, and they were not an army, but he would be at war until their journey, or their lives, ended. Or his did.

But in Nenyane, in Nenyane's swordsmanship, he found what he had lacked since his very first encounter with the demons: strength. The ability to fight and win. He was no longer huddled in the forest; nor was he huddling in the valleys of Averda. His sword did not bounce off demonic limbs.

Could he die?

Yes. But that had always been the case in any battle, any skirmish, any war. No man who lifted sword to kill—in defense or offense— could expect to be invulnerable. No wise man. But in his journey through Breodanir, Gervanno had become the soldier he could not be in the Averdan valleys. His presence in this narrow, winding field could make a difference.

The old woman who had granted him the weapon he bore had implied that his sword was effective because of Nenyane's presence. But the sword he had found in her box of odds and ends? That blade could harm his enemies should Nenyane be absent. The strength of his years of training and experience could, once again, be of value.

Nenyane was present. Where Stephen was, Nenyane either followed or led. The use of this new sword would, therefore, prove nothing. But he followed his instincts, as he always had. In any other circumstance, his instincts would have broken free of their visceral shell to scream, sergeant-like, in his ear: only a fool took an untried, untested blade into battle if he had any choice at all.

But the circus itself was a child's dream, and demons—until Averda —a child's nightmare.

He no longer lived in the world he once knew. Even should he return to his former home, his experience in these northern, foreign lands would shadow the familiar, changing it in subtle ways. It was time, then, to develop and trust different instincts; to build on what he had trusted to this point. He had no intention of remaining in the distant South if Stephen and Nenyane did not.

He had no intention of allowing them to walk the road to his home-land alone. But to walk it at all, Stephen had to survive. Gervanno leaned into the breeze. It had been so slight when they had left Hansleigh, it could barely be felt. It was stronger now.

The mage had leapt into the folds of that breeze as he did when he prepared for battle; the wind had carried him beyond Gervanno's sight. Of the people present, none worried for the mage except the sword master. It seemed inconceivable that the mage could perish; indeed, in the many, many glimpses of possible death Gervanno had seen, the mage's had not been among them.

The wind picked up as they ran; it grew strong enough to carry leaves and small branches, some of which Gervanno felt as a sting against exposed cheek. That was all the warning Gervanno and his companions were offered: the howl of the wind.

It was enough.

The trees did not change. The forest itself did not immediately become different. The earth beneath his feet retained the same hint of dampness that softened the impact of running feet. But the wind began to howl, and they ran into it; it did not push their backs.

Gervanno did not possess Maubreche sensitivities, but he knew, between one long stride and the next, when he had at last left the forest claimed by the circus master Nenyane called a god.

HE HAD LOST sight of Meralonne the moment the wild wind had carried him in his forward flight; the mage moved far more quickly than the scent-tracking dogs or their various masters. But he now saw the platinum hair and the brilliant, reflective shine of the mage's armor. The wind was storm all around him, but he stood in the eye of that storm, his blade like a flash of captured lightning.

His was not the only blade present, nor the only blade that retained unnatural, brilliant light. Arrayed before him, around him, torn by wind and sustained by flame, stood the enemy.

Stephen's dogs froze in place, retreating at their Hunter's silent command. To his side, he could hear the sound of drawn blades: Max and Alex. Stephen drew sword as well. Nenyane's blade was silent, but she carried one, and if it did not glow with unnatural light, it was the equal of the mage's.

Gervanno's hand trembled on the hilt of his sword; he did not yet draw it.

The Widan, in the Dominion, relied on the arcane arts they had mastered when they entered combat, should they enter it at all. Clearly the Northern Widan were different. Meralonne's true weapon was the sword he carried.

There was no sign of the bard. Leial barked; Gervanno bent his knees to set the dog down, his gaze fixed on the demons Meralonne faced. There were three who wielded blades of fire, but beyond them were more; Gervanno knew them as his opponents. Only two of the three Meralonne faced appeared human to Gervanno's eyes; the third could not be mistaken for a human on any but the darkest, cloudiest of nights.

Nor could the demons at their backs; they were bestial. Some stood on two legs, most did not; their claws caught and reflected the mage's light. And the demonic fire.

"Gervanno—Stephen is in your care," Nenyane said. She did not turn to look at the cerdan; her gaze was upon Meralonne.

No, he thought; it was fixed on the demons themselves. When she leapt, the wind carried her, as it carried the mage, as if her weight was familiar. It touched no one else in a similar fashion. Here, Gervanno could see that the wind and fire fought, but air was difficult to grasp.

People were not.

Fire flared, as if it could see; it moved toward the dogs and the Hunters as if it, too, were a soldier in search of an enemy.

He lost sight of the Elseth brothers, and inhaled sharply. They had not survived in some of the glimpses of dread future; they had survived in others. He had not seen the cause of their deaths, just the fact of it, the bodies, the loss of subtle movements of chest, of eyes.

But Stephen of Maubreche had not survived in all of those glimpses either.

He therefore left Nenyane and Meralonne to their battle and shifted the net of his awareness, his focus. He did not care if the dogs perished here, but he was not Hunter; they were not, in any fashion, kin. In his vision, Leial had not been among the dead, but Leial had never been a soldier.

He had not seen, in all of his visions, what had struck killing blows —but he knew, now. Demons. Demons had destroyed one of his lives; he thought, at the time, that they had destroyed everything. Everything he believed about himself. Every oath he had sworn to himself.

If he had lost that life, and the people and duties that had slowly given it meaning, he had not died. He had clung to the duties that remained him: Silvo's sword. Word of the demonic attack and its destruction of Evaro's caravan. He had to carry both word and sword, to the West and to the South.

Carrying those final duties, he had met Stephen and Nenyane, and that had altered the course of his life. It had renewed something in him, offering him a different duty, a different life: a third, by the Lady's mercy. He would not leave it unless and until he was dead.

He had been lost. In Maubreche, he had found himself. It was not an act of atonement, to serve Maubreche. It was not an act of cowardice. He had not simply bowed to pressure or command. In its entirety, it was his decision. If, at first, it aligned with the wreckage of his life in the wake of the caravan's destruction, it had become far more than a simple act of convenience—he would be paid, and coin was necessary in any country.

Here, sword in hand, he could become the swordsman he had once greatly desired to be. His sword master was Nenyane. She had no sense of the forms of respect and obedience that must come as a bond between master and student. But all such forms, all such signs of respect deserved—and given—were irrelevant to Nenyane.

Only the blade itself mattered, and she raised hers. It was not her ability to stand—to run—across the air itself that made her a sword master; it was not the fact that the swords of the demons, which seemed to be more fire than steel, struck her sword as if they were the basest of mortal metals. She could stand and fight her enemies in *any* terrain, and her weapon, unlike the blue fire of the magi's, was a weapon that Gervanno or any of his kin might lift in battle.

The circus had unsettled him. The missing daughter of a stranger had remained with him, her name echoing in memory, although—until this morning—he had never heard it before. He had not expected to enter the circus when he had arrived in Hansleigh. Entering it, he had not expected to see a small town, its vibrant colors a strong reminder that this circus was almost a dream. A dream better suited to the childhood he had struggled so hard, so long, to abandon.

He did not expect the seer's vision, although Gervanno was the one, in the end, who had sought some glimpse of magic, as if the child he had been had lingered, no matter the effort he had made to distance himself from that boy.

He did not expect to find a new sword. Even had he found an artisan capable of crafting the ideal sword, the artisan would not have been able to craft it in one day. Discussion about the desired sword would take hours, and negotiations for the cost would add to that delay. In the Dominion, men carried swords. Swords were costly. As a young cerdan, Gervanno had spent everything he had to purchase a decent sword.

The sword does not make the man. The man makes the sword. Do not forget this.

He could not afford more than decent. Men of wealth, Tors and Tyrs, could afford *good*. Gervanno's sword had been good enough. It would always be good enough, unless his efforts on the field of battle proved so valiant, so visible, he was rewarded with a sword, from such Tor or Tyr, that he could never afford on his own.

That childhood dream had died as the boy grew into a man, and the man observed the truth of the world. Lesser swordsmen, born to wealth and power, wielded such swords. He had shuttered his heart, lest envy sour and break him; he had seen it happen again and again to other men, some of them friends, some comrades, and some juniors under his command.

Envy destroyed even the small flickers of joy and pride a man—not a child—could attain. He did not choose to carry it; did not choose to feed it. In his youth, he had found it far harder than he did as an adult; he had grown into its absence.

His sword made no sound as it left its sheath. The surface of the blade's flat reflected fire and lightning. But it reflected sunlight as well, a sunlight unfettered by the shadows of trees, branches, and demons.

He at last drew blade—new blade, gift of circus and the embers of childhood dream, for who would otherwise carry an untried, untested blade into a battle that had ended, again and again, in death?

From this moment on, envy would be forever beyond him.

CHAPTER TEN

The flat of the long, curved blade reflected fire and lightning as if gathering both. The reflection itself, he might have expected; the mage's blade, the blades of the three demons the mage now faced, dominated the sky immediately above the Hunters.

But the sword reflected sunlight, as if the sun were at the sky's height, unfettered by trees, by clouds, by demons. The light was white gold, and it ran the length of the steel, from hilt to tip. Had Gervanno been at war in the desert—and no rational man chose the desert sands as their battlefield had they any choice—he might not have noticed, for there the sun did reign.

The light was not the sun's light. He felt a shiver of anticipation; it was tightly entwined around the fear that fueled caution.

When the demons that gathered around the edge of a storm of wind and fire began to move towards the Hunters, Gervanno shifted position, both of feet and blade, bending slightly into knees.

The demons on the ground sought—just as the Hunters—to avoid the aerial conflict; they did not seek to avoid combat. So many of those who claimed to be powerful exercised their power on those they deemed weak. Demons were no different.

Only their judgment of strength and weakness was questionable. To demons, mortals were weak, irrelevant. Gervanno, being mortal, did not dismiss mortals in the same fashion. Perhaps that was their single advantage on any field the demons took: mortals were underestimated. Even here, the demons considered the mage the real threat.

Overestimation could also become a weakness.

The lesser demons could destroy a town, should the townspeople have little familiarity with demons or military arms. One such creature might kill tens, or hundreds, if left unchecked. But they could not as easily kill Gervanno di'Sarrado. They could not simply disregard Maubreche or Elseth.

Gervanno's sword was long, the arc of its slash, wide. He was guard; Nenyane had joined Meralonne because Gervanno was present. He therefore stepped forward, stepped in front, of the four Hunters, speaking only a single word: *flank*.

Stephen did not send his dogs to fight. He had, in the streets of the King's City. Here, they retreated as Gervanno faced the first of the demons in its overeager approach. He had oft wondered if demonic appearance had been chosen to instill fear in mortals, for this creature was not quite beast and not quite man. It ran on four legs, but the forelegs were arms, and clawed, and its face was reminiscent of a man's —if a man's jaws could be distended by two feet or three when they opened. Fangs were oddly white in a face that was otherwise grey, the very pallor of death.

But the wilderness called demons the dead, as if they were animate corpses.

Could the dead die again? Or did they simply face destruction? He did not know. It did not matter. His sword swung; the demon lifted claw to parry it. His strikes had been parried in similar fashion before. But this time, the blade severed claws and part of the creature's hand; it roared in rage, pain, and—to Gervanno's ear—surprise, black eyes widening as part of the limb fell away.

Gervanno pressed forward, shifting in place to parry the demon's counterattack.

There was no third attack; Gervanno parried and continued the sword's motion, severing limb at what would, in anything living, be the shoulder. His blade shifted; the demon attempted to leap back, but it had no room in which to move, for its comrades had leapt to join the fray, and they were too close.

The demon, blocked from behind, lunged forward, attacking now with its jaws, its great fangs.

Half of its face fell away as Gervanno's sword sliced through those open jaws. The demon's body became ash, and the wind—howling and wild—blew it away in a fury Gervanno could almost hear.

He did not pause; the demons slowed, the slowness implying fear. They spread out, as if seeking the weaker mortals—the humans, not the dogs. Gervanno could not face them all, but Max and Stephen's presence made it far harder for the demons to flank or surround him. Here, the dogs helped. If they did not move out to attack or to harry the attackers, they provided multiple sets of eyes, multiple viewpoints.

Gervanno, accustomed to only one, paid attention to peripheral vision. When the next demon closed to attack, another joined him. One was fully bestial, one was almost human in initial appearance.

Two to one was never good. Three to one was death, if Gervanno could not retreat. He did not retreat. He waited for the demons to approach, waited for the right moment to step forward, to turn to the side as the four-legged creature leapt, and to reduce the number of opponents to a single, human-like demon as he removed the beast's head from its body in a diagonal cut.

Blood hit his chest, his arm, like a wave—it was warm, red, very like the blood of mortals. But it, like the demon's corpse, became ash and memory as the demon died. Demonic blood did not corrode his sword. Perhaps nothing would.

The second demon attacked the instant his blade had begun the arc that passed through the first demon's neck. Had the sword encountered resistance, Gervanno would have been defenseless. It had not. He continued the motion of sword, once again sliding sideways to avoid the enemy's thrust. This enemy, unlike the more bestial ones, was smarter. Gervanno had feared magic, for against Widan arts he had little defense.

The hand extended, growing claws. Those claws, hard ebon tendrils, shot outward, extending toward Gervanno's chest, while the demon itself remained out of reach of Gervanno's blade. He brought his sword up; the edge caught light, the flat as well, although the light was different in color and intensity.

The demon roared in pain, in rage, as if the two were one. Perhaps for demons, they were.

The claws retracted, but Gervanno had clipped three; the sound of those claws as they struck earth had almost been a peal. The fear that demons engendered in any rational person was almost entirely absent.

Whatever his enemy was—or had once been, when alive—was irrelevant.

The demon wished for Gervanno's death. Gervanno wished to survive. In the immediate combat, there were only two options. Kill or be killed. He could not safely retreat. If he destroyed the demon who attacked him, others would step into the gap ash and wind made of the creature's body. Had he been alone, he would be dead.

He was not alone.

MAX HAD UNSHEATHED his sword before Gervanno had drawn his. Max was not a great swordsman; in Nenyane's opinion, his sword skills were passable. Barely. In their early years, Max had found this offensive—until they had first crossed blades.

Had Max been a different person, his pride would have driven him forward; he was Maxwell of Elseth. He'd recognized, instantly, that Nenyane—a *girl*—was a master. There was no work, no blessing, no training, that would ever bring him to her level. Something about Nenyane's skill spoke to Max with utter, certain finality.

He knew two things on that day. The first, he had never seen a weaponsmaster capable of defeating this pale-haired child; and the second, that she, controversial beyond compare, would be Stephen of Maubreche's huntbrother. No words spoken against her, no attempts to displace her, no matter how kind, would shake that fact.

She was Stephen's. Stephen was hers. Her choice. On Stephen's behalf, all of the power and skill Max had seen on that long-ago day, would be wielded.

Alex had disagreed, at first. Alex, the favorite grandchild, had absorbed far more about Breodanir's politics and the battlefield of the purely social. Alex had pointed out all the ways in which Nenyane would be a disaster for Maubreche's oldest son. Even seeing her fight, he had argued.

He did not disagree that Nenyane was *attached* to Stephen; could not disagree with Max's assessment of her skill, having seen the two spar. But he believed that Nenyane would serve Stephen *and* Stephen's future huntbrother. Max, younger then, had argued; the argument had grown heated. Nothing Alex said could shake his brother's certainty.

It was Alex—whose certainty, built on purely external, social concerns—who had broken.

This didn't mean that Max didn't train; he did. As that arrogant child, he had believed swords were almost pointless for Hunters. He knew he could never reach Nenyane's level of absolute mastery; he knew it was not required of him. But he believed, on some instinctive and unspoken level, that her presence, her existence as Stephen's hunt-brother, implied that skill with sword would be necessary.

Completely, utterly necessary.

Alex accepted this, and Alex had trained. William, the oldest, had found it almost a frustrating waste of time and had said as much to their father and mother. Their mother had agreed; their father had not. Gilliam seldom spoke of his life with Stephen of Elseth, the hunt-brother he had lost decades past. But Gilliam had blessed the extra lessons, his expression almost haunted. Their mother did not argue with their father.

Steel.

Steel had remained behind and to Max's side, which was otherwise exposed. No demons occupied the forest to his dog's—*his!*—side, but Steel was alert and wary. Max slid behind the dog's eyes, the shift brief. He did not send Steel out; Steel was needed here. Steel would guard; if demons moved to flank them, the dogs would notice immediately. Only one of those dogs was his, but one was enough.

Max had taken swords from the circus. One long, and one shorter; it was the longer sword he drew now. In his hand, it felt like a sword. A normal sword. To Max's eyes, Gervanno's weapon was different. The obvious difference—the single edge of the slightly curved blade—was not what drew his attention. Instinct told Max that Gervanno's sword, and the sword he himself had pulled from a box too small to contain it, were not the same.

Max's sword suited Max's experience and ability.

Gervanno's sword suited Gervanno. The Southern guard was not equal to Nenyane in skill—but he was perhaps the closest Max had ever seen. To Max's eye, Gervanno's skill had grown in the time the Southerner had traveled with Stephen and Nenyane; Gervanno was Nenyane's chosen sparring partner. Her endurance was legendary: she could work with Stephen for an hour, without break, and then turn immediately to Gervanno and demand he do the same.

Gervanno never declined.

But the result of that sparring and the lessons inherent in them could be seen now. Gervanno formed the tiny vanguard of their party; he had dispatched one demon almost before Max was aware that the creature had launched its first—and only—attack. Max then injured the demon who had attempted to take advantage of the theoretical gap in Gervanno's attention.

Had there been only two, Max would not have been concerned; there were far more than two. He did not take Nenyane or Meralonne into account; their battle was a different war, a different conflict. It was aerial, and nothing the Hunters could do could contribute to victory; at best, they could avoid becoming a distraction.

To do that, they had to survive.

Steel noticed the movement of demons—two—at the outer edge of their loose, defensive grouping. They were closest to Max.

Be careful.

Max did not reply. He had turned, adjusting his stance; he moved, his steps utterly silent, as if he were at the midpoint of a complicated hunt. His steps disturbed no small branches or plants; the wind had already lifted natural debris into its raging folds.

The demons were called the dead by those creatures in the wilderness who lifted voice with words. How did the dead see? By what did they track? How did they hear?

He knew that they could—and did—die, but they left no natural corpses. The only evidence of their existence that remained were the injuries—and deaths—left in their wake.

The forests that surrounded the Free Towns were not Breodanir's, but they nonetheless felt familiar, comfortable; this was the terrain that Max best knew. He understood the cunning of the forest's hunted; understood how, if one was reckless, the hunted could become the hunter.

Boast after the hunt is finished, his father had once said. *If you must be crass, boast before. But never, ever boast during the hunt.*

We can't, Alex pointed out. *Who would we boast to?*

Yourselves. And that is the most costly of boasts.

Max readied sword, using trees for cover, borrowing Steel's vision as the dog crouched low to ground on front paws.

Two, he thought. Both of these demons moved on four legs. Their claws were a threat, but the most significant weapon they wielded was their jaws. The jaws could, and did, extend, growing in size both unnaturally and quickly, as if physical form were fluid and theoretical.

Demons had been no part of his much-begrudged book lessons, or he would have paid attention. Not until he had been sent in theoretical disgrace to the King's City, had demons entered the curriculum.

But Max had never been the ideal student for book learning. Experience was Max's most effective teacher. The encounter with demons in the streets of the King's City, the battle that had followed later, at the inn, were etched into memory—physical and internal. What he now saw would add to his knowledge.

He had no answer to his question about how demons tracked their prey, but they clearly did; they came to him, unerringly. And, instead of employing the forest geography to their advantage, they simply bit *through* the trunk of a tree.

Max saw the tree teeter; he was certain Stephen was aware of its incoming fall. The demons were clearly aware of his position. He raised voice to offer Gervanno a warning, breaking what remained of his silence. Gervanno had only one set of eyes with which to observe the shifting landscape.

No acknowledgement of the warning was given but one: Gervanno shifted position, moving three or four feet to the side of where the tree would fall. The demon he faced did not follow; it attacked from range, the length of extended claws like slender, curved spears. More, Max didn't see. The demons knocked another tree out of their path, but its fall would not immediately endanger the Hunters.

The danger was more subtle. The trees were old, the trunks, tall. Their fall could create a box within which movement would be curtailed. He wondered if even his thoughts could be heard.

Trees fell; Steel watched the forest, gaze darting between the trees and the position of the demons. On the far side, nearest Stephen, those creatures that could not bypass Gervanno safely chose to use their jaws —or arms—to break the great trunks of old trees; to push them in the direction of their enemies.

They fell slowly at first, but gained speed as momentum grew.

The demons could bound over the barrier made by the trees, as their fallen trunks began to restrict the shape of the battlefield. Max could, with effort, do the same—but not armed. Alex and Stephen

MICHELLE WEST

were in a similar position. Gervanno simply shifted in place, avoiding the trees.

None of the four could avoid the fire that sprang up around the fallen trunks. The fire was not natural, given the speed at which it grew. But the storm of wind that came roaring into the burning, haphazard enclosure wasn't natural, either.

The demons were swept off their feet, shunted in all directions. Max kept his footing, as did Alex; two of Stephen's dogs did not.

Wild wind. Wild flame.

They had enmity of their own. Max could not shout to be heard in the sudden din of the storm. Above his head, lightning flashed, red and blue, and the storm had a momentary voice.

"Stay your ground. The fire will not touch you if you remain as you are standing."

"The dogs!" Max shouted in reply. He recognized the voice. He could hear it so clearly there might have been no other sound in the forest.

"The dogs will be safe."

Kallandras of Senniel had found them.

NENYANE HAD NOT EXPECTED Illaraphaniel to be so pressed. The air was his to command, and the demons he faced—*Kialli* all—were not, in life, his equal. Such a fight, three opponents to two, should have been over almost before it started, given Illaraphaniel's power; he was among the first of the princes. These creatures were not.

But here, his lack of shield proved a much bigger disadvantage than Nenyane, who fought without, could have foreseen. Her own combat was also hampered, as she was compelled to become the prince's shield. She could parry the *Kialli* blades with ease, and respond in kind, but the need to parry two of the three swords at any one time was far more constraining.

One of the *Kialli* lost their shield arm, which made the combat simpler. Without a shield to block Illaraphaniel's blade, the odds became even; the ash of dissolution was devoured by the wild air. She focused on shields. Her sword was not equal to the task of destroying them; Illaraphaniel's could be, but not without a greater expenditure of power than would be wise when facing two enemies.

One more, she thought; one more and she could join Stephen. The demons on the ground were almost insignificant in comparison to the *Kialli* here, but Stephen was not a firstborn prince of the White Lady. What Illaraphaniel would barely condescend to notice could end Stephen's life if he were unlucky or careless.

Nenyane was huntbrother because Stephen was Hunter. But she did not love the Maubreche dogs the way Stephen did. Their deaths, while regrettable, would not break or shatter anything inside of her. They would harm Stephen. She had never approved of Stephen's use of the dogs. She had even argued against it; it was one of the few times Corwin had lost his temper with her.

They're a weakness! she had shouted.

They're our strength!

Cynthia had intervened before they had come to blows, probably because a grown man and a child punching each other was against the dignity of a ruling family. Nenyane had never been in danger. Nothing Corwin could do would hurt anything but her dignity, and given Nenyane, not even that.

Cynthia, of course, had not believed that. But Corwin had always known. Since the day he had chosen to test her skill with a sword before allowing her to teach Stephen, he had known. And he had made the decision to trust Nenyane with his oldest son.

There had been wrinkles in that plan. He had never intended that Nenyane become Stephen's huntbrother — but he had never intended to separate Nenyane and Stephen, either. Nenyane didn't care about being huntbrother. Knowing that Corwin was willing to trust her with the most important of Stephen's lessons, she was willing to undertake the responsibilities of the dogs.

But she had never been happy about them.

Robart had once accused her of being jealous of the dogs.

It wasn't jealousy. She knew, viscerally, that the path she and Stephen had to walk was inimical to the dogs. Stephen would lose them in ones and twos, and his focus would be on their protection, not on their utility. You couldn't use a sword if you were afraid that any blow you struck, any blow you parried, would chip or damage the blade.

She felt that shift of concern, the sudden, sharp fear, that was given only to the dogs.

She focused on the demon she faced with renewed intent.

STEPHEN HEARD KALLANDRAS CLEARLY. Anyone the bard intended to bespeak had. But he had lost the use of four dogs, and Pearl was enraged. They weren't dead, but their vision was such a chaos of unintended movement that he could not look through their eyes for long.

Kallandras had said the dogs would be safe; he had to trust that.

But here, the wind was a force that could barely be endured. Fire rose as if it were a physical body that the wind intended to tear to pieces; he felt its heat as it passed above and around him. If it attempted to cling, the wind's attack prevented fire from finding purchase on the Hunters or their remaining dogs.

The trees, however, continued to burn, and the fire that had wrapped around fallen trunks leapt toward standing trees in an attempt to fortify itself, forming a ring of fire. Stephen was on the inside of that ring. He bent into his knees, retaining his footing as the wind howled. Max and Alex did the same.

Gervanno fought; the demons could pass through the fire as if it were simple air. They could not, however, stand against the wind with any ease. Only three of the creatures stepped through the flames—all of them mortal in general form. None looked human.

Gervanno's sword passed through the first demon; a cutting blow, not a thrust. The demon's eyes widened as it was bisected in place. If the demons weren't hampered by fire, their vision was.

Max, watching, nodded as if to himself. As most Breodani did, he relied on thrusting, on a stabbing motion, rather than slashing or cutting. Gervanno's sword was the opposite, and they could all see how effective it was. They could also see that they were not, and would likely never be, Gervanno's equal.

But Max shifted stance, and when the next demon emerged from flame, he brought the blade down in an arc, cutting hand from wrist just as long claws emerged from its fingers. The demon roared but did not dissolve the way Gervanno's opponent had. Instead, it retreated back through the fire, where Max could not follow. Not easily.

Don't even think it, Alex snapped, genuinely angry. *Kallandras has taken care of most of the demons on the ground—running after them is just asking to die.*

I'm not an idiot, Max replied, with just as much heat as Alex had spoken.

Not usually, no. But it takes work for the bard to do this. It costs him. He can't control the wild wind the way you or I control dogs or swords. Don't make his work any harder.

Max was surprised enough that he stilled. *I haven't moved my feet. I've stayed my ground, as he asked.*

ALEX SAID NOTHING FURTHER. He was tense, and he didn't have the advantage of Steel's eyes, but he had always had a second pair of eyes with which to view the world. He could see what Max saw. He could see it without effort. He, too, had been trained in the handling of dogs; he, too, could work with a full hunting pack of eight.

But to Alex, the dogs were not natural, extra limbs. Not in the same way. He had been surprised when Stephen separated Steel from his pack and offered the dog to Max, but the surprise was secondary to the immense sense of gratitude.

Beyond the area the Hunters and Gervanno occupied, the wind grew wilder, as if the bard had unleashed it everywhere in the forest that did not include them. Above the wind's howl, the roar of fire could be heard, and in it, Alex could almost hear syllables.

He wasn't surprised when Kallandras came to ground, although he hadn't seen him in the air. The bard was pale, jaws clenched, eyes narrowed in an otherwise calm expression.

Alex and Max shifted in place; the bard had landed in the center of the Hunters, farthest from Gervanno.

"Call the dogs in," Kallandras said.

The dogs came; Stephen did not otherwise reply.

"Hold your ground here. The three above were not the only demons of power in this place."

There were now only two, but Alex did not correct him.

"If Adala and Trevor came this way, we had best hope they made use of their head start. If they encountered the gathering forces of the demons, we will not find them alive." His pale skin glistened with sweat. His left hand was bleeding.

Gervanno was sweating as well. His was the only sword that continuously attacked the demons, but he had slowly backed up until he, too, stood within the confines of the eye of this particular storm.

If Alex had considered the wind to have been unleashed prior to

Gervanno's careful retreat, he had been wrong. Only when Gervanno was within the physical space they all occupied did the wind truly become wild.

Wind storms were rare in Breodanir. Alex knew that wind could topple trees or their branches—but the trees toppled were old. He had read about the damage falling trees could cause, but he had never seen it personally.

Had a town been anywhere near this storm, buildings would have been flattened had they been built within the range of falling trees. No, he thought; they didn't have to be close. The massive trees, uprooted by wind and scarred by fire, were tossed in the wind's currents as if they were delicate branches. Their shadows did not pass overhead.

Meralonne could summon the wind; he could, and did, fight while standing in its folds. The mage did not seem to suffer the ill-effects such control caused the bard—but if Kallandras could speak to the wild air as Meralonne did, Meralonne's was the greater control.

Nothing caught in the storm of Kallandras's making touched the aerial combat above.

Alex watched as two enemies became one. He could not hear a word the mage said; nor could he hear the demon's response. But the odds tilted in the mage's favor; the mage had Nenyane. Nenyane was a blur. She, too, could fight while standing in air. She had never summoned it as Meralonne did, but she had no difficulty wielding sword in the groundless battlefield.

She did not immediately land, perhaps because Kallandras's storm continued unabated around them. Instead, she darted forward, vanishing briefly from view as unmoored debris formed a visual wall between them.

"She's scouting," Stephen told them.

"Is she looking for Adala?"

He shook his head. "She's looking for other demons."

"Have we managed to deal with these ones?"

"Mostly. Some of the demons on the ground chose to flee—but they scattered. She can pick them off easily. But one in particular seemed to be running toward something, rather than away from us. That's the one she's worried about." He grimaced and closed his eyes.

Alex and Max could easily view the world through each other's eyes. Stephen and Nenyane seldom did. Nenyane said she had no trouble with it. Stephen said it gave him headaches. It was the other reason Lord Maubreche had sought a traditional huntbrother for his oldest son. He felt that the level of difficulty such a natural bond caused his son was an indication that Nenyane was the wrong choice.

But Nenyane was huntbrother. And if Lord and Lady Maubreche were content to view her as an orphan in need of family, Alex and Max never had. Neither had their mother. Espere did not love Nenyane, but neither feared nor loathed her. She considered Nenyane safe—for Stephen. Only Stephen.

Alex accepted this. Stephen's eyes didn't see what Nenyane's eyes did and could. But that was fair. Nenyane was not a normal child. Not a normal woman. Neither Alex or his brother were confident that they could track Nenyane. She had only the faintest trace of scent, and most of it was actually Stephen's.

She didn't speak through the Hunter bond except at need—and Nenyane's version of need could be disastrous. She did look through Stephen's eyes the way the Elseth brothers looked through each other's. It was Stephen who avoided doing the same.

But he could and did. He closed his own eyes to do it. Max and Alex sharing two viewpoints caused no confusion to either of the brothers. Two sets of eyes were natural; normal. Alex wasn't certain what the world would look like had he access to only one. Neither brother lost track of themselves when seeing what the other saw.

Stephen cursed. As curses went, it was mild; it might have caused Alex's grandmother to raise a brow, no more. But Stephen seldom cursed. Nenyane did it all for him.

"Stephen?" Kallandras's hands fell to the hilts of his weapons. Only when he touched them did they become visible to Alex's eyes.

"Tell the mage," Stephen said, turning to the bard. "There's a greater gathering of demons to the southeast."

"Are they moving?"

"Not yet."

Kallandras exhaled; his lips moved silently. "How many does your huntbrother see?"

Stephen hesitated. Alex could guess why. "Nenyane's sense of what's dangerous isn't like the rest of ours. It's more like Meralonne's. In her eyes, there's only one that's significant."

None of the Hunters considered the demons they'd been fighting before Kallandras intervened to be insignificant.

"How does that demon compare to the three she fought here?"

"She recognizes him."

THE WIND'S STORM BANKED. Fire was nowhere in evidence. Meralonne came to ground to one side of Kallandras. To Alex's surprise, the mage's armor had been dented.

"Where is Nenyane?"

"She's scouting ahead," Stephen replied; the question had been asked of him. "She wanted to pick up the stragglers before they escaped to other towns or settlements."

Meralonne nodded.

"But one of the demons wasn't running away from the wind's wrath; it was running to what she now supposes is the main body of their forces here."

"There was significant power here," the mage replied. "This would, in other such incidents, be considered the main body."

Alex would certainly have made that assumption. "What do you think they're hunting here?"

Gervanno cleared throat; it was a soft sound, meant to garner minor attention. Once the cerdan had that attention, he said, "The caravan with which I traveled was apprehended on the road; we were making our way to the King's City.

"It was destroyed almost to a man. We had no Widan with us, and no sword master; Stephen was safely ensconced in Maubreche. But they came in similar numbers; some were mounted. They were hunting, they said, for a sword." He sheathed the one he carried. "Perhaps they hope to force their way into the circus lands to find this one."

Meralonne pinched the bridge of his nose. "I assure you that is not the case. Oh, the sword is well-made, and against the enemies we face on this road, it is perfect. But it is not otherwise so significant that they would risk their forces for it. Stephen, tell Nenyane to retreat."

Stephen hesitated. Which must mean that Stephen had already tried that, and she'd failed to hear him. "She asks if you remember Ishavriel. I'm sorry," he added. "Those are her exact words—she demanded that I repeat her question word for word."

"He is here?"

"According to Nenyane, yes. If the demon running toward Ishavriel reached him, he will know we're here."

"My apologies for doubting her. Her memories are not what they once were."

"She wants to attack him. She isn't."

Alex whistled.

"Tell her to come back. Remind her that she has suffered injuries, purportedly at the hands of *Kialli*. It is why she was brought to Maubreche: to recover."

Alex frowned. He watched the mage, and only the mage. Meralonne's face was almost absent all expression, but some unnamed emotion moved his eyes and the corners of his lips.

The wind shifted direction, carrying Nenyane of Maubreche in its folds. She leapt clear of it, landing so lightly in front of Stephen and Gervanno she might have weighed nothing at all. Her eyes were flashing, her hands curled into fists; she carried no sword.

"Did the demons have a human captive?"

Nenyane shook her head.

Stephen's dogs once again moved toward their master—and toward the items he'd taken from Adala's room. He held one in his hands.

Max lifted brows in question.

"We need to move, and we need to move quickly. If we return to Hansleigh, we might be able to enter the circus grounds again. I'm not sure there will be any safety in that, now. Or we can do what we set out to do. If Adala's scent passes through the body of the demonic forces..." He glanced at his huntbrother. "I won't know until the dogs start tracking again."

"If it looks like it does?" Nenyane's glare slid off Meralonne.

"We'll have to hope that the demons are unintentionally on a collision course with Adala, and we have a chance of reaching her before they meet."

"And if she's already dead? If they found and killed her?"

"We can discuss it, then."

ADALA'S SCENT CONTINUED; she had moved into the forests south of Hansleigh, beyond the reach of the circus master's lands, but had traveled to the southwest. The demons were directly to the south of where their forward party had clashed with Meralonne and Nenyane.

They weren't on the move; they were gathered, waiting for something. But they knew their scouts had encountered resistance. There's no way they missed that. Nenyane kept easy pace with the dogs. She spoke through the bond instead of shouting, which would have been her other option. *They'll be able to track us—or track Meralonne—should they feel the need.*

Will they notice anyone else?

She had no immediate answer, but the question occupied much of her thought as the dogs moved in silence with a renewed sense of urgency.

Stephen's. They might be peripherally aware of Nenyane's, but as always, it was Stephen that drove them. They moved more quickly than they had the first time, but Kallandras joined them on the ground. Meralonne took the rear. He, too, chose to move on the ground, and any breeze they felt in passing belonged to neither mage nor bard.

Nenyane thought the caution a waste of time.

They're probably preserving strength, Stephen told her.

She disagreed. *The bard shouldn't fight again for at least a couple of days. He's well beyond preserving strength. If we could send him back to the circus, that would be best.*

Do you have any idea how to get them to open the gate again?

She didn't.

If we find Adala and Trevor, and if we can convince them to return, we're going to have to head north, across the circus lands.

Let's just hope we find them before the demons do.

IT WAS MAX, absent lymer, who saw the first sign that someone had passed in the direction the dogs led. Almost no one could pass through heavily forested land and leave no trace of their passing. Alex could. Max, in theory taught the same way, could not. The Maubreche Hunters were, like Max, less capable, although Max privately believed the lack was due to Nenyane. If she could be bothered, she would have been at least as competent as Max.

But their quarry—in normal hunts, or this one—weren't trained to leave no hint of their passage across the land. Nenyane, therefore, felt the effort to pass without trace was not worth the concentration.

Nenyane felt much in her life was not worth the effort. Only Stephen, and his safety, moved her.

Alex disagreed. *She'd fight to protect any of us.*

She wouldn't care about the dogs.

To that, Alex offered no argument. He examined the broken branches — twigs, really — at shoulder height. Max had noticed first. He had noticed, as well, the bent stalks of forest weeds.

Two people; one heavier. There, and there.

Alex nodded. They had come to a stop to briefly examine Max's findings.

"They're close."

"And the demons?" Max looked to the mage.

The mage said nothing.

On the first day he had seen Stephen in the King's City, Max felt he had understood why both he and Alex had been sent there. Their mother didn't care. Their father did, but had agreed — and he had to know, better than anyone, that schooling in the King's City would change nothing for his two youngest sons.

But here, in this forest on foreign soil, the wind at the command of two men, and an uncounted number of demons somewhere in the distance, he felt that certainty far more strongly. This was what he and Alex were meant to do. This was why they had left Elseth.

Demons had plagued his father and his father's huntbrother as they made their trek to the heart of the Empire.

Stephen of Elseth had died there. He had died *because of* the Hunter's Oath. Their Stephen would not die while Max and Alex lived.

THEY FOUND OTHER SIGNS; the lymers no longer needed to be reminded of the scent for which they searched. Meralonne uttered no warnings; the demons were not in immediate pursuit. They were, in Meralonne's opinion, concerned with Hansleigh and the circus master.

In the mage's opinion, the demons didn't know that Adala was the circus's weakness. Had they, the girl would almost certainly be dead. How could they know? Even questioning the townspeople in the absence of the circus wouldn't give them that information. The townspeople couldn't share what they didn't know. Only the circus people did, and there was no way for the demons to reach them.

Not yet.

Stephen did not sound horn; the dogs did not bay. Steel was likewise silent. They used the lessons of the hunt to which they'd been
trained all their lives, but it was not that hunt. The difference was
important.

Max knew the moment Steel knew—Steel who was now a pack of
one. Or three. He hadn't called Hunter's trance here; he had entered
that state when they had run across the first of the demons, and left it
when the demons were no longer a fighting concern. As Kallandras
did, both of the Elseth Hunters now husbanded strength.

Stephen had done the same; only Nenyane moved, in the end, at
peak power. She was huntbrother, not Hunter; the ability to call trance
was not hers. In Nenyane's case, she had never required it. Even at the
jog they'd kept as they followed the townsfolk's trail, she remained
unwinded; no sign of sweat or exertion touched her.

Ahead of the dogs, but seen through Steel's eyes, Max could see
two people's backs.

TREVOR WAS a head taller than his companion, and half again her
width. Adala would have been considered petite, even in the Dominion; had he not known her age, he would have assumed, at visual
distance, that she was a much younger child. Only when she turned—
as the dogs and the Hunters came close enough to draw her attention
—would he have revised that opinion.

But Gervanno knew her age. She was a young woman, not a child,
and the young man by her side—who drew, of all things, a dagger—
was her age. As the dogs moved to ring her, no doubt at Stephen's
command, she put a hand on Trevor's arm; her lips moved, but
Gervanno could not read them at this distance. Had she been speaking
Torra, he might have.

It was Gervanno upon who the Hunters now waited, and it was
therefore Gervanno who stepped forward between the dogs, his own
much smaller dog in arms. He had set Leial down to fight the demons;
he had lifted Leial when the Hunters once again picked up Adala's
trail.

His life had been a soldier's life, not a parent's; his duties had
seldom involved civilians, except in the worst of the atrocities of war.

The lack of social skill suddenly mattered as he met the gaze of Adala: a blend of apprehension and anger.

Kallandras of Senniel joined the Southern cerdan. The bard was pale, but his expression showed no sign of pain or fatigue.

"We have come to find you," he told the two, his voice gentle and soft, his words nonetheless clear.

Adala's eyes narrowed. "My father sent you?"

Kallandras shook his head. "My companion visited the pavilion of fate and fortune." He then turned to Gervanno.

Facing two desperate children, the cerdan found his voice. "I was offered a glimpse of the future; I did not expect to be offered a glimpse of many such futures. In almost all of those futures, Hansleigh was destroyed. The townspeople were killed and their bodies lay in the streets; I did not, in those visions, search homes."

Trevor was frozen. Adala folded her arms, her eyes narrowed to slits.

"Evayne a'Nolan was the fortune-teller." Kallandras told the girl.

If the name meant anything to Adala, Gervanno saw no sign of recognition in her expression. "And so you came to find me?"

Gervanno nodded, although the girl's gaze was upon the bard. Leial barked, the sound almost a whine. This caught the attention of both Adala and Trevor. Leial was not a Breodani hunting dog, and Leial's position — in Gervanno's arms — rendered any threat he might have posed moot.

"Your father did me a favor," Gervanno then said. "I sought to return that favor in kind."

"We left Hansleigh for a reason."

"Yes. You were summoned to the circus. You were invited to join it."

"*Invited.*" Her tone made clear what everyone present had suspected. It was not an invitation; it was a command. She had been drafted.

"You knew the circus would arrive in town. You must have known. Summonses such as yours come before the circus arrives."

She nodded, glancing to the side as if seeking an exit through which she might run with little warning.

"Trevor was not so commanded."

"If I had been, we would have gone together," Trevor said, speaking for the first time. His gaze was less hostile than Adala's. As most men with greater height and size, he was accustomed to allowing the fact of his physical presence to speak for him. Adala lacked that advantage, but had honed tone and temper in its place. Of the two, Gervanno's natural instincts made the girl more of a threat.

"We are all foreigners," Gervanno said, when it was clear Trevor would not immediately continue. "We therefore know very little about the circus. But we now know this: the circus does not visit until and unless the Free Towns are in peril."

Adala's silence shifted in texture as her shoulders gathered. She was bracing for a blow, although no one here would strike her deliberately.

"On our search, we encountered what we believe the threat to Hansleigh to be, this time." Physical blows, however, were unnecessary. It was not clear to Gervanno whether or not Adala knew or understood what that threat was. It was clear that she understood the existence of threat.

Trevor glanced at Adala; Adala did not look away from Gervanno. She straightened out, drawing herself to her full height. The height was not impressive; her determination, her will, was. It had not been Trevor's decision to run away. Gervanno had suspected as much, and was not surprised to see that suspicion confirmed.

"Hansleigh is no longer my home," Adala replied. "And the threat Hansleigh faces is no concern of ours." Before Gervanno could speak, she added, "Hansleigh abandoned us first."

"Hansleigh did not abandon you. Your father was very worried."

"My father wasn't worried about *me*," she said, voice low, words like a spray of arrows from expert archers. "He was worried about himself. He was worried about his inn. He was worried about his employees. Maybe even the rest of the family. But not me. Not me. The minute he knew about the *invitation*, he had already given me up as lost. I was no longer a member of the family."

That had not been what Gervanno had seen in her father's eyes. Or it had not been all he had seen. Adala had lived her whole life under the auspices of her father; he could not argue that a stranger of less than a few hours' acquaintance somehow knew him better.

"Trevor's father was likewise worried," he said.

Trevor flinched. If Adala had chosen to give up Hansleigh in its entirety, if she had convinced Trevor to follow, Trevor was not as angry, not as certain, as she.

Gervanno had learned, with time and bitter experience, that one did not interfere in the love lives of one's compatriots. He had seen love start, and had seen it end—but endings were never simple, never clean. One could craft a bowl, heat it, cool it. But when the bowl was dropped and it shattered, the resultant shards could cut the careless, and the bowl itself would never be fully repaired. It could not serve the purpose for which it had been so carefully, deliberately created.

"Trevor's father *is* worried about his son. It is why we chose flight. We must move quickly, or we'll be caught up in things we can't survive."

So, she knew.

He wondered what her role in the circus would have been, or might be in future. The townspeople believed that those who were skilled, those whose talents were easily, visibly seen, could join the circus; they believed it was an honor.

Adala did not.

Trevor turned to her; she kept her profile to him, glaring at Gervanno. "What will happen to Hansleigh? If the circus is in town, all of Hansleigh should be in the circus grounds."

Trevor was the weakness. He had, in Gervanno's opinion, followed Adala because he was in love with her, and the passionate love of the young could not be equaled. But his fear of separation, his anger at the certainty that it would occur, had not destroyed or fully displaced love for his family or his friends. He had made his choice, yes.

But his choice had been simpler: follow the love of his life, leave his family and friends behind.

Had the choice been between his love and his family's certain deaths, Gervanno thought the boy would have faltered. Would falter now. He was less certain of Adala; she had clearly chosen pain and anger as her shield. While she could dwell behind them, she could avoid thinking about the cost of any decision she had made.

Or would make.

Hansleigh was not his home. Adala was not his kin.

Demons, however, were his enemy; they were the enemy of any living man.

"Trevor," he said, coming to a distasteful decision. "What are you told about the circus? We are, as I said, outsiders; we travel through the Free Towns, but we do not make them our home." Having made the decision, he softened it, in preparation for what must follow. "I traveled to the west, to Breodanir. If you must flee, Breodanir is safer than the border to the South, which is my homeland.

"But I traveled as a caravan guard, and my caravan was destroyed, to a man, by demons who came to the merchant road. Not a single life was spared; I alone escaped detection. I traveled to the capital of Breodanir to discharge the duty of informing those in power of that demonic attack. Demons then attacked that city, but there was power in the city to repel them, although many died there."

Trevor's silence was tinged with fear, Adala's commingled with fear and fury.

Into that textured silence, Gervanno continued. "The circus came to town. We saw posters, and heard mention of it, but intended to avoid it, for we have duties in the East. One of the caravan masters I knew convinced us that, if the circus is called, it is called for a reason and we must attend, if we valued our lives. It was a commitment of a day's time, but we trusted the advice given."

"You're not at the circus now," Trevor said, the statement a question.

"It was in the fairgrounds of that circus that we encountered the seer. I chose to look at the crystal ball she carried. And there, I saw both of you. I saw Adala. I saw Trevor. And I saw my compatriots—those of Breodanir who now travel with me to the Empire.

"In most of the glimpses of the future I was shown, you were dead."

Trevor paled. Adala did not. "What of it?" she demanded.

"They were not the only visions I saw. You must suspect that we would not have risked our lives simply to secure yours; if I feel a debt to your father, it is not a debt great enough to encompass the lives of my companions."

"What did you see?" It was Trevor who asked. Adala once again placed a hand on Trevor's arm, but this time he didn't seem to notice it.

"In every instance where you were both dead, so, too was Hansleigh. The streets of the town were littered with corpses, and the air, the cries of those who would soon join them. The circus, the gate to the circus, was gone. And the demons that I have faced time and again wandered among the corpses, searching."

"But—but the circus is performing," Trevor said. "The town should be empty!"

"That is what we were told. That is what the townspeople believe. They wander the circus grounds, partake of the offered food and trinkets, and anticipate the performance. They are without fear, saving only your parents, who know you have not joined them."

Trevor turned head to look down at Adala. She was silent, but she, too, had paled.

"You believed they would be safe. You believed it was only your own lives at risk."

"We knew there was a risk that we wouldn't be." It was Trevor who answered. "The circus—as your merchant friend said—is called for a reason. It's called during possible disasters. There are stories about the circus emptying, and people returning to damaged homes. But the people of Hansleigh were safe.

"Those who ignore the call to the circus are not guaranteed to survive."

"That is what we were told," Gervanno replied.

"Then why are you here?" Adala demanded.

"I could not interrogate the fortune-teller. I would have, but she chose to walk away when confronted by those with whom she had prior acquaintance. We could not follow. She did not offer advice on what I had seen in her crystal ball." He exhaled. He had already made his choice, but choice was never simple.

"I believe your death will weaken the circus substantially. It is because you have walked away that the circus will be unable to offer a defense against our enemies. The circus grounds, which contain the people of Hansleigh, will withdraw and the people will be left in Hansleigh's streets.

"There is a small army of demons that stands just outside the borders of Hansleigh's forested land. When the circus retreats, those demons will enter Hansleigh. The Free Towns have a constabulary force; retired soldiers form part of the citizenry. There is no power within the Free Towns themselves that can stand against the demons who are gathered, waiting.

"I do not understand the compact the circus master made and has made with the people of the Free Towns, but if you flee now, Hansleigh will certainly perish."

Trevor turned to Adala; Adala met, and held, Gervanno's steady gaze. Her face had paled, but her expression was more rage than pain; there was a fury of ice in it. Her hands had become fists.

Had she known? Had she understood what she risked? If she had, Trevor had not, as Gervanno expected.

"And you've come to drag me back?" she demanded.

"Adala—"

"No. As strange as it sounds, no. We have come to walk the narrow path that leads, in the end, to your survival—because without you, the circus will not stand. It will survive—but it cannot both survive and protect."

"Gervanno," the Northern Widan said. "The time for talk is coming to a close. The forest is burning, and the wind has noticed."

Nenyane nodded.

Stephen, however, shook his head. "Unless we mean to take them, captive, to the circus, talk is what we have."

"The demons will move," she said. "They are moving, now."

"They're moving toward Hansleigh, not away." It was the bard who spoke. No one asked him how he knew; they felt the shift of the breeze around where they stood.

Alex moved to the bard's side; Alex spoke, the words a whisper of sound lost to the movement of air, the Elseth Hunter's brow furrowed with open concern.

"There is no safe place in which to continue this discussion," the mage said.

Nenyane appeared to agree, until she spoke. "Were you listening to the circus master at all? He will not take her if we drag her to the circus gate; it will not open. He has said that his circus—the heart of his lands—is dependent on choice. Choice is offered, choice is accepted. If Adala does not choose the circus, it doesn't matter if she survives to reach it."

"And he'll let every other citizen of Hansleigh perish?" Stephen's tone was incredulous.

"Yes. If Adala does not choose to join the circus, the town will no longer be protected. I am uncertain that this will be the circus master's desire. The circus itself will survive. But the circus master will close the gates to the heart of his power."

"Why are you so certain?"

"He's a god. It's what gods do. It's not that he doesn't care about humans—in the Free Towns and in the heart of his domain—but it is how he expresses that care. Adala has a choice."

"I made my choice," Adala said. "If I hadn't, I wouldn't be here."

Nenyane nodded.

It was Trevor who stepped forward, face white, hands trembling.

As Gervanno had known he would. "I didn't. I chose love — I wanted to be with you forever. I thought they'd be fine. But I can't choose all of their deaths — the people I love, the people I like, even the people I hate."

Adala said nothing.

"I can't go with you if it means everyone will die."

CHAPTER ELEVEN

"I t will make no difference if *you* return," Nenyane said. The youth was in pain, but Nenyane had never been the heart of compassion, and here, demons in the near distance, the lack was evident.

"This isn't a choice," Adala said. Trevor's words had hurt her; she had lost the rigid physicality of defiance.

"It is," Nenyane replied. "It is your choice to make."

"How is it a *choice*?" Her voice rose, her eyes widening; echoes of pain informed every syllable. Pain, anger, and the beginning of loss. "Join the circus or everyone dies? It's *a threat*."

"No. It feels that way, because the choice is a terrible one. But the god will not cage you; he will not capture you and drag you back. He will not sacrifice you on any altar of his making, or your own. His lands will survive, regardless. If the demons manage to encroach upon the circus, there *is* power there to defend the lord's lands. But that power does not—and I believe cannot—extend beyond the circus itself.

"Could it, Hansleigh would be a very different place."

Meralonne stepped up, onto the air; it carried him. "They will come, soon. Nenyane, Stephen said you recognized our enemy. You named him."

"I knew him. I knew him as Ishavriel," she replied, although she did not look away from Adala.

The mage nodded. "Kallandras, remain with the children."

At any other time, Nenyane would have argued against the use of the word *children*. She did not offer argument now. Instead, she too stepped onto the air, rising above the ground.

"Not you. Remain with Stephen."

Nenyane glanced at Gervanno. Gervanno hesitated. She marked it. "Against the demons you have already fought, I stand little chance," Gervanno finally said. "Against the others, yes."

"We intend to close with the leader," she said. "If we draw their attention, they may split their forces in a similar fashion."

But Gervanno shook his head. "I have been in Maubreche. The demons seek many things. Perhaps their intent is to destroy the circus itself. Perhaps not. But they seek a sword, and they seek Stephen's death."

"They don't know we're here."

"They don't know yet. Or didn't know. This is not the time to fight or travel separately." When Nenyane failed to reply, he said, "I am not confident in my ability to preserve Stephen's life. Were the enemies we face different, I would be — but even in that case, confidence in battle is always built upon a foundation of luck, good or bad. I do not yet have enough experience with demons that I trust my natural reflex." He watched her hesitate.

"When the caravan I traveled with was destroyed, it was all of an instant. People were reduced to ash. Metals melted and hardened. There is literally nothing I could have done, sword in hand, that would have protected the caravan.

"I have watched you fight. I have watched Meralonne. I have watched the bard. Were the three of you to have been present on the day our caravan was attacked, it would have survived. We would have taken losses, but not the way we did.

"You recognize your enemy; I do not. If you cannot fully engage, if you cannot hold him in place while we seek to make our escape, we will perish." He spoke dispassionately, his voice dry; he offered Nenyane unadorned facts, as if death were simply another choice that must be considered in the immediate future.

She stepped down from the air, her feet once again touching the ground.

None of the Hunters had spoken a word.

"How will the demons reach our people if our people are in the circus?" Trevor asked, his voice shaking, the syllables almost breaking.

"They will attack the circus itself," Nenyane replied. "There are gates that open to allow residents entry; the gates are illusory. They are physical, yes, but they are not the actual gates beyond which the circus dwells. Think of them as a drawbridge."

"A...what?"

"Some castles have bridges they can lower. Wagons, carriages, foot traffic—the bridges are designed to support their weight. The bridge is lowered, and people enter the castle. But if the castle is being approached by enemies, the bridge isn't lowered; there's no easy way to enter. The bridge takes a while to lower safely.

"The circus grounds are created *on* that bridge. Only those who are invited to join the circus can enter the castle itself. If the bridge is attacked, the circus will lift that bridge. It won't matter whose standing on it. When the bridge is gone, people will once again be standing in Hansleigh."

"But the people—"

"Yes." Nenyane fell silent. She seemed, to Gervanno, kin to the circus master; her words were unadorned by even the simplest of emotions. He did not consider the circus master's choice to be a choice. Nenyane did. "What will you do? We have come this far to find you, but in the end, if you do not choose to return, it is a waste of our time."

Trevor closed his eyes. He stood thus, absorbing everything he had heard. The youth had chosen to leave the comfort and safety, the certainty, of home; his love for Adala was evident in that decision. On the day he made that decision—and Gervanno was uncertain of how long ago it had been made—he had chosen love of Adala over love of anything else in his life.

But that choice had been made when he could assume that the town would remain as it was. The people who faced the unknown were meant to be Adala and Trevor. Demons had not been part of his choice.

The safety of Hansleigh, however, was tied to the circus master, the lord of these very strange lands. Trevor had to have known that the presence of the circus presaged danger to Hansleigh, even if he could not predict what that danger would be.

"If I go back," Trevor said, "could I change anything?"

Nenyane shook her head. "You were not asked to join the circus. If you return alone, you will die."

"And Adala won't?"

"I cannot answer with certainty, but I believe if she continues to flee as she planned, there is a chance she will survive. She was offered a choice. She made it. But she has time—scant time—to reverse that decision."

"And if Adala returns?"

"If she returns *in time*, neither you, your families, nor your town will perish." The sword master offered no advice; she explained the options as if the consequences did not matter. Gervanno wondered if he would ever be as unaffected. He had always yearned for that detachment; on rare occasions, he could find it. But he could not remain at its center, above or beyond the currents of life and the emotions life engendered.

"And if we both flee?"

"You have some chance of surviving." The town would not. Nenyane did not reiterate this fact; she truly did not seem to care.

"If I go back," Adala said, to Trevor alone, "it's over. We'll be separated forever. I'll be wed to the circus until I die."

Nenyane said nothing; instead, she turned to look over her shoulder. Her eyes narrowed. "Kallandras, can you hear them?"

The bard nodded.

She turned to the Elseth Hunters. "We have no time for this. If she will not return, we must put distance between the demons and ourselves. Every minute that passes increases our risk."

Gervanno agreed. He better understood the futures he had seen in shattered glimpses. In most, they were dead, or soon to be dead. Adala and Trevor were dead. Alex and Max. The bard was injured, the mage absent. Nenyane remained in those visions where Steven was not dying. But in some, Stephen joined Max and Alex.

Gervanno was a stranger to Adala and her young man; he was no part of the story they had built, day by day, into a love that defied custom, convention, and even command. His role, now, was to break what they'd built; he could not nurture it, could not encourage it.

He, who had surrendered all courage, all honor, on the road at the edge of Breodanir, could not judge them.

Trevor swallowed.

Gervanno understood, then, how cruel choice could be. Were it not for Gervanno's visit with the seer, the two would have continued on their way, certain in the strength of their love; they would have struggled with that love and commitment as a foundation for the future, no matter how shaky that future might be.

They would not have thought of themselves as monstrous. They would not have equated love with the slaughter of every other person they had ever known. They were not Nenyane. He could not imagine the sword master in love; he could imagine that she would walk away from the entirety of a town in pursuit of the things that did matter to her. She would not judge herself harshly should every other inhabitant die. Their lives were not hers to bear.

Only Stephen's was.

He was certain that neither Adala nor Trevor had traveled far from Hansleigh in their span of years. They were not Nenyane.

Trevor turned to Adala. She was red-eyed, although her tears were otherwise silent. "It's not my decision to make." His voice was low.

"And if it was?" Hers was sharp.

Ah, Trevor was young; he hesitated. If he had an answer, he struggled to frame it in words that would not hurt her. Would not hurt them. He did not understand that the absence of words was damning. Maybe, as he aged, he would. Maybe he would not.

Trevor surprised him. "If what they say is true, and if my presence could somehow preserve the circus, and with it, my family, I would return. But I'm not the necessary one." Some bitterness, there. "I've never been the necessary one—not to anyone but you. If you choose to return, I'll go with you. If you choose to keep running, I'll run with you."

"So you'll leave it all up to me."

"Because it *is*." The slender thread of Nenyane's patience snapped. "It's *your* choice. Your decision. Your consequences. He's willing to let you make it because he knows that. He's not trying to talk you into anything. He's not trying to pressure you—the demons can do that just fine on their own. But we need you to choose *now*, because what we do depends on what you decide."

"You can just leave," Adala snarled, pushed by too many things.

Nenyane turned to Stephen. Stephen, however, was studying his feet. Or the ground. Or perhaps the viewpoints of his dogs. The Maubreche Hunter was not comfortable being here; no more were the Elseth brothers, although Alex appeared to be paying attention.

Kallandras turned to Adala. "My companion is brusque, but she is not wrong. The demons are on the move. Our party's scout can distract them, but he is uncertain that that will delay them for long."

Stephen knelt. He placed a hand against the forest floor.

Nenyane's eyes flashed silver; she drew her blade. Her gaze snapped away from the two runaways.

Max turned to Stephen. "What is it?"

"I don't understand," Stephen said; he had closed his eyes. "Something is happening to the earth, here. It's not like Breodanir's demesnes, but..."

"But?"

"It almost feels like someone is attempting to claim land the way Meralonne did just before we arrived in Hansleigh."

"Is it Meralonne?" Alex asked.

"I don't know. But it feels like the earth is trying to speak."

Nenyane cursed. "We need to move. We need to move quickly. The dead can't bespeak the earth. The earth sleeps. But if the earth is awakened, if it's aware of the presence of the dead, it will stop at nothing to destroy them. We won't survive it."

Gervanno was certain Nenyane would. He was mostly certain the bard would. But the Elseth Hunters and the Maubreche dogs would perish. As would Adala and Trevor. He frowned. Perhaps Adala, gifted in some fashion that the circus master could recognize, would survive.

It was Alex who spoke to Stephen. "Is the ancient earth waking because someone is attempting to make themselves lord of this land? Or did Meralonne attempt to wake the earth?"

"I don't know. I heard the voice of the earth in Breodanir. I saw the damage it could do. It's not aware of the creatures that live on its surface. But this reminds me of the night before we walked into Hansleigh." He turned to Nenyane. "Who is the demon Meralonne is facing?"

"I told you—Ishavriel."

Alex winced. "We heard the name. We don't know anything else about him."

"At the dawn of the White Lady's court, he was one of the firstborn princes. He rode with her when she hunted. He was a power akin to Illaraphaniel, in that ancient world. The dead do not retain all of the power they once claimed when they lived, but they retain knowledge and memory when they so choose. *Kiallanin* is one of the ancient words for memory.

"He retains memory and power. He is, on his own, almost equal to Meralonne at his full power. It is he who commanded the demons we faced in our attempt to reach Adala in time, and they were not insignificant. None of the demons will be insignificant to most of us. But Ishavriel is not insignificant to Illaraphaniel."

"I'm not sure it *is* Meralonne," Stephen said.

"Who else could it be?"

"You can't tell?"

"No one has made their claim yet; I hear no lord's name in the wilderness."

Nenyane looked worried. "But he can't make that claim without being heard. Ishavriel will know."

"I don't think it's Meralonne," Stephen repeated, his voice falling in volume until the mage's name was a whisper of sound.

To his surprise—to the surprise of all present, save only Adala—it was Trevor who spoke. "It's the circus master," he whispered. He might have said *it's God* in the same tone. The blacksmith's son turned to Adala and caught both of her hands in his; his knuckles were white.

She was silent as she met his gaze, her forehead creasing at what she read in his mute appeal. She understood what he was now asking, and understood, as well, that he could not find the words to state it more clearly than this. Between the two, it was Adala who seemed fearless.

Gervanno turned away. In his youth, it had been very difficult to spend time alone with a woman of adult age. To do so courted rage on the part of the girl's family. He had discovered that this was not the case in the Empire, or what he had seen of the kingdoms; he had found it shocking at first, but had kept the expression of shock to a minimum.

Sylvia, on the other hand, had noticed; she found it amusing. But she would not have been traveling in the fashion she did were the caravan confined to the South. The entirety of her bearing had echoed the Voyani, and the Voyani had never been considered respectable. Still, she was married and Evaro, her husband, clearly approved of her presence by his side. The guards from the South, therefore, had no cause to judge.

But he wondered, seeing Adala and Trevor, if the forced separation was not a mercy. He himself had never fallen in love in such a desperate way. He had envied that love, as a youth. He did not envy the pain.

Adala was right.

This choice was not a choice, in Gervanno's opinion. It was a threat. *Do as I ask, or everyone and everything you once loved will perish.* It was not the circus master who would destroy them, but it might as well have been.

"You can't go back," Adala said, voice thick, hands as white-knuckled as Trevor's.

"I have to. I have to try to warn them."

"Weren't you listening to anything they said? You'll die. You'll just die!"

He lowered his chin. "I'll die anyway," he told her. "I'll spend every day of the rest of my life knowing that my decision killed them."

"It's *not* your decision. You just said that." Her voice was just as low. "It doesn't *matter* if you're there."

"No. I know. But I know that, if it weren't for me, you'd've joined the circus. You might have even been happy to be invited. I know you're the important one. How could I not know? I've always seen it in you. If we were special at all, it's *because* of you." He meant the words. In the face of her anger, and the seeds of a sense of betrayal, he found the courage to speak.

Death required courage. The risk of death required courage. If one could not accept the risk, if one could not acknowledge all of the ways in which intentions could be derailed, survival was more difficult, not less.

But not all risks involved death. And men were cowards at heart. He knew neither of the two well enough to judge, but he thought, had he been a girl, he too might have found cause to love this youth.

"I didn't want to lose you," she said, anger a vibration at the heart of the words.

"I never wanted to lose you. I know I don't deserve you."

"I was willing to walk away from Hansleigh."

He nodded. "So was I. I was willing to walk away from anyone or anything but you."

"And now?"

He said nothing. But it was clear that Adala had chosen the harshest of breaks when she made her decision. The act of abandoning the circus was a declaration: the people she had once loved, she would no longer love. Their fate and hers were sundered.

Trevor's decision was similar only on the surface.

And perhaps Gervanno was being unfair. Leial barked at Adala. She frowned and glanced at the dog Gervanno held in his arms. Leial's tail began to thud against Gervanno's chest. He set the dog down.

Adala knelt and opened her arms, and Leial bounded toward her, leaping up with both paws and washing her face in happy abandon. "You brought your pet?" she asked, without looking up.

"He followed us. I had asked someone to keep Leial safe in the circus while we began our search."

"I had a dog, until a year ago."

Trevor remained by her side. Hers was the only external opinion that affected him, or would affect him. But he did not speak until she had finished petting Leial. Gervanno was surprised when she lifted Leial from the ground. He had seen smaller dogs, in far richer surroundings; in his life; Leial's weight was not entirely trivial.

Then again, if Adala worked at the inn, she regularly lifted trays that weighed almost as much.

"I don't want to go back," she whispered. "I've only had one dream for the past year, and I don't want it to die." She didn't look at Trevor as she spoke.

Trevor closed his eyes briefly.

Gervanno understood. There was very little that could make people as uncomfortable as the grief of others, especially those whom one loved. The desperate urge to do something—anything—to make the person feel better warred with the certain knowledge that nothing could.

"But I don't want every man, woman and child in Hansleigh to die, either." She looked to Nenyane. "Are you certain that if we choose to return, Hansleigh can be saved?"

"No. There are no certainties in war. I'm merely certain that if you choose not to return, they will die." She was restless, now; a different wind lifted hair that was as silver as the Northern mage's. But her eyes had been on Trevor since he had mentioned the circus master.

"In as much as it is possible for a being such as the circus master, he cares about the residents of the Free Towns. This attempt to claim land that is not the wilderness should have been vain and foolish. These

lands are mortal lands; they are not meant to sustain or serve one such
as he.

"But if you felt it, if you were aware of it, the lands in which you
were birthed are not mortal lands, no matter their seeming. The presence of the wilderness has grown stronger even in the past year, if the
lands can feel and hear his name at all."

Gervanno frowned. He glanced at Nenyane; she was master here,
and he, student; he did not argue or attempt to correct her. But he
understood that, on the outer periphery of Hansleigh, the man she
called Illaraphaniel had not only dared to claim land as his own, but
had done so. If he understood what had occurred, the land itself had
wakened to the Northern Widan's command. Could the circus master
be expected to do less?

Perhaps it was because the land itself, the space over which Illaraphaniel asserted authority, was so small it was all but insignificant in
the wilderness. Only those who crossed its borders might be aware of
it at all—Gervanno was not certain he would have noticed, unless he
fled inclement weather and that weather vanished between one step
and the next.

Nenyane's expression gave little away. Stephen had noticed something. But he had not noticed it the way Trevor had.

No, Gervanno thought. Trevor was of the township. Trevor was
some part of the circus master's lands. He wondered, then, what the
people of Hansleigh knew. Perhaps there was a compact to be upheld,
similar to that of the Hunters—some ancient vow, some oath or custom
that outsiders such as the Hunters and Gervanno himself would not
know.

Still, Trevor waited. If he had decided he must return—and perish
with the rest of his kin—he waited for Adala. Nothing could force him
to abandon her here. But something had forced him to abandon her in
future, and they both knew it.

This island, this moment in which they all stood, was now a crumbling foundation. The future they had envisioned had ended; they
could no longer walk toward it. She knew. She knew what his choice
was. She knew she could simply walk away. If she did, Trevor would
return with them—Trevor, who had not been invited to join the mythical circus. Trevor, who would never be allowed to step into its pretty
cage.

He would not force her to return. But his choice would. Perhaps, to

Adala, death was preferable. Dead, she would not struggle with the pain of loss and absence. Dead, she would not regret or resent. Gervanno had seen such tragedies in his youth. He had not understood it, then.

But her death, should she remain here, would affect not only Hansleigh but Gervanno's party as well. She turned to Trevor; he reached out with a hand. Both of hers were occupied with Leial, as if Leial had become a shield, a way of rejecting what she clearly wanted to take.

"Is it so wrong?" she asked Trevor. "Is it so wrong to love?"

He shook his head.

"It feels wrong," she told him. "I wish I had never loved you at all."

He flinched, but accepted her words. "I wish, for your sake, you hadn't. I never deserved it. I never deserved you." He lowered his hand and turned to Nenyane once again. "Can you get us back to Hansleigh safely?"

"I told you—there are no guarantees in war. The circus master is attempting to expand his reach, but these lands don't respond well to that interference. Such resistance is built into the very compact upon which the gods agreed when they chose to leave this world. He should not be able to touch these lands at all."

Meralonne did.

Meralonne is of *this world. He never left it. He was not party to the covenant of the gods.*

"In the Free Towns, it wouldn't be an issue—but here, his influence, his power, are spread too thin." She frowned. "It implies that he knows where you are."

Trevor and Adala shared a glance. It was Adala who replied. "We'll follow your lead from here, and maybe we can explain what shouldn't be explained to outsiders."

"We can't—"

Adala's frown was sharp as she glanced at Trevor. "If they were sent to find us, if they were meant to risk their lives against the enemies of the circus, they have a right to know."

"If you must speak of it," Nenyane said, "speak later. We've wasted too much time here."

Her sentence was broken by thunder. Thunder in a clear sky. Clouds had gathered at only one point, but to Gervanno's eye, the sky itself was an odd color. Blue, yes, but tinged with pink and purple, as if sunset had magically, instantly arrived.

Nenyane's eyes widened. "That *fool*!" She turned. Turned back. "Gervanno. Alex. Max." She did not give them orders, but the orders were implied by the name she had not spoken. This time, when she leapt into the air, Kallandras made no attempt to stop her. He, too, had turned toward the sound of thunder.

Alex turned to the bard. "Who do you think she was calling a fool this time?" He lifted his pack, shouldering it as Max did the same.

"Meralonne," the bard replied. "The mage has momentarily lost his temper, and she believes this is not the circumstance in which to do so —things lost might never be found again. Come. I know the way to Hansleigh, and I will lead us in Nenyane's absence." As he spoke, he drew two weapons. "Stephen, remain as close to Adala as possible. Trevor, have you any competence with the sword at all?"

"Only forging them," Trevor replied.

"Then remain near Stephen and Adala." The bard did not take to the air; did not attempt to call the wind. He had done so once already, and was still pale from the effort. He led. They followed.

Gervanno, however, approached the two: the girl angry, the boy fearful, and both sorrowing. "I do not understand the purpose of these," he told them, for they both looked to him when he cleared his throat. He retrieved the two rings he had taken from the stall of things lost and found. They were warm in his palm, as if their single rubies were captured fire, tamed in such a way that they would not burn.

"In one of the futures I was shown, you wore these rings. I do not know their purpose. I saw them in the circus, and I saw them in vision, and I assumed they belonged to you."

Trevor frowned and glanced at Adala.

Adala stared at the rings in Gervanno's palm. "They don't belong to us, or to me," she finally said. "Neither of us earn enough yet to buy anything so grand." Her expression flickered as she spoke the words, briefly touching the memory of the dreams such rings might have implied had the circus not come to town.

"They belong to you now, if you will accept them; they are the circus's gifts, not mine." He knew how much that would weigh against Adala's acceptance, but felt it important that he not lie to this young woman.

"Where did you find them?" Adala asked, voice low.

"In a stall bearing the banner *Lost and Found*."

"Many things make their way to the circus," she whispered, as if repeating a story she'd heard as a child. Her hands shook. "Tell me, you have seen the future: did these rings somehow help us survive?"

"I do not know. But I do know, in the very few futures in which you both survived, these rings were upon your hands."

"And you didn't think to keep them for yourself or your companions?"

"No."

"Why not?"

"I considered them yours from the moment I saw them in the circus stalls. If they cause you or Trevor harm, I did not see it—but I cannot be certain that they didn't or won't. I know only that, in those futures in which you survived, you both wore them."

"There was no future you saw where we lived without?"

"I was interrupted in my scouring of the crystal. I do not consider the rings to be normal in nature. There is something about them that implies magical arts. In my experience, there is always a hidden cost to gifts. I will not pressure you to accept them, because I did not see—and cannot see—what that cost might be. I only know it is not mine to bear; it is yours in its entirety."

Trevor, however, stepped forward and grabbed both rings from Gervanno's open palm. He turned to Adala. "I'll wear one," he said.

"You hate rings."

"I don't hate them—I've just never worn one before. There are just other things I'd rather spend money on. But these are a pair. And if we can't..." He fell silent.

Adala met his gaze and held it; neither looked away. If this was a contest of wills, it would not be lost by either of the two—but more than will was involved. Pain, anger, betrayal, loss—but beneath it, the cause of those things: the love, the dreams of a future in which love would flourish, not wither.

The certainty that it would.

Adala swallowed all of it, and held out one shaking hand. Trevor very awkwardly put the ring on her finger, as if it were a troth ring.

Gervanno was uncertain what he had expected when both rings were donned; he had the vague hope that both of the wayward children would simply vanish, returned to the safety of the circus environs. It was an unvoiced hope, barely even to himself, and it died; the rings remained on shaking hands as they turned, at last, to face their pursuers.

They had abandoned all of their own bright hopes. He thought they had perhaps one left between them now, and it was bitter.

———

ALEX COULD FEEL the difference in the earth beneath his feet. It was subtle; he should not, in his own opinion, have been able to feel any difference at all. But there was a warmth radiating up, even through the soles of his boots. He did not hear a name, as Nenyane sometimes did or could; had it not been for Trevor's reaction, he would not have made the attempt to listen at all. He was tense, as was Max; Max had called trance, and scouted ahead with Steel's aid.

Stephen sent Pearl with them—or rather, allowed her to go. Alex could appreciate the King's lymer, but understood why she, of all dogs in the royal kennels, had been given away; she was difficult. It was her tendency to be oppositional. Alex believed that any other Hunter would have failed to handle her at all. But Stephen's charisma, where hunting dogs was concerned, was unequaled. She obeyed Stephen because, on some intrinsic level, she recognized Stephen as her master. As the leader of the pack she had only barely joined.

She did not fight him, now. She understood that they were all a hair's breadth from utter disaster. If she was displeased, she would make Stephen pay when disaster did not loom so close.

The trees they passed looked like the trees through which they'd tracked Adala and Trevor, but the undergrowth was different. Alex's only concern was that the claiming of the land—as if it were wilderness —would change its geography enough that knowledge of the forest they'd traversed would be rendered irrelevant. Finding Adala was half the battle. Returning her to the circus was the other.

Thunder sounded beneath the clear sky, a roar of sound that almost seemed to contain syllables. Thunder replied, but this second roar was uttered by a voice he recognized.

Meralonne.

He did not turn to look over his shoulder. "Stephen?"

"Meralonne is fighting," the Maubreche Hunter replied. "If we go to his aid, Nenyane will be unforgiving, if we survive."

Alex had expected no less. *He is buying us time,* he told his brother, who wanted to turn back. *If we head into a small army of demons, we'll waste it.*

You heard him, Max countered. *That's not a staying action.*

No. But Alex had the sense that Meralonne would not appreciate any witnesses to what was clearly his pain. He could tolerate Nenyane for reasons that had never been entirely clear, but Nenyane was unlikely to be affected by Meralonne's anguish at all. People's pain generally passed beneath her; she couldn't quite see the point of it.

Stephen was the exception, and even Stephen was subject to her wild impatience.

Just let us get back to Hansleigh. Let them get back without losses.

NENYANE DID NOT REMEMBER Ishavriel as Illaraphaniel did. She had encountered the demon before; she knew he was a genuine threat. But she did not see him as Illaraphaniel did; she had none of the Arianni's memory. It was perhaps the first time she thought lack of memory might—just might—be a kindness. Anger at herself followed the fleeting thought.

Ishavriel did not take to the air, there to join Illaraphaniel in combat; he remained bound by gravity, ringed in fire. But she noted that he, as Illaraphaniel, fought without shield, both hands on the hilt of his burning sword. His armor was kin to Illaraphaniel's, and the backward fall of platinum hair almost the same. They might have been brothers.

Ah. They had been brothers, in the distant past, before they were sundered by love and death. Driven by it, moved to hatred and its madness.

It was not the first time Illaraphaniel had recognized the *Kialli*.

It would not be the last, she was certain. But something in this one caused him to lose all reason. Nor was he the only one.

"She *killed them*!" Ishavriel screamed. "Can you not see? She killed them, three of our brightest, our best—*that* was the reward for their endless service! They chose her, and they perished!"

"They chose to disobey her, who should have been revered above all else! Would the *lord* you chose in her stead not do the same?" Their clashing blades, the rage of the wind and the fire, underscored the words that Nenyane could nonetheless hear clearly. "I *will not* fail her again!"

In this battle, Nenyane did not serve as shield; could not. Nothing could come, strategically, between these two. Had Ishavriel been the only *Kialli* of note in her eyes, she would have left the field. But she could not now leave; the other demons—lesser in all ways—would no doubt follow, and she could not lead them back to Stephen.

She wondered if that was one of the many deaths Evayne had shown Gervanno. She did not trust Evayne. Would never trust her. Stephen believed that Evayne had saved her life; brought her, shattered in more ways than one, to Maubreche. Nenyane acknowledged the truth of this, but felt no gratitude for it. Evayne had rescued her because she served a purpose—but it was Evayne's purpose, not Nenyane's, who remembered almost nothing.

And if, in the end, that purpose killed Nenyane? Or—far worse— Stephen?

Evayne would not care as long as the purpose was served.

She hadn't given Gervanno his visions to save Adala. She wished to save Hansleigh, or the circus, or something in the circus, and it didn't matter to Evayne who, or what, she sacrificed in order to achieve that. They could *all* die if they had no other purpose and she would not grieve. Would not hesitate.

Nenyane was never far from anger. Stephen was not comfortable with her rage, and it was for his sake alone that she attempted to keep it under control. It was the one disadvantage to the huntbrother bond: no matter how far away he was, he could sense it.

But he could not be injured by it.

If Ishavriel was not to be her opponent, and unless Illaraphaniel perished here, he would not, there were no lack of demons under the *Kialli's* command. Some were almost beneath notice; they were very like the Breodani dogs. Some were significant; they seemed irrelevant only in the presence of Ishavriel.

The lesser demon-kin could not kill her. They could injure her, but although theirs were the greater numbers, they could not all attack at once. They could attack from behind. Or try; she was far more agile than they. Those who ran on four legs did not generally use the magic that graced the powerful among their kind. It was beyond them.

But some were far closer to Ishavriel in form and power. She had already fought three, by Illaraphaniel's side.

She gazed out at them, from the folds of the wild air; they did not seem to see her at all. They, like she, felt compelled to witness the battle between the living and the dead, two men who had loved and served the White Lady. Only one had chosen to betray her.

Most of the demons who watched did so mutely, flickers of the memories they had willingly abandoned transforming their expressions, where expression could be easily seen. They had chosen to forget. They had taken comfort in the forgetting.

Illaraphaniel made them remember, for as he fought, the appearance of simple, mortal mage vanished; gone were the road-stained robes, gone the medallion that marked him as a simple member of the Order of Knowledge. Summer enshrouded the whole of his being, saving only the blue ice of his sword's light: he was limned in gold, and standing thus, fighting thus, Winter was the myth.

He was one of the firstborn princes of the ancient court.

He could never be anything else.

They remembered, who had forgotten by their own choice. And those who had not made that choice remembered the visceral truth of Illaraphaniel in this, or any other place. They whispered his name, or mouthed it; long jaws, short, lips the shape and size of a man's—for a moment, he was the only thing they could see.

But their commander was not Illaraphaniel.

Their truth was no longer mired in the firstborn princes of that court, long abandoned; the hush into which they had fallen could not last. They had already destroyed themselves; they had abandoned everything they had once been. The pain of loss did not engender regret—ah, no, it probably did. But nothing could now change. They could not return to life. They could not remake what had been both made and broken. What they had once been had been created by the White Lady, and their deaths had not returned the power of that making to her.

Even had she the desire, she could not therefore remake them; could not birth them anew.

Something in Nenyane struggled, as if memory was captive, caged, and desired freedom. From that struggle a single thought arose: the White Lady could no longer give birth. There would be no more of her kin.

She turned away from the splinters of memory as the demons,

forced by less shattered memories of their own to face their endless, ancient loss, sought a target for their rage.

STEPHEN STUMBLED ONCE; it was physical. Distracted by Nenyane's thoughts—he did not dare to attempt to see what she saw—he had failed to notice an obvious root. It would have been embarrassing had his father been present; it was not, now.

"None of the demons have noticed us," he said. Had they not encountered demons while they tracked Adala and Trevor, he would be far less concerned. Nenyane and Meralonne had dispatched over half of their attackers, and Nenyane had considered at least three to be significant. There should have been safety in those deaths.

Breodanir did not fight wars. Its lords and scholars studied them. Stephen remembered military terms because he applied them to elements of the hunt. If the demons they had faced had been a scouting team, the main body from which they'd been sent was an army.

Stephen understood Nenyane's shock. Meralonne had meant to draw their attention. He had meant to buy time. But his arrival upon that field of battle had seen that intent change from the moment he laid eyes upon Ishavriel.

He knew Meralonne was not human. Was not mortal. Nothing emphasized that fact so clearly as his literally thunderous rage. He knew the mage could command the wild air, and the air obeyed; such obedience did not seem to exact the same cost for the mage that it did the bard.

But Stephen wanted to turn back. Running away—for they had picked up their pace to a jog—felt viscerally wrong.

Don't even think it, Nenyane snarled. Had she not spoken through their bond, her words would have been lost to thunder, the crash of syllables so intense they failed to cohere into words.

Trevor stumbled. Adala set Leial on the ground and took his hand. He did not pull away. Instead, he righted himself, tightened his grip briefly, and turned, once again, to follow the bard's back.

The bard might have been a Hunter, given the grace and ease of his movements as he led; Adala did not look back.

It would have been a miracle to run through this demon-infested forest without an encounter. Stephen didn't expect miracles.

He was not disappointed.

To the left, Brylle picked up the cloying scent of death, saw its shadows, and leapt—at Stephen's command—ahead. Behind Brylle, crashing into the trunk of an older tree, was a demon. Or a monster. Demons did not have a single, identifiable form—but their scent seldom varied.

Patches and Pearl were ahead, almost flanking Kallandras; Patches veered, turning back toward her master.

Stephen shouted a warning. But the wind changed course and direction almost the instant the demon collided with the tree. The demon righted itself instantly, or made that attempt; its claws had broken bark, and the friction of withdrawal slowed it.

Had there only been one, Gervanno, blade drawn, would have made quick work of it.

These were not creatures Nenyane considered dangerous or significant—not when she was present. But she was not by Stephen's side. He felt her alarm as a bloom of emotion, both visceral and distant.

If Adala and Trevor had needed proof of their claims, they had it now. Trevor was wide-eyed, almost panicked. Adala, however, was grim. When a demon landed—or attempted to land—in their midst, she yanked Trevor off his feet, to the side. Gervanno's blade bisected the demon before it could do the same to Stephen.

It shrieked in pain. Or surprise.

Ash swept across their faces an instant later. They had no time to feel relief; they did have time to arm themselves. Stephen bore sword— the straight, double-edged blade of the North; Gervanno wielded the longer curved blade of the South.

Into their midst, once again in the air, came the bard. He wielded two weapons Stephen had seen only in his hands. The Breodani did not wield them.

Patches and Brylle could see other demons. Brylle joined Sanfel. The dogs had slowed; they no longer needed to sprint to catch up. Sanfel caught two to the left, or three; the demons moved so quickly, it was hard to count. Stephen didn't make the effort. Instead, he reached for the King's dogs—or rather, the dogs the King had gifted him. Patches and Pearl remained to the west of the group. Senshal and Corran, he sent to the right.

Marrel took up position to the east; he was joined by Steel. Stephen could sense Steel, but could not command him, in theory. He made no attempt to do so. Max understood where Steel should be; there were only eight dogs. What Marrel could see, Steel could see.

Stephen did not call the Hunter's trance—not yet. Gervanno's sword was in motion; the Southerner stood just ahead of Adala and Trevor. Max and Alex took up position behind Stephen; they were both armed. Alex was slightly better with a sword than Max, but the difference in a fight like this would not be noticeable.

Had Kallandras not been present, Stephen would have entered the trance state immediately. He chose to husband that energy; if the fight was long, he might need it. Alex and Max could stay in the trance state for far longer than Stephen, but typically tended to share its burden; Alex would enter the trance state, and Max would remain outside of it, until Alex was flagging; Max would then call the trance and Alex would leave it.

GERVANNO BENT slightly into his knees as he listened. The dogs were silent; their movement was not. The Terreans had forests, but the Tors and Tyrs did not engage their enemies in those forests; for the most part, the Tors were mounted, and mounts did not maneuver well in that terrain.

"**Two to the left. Three to the right. None approach from the west.**" Kallandras, airborne, spoke directly—and clearly—to Gervanno. Given the movement of the Hunters, they were already aware of the demons. They had their dogs. Gervanno's dog was now hiding behind Adala. Gervanno stepped neatly to the right of the group, moving in such a way that Adala remained at their center.

He could see the sharp, moving shadows as they approached. Three. He could not orient himself to narrow the field; he could use trees as cover, but the demons could move around those trees. Or bring them down completely.

There were too many. Max, Alex, and Stephen were armed, and they could defend themselves against one—but not with certainty.

Kallandras remained in the air. The air did not pull the demons from the ground, and Kallandras did not land. Instead, he surveyed the battlefield and passed necessary information to those who had to fight on it. Gervanno had seldom received battlefield communications that had been this clear, this relevant, and this timely.

The demons were driven, almost frenzied, in their attacks; much more so than they had been during their first encounter. There was a desperation to their movements that made them careless—or perhaps it was just the natural arrogance of their kind.

The sword that had been lost, the sword that had remained in a box far too short to contain it, had been found by Gervanno di'Sarrado. It was far lighter than his previous weapon, but it fit his hand as if it had been crafted—by artisan and experience—for no other's. He had adjusted to the lesser weight the first time he'd drawn it, but some of his instincts had been honed by the use of a more traditional blade.

If the blade was light, it was sharp, its edge deadly. Demons lost limbs. Two, three. They did not seem to learn from the deaths of their comrades, or did not learn quickly; they had a tendency to block with their hands or claws.

He took advantage of that, dispatching his enemies, blood becoming ash that did not tarnish or threaten the blade itself. But there were *too many*.

He could not keep track of Max and Alex, and gave up on the attempt.

He assumed Trevor was Adala's problem. That left Adala and Stephen himself. The young woman's life was the price for the safety of Hansleigh. But Stephen's life was the task set him by Nenyane. Could he choose but one, and only one, he would save Stephen.

He was not certain he would have the opportunity to choose even one. He would do what he could until Nenyane returned.

NENYANE DID NOT RETURN. She knew a small party of demons had broken away from the main body, which was otherwise almost enspelled by the memories the presence of their long-ago firstborn prince evoked.

She knew what Stephen faced; knew that Adala and Trevor had decided—barely—to return to Hansleigh. If they survived.

Gervanno. She did not pray; she had never seen the point of speaking to those who could not hear or did not listen. His name was as close as she came. The demons that had broken away were not a threat in any fashion save number.

She did not leave. She did not rush, headlong, toward Stephen.

Until and unless a more dangerous demon left to join the others, she would choose to make her stand here; here, where she could whittle down the numbers of the insignificant in the shadow of the only truly important combat on this field.

Illaraphaniel was trapped in the rage and pain of betrayal, as if it had happened yesterday. As if rage and pain might somehow change the past itself, as if demanding a *reason* would ease that loss. His pain was familiar to her, although she could not recall seeing it so clearly before.

Nor did she have the time to struggle with memory and the self-loathing the attempt usually brought. She danced to avoid claws and snapping jaws; the demons bound to ground leapt up, and up again, their teeth snapping shut on nothing but the air that was her support.

She knew she could be injured—gravely, almost mortally—but had never *felt* it, had never feared it. She feared only one thing, had feared only one thing since her childhood in Maubreche. She had devoted the whole of her life and her attention to avoiding that fear: Stephen's death. How, then, had she left his safety in the hands of a man of such short acquaintance?

But no, Alex and Max were there as well. Neither were the equal of Gervanno when it came to the blade, but their loyalty was unquestioned. Between the three, if Stephen could be safe, he would be safe. She chose to fight here to lessen the numbers that might be sent to aid their brethren. She chose to make a stand in the wilderness that was, even now, encroaching, because on some visceral level, it felt *right*.

There were two ways to protect Stephen from a small army. The first was by his side. The second? Destroy the small army.

THERE WERE TOO MANY. They moved too quickly. The Hunters did not flee; nor did Adala and Trevor. But it felt as if they had chosen not retreat but flight; the demons were a blur of movement in Gervanno's peripheral vision. Were it not for the bard's shouted calls, Gervanno would, at best, be maimed; at worst, dead. As he responded to Kallandras's words, he better understood the advantage Imperial armies had, even in terrain better known and understood by the generals of the Dominion.

Information did not normally spread easily—or accurately—in the heat of battle. Not like this.

———

STEPHEN FLINCHED. Pearl had been injured by one of the demons as it passed her, heading toward the loose grouping in the heart of their formation. Patches had dodged a similar blow, but Pearl had been clipped by the sweep of demonic claws; the demons did not remain to finish the dogs off, or he would have lost them both.

Marrel, he commanded to flee; he hoped Max did the same for Steel. The largest influx of demons came from the east, where those dogs were keeping watch. He did not attack the demons through the dogs; he might have, had there been only one or two.

But there were more. And more; enough that they broke through the trees. They did not choose to topple the great trunks this time.

At his back, Stephen heard Trevor curse, the single word carrying the fear anyone unfamiliar with the demonic must feel when confronted by the truth of its existence.

Adala was silent. Utterly silent. Or so it appeared at first. But something akin to curse joined Trevor's single word; it was longer, but far quieter.

———

ALEX HEARD IT FIRST. It caught his attention, although in theory it was softer than the snarls and threats of demons. The demons that slid around trees that might, in other circumstance, be used for cover, spoke. Every word was audible; every word was clear. It was perhaps the thing Alex found most disturbing about the demons.

"You will die here. You will die slowly and in pain. You will yearn for death when it finally comes." Speech of this nature came as naturally to the demons as breath to Alex. Perhaps it was because he listened. Max did not hear the words, or did not regard them as anything other than bestial grunts. The fact of the demons, the fact of their intent, would be clear to his brother, even if no words were spoken.

But Max heard Adala's tremulous cadence; he realized then that neither he nor Max understood the language in which Adala spoke. She was, given the way the syllables rose and fell, crying. Not weeping

—that would have destroyed cadence utterly. But the words were spoken as if her throat was now thick with tears that she must control, if only barely.

She whispered a name before she started: Trevor. And she whispered that name again when she finished. Trevor was the entire world in that moment; Alex felt the truth of it. He did not—could not—turn to look. Could not see if Trevor heard what he heard.

But he could see the moment her words, spoken with such difficulty, took effect, and he understood two things, then. The circus master had laid a tenuous claim on these lands, or so Nenyane and Meralonne had assumed. They were wrong.

It was not a claim on the lands themselves. It was a promise—or threat—to one of his own: Adala of the circus. She was the anchor here. She was the point around which that tenuous and strange control began.

She knew it, too. Or knew why she had been summoned, why she was of value to the circus. She had rejected it utterly, and it had led to this: demons, in the forests outside of Hansleigh, who intended to destroy the circus itself. They could destroy Hansleigh—and the rest of the Free Towns—in no other way. And they would start with Adala. They would start with Trevor.

The others didn't matter to Adala.

Or perhaps that was unfair. What Alex heard—what Max did not hear—were the strains of music, a voice lifted in song, a verse forced from lips that had chosen never to utter them. They were out of place, here; they were a song that would not have been out of place in the circus bazaar, carried by voices of enrapt and delighted children.

Almost, he could hear the strains of other instruments join her, and those instruments carried the tune she had begun when her voice faltered, as if offering necessary support. Alex thought she had finished when she once again spoke Trevor's name, but no: she had paused for breath. For a deeper breath, a more certain commitment.

When she resumed, when she found whatever determination she required, her voice was stronger and far more certain. He could not understand the words; Max could only barely hear them *as* words.

But the demons could hear what Alex could not.

And the forest could hear it as well.

CHAPTER TWELVE

The shadows of branches and boughs that crossed the forest floor began to move; had they not moved slowly, Alex might have mistaken them for new demons entering the fray.

But the shadows reflected the trees themselves; the *trees* began to move, hesitantly at first, or slowly, as one might if woken from long slumber with little warning. They had no faces, but had they, those faces would have been turned to the point beyond Alex and Max's backs: to Adala of Hansleigh, born to an innkeeper, and destined for the circus she had desperately wanted to flee.

Alex agreed with Stephen, not Nenyane. If this was what Nenyane called *choice*, she was wrong. What choice could there be between losing everything you had ever loved by serving the circus, or losing everyone you had ever loved in the act of protecting it? Either way, Adala faced loss.

But she faced demons now, the truth of the threat immutable. There was no lie she could tell herself that could lessen guilt.

The earth beneath Alex's feet began to tremble; the demons could maintain their footing more easily than the Hunters, having four legs and bodies that seemed to disregard gravity, if they could not rise above it entirely.

He had seen this happen in the wilderness outside of Bowgren; he knew the trees would move, and the earth beneath their feet dip and break. He shouted a warning—to Stephen, and to any who might be listening.

"I have them, Alexander. It will not be long now. But our enemies will know."

Trees did not bend. They did not bow. Their branches did and could, in windstorms and gales. But these were not mortal trees, not the trees rooted in the forests of Alex's youth. One branch fell—literally fell—and crushed two of the demons facing the Hunters in an instant; ash billowed around the trunk of the fallen branch.

He had not moved, almost frozen; branches fell to his back and side. *Max.*

I'm fine. At most, I'll have to remove splinters. Max hated splinters. It was an odd thing to think while surrounded by demons and moving trees. *The bard has Steel and Marrel.*

Adala's words, Adala's odd, lilting song, continued, gaining in strength and volume, as if the sight of the trees and their weaponized branches shored up her faltering conviction.

The demons roared, their claws piercing bark.

Sap flowed as if it were blood, its color gold as it fell. But the demons fell more quickly; they fell to branches and to swords, for roots ripped themselves free of the earth to entangle and hold the demons in place. Frozen, they weren't harmless; they could extend their arms and jaws. But the loss of mobility made them far, far easier to target. Gervanno made short work of them; Max and Alex helped.

When the wind slowed, and the bard once again touched earth with both feet, the combat was over for the moment. Stephen called the dogs in, and Kallandras returned the two he had pulled up into the folds of the wild wind.

Steel was not happy. Marrel was angry. Both, however, were alert. It was Max who calmed Steel, Stephen who dealt with Marrel.

Alex watched Adala. She fell silent as the wind did, lowering both of her trembling arms.

"We must away," Kallandras said, his voice soft and simultaneously completely audible.

Adala shook her head. In bitter, exhausted words she said, "Not yet."

What the bard heard must have been more than simple denial; he did not argue. Trevor's hands were at his side, but he shadowed Adala, his expression a mixture of helplessness and determination.

"Can you see them?" she whispered.

Trevor said nothing. Alex, however, turned toward the trees she faced. He knew they weren't normal trees, and wondered if this was the reason the circus master had, unasked, attempted to extend his lands beyond the borders of Hansleigh.

He hadn't expected the trees to answer. He knew they had moved; he had seen their branches and roots, seen the way they ended the frenetic combat.

But the tree that Adala faced moved in an entirely different way; as if it were clothing or curtain, the bark was pulled back to either side, exposing the new wood that lay beneath it.

That wood was gold in color. Gold implied warmth. Someone had said it was Summer in the wilderness—Alex thought it Nenyane or Meralonne, but could not immediately recall.

A person stepped out of the heart of the tree's trunk. His eyes were green—the color of new leaves, new buds—and his skin was gold and yellow. His hair was green—a swirl of vines from which leaves sprang even as Alex watched.

"So," he said, looking down at Adala. He had to look down. He was well over six feet in height, possibly closer to seven. In life, Alex had never met a person this tall. "The time has come. We hear you, daughter of Neamis, and we fulfill our ancient oath."

Her eyes were wide as she met this forest denizen; tears had not fully dried on her cheeks, but there was wonder in the brown eyes that met eyes of the purest green.

"What promise?" she whispered.

"The lord of your lands is not the lord of ours; nor was he. But it was not in his nature to subject those who were rooted in his lands to enforced servitude; nor was it his desire that we offer obedience born of the adulation that might naturally result in his rulership.

"We slept, as we knew we must. Sleep did not destroy us, as it no doubt did so many of our ancient kin. The gods were not kind. Do you not know this, child of Neamis?"

Adala shook her head, as if a simple *no* was beyond her.

"I see. Perhaps he expected that you would. Come. I hear the peal of distant bells, and the voice of your lord has been raised. I have not heard that sound, sleeping or waking, since my own childhood. The dead walk here. It is not safe for you or your companions." Thus speaking, the man frowned and turned toward the east. He fell silent, as if his gaze could pierce the trees that stood between them and the rest of the demons.

"We were not commanded to serve," he said, when he finally spoke again. "It was asked of us, as a boon. In return, he promised that the long sleep would end; we would not sleep unto death as so many of our kin would. A slender promise. We would wake, and we would come to the aid of his children when such need arose, and thereafter, we would be free.

"I perceive that you are that child. But you travel with strange and dangerous companions."

Adala glanced at Trevor.

"They are not your companions, then?" He turned to Gervanno. "Perhaps apologies are due; I did not mean to interrupt your contest."

"We are grateful for your intervention," the swordsman replied. He had not sheathed his weapon.

"I see. Gratitude is ever what it was." But he smiled as he spoke, and his eyes reflected a light that touched nothing else in the forest. "Come," he said. "We have made our vow, and we will now fulfill it."

As he spoke, the trees surrounding the Hunters began to shift in place, just as this first tree had done. From the trunks of trees a dozen people emerged; each had skin of gold, some darker than others, and each had eyes of pure green. None appeared to be armed, and the trees themselves remained rooted.

Alex could not doubt their ability to fight; he had seen demons crushed in an instant by the weight of the branches they had dropped. But the trees themselves did not move.

"The boy is worried for us," one of the newcomers said, amusement warming her tone.

The first tree frowned. "Worried? For us?" He turned immediately to Alex, as if Alex's fears had been spoken aloud. "You?"

"Can you not sense it?" she said.

"No. But the child of Neamis is louder, where I stand. What worries the child?"

"He is not of Neamis," she replied, "but I believe he is concerned that, if we part from our trees, we will be as helpless as he."

Alex did not consider himself helpless. He did, however, consider himself politic. He swallowed all defensiveness, and nodded.

"The young are bound," the first tree said, speaking to Alex, not Adala. "And the very, very old, by choice. The old are canny; they cannot be destroyed until and unless their body is found. But they range far when they choose to travel, and they learn the ways of the land above the earth.

"We may move, and we may return."

"But if the trees are destroyed—"

"Yes. If the trees are destroyed, we will perish. But you will find that we are not so easily felled as mortal trees. If even a seed remains, we will grow again in the fullness of time. The earth hears us, here." He turned once again to Adala. "What would you have of us?"

For a long, long beat, she did not answer. When she did, her voice held no wonder, no awe, and very little hope. "Help me return to the circus."

"Very well."

STEPHEN TURNED TO THE EAST, where Nenyane now fought. Nenyane and Meralonne. His dogs ringed him; Alex and Max stood by his side. It was Alex who turned to Gervanno. "We didn't see what you saw," he said. "If Adala and Trevor have the trees as guards, should we join Nenyane and Meralonne?"

Gervanno did not answer immediately, but he, too, had turned to the east, where lightning flashed, blue and red, in a pale, violet sky. Gervanno had not put up his sword; Max and Alex had. Stephen's was also sheathed; he had sheathed it the moment the first tree had emerged to stand before Adala.

"She is buying time," Gervanno said.

"Yes. But she didn't know that there were circus guardians planted in these forests, awaiting a call."

Gervanno's answer was slow to come.

Kallandras's was not. "She is buying time, as is Meralonne. They will not thank us if we join them; we will be a distraction. We will not be an aid." He was pale, strands of his curling hair plastered to a forehead damp with sweat. "I do not dare ask the wind's aid there, so close to the fire and the angry earth. If Adala reaches the circus, we have achieved our goal.

"If she does not, Hansleigh will perish."

Gervanno did not move. Nor did Stephen.

The bard closed his eyes. His lips moved, but no sound escaped them — no sound meant for Stephen's ears. Or Gervanno's.

"Nenyane asks that we leave, and move as quickly as possible."

"And Meralonne?"

"Has not replied. I am not certain he heard me at all."

Stephen then turned to the beings who had come from the hearts of the trees in this forest, made strange by pale, lilac skies. "The vow you offered," he said, voice low. "Was it sanctified?"

"It would not be a vow, otherwise," the man who appeared to be their leader said. His voice was warm and gentle, so at odds with his purpose. "But I perceive you are the son of the Oathbinder. You must know well the cost and burden of oathbreaking." He waited for an answer that did not come. "We hear Illaraphaniel's cry of war in the distance; we must away."

             ———

IT FELT WRONG TO HER. It felt wrong on every level. Stephen moved, and his annoying, burdensome dogs moved with him, as if they were extensions of his body, limbs so natural in their use he couldn't imagine life without them.

She knew this battle, knew this battlefield, although she had never stood in this forest before. The dead were the enemies she had been raised to fight, and the familiarity of the combat, the *rightness* of it, let no room for doubt.

But Stephen was not at her side. Stephen had not stepped onto *this* field. She had sent him away. She had *asked* that he leave. She knew how much he hated it, and she had fallen silent when his urgent question reached her through the bond they shared.

He called it the huntbrother's bond, or the Hunter's bond.

He was wrong. She had never corrected him.

Wind caught ash and lifted it in a small cyclone of moving air, as if ash were meant to be a wall, a defense. The demons did not care. Those who perished did so too quickly for their pain or horror to linger. They were cunning, clever, and dangerously greedy; they did not work in concert except at the will of their lord.

Their lord on this field was Ishavriel.

Ishavriel's grief and rage blanketed them all; their attacks grew frenzied, but none raised claw against Illaraphaniel. If they had chosen to surrender the pain of memory, they recognized him nonetheless; they felt loss and sorrow and yearning, but all were unmoored. They did not know or understand *why*.

In that way, and that way alone, Nenyane and the demons were alike.

All of their ancient pain fueled their attacks, but by their own choice, those attacks were almost mindless; they hit each other, their claws causing more damage to their kin than they did to Nenyane. But their numbers seemed endless as she stood her ground. The demons closed in on all sides; trees had been felled so that they might.

Lightning flashed red, red, red, and then blue—and the blue seemed to cover the entirety of the visible skyline.

Stephen moved further away.

HE MADE no effort to ignore his huntbrother. He did not naturally view the world through her eyes—it was painful and costly. But he had done so on a battlefield in the wilderness, freeing the denizens of that ancient land from their enslavement at the hands of their lord.

Then, he had literally held onto Nenyane. He could not do that here. Could not do it unless and until the demons were dead, or their lord signaled retreat. He wondered if their attack on Hansleigh was aimed at the circus master, or if—and this was worse—they had known that Stephen himself would be present there. Demons had come to Maubreche before, seeking Stephen's death.

They had perished. Nenyane, however, believed that they could not truly die. They would return to the Hells, weakened and far less significant. They would return to the mortal world if summoned, lesser in power, lesser in significance; they would retain information they had gained during their prior visit.

They would therefore know that the person who had "killed" them was Nenyane. Or Meralonne. Or Kallandras. Gervanno.

The dogs moved quickly, but they moved with purpose. He glanced through their eyes; the forest through which they traveled was devoid of demons, but not of life. He glanced up at the sky on the horizon; it was blue. But across the whole of that sky, lightning continued to flash, and the earth beneath their feet trembled.

The forest guards could, and did, bespeak the trees that otherwise seemed natural, but it was subtle. Roots did not cross their path. Branches did not hang at the level of their eyes. Birds complained, but even those complaints were somehow gentled. They flew to safety, as startled birds oft did—but safety was ahead, not behind.

Nenyane was now behind.

She had never feared demons. She hated them, and it was work to control the intense, visceral response; she did the work. Stephen could not easily survive what Nenyane could. Not then. Not now. She had never been injured by the demons they had faced in Maubreche. Scratched, yes, bruised once—but Stephen retained far more bruising from their sparring then Nenyane had from combat.

She believed she was invulnerable. He believed it as well. Or would have, had it not been for her arrival, as a child, in Maubreche. She had been injured badly enough that she could remember none of that childhood; the loss of memory had been frustrating. Only in the past year had the frustration grown so large it could swallow the whole of her concentration.

But she had wept in the Queen's gallery. She had wept. Buried in her memories, lost to her conscious recall, was a sorrow so profound it had devoured all of her ability to think, to move. From that moment on, he had been afraid: afraid of the memories she had lost. Afraid that they might return to her in a place and at a time where immobility caused by grief would lead to her destruction.

He was almost comforted by the familiar, wordless emotion that traveled between them. Nenyane was annoyed.

Nothing enraged Nenyane except demons. But many things annoyed or irritated her. The dogs. His brother. His mother's rules. His incompetence with a sword. He felt at home in the mundanity of it.

He wanted to turn back.

He did not. He knew that, should he turn back, Nenyane's focus would be split. There were two things that moved her. Demons. Stephen. He would split her focus when she could not afford to have it split, because if Nenyane considered the demons almost irrelevant, she knew they could—with luck—injure or kill Stephen.

He hated to be so weak that he was nothing but liability. In hunts, because she handled the dogs so abruptly, he never felt that way. But hunts, while dangerous, were not guaranteed to kill him. There, he had expertise and inclination that allowed them to stand as equals. Here, in this emergent wilderness, those skills were all but insignificant.

She had left Gervanno behind, not for Gervanno's sake, but for Stephen's. Gervanno, who could fight at her side well enough she didn't worry when he joined her. The Southern guard understood her skills, understood the natural ebb and flow of her bladework, in a way Stephen did not, although Gervanno had known Nenyane for mere months, and Stephen had known her for over half his life.

He shook his head and focused. Pearl, slightly ahead of Patches, had slowed in her forward progress.

KALLANDRAS'S HAND BLED. The weight of the ring he wore absorbed elemental rage; it allowed him to bespeak the wild air, to cajole it, to make requests of it. But if those requests could be heard, the wilderness did not respond well to mortal lords; by taking to the air, Kallandras declared himself in the wilderness.

In mortal lands, the effect was not nearly so pronounced, but the use of the wind had always been costly. Had he been a youth again, he might have perished here, but he had learned the differences, for he had crossed the hidden paths before. The Winter Road.

In his youth, newly separated from the brothers to whom he had sworn both life and life's breath, he had been reckless with pain. He had hated Evayne a'Nolan, then. But from this distance he understood that she was no different from Kallandras himself. She, too, had made the choice to preserve the people she claimed to love, and she was dark with resentment and anger.

An echo of that could be seen and felt in Adala. An echo of his youth. An echo of Evayne's. Perhaps Evayne had reached out to Gervanno for that reason. But no. If she felt sympathy at all, it did not drive her and could not stop her. She understood well what *choice* meant to the gods. Gods did not offer that choice as extortion, but it was.

Do this or everyone you have ever loved will die.

If Adala could make that choice to leave—and she might have— Trevor could not. Those two were bound by love, and love would not last. It would become ash and scarring in the face of the war that had already begun its spread across these lands. Her choice was not a choice at all.

Nenyane believed it was. It was not a *good* choice, but it was none-theless hers to make.

Kallandras had faced Adala's choice, in a slightly different context. But the person who had offered him this choice, bitter and angry and uncertain, had been mortal. Evayne understood the cost to Kallandras and, in her own rage and pain, didn't care. Had she not been forced to make the same choice? Why should she suffer alone to win this war?

It was better for her when she had been driven by both anger and the ignorance of youth, for she *did* understand what she was demanding of Kallandras—and he was not the only person who would be offered the same choice. Everywhere she walked, she left pain and loss in her wake.

She had not, to his knowledge, visited Adala. Perhaps that was the only kindness the circus master could offer, if that being could perceive kindness at all. The bard was certain Nenyane was correct: the circus master believed in mortal choice. Perhaps lords such as he could not perceive or conceive of the love that could and did arise between mortals.

Adala made the bard feel young again, and his youth had not been kind. Her choice would cost her Trevor, in the end; Trevor would be forced to lead a normal life. Adala would be part of the circus. They would not marry, they would not bear children, they would not face their separate lives together.

But Trevor would not hate her. He would not long for her death, would not dream of causing it by his own hands. She would not become a permanent story of unprecedented abandonment and betrayal. The totality of her passionate, almost frenzied love would become, in the end, elegiac; she would have regret in its place, and resentment. And perhaps she would, in the end, have some semblance of peace.

Kallandras would not have believed, in his distant youth, that he could *survive* the separation he had chosen; were it not for the survival of his brothers, were it not for a *chance* of that survival, not a promise, he would never have left them. He had chosen them for himself; he had struggled to pass their many tests, and he had made certain that those who had entered the labyrinth had done the same.

And yet, they were almost gone, those closest of his brothers, their lives taken by the deaths assigned them by their Lady. Ah, no. By his own hand, who had sacrificed everything to preserve them. They had come for him as if to redeem themselves for ever believing in him at all.

He watched the forest guardians as they moved ahead. They treated Adala's companions with respect, but it was Adala who stood at their heart. She had seen the demons, perhaps for the first time; she understood, or thought she understood, what forces would sweep through Hansleigh if the circus itself could not hold.

It would help. Knowledge and experience could become anchors. Kallandras had resented—had hated—Evayne for a decade. But, as the forces she had prophesied began to make themselves known, he had felt not dread but relief.

His choice had been necessary. He had not based it on a lie. The Lord of the Hells walked the mortal plane, and intended to make it his own in its entirety. No other gods would be worshipped. No other gods would be obeyed.

Those who stood with the gods to whom they had dedicated their lives would be the first to fall.

He had longed in his youth to let the war unfold, its consequences made clear. He had thought it might offer an echo of redemption; he knew he could never return to his brothers. Even were the reasons for his choice proven true, he had betrayed them. He had not sought the permission of the Lady. Had not killed at her command, and only her command, as his brothers must.

Could he not hear his brothers, and those who would have been welcomed as brothers had he not deserted the labyrinth, he might have known peace.

He wondered if Adala believed she ever would. All of her plans for the future had seemed so strong, so certain; they were shattered now, and the pieces could not be retrieved and somehow made whole.

Every person present knew this. Trevor knew it.

Nenyane did not. Would not. Kallandras had wondered, observing the Maubreche huntbrother, who she was, where she had come from. It was only in the wilderness that Nenyane of Maubreche truly came into her own.

Had they not been in careful retreat, Kallandras might have armed himself with lute, not weapons; he might have offered Adala a song that would speak to her experience, because it came from his own. But perhaps not; weeping made movement difficult. Kallandras's years in the second school of his choosing—Senniel College—were when he had learned how to keep those tears at bay when he sang. Adala had not learned yet.

ALEX DID NOT UNDERSTAND the path the forest guards chose as they headed toward Hansleigh; it seemed to be longer than necessary. The direct approach they had taken to reach Adala had been shorter. He knew time was of the essence.

"There is only one path," the leader of the wild guards said, when Alex asked. "Only one path we can traverse in these lands. Perhaps to your eyes the path is imperceptible; you are mortal, and free to walk in any direction.

"We are not. Were it not for the narrow path we perceive, we could not walk in these lands at all."

Alex glanced at the bard. Normally he would direct his silent questions to Nenyane, but she was absent. The mage was absent as well. But given things they had said about the wilderness and the lords that ruled there, this seemed strange. Alex could easily leave the path and return to it; he had tried. Max had been less than patient with the brief experimentation, but allowed it.

He could walk directly beside some of the moving trees. They could not join him. They could not easily reach an arm across a path Alex couldn't perceive. But this wasn't how the wilderness worked, in theory. In Bowgren, or in Margen, they could see the change in the land as they approached it, but once they'd stepped into the wilderness, the demesnes were gone. Only the wilderness remained.

That was clearly not true of these lands.

"We might reach Hansleigh more quickly," Kallandras told Alex, "but without Adala's presence, it would be pointless. If the guardians believe they can reach Hansleigh following a path laid down for them, it is better to follow their lead here."

Adala said nothing.

The only thing that indicated the path was not quite in the real world was the color of the sky directly over their heads.

THE GUARDS CAME to a stop before Hansleigh was in sight. The Hunters remained within the periphery of the guard's formation; the dogs did not. But Gervanno watched the dogs return from their positions outside of the main, moving body.

"Why have we stopped?" Kallandras asked; he could speak very softly, but his words, as always, carried.

The head of the guard glanced back at the bard. "There is an obstacle in the road; we are uncertain if it is a threat."

Gervanno moved toward the front of the formation, sword in hand.

"Well met, well met," the obstacle said. His smile was exquisitely sharp. His clothing would have been out of place in Hansleigh; it seemed almost outlandishly ostentatious in the forest.

Kallandras glanced at Gervanno, and then stepped forward.

"Well met, ATerafin." The bard offered the obstacle a perfect, if brief, bow. "You are walking a very strange road for one so dressed."

"I was not given time to change into more appropriate clothing, and I admit I am likely to be missed. This would not be the day I had planned, but I was commanded to attend a gathering of an entirely different nature."

Gervanno exhaled. He then knelt as the golden fox came out from behind Jarven. "You look well," the fox said to the cerdan. As expected, he approached Gervanno; Gervanno scooped him up in one arm and rose. "But I see you have an unusual weapon. Where did you find it?"

Gervanno could not fight while carrying the fox, but did not expect he would have to do so while he served as the elder's transport. To his surprise, the forest guard offered the fox no greeting or acknowledgement; they were wary in exactly the way they might—and should have —been had a demon attempted a conversation.

Adala and Trevor were staring at the fox. And at Gervanno, who carried him. Jarven ATerafin seemed almost irrelevant in comparison. Gervanno understood, but of the two, it was Jarven around whom caution must be practiced.

"How have you traveled here, Eldest?" Gervanno asked, his tone respectful, his question soft.

"We have permission," the fox replied. "But as you surmise, there was difficulty. My Lord sent me, and I felt it would be good exercise for young Jarven."

Jarven was not young. The fox sometimes referred to him as a cub, but nothing about Jarven—even his controlled recklessness—spoke of youth. He was a man in his prime and he was dangerous. Gervanno understood that the fox was the greater danger; the fox was master, Jarven student. He believed it, but perhaps the fox was like a natural disaster; one did not bespeak the rain storm. One could not control it.

Jarven was a man who could stand among the most powerful of Tyrs. He was the type of man Gervanno had been trained to observe, serve, or stand against should the need arise.

Gervanno had not been happy to see demons; indeed, he had left his homelands because he never wished to encounter demons again. But something about Jarven ATerafin was worse. No man could become a demon; no man could become an elder in the wilderness. Absent the strange, wild magic that Gervanno had encountered since the utter destruction of Evaro's caravan, Jarven was the most dangerous person present.

Jarven's eyes, as they met Gervanno's, were narrowed with what seemed to be amusement.

Kallandras was diffident, neutral, but his bearing had shifted the moment Jarven ATerafin had appeared on the path What Gervanno sensed, Kallandras sensed as well.

Jarven's gaze remained longest on the bard. He barely glanced at Adala or Trevor, and he treated the forest's guardians as if they were simple cerdan; they were all but invisible. Gervanno could not have done the same, but perhaps from the outside, he would have appeared just as accepting and indifferent.

"Gervanno, I asked you a question." The fox's voice had dropped into a register more suited to growling than speech. Leial barked, his voice hitting the higher register, as if he were frightened, but had decided to stand his ground.

"Apologies, Eldest. I had not expected to encounter you here, of all places, and I am perhaps distracted."

Adala had turned to the fox the moment it had started to speak, and her eyes remained round as she stared.

"I found the sword upon the circus grounds."

"Ah. You entered the circus?"

"Upon the advice of a merchant acquaintance, yes. She felt that if the circus opened, it was vital to our survival that we attend."

"And you chose to take her advice. I am uncertain that my own cub would display such wisdom."

Jarven's smile tightened but did not vanish.

"The sword, then?"

Gervanno frowned. "Do you recognize it, Eldest?"

The fox did not answer. Or perhaps the fox expected his own questions — and their answers — to take priority over Gervanno's.

"The circus is a place of many of pavilions — at least before the performance begins. In one of those pavilions was a stall bearing the banner *Lost and Found*. The woman who ran the stall had a small table, and on that table, a wooden crate. One far too small to contain such a weapon."

"She had been waiting for you, then?"

Gervanno frowned. "No. I believe it was Maxwell on whom she waited. Maxwell, however, was joined by his brother, Alex."

"And you found them?"

Gervanno nodded. "She seemed surprised, but I inferred that anyone who could, and did, find her stall was free to peruse lost items. This was one such item."

"And you chose it? It did not choose you?"

The question made little sense to Gervanno: it made sense to Jarven; it made sense to Kallandras. "I chose the sword. The stall owner believed that it would serve me well on the road we must take." He hesitated, and then added, "She believed it would cause injury to demons in a fashion normal steel might not." He did not add that Nenyane's presence somehow elevated his ordinary sword, in that woman's opinion.

"Eldest," Kallandras said, voice grave. "We are delighted and exalted by your company, but we must make our way to Hansleigh without delay."

"Yes, I see," the fox replied, voice cooler. "I am to travel with you."

"Might I prevail upon you to allow Adala to carry you? Gervanno's sword has been used, and his sword arm is essential if we are to encounter the dead upon this narrow path."

"You may not." The fox turned head to Adala, studying her, his nose twitching in minor disdain. "I will not allow harm to come to Gervanno."

"It is not for Gervanno's sake that we have ventured this far," Kallandras replied. "But your student is present; surely he can take Gervanno's place."

The fox growled. Gervanno saw no peaceful end to this argument.

He understood—had understood the moment he caught sight of the fox—that he would, once again, carry the elder.

The fox glared at Gervanno's new sword. He growled at it, his weight increasing with the depth and resonance of the sound—a sound too large for his body. Gervanno had experienced this before; he knew viscerally that the fox was not a fox. If it hunted, it did not hunt chickens.

"Eldest, might we continue to speak while we move?"

"Yes, yes. I would like to take that sword and put it somewhere safe," the fox added. It was not a command. Had it been, Gervanno would not have obeyed, and perhaps the fox understood that. There was only one price to be paid for obvious and open disrespect, and at this moment, the fox did not wish to end Gervanno's life.

"You have seen this sword before?"

"Or one very like it," the fox replied. "Until I see it in action, I cannot be certain."

And when you are? Gervanno did not ask.

THE FOREST GUARDIANS were aware of the fox. The golden creature had been the reason they had stopped on the road that had been defined in a way invisible to the eyes of those who followed. They clearly did not trust the fox; one guard always stood between Adala and the elder.

Adala could not mistake it for a fox; could not mistake it for an animal of any kind. Its fur glowed and shimmered in a way that made its form almost indistinct if she looked at it for too long. The trees—she could think of them in no other way, although nothing about them resembled the trees from which they had stepped—seemed to recognize the fox. They did not attack the creature, but made certain to keep their distance.

Or to keep her separate.

She glanced at Trevor. He had taken her hand; they might have been walking in the quiet stretch of paths outside of Hansleigh, seeking privacy that a crowded inn or the smithy could not provide. On those walks, the future had formed. Desire and love had been hesitantly, and then passionately, built. This would be the end of it, the walk colored by echoes of all others.

They were not alone, now. They would not be alone while they headed to Hansleigh, surrounded by guards from different lands, different countries. They weren't walking toward their death, but to Adala in the moment, death might have been the better option. Her death. Not Trevor's. Even now, even knowing that he could not walk away from the destruction of the town that had been their home from birth, she did not desire it.

Did she feel betrayed?

Yes. Yes and no. She accepted that she loved Trevor. But part of that love was the acknowledgement that he was who he was. Had he been the type of man who *could* walk away, choosing his own desires above all others, she would never have loved him at all.

And maybe that would have been better.

Had she never loved, she would never be in this much pain. Had Trevor not existed, she would have happily walked from the inn to the circus. Maybe that had been a child's daydream — and maybe because it had been, the *idea* of walking away from everyone she had known and loved in her life wasn't so strange, so wrong.

No one who joined the circus returned.

Sometimes, families could find their sons and daughters on the circus grounds, after they'd become circus, not town. But the circus seldom performed, and it was only when it did that those lost sons and daughters could be seen. They did not return to the town after joining the circus.

Adala had heard stories. *Everyone* in Hansleigh heard stories. Soon, she would join one. She would become that lost child, that source of pride and possibly sorrow. She would see her parents only when the circus performed — if even then.

And they would grow old. She would not. Time would move them past her. Time would move Trevor past her as well. He might love her now — no, he *did*. But love would be starved as time passed. He would grow older. She would see him perhaps once a decade. And one day he would come to the circus at someone else's side. One day, he would walk hand in hand with a different woman. Someone who was not Adala.

She *hated* the circus.

She had wanted one thing in her life. She had given everything to a dream that *could* become reality. And it was something, in the end, she could not have. Death could have him — and would, even if she joined the circus, in the end — but not Adala.

His hand tightened, as if he could hear her thoughts. Of course. He was Trevor. He knew her well enough to know how she felt.

She wondered how he felt, as she briefly tightened her hand. She had thought about her own loss, her own pain — they had seemed so large they could engulf her. She hadn't considered Trevor's loss. She glanced at him. His face was pale, his jaw set. He didn't speak. But he was Devon's son; words came slowly and seldom. He had been content to listen to Adala, from whom words bubbled as if they were breath.

He would not listen again. She could not speak; if she did, she'd cry. If tears began, she'd weep, and in the worst case, she'd descend into pleading and begging. There were demons in the forest. There was a talking golden fox. There were the hearts of trees, following a path that only they could see.

But that wasn't true. Adala could see it as well. Adala, who had been commanded to attend the circus master. Adala, who had been invited to join the circus. The choice was hers. That was part of the story of the circus.

She must already be part of the circus; she could have followed this path without guards, strangers, or their many dogs. Without Trevor. She almost let go of his hand. She was hurt; she had always been more easily hurt by the world than Trevor. She didn't want him to be in pain, but conversely, she wanted to know that he was suffering, too. That the suffering — like prior joy — was a bridge between them, a land across which they walked and in which they lived.

She struggled with the impulse. She could lash out — she'd done it before — but that would make their final hours together a misery of anger and pain, nothing else. But that's what it was, wasn't it? Misery, pain, loss. That's what was left.

No. No, if this was to be the final chance she had to make memories of Trevor, that wasn't what she wanted.

In the distance, she could hear music.

But in this forest, she could hear the fox. She'd thought the fox had spoken to her at first. Its voice was so clear, it was almost overwhelming. But no; it spoke to the guardians, and then to the man who carried the form it had chosen.

A bitter wonder rose in her, something akin to awe; she felt it, grudging at first, with each step she took. But she could not look away from the fox when it spoke. She found she had to concentrate to pick words from the flow of many syllables. The fox's voice wasn't meant for her, for Trevor, for anyone in this strange gathering.

But the man who had arrived with the fox on the road, almost forgotten in the fox's presence, could also hear the fox clearly. He, too, was oddly haloed in light of pale gold, as if he reflected the majesty of the creature that did not belong in circus lands.

He spoke once. His words were a whisper of sound, at odds with the smile that followed them; he sounded almost feral. The trees disliked him, but had they not, Adala would have kept her distance, regardless. Men like this one had passed through her family's inn before. Their certainty in their own power—and the respect that power was due—could become problematic.

Such customers were served by her father, for the most part.

But this man...this man and the fox were connected, for all that the Southerner carried the fox in one arm. She closed her eyes, exhaling slowly. Opened them to see the fox's gaze fully on her own. Its eyes were an odd color; silver, then gold, the two colors blending and separating as if struggling for dominance.

"You walk a difficult road," the fox said.

Adala's gaze had been drawn to the fox before he spoke; she could not break it. Had he been the ostentatiously dressed man, she would have turned her face away and failed to acknowledge the words with anything but a nod. She'd learned that much, working at the inn. But she could not put off the fox in the same way. He was not a difficult, arrogant man; he was not a man at all.

Still, she struggled to find words. "It is not a road I chose," she finally said, voice low.

"It is, indeed, a road you have chosen; else why would you walk it?"

"Why are any of us walking it?" She kept the edge from her words, but it was a struggle.

"They walk it because you must walk it," the fox replied. "Gervanno walks it because he chose to find you and escort you to protect you from the dead that now wander at will through the mortal forests. They cannot yet walk the lands of your lord—but I perceive that your absence is the gap in the wall, there.

"They do not know it yet; Illaraphaniel's rage has drawn their attention. But if even one of any note realizes what you presage, your survival is not guaranteed. Do you know that these forests reject even one such as I?" The question was conversational in nature.

"How so? You are clearly here." Adala kept her voice soft, her tone pleasant. She was genuinely curious.

"The circus lands were not created for my kind. To walk these lands at all, permission has always been required. I have become a guest. Is that the correct word? A guest. I will serve as a member of the audience, should the circus perform. My Lord ordered me to bear witness.

"I perceive that you suffer as you walk this road, and I will offer you comfort."

She stiffened, then. She had never encountered talking animals before, not in anything save the stories told around the inn's hearth when dinner was done. But in those stories, the animals were capricious; they were just as like to end a life as to save it.

"The circus as it stands now is coming to an end. The long task of the circus master has almost been completed. Your presence will preserve it for a scant few years, but those years are the years that define its purpose."

She stumbled. Trevor did not. He righted her, briefly throwing an arm around her to prevent her fall. "Why are you telling me this?"

"It is a message from my Lord. I do not understand why she believed it would ease your pain in any fashion; you are of the circus. The loss of the circus is now your loss." He licked his paw. "My Lord is Sen; she sees almost as the Oracle sees. Ah, but I perceive neither word has meaning for you yet.

"If the circus falls now, it has failed in its ancient choice and charge. She bids me tell you it is a heavy, heavy burden that has nonetheless been carried. It must travel to its destination, and against all odds, it has not faltered. But the time is coming when that destination will be reached, and the burden can be—honorably—set down.

"No single person could carry its weight, be they even gods of the old world. Perhaps especially not those gods, who were so easily distracted by war. Carry it, my Lord says, the last few feet, the final few inches."

She felt hope, then. It was a hope she should not cling to, should not struggle to preserve; it was only in the absence of hope that she could shoulder despair and move forward. But in the moment, that was a lie; she could move forward because Trevor carried part of her weight.

"Understand that she is *my* Lord, but she not *the* lord who rules these lands. She can promise you nothing; she can offer you nothing. Nothing," the fox added, "but this. If the weight you have chosen to carry becomes too much of a burden, you may come to her lands and live in her city; there will be a place for you should you so choose."

"And will she want what the circus master wants?" Adala's words were harsh, too quickly spoken. She knew better, but couldn't keep resentment out of her tone.

"I cannot, in truth, tell you what she wants," the fox replied.

Adala's eyes narrowed. "Speak truth, as you have been, or do not — " she stopped herself, but only barely.

The fox's brows rose. "Ah, I see. I see some part of why you are called. It is unusual to find one who can hear truth, and I have never personally found it relevant. In the wilderness of my youth, the only truth that mattered was power." His smile revealed several white, sharp teeth. "And the wilderness is returning, child. In such a time, boldness is oft rewarded by death."

Trevor slid an arm around Adala's shoulders; as always, he left words to her.

"But you have a different gift. When you speak to the wilderness, it hears your voice; when it speaks, you hear it. Judge truth or lie as you will. You are under no geas of my Lord's making, and face no consequences should you refuse what she offers."

"But she sent you to meet me."

"She sent me to serve as escort. She perceives import in this place. If my Gervanno was given a glimpse of the possible future, it is an echo of her power. Do not allow her sense of your importance to cloud your own; you are a mortal. You have a duty. It is to escape that duty that you fled, but escape in this landscape is death.

"Yours is not the only life with which she is concerned; I would argue that her concern for your survival is lesser in every way. But she, too, is mortal. Her roots — such roots as mortals may plant — are not my own. She feels sympathy — that is the word, yes?" The fox exposed gold and white throat as he looked up to the man who carried him.

The man nodded, and the fox's gaze once again returned to Adala.

"She feels she has faced a choice very similar to yours. I do not see it, myself."

"Eldest," the other stranger said. To Adala's eyes, the man was old —the oldest person present. But there was an odd vitality to him that implied that the ravages of age, seen so often in Hansleigh, had not touched him at all. "We *are* mortal, and time is passing quickly."

"Jewel desired that I speak with this girl," the fox replied.

"And you have. But if more speech is to be offered, might I respectfully suggest it be offered when we have reached Hansleigh?"

"I am bored, Jarven. At the very least we might dispose of some of the dead—those that survive Illaraphaniel. You need the practice," the fox added, sniffing.

"I am certain I do," the man replied, the genial smile around his mouth never quite reaching his eyes. "But if this matter is of great import to our lord, we should perhaps see to it first."

The fox exhaled as he turned, once again, to face the older man. "Do not interrupt me. I am almost out of patience; you know I found this road excessively *trying* to walk. Even now, it is so slender I might *be* auditioning to become a tawdry performer in some other lord's entertainment."

The man bowed, the fox's glare upon his fully bent back.

Adala held breath, and not just because the forest guardians had stiffened at the shifting tone of the fox's voice. She had not feared the fox the way she had the demons, but knew, in this moment, that that lack of fear had been due to her own ignorance.

"But I perceive Gervanno is at least as concerned as you claim to be," the fox said.

The guardians birthed from trees exhaled softly, as if they once again had permission to breathe.

"He is not what you are, and perhaps you are correct. While we play, mortals will perish, and it is clear our Lord has some need of at least a few of them."

ALEX'S GAZE moved across the whole of their gathered party. He wanted to speak with the trees; he wanted to listen to the fox. He, like Gervanno, wished to avoid Jarven; there was something about the man that made turning one's back extremely difficult.

Kallandras both knew, and did not care for, Jarven ATerafin; that much was clear, although the expression of that dislike was very subtle.

Max had missed it entirely; Alex was almost certain Stephen had missed it as well. Nenyane was Stephen's chief source of suspicion, and she was engaged with demons. Demons who had attempted to end Stephen's life on more than one occasion.

The bard did not seem to mistrust the trees in the same way he did the man, and he treated the fox with a deep and genuine respect— enough so that the fox barely noticed the bard at all.

The fox spared no attention for Max or Alex, and none for Trevor or the Breodani dogs. But after he had spoken with Adala, he turned toward Stephen.

"I see your companion has chosen to remain on the field of battle. How unexpected." The fox once again lifted its head to catch Gervanno's eye. "Did she expect that you would somehow keep him safe?" There was a hint of incredulity in the question.

A different man would have found it irritating or offensive. Gervanno's respect for Nenyane, however, was boundless; he took none. He did not believe that he could ever be her match. To be told that the idea was possibly ludicrous was, to Gervanno, a simple statement of fact.

The fox sniffed, as if the comment had been a test. Alex thought it a waste of time; Gervanno was a man who was all but impervious to such tests. His character was not subject to them.

"I asked you a question."

"I believe she considered the possible dangers, and chose the lesser. She knows the value of my sword, and she trusts I will not desert Stephen of Maubreche while I live. We stand in the wilderness, and I have been told it is folly to expect safety here."

"By her, no doubt."

Gervanno nodded.

"I cannot understand why the gods of old placed so much faith in your species. You are frail, your lives are short; I have often thought you very like the flowers your people spend so much time and care cultivating. They might have beauty to the eyes of the gardeners, but they are destined to blossom for only a brief time."

"It is the nature of flowers," Gervanno replied. "But perhaps you have lived so long, and seen so much, you are inured to beauty in a fashion we, in our decades, cannot fully be. We yearn, in our fashion, for things that we find beautiful. And we hold those memories during times when nothing of beauty can be found or seen."

"You are a very frustrating young man," the fox replied. "But perhaps, in a fashion, wise. We do not let go of things we find beautiful where we have any choice at all." His voice softened. "Sometimes we do not have that choice; I have learned this, in my long, long life: we might keep mortals captive to preserve them, but captivity destroys what we desperately desired to save.

"As you say, it is best to experience the moment that we know will pass. Perhaps it is knowledge that the end is imminent that makes the moment itself more precious. One cannot simply wander away and return at one's leisure."

Gervanno had not said that.

"We will therefore move. Now."

Alex looked to the guards who surrounded Adala. They began to walk.

Chapter Thirteen

The elder had understated the difficulty of travel. Jarven, not one to whine unless it suited his purpose, had not chosen to correct the impression the elder had left. He was dressed for a meeting of social import, but social activities had become increasingly irrelevant in the new world into which he had emerged.

Still, the clothing was inappropriate for the occasion; expensive, if understated, and less flexible than he would have liked. He had had time to relieve himself of jacket, which would have been the most constricting, but had not had time to arm himself beyond the daggers he habitually carried.

This was irritating, but not a cause for anger.

Gervanno di'Sarrado's presence was.

It would not be the first time in Jarven's long life—although *long* was fast becoming contextual, to his detriment—that he had competed with others for a position he desired. But it would be the first time he had entered such a competition with a man who was not even playing the game.

The fox's interest in Finch, he accepted; Finch was Jewel's, and Jewel was lord.

The elder's interest in Gervanno had no such roots, no such grounding. Gervanno was an almost deplorably upright man, and had no desire for any entanglement with the fox and what the fox represented.

Jarven might have attempted to speak with The Terafin prior to the alteration of Averalaan; he could not do so, now. The fox would know, and his service to the lord was unlike any service The Terafin had been offered before. Even at this distance, the fox could hear her name, as if the fox himself were rooted in the wilderness Jewel Markess ATerafin had claimed.

The wheels of commerce ran smoothly within Averalaan; the Twin Kings still ruled. The fox, however, did not acknowledge any ruler save Jewel. He allowed Jarven to do so *because* Jewel did, but otherwise paid little heed to the social rules that governed the Empire. He did not, however, allow Jarven's interaction with imperial society to eclipse the needs of his Lord.

When Jewel called the fox, the fox obeyed.

This time, the fox chose to command Jarven to attend him. Jarven had therefore been forced to offer regrets and walk instantly to where the fox waited. He had carried the fox, just as Gervanno now did, into Jewel's presence.

She was not what she had been. He was not one of her inner council, to see her in those hours when she made the attempt to appear so. That young woman would never have called upon the elder. The one who did, although she sat upon the throne in the audience chamber, was not the Jewel he had observed.

He noted, however, that Haval stood to one side of her throne. The wilderness acknowledged Haval as Councillor. It did not annoy Jarven; it mostly amused him.

Jewel paid heed to the convention of Imperial fashion in this room when she chose to use it in the absence of her den. The fox allowed Jarven to set him upon the stone floor. Delicate paws closed the gap between ruler and ruled, until the elder was almost touching Jewel's knees.

She gestured, silent. Floating lights approached her; were it not for their odd color they might be mistaken for fireflies at a distance. But their wings were too distinct and their movement too direct; they did not float, but gathered and cohered. Jewel had not spoken a word. In her open palms, disparate light became one light, something that most resembled a crystal ball. It trembled in her hands.

The fox looked at what she held for a long time. He remained motionless until Jewel once again adjusted her hands, and the ball of light scattered into its disparate parts.

"Jarven," he finally said, without looking back. "We will be leaving immediately."

Jarven did not ask for time to properly dress or arm himself; there was an undercurrent of rumble in the fox's statement that made of it an absolute command. He did look up in an attempt to catch The Terafin's eye. She merely nodded.

And so he had entered the wilderness of Terafin that so few of the citizens of the Empire could traverse. Many of the city's people had seen it, on the day the entire landscape of Averalaan had transformed so dramatically. But they did not return to it. Most did not make the attempt, but the young, and those who wished to prove they were fearless, would.

Jarven might have been one of them in his youth.

The fox did not insist that Jarven carry him; Jarven made the offer by kneeling before his chosen master.

"We do not have time for this," the fox snapped. Jarven rose instantly.

He had expected that passage through the wilderness would be difficult, but he had become accustomed to such travel. He had not expected that he would, in the end, be reduced to following his master's lead. He could barely *see* the wilderness; he could not see a path through it.

The fox had to turn back three times to find Jarven, which predictably annoyed him. He did not point out that the fox had yet to confer the rest of his power, such as it was, and that perhaps, had he chosen to do so, Jarven might find the way far more readily.

But even the scent of the fox was easily lost.

"I told you it would be difficult; it is why we had no time to waste. Even I find the passage tortuous. Had we time, you might travel the way mortals do; we do not."

"Whose lands do we now cross?"

The fox did not answer, not directly. "If you cannot hear the name of the lord, it is for the best."

Jarven had never appreciated this type of condescension. "Best for who?"

The fox chuckled, his voice clear although his body could only be seen as a glimmering of golden light. "We do not walk in the wilderness, here; we follow its ghost and its echoes. These lands were always an oddity, and most of my kin did not willingly enter them; their lord means us no harm, but your earthquakes mean you no harm when they happen, either.

"Come. I do not wish to be late; it is to avoid tragedy that we travel in haste."

The fox did not, of course, share the possible tragedy with Jarven. Nor had The Terafin.

There was very little Jarven loathed as much as his own ignorance. It was to alleviate ignorance that he had charted this new course, at what had once been the end of his life. He was curious, if inconvenienced; he could finesse his sudden absence should the need arise.

But when they had emerged from the terrible fog that surrounded their entire trek through these lands, and he had seen Gervanno di'Sarrado, he had fallen silent. Silence, when angry, had been the hardest of the lessons he had taught himself in his distant youth.

He did not doubt that The Terafin had seen a possible tragedy; did not doubt that her reasons for attempting to avoid it would serve the interests of the Empire—or the mortals who dwelled within it. He could not doubt it; he caught sight of Kallandras of Senniel College, and the barely visible band of Hunters with whom he traveled.

But the first thing he had seen when he stepped onto a road that was clear and bright was the Southern cerdan. Even the *arborii* had failed to catch his immediate attention.

He considered Gervanno's death. He did not think he would survive being the cause of it, but there were subtle ways to kill a person. He knew most of them. He could not arrange any of them while Gervanno carried the fox, however, and the fox had insisted that Gervanno once again take up the burden of his presence.

Jarven understood. The fox accepted Jewel's command, but his *concern* was this almost irrelevant Southerner. He would have carried out his duties, even in the absence of Gervanno, but he was engaged with the orders because this man was present.

What, of value, did Gervanno offer the fox?

Jarven could see very little value in his presence. Perhaps, had he believed the fox was attempting to increase his standing with the mortal public, Gervanno could be of use. He was the type of man that showed well to those with little power and no easy way to gain more of it; by elevating Gervanno, one could show a type of respect for the honor that Gervanno radiated.

The wilderness did not prize such honor.

The language of the wilderness was a language Jarven understood: power. Gervanno had almost none. He had his sense of duty: tarnished and frayed by experience in war but not, clearly, broken.

The fox's stated interest in Gervanno was slim, but it was clear the eldest was drawn to Gervanno. He had not offered the Southerner what he had offered Jarven, his student. Nor had he demanded from Gervanno what he had demanded, in blood and pain, from Jarven.

But he had bitten Gervanno, on a road Jarven had not traveled. Bitten, not in an attempt to wound or kill, but to confer some trace of himself. Gervanno had not suffered during this strange infusion; the bite had barely pierced skin. But it *had* pierced skin. The fox could now find Gervanno on any road the Southerner walked, his presence much stronger when he stood in the wilderness.

The fox professed a minor interest in Gervanno; Gervanno was the type of man that Jarven had not, and would never, be. Had Jarven been that man, the fox would never have taken an interest in him; he would never have chosen to confer and imbue him with some portion of his power. He would never have chosen Jarven as his cub.

And yet, here they were, admittedly at Jewel's request. Jarven had often failed to fulfill requests that did not benefit him with the previous Terafin. The fox, sly, cunning, and self-absorbed, did not. Not when it came to Jewel. Jarven had, therefore, been forced to treat The Terafin with an unheard-of respect, and it chafed him.

He was a capable liar; it had not caused him difficulty in the past. But it was the nature of lies: they were meant for other people. Not himself.

He therefore did not lie. The fox had waited for Gervanno to notice his presence, and the fox had demanded—silently, for he had taken for himself no right of command save that of power—that Gervanno carry him. He rested in the cerdan's arms now.

Jarven understood threats.

He had clawed his way from the streets of the hundred holdings to a position of prominence in the Merchant Authority as the head of House Terafin's merchant operations. Prior to Terafin, he had served

the Kings, until boredom and frustration had caused him to train a
successor so that someone else could bear the royal shackles.

His rise had not been without bumps and interruptions. He had
had rivals—of course he had—men and women who desired the position Jarven himself desired. He had evaluated them all, had made
choices based on his own expedience and the needs of the House of
which he was a member. Some, he had removed. Some had bowed out.

He recognized competition, although it had been years, perhaps a
decade, since any of note had arrived. At his age, those who wanted
what Jarven had were content to wait his death, assuming it *must* be
soon. Better that he die naturally than they sully their own clean hands.
Jarven would not have waited in that fashion.

He recognized in Gervanno a rival. A competitor.

And yet, not. Were Gervanno to be offered what Jarven had been
offered, the cerdan would refuse. Politely. Respectfully. But the answer
would be no. It was for that reason that Jarven had not previously
considered him a threat.

He accepted now that Gervanno was. And what a pale, toothless
rival he was. He recognized power, but did not desire to own it, to be
it. He obeyed the fox not because the fox was his master, but because
the fox could end his life. And yet, there was no fear of the fox in him
beyond what was prudent.

Such a man would barely be worth Jarven's attention, should he
wander into Averalaan or the Merchant Authority. Had he appeared at
the Terafin manse, Jarven would not have known of him at all, so
harmless did he appear. Jarven understood that Gervanno was not a
rival in any genuine sense except one: he had piqued the fox's interest.
By simply drawing breath, he drew the fox's attention—ancient and
wild and almost immoveable.

He had been no part of the fox's plan. Crossing paths with
Gervanno in the wilderness, at the borders of Breodanir, had been an
accident; a scouting encounter. When their work had been done in the
King's City—ah, no, when Jarven's goal was frustrated, and his quarry
had already pulled up roots and fled—that should have been the end
of it.

But The Terafin considered Gervanno's *companions* people of note,
of grave import. In order to succor those companions, the elder had
been sent to the Free Towns. To Gervanno and his ilk. To Kallandras
of Senniel, harbinger of disaster and death. To Meralonne APhaniel,

whose voice in the distance was so loud one could be forgiven for assuming that the lands upon which they now stood were, in their entirety, his.

Or perhaps the fox made his choice deliberately. He, like Jarven, had a dark sense of humor; he liked to see Jarven discomfited, unbalanced. Perhaps this was simply another of his infernal tests, but a subtle one.

Jarven watched the fox and Gervanno. It did not feel like a lie, but it did not feel like the entirety of the truth, either.

"I am tasked with the protection of these people."

Jarven glanced at the bard; he did not need to feign surprise. It was very, very seldom that he heard the bardic voice —who would dare to use it against an important member of House Terafin?

Kallandras of Senniel did not continue to speak thus; he made no threat, offered no negotiation. His words were both wall and warning. Jarven did not bother to reply.

ALEX DESIRED a stretch of time in the wilderness during which he could stand and move in wonder and awe, could explore living legend, living myth, separating truth from the attenuated echoes left only in children's stories. At the heart of those early stories was wonder.

And death. Children's stories could be remarkably bloody. Perhaps that was why legend and myth were all that remained: the truth was far too terrifying.

Here, surrounded by walking trees, a talking fox, and the thunderous sounds of Meralonne at war, he could not pause, could not absorb, could not take notes. Alex was, when left to his own devices, an inveterate notetaker.

Still, he noted the tension in the trees when Jarven ATerafin and the talking fox had suddenly intercepted them on the narrow road that only the trees could see. He noted the way they drew Adala further into the odd, moving clearing they formed.

She had been the object of their vow, or so they had said. It was to bring her to Hansleigh that they had been planted. If they noted Stephen, he was mostly irrelevant. Adala was not. Alex had been uncertain what choice she would make when she had been found, but their ominous words had somehow brought her comfort.

He, however, heard only the death of Hansleigh in the near future. In the future that would happen, even if Adala somehow made it back alive today.

The skies flashed red, white, red; the earth beneath their feet almost buckled.

Alex turned to Stephen, then.

Stephen was white. "There are—there are too many." His voice was a whisper. The dogs gathered instantly, ready for battle—but the battle was distant. Stephen could not turn and run; he could not make it in time to intervene in whatever it was he saw or heard.

Gervanno turned to Stephen, fox in arms temporarily forgotten. He was tense now, but not as pale as Stephen. "What do you see?" he said, his voice a bark of sound, a soldier's command.

"The dead," Stephen replied.

"Meralonne?"

"He is still fighting. One other has joined the battle against him; normally Nenyane would come to his aid. But there are too many demons on the ground. She says there must be a door or a portal somewhere nearby."

"Near to her?"

Stephen nodded. "She doesn't know where."

"Does she need us to find it?"

He winced. "No. She needs to know we're safe." The words were bitter. "She's not yet overwhelmed, but I don't think she can do this forever."

Alex touched Stephen's shoulder. He understood Stephen's visceral need to go back, to stand beside her. But he understood that that wouldn't help Nenyane. Nenyane had always been unusual. Alex had never seen her injured. Stephen? Yes. Hunters faced injury and the possibility of death during their normal hunts.

Nenyane never had, and in theory the risk to Nenyane should have been far greater. Stephen had access to the Hunter's trance; hunt-brothers did not. But Nenyane's endurance was far beyond Stephen's, Max's, or Alex's. And if Nenyane told them to run, if Nenyane demanded they protect Stephen, Alex was comfortable obeying. He didn't expect Stephen to be as comfortable. Although Stephen knew her best, Nenyane was still his huntbrother, and deserting his hunt-brother was never going to be easy.

Had Stephen turned back, Alex would have followed, as would Max.

Gervanno prevented it.

Gervanno had been given a single task. To protect Stephen in Nenyane's stead. In theory, Gervanno was a Maubreche hire; it was Stephen who was master here, in any legal sense. Not even Stephen believed that legality carried weight with the Southern swordsman.

"She thinks the demons are tracking us," Stephen said, raising his voice.

The forest guards did not acknowledge his words in any way but one: they began to move more quickly.

NENYANE COULD NOT PREVENT demons from peeling off the main body of the army at the edges. She could, and did, prevent them from fleeing when they were within sword's reach, but there were far too many to easily control. Their numbers had not diminished; they had increased as she stood her ground.

Increased, as Illaraphaniel's battle with Ishavriel continued.

Awe and terror were emotions Illaraphaniel had always evoked; she had no memory of Ishavriel as a living prince of the White Lady's court. He was, had always been, traitor—and his treachery, as a handful of other defections, echoed down the ages. It could be seen in Illaraphaniel's broken rage.

She had not expected Ishavriel's rage to be as intense; she had not expected the pain of his ancient, permanent decision to scar him, just as it had his lost brothers. He had *chosen* to leave. He had chosen to abandon. The desertion of Ishavriel and those who joined the Lord of the Hells had injured the White Lady; she had lost much of her power on the day they had broken with her.

And yet, she could hear in the undercurrents of his voice—a voice too loud, too thunderous, to contain subtlety—a pitiful, consuming desire. The White Lady was lost to him forever—by his own will. She could not understand the pain he felt. Could not understand the rage and envy and broken love that Illaraphaniel invoked.

Ishavriel was dead.

Illaraphaniel was not—not yet. But in Illaraphaniel's voice, as thunderous, as Ishavriel's, she heard the same pain—as if pain were a theme that could only be fully shared by those born to, and of, the White Lady.

She could not catch Illaraphaniel's attention; she tried only once. If numerous demon-kin of little note joined their brethren on the ground to perish there, they were barely a threat. Not all of the demons who joined the battle were insignificant.

None had the power of Ishavriel. None had the authority.

But one unfurled wings of fire that spread across the horizon, and fire began to consume the forest. That one looked up, his face pale and similar in structure to the two combatants who ruled the air; his lips moved, his brows drew together.

She could not hear his voice. Could not hear his words. Was peripherally aware of his displeasure as clouds of ash muted his visage. She had no name to give, no name to attach to this *Kialli*. He looked up, his gaze fixed to Illaraphaniel, as all demons did when they entered this forest.

But when she next saw clearly through the detritus of the dead, she met his gaze. It was Nenyane to whom he now looked. His eyes narrowed briefly, as if in confusion—but when they cleared, recognition and intent remained.

He cried out a word. Two. Three. The sky filled with wings at his command.

She remembered, then, Gervanno's story. She remembered the words he had spoken of the night in which the merchant caravan he guarded had been destroyed to a man. Gervanno had survived. Only Gervanno.

What had they been looking for?

WHEN STEPHEN CAME to a stop a second time, the whole of his body stiffened; he might have stumbled had Alex not reached out to grab his arm.

Gervanno turned to Stephen, almost a step behind. Whatever he saw in Stephen's expression caused him to turn, to look back. The fox was in his arms. The fox and the sword.

"Stephen, what is it, what's changed?"

Stephen struggled to speak. "Nenyane—Nenyane thinks there's an open portal in the mortal lands. Some way for demons to come, quickly, to the lands outside of Hansleigh."

"A gate from the Hells?"

He shook his head. "A gate from the Northern Wastes. A gate from the Shining Palace. Demons are joining those on the field. Meralonne is—Meralonne has the attention of their commander. But a demon of power has just joined the battlefield." White now, Stephen struggled to take a deeper breath. "Nenyane doesn't recognize him."

"Meralonne is in danger?"

"She doesn't recognize the *Kialli*," Stephen repeated. "But he's recognized her."

"What?" Two voices. Gervanno's. The fox's.

The guards had come to a halt because Adala had ceased her quick walk. She turned to Stephen. He understood, then, why the circus had claimed her. She had taken trees in stride, and demons seemed an almost inevitable obstacle to her return. It was her voice, her call, that had, in the end, woken the trees themselves, reminding them of a duty so ancient she could not have been consciously aware of it.

"Can she see the portal?" It was the fox who asked, his tone barely shy of demand.

Stephen shook his head. "There's too much dust in the air, and too many demons. But the new *Kialli* lord has summoned winged creatures."

Gervanno paled.

"Nenyane doesn't think those creatures are demonic in nature. She doesn't think they're dead."

THE GUARDS TURNED to Adala in silence; she could almost hear creaking, although none spoke. The fox was glowing so brilliantly in her vision she had to squint to see him at all. But the man who carried the fox seemed to shroud that light where golden fur came into contact with human body.

"Gervanno."

The man described winged creatures. He used a word Adala both understood and failed to recognize immediately.

"That is impossible. You have clearly never seen a dragon," the fox replied. He was irritated. Irritable. "Did you see scales?"

The man was silent, so pale he might have come from the distant North, not the South he claimed as his birthplace. "No. No scales. But wings far larger than even the largest of the birds I have seen. Their breath was fire. They did not speak. The skies were dark with their wings in the day's light."

The fox cursed. Adala, no stranger to foul language, given her life in the inn, was nonetheless shocked.

She had fled Hansleigh, and the circus, for the sake of love. She understood in a way Trevor did not that the circus would devour her. Had he been invited to join the circus itself, she would never had chosen to leave.

Even when told that the survival of the entire town depended on her, what she had felt in the moment was resentment, not love. Resentment of Trevor, who made the choice to deny her because he could not sacrifice the town on the altar of love. He had believed that their flight would allow them to be together.

He had not believed it would doom every other person in his life for whom he had cared. Never returning was one thing—although perhaps he had not understood that, in choosing Adala, he might never see his loved ones again. But when he *had* understood the consequences, he had not chosen Adala.

But Adala had not understood either.

Not until this moment.

She had believed that she could escape with Trevor—the only thing in this life she had ever truly wanted. All of her planning, all of her intent, had been focused on preserving that precious emotion; she intended to keep love alive for as long as she possibly could.

And it had come to this.

Was it so selfish to want to love and to be loved? Was it so terrible that this must be its consequence? Why did love exist *at all*, if this was its outcome? For she could hear the earth beneath her feet. Could hear the words carried by the breeze; could hear the water in its brooks. She could even, at this remove, hear the fire.

She knew what the wind now carried aloft; she could all but see it herself, although the branches of the forest obscured clear sight of the skies themselves.

She knew why the circus had called her.

In truth, she had expected it. The circus didn't call children. Children were not expected to be able to choose wisely, or at all. She knew.

She had asked. She had *demanded*. But the circus had not opened to perform in all the years of her childhood; it was myth, legend, daydream.

Only as she left childhood had her daydreams grown to encompass more than the circus. As a child, she had yearned to be *special*, because being special meant she was worthy. No, it meant she was *more* worthy. She saw that now in the children who were the age she had once been. Being special meant being more loved. Being more worthy of love.

Trevor's love did not depend on that elusive quality. Trevor's love made her feel so special no other love was required. Daydreams of the circus withered; daydreams of Trevor took their place. She forgot about the things that had once made her feel special. They were things that might be considered worthy of the circus.

She wanted, instead, to be a person worthy of Trevor. Trevor didn't need special. He didn't need anything but Adala. Trevor was what she wanted from life. She was what he wanted. Between them, they could build a small, normal world for just the two of them. She could see that future in the distance, and every word, every kindness, every declaration of love brought their future closer.

Into that new dream, the dream in which she was simply Adala and special only to Trevor, came uneasiness. She did not doubt Trevor — that was the miracle of Trevor. He loved her. She knew it. She didn't chase love. She didn't have to prove herself worthy of it. His presence was steady, comforting, and sometimes almost electric.

It wasn't Trevor that filled her with a quiet but growing anxiety. It was the daydreams of distant childhood, the ones she'd discarded as she left childhood behind. She'd discarded them. They had no place in her life. But some dreams didn't end when you wanted them to end. And some dreams took a turn that led to nightmare; you could feel the change in the air and the landscape, but you couldn't prevent it.

News traveled through Hansleigh and its inns. Merchants and bards and travelers sat at the tables Adala served, exchanging stories. Stories of the strange turns the road could suddenly take. Stories of guards who were lost to the caravans with which they traveled. Strange and terrible screams in the night, or worse, in broad daylight.

She was no child now. She knew — it had always been whispered — that the circus was called when things were too dire, too strange.

No. No. It couldn't happen now. Adala hid everything strange about herself. She tried so very hard *not* to be special. Not to be noticed. Not now. Not *now*.

Because every citizen of every Free Town understood one thing: those the circus called, they kept. The circus became their home. The circus became their family. The loss of family had not terrified her when she had been a child. Her daydreams had not involved abandonment. No, she had assumed that her family would come to see her at the height of the circus's glory, and they would be *so proud*. They could tell her aunts and uncles and their friends that Adala was their daughter.

But the people who joined the circus? They didn't return.

She had listened to the bright and shining stories of the circus as a child. No one shared the dark stories, the horror stories. No one spoke badly of the circus, as if it were the only taboo known in Hansleigh. Adala didn't search for *bad* stories. What she wanted was cold, hard facts. What she needed was the truth.

She stumbled; the forest guards urged her forward at a faster pace than she could maintain. The strangers didn't have the same trouble, but she couldn't resent them. She could—and did—resent herself. Trevor caught her before she could fall.

He didn't speak.

He knew she'd be aware of the change in the shadows across their path; knew she would hear the raucous cries of winged creatures that were not, had never been, birds. Against pursuers on the ground, they could make a stand. Their pursuers, therefore, came from the air.

GERVANNO UNDERSTOOD, at a glance, that Stephen was now worried for, afraid for, Nenyane. Something had arrived on the battlefield, some fell reinforcement, that threatened the sword master. Had it not been for the sudden darkening of sun across earth, where it had broken through the treetops, he might have turned back.

But he recognized these shadowed movements, and had he not, he would have recognized the cries of the creatures whose wingspans were surely created to block light. He did not freeze; he did not stumble. But a darkness was growing within him, a chill, a cold certainty.

Survival had never been guaranteed. Perhaps his life since the death of Evaro had been a fever dream, a final dream; he had not escaped notice. He had not survived. What reality involved so many demons? What reality encompassed the land of three moons and perpetual night? In what reality did a talking, golden fox exist?

What reality could produce Nenyane of Maubreche?

He was brought back to himself when the fox he carried bit his hand. The pain was sharp, if momentary; he had had worse injuries. It was the equivalent of a slap.

"I see," the fox said, its voice far lower than its norm. "We are unlucky today, but I better understand why my Lord chose to ask me to intervene. Do not lose yourself here, Gervanno di'Sarrado. Not while you carry that blade. Jarven."

Jarven ATerafin immediately joined the fox, matching Gervanno's interrupted stride. The group slowed almost to a halt.

"We cannot afford to stop," the fox said. "Nor can we afford to wait. Tell me, Jarven, what do you see in the skies above?"

"I was never a zoologist," Jarven replied. "But were I to hazard a guess, I would say wyverns, in the Old Weston tongue."

"How many?"

"Perhaps a dozen."

"That is a very inaccurate number."

Jarven nodded.

"Do you understand their speech?"

"It is not, to my ears, speech at all."

"Very good. Tell me, do any of these wyverns have riders?"

This question, Jarven took longer to answer. It was therefore Gervanno who said, "Yes."

"They are about to set fire to the forest, or at least to its undergrowth," the fox told them. "At the command of the one who rides. If he is gone, they are likely to disperse."

"Likely, Eldest?" Gervanno asked.

"They may be maddened. Wyverns are not like the forest or the wild elements; they can be raised and trained. They do not have roots with which to ground themselves. But this is not a good sign. Our enemy is either bold or desperate. It is in our interests that it be the latter. I would suggest that we now focus on finding—and destroying —the person in command of the wyverns."

"Do they serve voluntarily?" It was Stephen who asked.

The fox sniffed. "Does it matter?" Before Stephen could answer, he added, "It is *very* likely that they are coming for you, child. They do not need to kill us all if you are dead."

"Why?"

"Because if you are dead, she will not be able to stand and fight. The ignorance of mortals is oft astonishing, even to me, who has seen so much. There is risk, regardless; we are moving away from her, not toward. There is wisdom in that decision. She might find you if you are safe and alive. She will not be able to preserve you on the field she has chosen. Not yet."

"Eldest," Stephen said, voice soft. "Who do you think she is?"

The fox shrugged. "Come, Jarven. Gervanno. Let us test your weapons and your skills."

"Eldest, I cannot fly."

"No, of course not."

"I cannot command the air to carry me; there is only one among us now who might, and he is all but spent."

The fox growled. "Will you waste time with petty, pointless arguments?"

Kallandras looked up to the sky. His lips moved; Gervanno could not hear his words. "I can scatter the wyverns," he said, "but I cannot bring them down. Ser Gervanno is correct. I do not have the power to do what must be done. I might make the attempt, but I am likely to lose consciousness well before it succeeds.

"The wind will not come to the aid of the dead. If a *Kialli* lord rides the wyverns, he might be hard-pressed—but so, too, will we. The earth here is almost awake, and the wind can only barely be prevented from hearing its voice and its challenge." Kallandras then turned to the fox. "If the wind can hear you, it is your voice that must entreat it."

To Gervanno's surprise, Adala cleared her throat; she meant to get someone's attention.

ADALA HAD DONE everything she could to deny the things that had once made her feel so special. She had not *listened*. She had not spoken. She had not acknowledged the things she could see that no one in her family, no one among her shifting group of friends, could see. She did not speak of the circus.

She had learned what she had most feared from an old woman who was willing to speak with her. Mrs. Wheeler had seen the circus perform, not once, but four times. Four times, and she was certain she would live to see a fifth.

Mrs. Wheeler had never been among the blessed. She had never received the invitation to join the circus. She had never been exalted. Those who had were necessary. They were *needed*. Some hint of distant envy had informed the old woman's voice: some desire to know what it might be like to be needed. But the envy was so far away it had almost felt like nostalgia, like momentary daydream.

She'd been needed enough, in ways that had nothing to do with the circus—inasmuch as the Free Towns had nothing to do with the circus.

Occasionally those who migrated to the Free Towns from various kingdoms or countries joined the circus, but they were few; Mrs. Wheeler didn't know how they received their invitations, if they received them the normal way. The normal way was a letter, if the receiver could read. Those that couldn't received a visit from someone in bright circus garb.

Adala could read.

Mostly, it was those born to the Free Towns who were so blessed. Or cursed. Mrs. Wheeler's sister had joined the circus. The old woman had chuckled at her own envy, for she was the younger sister, and Daisy—the invitee—the older.

"I should have known," the old woman said. "I could see my parents' pride. I could see their excitement. I was too young to look beneath them, so caught up in my own envy." Her eyes were an odd shape as she spoke of that time; narrowed, as if in pain. "But I hear it now. None of my children, and none of theirs, were called to the circus.

"But Daisy was. She was excited—she'd always been excitable— and she bounced around town telling anyone who would stand still for long enough that she'd been asked to join the circus. They listened. Some even stopped and turned back. Everywhere we went, for two whole weeks, she was the center of attention.

"Anyone who lives in the Free Towns—not just Hansleigh—can receive the invitation. We take pride in our town, and sometimes those who travel between them carry word. How many of our own are deemed worthy of the circus. How many of Evanston's or Callenton's." Mrs. Wheeler shook her head. "I don't remember what the count was that year; I'm not sure I even paid attention to the friendly competition.

"But even if there had only been one such invitee, it would have been Daisy. I don't think I understood it, back then. But my parents did. They made the most of Daisy during those two weeks. They treated her like a queen. I was young enough to resent it, the first time the circus came to town in my life.

"And I regretted it."

Adala had listened. The old woman's words had sunk roots, sunk teeth, into her thoughts. "Why?"

"Daisy didn't come home when the circus performance was finished. I didn't see her perform—I'm sure she didn't that year, she was so new. But she didn't return to us. And after the circus was gone, I understood that she never would. My parents had known. The moment Daisy received the invitation, the moment she'd opened it and raced around the house squealing, they'd known.

"Those two weeks? That was all the time they'd have left with her. I think they wanted to give her everything they could—a lifetime's worth of everything in two weeks. Because they wouldn't be able to give her anything again. They didn't explain it to me. I don't think they trusted me to keep it to myself. She was happy, and they wanted her to *be* happy, at home, while she still could."

"Did you see her again?" Adala asked. It was the reason she'd come: to ask this question. She hadn't raced around the house in joy. She hadn't bragged about the invitation. She'd told no one.

"I did. It was ten years later. Ten years before the circus came to town again. I'd married, by then. I had two children of my own, both young and exhausting. I was tired, and I almost wanted to stay home and miss the circus entirely."

Adala's brows rose.

"You'll know what it's like, in time. But no one misses the circus when it comes to town, and there are reasons for that. I went. And it was in the pavilions before the actual performance that I saw Daisy again.

"She saw me. She saw me with my children and my husband. I knew her the moment I laid eyes on her; I think it took her a moment to recognize me. She'd missed ten years of my life. She hadn't watched me change and age day by day. She wasn't there at my wedding. She didn't know she'd become an aunt.

"She hadn't changed at all. She kept her hair a little shorter, but nothing about her face had changed. She looked the same, to my eyes, as she had the day she'd left. It's why I knew her. I wanted to talk to her. I guess she didn't want to talk to me — she disappeared before I could reach her.

"Time changes all of us. It doesn't change the circus."

Adala didn't ask Mrs. Wheeler if she'd been certain that the girl she saw was Daisy. She hadn't needed to ask.

"The circus came to town again five years later. Maybe six. Tea's getting cold," she added. Adala rose to set the kettle boiling again, while Mrs. Wheeler waited. "My kids were older, and excited — as if this was their first circus, not their second. Well, it was first for the last two. We entered the circus. I didn't see her immediately — but I did see her when we were seated.

"She was as far away as the sun. But beautiful, the way she'd always been beautiful: lively, bright; reaching, always, for attention. She looked happy. No, she looked radiant. She was the heart of what I remembered; time had worn off the edges of envy, the need to somehow compete. She was Daisy. I was me.

"I didn't tell my children who she was. I didn't want to answer the questions that would follow. Daisy was far too young to be my sister. They knew they had an aunt in the circus. They assumed she'd be an older woman, like me.

"I didn't speak to Daisy. I didn't try. She had her life. I don't know that it made her happy. I had mine, and it did make me happy, some of the time. Unhappy others. But that's the way of life. No life is lived without tears."

"It was another ten years — eleven, maybe — before the circus came to town again. My oldest children were the age Daisy was when she was invited to join the circus. We went, as we always did. Robert volunteered to join the town crew to sweep inns and homes for people who'd somehow missed the announcement.

"She was there, again. She was performing. She looked maybe a year or two older than she had when she left. She didn't see me in the audience. I'm not sure she really *saw* the audience, mind. She knew we were there. She knew we'd be watching."

"So you didn't speak with her."

"No. I didn't try. She was the age of my oldest. She'd spent all her life, from the moment she left us, in the circus. What would I have to say to her? I could tell her she'd become an aunt four times, but she wouldn't know my children. I could talk about our parents — but our parents at the time were older as well. Their worries and their lives might have some overlap with her memories, but the facts of their daily lives wouldn't."

"Did your parents ever try to talk to her?"

Mrs. Wheeler frowned. "I don't know. I never asked. They never asked me, either. They saw her perform. I think seeing her on stage comforted them—but that's a guess on my part. Had Robert joined the circus, and decades later I could see him happy and strong, I'd be comforted. But I'd know that he could never, ever come home."

"So you never spoke with her."

The old woman shook her head. "Not even the last time the circus came to town. I saw her not on the stage, but in the pavilions—a tidy young woman offering hospitality to the visitors. I wanted to tell her that our parents were dead. But they had no last words for her. Nothing to offer or share.

"And telling her that would have changed nothing. Maybe she'd cry. Maybe she wouldn't. But it's not like I could send a letter asking her to come for the funeral, either. She was circus. They weren't. They'd said all their goodbyes to their daughter before she'd left them.

"I hadn't." Mrs. Wheeler's smile was complicated. It didn't brighten her expression at all. "But the circus is coming. I can feel it in my bones. My children have children of their own—those that married, at any rate. They feed themselves. They care for themselves. My husband crossed the bridge years ago. I don't have to mind them. I don't have to take care of them.

"I'm going to find her this time. I'm going to say the goodbyes I was too immature, too petty, to say then."

"Will she recognize you?"

"I don't know. In her shoes, I wouldn't. But I'm not going for her sake; I'm going for my own. The regrets are mine, after all."

"ADALA?" It was Trevor who called her back from her memories, a place she shouldn't have gone when so much was in turmoil.

"I will speak to the wind," she replied, turning to the bard, her expression grave.

SHE COULD ALWAYS SPEAK to the wind. Before she could speak to *people*, she could babble, and the wind heard her voice. She could speak to the fire, small and large, but she didn't like the fire as much, because fire burned.

The first time she had seen a windstorm, she realized wind could cause damage. But it did not damage Adala. Instead, she *flew*.

Her parents knew. Of course they knew. They didn't tell her to hide it — she learned that late, too late. But she suspected that there was no way to hide; how did one hide from the air? How did one hide from the lord of the circus, whose mysterious lands were an integral part of Hansleigh?

She was older when she heard the trees. Older still when they could hear her.

It was only when she was old enough to work in the inn's main dining room that she heard drunken stories about *magic*. She had never considered simple speech magic, before. How could it be? She was no mage. What mage carried plates in an inn?

Still, she knew she was special. She'd known she was special. She'd known that the circus was her destiny, her future home.

It was only when she grew close to Trevor, when she realized she loved him and wanted to spend all of her future by his side, that she understood what a curse destiny could be. She stopped speaking to things that shouldn't naturally hear human speech. It had been hard, she could admit that now — but nothing had been as terrifying as the thought of losing Trevor.

Still, she'd had hope. She had hope until she listened to Mrs. Wheeler's story.

She couldn't just sit still. As stories about the shifting roads, the mysterious disappearances, and even whispered tales of demons became more common in the inn's dining room, with its blend of residents and strangers, her apprehension grew fangs.

Had she not made a plan, she would have been a wreck. But she *did* plan.

"CAN YOU?" the bard asked, as Adala turned her face toward the treetops, and the breeze that moved them.

"I think it's different from what you do," Adala replied.

One of the guards stepped between bard and young woman, but Adala shook her head. "He won't stop me."

"No," the guard said. "But now, you *must* stand as we stand—or consent to be carried. The wind will not hear you if you are not standing in the lands of your birth."

Adala raised her arms, and the guard lifted her, carrying her as if she were a child.

IT WAS CHILDHOOD SHE ABANDONED. She'd spent enough time in the inn with its various customers; she understood the *theory* of escape. She had no intention of fleeing without purpose. Without notice, yes. But if they ran without any plan, they might starve before long. She knew it wouldn't be *easy*, but all she cared about was *possible*.

She knew she couldn't hide in the town itself. She couldn't simply wait until the rest of the town emptied, heading toward the circus. That would have been best, but the circus came to town when the town itself was in danger. It was that danger that she and Trevor had to avoid.

All her plans. But the fear that should have dogged them both was brightened by both commitment and excitement. They were determined, having made their choice. They would be together. They would live together. No one could stop them.

No one, Adala thought, as dreams crumbled to ash and the wind swept them away, but Adala and Trevor themselves.

She had woken the trees. She had called upon the talent to which she'd been born. She'd known the trees would respond. She hadn't expected what they *did* do, but she'd expected they would help somehow.

She lifted her voice, calling the wind, singing—as she often sang in a childhood so far removed she could barely remember it at all—because song could carry sentiment in a way simple words could not. The arms that carried her were hard, solid; they *felt* like wood.

She had never tested the effects of that song, hummed quietly throughout parts of her working day, beyond the loose borders of Hansleigh. But she accepted as truth that it was only in the lands the circus master had granted the Free Towns that the wind would, or could, hear her.

The bard could make himself heard anywhere—but apparently it was costly. It exhausted him. He had learned to use the wind in combat, as if it were a complex, subtle weapon.

It had never exhausted Adala. The wind listened. Did it obey? She couldn't remember. The wind was her invisible, childhood friend. Children could boss each other around without thought or much deliberation. Adala did not recall attempting to do that to the wind.

She did not do it now. But she felt the wind. She heard the wind. And she saw the winged creatures slowly black out the sky. The trees were stiff, silent; they did not scream or flee. But some wanted to run back to the trees in the forest that were now far behind them.

The winged creatures breathed fire. Exhaled it from above. This wasn't a fire that could hear Adala speak, but she didn't try to coax or command it. She knew she would fail. Crowns of trees became crowns of flame wherever their enemies exhaled. She was horrified; she knew where her guards came from. But the wyverns concentrated on clearing the obstruction just beneath where they flew, and the rooted trees were farther away.

She lifted voice, lifted song, beseeching the wind as she did.

Above her upturned face, the wyverns faltered, their formation breaking as the wind took up Adala's song, and returned it to her, joining the ebb and flow of her breath as if her breath was all of the wind itself.

No one interrupted her. No one attempted to tell her what she must —or must not—say. They watched, almost enraptured, this tiny audience that should have been standing in the safety of the circus itself.

The wind's voice was not the only voice she could hear; it wasn't the only voice to join her song, strengthening it with harmonies that sent a sweet shock from her ears to her spine. She stood at the periphery of a chorus, and she turned toward it instinctively.

There was the circus; she could almost see it in the distance, as if trees and forests and distance were a lie. A lie she'd told herself all her life. A lie she desperately—so desperately—had wanted to believe.

KALLANDRAS TURNED TO TREVOR; Trevor, shadowed as they were all shadowed by the great wings of flying serpents, was smiling. Tears trailed down his cheeks, but they were silent; he did not sob.

He was staring at Adala, and only Adala; something about her song had caught and held his attention, as if it were a voice he had yearned for all his life. To hear it now was an unexpected gift, and it had always been the unexpected gifts that elicited tears from the audience.

Even Kallandras could hear her song. He could hear, above their heads, the wind's voice; the wind *was singing*. It did not fight Adala; she did not need to cajole, to manipulate. She did not need to tell the wild air what to do—the wild air responded instinctively. Were there enemies in its path? Yes. But they were Adala's enemies, and the wind swept them away as if they were gnats, or less. As if they were beneath notice.

This wild air was not something Kallandras could touch or bespeak. At best, he could avoid its notice, and he did so, now. The earth beneath their feet did not rumble; it did not threaten. But it, too, seemed to thrum as Adala sang.

Her voice was not strong. It was not trained. It would not—or should not—carry.

What had the circus master made of these lands and the people who were born to them? Common wisdom—even ancient, common wisdom—made clear that mortals did not and could not command the wilderness; they could not, without intervention, bespeak it at all. Had Kallandras not worn one of the five rings, the final making of Myrddion, he, too, would have been beneath the element's notice.

The tree that carried Adala glanced at the bard. "We must move, now. They cannot yet attack us, but one of the dead is carried above. If he lands, she will be in danger."

STEPHEN MADE no attempt to speak to Nenyane, but he'd never had the need. What he knew, she knew, unless she was angry enough to deliberately ignore him.

She therefore knew about the wyverns; knew that they had appeared in the skies above the Hunters, and knew that Adala had—somehow—called the wild air. She did not speak, did not question him; by that he knew just how hard-pressed she was. But she was grateful that the *Kialli* lord she did not know had chosen to hunt elsewhere. She had feared—momentarily—what the outcome would be should he join Ishavriel.

Ishavriel had not desired a victory gained in such a fashion. She was certain.

She wanted to leave Meralonne; she wanted to race toward Stephen. She did not. As if Meralonne—as if Illaraphaniel—defined the battlefield itself, she could not desert it, not yet. But she struggled.

Stephen did not struggle in the same way. The guard who now carried Adala set the pace of their retreat as Adala's voice dropped to a murmur. If she could command the wind, she seemed both surprised and frustrated at the area of affect over which she could assert control. Directly above the path they walked, the skies cleared; the wyverns recovered to either side of it.

The forest guard had said that she must advance only on the path they could perceive; they had said it was narrow. That narrow gap extended to the sky and to the wind that willingly obeyed her. The wyverns could not be moved beyond that narrow area, not by the wild air. They adjusted their attacks, their fire coming in at a steeper angle; Stephen could hear the commands given them, although he could not quite distinguish words. Something in the voice chilled him; something in its folds scraped against thought and instinct.

Your instincts. Nenyane did not explain further.

The creatures weren't demons. They were, in some fashion, alive. They could fly in the skies above normal, mortal lands—demonstrably. But they obeyed the command of one of the *Kialli*, and he was high above the ground, carried aloft by the wyverns. They could not breathe their fire across the treetops above the path Stephen's eyes couldn't distinguish from the rest of the forest.

They could, and did, set trees to either side of that path alight. Those trees could fall across the path; nothing prevented it. Alex could, and did, cross the boundary that didn't seem to exist for the Hunters, their dogs, or Gervanno. Gervanno, however, kept to the path, following in the footsteps the guards laid down. Where they could not, or did not, step, the cerdan would not step.

Fire burned the treetops, and traveled down their lengths, but it burned slowly; the wyverns could not bring the trees down with that breath alone.

Stephen was surprised that no wild, elemental fire joined their breath—but perhaps it couldn't. Perhaps, on this path, the elements obeyed only those beings who served the circus master, the lord of these lands.

He had so many questions, but only one was relevant: could they make it to Hansleigh in time?

———

GERVANNO'S QUESTION WAS DIFFERENT. He understood Adala's import; had he not, they would not now be running beneath skies darkened, constantly, by almost black wings. He kept his eyes on Trevor's back. Trevor jogged between two of the trees, as close to Adala as he could be. The boy was not accustomed to battlefield retreat; he looked up, constantly, and stumbled twice because he could not run while doing so.

Gervanno did not blame the boy. He was not a soldier; he was not trained to be one. He was a blacksmith, a blacksmith's son; his skill was not martial in nature, but war required blacksmiths.

War required farmers.

War required soldiers. Those soldiers came from the ranks of the untrained. It was in their training, in their arming, that armies were created. But armies were imperfect because people were imperfect. Training Trevor was not Gervanno's duty; it was not his responsibility. But seeing him to Hansleigh alive now was.

It was secondary to Stephen's survival.

It was critical to Stephen's survival.

The fox growled. He had not allowed himself to be set down. "No," the fox said, although Gervanno had not spoken. "The path is troublesome here; it is far easier to traverse it in the fashion I have chosen than it would be on foot.

"But if the wyverns seek to land, set me down then. You will not be able to fight effectively against such creatures if you cannot use both of your arms."

"You speak of their commander."

"I do. I am uncertain that he will be able to land safely on the road we now travel, but as the mortals have proven, these lands are tied to the lands in which they otherwise live. It is quite possible that he could attack without ever crossing the faint border."

Gervanno said nothing. He knew that, should the creature land, they were dead.

No. No. Things were not the same, now. Evaro's caravan had been guarded by men who knew little to nothing about demons. By his side,

Kallandras of Senniel ran. So, too, all of his companions in the wilderness that had threatened Bowgren's very existence. He had faced creatures that would not have existed in the worst of his nightmares, and he had survived.

They had survived.

But even thinking it, Nenyane came to mind and stubbornly remained there: she was absent.

SHE MOVED ACROSS THE BATTLEFIELD, well aware that wars were not pretty, scheduled occurrences; they were not balls or teas or audiences with the powerful. They occurred where and as they occurred.

Above her, red and blue light continued to flash, and the skies were almost purple overhead. But the one *Kialli* she had feared had not remained to fight; he had summoned his wyverns, and he had sent them across the contested skies. They were not dead; they could traverse the wilderness with far more ease than the demons might.

She knew that demons were, in some fashion, eternal, but they were not invulnerable. Kill their bodies, and their essence returned to the Hells, there to wait a second summons. Or a hundredth. That they moved at all was a testament to the lives they had surrendered to join the Lord of the Hells.

Dust flew in the wake of her sword; the flat of her blade caught and reflected the true swords of the Arianni above: blue and red. Alive and dead. Sworn and foresworn. Pain persisted long past the point of death for those who had chosen the Lord of the Hells.

She moved further from them, through the ranks of the dead; none were strong enough that she needed to come to a halt to stand her ground.

There was a portal here; there must be a portal here. Or perhaps just beyond. She could see, could sense, a space, a gap in the demonic formation. Leaderless, those who had chosen to surrender all memory to avoid their eternal pain, the demons drove themselves forward seeking sustenance: seeking to cause the pain that fed them.

They would not find that pain in Nenyane, or from her.

But they would not find true death, either. Could she, she would have ended them completely; it would not have required thought. But perhaps that would have been a kindness, and Nenyane had never felt a need, a desire, to be kind. That had never been her duty.

Above the heads of the demons, many of whom now resembled nightmare dogs, she could see the glimmering magic, a strange rent in the air, framed by a semi-circle that resembled tarnished silver: it was mostly black, but some hint of light broke through the odd formation.

Standing in that portal, arms crossed, was a woman Nenyane had never seen. Her dark eyes were narrowed to slits, her hair was wild, and her expression was almost...petulant. Of all things she had expected to find this close to the portal, a mortal woman of middle-age was not one.

"I want to go to the circus!" she shouted. "You said we would go to the circus!"

CHAPTER FOURTEEN

T he woman's voice was an odd combination of whine and shout; Nenyane was certain it would carry across the whole of the battlefield. She wouldn't have been surprised had the woman stamped her feet like a furious child.

But if she felt she would not have been surprised, she was proven wrong; when the woman opened her crossed arms, her hands were fists, and she *did* stomp the ground, shouting. "I want to see the circus!"

Demons flew—some literally, some figuratively—as she gave way to fury. A tantrum of this nature was *not* something one encountered on the battlefield, unless that field had somehow grown to encompass civilian villages, civilian children. This one had not.

Fire sprouted from the woman's fingers, a punctuation to her anger. That fire devoured the demons who now had two enemies to face: the woman at their back—the woman who, to Nenyane's eye, was the anchoring support for the magic that held the portal in place—and Nenyane herself.

It was from the portal that the demons had emerged—and more had seemed, before she set eyes on the woman, likely to follow. But nothing came out of the portal behind the almost shrieking mage. Had Nenyane been among the horde of demons awaiting transit, she would have avoided coming anywhere near the woman's fury.

"You promised we could go to the circus!"

Each syllable was a storm; the sound of her voice all but overwhelmed the sounds of *Kialli* conflict and broken, shattered kinship. The ground trembled with her rage; had Nenyane been a different person, she might have stumbled, might have been driven to her knees. The demons were.

She had no qualms about taking advantage of their momentary vulnerability. This woman was not her comrade-at-arms—she was theirs.

She must be theirs.

The shape of the portal shifted; it shrank as fire consumed demons. Nenyane cut them down, but they didn't fear Nenyane in the way they feared the stranger. Nenyane had seldom worried about demonic pain; she had sometimes wondered if demons felt pain at all. But they must; the death Nenyane offered and the death the woman offered were different, and clearly Nenyane's was less terrible.

But she understood why. There was something about this woman and her shrieks that spoke of, that implied, power—a power so great, so majestic, she might not have been mortal at all. Had she not spoken recognizable words, had their content not been so immediately accessible, even Nenyane might have stilled for a moment. But the woman didn't appear to notice Nenyane at all.

It was almost as if the killing of demons was so natural, so expected, that someone doing so at the back of the growing army was irrelevant.

It was not irrelevant to the combatants.

From across the field, from above, it, a single word fell like sudden storm.

"*Anya!*"

THE MADDENED mage looked up at the word. Ishavriel's voice had caused a ripple across the field of battle, as if it were storm, and the ground-bound combatants were stalks of wheat. It invoked only displeasure from the mage. She *stomped her feet*. "You *promised*!"

Had Ishavriel not been locked in combat with Illaraphaniel, the woman would be dead.

But he was and she knew it; there was something about her that reminded Nenyane of the servants' children—and Robart—in the

Maubreche manor. Ishavriel was distant, and he was occupied with work he could not safely avoid. She wanted his attention. His work could *wait*; her demand could not.

Nenyane revised her opinion. There was no child in the Maubreche manor who could behave so poorly. Not even Robart at his worst, just barely out of toddlerhood, could have managed the spectacularly poor judgment this woman now showed.

She lashed out with clenched fist; her fist hit the defining line of the portal.

The portal buckled, listing instantly to the left.

"Anya!"

She hit the right side, a more deliberate blow.

Nenyane had intended to find the source of the growing army of demons; she had planned to take down the mage—or mages—responsible for what she assumed was a gate. There were too many demons on this field; she could not stop them all. She could, however, stop their numbers from growing.

It was a risk, the decision too swift to be called calculated. She fought her way through demons toward the possible source of their incursion, intending to destroy it. No action had been necessary on her part. No demons would emerge from what had been a large, standing portal. It was gone.

The mage did not notice her at all. How much power must one have to fail to notice an enemy of Nenyane's caliber?

But no. No, this was not about power. In Robart's childhood years, power was no part of the equation. To Robart, all of the power resided in the hands of his parents, and his rage that they chose to withhold what he desired did not allow for simple thoughts about the consequences of his behavior; consequences implied the future, and he was so wed to his broken fury in the moment, the future might not have existed at all.

This woman was very like that child. Nenyane had disliked Robart when she had first arrived at the manse. The boy was loud, he was feeble, he was a brat with no sense of right or wrong. The most Robart could do, should things descend into a state of war, was divert the attentions of the adults who *could* fight it.

Robart had been selfish. He had been messy. He had had no sense of what he should, and should not, touch. Even Robart's voice had bothered her—it was so high-pitched, always teetering on the edge of whining. Nenyane hated whining.

But Robart was precious to Stephen—Stephen, who had been just as irritated by his brother's random behavior as Nenyane had been. When not irritated, Stephen even managed to find some joy in Robart's existence; in his ready smiles, his laughter, his wont to trail after Stephen no matter where Stephen went. Some of Robart's worst tantrums involved the drill yard; Robart was considered far too young to safely observe Stephen's lessons.

He had thrown himself on the floor, pounding, kicking, and screaming until he ran out of breath and was forced to inhale. It had been a truly annoying spectacle.

This woman, this Anya, at least spared Nenyane that. She did not throw herself across the forest floor; she did not punch it and kick it and wail wordlessly until she was exhausted.

But she, too, seemed immune to consequence. It was her pain, her disappointment, her demands, that were of import; Nenyane wasn't certain the woman *saw* anything else. She certainly didn't see Nenyane, moving toward her, armed. Nor did she see the empty space immediately within range of the arc of Nenyane's moving sword.

Still, Nenyane knew this woman was a grave danger. Knew it intellectually—how could she not? The stranger had built the portal that she had also, in fury, just destroyed. The demons had come through that portal. Not even Illaraphaniel could hold a portal of this nature in place for long.

What she had done once, she might do again. She was a true threat. But, all her screaming and whining aside, it was viscerally impossible to think of her that way. Nenyane, who never hesitated on the field of battle, hesitated now.

Hesitation was death.

The screaming woman had—clearly—created the portal through which an army had passed. If she could do it here, she could do it anywhere. She could do it in Breodanir. If.

The woman didn't seem aware of Nenyane at all. Nenyane bisected a demon, and as ash cleared, she leapt.

WHAT STEPHEN FEARED as he ran at a jog through these unfamiliar forests was not Nenyane's death. She had faced demons in Maubreche before; they had both been children, although childhood would not contain them for much longer. Stephen had never seen her injured. When she had first arrived, it had been clear that her life *could* be threatened—but nothing that had happened since that day could explain to Stephen how.

It was the reason he had refused to allow her to swear the hunt-brother's oath. She had wanted to, not because it was a public declaration of her loyalty to her Hunter, but because refusing to do so would cause unnecessary noise: first, from their family; and second, from the priesthood and any other Hunter Lord who felt he had the right to offer unasked-for advice.

She hadn't understood his decision, although perhaps that was unfair. She understood the significance of the oath; she understood that it was a *true* oath, sanctified by the Hunter God. She just didn't care.

If she could swear that she would die in his stead, why should it matter? She had every intention of doing just that. It changed nothing.

But it did. To Stephen, it did. Being oathbound was the *only* way he could imagine Nenyane dying. She could be foresworn. If she were, Stephen's desires, the desires of the priesthood, the desires of their parents, who had grown to love the prickly, blunt orphan, would count for nothing. Stephen might call upon the god who was his father, and the god might arrive—but no one knew better than Stephen that even Stephen's pleas to invalidate the oath would not move the god at all.

If Nenyane wanted to swear the huntbrother's oath, she could do it in private; Stephen would have no ceremonial part in accepting it.

No, it wasn't her death he feared. It was this. It was Nenyane, so focused on battle she could see almost nothing else, killing *people*. If demons had once been people, in a past so ancient its truth existed only in myth or story, they were not people now; they were walking, intelligent corpses. They were creatures who desired Stephen's death.

She could cut down one, or ten, or several dozen; it did not bother Stephen at all.

Nor would it bother her Hunter if she could somehow cut down the wyverns who were literally blackening the surrounding forest—and the wyverns *were* living beings. He had barely blinked when she had killed the assassin, a hair's breadth before the assassin could end his life.

He reached out for her, shouting, the bond between them almost a physical constraint.

Nenyane's reply was wordless, visceral—a snarl of emotion. She pushed back. Stephen almost stumbled, but maintained both footing and concentration as shadows clipped the path down which they ran. If the wyverns could not fly directly overhead—and Adala ensured they could not—their wingspans were large enough they could still shadow the path.

He grimaced. He could not afford to fully look through Nenyane's eyes. It always took concentration, but as the physical distance between Hunter and huntbrother grew, the need for concentration deepened. He didn't need to look. He understood what she'd intended when she began to fight her way to the back of the demonic horde.

He understood what she'd found. He knew that she faced a woman who was now having a temper tantrum—one that Stephen himself would have found surprising, given where the woman was standing. All of this was clear in her thoughts; he could hear what he could not take the risk of forcing himself to see.

He knew when their thoughts diverged; knew when her focus shifted; knew when she'd reached a decision.

Nenyane, no! Don't kill her!

She was instantly angry. She was beyond angry. *She brought the demons!*

He did not argue facts with her; he did not offer possible, nuanced explanations that would make the woman less of a threat. Nenyane was far too certain about what she'd seen. On some days in his youth, he'd wondered what it would be like if Nenyane were like the Maubreche dogs. She'd been pretty angry about that, as well.

They'd ended up brawling, one of the few times it had happened, and when the reason for the fight was finally discovered, his *father* had been furious—at Stephen. His mother had argued that Stephen's age should be taken into consideration. So had Arlin.

How angry would they be, now?

What would Corwin say to him? Would he agree with Nenyane? Would he agree with Stephen? Would he demand that something that could summon a small demonic army be destroyed? Had the woman *been* a demon, there would be no argument. Had Stephen been by his huntbrother's side, there would be no argument.

Stephen would not have killed her unless and until she attempted to kill him. Because she *wasn't* demonic. She was a person.

If I waited, it would be too late.

And if you killed —if you could *kill —without cause, it would a different kind of too late!*

You're not here —it's my *decision. Or are you afraid I'll become a murderer?*

What does that even mean? He did stumble. His dogs had shortened the distance they kept between their Hunter and their running positions, tightening their formation as if proximity were necessary. They could not *see* the threat their master felt, but they were aware that he felt it.

We were made for war —and this is war. There are no bad guys or good guys —there are survivors. Where she stands, there won't be survivors. The demons know it. If you were here, you'd know it. I can end her here. You'll regret it if I don't.

He would regret it if she did.

She was right. He knew she was right. He could not argue against the facts that drove her. The screaming child in the body of an adult Gervanno's age was a true threat. Nenyane believed that, were it not for her, the demons that gathered outside of Hansleigh would not be there in the numbers they were.

A handful would have been enough to destroy that town. It would not be enough to assault the circus. But demons were not humans; perhaps they did not know. The wilderness rejected them utterly, save where a lord accepted their presence as allies of convenience. The circus master would never be such a lord.

But the circus master *would* accept the presence of the mage, if Nenyane did not kill her.

Don't kill her, Stephen told his huntbrother. *Please, Nenyane —she's a child.*

She is not a child. She's at least twice your age. But Stephen, were she, and were she capable of unleashing a demonic army in the middle of Breodanir, would you make the same demand?

Yes. Yes. And more confidently. *Please.*

It'll be on your head, not mine. You know what I think is smart, here.

Yes.

NENYANE AND STEPHEN could have stood side by side, shouting their argument, fists clenched as if they were, once again, children in Maubreche, for all the stranger—Anya?—would have noticed.

Nenyane was grateful Stephen was moving—still moving—toward safety. It was fast becoming a questionable safety. In any other domain, the rule of the lord was law, and it was a law that could warp and twist every aspect of that lord's lands.

Here, it was different. She knew it, but could not put it into words. Nenyane had been *accepted* into the circus's territory, but only because she was Stephen's huntbrother. Had she arrived on foot, alone, her memories shattered and her future uncertain, she was almost certain she would not have been allowed to pass through the circus gates.

She could not be certain. What Illaraphaniel had felt before they had entered Hansleigh, Nenyane herself had not felt.

Had the lord been absolute, Adala would not have fled; she could not. Her absence would possibly be the ruin of the circus; it would allow for the deaths of all of Hansleigh's people. Yet he had insisted that choice be Adala's.

Stephen did not consider it a choice; nor did Gervanno. Alex considered it extortion.

Nenyane saw it as a choice. Illaraphaniel saw it as choice. The bard was utterly silent; she could not tell where he fell.

Nenyane knew choice. She understood it. She had made her choice the moment her feet had first touched Maubreche soil, and that decision had never wavered. It would never waver while Stephen lived. But to Stephen, that had been a choice.

And to Stephen, now, Anya was a choice. Nenyane could kill Anya now, or she could leave her, fleeing while the distant Ishavriel's rage and fury grew. She had no doubt that the woman in full throes of hysterical tantrum would do more harm—or at least as much harm—as Nenyane herself could.

Perhaps Ishavriel would kill her. But, had that been likely, she would already be dead. Perhaps her power—which was almost blinding in its density, its intensity—prevented that. Or perhaps she could, like any other young child, be cajoled. Perhaps the desire to *be* the good child, and receive the love given to a good child, was Ishavriel's lever.

She wanted to kill Anya.

But she, too, did not want to break any part of the binding that

held Stephen to her, that held her to Stephen. Not all of the bond was
pragmatic. Oaths were sworn by people, and people were emotional,
their emotions layered upon shared experience, that experience
becoming foundational knowledge.

Stephen could not prevent her from doing what must be done in
any way save this: he could *ask*. He could tell her, without words, what
would break — and she could decide whether or not the break would
damage things irreparably.

She did not put up her sword; that was suicide.

But she did leave it in one hand. The other, she almost hesitantly
extended to the woman who was still rolling about on the ground in
tearful fury.

Fine, she told Stephen. *You win.*

He said nothing; she was irritated at the relief that washed
over him.

Nenyane exhaled. "Anya?"

The woman did not hear her, so focused was she on her unjust
deprivation.

Nenyane tried again, to no effect. She drew closer; she did not wish
to raise voice because Ishavriel and Illaraphaniel remained locked in
combat, but Ishavriel was aware of Anya. If Nenyane spoke too loudly,
he would be aware of her. Ah, no; he was already aware of Nenyane.
He was not aware that she now stood within sword's reach of Anya,
and she didn't want that attention yet.

"Anya?" The third time she spoke she was almost leaning over the
prone woman, whose screams had, for the moment, quieted into heart-
broken sobs. She rolled over then, her eyes widening as she looked up
at Nenyane. At the empty hand Nenyane held out, a wordless offer of
help. It was the empty hand she saw first; the sword hand, second.

It was the empty hand to which she responded. "Yes?" She placed
one of her own hands across Nenyane's. Had she desired Nenyane's
death, she could have achieved it in that moment. When their hands
touched, when their skin touched, Nenyane felt a shock of terrible elec-
tricity: a storm of magic, a power so vast, so deep, it was an ocean.

Were it not for Stephen's presence, she would have pulled away —
at the very least. But he was there, assessing, when he should have
been running.

Anya's hand tightened, and Nenyane put weight into her own,
pulling the older woman to her feet. Her dress was dirty. It was also

unusual, the fabric an odd blend of sheen and matte in shades of purple. It was *not* a dress for a battlefield, if there'd ever been such a thing. Nor was it a dress for a ball, at least not the Breodani balls with which Nenyane was familiar.

The skirt was cut and sewn so it fell in a full circle which would allow for free movement, to a point; it was too long to run in.

"Who are you?" Anya demanded, her expression almost ludicrously shifty.

"Nenyane."

"Why are you here?"

Nenyane shrugged. "I don't like demons."

"Me either. They're fighting," she added, looking to the sky.

"They are," Nenyane replied. She had given her choice of words into Stephen's hands, and he guided her. She would never have spoken to the most powerful mortal mage she had ever encountered this way, otherwise. "But you said you wanted to see the circus."

Suspicion warred with greed, but greed won. Stephen was right. Something about this terrifying woman was a child. If one disregarded her age, there was something more than child behind those bright eyes; a flicker of a different awareness, a different understanding.

You don't understand how dangerous she is. She didn't ask Stephen to change his mind. He wouldn't. She cast a backward glance to the two who ruled the sky. The portal was gone. There was a possibility this mage could recreate it—but not instantly, not immediately. Nenyane didn't want her to try.

"Where did you get that ribbon?" Anya asked. Surrounded by demons, beneath the flashing red and blue that formed their sky, it was the ribbon that drew her attention.

"The circus," Nenyane replied. There was no lie in the words. Nenyane was uncertain whether or not Anya would detect a lie, but knew that she could not easily survive if she did and chose to take offense.

Humans did not rule in the wilderness.

Nenyane was certain Anya could, should she understand the wilderness and desire to be lord.

"He promised I could see the circus," Anya said, brows folding and eyes narrowing. The hand that held Nenyane's tightened; the free hand balled into fist.

"He came to destroy the circus," Nenyane replied. "So he didn't lie."

"Destroy it? Why?"

"Because the master of the circus doesn't like demons either."

"No demons?"

"No demons in the circus."

"He said I could see the circus," Anya repeated. "He *said I could*."

"If the demons mean to destroy it, you would see the circus — but it wouldn't be any fun, then."

"I don't like demons."

"Do you like circuses?"

Anya smiled and nodded. "I *like* the circus."

Nenyane frowned. "You've been to the circus before?"

"Of course! When the circus comes to town, *everyone* goes to the circus. Didn't you know?"

"I only learned that today," Nenyane replied.

"But why are you here?"

"Because some of the townsfolk weren't in town when the circus gates opened."

Anya's eyes widened. "They'll die!"

Nenyane nodded.

"But you won't."

"No, Anya. I won't die. Did you want to come with me to the circus?"

"Yes." She did not let go of Nenyane's hand. She looked past the demons. "Do you know how to get there?" Before Nenyane could answer, she said, "I do. I know. I remember."

"Should we meet up with the townspeople?"

"I don't know where they are," was the hesitant reply. "But you said you came to find them?"

"We did. My friends found them. I stayed to kill demons."

"Did they desert you?"

The whole of Nenyane's body stiffened at the sudden shift of tone. It was a reminder that the rage of a child could be all-encompassing and endless. Mortal children, however, did not have — would never have — the power that Anya did.

"No," Nenyane said, the word swift, the tone urgent. "No, they didn't. I'm the best swordsman they have, and the townspeople can't fight demons. I offered to stay. I told them to leave. If they stayed, the townspeople would die, and we would have left the circus for no reason. They didn't desert me," she said, forcing herself to speak more slowly. "They would never desert me. But someone had to stay to keep the demons away from them."

"You're not angry?"

"I'm not angry. But if my friend had insisted on staying, I would have been. At him."

Anya's frown was almost etched in steel. "Him?"

"He's my brother."

Her frown cleared, then. "You should find him."

Nenyane nodded. She turned toward the demons; they were circling, but they had not attempted to attack again.

Anya made clear why. She had one hand free, but the gestures that many mages relied on to cast spells of power were not necessary for Anya. Fire was her weapon, here; it flooded out from the tips of her fingers in a burst of orange, red, and gold. The damage Nenyane's blade could do didn't come close. Nenyane didn't think Meralonne at the height of his power could have destroyed as much.

"I won't let the demons hurt you," Anya told Nenyane, her voice both soft and determined — as if it was Nenyane who was the child, and Nenyane who was in need of protection. As if she couldn't see the sword in Nenyane's hand at all.

In the storm that raged above, Ishavriel shouted a single, enraged word.

Anya's name.

THE SKIES WERE the grey of charcoal and flame and wide, wide wings; the wyverns did not land. Adala's forest guardians thought the wyverns could, but if they landed here, the guardians were safe for the moment.

"We should not run," the fox said. "I have told you this before. Running is what prey does. Surely you must be aware of this: it is still-ness that fails to attract their attention."

Gervanno did not stumble.

"You understand this truth on an instinctive level," the fox continued. Gervanno did not spare breath to argue; he knew a lecture when he heard it, and no teacher of his youth wished argument. The only time words were required were when a question that demanded an answer was asked. The fox had not yet asked.

Had he, he might have told the fox that there were situations in which men retreated, surrendering a field they could not win. This was such a field; it was a small miracle that the Hunters and their companions had survived thus far.

A small miracle offered by a young woman who had fled Hansleigh in the hope of building a different life with the man she had chosen. The wind did not obey her commands the way it might have obeyed the bard; none of the party were lifted off their feet, and none flew. The bard did not attempt to take combat to the air, even though he could; Gervanno had seen him in his martial flight.

"They cannot land on this path," the fox said, as if divining the whole of Gervanno's thought in a glance.

To the side, trees burned from their crowns down; the forest would be a smoking ruin everywhere but where the guardians ran. The Hunters and their dogs followed them. Trevor jogged beside Adala, and the trees allowed it. No one else ran in the center of their formation now.

Jarven ATerafin kept pace with Gervanno.

They were interrupted only once by a cry of rage that shook even the wyverns in their flight; it threatened to shatter the sky, if that were possible.

"When I tell you to put me down," the fox said, "do so immediately —but keep running. Do not deviate from the path or pace set by the *arborii*. Do I make myself clear?"

Gervanno nodded.

"We may have more difficulty in the immediate future. Jarven."

Jarven ATerafin nodded as well. His expression implied irritation, not anger. Gervanno would not have dared to speak to Jarven thus, but Gervanno was not, and would never be, Jarven's master. Jarven faded from view; he did not peel off, he did not stop. He simply, and slowly, vanished.

"Jarven can take care of himself," the fox said, although Gervanno had not spoken. "If he cannot survive something as simple as this, he will never survive what he desires in the future. Are you concerned?"

"He is a man of power," Gervanno replied. "I am not."

"Power is subtle and contextual. He is not yet what he wants to be, and he is therefore tested." The fox's voice was grim but amused. "You do not desire what he desires. Were you to face him as he is now, he is not guaranteed to be the victor, unless he chooses subterfuge—but that is not beyond him.

"I, however, do not wish to engage in that contest. Where outcomes are certain, they are boring. Jarven's future is not certain. Do you wish to warn me that he is a danger?" the fox chuckled. "Were he not capable of being at least that, I would never have taken him in." The fox fell silent, gaining weight.

Gervanno slowed.

"What I like about you," the fox said, as Gervanno knelt to set him down, "is your lack of words, or rather, your lack of need to hear them. My cub has alerted me to a possible danger. Given Illara-phaniel's absence, it is by far the gravest danger we have faced today."

We.

It was Stephen who turned. "No—she's not a danger."

The Southern guard turned to his titular master. "She?"

"Nenyane is bringing a woman she discovered on the battlefield."

The fox's eyes rounded, brows rising so high they would have vanished into hairline had he been a person.

"A woman? Is that *all* you have to say?"

Given the boy's expression, Gervanno would not have been surprised if it was. But the Breodani, while ruled by their matriarchs, were not from the South.

"What would you add, Eldest?"

"The so-called woman she *discovered* on the battlefield is the biggest of the dangers we might face today—and that would include the wyverns and the *Kialli*."

Stephen exhaled. "She's from the townships," he said.

The forest guard slowed so as not to create a larger gap between Adala and the stragglers.

One of the guards turned back to join Stephen. "Please repeat that."

"The woman is from the townships. She wants...she wants to go to the circus."

"Are you certain?"

Stephen nodded.

The guard then turned to the fox. "Eldest, if Stephen is correct, you are not to harm the stranger—not here, not on this path. If you feel you must confront her, it is necessary for your safety that you do so beyond the path we travel." The voice was grave.

For the first time since the fox had crossed their paths, Gervanno's arms were free. The fox, however, chose to trust the guardian, and made it clear that Gervanno did not require two arms. He walked to the cerdan and placed a paw, rather heavily, across his right boot.

Gervanno lifted him, scanning the forest for some sign of Jarven. And waiting for a glimpse of Nenyane.

***

STEPHEN UNDERSTOOD WHY THE FOX, sight unseen, considered Anya the gravest of the dangers they might face as they tried to make their way to Hansleigh. He had not seen her, but he had heard her wailing fury. He had heard every reaction she'd engendered in his huntbrother. He knew that she had created the portal through which the demons had traveled. It was hard to believe that she could be such an exceptionally powerful mage and still have a screaming tantrum as if she were less than four years old.

If she lost her temper here, it would be, in the end, on Stephen. Any deaths would be on Stephen's head; Nenyane had wanted her dead. Nenyane had intended to kill her while she was screaming in thwarted rage about a *circus*.

But even so, he had chosen to take that risk.

"I don't think she likes men," Stephen said, into the silence of anticipation. "If we need to approach her, it's best that Adala—or Nenyane—do so."

"And if we cannot?"

Stephen exhaled. "Anya is her name—or the name she's called—and she can take care of herself. If Anya wanted, she could torch the whole forest without thought."

"You said she desires the circus?" It was the bard who asked. He had joined them so silently that Stephen hadn't been aware of his presence until the moment he chose to speak.

"She was apparently promised she could visit it." Stephen frowned. "Do you know her?"

"I know of her. Who made that promise to her?"

"She didn't say."

"What did she say?"

"She wanted to see the circus. She was promised she could go to the circus. She was furious because she wasn't at the circus yet."

Kallandras did not seem surprised. At all.

"But it became clear as she became calm enough to converse that she's seen the circus before—she said that when the circus came to town, *everyone* went to the circus. I think she's from the townships."

"Did she run? Did she run away like I did?" And last, Adala joined them.

Stephen had no idea. Nenyane hadn't asked—and did not.

It was the forest guard who carried Adala that answered. "No. Can you not sense it now? She is not a force that the circus master could safely contain. But she is of the townships, as Stephen presumed. We cannot hurt her."

"I do not serve your lord," the fox said, from his perch in Gervanno's arm. "I most assuredly can should it be required."

"Eldest," Kallandras said, the word inflected in such a way that it contained depths of respect and acknowledgement that Stephen was uncertain he could produce. "Fate unwinds in its own fashion. Perhaps this woman, lost to the Free Towns, is necessary to the survival of the circus itself. I ask, as boon, that you stay your hand unless she attacks you directly.

"I ask further that you take no more offense at her words than you would that of a child new to walking; she does not understand the currents of respect that the wilderness demands."

"Ah, but she does," the fox replied. "In the wilderness, it is the greater power that demands respect, in the end. Only those with less power are forced to placate." His teeth gleamed bright as he chuckled; they made the forest seem gloomy and shadowed, for all that fire burned above and the sun was at its height.

It was clear to Stephen that Gervanno wished to continue their forward jog. Stopping to chat in the middle of a strategic retreat was not wise. Stephen had never been at war in the fashion Gervanno had; he had been trained in martial arts, and schooled in the history of war, the clash of armies, but he had experienced none of it himself.

Not in the world in which he lived.

The cerdan was not afraid; he was not panicked. But he was tense, and his eyes did not leave what the forest guards called the path.

THEY HEARD the strange newcomer before they caught sight of her. Her voice was shrill and slightly nasal; had there been birds to startle, they would have fled at the sound. She had not learned to walk silently; indeed, as she approached, she stepped on branches and cursed when twigs caught on her hair.

Listening, one might have thought she was alone, but that impression would not have lasted; she was clearly talking to—or at—someone. She was babbling in excitement, with brief bursts of irritation.

The guards stiffened, as if they were attempting to plant themselves, at the sound of that babble, at the words that emerged. There was an eager, vital joy in the woman's tone. Even her irritation at twigs and slender branches didn't quell that.

It was, therefore, a surprise to see her in person. She walked, occasionally jumping on the spot as if her excitement must be shed in some fashion or it would overflow, her hand in Nenyane's.

Nenyane looked as amused as she felt; her lips were a thin line. She'd never liked children, even when she had been one. She never *hurt* them; she never considered them a threat. But this type of battle was exactly the reason she avoided having to mind them where it was at all possible.

Good job, Stephen told her.

Her response was sour but wordless.

The fox remained in Gervanno's arm, ears twitching as Nenyane's companion came into view. The guard that carried Adala remained standing. The rest of the trees did not. They bowed, the motion supple and at odds with the trees from which they had come. Alex moved closer to Stephen.

Kallandras stepped back. Stephen was not surprised to see that the bard no longer carried weapons in his hands; he *was* surprised to see the lute that was cradled in those hands take their place. The bard began to strum its strings, although he did not join voice to song, not yet.

Anya came into view.

Her babble stopped, as did she. Nenyane, however, spoke, voice low enough that only Stephen could hear what passed for encouragement from his huntbrother. The content of her chosen words had always been important to Nenyane—but tone and finesse of sharing that content had never mattered.

Still, this newcomer nodded, frowning. "Are *they* yours? I don't think they're yours."

"In the sky?"

Anya nodded. Her face didn't match her voice; her very adult body did not match her demeanor. Nothing about her suggested power except her presence, her survival. Nothing until she frowned.

"Oh, that's right." She lifted her voice. *"Go away! Go away right now!"*

Gervanno stiffened, but the forest guards had not yet unbent. If they'd been attempting to move just beyond the edge of the wyvern's notice, this newcomer had made clear exactly where she stood.

Nenyane shook her head.

To Gervanno and the Maubreche Hunters, Stephen said, "Nenyane says, 'Watch.'"

"I *told you* to *go away!*" Anya clutched Nenyane's hand far more tightly, as if she meant to bunch her own hands in angry fists, and had forgotten that one of them was entangled with someone else's.

She raised her arms, still forgetting that Nenyane's hand was caught in hers. But some attempt at movement made her frown at their joined hands. She let go.

From ground to sky, fire blossomed, rising as if it were inverted lightning. It was blue and white, but at this distance Stephen felt the flash of its heat; he instinctively stepped back.

The trees that had bowed remained bowed; this newcomer had not given them permission to rise. Stephen thought she was barely aware of them at all; her attention was given to wyverns. And that attention was brief.

The skies filled with the sound of living screams. None of them were Anya's. To Stephen, the older woman was not enraged; her anger carried the strong undertone of petulance. Had she been an over-tired toddler she could not have sounded more childlike.

Stephen had never wondered what the world would be like, should toddlers be given the power of gods. He wondered now, breath held.

Nenyane, however, was not concerned. Power had often concerned her, but only when it was aimed at Stephen. That Anya had power was evident, but it had been evident to his huntbrother from the moment they first encountered each other. Nothing Stephen could do—ever— could equal what Anya now did: she brought the wyverns down.

Trees were crushed by their sudden weight, the momentum of their fall, and the thrashing of their wings and bodies as life bled from them.

One winged creature avoided the fire she wielded. Not a wyvern, but a creature that sprouted wings nonetheless. His cry was not wordless, but Stephen didn't understand the words he shouted. He did recognize one of them. *Anya.*

See? I told you. Watch.

"GERVANNO, PUT ME DOWN. NOW."

Gervanno obeyed, but his gaze did not move. He could see the bent trees; could see the tree that had chosen to guard Adala, standing with the girl in his arms.

The fox's feet touched the path; a brief grimace of distaste rippled across the golden brow. "Do not attack her. If she attempts to attack you, defend without attempting to strike her."

"What will you do, Eldest?"

"I will speak with her," the fox replied. "I will survive it."

For the first time since Gervanno had encountered the fox, he was uncertain. Many of the wyverns that had plagued them were dead — dead or gone. Even the demon that had commanded them was no longer seated.

He knew of the Widan. He knew of the Imperial mages. He had seen both on battlefields. He had never seen anything like this Anya before. He did not know how to approach her, should approach be necessary, but he knew he could not do so while armed.

He glanced at Nenyane for guidance. She was not armed. He therefore sheathed his sword, and waited.

"These are your friends?" Anya asked, turning once again to the sword master.

"And family. One of them."

"Which one? Oh, you mean the god-born boy?"

"Stephen of Maubreche, yes."

"Is he important to you?"

"Very."

Anya frowned. "They want him dead, you know." The words were almost conversational.

"Is that why you came here?"

Anya shook her head. "I came to see the circus." A querulous note entered her voice. She turned then, gazed at the bent trees, and said,

"You may rise." As if beings of the wilderness were part of her daily life, and almost beneath her notice.

Only when given permission did the guards unbend.

Nenyane did not introduce anyone else by name.

"Are we going to the circus now?" she asked, as if nothing else was relevant.

"We are." Nenyane exhaled. "We think the demons want to destroy the circus."

Anya's brows, peppered with flecks of white, rose. "They want to destroy the circus?"

Nenyane nodded. "That's why they came here in such numbers."

The most powerful human Gervanno had ever encountered snorted. "That's impossible. Demons aren't very smart," she added. "They *think* they are, but they aren't."

"I think they told you that you could go to the circus *because* they meant to enter it themselves."

The magi's jaw dropped. "That's *impossible*."

"Why?"

"They aren't people," she replied. "Only people can enter the circus."

"Only people," the fox said, "And those who receive the circus master's permission."

Anya looked down at her feet; the fox had not chosen to shed his smallest form. He looked up, his whiskers twitching.

Anya crowed in wordless delight. "You have a talking animal!"

Gervanno froze. Alex inhaled sharply. Stephen did the same, but he relaxed. Nenyane wasn't worried about the fox's pride. Had Gervanno —had anyone present, save this Anya—spoken the same words to the fox, they might have perished.

"I have chosen to travel with them, for a time; I, too, would like to see the circus, but it is not as simple for one such as I. Would it bother you if I traveled with you? I shouldn't like to be told to go away."

Anya knelt in front of the fox, the joy of discovery in her expression; she was truly delighted. Once again, Gervanno was reminded of the village children in his distant homeland.

She did not answer with words. Instead, she swept the fox up, into her arms. Once again, a ripple of held breath traveled across the gathering. The fox, however, did not complain.

"You are a very bright, very interesting human," the fox said.

She was pleased. She turned to Nenyane, beaming. "I can let you carry the fox if you want." This was said in the tone of a child who knew she should share, and who made the offer, but who really didn't *want* to.

Nenyane's smile froze on her face. "Thank you for the offer, but no. There are demons abroad, and I need both of my hands to properly wield a weapon."

"Why do you need a weapon?" Anya asked, genuinely confused. "You have me!"

"Perhaps she doesn't want to be presumptuous," the fox said. "But I would rather spend time in your company than hers."

This pleased Anya greatly. "I'm sure you'll be allowed to visit the circus," she told the golden animal. "You're with me." She then paused to look at the trees.

At Adala.

"Oh!" she said, her smile deepening. "You're circus!"

Adala had watched Anya from the cradle of the tree guardian's arms; she was surprised to be noticed. "How can you tell?"

The question clearly made no sense to Anya. "What do you mean?"

"I was summoned to join the circus," Adala replied. "But I haven't made it there yet." She frowned. "Were you called to join the circus as well?"

Anya shook her head; a shadow crossed her face. Anya's childlike cadence halted; her expression became instantly far graver. No one wanted to be in her presence should it remain there; the gravity seemed to tilt toward rage. They had seen her rage at the wyverns that had destroyed Evaro's caravan to a man, with a single exception.

Had she been traveling with them, Evaro would have survived; it was the wyverns and the demon who would have perished.

But he understood that their survival afterwards might not have been guaranteed; if this childish older woman grew fretful or irritable, she might end the caravan in an instant. Having spent some time with his sister's children, Gervanno knew that such irritability was common, but not entirely predictable.

The fox nudged her stiffening hand, and delight returned. Adala did not ask again. Neither did Alex, the one most prone to seek answers to questions.

Gervanno understood, now, why the fox had approached Anya in the fashion he had. Anya was a power, but respect, as Gervanno had often been told, takes many forms and guises.

"Maybe they knew," Anya said to the fox. "Maybe that's why they thought they could attack the circus." She exhaled and looked to Adala again. "You shouldn't be here. You really shouldn't be here."

Adala met Anya's gaze as if the woman were not, and could not be, a threat to her. "No," she agreed, voice thick. "I shouldn't. Will you help us?"

Anya beamed. There was no other word to describe her expression. "We'd better hurry. I don't like demons. I mostly kill them." Her expression stiffened; she looked over her shoulder.

"No!" she shouted, although to whom or what was unclear. "You *promised* I could go to the circus! *He* promised! I am *going*!"

Her arms around the fox tightened, as if she'd forgotten she was carrying anything in them. The fox, however, said nothing.

Gone was the silence of intent and caution. Gone was *any* silence. Anya was chatty. Endlessly chatty. The trees did not speak to her, but she accepted their presence as if they were rooted and mute. She spoke with the fox, for the most part, although she sometimes shot a question at Nenyane, as if she was afraid Nenyane would feel left out.

Adala had been identified; her role was clear. Anya did not seem to notice Trevor at all. Adala made no attempt to introduce him, no attempt to draw the woman's attention to him. As if she understood that Anya was both savior and death, two sides of a spinning coin that had not quite come to a stop.

Trevor made no attempt to introduce himself, either.

"It is best that way," the fox said, his voice very soft. Anya noticed that the fox looked, briefly, in Gervanno's directly; she tightened her grip on the fox, as if afraid someone might take him from her.

No one present would be so foolish. Had they been inclined to dismiss the woman because she was childlike, even simple, the destruction of the wyverns made clear what the cost of that dismissal might be.

The rainless thunder and lightning at their backs receded. They had been of great concern to Gervanno, but Nenyane had returned to Stephen's side. The Northern mage had not. The Northern mage was not Nenyane's equal in his handling of a sword; he was, however,

Widan without parallel. Nenyane had chosen to leave him, retreating from the field. But Nenyane had brought a one-woman army in her wake.

"There will be no more demons," the sword master told Gervanno. "Not today."

"The demons they've already gathered are more than enough," Stephen added.

ADALA KNEW, the moment she set eyes on Anya, that the entire company teetered on the edge of oblivion. She knew it before Anya, in a rage that seemed petulant, had destroyed the fire-breathing creatures that hovered to either side of the circus guard.

She could see, in Anya, the shimmering luminosity of power, but what her eyes saw was almost irrelevant. She could *hear*. She could hear the rising, discordant chorus of Anya's power. She could almost taste the color of that sound—which made no sense.

Adala could not sing to Anya, not in the way she could to the elements. She didn't so much sing *to* them as sing *with* them, blending her voice in harmony with theirs until their voices were one. Then, she might ask them to do her bidding, and they would respond as if that bidding were their own desire.

She could not sing in any fashion this woman would hear; could not add Anya's complicated harmonies to her natural song. The voices of the elements would not, and could not, reach Anya. But Anya had looked at Adala, and Anya had instantly known: Adala was circus.

Adala, who had been willing to walk away from the life she had known, as long as she could walk beside Trevor.

What had Anya seen? Why had it been so clear to her, when no one in Hansleigh could discern a difference? When even Trevor, who knew her better than anyone, couldn't, until she'd told him herself?

She wanted to ask, but she'd heard the way the torrent of sound that was Anya suddenly lurched and shifted. It had shifted in a far less dangerous fashion when the woman had lifted her arms and blasted the flying creatures from the sky. Anya could not risk strengthening that deepening gulf of sound. She was certain that none of them would survive.

Not the circus guards. Not Trevor. Not the others who had come to escort her back to the captivity that would destroy all chance of the love she had come to desire.

It was Trevor's presence that stayed her, that silenced her. Some part of Adala might not have cared if she had joined her voice to the rage that rested to one side of the genuine delight Anya offered the world. It was such a familiar song, it might have been Adala's: the death of love. The loss of trust. The terrible pain of endless captivity.

THEY DISCARDED silence as they moved; if caution was required while accompanying Anya, the fox had dismantled the need for much of it.

Nenyane had never liked the fox; she had never liked his student. She did not trust either. Were it not for Gervanno, her natural inclination to avoid hostility in the presence of power would have been broken. The fox wasn't *safe*.

But if she were honest, it was the fox's interest *in* Gervanno that rattled her. Gervanno was not of the wilderness. Only his sense of duty brought him here. Gervanno was not her equal, but he was close, and Gervanno could be trusted. She could move from Stephen's side for brief periods of time, as long as Gervanno was present; she could rush ahead to scout, and Gervanno would remain, sword drawn, ready to put his life on the line to protect her Hunter.

Only when the fox interfered did his focus shift; he, too, sensed the fox's power, and he offered respect. Respect, however, verged dangerously close to obedience.

But the fox, here, was essential. The fox had somehow known. He could approach Anya, and absorb Anya's gushing delight. His decision to allow Anya to carry him meant Anya's focus was on that delight. It had been broken only twice: with the wyverns, which was to their advantage, and with Adala, which had almost been disastrous.

In all her time in mortal lands, Nenyane had never encountered a person like Anya. She had no desire to ever encounter her again. Her power was immense. Lesser gods might have been possessed of the same strength, in the era when gods walked the world. And lesser gods, slaves to their essential natures, might have been just as capricious.

But none of the gods would create what Anya had created in the forests — the mortal forests — outside of Hansleigh. None would build a

portal through which demons might pass, and in number. None,
save one.

Ishavriel had called Anya's name. Ishavriel was angry.

Anya had flinched, but instead of collapsing in the fear one might
expect, she found her own rage, and shouted back. Nenyane had
brought her because it was clear Anya had once been of the Free
Towns; Anya *knew* the circus. She knew of its existence. She had visited
the circus before.

Anya recognized Adala *as* part of that circus. Nenyane, who could
see what Stephen often couldn't, couldn't see anything remarkable
about Adala at all. But Stephen had. Adala had called the wind, and
the wind had come.

The world was growing strange and wild, and the wilderness was
predicable only in that it was unpredictable. Between one step and the
next, across a border invisible to the eye, the world could shift and
change, and things unseen could be revealed.

Anya was like an echo of that wilderness, but wrapped into a single
person.

Nenyane didn't want to be indebted to the fox, but she accepted
that the fox's insight into this very disturbing mage would serve two
purposes. It would allow Anya to accompany them without fear that
their company would meet the end the wyverns had, and it would keep
Anya happy.

Unhappy Anya was ruin and death.

THE WINGED DEMON did not approach the party again.

Kallandras had listened to Adala when she had taken brief
command of the wind. It was an approach he had never considered;
she had blended her voice so perfectly with the capricious song of
elemental air that they were almost indivisible. It was in the harmony,
that blending, that her power lay: when the wind moved at her desire,
there was no resistance. The wind did as it pleased. If it pleased Adala,
it was irrelevant.

He had borne the ring of air for much of his life, and used the
power carved and tempered into it by an Artisan without equal. But
the use of that power was costly, had always been costly. If he was
given time, he might try Adala's approach.

To do that, they must survive. Survival depended on Anya.

Kallandras did not watch the sky; he kept pace with the party, but his fingers strummed lute strings. He did not sing; it was not required. Anya was genuine in her emotions. The bard heard anticipation and delight in her voice. Only when she had shouted at the wyverns had that shifted—but what he heard in that moment was not what the rest of the party heard, with the possible exception of Adala.

Anya had swallowed rage and pain and betrayal; she had consumed it. In turn, it had almost consumed her. Delight was not the source of the terrifying power she had unleashed. His music was quiet, calming, wordless. He would not have been surprised had she failed to notice it at all. But the fox did, and the fox nodded a subtle command: continue to play.

Kallandras played. It was not the battle he had been prepared to join, but it was one he knew well. All of the Senniel bards—talent-born or no—had been trained to calm crowds, to draw attention and to hold it. They could ease a mood, if necessary; they could embolden weary soldiers in a similar fashion.

They could make themselves heard, should the need arise. Here, it did not. Better to leave Anya in the fox's care, for she was, although she carried him.

She did not seem to see Kallandras; she barely glanced at Gervanno or the Hunters. She noticed Nenyane, she noticed Adala, and she noticed the fox.

It was far, far better not to draw her attention; Kallandras murmured this truth in a way she would not hear.

Alex nodded, as if he had drawn the same conclusion; Max grimaced.

The dogs did not find her a threat. They were not worried about her presence at all. Even when she had swept the wyverns from the skies above, the dogs' attitude did not change.

"I WANTED TO JOIN THE CIRCUS," Anya said to the fox. "When I was little. I wanted to be part of it."

"You were never called?"

"No. But someone visited once, before I ran away."

"Someone from the circus?"

She nodded. "To tell me that I couldn't be part of the circus. I was meant for bigger things. That's what she said. Bigger things."

"I think you are far too powerful for the circus," the fox said, his voice soothing and respectful.

"I don't know. I'm not sure about the bigger things. Bigger things mean people are always trying to tell me what to do. I don't like it."

"No, I imagine that is frustrating. Why should those with far less power and competence tell the powerful and significant what they *should* be doing?"

Anya brightened. "You think so?"

"Of course I do. I am not attempting, in any way, to tell you what to do, am I?"

Nenyane grimaced. Stephen could hear her grinding her teeth. *I really want to kill him.*

No you don't. But yes, he's frustrating and disingenuous.

He's dangerous.

Nenyane, so are you. So are Meralonne, Kallandras, and Gervanno.

He's lying.

He's flattering her. It's not the same.

It's exactly the same.

And we're grateful for it. Ah. Stephen understood the problem. Nenyane wasn't grateful for it. The very idea that her continued survival depended on such cloying flattery was offensive and insulting. She'd often been like this, especially when introduced to the ruling Hunter Ladies she so disliked.

If she's with us and she's happy, the demons won't be a problem. We can arrive at the circus in time for Adala to join. He exhaled. *I'm not certain why the circus master believes Hansleigh will be safe once the circus performance ends —the demons will still be in the forest, and the town can't stand against the demons on its own.*

We'll deal with that when we come to it.

Stephen frowned. *What is it? What's wrong?*

Nenyane shook her head.

Is it Meralonne?

She didn't answer.

CHAPTER FIFTEEN

The jog the party had kept slowed to a crawl; the group's speed was centered around, and therefore dictated, by Anya. While she was excited to be on her way to the circus, she was focused on the fox. Close one's eyes, and one might have heard a child who couldn't squelch audible signs of excitement.

One might be wandering in a forest in weather just warm enough, taking a leisurely stroll after the day's work was done. One might not even notice the lack of birdsong and bird aggression, as above one's head small struggles of dominance usually took place.

Anya broke silence simply by talking; her words were quick, the syllables running together as if speech were a constant stream. The fox became small stones standing in the stream's current without ever impeding its passage; his tone was coaxing, almost gentle.

Max knew Alex didn't like the fox. Nenyane was, for Nenyane, careful and polite, but she couldn't stand the fox, either. Gervanno di'Sarrado treated the fox as if the fox were a lord; he seemed respectful, but the fox demanded far more of Gervanno than he did of either Kallandras or Meralonne, both of whom also treated the fox with respect.

Stephen did not interact with the fox, for good or ill—probably because it would set Nenyane off. She made a point of standing between Anya and Stephen, probably because Anya carried the "talking animal." Max was almost certain that no one else would have survived that delighted exclamation.

No, Alex agreed. *It suited the fox's purpose, so he tolerated it.*

Yes, but what's his purpose? That was the heart of Max's ambivalence.

Alex didn't know either, and made no guesses. There was something about the fox that both drew and repelled Alex's attention—as if he felt he *must* look, but conversely, must not look, at the same time. Anya, however, was a shadow, subtle but vast.

Max didn't see her that way, but accepted Alex's view: he had seen her destroy the flying, fire-breathing beasts as if they were gnats or mosquitoes. She wanted them gone. When they didn't immediately obey, she got rid of them. And it was effortless on her part; it appeared to require no thought, no control. No self-control.

Max was competent with a sword. Alex was better. Both, however, had worked to achieve the mastery they had. It wasn't good enough for Nenyane; it was acceptable, but only barely. Had it not been for Gervanno, she would have demanded that they continue to train. Perhaps Anya, in a distant youth, had undergone similar training.

Alex found it difficult to believe. There was a wild force in Anya that was contained—but only barely—by the form of a woman of middle age. He had sensed the same in the fox, but in Anya's arms, the fox could barely be sensed at all. As he walked, Steel by his side, he knew they were approaching the town they had left. The trees walked single file for this last leg of a path only they could see, but that path still remained embedded in the normal forests in which they might hunt should the need arise.

They emerged from the forest on the south side of Hansleigh.

Alex called an immediate halt, his voice loud with urgency.

The forest guards, however, had stopped just before Alex shouted. Some of Hansleigh was on fire, and the streets were not empty. Although fewer in number than they had been in the forest, demons walked the town's roads.

Alex understood, then: the circus performance kept the townspeople safe. It did not encompass the empty town itself.

Nenyane's sword was in hand as she leapt toward the town, her feet barely skirting ground between her enormous jumps.

"I would not have counseled that approach," the fox said.

"Oh?" Kallandras, often the first to take to the air, had not moved. Nor had Stephen; Nenyane had left him with Gervanno.

Gervanno, however, drew sword. He did not leap as if weight itself were inconsequential, but he followed Nenyane.

Of course he did. Nenyane had given him no command to stay behind. She considered Stephen, surrounded by moving trees, the fox, and an unbelievably powerful mage, to be safe.

And if she did not demand that Gervanno remain by Stephen's side, there was only one other place for him: by hers.

"Do not worry for Gervanno," the fox said; he did not turn his head, and Max could not be certain to whom the fox spoke. He assumed it was Stephen. "She is the master he would choose to serve until even breath was beyond him. Almost, I envy her."

"Who is your master?" Anya asked, the thought clearly occurring to her only now. Or perhaps it was the fact that talking animals did not have masters in the stories of her childhood; they hadn't, in the childhood stories Max could stay still to hear. Alex, however, had always listened. Always.

"While she lives," the fox replied, "she is the great Sen of the city of Averalaan."

"Sen? What is that?"

"Perhaps, if we travel together for a time, you will know. But the *Kialli* consider her one of their most dangerous enemies, and perhaps you will face her as foe, not as friend. I perceive you have lived in a land ruled by the dead—and their lord. But you were not born to the dead.

"You were born to the Free Towns. You were born to lands over which the circus master presides in some subtle, minor fashion."

"I wasn't called to the circus," Anya said.

"No, child. Of course not. No master with any wisdom wishes to have a servant more powerful in all ways than himself. The circus master rightfully feared you would shine so brightly the rest of the circus would be irrelevant."

It was both flattery and truth.

That's why Nenyane doesn't like him.

Max shook his head. *It's Gervanno. She can't claim him—not in any normal, legal way. She's huntbrother. Her life is Stephen—and it is Stephen. It's why Father trusted her. It's why we trust her. She's not the perfect, traditional huntbrother; she can't navigate the political and social spheres with any grace. If any huntbrother could protect his Hunter from the Hunter's Death, it would be*

Nenyane. But she's drawn to Gervanno and she doesn't want anything to take him away.

Alex wasn't as certain, but acknowledged the bond that had grown between the two swordsmen in such a short time, given one of the people was the prickly, dismissive Nenyane. *Should we join them?*

Max shook his head. *She didn't tell Gervanno to stay because we're here. The dogs are here.* He grimaced. All demons were dangerous to the merely mortal. They weren't a danger to Nenyane.

They weren't a danger to Anya, but Anya frowned; she looked up from the fox to see Gervanno's back, and from there, the burning buildings. Her jaw dropped; no words escaped her open mouth.

Max repented. Nenyane and Gervanno should not have headed into the town. Anya's rage was instant. He had never watched the magi carefully until circumstance had forced him to travel alongside Meralonne APhaniel. Meralonne's magic was not Anya's magic.

Rain—if something so instant, so violent, could still be called rain—fell in torrents. If the fire were natural fire, it would be extinguished. If it were not, Hansleigh might suffer more damage than the demons had already caused. Even thinking of it, Max held breath, as if waiting for the confirmation of looming disaster.

From the heart of the storm, a voice emerged, and it spoke a single word.

"Anya!"

"Gervanno, avoid the fires. Avoid them at all costs." Gervanno recognized the bard's voice; he felt it as a physical touch. Not a blow, not precisely, but almost a command. His body responded; he moved. He could see Nenyane; could see her slow. He assumed the bard had spoken to her, as well.

No one could command Nenyane without her permission, but the bard did not speak thus without cause. She pivoted, leaping to the side; she landed just in front of Gervanno, lifting an arm. He came to a halt, sword readied, as the storm's rain suddenly fell. It was far too contained to be natural, and far too violent.

"Anya," Nenyane said to Gervanno, lifting her voice to be heard. She exhaled, but made no move to turn back. Nor did she put up her sword or dismiss Gervanno. Her expression, as she stared into the flood of water, was focused, intent. The water had not killed the demons. Not all of them.

She closed her eyes very briefly when a single word came out of the heart of the unnatural storm. **Anya.** Anya's name, wrapped in a rage and fury that might equal Anya's.

Gervanno did not speak, did not ask. He understood that this voice was the reason she had leapt, instantly, toward Hansleigh, leaving behind the Hunters, the fox, the mage herself.

"Well, this is going to be tricky," a familiar voice said.

Gervanno grimaced as Jarven ATerafin made himself known. Nenyane did not condescend to acknowledge him at all.

The water's torrential flow was suddenly wrapped in fire; steam rose as Anya's storm was burned away.

"I do not believe this is our fight," Jarven continued, when neither Nenyane nor Gervanno spoke.

"Your fights, at the moment, are his fights," Nenyane snapped.

"That is harsh. Surely we all share the same enemy?" Jarven's eyes were bright—too bright. The smile that crossed his face was a smile Gervanno had seen before, on the faces of different men: men who were so certain of their power, transgression did not exist. Power was not responsibility for men such as these; it was not even a goal. It was what they were.

Jarven was hemmed in by the fox, but the fox was not human. Not mortal. The concerns of the fox stayed Jarven's hand; they curtailed his freedom. Jarven obeyed—for now. Else he might never have joined this battle at all.

Nenyane did not answer. Instead, she bent into her knees, and before Jarven could comment, she leapt up, and up again. This time, she found purchase in the air as the fire began to bank.

———

FOR THE FIRST time since Anya had arrived, the tree that carried Adala set her—gently—down. Down, where her feet touched the earth at the end of the path the trees had followed. She reached for Trevor's hand and clutched it tightly; he did not withdraw. He never would, if given a choice. She knew. How could she not? He had been willing to give up his life and his future in Hansleigh in order to build one with her.

But he hadn't been willing to give up their lives—the lives of the people he had known and cared for all his life—to build that life.

And in the end, she hadn't been willing to surrender his. She accepted the truth, as flames, reflected in her open eyes, shifted their color. Had Trevor been the type of person who could easily walk away —who could walk away at all—she would never have loved him. She wanted his love. She wanted to be the most important person in his life. Maybe even the only person in his life.

But if he could abandon all others to death, he wouldn't be Trevor.

If she could abandon him to death, she wouldn't be Adala.

She was neither wordless nor silent, but none of her words were meant for Trevor. None were meant to encapsulate the sense of loss, the bleak, empty days of the future that now stretched ahead of them both.

They were meant for the fire. She could hear the fire's voice. When she stepped off the narrow path that had led them from the forest to the borders of Hansleigh, she knew she was not stepping out of the forest; she was not stepping out of the wilderness.

No, she was stepping into it. She was standing on it. She was home. Hansleigh had always been, on some visceral level, circus. She had been summoned to the circus; she had fled before the day she was meant to join it. Joining meant leaving the Hansleigh of her childhood and youth, which would not have been a sacrifice.

It meant leaving Trevor, which seemed, in those terrible weeks, to sacrifice *everything*.

And now?

Now, she could hear the song of earth and wind and fire. The water, Anya's water, she did not hear in the same fashion. She could hear the voice that drove the fire, but fire was one of the elements that those who visited to announce the circus could bespeak. They could juggle with fire. They could breathe it. In their hands it was spectacle, mystery; in their hands, it was safe.

The voice that compelled the fire here was not safe. She hated the sound of its discordance; it did not sing fire's song, but its own, and its own was ugly to her ears.

She knew of the bard-born; she knew of the talent-born. It would be impossible not to hear the tales that circulated in the dining room of the inn—and in the halls, and at the front desk, wherever people stopped to chat. She knew the bard was talent-born; she could hear the vibration in his voice when he sang. She did not hear it when he spoke.

She heard it now, although the words, not meant for her, did not reach her ears.

She saw the glint of diamond on his thumb, a finger red and swollen, as if burned and only barely healed, the new skin thin and shiny.

"Bard," she said. "It is not yet your turn to sing."

He turned to her, his expression neutral; his gaze met, and held, hers.

With a smile that was bitter, she said, "This is a circus town. It is ours, in the end, not yours."

"Ours?" he asked.

Adala turned to Anya. "Ours. Anya is from the towns."

Anya nodded. "Not Hansleigh," she added.

"The Free Towns are the Free Towns; the circus comes to all of them." Adala parroted words she had heard since childhood. They were words that she had never attempted to verify; her family didn't travel. They minded the inn and played paid host to those who did and could. She had daydreamed of many things when a child; one had been travel. She had desired to see the world.

Her parents, overworked and busy, had not been indulgent. The world beyond the Free Towns was a difficult, dangerous place. It was like their stories of the monsters under the bed, which only woke at night but could eat the feet of the unwary.

All stories meant to frighten children.

But some stories contained a kernel of truth: she saw that clearly in this moment, because parts of Hansleigh were burning—or had been burning. Anya had guttered the natural fires, but the heart of the fire remained; it was no longer interested in empty buildings.

It moved toward Nenyane and the Southern sword master. The desire to burn everything in its path had been honed to a point; the fire traveled as if it were a spear.

Adala sang. She found the voice of the fire first, but it was not the only voice she could hear. She could hear them all. She could hear them more clearly than she had ever heard them before. She didn't know why. She'd spent the last few years desperately hiding any hint that she could.

Desperately avoiding the truth that maybe she'd known, even as a child. She was circus. The circus did not own her—yet. But it was part of her. Part of what and who she was. It was the part she'd denied. It was the part she'd neglected. She'd chosen Trevor. The circus had chosen her. That's what she'd told herself. The circus had chosen her.

But she was wrong.

The circus was part of her. She was, as Anya had said, circus. She lifted her voice, and years of hiding, years of fear, melted away. She could not have what she wanted. Could not have the love that she craved and dreamed of for what felt like a lifetime, although it had been less than a year.

She could have this. She could speak freely. She could sing freely. She raised voice in a song even the bard-born could not sing.

WHAT KALLANDRAS COULD HEAR in her voice, no one else could, although it would have been impossible not to hear her. The Free Towns had always been an enigma. When the Empire had expanded its borders, it moved north or south; it moved to the west, and came to a wall there. The Free Towns had the militia one might expect of such towns; they were not city states; they were not overtly wealthy.

But in spite of this, the townships had remained; there was a reason they were called the Free Towns in the kingdoms to the west, and in the Empire to the east.

He heard it now. He had never heard a song such as this, who had spent his adult life studying, learning, and performing. Humans could not control the wild elements; this was common knowledge. Kallandras could because he wore one of Myrddion's five rings: the ring of diamond. The ring of air and wind. He could command, should command become necessary, but it was costly; far better to cajole the wind. The wind did not struggle often against that gentle urging; only when faced with the wild fire, earth, or water, was it necessary to exert the control the wind hated.

Adala did not exert control in the fashion the rings of an Artisan allowed. She did not exert control the way the *Kialli*, hidden by rising steam and smoke, did. When she sang, he could hear the wind in her voice: the wildness of it, both gentle and keening. Kallandras heard wind first, because he knew it best; he wondered, briefly, if the ring he wore could be used against her. But it was not just the wild air that was contained in her song; it was the music of earth, of water, of fire. She did not cajole, as he cajoled. She could not command as Meralonne commanded—or as the *Kialli*, still obscured by steam, must.

For a moment, she was the wilderness. She, a human girl, born to the Free Towns, which had never, on the surface, seemed remarkable. Evayne a'Nolan had been born in the Free Towns. Or raised in them. She, like Anya, had never been swallowed by the circus.

He understood why those born to the circus were called to it, but wondered what Adala might make of herself outside of the realm of the circus master. Would the power that characterized her voice and song fade to nothing in lands that the circus master did not rule? If not, the Free Towns were likely to become far more significant to people who ruled across the continent.

But she would never know, would she?

We're always given choice, a bitter voice from his distant past said. *But all choice has consequences. Tell me: if you're asked which hand you'd rather lose, right or left, when a power far greater than your own is asking, is that really choice?*

He shook his head. How different, in the end, was the choice Evayne had offered Kallandras in his youth? Adala was the age he had been when he had first been offered the choice. He could have killed the young Evayne. He could have killed her with ease. Had he not been bard-born, he would have, for she knew who he was and clearly knew where the ancient labyrinths of the brotherhood lay.

But he was bard-born. He had stayed his hand because he had heard the truth in her voice, her words. She believed them. She *knew*. He could see her clearly now because he was older; he had passed through the scorching fires she had caused him to set; he had made his choice. And only now could he viscerally feel that the truth he had acknowledged *was* true. What had been offered with such resentment and pain in a youth he could no longer touch, was offered now in earnest.

And she would come to him, as the child she had once been, caught in the youth he had finally escaped. She would come in grief and pain. She would come nursing invisible wounds; the visible wounds did not take root in her the way the emotional losses did. He had never been a kind child; she had.

As a woman, as an older woman, she was a power to be reckoned with. If Kallandras could have killed her with ease on the day they had first met, he was uncertain he could kill her now—and if he could, he would by relying on the decades of experience and trust she felt for him. But if she perished before she had finished walking her solitary road, all of his sacrifice might be in vain.

They were tied together by the fate she sought to deny. If their roads diverged, it was only in the small details; the larger goal never changed. For either of them.

Adala was, for a moment, walking the same path as Kallandras. She faced the same enemies. But she did so under the watchful eye of a god: the circus master. The lord of the Free Towns. She had been born here, raised here, and touched, always, by the lands fashioned by that master. They were not wilderness in any way Kallandras understood, but they were claimed. They were owned.

He did not hear the circus master's name when he walked the streets of Hansleigh; he did not hear it when he walked within the borders that defined the town. But he heard a hint of a greater power in Adala's voice, now. Bitter birthright, but beautiful enough his fingers on lute strings fell momentarily still. When they moved again, they moved in harmony to her song, which was far more difficult than at any other time; he had sung duets with creatures immortal and ancient, joining his pain, his experience, to theirs in perfect harmony.

Adala's voice defied that skill. It defied the lessons of Senniel. It defied the lessons of everything except the battlefield. He stopped, then. There was a brief hush in the air, as if the sense of combat had been noted; he did nothing to disturb it.

He was not certain Adala had even noticed. The fire banked as she sang; the wind caught Nenyane mid-leap and carried her weight, as it did when Kallandras bespoke it. Only at great need did he command— but in this long battle, need was never far away. He wondered again if he might do as Adala did if he had the time to listen, to practice. But something in her voice contained an echo of other, something that did not exist in the talent-born of his acquaintance.

He heard it in Illaraphaniel's voice at times, and in the resonant voices of the *Kialli*; he heard it, strongly, in the fox. He heard echoes of it, attenuated and cold, in Jarven ATerafin's voice.

He now knew that the Free Towns were protected by the circus; he understood that some of their residents were drafted into that circus, sacrificing their lives to its service. Adala was, or would be, one. But if the power was granted with acceptance of that summons, the certainty in her voice—the nuance of delight, and even of homecoming—should not have existed. Wonder, yes; perhaps a tinge of awe—but familiarity? No.

She painted the aural landscape with all of the strands of herself, her experience, her delight, her sorrow, and her acceptance.

The wilderness turned toward the sound of her voice as if it was their own, as if the elements recognized a fundamental part of themselves in what they heard.

To the eye, she was a young woman from the Free Towns, her clothing in good repair, but otherwise unremarkable. Nothing about her would have demanded attention, nothing about her would have offered warning; she would have been one of the protected, not one of the protectors, if he noticed her in the crowded inn at all.

He could not join voice to her voice; could not pick up strands of her song to change the feel of the weave of the rising chorus. He could listen. He could hear. He could bear witness.

He had lifted voice in the wilderness before, a voice bright with power and dark with battle and muted in elegy. But he did not sing to the wild elements, or did not sing with them. He could not find the necessary connection to their voices, their will, their thoughts; they were, and remained, opaque. If the elements had emotions at all, he was only barely aware of them, and much of that awareness involved rage.

Adala could hear them. She could hear them clearly.

Had Anya been any other townsperson, Kallandras might have risked asking if she could hear what Adala could hear; she was not. But perhaps her answer to that question could be found in her first greeting of Adala: *you're circus.*

What Anya had seen, he could not see; the delight of the older woman's declaration was tinged with a hint of childhood awe. Kallandras had not been born to the Free Towns, but knew the circus was held in high regard; it was almost mythical, and yet—when it so chose —approachable. It was both other and their own at the same time.

What had the circus master created? What subtle changes had been made in the mortals who inhabited lands he had never fully left?

He could hear the answer in Adala's words. She was mortal, human, desirous of love and family and a life that Kallandras would never consider normal; that had been her dream. It had been his, as a very young child: the desire for love and family. His answer, his realization of that daydream, had not resembled hers in any fashion. She had attempted to flee Hansleigh, and the circus that was, if Anya was correct, her birthright. She had lived a life informed by Hansleigh's excellent mimicry of a normal life, and she had made a choice: flee.

That had been his choice as a much younger child as well. But he had not fled to keep a dream alive, to make it real. He had fled to survive. He had fled with no assumption of hope, of joy, no belief that the life to which he was fleeing was better than the one that had ended without warning.

And he knew these thoughts — farther and farther from the life that had he had built in the wake of loss and fear — emerged because Adala's voice invoked them. There was a purity to her song that implied refuge, sanctuary — a sanctuary free from the constraints and experiences of mortal life, mortal loss.

But threaded throughout her song was a sorrow so deep, so wide, the two were in balance: eternity and grief.

Were she not mortal, were she not human, the song might continue forever. But if the lord of the circus valued humans and human choice, he valued them the way the Oracle did: without mercy, without consideration for the individuals in question. He did not, in Kallandras's estimation, value people at all; he valued their theoretical survival as a race.

Given the enemy and the war they now faced, perhaps this was the wise choice, the correct choice. But no human could stand forever as Adala stood now unless they could be trapped and contained in this moment. Humans did not and could not live in isolation, and the contact with others, the experiences shared, would mar the youthful perfection of her song.

He could not sing as she sang. He could never have sung as she sang. The beat and timing of her notes, the sudden shifts in melody and tempo, were almost cacophony; to the trained, the taught, the schooled, they would make no sense, and instinct would guide those students to shift and change the song itself until it skirted the edge of paradigm without every fully departing from its structure.

That structure, the wilderness did not hear; it was not a song meant for mortal ears. Not a song meant for mortal voices.

What had the circus master done to the humans he sheltered, that someone like Adala could be born?

The wind heeded her. The fire banked. The water — for she had called water—gentled fire without extinguishing it. Even the earth, rumbling beneath their feet, stilled.

The demon roared in rage and anger. He had expected some conflict, but Meralonne was not present, and all others who stood in the near-empty town were merely mortal. Anya, however, had caught his attention, and Anya could not be considered irrelevant or powerless.

If the *Kialli* had heard Adala's song at all, he gave no sign.

Nor, Kallandras realized, did anyone present. Anya understood that Adala had done something because it was part of being *circus* to her. Nenyane did not return to be questioned, but Nenyane was unlike Alex: she knew what she knew, and did not question it.

He readied weapons as the natural cacophony of enraged elements quieted, and glanced once at Trevor.

Ah. Trevor could hear. Tears left tracks across both of his cheeks; he made no attempt to staunch their flow, nor to hide it. Trevor *could* hear. What he heard, he seemed to understand. There was a hint of pride beneath a far larger expression of loss, and the love that had caused him to make the same choice Adala had made.

He knew, when she lifted voice, that Adala would never leave Hansleigh.

He knew that he was not of the circus, not born for it. He knew that Adala's song, Adala's gift, was offered in part for everything that she had surrendered to return to this place—and that he was the largest part of it. But he knew, must know, that the song she offered was not a dirge.

It was a homecoming. There was both pain and joy in it, a tremulous reawakening to the things she had denied, rejected, pushed aside. Kallandras knew this as well. Had it not been because of his talent—a curse on his family—that he had lost the life he had lived to that point? He had hidden it, turned away from it, denied it—until the moment it had become his strength.

The losses were undeniable. They were part of a past that could not be changed, part of the weave of history that led, inexorably, toward the future—a future of certain war and death that, nonetheless, contained the faintest thread of hope. It was the hope he had followed, bitter though it had been.

It was hope he heard now, although it was not his voice that carried it, lifting it, threading it around a wilderness that even the gods in their later years could not fully explain or comprehend.

He offered Adala the briefest of bows, and turned toward the wind —wind she did not command—leaping into its folds toward the unfolding wings of the *Kialli* who had come to destroy the town, and any who might seek entrance to the circus from its empty streets.

Here, however, the fire would not be in the *Kialli's* hands. If the fire could not be commanded and controlled, the fight to control the wild air was also absent. The earth would not be enraged by sentient flame; the ground would not break beneath their feet or the foundations of the homes and buildings that comprised Hansleigh.

Here, all combat would be by the sword.

HE READIED HIS WEAPON; Nenyane had never lowered hers. But Nenyane did not move toward the demon; she stood in the folds of the air, tense, as if waiting.

Anya did not wait. Kallandras was not a mage; he had worked alongside mages as messenger, as many of the bard-born did. He had relayed orders from commanders to those mages, changing the shape of combat.

Anya did not speak. She did not shout. Had she, Kallandras was uneasily certain she would have expressed rage about the *Kialli's* interference in her plan to see the circus. Her words were childlike, simple words, as if those sentences, that communication, were the only ones available to her.

Beneath her words was constant rage, interrupted by an odd delight. She had seen Adala clearly, and hints of joy brightened her voice, her eyes, even her gestures. She was perhaps the most powerful mage Kallandras had ever seen in action, but she had the impulse control of a young child. She had come in the lee of *Kialli*, and it was clear the demon they faced had recognized her.

The demon lifted hand; he did not carry the red sword of the *Kialli*, but instead, a whip that glowed the same red as the more common swords the *Kialli* wielded.

Nenyane was on the move as the whip's tongues stretched and extended—but she leapt to the side, in the air, and the tongues of red traveled past her toward Anya.

No—toward Adala.

The trees stood in the way; one reached up and out and lost the grainy arm it had lifted in her defense.

Kallandras leapt; the air carried him, moving him quickly toward his intended destination, as if it understood the bard's imperative. For the moment, they were one and the same. The demon's attack was meant to free the fire from Adala's constraint.

The fire, however, like the wild air, had no desire for that freedom. Had the whip been composed of wild flame, its tongues would not have traveled toward the demon's intended target. He was uncertain that fire would attack the *Kialli*, but his own experience with the wild air implied that such an attack was a possibility.

It would not be a possibility now. Kallandras's subtle attempt to bespeak the wind had been entirely unsuccessful. This had not happened in the past; the wind might resist him, but it had always heard his voice. Now, he was all but certain that the only person it could hear was Adala, and while Adala lifted voice in an almost alien song, it would hear no one else.

The *Kialli* also understood this, and roared a name: *Anya!*

A command: *Kill her!*

There was no world in which Kallandras—bard-born, talent-born, trained to song and death—would have uttered that command. No world in which he would have used the power that had cursed and graced him against the mage.

Her response was swift and loud; the vocabulary with which she replied was simple, primal; a toddler might have shouted in just such a fury when their beloved family denied them their desire. It was the fury of a child who, disappointed beyond measure, nonetheless felt entirely safe.

She could not and did not expect the demons to love her, but she did not fear them. She believed they could not injure her, could not damage her, could not cause her pain. All this, he heard in her words.

And more: there was no pain the *Kialli* could cause that could be measured against the pain she carried within her; she almost burned with it, it was so clear. Beneath the angry petulance all others present could hear, was a pain so deep, so vast, so vital, she might be dying of it even as she lifted arm.

It was loss. It was betrayal. It was—ah.

Kallandras gained the air directly in front of Adala. To Anya—to Anya alone—he said, "**I will protect the circus.**"

She did not reply to Kallandras; she was focused entirely on the *Kialli* who had dared to command her. The fire that would no longer hear or obey the demon lord came to Anya's hand in a ball of moving flame; she held it above her palm, her eyes narrowing.

When the tongues of the demonic whip lashed out again, she threw the fire up; it hovered above her head, almost at a level with Kallandras. Had she been any other mage, he would have assumed that he, as ally, was safe. She was Anya. He wasn't certain she was aware of him at all. But she was aware of Adala.

Many were the lessons taught him in labyrinths in which he had come of age; one of them was survival. He stepped from the air that bore his weight so willingly; he armed himself as he came to the ground in front of Adala.

The whip snapped; the fire blossomed. He could feel its heat, but it had no voice; it was an artifact of magery, not a wild sentience, and it spread above them all, a slender shield. The whip pierced it with ease —but its tails slowed, as if momentum was devoured by the mage's fire —a fire that then traveled up the whip's almost immobile tendrils, toward the demon that wielded it.

The demon roared in fury; the whip snapped back in his hand as he reached for, and raised, his shield—a shield that had not come to his hand until that moment. From the smoking ruins of the building the demon had destroyed came other shadows, dark and quick, obeying the command of their master. They raced across the empty streets toward Anya. Toward Adala.

They would not come close to reaching either.

Nenyane, observing at a distance, moved; as she did, Gervanno moved as well. The Breodani dogs were tense, but they remained by their Hunters, as if waiting orders that did not come.

Kallandras did not join the two swordsmen in the streets of Hansleigh; he felt no fear at all for Nenyane or Gervanno. Had the *Kialli* entered the fray, he might have—but Nenyane had understood, the moment the demon began to speak, that he was not her target. She had avoided closing with the *Kialli* at all. If she could survive a demon with relative ease, she was far less confident that she could survive what the mage might throw at him.

And wisely so. Anya did not speak; the demon shouted her name again, and a third time. But lightning followed fire; it struck the shield the demon raised, illuminating the creature's wings.

"You will not survive this!"

Demonic wings spread, shadowing Hansleigh's daylit streets. Had Kallandras control of the wild air, that would have been a tactical mistake; he did not. Adala's control was not honed for combat; the wind which had carried Kallandras willingly to her side did not reach out to batter and buffet the demon's wings.

But it did carry the ash of demonic bodies as Nenyane made short work of the lesser demons commanded by the winged *Kialli*. As if it were fog, those ashes dispersed, lowering visibility.

Demonic shield shattered, as if it were fine, brittle glass.

The demon pushed himself off the ground, the wings lofting his body above the town at astonishing speed. As if the *Kialli* understood that this was where he must meet his end on this sojourn in the living world, he abandoned weapon. Into the curve of an ebon palm came a horn in the weapon's place.

Kallandras would have told Nenyane to destroy the horn before it could be winded, but the Maubreche huntbrother was not fast enough to close the distance between them. Anya snorted, fear entirely absent from the sound; she was almost disgusted.

Could Adala command the wind, the wind might have contained the note the horn sounded, preventing the call from reaching the ears of those for whom it was intended. She could not, or did not.

Kallandras turned to Trevor; he did not want to interrupt Adala's song. "We need to enter Hansleigh quickly. The allies of that creature will come at its call."

Trevor nodded. "I don't know if the circus gate will still be there — I've never missed the circus before."

Anya brought both of her hands up, and then down, in a single almost graceful motion. In the distance, the wings of the demon crumpled. "It doesn't matter," she said, although she was watching the sky with smug satisfaction. "Demons can't enter the circus." She frowned. "I don't think the trees can, either."

"Nenyane, Gervanno, we are moving toward the gate, now. Kill as you must, but move to join us."

IN THE CENTER OF HANSLEIGH, a gate stood. It was attached to no walls, no fence; it could be approached from front or back. It did not open as they approached.

Anya looked to Adala as the trees set her down in the cobbled streets of her home. "We cannot go further," they told her. "But tell the lord that we have fulfilled our ancient vows."

Adala glanced at the trees, and then at Trevor; her attention was split between them, but the song she had sung until this moment quieted; she could sing or she could speak, but she could not do both simultaneously. Trevor took her hand in his, although she had not raised her own. Together, they approached the gate. Adala lifted hand to touch it.

The gate did not open.

Nenyane had kept pace with Gervanno. Stephen watched her progress, but after the *Kialli* fell to ground, the smaller demons under his command had scattered. To villagers, they would be as deadly as the greater demon; to Nenyane, they were almost as relevant as rats or mice.

Trevor touched the gate; the gate did not open.

"Adala?"

She shook her head. She had made the choice to return, but that choice would be irrelevant if she could not reach the circus itself.

Disappointment touched the fey mage's face, folding into the lines of a frown. She was not—yet—angry. "We can't be too late," she said, the words almost a whisper.

Stephen knew they did not want this woman to become angry. But he made no attempt to reassure her, either; he had seen his share of dangerously tired young children in his manor life, and their tantrums, while unpleasant—and sometimes, oddly amusing—could not kill. He had the sense—had had the sense from the moment Nenyane had first encountered her—that the magi's tantrums would destroy the entirety of Hansleigh, and she would not even notice until she was done.

———

GERVANNO EXHALED. He walked to the gate, gently stepping to one side of Trevor, the blacksmith's son. From his pouch, he withdrew a second chance: a gold coin. What had the woman said? Those who had served the circus for a long time could, on occasion, distribute tickets to guests they chose. She had chosen to gift one to Gervanno.

As if she could see the need for it. As if she had understood the task he would undertake.

"Meralonne's not here," Alex said, as Gervanno approached the gate. Gervanno glanced at the Elseth Hunter. Alex had always been perceptive.

"Illaraphaniel is possibly the only one of us that could survive should the circus not enfold him," Nenyane replied. "He is *angry*. He will not come if called." She turned to the bard; the bard offered her a minimal nod. "Gervanno?"

He approached the closed gate. He lifted the coin that the woman in the stall had given him. He touched it to gate; the ticket began to fade from view, becoming transparent and intangible as he watched.

His gaze was on the vanishing coin, even the feel of the heavy solari between his fingers barely lingering. The bars of the gate began to fade as well.

At his back, Anya crowed with wordless delight and relief. It was not too late. She had not missed the circus. She was the first to run through the open gates.

Adala's expression, when he glanced in her direction, was far more complicated, but she had turned to look at Trevor.

Gervanno offered them what respect he could; he waited. Waiting, he could see echoes of many couples he had known and observed as a child in his hometown; he had never understood the point of coupling, of falling in love. It seemed, to his youthful eye, to cause nothing but pain.

But joy was private. He was certain Adala and Trevor had experienced joy, and husbanded it between themselves. Had it been worthwhile? Had they never come to love one another, there would have been no break in the duties to which they were born; Adala would have joined the circus, as she was meant to, and perhaps the circus itself would not now be endangered.

He had not been told much about the circus, but what he had heard allowed him to infer. The circus was built upon the foundation formed by humans born to the Free Towns. He suspected that those called to the circus were essential to its survival. How many, after all, could turn aside from that call before the circus lost whatever power was necessary to sustain itself?

How long would the Free Towns stand without the circus?

Trevor opened his arms; Adala leapt into them. They closed around her slender body and trembled there—or perhaps it was Adala who trembled. They both understood that, when they passed through the gate, Adala would no longer be a young woman in Hansleigh; she would forever be part of the circus. She could not visit Trevor; he could not visit her.

Not unless and until the circus performed.

Watching as they slowly stepped into the known and unknown future, Gervanno was surprised: an echo of the past returned, as it sometimes did, without deliberate attempt to recall it.

Do not attempt to stand in two worlds.

His Oma had said this, speaking not to Gervanno but to an older cousin—an unmarried woman, edging close to the age where that would become her permanent state.

There is only one world, Oma. I stand on two feet.

You are trying to stand on the border, child. Do not. This is your home. We are your family.

Gervanno did not understand why his Oma had said this—but that wasn't unusual. He agreed with his cousin, Emma. There was only one world.

I will not surrender my art, Emma had replied, hands folding into fists and resting firmly on her hips. She looked like a young version of their Oma, but if Gervanno had been a child, he'd been wise enough not to make the comparison aloud.

Your art won't keep you fed. It won't keep you warm. Where will you get the money required to buy your paints and pigments? What will you use as barter?

The work itself.

Abandon that, girl. It is a conceit. It is a passing fancy. If you cannot understand your place in the world, you will lose it. Do not attempt to stand in two worlds.

There is only one world, his cousin had replied, the tone making the repetition different.

Looking through the open gate, Gervanno shook his head. His cousin would have been chagrined; his Oma, worried. Very worried. The worlds of women and men did not often overlap in the Dominion. Gervanno had no idea what his Oma knew, if she knew anything beyond the vague anxiety caused by superstition.

He heard her words from a remove, and understood that there were far more worlds than one.

"Gervanno," Nenyane snapped.

"I will wait until everyone else has safely entered the gate," he replied. "I do not want to take the risk of having the gate close once I enter. The ticket," he added, "was mine." He gestured at Alex, and Alex nodded; he and Max passed through the gate. When their feet left the streets of Hansleigh, they vanished from sight.

Stephen followed, his dogs at his heels, and Nenyane glared at Gervanno before she followed her Hunter, as she was duty bound to do.

Meralonne would not arrive at this gate. Gervanno accepted Nenyane's assessment as fact. That left only the trees and the golden fox.

The trees, however, returned to the border of forest and town; they had carried Adala into the streets, but did not remain in Hansleigh. "Did you see what became of Jarven and his fox?"

"I did not," the bard replied. "But I do not believe the fox would be welcome in this place. Where the fox cannot pass, Jarven is unlikely to follow. Whatever his duty is, it is not ours."

"Why would the fox be forbidden these lands?"

"There is nothing human in him."

"And Jarven?"

The bard answered with obvious reluctance; it seemed exaggerated to Gervanno, but nonetheless genuine. "Jarven could probably pass through the gate. But he is unlikely to be fully welcome. He has sworn his oaths; he has made his alliance."

"So have the Hunters, but they are welcome."

Kallandras nodded. He then passed beyond Gervanno's questions. Gervanno stood alone in Hansleigh's empty streets.

"HE IS NOT WRONG," a familiar voice said. "And he is not right. That is the nature of mortality. You are not a race for whom absolutes apply, although your social customs often dictate that they must."

Gervanno looked down to see the golden fox. A grey patina of dust —no doubt from the broken stones and buildings—dimmed the sheen of his coat as he padded toward the cerdan. "This war was not my war in times past. It is my war now because the Lord to whom I have pledged allegiance considers it the heart of her own war. The lord of these lands is unknown to her, but not unknown to me.

"Do not trust the gods, Gervanno. You were raised in lands which claim only two: Sun and Moon, Day and Night. In the South, the gods are above your voices, beyond your reach. They exist, and their displeasure—or pleasure—is both unknown and unknowable. You are not succored by them; you are not swayed by them except in the most modest of fashions.

"Do not trust the gods. Do not trust the Firstborn."

Gervanno said, "Eldest." It was not an agreement, but an acknowledgement.

The fox butted Gervanno's shin with his head. Gervanno understood the wordless command, and knelt immediately. The fox leapt onto his lap, and Gervanno gathered his almost insubstantial weight in one arm. "I wish to visit this circus."

The cerdan froze.

Whiskers twitching, the fox chuckled. "The lord of these lands is not a lord who desires to be seen; his touch is so light mortals have failed to recognize it for what it is. He does not interact with those born to—and of—the wilderness, and he does not grant passage into the circus realm. It is, I believe, the seat of his power.

"So I wish to experiment. I believe his rules are clear: only humans may enter the circus grounds. But I also believe, having observed the young townswoman, that it is not an absolute. The mortals who are called to the circus are not entirely human, and they are clearly not prevented from entering.

"You are not entirely unentangled, either, but you were allowed entry. You were gifted a sword, and obviously more, while you wandered the seat of power. I will have you carry me through the gate while it remains open."

"And if I cannot enter while bearing you?"

"Then I will have to find a different method of requesting an audience with the lord of these lands."

"Why is the audience necessary, Eldest?"

"Because my Lord is Sen, and her vision reaches even the most distant of lands."

"Did your lord send you on this mission?"

"My Lord seldom commands," the fox replied, which was not an answer.

Gervanno did not press for more.

"If you continue to hesitate, you will lose your opportunity. Can you not feel the shift in the wind and the earth? The child has passed, and her voice no longer harmonizes the wilderness. They will come, and the gate will be shut and barred. Unless you wish to flee now — when I might guarantee your safety — you must risk carrying an uninvited guest."

Gervanno did not argue. He could not dump the fox in the streets; he barely considered it an option. He understood power and its subtle applications, but it had always been true that the lord he faced was the greater danger than the lord who occupied a distant city. Only when that distant lord was one to whom he had sworn vows of honor was there ever a contest.

He stepped through the open gate.

———

HIS FEET DID NOT TOUCH the cobbled, pristine streets of the circus and its many pavilions. He entered, instead, a small copse of trees that were far taller and wider than he. His arms contained the golden fox; in the distance, he could catch the faint strains of instruments and music. He could almost hear voices, or what sounded like voices to his ear, but words were blurred and indistinct. They were raised in song.

In song that felt familiar, although it took him a moment to untangle that sense of familiarity. Adala's song had sounded very much like this, although no instruments had punctuated the odd, unintelligible syllables.

He stood for a moment in the shadow of the great trunk of the nearest tree. He was only slightly surprised when a man stepped out from the enfolding bark of that tree. This man was very like the guards that had emerged from the trees in the forest outside of Hansleigh to carry and protect Adala from anything that might harm her. But he was taller, darker of skin, and his eyes were a green so bright they seemed lit from within.

"Gervanno di'Sarrado, I greet you."

Gervanno bowed — or began to bow; the fox caught the mound of his palm in his pale, sharp teeth.

"Eldest," the man said, as Gervanno straightened. "You will forgive my lack of manners. Gervanno di'Sarrado is our guest—and one to whom we owe a great debt as of today. We assumed that proper manners would be of little relevance to you, who has entered our lord's land uninvited at this time."

The fox eased the pressure of small teeth. "I am not interested in treating with you; it is to your lord I wish to speak."

"Surely you must understand that at such a time, our lord is much occupied. He is the circus master, and the circus is open to mortal guests."

The low growl in the fox's throat caused Gervanno's arm to tremble.

"We ask your understanding at this time, Eldest. Gervanno must return to his friends, and you must wait until the performance is over." Before Gervanno could speak, the tree said, "It has not yet begun; you have time."

"May we join after the performance has begun?"

"It is frowned upon, but the circus master is aware that pressing emergencies for visitors—such as reclaiming young children—oft make that necessary. You are not such a child, but I believe an exception could be made for you. If you are ready, you will not be late."

Gervanno nodded, but the tree made no move to leave.

"The eldest, however, is not part of the audience; those in the audience are mortals."

The fox almost spit. "And the child that travels with the Hunters? She is considered *mortal*?"

CHAPTER SIXTEEN

The tree fell silent for a long moment.

The fox bristled; he grew markedly heavier as he rested in Gervanno's arms. The tree did not appear to notice the elder's growing displeasure. Artifice. Artifice or certainty that the consequences would be irrelevant.

They would not be irrelevant to Gervanno.

"What the lord allows, he allows; she travels with mortals. When the circus opened to offer entry to the villagers of the Free Towns, she passed through the gates without difficulty.

"She is of their world, Eldest, in a way you or I are not. Take umbrage, if that is your desire — but understand that it should not be taken here. Ser Gervanno, if you wish to rejoin the Hunters to whom you owe your allegiance, you must set the eldest down. The circus master will not allow his passage."

Small, sharp teeth once again closed around Gervanno's hand in warning, but the fox was angry now, and blood, however little, was drawn.

"I see," the tree said, its voice a rumble equal now to the fox's when the fox was in a different form. "Understand, Eldest, that you cannot claim this one; he is not, and will never be, yours. Release him."

The fox was prideful. Had Gervanno any authority, he might have attempted to intervene; he did not. The fox growled, but did not release his hand. The fox might be an ancient, wild force, but even he could not easily speak with a full mouth—in that, at least, he was like any other living creature of Gervanno's acquaintance.

"Ser Gervanno, what would you have us do?" As the tree spoke, others gathered from this copse, leaving bark and roots behind.

"The eldest has come to my aid before. Were it not for his intervention, I would not be here at all; I would be lost in the wilderness. I would not have met my current master; I would not have met my current teacher. I would never have come to the circus at all."

"Had you not, the circus would be far more endangered," the first tree replied. "But the eldest cannot accompany you, and you must return. Here, the eldest might remain until the circus performance draws to its close. But there is only one place, in the circus, that the eldest might stand—and it is not to perform for the delight and awe of mortals that the eldest exists.

"If we have given offense, Eldest, we apologize. But the circus child returned to the circus grounds almost catastrophically late. As you must be aware, these lands in which we stand are at the heart of the high wilderness; it is here that our lord takes his rest. You might stand here, as we stand, and converse; you might leave the woods we gird and explore his hospitality. But Ser Gervanno cannot accompany you."

The fox released Gervanno's hand. "He has risked much for the sake of your lord and your lord's plans," he said, his small teeth reddened with Gervanno's blood. "And you make a grave mistake if you assume I have no interest in his existence."

"You clearly have some interest," the tree replied. "But that is not what I said. You cannot own him. He is not yours. We are aware that you have, from time to time, dabbled in the fates of mortals; you have raised some handful as your own. This one will never be that. What you offer, he does not desire; what you demand, he cannot give."

"Do not believe you can sunder the bonds I have made," the fox growled. "Did you not hear the mortal? He owes me a debt. Were it not for that debt, I would not be here—but neither would he. And it is his will that brought your circus child back to the fold."

"Ser Gervanno, do you serve the eldest?"

"I am too humble an existence to be servant to the eldest," Gervanno replied. Humility had always been an acceptable escape—a way of saying no to the powerful without causing any loss of face. He assumed the fault.

"And too humble to serve our lord," the tree replied, a hint of amusement in the words; he understood Gervanno's intent. So, too, the fox.

Silence enveloped them all. It was the fox who broke it.

"Very well. But tell your lord this: if this man is not mine, he is of *great* interest to me. I will hold your lord—and all of his lieges— responsible should this man die before his time. Mortal time is fleeting enough as is. If Gervanno were wise, he would quit this place; in my Lord's lands, he would be safe."

"Eldest, if he were wise, you would have no interest in him all. But perhaps you better understand my lord's fondness for mortals—they are varied and unpredictable. They are born and they perish. Some are never seen, and some glow so brightly ere their end they are like the sun itself.

"It was to protect such light, such shadow, such brief lives, that our lord made the choices he did, and he has remained true to those choices. While Gervanno remains within the circus boundaries, he will be as safe as he can be."

"The world is changing as we speak," the fox replied.

"That is the nature of life."

"Does your lord regret?"

"If he does, he does not share those regrets with us; we are, as Ser Gervanno, too humble an existence in comparison."

"What are you waiting for?" The fox snapped, sounding peevish rather than furious. "Put me down. It has been long since I have been entertained in the seat of a god's power—even one as reticent and slight as the circus master."

"You forget in whose lands you now walk," the tree said, a note of warning in his tone.

"I? I do not. Were your lord so easily offended by the lack of obse-quious respect, he could not be what he is."

Gervanno knelt and set the fox down on the forest floor. He rose when the fox made no further complaint, noticing the way the earth sank beneath paws that appeared far too dainty to cause such impressions.

"If you would," the tree said to Gervanno, "follow me. I will lead you to the circus grounds."

ONLY WHEN THEY were well quit of the fox and the copse of trees did the tree speak. "I cannot continue to guide you beyond a certain point."

"The circus—"

"Yes. It is possible for my kin to stand within the circus grounds—indeed some handful of us are planted there, as they are within the Free Towns. But until the lord's reign ends, he wishes to hide the wilderness from those who were nonetheless sheltered and protected by the thinnest of its roots.

"I will tell you now, that one of your companions attempted to enter the gate you—and you alone—were given the opportunity to open. He failed to enter; the circus would not accept him."

Gervanno frowned. The frown did not clear when he raised head. "Jarven."

"That is not the name—not the only name—we hear. But yes, it is among them."

"You do not consider him human."

"It was not his desire to remain so. He bears the blood of the eldest, and the will, the intent. Such covenants were once far more common, in an age where there were no mortal lands."

Gervanno lifted a hand; the wounds from the fox's teeth were slight, but visible.

"You do not wish to ask the question foremost in your thoughts." This amused the tree. "If the eldest chose to intervene, if he chose to preserve your life, he almost certainly felt it necessary to mark you in some fashion. It is subtle, and given your various companions, such subtle signs might be easily missed in any other land."

"But such a mark would not prevent me from entering the circus."

"No. It is a mark; it is not a binding gift. It is not something you chose."

"And Jarven?"

"As I said, he has no desire to remain what he was. It is not experience and time that has produced his current power. It is the eldest. Jarven chose. You did not."

Gervanno nodded.

"I see that I have not fully answered your concerns. You must share them; I did but guess. No offense will be taken."

"Stephen of Maubreche."

"The god-born have existed since mortals have existed, in great or lesser fashion; they have become necessary conduits since the gods chose to leave the mortal plane. But they are mortal, they are human."

"And the bard?"

"It is the same. The power that gilds the voice of your friend is a power to which he was born. Not all mortals contain such power, but he is one. So, too, the troubled child, but perhaps she is not your concern."

"She is a concern, Eldest—but it is not for her safety I fear."

"No. She is wild and perilous; her talent is far too large for her. It is a wonder that she has survived at all."

"The fox spoke of one of my companions as if she were not mortal at all—and you did not deny his words."

"Ah. Tell me, how do you know that one?"

"She is huntbrother to Stephen of Maubreche—the god-born child around whom the dogs gather."

"And huntbrother has a meaning to you that it does not have to one such as I. Is it a sworn bonding?"

Gervanno did not know how to answer, but understood that he must make the attempt. "It is a binding, but it is not sworn in the same fashion that the Breodani swear. She and Stephen are two halves of a whole. She..." He almost said *serves*, but it was the wrong word. "Protects him. It is her greatest priority."

"I see. A mortal boy, again. I was not certain I could answer your question when it was first asked. I will answer it now. She is not human, but she has chosen humanity; she will remain by Stephen's side until he—or she—is dead. She is, in any sense the wilderness understands and accepts, Stephen's. Part of him, like a limb. No human visitor has ever been asked to surrender a limb as price of passage." The expression on the tree's face shifted as he spoke, his voice gentling.

"You have not asked for advice, and I should not give it—but I have spent almost all of my life surrounded by the lord's various mortals. Be wary, Ser Gervanno, of the Hunter's sword master. No, I do not imply malice on her part.

"But the answer to your question is this: just as you did not choose to become the fox's cub, and the bard did not choose to be born to the wild power of song and voice, just as Stephen of Maubreche did not choose to be born the son of Bredan, his companion did not choose her birth or her awakening.

"My lord is not human. He is not mortal. But he values choice as he perceives it. Lack of choice does not accrue blame or rejection."

Gervanno was well aware that the lord's interpretation of choice was not choice in any true sense—but it was also an interpretation with which he was very familiar.

"She will not choose you. She *cannot* choose you. Do not covet what you cannot attain." The words were harsh, the tone like summer shade. "But I think it unlikely that this will be a danger you must face. The eldest has grown fond of you in such a short time. Do you see the gate at the end of this path?"

Gervanno nodded.

"Pass through it. It leads to the circus."

"And not to Hansleigh?"

"There is no gate that leads to any of the mortal towns from this place. Our lord favors choice. We must therefore prepare for the consequences of choices we ourselves do not make. The children do not always choose at our convenience. Adala is not the first of the children to disavow the circus. She is not the first who chose to walk away.

"Were it any other time, things would not be so dire, but—a different god now walks the mortal lands, and the consequences of mortal choices might doom us all." Even speaking these words, he smiled. "It is a long, long tale, and in your lifetime—should you survive —you will see its end.

"As will we, who were planted and who grew in this ancient soil. I will not tell you to be wary of the fox. I will, however, tell you that, in cases where your survival is the only concern, you can trust his intent. It is not his desire to entrap you; if he offers you shelter, reject it if he is unwilling to offer his word that your companions will be safe.

"But do not trust him beyond that." The tree offered Gervanno a solemn nod. "We are in your debt," he said, as he lifted his chin. "You brought our stray hatchling back to the circus. Whether she has arrived in time or not does not lessen the debt—for without your intervention, she would not have arrived at all."

THE GATE LED, as promised, to the circus grounds, but he heard nothing, saw nothing but cloud, until both feet were on the other side of the gate. Then he heard the music that had been oddly disjointed, distant snatches of sound; he saw the pavilions and their flags, and streets that were once again crowded.

In such a crowd it should have been difficult to find his companions; it was not. As if the crowd were forest, the natural gaps formed between people led him toward his Hunters and Anya.

Gervanno expected the hunting dogs to notice his presence first. They did not. They were engaged in what appeared to be a growing argument between Nenyane...and the mage. The mage who had not traveled with them from Breodanir to Hansleigh; the mage who had recognized some intrinsic part of Adala's nature.

He approached with care, but did not draw weapon. This was not a place for the type of battle that required it; there were no demons in these streets. The circus master promised safety and succor to the residents of the Free Town—and their guests.

He couldn't hear the argument until he was closer, but he moved as if no such argument existed. It was a trick he'd been taught in childhood, in the distant South. Intervention was never safe, and it must be measured, the risks understood, before one could.

Interfering with family was safe; interfering with friends was relatively safe, although friendship might be lost. Interfering with strangers was almost never done. But in the villages, there were very few strangers, and many of those were men of power.

Anya was a person of power. She sounded, when she spoke, like a younger child, one who had moved beyond the babble of attempted speech to speech itself. Her outbursts—of delight or rage—were spontaneous. Unthreatening.

But her power was not. If use of that power accompanied those outbursts, she could become a natural disaster. There was nothing about her that implied careful reasoning, strategy, or even an awareness of the damage she could do—as if she were, in truth, a young child in the throes of tantrum, and not a woman full grown.

Nenyane was not the most patient of people, but it was not Gervanno who could curb the expression of that impatience; it was Stephen. Stephen, however, stood back, farther behind his huntbrother than the norm.

The first person Gervanno reached was Kallandras. The bard lifted hand, not in greeting, but in request; Gervanno came to a stop, asking Kallandras a question with simple expression alone.

"Anya wishes to visit the pavilions; the pavilions are closing."

"Nenyane points out that her intent—to visit the circus—has been fulfilled, and even if it hasn't, Anya isn't the boss of the circus. Those were her words. Anya did not appreciate them."

"Stephen hasn't intervened."

"No, not yet. In my opinion, that is wise. But that is not, I feel, the heart of the argument."

Gervanno waited.

"When we passed through the gate, we entered the circus grounds; they were as you see them. Nenyane was not pleased that you failed to follow. Anya did not notice your absence. But she did notice that, while Trevor remained with us, Adala did not."

"And that lead to pavilions?"

"Anya's assumption was that Adala had run ahead to enter those pavilions—which were closing. She seems to have taken a personal interest in Adala, and she wished to follow her. Nenyane pointed out that she was making assumptions about Adala's actual destination, and Anya, wishing to perhaps prove a point, demanded the right to search for Adala.

"As the pavilions themselves—with the sole exception of the one offering food and drink—are closed to visitors in preparation for the performance, she was unable to do so."

Gervanno winced.

"And thus the argument. If she were, in fact, a child, the diversion would have worked. She is not. She wishes to find Adala. Now. She has not yet lost her temper, but it is perilously close."

"Does Trevor know where Adala has gone?"

Kallandras shook his head. "I think he has not joined any argument because Anya seems strangely hostile to him—but what she wants, he also wants."

Gervanno exhaled. "The circus, I am told, can take care of itself. But I have a strong suspicion that it will not be safe for the townspeople if Anya actually loses her temper." He watched the crowd's reaction. Some were curious; some leashed curiosity and stood at what one could presume was a safe distance. It was clear that none of the townsfolk had seen Anya's magic, given what that safe distance was.

The crowd would be safe if Nenyane lost hers; she would stomp off, hands in fists. She would not attack Anya; she would not offer the mage violence. Not unless Anya's temper threatened Stephen.

"*I want to see Adala!*" Anya's hair began to rise.

Kallandras stepped forward.

"No, bard. You are a guest. The responsibility is mine."

Gervanno turned; the circus master, in his neat, dark clothing, stepped past Kallandras toward the woman who had just screamed in rage, her hands in fists.

"Anya," he said. From this distance, his voice was clear as a bell struck in silence.

Nenyane fell silent—everyone did. Awe tinted that silence. The circus master himself had stepped into the streets. Did this mean the performance would start soon?

The mage turned to the circus master, her eyes narrowing; they seemed, at this distance, to be almost red, as if reflecting a fire that Gervanno's eyes could not perceive. Her anger was arrested, the words cut off before she finished them.

To Gervanno's surprise, she bowed, her bow very low. A child could not have managed such perfect precision; there was genuine grace in her movements.

"It has been many years since we have sensed your presence in Evanston. You have wandered far."

"I wanted to join the circus, once," Anya said, still bowed.

"Come, child. Rise."

"But I was never chosen. Never."

"The power to which you were born was not a power of, or for, the circus. Are you not aware of how powerful you have become?"

She did rise, as bid; a hint of the child she had once been remained in her expression. "I'm powerful," she replied, smiling.

"Too powerful for the circus."

"But not Adala."

"No."

"I could tell she was circus," Anya continued.

The circus master smiled. "Did she tell you?"

"No—I could see it."

Silence again. It was the circus master who broke it. "See it?"

"It has a taste. It smells of circus. Adala felt like the circus. I could hear her even when she didn't speak."

"And can you see her now?"

"I *want* to see her!"

"Can you tell me why?" His voice was gentle, patient.

Anya shook her head. "I found her!"

No one corrected her.

"Adala is being welcomed into the circus as our newest member," the circus master told Anya. "It is not a ceremony that is part of the circus performance. Perhaps you are unaware of the difficulty the circus presently faces." There was no sarcasm, no doubt, in his tone.

Nenyane snorted, regardless.

Anya frowned, her attention drawn—for the first time—from the circus master and her own desires. What she saw in Nenyane's far less guarded expression caused confusion.

"What?" Nenyane's tone was almost a howl of outrage. "How could you possibly be unaware of the danger to the circus? It was your portal!"

"My portal?"

"Or whatever you want to call it. The *Kialli* meant to destroy the circus—you must have understood that."

"No!"

"Why did they come here at all? Why did they come at this time?"

Anya frowned. "They said they were coming to visit the circus."

"And you made a portal so they could all come here?"

Anya's eyes shifted away from the circus master. Away from Nenyane. Gervanno had seen exactly this behavior from children, newly come to the concept of lying. They weren't *good* at it. They were bad at it in exactly this fashion.

"They're not allowed in the circus. They're not like us. I didn't think they could hurt the circus!"

"So you came because they told you the circus would be performing, and you wanted to visit the circus."

"Yes!"

"Even if they can't hurt the circus, they can destroy all the towns. And that hurts the Free Towns."

"It damages the circus," the circus master said, "but the damage is more subtle; its cost is less immediately obvious. There is a reason that the circus opens its gates. During the performance, those who do not perform leave the circus grounds to guard the towns. In the past, they fought human armies or bandits.

"Against demons such as those you have brought to the borders of my lands, the battle's outcome is far, far less certain."

Anya frowned.

"Adala is necessary; she is, as you surmised, circus. But she is not yet trained to perform; it has been our custom that performers do not take to the stage while they have living family in the towns. It is, therefore, people like Adala, whose attachment to their former homes is strongest, who will be tasked with defense.

"You have allowed passage to an army my children have never faced. The circus will perform. It must perform. But the safety of the circus has been threatened by your actions."

Anya's expression shifted between anger and tears; Gervanno held his breath. Had he the ability, he would have stopped Nenyane; he did not even dream of attempting to stop the circus master.

"I'm not a demon," Anya whispered. "I would never hurt the circus!"

She did not lie. But the temperament of children had always been fickle. Anya looked past the circus master to the varied pavilions, most of which were closing as the performance approached. There was a terrible, painful yearning in her expression; he could only barely see her as a woman full grown.

The circus master turned to Nenyane, of all people. "If you would guide Anya through the pavilions, I will allow her to visit them; they will be quiet now, and the damage she might do, lessened."

Nenyane was not circus. Would never be circus. Nenyane professed to have no patience for children. It had never been necessary. Stephen and Alex were both fonts of endless patience.

"I don't want to leave my Hunter," Nenyane finally said.

"No, of course not. But there will be no productive discussion until Anya has visited those pavilions."

Gervanno doubted that there would be productive discussion at all. Anya was too much like a child.

"Adala?" Anya asked, although her expression was once again far more cheerful.

"She cannot speak with you yet. But perhaps, once you have finished visiting the other parts of my circus, she will be ready. You are not circus," he said, repeating his former words in a much gentler tone. "And your presence may harm her."

"I wouldn't hurt her!"

"Not deliberately, no."

Alex entered the pavilion on the heels of Nenyane and Stephen; Max pulled up the rear. Max found Anya extremely unsettling; he was unwilling to fear her, but that took effort. It wasn't her power that discomfited Max. It was the fact that she sounded like a child.

Alex and Max had been children together. They had fought, made up, fought, and explored in fashions their grandmother considered dangerous. But neither of the two could do damage on the scale Anya could when they lost their tempers.

Alex trusted the circus master enough that he could comfortably accompany a party that included Anya. Max did not.

You saw what she did to the demons.

Alex nodded.

You saw what she did to the airborne creatures.

He had. But as both demons and wyverns would have killed them all had they been given the chance, Alex considered it a positive.

Max considered Anya a weapon, a double-edged sword. His own sword, newly acquired, wasn't sentient; it was unlikely to injure him in an unforeseen fit of pique.

Nenyane's not afraid of her, Alex pointed out.

No. But Nenyane's different. She's likely to survive if Anya throws a tantrum.

Anya was not throwing a tantrum now. The first pavilion they entered was one centered on food. All of the pavilions had offered refreshments, but only one had offered nothing but food. Her expressions of delight were tinged with yearning and greed; Alex had no need to be close to her to hear her exclamations. There was something about her joy that was almost infectious; had it not been for Max's natural suspicion, Alex would have accepted it at face value.

He would have accepted it because it was genuine.

The traces of what she'd eaten remained on her lips, her cheeks, even the edge of her chin; her hands became sticky with foods both sweet and savory. If she was accustomed to forks and knives, there was no sign of it, given how little she used them.

It was Nenyane who gave up in disgust, and accepted the warmed hand towels people in the stall handed Anya—who had ignored them all. It was also Nenyane who impatiently but gently wiped the mage's face clean, which was a losing battle. Anya's stomach was, apparently, bottomless, and new food crumbs and sauces were smeared across her face almost the moment Nenyane had finished cleaning it.

She was so much like a child. So much. How had she come to work with *Kialli*? Why had she allowed a demonic army to enter these lands from wherever it was they now dwelled?

She didn't care about the army. She didn't care about the towns. She cared about coming here. That's it.

Alex didn't believe she intended harm to the circus.

Of course not, his brother snapped. *But she wasn't aware of the harm that could be done. She believes that she will get what she wants—and be safe. I'm not sure she thinks about the safety of other people at all.*

Alex disagreed. Children did—and could—consider the safety of precious few people, but that consideration existed.

Yes, but none of us are her mother.

Where did she live? Could a human—even one as powerful as Anya—live with demons? Could they survive?

Maybe she's one of the demon's pets.

Alex considered Max's words. *Would you try to keep her as a pet?*

Max recoiled. *She's human.*

She is. But you'd never keep her as an ally. If she chose to fight by your side, it would be in the moment—that's the only time it would be safe.

Or maybe you'd need to make her believe that your enemies were her enemies. You could try to focus her that way.

Sure. And it would work for a little bit—but she's a child. She'd get bored. She'd want to do whatever it took to alleviate boredom.

Like visit the circus?

Alex conceded. *Like visit the circus. You win.*

We weren't even fighting, Max replied. But he flinched as Anya's delighted laugher swept across the entirety of the tented area, magnified and echoing, as if trumpeting delight and joy into every quiet corner of the circus would somehow preserve it.

"You have my apologies," the circus master said; both Elseth brothers startled and turned, but neither drew weapons. Max didn't call Steel back, either. "I am the master of the circus, as you are aware. But the circus is not simple entertainment—as you are also, no doubt, aware, if in a lesser way.

"Anya a'Cooper was born in the Free Towns. She came of age in the Free Towns. She was not meant for the circus—although a thread of that is woven into her being. Her power was far too great; had she taken the advice she was given, she would have become a mage without parallel at a moment in history when such power is required if mortals are to survive beyond the tiny enclaves they once called home.

"But she made Adala's choice."

Max frowned. Alex, however, understood. "She ran away."

"With the young man who had become the object of her affection, yes. It was too late before that point; I had fully expected that, in the absence of the mage-born who might better teach her to handle and release the power she was building, she would perish. It is not the first time it has happened; it will not be the last.

"But she left the townships. If she subsequently faced a catastrophic failure, her town would not be destroyed."

Alex's frown deepened as he considered the words.

"The young daydream of power," the circus master continued. "But power is dangerous if it is not carefully handled. In the minds and bodies of the mage-born, power accretes; if there is no clear way to release it, one of two things might happen. In Anya's case, both were likely. She would damage her mind significantly, and she would destroy her body—and everything within range of the blast—when her body instinctively forced that power out in a vain attempt to preserve itself.

"I do not know where she was found. Were she not one of my scattered children, I would have denied her entry to the circus grounds. But she was, and is. You are wondering if it is safe to have her here. The answer, if you desire certainty, is no. But she will not willingly or knowingly imperil the circus.

"I believe it would be safest if she and Adala remain separated at this point. I am uncertain that Anya's rage will not be Trevor's death—and should she make the attempt, I will have to destroy her. If that is possible."

"Why Trevor's death?"

"Anya ran away with her young man. She was betrayed, and she therefore holds a burning hatred of claims of love. She will not trust Trevor, of course; she will believe that Adala should hate him. But something in Adala resonates with Anya, and we do not wish to trigger it."

None of this felt like reason for apology. Max's attention had drifted; Alex's had sharpened. Only one of them had to understand what was being said.

"Alex of Elseth, I would consider myself in your debt if you could contain the two most difficult members of your company, where it is at all possible."

He could think of only one, but responsibility for Nenyane's temper was generally Stephen's. "You don't mean Anya, do you?"

The circus master did not reply.

"Anya isn't part of our company—she came with the demons."

"Is that the whole of your objection?"

Alex shook his head. "You must know, you must have noticed, that Anya doesn't interact with men. The best I think we can hope for is a passing gaze; we become part of the landscape, something she passes by or over. There's a reason she spoke with Adala, and a reason she speaks with Nenyane."

The circus master nodded. "Adala should have been present at the circus almost two weeks before we opened our gates to visitors; she was not. I will do what I can to keep Trevor far away from Anya. His death will not hurt the circus directly, but it will severely damage Adala's commitment, at a time when the circus cannot afford it."

"Demons can't enter the circus," Alex whispered. The last word tailed up, making a question of the statement.

The circus master said, "That is the belief, yes. Belief, here, has a weight, a potency that it does not, beyond these borders. Remember it. Remember it, should you survive and pass into the wilderness, high or low.

"Anya will be occupied for the moment. If it is possible to keep her occupied and in this joyful state, she might join the audience when the auditorium and the stage are ready, if they are ready in time."

"In time for what?"

"The performance, young Hunter." The circus master smiled. "Go, now, or you will fall behind."

———

IT WASN'T hard to find Anya again; her voice could be heard anywhere beneath the ceilings above their heads. Alex was certain they'd be heard outside of the pavilion. Anya was attached to Nenyane's arm—clutching her sleeve like a young child who was afraid to lose a parent in a crowd.

There were no crowds, now. The stalls were empty of visitors, although those who tended the stalls remained. Children had snuck back into the pavilion, which was theoretically closed, and they were followed by their parents—or grandparents, aunts, uncles or older siblings—making the buildings seem less empty.

Anya noticed; she waved at young children, often with food in her hand; the very enterprising chortled and toddled toward her. She smiled at the elderly; the only time her hand left Nenyane's arm was to offer an old woman support when she almost tripped.

Now, looking at her back, Anya seemed like a village girl on the edge of adulthood, which might remain permanently out of her reach. Nenyane's sleeves became her napkin, but Nenyane didn't seem to mind that. Alex thought she probably hadn't noticed. Crumbs weren't dangerous. They weren't poisonous, and given the list of possible dangers Stephen faced, they probably blended into the dust and debris of their journey to return to the circus.

Seen now, Anya wasn't a threat. And that was the problem with Anya. Lack of threat could morph, unpredictably, into death and destruction, dependent entirely on a mercurial mood and triggers none of them knew well enough to avoid.

But the circus master had heavily implied that Anya's power might be needed to defend the circus itself. Alex would have much preferred the mage—APhaniel—as the source of last defense, but the mage had not returned to them. Even had he, he had been wary enough of the circus and its master that he was unlikely to take a step onto the circus grounds themselves.

Anya, however, was here. There was no question that she would have the right to enter the circus, and no question that the circus master considered her a guest of import. The pavilions had ceased their closing operations, and the circus performance—which Alex inferred had been delayed—would be delayed further if she was to be kept happy.

But even so, it was Alex who approached Stephen—not Nenyane, but the end result would be the same. It was Alex who suggested, after some hesitation, that Nenyane should lead her to the pavilion that contained the very unusual lost and found, if she was willing to go.

She was willing to follow Nenyane, but Nenyane found watching her eat—volubly and messily—entertaining, and Anya stopped at every single stall. Nenyane didn't hurry; indeed, she seemed to be seeing these stalls for the first time. Maybe she was. Nenyane's visceral dislike of simple entertainment in the lee of looming war had colored everything. This second time, she was more deliberate.

"Nenyane thinks it's important," Stephen told the Elseth Hunter.

"So does the circus master," Alex replied, matching the near-whisper in which Stephen spoke.

"You spoke with him?"

"He suggested that I follow Anya and keep her distracted." He felt Max's warning, wordless, and fell silent.

Anya had moved toward Stephen—and therefore Alex—as Nenyane moved. She dropped a hand to pat one of the dogs; Pearl, as it happened. Pearl, ever sensitive to the hierarchy of attention and affection, drew attention simply by walking; Anya was willing to give Pearl what she all but demanded. If Pearl had become aggressive or defensive, Alex wasn't certain Pearl would survive.

The dog, however, seemed delighted by Anya's attention, and that held the chaotic woman in place for several minutes. When she rose, hand still absentmindedly clutching Nenyane's sleeve, she yawned. It was neither subtle nor ladylike, although Alex had expected neither.

Alex glanced at Stephen; Stephen nodded. They shared no Hunter bond, but years of experience textured the silence between them.

Stephen followed Alex as Alex began to move. Nenyane would follow Stephen, when Anya was ready.

Gervanno and Kallandras had not entered the pavilion at all.

———

GERVANNO DID NOT ENTER the pavilion on Alex's heel. He knew where the Hunters would eventually emerge—unless Anya lost her temper—because there was only one way to both enter and leave.

Stephen found his absence odd. He had known Gervanno for a relatively short time, but in that time, the Southern guard had become an integral part of daily life. There was little routine in that life, and perhaps that's why he had become an almost natural addition. His presence marked the boundary between life in Maubreche and life beyond it.

He was technically a Maubreche guard, but that was a polite fiction.

It isn't a fiction, Nenyane said.

It was. Free of contracts and the pay that resulted, Gervanno

would follow because of Nenyane. The two—Gervanno and Nenyane
—found joy in the sparring that Stephen considered a necessity to be
endured. He wished he had a tenth of Gervanno's enthusiasm.

So do I.

Stephen shook his head, smiling at her tone, at the sound of her.
Alex wants us to go the pavilion with the lost and found stall.

Why?

*I'm not sure. The circus master wants Anya to be distracted and amused
until the performance starts.*

Mention of the performance didn't sour Nenyane's mood. *Does he
know who she is?*

I'd guess he'd have to, to ask that. She seems to like you.

Nenyane nodded, but failed to find words. Anya had visited every
single stall in the pavilion before she was satisfied. Given the speed at
which she had eaten, it was a wonder she could walk at all.

Nenyane followed Stephen, who let Alex take the lead. Anya took
it back, tugging Nenyane toward the pavilion of Fortune and fate. As it
was where Alex wished to lead her, neither Stephen nor Alex objected.

Nenyane made one attempt to divert the mage, and when that
failed, surrendered. Anya didn't appear to notice the Hunters or
Gervanno, but she was unwilling to be left alone, as her grip on
Nenyane's sleeve made obvious.

The skies above the streets of the circus were clear—Stephen imagined they always were on the days the circus opened. The color,
however, had changed: it was now an amethyst, paling as it reached for
the sun—or what should have been the sun. No sun reigned in those
skies. What rested at the heights was a pale, silvery moon—as if
evening had fallen but was kept at bay at the will of the circus master.

Anya didn't notice the sky.

The people gathered in the streets did. Kallandras, lute in arms,
began to play—his music soft enough that it could be submerged in the
noise of crowds, but loud enough to be heard. The bard did not sing.
Stephen had seen Kallandras perform in the dining rooms of inns.
There, he was a bard from Senniel College in the heart of the Empire;
he engaged, he chuckled, he responded to his audience. His music was
meant to entertain, to move, to speak to shared experience.

Stephen was certain the bard could do that with his eyes closed.
This, however, was different. There was a frown of concentration, and
a slip of fingers, a breaking of what might be melody, and a return to it;

there was no rhythm to the flow of notes. It was almost as if the bard
was composing as he walked, and the piece itself was difficult, almost
atonal in places.

It was not music played to please a crowd. It was not, perhaps,
music at all, just the beginnings of what might, if not abandoned,
become a song.

Anya heard it and paused, turning her head in the bard's direction,
her grip on Nenyane's sleeve loosening. If Kallandras noticed the shift
in attention, he gave no sign of it. But what Anya heard was clearly not
what the Hunters heard; she started to hum.

Stephen exhaled in relief.

She's not that *skittish*, Nenyane snapped.

*She's from the Free Towns. Maybe even the townspeople would hear some-
thing in Adala's song that the rest of us can't.*

To Nenyane, that was a reasonable guess. Humming, Anya tugged
Nenyane's sleeve, and they began to move again.

GERVANNO HAD no desire to enter the pavilion of fate and fortune,
having entered it and left it once before. Anya lingered in the streets to
listen to the bard before she remembered where she'd been heading.
She had not mentioned Adala again. Glancing behind, Gervanno could
see the circus workers closing the pavilion Anya had finally left; he
imagined awnings and booths being dismantled the minute she had no
more use for them.

He was grateful for the absence of Trevor. Anya was easily
distracted, but her desire to find Adala could return without warning.

Whatever it was Adala was now doing, he hoped she would
complete it successfully. He did not like the color of the sky, having
seen it before, and felt certain that the shift in color, from natural blue
to purple, implied that time was, as the forest people had said, of the
essence.

Anya and Nenyane entered the pavilion. Gervanno chose to wait
outside the entrance. Any hint of childhood wonder, any nostalgia that
arose from it, had been crushed and broken by where that glimpse had
led; he did not wish to subject himself to any further responsibility.

Kallandras, however, followed, keeping pace with the hindmost of
the dogs.

Left alone, Gervanno found his gaze drawn to the sky; it was beautiful and it was wrong. The skies, upon entry to the circus, had been the clear blue of cloudless day; the clouds that had scudded across Hansleigh's skies had not been granted entry.

No one could mistake the circus for a natural place—no visitor, no outsider.

But Gervanno and his companions were not the only outsiders present. Looking through the gathered crowd, the cerdan caught sight of a familiar woman: Eva Juwal. He glanced toward the pavilion's interior, and then toward the Imperial merchant. The circus master had not tasked Gervanno with Anya's care; he had given that duty to Alex.

No harm would come to Stephen in the pavilions here.

Gervanno left the entrance of the building and headed toward Eva. She was surrounded by her own people: a dozen guards, perhaps fifteen; a younger woman; and a man Gervanno's age, the latter bearing scars very similar to Eva's. Eva's past was not well-known, although she attracted stories because she could so credibly sit at their heart.

He caught her attention. The guards she employed did not notice him; had he intended to kill Eva, he might have managed it. He wouldn't even be guaranteed to die after the attempt.

Her companion felt familiar, but Gervanno could not place his face. If they had met, it would have been along the merchant roads, at one of the inns or merchant compounds provided for their use. The man did not speak, but Gervanno did not speak much either. It would have been hard to wedge words of his own between Evaro's—the man could talk for four hours straight without apparent need for breath.

Eva noticed Gervanno. "I see you made it in." She smiled, the smile sharp. Nothing about Eva was soft.

"There was some difficulty. But we made it in time to witness the performance." He glanced, deliberately, at the sky.

Eva noted the direction of his gaze.

"You've been to the circus before," he said.

"I have. When the circus performs, the towns empty."

"Have the skies ever been this color?"

Eva's eyes narrowed almost to slits. "No."

"Has the performance been delayed to this extent in your prior visits?"

Eva's hesitation was marked, but she answered. "No. By now, the pavilions would be dismantled, and the stragglers ushered into the

line." Eyes still narrowed, she said, "What's happening? You said you
had some difficulty."

Gervanno nodded.

Eva slid from Weston, her mother tongue, to Torra. Most of her
people would understand her, but the townspeople were unlikely to do
the same.

"What was the difficulty? Does it have something to do with the
sky?"

Eva's advice had driven the Hunters to the circus. Were it not for
Eva, they would likely not have entered the grounds when the gates
opened.

"I hoped you might answer that," Gervanno replied, relenting. "I've
seen skies like this before—but only since the roads themselves have
become strange and unpredictable."

Eva whistled. "You survived a turning?"

"Barely." The weight of the single word was a wall. Eva understood
it, and asked for no more.

"Do you know why the performance has been delayed?"

Gervanno exhaled. "One of the people called to join the circus ran
away. She decided to return, but arrived an hour ago. Perhaps longer,
now."

Eva's brows rose, widening the contours of her eyes before they
relaxed into their normal, narrowed shape. "She decided to return?"
Eva mimicked Gervanno's voice exactly.

"She is, I am informed, *circus*. Until the last moment, the decision to
return or run was hers. She was not dragged back by force—I am not
even certain that's possible."

"Fool of a girl. If she was called, she knows better."

Gervanno and Eva were of an age. Both were far from the dreams
and desires of the young. The dreams that had gripped Gervanno as a
young man were not the dreams that had moved Trevor to leave his
family and his life.

"Would you have gone, if called?" he asked.

"Yes. Wouldn't you?"

"Nothing like the circus existed in my childhood home."

"Not an answer."

Gervanno smiled. "Yes. You have not seen skies of this nature
above the circus before."

Eva shook her head. "Are we going to need the weapons we didn't bring with us?"

"I do not know." He glanced up again. "Nor would I counsel you to retrieve them."

Eva's eyes narrowed further; they almost seem closed. "What waits us in the streets of the towns?"

"Demons. You have not attended a circus in which those called to serve failed to arrive?"

"It would never be announced. If they failed to answer the call, we wouldn't have known." Eva exhaled. "This brings back memories—and I don't need them. But the turnings, the transformation of the merchant roads, the losses of whole villages in the kingdoms—those never happened, either. Is that what you came to ask?"

Gervanno nodded.

"I won't ask how you know what awaits us. I won't ask how you found our missing circus person. I won't even ask how you got back in. But it's clear to me the circus master intends you to do something to protect and guard the circus. The performance hasn't started." Her voice lowered at the last sentence. "It *has to start*.

"You don't understand. Fine. But every person born to the townships understands—and the fact that the performance has been delayed is beginning to cause alarm. Get that fancy bard of yours out here. Do what you can to keep the crowd calm or excited in the *right* way."

Gervanno nodded again. It did not occur to him to argue with Eva Juwal. Only the very young would have tried.

THE INTERIOR OF THIS PAVILION, unlike the food pavilion, was somber and almost silent. The stalls that had offered refreshment had been taken down. The atmosphere of the halls in which fortune-tellers offered glimpses of the future was all that remained.

Alex saw no other visitors.

The people sitting at chairs on the other side of tables wore robes, some embroidered in a way that symbols caught light, as if they were stars in the depths of night sky. Anya passed them by, almost unseeing. Instead of walking slightly behind and to the side of Nenyane, she dragged Nenyane along in her wake. Her entire demeanor had changed the moment they'd entered the pavilion. She no longer grazed; she barely noticed what she passed.

She was looking for something or someone specific.

One of the oldest of people seated rose as Anya approached. Anya failed to notice her. Alex noted that, while there were men on the other side of some of the tables, none attempted to draw Anya's attention to themselves.

"There you are, child," the woman said quietly.

Anya stopped so suddenly Nenyane collided with her.

"Katie? Katie is that you?" Anya whispered.

"Anya," the woman replied. "You remember me. You remember my name."

"I got in *so much* trouble because I called you Katie—my mother said it wasn't right. Because you were important."

"I remember your mother." The woman left her stall and came to stand beside Anya. "She loved you very, very much, but she was often nervous around other people."

"Is she here?"

"No. She was never called to serve. But most people with young children aren't called. Only when the children are old enough—if they ever are—are we asked to leave them. Most of the people who are asked to join the circus are younger than I was. But my marriage and my firstborn came two years before the circus performed.

"I was allowed to raise them, first."

"What about Peter?"

"Peter was not called."

"I wasn't, either."

"No. We can't tell," the woman continued, when Anya fell silent. "None of us could tell who might—or might not—be called. There were bets. Games. Braggarts who turned out to be wrong. Or right. But we had our own hopes and dreams. Fate isn't always kind.

"By the time I was called, my girls were old enough to be envious and excited. They knew they weren't supposed to tell anyone until the circus opened—but they had friends, and they were about to lose me. They had to find *some* joy in it."

"You can't go home?" Anya asked, as if she didn't know the answer.

"No. Not while the circus is needed." The woman lowered her head. "I don't usually work in the stalls. The circus can be so overwhelming to newcomers—and I'm a relative newcomer. It's a big adjustment, and it's made harder if we see, or are seen, by our families, our friends." She glanced past Anya to the Hunters. "Or our former pets."

"But you're here."

Katie—Alex felt uncomfortable thinking of this woman as Katie, but had no other way to address her—nodded. "I'm here because you're here. The circus master told me that if I chose to meet you, I could." She held out both of her hands.

Anya placed her own on top of them. It was the first time since they'd arrived that she'd willingly let go of Nenyane's arm.

"I know it's been a long time since you left the towns," Katie continued. "But they were your home. I hope..." the woman exhaled. "I hope they still are."

"I don't live there," Anya replied—but the words were a whisper.

Alex felt the hair on the back of his neck begin to rise. He stepped in, smiling, as if both Katie and Anya were extremely proud, extremely prickly ruling Hunter Ladies. "Might we visit your stall? Anya was very interested in the pavilions—she came all this way to visit the circus again.

"I apologize for our lack of manners—we didn't want to intrude. I am Alexander, and this is my brother Maxwell. We hail from Elseth, in the kingdom of Breodanir to the west. Nenyane and Stephen are from Maubreche."

"And your dogs?"

Alex's smile was deep and genuine. "My brother's dog is Steel." Steel lifted his head at the sound of his name, and padded forward toward Katie. Katie's hands were occupied. "The white dog closest to Anya is Pearl, and she feels her introduction is the only vital one."

Katie chuckled. "She's a beauty—no wonder she's conceited."

Alex continued down the list of Stephen's dogs. He met Katie's warm, friendly gaze, his own silent and pleading. As if she understood, Katie did not ask Anya to consider the towns her home again. "Do you tell fortunes here?" he continued, as Anya's face lost some of its rigidity.

"I do—but I am very new to it. People think, given my age, I should be old and seasoned. I should be more certain in my delivery. I've been practicing backstage since I first arrived. Anya?"

Anya blinked. "My fortune?"

"Come sit across from me. No, wait, let me get back to my chair.

The damn things are so uncomfortable—the circus master must think we have butts of stone."

Anya laughed out loud.

Alex froze. But the circus master, if displeased with the obvious disrespect, did not suddenly appear to correct it. Anya took the chair in front of the stall, and the Hunters, accustomed to social distance, stood back. Except for Nenyane, who had been studying Katie as if she were a particularly unique sword. She had started to move, but Anya had, once again, grabbed her arm, granting silent permission to remain.

"These balls," Katie said, pushing the obvious crystal ball to the side and out of the way, "aren't any good to me. I've been taught to incorporate 'em. That's the word they used. Incorporate." She rolled her eyes.

Anya's smile was deeper, it was genuine. The momentary clouds that had changed her expression were gone, as if pushed aside by a strong wind. She knew this woman. Or had known her when she had lived in the Free Towns. Alex was certain she didn't live in them now.

"Why do they think it's important?" Anya asked.

"It's what people expect. Little magics, small talents, are real—if they weren't, we would never be called. But people's belief, people's desire *to* believe, really help them. And us. So we tell 'em to look into the crystals, to think about their future, or even just to listen and wait —and you know how people are. If breathing required patience, half the town would drop dead."

Anya laughed again. "What should I do, then?"

"Just take my hand, and then—be patient. Let me see. Let me try to understand what I'm seeing. The real seers—they don't need touch at all. They can see *so much*. But they're rare and they're dangerous. Here, in the circus, we speak to the townies. We're not supposed to terrify them.

"We're allowed to caution them if what we see is bad. And they're willing to listen because it's why they come here at all. But it's like the touch itself builds a bridge."

"A bridge?"

"Between me and them. Or between me and you."

Anya hesitated and then placed a hand much more tentatively across Katie's.

"How does it work?"

"I don't know. I just...see a future. A possible fate."

"Is it good or bad?"

"It takes a bit. Patience, remember?" Katie's tone was sharp, but affectionate.

Anya was a child, trapped in a body that didn't reflect it. She couldn't sit still; her patience involved fidgeting in silence. But her expression was absorbed, eager.

"What if it's bad? What do you tell people?" In a different tone, she added, "Do you lie?"

"No. I'm not good at that—you know that. Maybe that's why I'm not really ready to sit here when most visitors come. But I don't want to see my kids."

"Yes, you do."

"I mean—I don't want them to see *me* right now. I don't know if they'll recognize me. I don't know if I'll recognize them. I wasn't young when I joined the circus. You recognize me because I almost look the same as I did the last time you saw me."

"But then they'll know who you are, too!" Anya almost jumped out of her seat.

Katie's hand tightened. "I'm not allowed."

Anya's face stiffened, her eyes and lips thinning. Her free hand clenched into a fist as it lay on the tabletop.

Katie shook her head. "That's always been true. Families take pride in having children considered worthy of the circus—but that's all they're left with: pride. Those who are chosen won't live with us; they won't cook for us or eat what we've cooked. They won't give us grand-children. I had my children before I was called. I had a family, and they were almost fully grown. And I deserted them. I left them with empty *pride*. But at least they were old enough to understand.

"It won't do me any good to see them. What if they're having trouble? What if they need help? I've got nothing to offer, but I'll desperately *want* to.

"Really, it's probably for our sake. The rules are what they've always been. I can see my family when the performance is finally underway, because they won't see me, then. But I've seen others do the same. The people who are happiest working for the circus are people who don't have family they can recognize anymore."

"Why? Why don't they?"

"Because their families live their normal lives, they grow old, and they die."

Anya's brows rose.

"And we're left behind. We're left behind in the circus created to protect those lives even if we can't be a part of them anymore." Katie grimaced. "Sorry, I shouldn't have said that."

"You always said things you shouldn't say. My mother told me that *all the time*."

"I liked your mother. She was always so nervous; you could say hello in the wrong tone and she'd jump six feet. But she was kind. She was helpful. She was so worried for you. I'd had my girls, and they were a bit older, so she'd come to me for advice. Why, I don't know; she found me intimidating."

"I know why," Anya said.

It was the first thing she'd said that seemed to surprise Katie. "Why?"

"Because you didn't lie. You didn't tell her it would all be fine."

"But that's what she wanted."

"Because if *you* said it, she'd believe it. But you didn't say it."

Katie inhaled. "No. I didn't. But how do you know what I said?"

"She told my dad. She was crying. I listened."

"When you were supposed to be in bed, no doubt."

"I was in bed, but I could hear her anyway. I listened because of the taste of the words — it was different from normal."

"Yes," Katie agreed. "It was." She closed her eyes once again, her head canting slightly forward as if she was craning to see whatever it was the contact between their hands evoked.

Her eyes opened, rounding in surprise; her mouth opened silently, as if she was attempting to grasp words that rushed past before they could be uttered.

"Oh Anya, child," she whispered, her hand white-knuckled around the mage's.

CHAPTER SEVENTEEN

"K atie—are you *crying*?"

Anya freed her hand from Nenyane's sleeve, and reached out to cup Katie's cheek in her palm. Katie was, indeed, crying.

"No, of course not."

Alex, adept at dealing with women in all stations of power, had always found tears difficult. Small children cried openly but accepted comfort readily, when they could be comforted at all. The women of Alex's experience often felt tears showed an appalling lack of self-control. To acknowledge the tears at all was to acknowledge what they did not wish acknowledged.

Women of power did not want to appear weak. They couldn't afford it.

Katie, as Anya called the woman at this stall, would have been at home in Breodanir.

"Why are you crying?" Anya asked, ignoring Katie's reply. "Who made you cry?"

The answer, to Alex, was obvious. Whatever Katie had seen while she did her job here had caused those tears. What she had seen of Anya.

Katie did not blame Anya; instead, she lifted the hand Anya held and wiped her eyes with the back of it. "Life sometimes makes me cry," she told Anya. "Some days, it seems like nothing but loss and pain. But

I'd never want all of life to be destroyed as a punishment for a few minor tears."

Anya nodded, expression grave.

"The towns were my home. They're the homes of my children, my children's children, the friends who survived without me. I was called to the circus," Katie added, rising. "And I came. But I didn't come the way you might have, were you called. I came knowing that I would be leaving my life behind.

"I had time to say my goodbyes. And I did."

"You didn't *want* to be here?"

"Oh Anya, I did. I gave up my home to protect it. I wasn't running away from it. I was running toward its future. But I've been here for years, and the circus isn't my home. My home is there. My home is in the crowd gathering before the performance begins. My home will be in the seats of the audience. My home, until the circus is closed, will be just in reach. I won't be able to touch it.

"Not the way I've touched you."

Anya ran around the table before Katie could leave. Without asking, she hugged the woman. Katie tensed slightly before relaxing.

Alex exhaled. "Ma'am, what can we do to help?"

"You brought our wayward child back. You found our Anya, and brought her back as well. I don't think we can ask for anything more." She returned Anya's hug before lowering her arms. "It was good to see you, child. I hope, in the future, you remember the circus and the townships the circus was created to protect. You weren't called to the circus because your fate is too grand for three large towns—but I ask that you remember us.

"If the circus falls today, all of my choices, all of my sacrifices, will be in vain; I would have been better off huddling together with my family while the end comes. Don't—don't forget us."

Anya was slower to release Katie, but she did. Her arms were tense by her side when she lowered them. "I won't. I *won't* forget."

Katie lifted a gentle hand, cupped Anya's cheek, and smiled. "I won't forget you, either. Here, should the circus stand, I will always remember this day. I'm being called away."

Alex had heard nothing. Anya, however, tilted her head as if listening to a voice not meant for the ears of outsiders. She was of an age with the woman whose hand slid away from her cheek, but age had not transformed her as it did most others. She was an eternal child.

"Katie!" Anya said, raising her voice as this small piece of her child-hood began to walk away.

Katie stiffened; it was brief. When she turned, her face was composed in a smile. The smile you'd give a child who was caught up in a terrible situation not of their own making.

"I won't forget! I won't let them destroy your life!"

Katie's smile dimmed, as if clouds had passed over the brief glimpse of sun. She opened her mouth, but closed it before words could escape. Alex could almost feel what remained unsaid. She wanted to offer comfort. She wanted to offer reassurance. She wanted to tell the child in adult clothing that it wasn't her responsibility.

Instead, she swallowed. "Thank you, Anya. I must go."

"I know. I know, I hear them. Gods are *so* noisy."

Alex was almost stunned at the casual—and disrespectful—mention of gods, but had long since given up on expecting basic respect from Anya.

Katie, however, surprised him. "They are. So very noisy." Her smile was both tremulous and simultaneously fond, but the fear in it changed its meaning. "I hope you get to see the performance."

"Will you be there?"

"I won't be performing on the stage, no. My gifts were never meant for a large audience. Even if they were, I wouldn't be the one chosen."

"Do you *want* to be?" Anya demanded.

Katie's smile was far more genuine. "No. I never liked people all that much. It's a wonder I had a family at all."

"My mother liked you," Anya said.

"I didn't say people didn't like *me*. I have to go."

"You should just say no."

"Can you say no when your god summons you? Can any of those who follow him?"

Anya shook her head, her shoulders curving inward. This time when Katie walked away, Anya made no attempt to stop her.

NENYANE COULD HEAR THE GOD. She failed to acknowledge it. She failed to acknowledge any authority she hadn't chosen for herself. But she managed—with the scions of the wilderness—to fail in a way that caused no offense.

She was on edge. She had watched the fortune-teller, had listened to the quiet conversation between eternal child and a woman who seemed of an age with her, and had waited in silence until all contact had been broken.

The only question she wanted to ask of Katie she couldn't ask without interrupting. She had therefore chosen to keep it to herself. Stephen, aware of his huntbrother's impatience, understood that, to Nenyane, Anya was a force of nature; a wild power. She wasn't human, not in the way the rest of her companions, saving only Meralonne, were. She demanded, by presence alone, the respect Nenyane would have offered ruling lords in the wilderness.

Nenyane wanted to ask Katie if her god summoned those who worked in the circus grounds often. If he summoned them directly before the performances the circus put on.

You already know the answer, Stephen told her. He, too, did not wish to discomfit Anya. Having seen her magery on display, and having watched her descent into childlike innocence and tantrum, he understood that the consequences, ill-considered—if considered at all—would be profound for the circus.

I don't, or I wouldn't want to ask.

The answer is clearly no. No, the god doesn't delay the performance. No, the god doesn't summon the circus workers.

You don't know that.

It's not a coincidence that the call went out upon Adala's return. We lost sight of her almost the moment we passed through the circus gates. Whatever is done to those who are called to join the circus, I'm certain it's not a simple explanation of new rules and new life. Adala was necessary. Had she not been, I don't think Evayne would have been here at all.

Nenyane tensed. She viscerally distrusted the seer-born woman.

We did what she needed us to do. Adala returned. Adala accepted—very late —the call.

That's all we actually *know.* Nenyane turned to Anya. "Is there anything else you'd like to see before we join the line to get into the biggest of the pavilions?"

Anya nodded, eyes narrowed, brow creased beneath dark hair that now showed signs of silver. Of physical age. She turned and began to walk. She followed the direction Katie had taken.

Nenyane's groan was almost inaudible; Stephen felt that, had it been loudly vocal, Anya would have failed to hear it. No one wanted

Anya to interfere in the circus investiture, if that's what it was. No one wanted Anya to confront a god.

Stephen was almost of a mind to leave Anya to her own devices. If the circus master was, as Nenyane had implied and Katie had finally confirmed, a god, this was his domain. Nothing the Breodani did could equal what a god might achieve, should a mage of incalculable power throw an arcane tantrum.

But where Anya went, Nenyane followed. Neither Stephen nor Alex interfered.

THE FIRST THING Alex heard when he exited the pavilion of fate and fortune was bardic song. He recognized Kallandras's voice, having heard it in the inns along the road. Warmth and familiarity radiated from the bard's tone, and that tone—soft in feel—carried easily above the scattered conversations of those who waited for the performance venue to open.

The streets were crowded; children, young enough to think an hour or two an impossible eternity, were running around standing adults as if they were simple landmarks. Adults waited with the patience children couldn't, but Alex could sense worry and restlessness in many of them. Where Kallandras's song reached them, the edge of that restlessness became blunted before it could give way to fear.

More than that, he did not observe. Nenyane had almost vanished from view, and the crowd stood in more of a huddle than an actual queue. Nenyane followed Anya; Stephen could lead Max and Alex toward them.

Anya seemed to be calmer in the presence of women or children; Nenyane was the only woman present. It was imperative that the mage remain calm, and the Maubreche huntbrother knew it; it was why she gave chase immediately.

The irony of the concept of Nenyane as comfort was lost on none of the Hunters. Nenyane was the least diplomatic of the four present; she was worse than even Max.

I'm way better than Nenyane, Max snapped.

Alex didn't argue with his brother. He could have; in their lives as Elseth Hunters, Max had been rude to the point of insult on dozens of occasions.

That's not rude, that's blunt.

Alex grimaced. He glanced at Steel, who kept pace with Max. Steel was an older dog, and far less likely to find the crowd disturbing or threatening, but the brunt of Breodani training involved hunting, not navigating crowds. In Breodanir, the villagers knew to give the dogs space, although the youngest of children often ignored this unspoken rule.

Anya, very like those young children, seemed not to notice the crowd at all; had she, she would have moved to its outer edge. Following her cost time spent in apologies for minor collisions. Anya didn't bother with them. To be fair, neither did Nenyane. Stephen and Alex were the most hampered by simple manners. Max managed to give a passing nod to them but allowed Alex to make his excuses, as he often did.

Katie had touched Anya's hand. Katie had seen some future loss, something that had almost made her cry. Alex knew very little about fortune-tellers. He knew very little about the magi, just enough to know Meralonne was not a normal mage-born servant of the Order of Knowledge.

He wouldn't have needed even that much knowledge to know Anya was in a class of her own. Had he been in charge, had he required the services of an extremely powerful mage, he would have searched the kingdom—and the Empire—in desperation before choosing to accept Anya's aid. She was not like a sword; she was not like a soldier. She could, with ease and disregard, destroy every person standing on a field of battle; sides would be irrelevant. She was guided by impulse, and that impulse, resembling a child's, was unreliable, unpredictable.

Alex was very worried. Demons weren't required for the destruction of the circus and the fabled protection it offered the townships. Anya was more than enough, and she was already here. He'd inferred that a god had created this place; that a god's power was entwined with the townships in some fashion. He knew less about gods than he did about magi, but they were called gods for a reason: they could, if one believed even an iota of myth and legend, destroy and reshape entire continents on a whim.

But he'd let Adala leave the town.

Adala's presence—or perhaps her absence—had thrown the entire circus into jeopardy. The god had not attempted to retrieve her. He had let the small consequences of human interactions make the decision.

He had allowed Gervanno to enter the pavilion of fortune and fate; what the Southerner saw there had led to their attempt to find Adala before she perished at the hands of demons.

The demons were beyond the circus gates, but they were present in great numbers. Perhaps they would destroy the towns, which would cause severe hardship for the townspeople. But living people could, with will, time, and resources, rebuild. Nothing could revive the dead.

Why didn't the god of this land expel the demons? Why did he allow demons to stand on the ground entwined with his power? What *was* this god?

Alex sped up. He didn't have to mind hunting dogs, and if he lacked their vision, their scenting abilities, he didn't require them; he could see perturbations in the crowd ahead. He could catch up.

Alex, wait.

Alex came to a stop, stumbling at his own momentum as he did. Max's tone implied immediate danger.

Look up, Max said, his tone spare and grim.

Alex was grateful that Max hadn't chosen to speak aloud. He looked up, although he could have just slipped behind his brother's eyes to see what Max saw.

A flash of lightning crossed the cloud-strewn sky—a sky that had been bright, clear azure when they had first set foot on circus ground. To Alex's growing horror, the lightning remained above them, irrespective of the passage of clouds; it seemed to shed light, to glitter, not as a bolt that flew at the whim of storm, but as a glimmering crack.

A crack in the sky.

NENYANE FELT the shift in the air; she felt a strange and growing dissonance. The air tasted of war, of death, of pain and loss. Anya, in whose wake she followed, paused her headlong forward rush; she looked back, and then up. Her face in profile was that of an older woman—a woman in the prime years of her power in Breodanir. She lacked the refinement, the grace, and the dignity that the Hunter Ladies used as armor, but there was a clarity to her gaze that was seldom present.

Nenyane followed that gaze to the height of sky.

"We must hurry," Anya told the Breodanir huntbrother, her tone lacking in demanding petulance. It made her sound almost like a different person. She reached out, caught Nenyane's hand in her own; Nenyane was surprised by the calluses she felt.

Anya began to run. She shouted twice: "Get out of the way!" People moved. Murmurs sprang up at their backs; some of the townspeople were annoyed, some concerned, some were shouting at what Nenyane assumed were their children, because some children must have been making an attempt to follow.

What do you see in the sky? Nenyane asked Stephen, as she ran.

Stephen's answer was long in coming. *The sky is cracking. I can see hints of night sky through amethyst. People are going to notice*, he added. They were running through a messy queue; the last thing they wanted was panic.

Tell Kallandras he must *keep people calm.*

I think he already knows that.

And if you see Gervanno, tell him to follow.

STEPHEN COULDN'T IMMEDIATELY SEE Gervanno, but he had the advantage of his dogs. Or the disadvantage. As people stopped, as people looked up in ones and twos, gazes were drawn to the sky, as if by inverted gravity. It meant people were less likely to notice the dogs in the immediate future—but more likely to panic in the moments to follow.

Patches found the Southern cerdan; he was in the company of a woman who looked, to Stephen's eye, like a seasoned mercenary. The lymer immediately leapt up on Gervanno, with both paws, barking.

The woman stepped back, but Gervanno turned toward Patches; Stephen met his gaze through the dog's eyes. The cerdan understood that he had been called to duty. He turned to the woman. "My apologies, Eva—I am apparently needed."

Eva's gaze, in the setting of scarred face, was grim. "You want help?"

"Keep people calm," Gervanno said, as another flash of lightning slashed the sky. "Or make them more terrified of you than the skies." He turned to Patches. "Lead. I'll follow."

THE CIRCUS GROUNDS had been composed of large buildings and people. Anya ran past them. The ground beneath Nenyane's feet grew muddy, although no rain had yet fallen on the circus itself. Beneath the mud, vines struggled their way free from the earth; Anya gestured at them and they burned.

If Anya had been of a mind to listen, Nenyane would have shrieked in dismay. There were ways to fight the wilderness and its lords' imperatives; this was not one of them. Nenyane understood that the lord's will had guided the vines; that the vines were meant to slow or stop their forward progress.

But the skies, the shattered appearance of things breaking, things yielding, implied that the lord's attention was elsewhere. What Anya instantly torched was not replaced. Nenyane could not see, beyond this mud-strewn path, any pavilions. She could see no sign of the circus workers, those called from the protected towns to serve at the lord's pleasure. What she could see was a wall. There was no gate; the stone was smooth and seemed, at this distance, to be all of one piece. It was meant to bar visitors from passing beyond it.

There was no door. There was nothing that implied that the wall protected anything; it curved inward, not outward, as if this were a final bastion of defense for those who now occupied the circus's streets.

Anya didn't see it that way. Of course she didn't. She let go of Nenyane's hand and lifted her own in a wild, oddly graceful sweep of motion. Nenyane leapt then, to stand in front of the mage.

"Wait, Anya!"

Anya's arms froze in the raised position. "For what?"

"You *could* destroy the wall—but the wall is clearly meant to protect the circus. It's important. We can't just break it!"

"They won't be able to *leave*," Anya said. "If this wall is here, they're trapped, too."

"The circus master can change that if he feels it's necessary!"

"But we need to *leave* the grounds. We need to be *there*."

"Be *where*?" Nenyane looked up to the height of the wall. The stone was smooth enough she doubted she could climb it; she might be able to reach its height if she focused and leapt. Anya was a mage; she could probably fly.

Anya's arms trembled as she glared at Nenyane. "Where *she* is. Where Adala is!" Her tone, ironically enough, was the one used when dealing with a truculent child. Nenyane had seldom been treated like a child in her life in Maubreche—the only life she clearly remembered. Physically, she looked younger, that was all. Anya was far younger in any way that counted than Nenyane had ever been, even as a silent, withdrawn child in the Maubreche territory.

"Adala is circus—you said that yourself. Neither you or I are circus. We don't want to be where the rites are performed. We do not want to be caught up in them." Nenyane made no attempt to force Anya to abandon her arrested gesture. Nenyane had very little chance of stopping her, and knew it. Persuasion—which had never been her strength—was her only option.

Alex thinks, Stephen said, *that Katie saw something when she touched Anya's hand.*

Of course she did. How is that relevant?

He thinks Anya may have seen something when she came into contact with Katie.

That's not the way it works!

The circus isn't normal. Nothing here is normal. Anya is definitely *not normal, not even for a mage. Alex thinks you shouldn't interfere with Anya too much.*

Does he think I should let her destroy the wall?

There was a moment of silence in which Anya's expression shifted, narrowed eyes changing the lay of lines worn there by sun and wind.

Here, in the privacy of the name-bond, the sound of the lightning that streaked across the sky and remained there, did not overwhelm the discussion. Stephen and Alex had to speak, but they spoke as softly as audibility allowed.

Anya's impatience showed in the trembling of raised arms, but she did not vent her growing frustration on Nenyane; her gaze passed beyond the Maubreche huntbrother to the wall she was trying to protect. To Nenyane's surprise, the raised hands became fists as Anya lifted her voice.

It was loud; louder than the thunderous lightning that threatened to shatter the sky. It teetered on the edge between demand and entreaty, between command and plea. The word was personal, emotional; Nenyane felt it almost as a name. She listened as Anya's voice broke on repetition. No; not break. The mage's voice seemed to split, the whole becoming separate strands of harmony that reminded Nenyane of a chorus, the voices soft or harsh, young or old—all, nonetheless, Anya's. Some elements of this chorus were stronger, more powerful. Some were soft enough they should have been over-whelmed.

Nenyane noted the moment that blood seeped from Anya's palms, hidden in the shape of fists. That blood trickled down the woman's exposed wrists, toward her clothing, as if it were the sweat of exertion.

She felt the sudden change in the earth beneath her feet, and almost leapt up to avoid it; there were no trees here, nothing in which she could find purchase. Soon, it wouldn't matter. The mists of the Between did not roll in; they did not become a fog that rose above knees to the height of waist or even shoulder. That fog was the ghost of a world, of many worlds, the only inheritance the gods could offer those whose voices could still reach them.

She knew.

She had known it the first time Stephen had entered the Between to bespeak his father, Bredan, he of oaths and covenants; of the gods, the closest to mortals with a single exception. That exception, without the Between as shield and mediator, now walked upon these lands.

"Child," he said, his voice a multitude of voices, louder and larger in every way than Anya's had been, who had demanded his presence.

Anya lowered her fists and turned to face the circus master—a man who no longer wore the tidy, authoritative suit of the master of perfor-mance. He did not gain the size of Bredan when Bredan joined his son in the Between, but in all other ways, his presence almost burned in its heat and radiance, in its many faces and many voices, in the shifting color of eyes that never stopped to claim one color and one alone.

"I told you, you could not be called to the circus. This is not the place for you."

"You couldn't keep me away," Anya replied, her tone so strident it would have been her death in a bygone era. Anya was not a woman to offer respect, except at her own whim. No, Nenyane thought, in utter silence: Anya was as direct as a young child might have been. She did not mean disrespect at all.

Nenyane was close enough to Anya to intervene, and she did, but her movements, graceful, were silent and as unobtrusive as they could be, given her intent to interfere.

"**Could I not?**"

Anya shook her head. "I'm town. The covenant of the Free Towns and the circus mean you can't reject me if I'm here and I choose to enter." She folded her arms, unaware of the blood that mingled with the cloth of her sleeve. "Some covenants can't be broken unless everything breaks."

"**Have you not looked at the sky?**"

Anya shrugged. "It wasn't a real sky, anyway."

"**And why have you called me, thus?**"

"To find Adala," was the prompt reply.

"**She is circus.**"

"Not yet, she's not. She will be. She's decided. She won't change her mind." Anya sniffed air, and lifted a hand as if to touch it. *As if she could.* Nenyane, aware of the wild elements, knew the air was simple air; nothing alive, nothing passably sentient, existed in its folds.

How does she know any of that? Alex wants to know.

If he'd like to come and interrupt her to ask, feel free, Nenyane snapped. *But you—stay where you are. Don't bring your dogs. Don't send them. Just— don't come here yet.*

"I came here to see the circus. It's been so long. I just…wanted to see the circus again."

The god waited.

"But I don't think that's why *they* came. I think they want to break the circus—and Adala is the reason they can. But soon, she'll be the reason they can't. It's complicated."

"It is always complicated," the god replied, in the familiar voice of the circus master. As he spoke, he assumed that form, clothing and all. Anya didn't appear to notice the change. "Mortals are delicate and complex; they are never all of one thing or all of the other. But perhaps that is true, in the end, of all things that live.

"You are correct. You were born in the townships, and my permission to enter my domain was granted you by the simple expedient of your birth. But you are not in full control of the power that is your birthright. I fear the damage you might do—without intent—should you be allowed to attend Adala. I fear the damage she might do to you, as well."

"Damage? To me?" Anya teetered between outrage and confusion. Perhaps because the circus master was a god, she allowed confusion to become the master. "She's just a girl."

"She is circus. Those who are called form the pillars of shelter for the townspeople. If you harm her, those pillars will fall." He lifted his head, gazing beyond the walls as if the walls did not exist. "The demons have come in number, although not in the numbers I was led to believe must follow. I sense the endless sorrow and despair of the *Kialli*. There is power, in their gathering. Our foes are not trivial."

Nenyane cleared her throat. "Anya destroyed the portal through which they meant to travel."

"Did she, now?"

"She is not fond of demons." But if Anya had destroyed the portal through which so many demons had passed, she had also created it. Nenyane kept that to herself, but without much hope. She was certain the lord of these lands already knew.

He once again turned to Anya. "You are almost a wild essence, a force that mortality cannot safely contain. You have paid that price. You will continue to pay it. Think you that I cannot keep my people safe?"

Anya said, "Can you promise that you can?"

"You are far too bold, child, but yes. Understand, however, that in your former lands—designed for mortals, built for their safety—mortals nonetheless commit murder. Mortals steal, lie, cheat. Mortals both weep and roar in fury. They die. They are allowed to *make* choices, and no choice is truly a choice if there are no consequences.

"Inasmuch as it is possible, the circus mimics your mortal lands; the lands intersect and overlap, but the touch of my rule is faint. Only when the circus comes to town is it as malleable, as elemental, as the wilderness itself, ancient and almost tamed."

"Adala's already made her choice."

"Yes, she has. But she is young and she is grieving. It is why there has been difficulty. But surely you must understand her pain and her fear. It is similar, in the end, to yours. She chose to flee the circus because to remain meant losing the young man she loved."

Silence, then.

It was a terrible silence. Anya's expression darkened, her eyes widening, confusion giving way to raw fury. "I will *kill him*."

Nenyane didn't understand.

"I *will* kill him."

The circus master shook his head. "Kill him, and you destroy the circus."

"I *have to* kill him," Anya said, voice a blended chorus of burning rage—and beyond that, immeasurable pain and loss.

Nenyane had met Trevor. In her estimation, the young man was besotted with Adala—enough to leave Hansleigh and the certain life of a blacksmith in order to be with her on the open, and unpredictable, road. Enough to abandon family and any other friend he had made in his life. Enough to protect her, where he could, and to share her suffering where he could not.

But he hadn't loved her enough to consign all of the past to blood and ash.

Nenyane had oft wondered what love meant. It was not a word she felt comfortable using. She understood *service*. She understood *loyalty*. She understood all of the shades and textures of *duty*. Stephen was her duty. Stephen's survival was the only true goal she had in life. Even regaining memory was a driving desire *because*, if she remembered more in this broken, changing world, she could be a *better* protector.

Stephen spoke of love. Stephen had spoken of love as a child. Stephen had spoken of love as an adult, one barely of age by Breodani law.

She had never really questioned it. She understood what it meant to Stephen, but knew, as well, that the word was subtle and complicated and meant many different things; it was entirely personal in context. What was frustrating to Nenyane was that everyone who used the word believed they knew what it meant.

Nenyane did not speak of love because it was unnecessary. She existed for Stephen. Stephen was her world.

Your world is not just me. You're a person; you're not a limb. You're not a tool.

...even if Stephen had other ideas.

But Stephen's love was not akin to Nenyane's sense of duty. At core, at heart, there were many, many things that invoked it. His family. Maubreche and its many servants. His dogs. Stephen might set out as Trevor had done. He would risk his life to accompany Nenyane in her search for the memories she had lost.

But he would not make that journey if his absence guaranteed the death of the other people he loved. He could not easily abandon those early ties and loyalties, that early familial love. He would be like Trevor: torn, almost immobile beneath the shadow of guilt. But were he not who he was, she would never have chosen him.

"What do you think he's going to do?" It was Nenyane who asked, not the circus master. The drawn expression on a face that was artifice implied that the lord of this small land knew what Anya feared.

"He'll desert her when she needs him! He'll betray her!" Each sentence rose in volume, rising as if it were the slope of a mountain she struggled to climb. "She'll be hurt. She'll be hurt enough she'll *wish* she were dead. And she'll wish he was dead, too. If she survives, she'll be forced to kill him. She might spend her *entire life* trying to find him and kill him."

"I don't think there is anything Trevor could do that would cause Adala to spend her life that way."

Anya's shriek was wordless; she'd spent the words, and they had not convinced Nenyane.

The circus master turned to the Maubreche huntbrother. "You are both wise and naïve. I would not have asked the question you asked.

"By circus rules, I cannot prevent Anya from doing what she feels she must do unless I end her life here. If I am forced to end her life, the essence of the circus will be severely, possibly permanently, damaged. I will therefore leave her in your hands."

"We need to find Adala!" Anya shouted.

"I will allow you to pass through the wall. It does not exist in the other direction; should you need to retreat to the grounds, you may return without my intervention." He turned once again to Nenyane. "You will not find peace within my lands. You will not find peace beyond them. Your duty, as Anya's, will be forged and fulfilled in the fires of different battles.

"But if it will put your mind at ease, you will find Illaraphaniel within the circus grounds; we have reached an accommodation of sorts. I will also allow your master to find you, should you feel it necessary."

"How will you know?"

"You are not of the towns, Nenyane of Maubreche; your respect is lacking." He did not answer the question. Instead, he gestured, and the wall rippled, as if stone were liquid, as if liquid could be moved into an exact, perfect shape, upon command.

A door appeared in what had been a single, seamless stone wall.

NENYANE APPROACHED THE DOOR, but before she could touch it, it opened from the other side. Standing in its frame was Katie. She looked exhausted, but her eyes brightened when she caught sight of Anya. Nenyane's wouldn't have. She might have managed to keep a grimace off her face, but only barely, and only if she worked at it.

"Come in, come in quickly." She looked beyond Anya to see the circus master, hands clasped loosely behind his back, his face a network of lines that implied some unnamed emotion. Katie nodded. "We can't keep the door open—there's too much at risk, now." Speaking, she looked up to see the sky, and the cracks that stretched from one horizon to the other.

"Is Adala safe?" Anya asked, as Katie held out a hand to her.

"She is."

"Is he there?"

Katie blinked. "He?"

"The boy. The boyfriend. The *reason* she was so late."

"Anya." Katie's tone shifted, the change familiar and surprising. It wasn't a tone of voice Nenyane had ever used, but she'd heard it often enough in Maubreche.

"I want to know if he's there, or if I have to go looking for him."

"You do not need to go looking for him. He is town, not circus. The circus master bears him no ill will. Nor do we, who have labored here so long. *Anya.*"

Anya's silence was almost frenetic. She fidgeted. She turned her head to look away from Katie, and then back, and then beyond her. She knew what the boy, as she'd called him, looked like; she had accompanied both Adala and Trevor back to Hansleigh. "I have to kill him," Anya whispered.

Katie's eyes closed; she inhaled slowly. "No, child, you do not. He is not the boy who abandoned you. He is not the child who fled while you could not. The only thing they share in common is they were willing to forsake their lives and homes for love."

"He *didn't love me!*"

I think we're in trouble, Stephen said.

No. Just—stay where you are. It's not safe here, not yet.

Why is she doing this?

Why are you asking me? Ask Alex. Later. Lightning once again flashed across the sky—but it moved at a crawl now, and its brief light lingered. Soon, there would be more cracks than sky. Whatever—or whoever—held the sky in place would be left holding shards and nothingness.

"Child," Katie said, for Anya's sudden outburst had not discomfited her at all, "He did. But he was —as you were—young. He wouldn't flee in terror now. Or would you rather he had stayed and died painfully?"

"Yes!" The word was so raw it was almost a scream. Katie did not move from the doorway. Anya had momentarily forgotten Adala, so focused was she on grief.

"You met Trevor," Katie continued, as if Anya's obvious distress did not touch her at all. "Do you think he could have survived attacking demons?"

Anya's pain made room for a derisive snort.

"Could yours? Could he have protected you—and himself—from the demons?"

"He didn't even *try*!"

"No. No, he didn't. But I will tell you this, Anya. If my children fled in terror when I was being attacked, and they somehow survived, I would not feel betrayed. I would not feel that their love for me was worthless. I would not hunt them down and kill them, after the fact. To me, flight would be almost a relief."

"It's different. He wasn't a child."

"Is Adala an adult to you?"

Anya fell silent.

"If she *is*, why does she need protection?"

"Adults die," Anya replied, but only after a long pause. "Even adults die."

"Yes. Could you defend yourself now?"

"Yes. I kill demons, too. All the time. But they just come back."

"Trevor won't come back. Tell me, Anya, if he had been torn apart in front of your eyes, would that have been better? I need you to think about that."

As if Anya were a stubborn child and Katie her mother—or perhaps her beloved aunt—Anya fell silent, caught in pain and fear and rage and fury for which there was no target, no outlet. She had no desire to rage at Katie. But she had no answer to offer, because the first answer was, clearly, *yes*. Yes, it would have been better.

Nenyane thought it might have been better for everyone else. The target for Anya's rage, the fuel for it, would be aimed solely at the lover's killers, not the lover himself.

"Come, then. But Anya, you must promise that you will not attempt to kill Trevor, or I cannot in good conscience take you to where Adala is."

Silence.

"Leave the decision of Trevor in Adala's hands. It is her right. The fate of the man who betrayed you is in your hands, now; let Trevor be in hers. She is becoming circus, as we all did, who responded to the call."

"But he's with her?"

Katie nodded. "It was her one request of the circus master. In her final moments as a child of Hansleigh, she wanted Trevor by her side."

Nenyane would have refused that request, had she been either god or circus servant. It was to keep Trevor in her life that she had planned and fled; to have him here, to have him bear witness to the final steps she took to sever that hope and that connection, was far too risky.

But Nenyane was not a god. She didn't think the way gods thought.

"Trevor is saying his final goodbyes. Adala is saying them as well. If you kill Trevor now, you will break her. It is *because* of Trevor, in the end, that she returned."

That clearly made no sense to Anya.

"He could not leave his family and friends to die. It would have broken him. Broken, he would break them both; he could not continue to love under the weight of crushing guilt. She does love him, with the ferocity of the young. She understood, the moment he knew demons waited to destroy all of the Free Towns, he could not both flee and continue to love her.

"Not as he had. Not as she hoped he would."

"But that makes no sense. Why would she come back, then?"

"Because she doesn't want to break him. She wants him to be safe. Oh, she wants her own family to survive, just as Trevor does. But it was Trevor's fear that was the decisive factor. She wants the last few minutes. Do not take them away from her."

Anya nodded slowly, some of the rage bleeding away from her expression. That left only bewilderment and tears, but the tears fell unnoticed by the mage.

They were not unnoticed by Katie. The woman lifted a hand to brush them away, every gesture gentle.

BEFORE KATIE DREW ANYA through the door, Stephen, Alex, and Max arrived. Shadowing their progress was Gervanno. Nenyane offered only the Southerner a curt nod.

"I don't know if you'll be allowed to enter."

Gervanno's nod was more formal, less curt. "If I cannot, I will remain with the waiting crowd. The circus people are now out in force, performing tricks and entertaining the queue; I will wait with them if the circus master does not see fit to allow me to do my duty to Maubreche."

"There are people who can fight in the crowd—but most aren't armed for it. They left their weapons behind."

"If it comes to an actual battle, they'll have weapons," Katie said, over her shoulder. She held Anya's hand as she walked, but made no arguments about Anya's companions. Or Nenyane's. Both Anya and Nenyane had been granted the circus master's permission. If the lord did not wish others to enter, they would not be allowed to progress.

The lord, however, did not interfere with humans. Nenyane followed Katie's lead. Anya had almost forgotten her presence, so invested was she in the older woman's.

Stephen's dogs made the entryway briefly crowded because Pearl insisted on going first. Going first wouldn't have been a problem, but Patches had returned with Gervanno. Pearl, therefore, waited until Patches rejoined the pack before asserting dominance in her usual, annoying way.

Stephen allowed a brief, but deep, hint of displeasure to show to Pearl.

Pearl, being Pearl, moved—but she was now sulky. The rest of the dogs, accustomed to Stephen, went through the door in an orderly fashion. Alex and Max followed. Gervanno pulled up the rear.

Through Pearl's eyes—of course, it had to be Pearl, as she had turned her head away from Stephen to announce her displeasure—he could see the door behind Gervanno vanish. They stood outside a curved stone wall, a demarcation that separated the guests of the circus from the heart of the circus itself.

But Stephen had not stepped into the wilderness. There were trees in his immediate view, but they seemed tended. Beneath their boughs was greenery—grass, and a hint of wild blossoms that were too deliberate in their placement to have taken root without planning.

Until they had stepped foot on the grass, this area had been occupied by some of those called to the circus. Stephen noted their age: none were young. Katie was perhaps of median age, with two notable exceptions: Adala and Trevor.

Adala was robed in shimmering green; she wore a crown of flowers, a wreath of vines. Her feet were bare, although toes could be glimpsed only as she moved, the robes were so long. They were too large for her frame, as if they'd been quickly repurposed, or as if the position she occupied was more important than the fact it was Adala herself who occupied it at all.

Stephen was surprised to see Trevor standing beside her, his hands by his side; when she moved, he followed, as if bound to her.

As if he desired nothing more than to be bound to her side forever.

He did not understand what Trevor was feeling, but knew grief when he saw it; who could be raised among Breodani nobility, and not have a deep understanding of loss and grief? Who could be son to Hunter Lords and face none of the consequences of the sacrifice power demanded?

As he so often did, he struggled to make comparisons between his own experience and Trevor's. What if he were standing in Trevor's figurative shoes, and Nenyane was wearing the robes that engulfed Adala? He had no doubt that given the choice, Trevor would choose to remain in the heart of the circus, at Adala's side. But Trevor had not been given that choice. He would not be given that choice. This, then, was the last thing he could do for the young woman he loved. This mournful, silent following, where he couldn't lift hand to touch her. This bearing of witness.

Trevor did not cry.

Adala did. Her cheeks were wet as she lifted her face; she glanced at Trevor and offered him a tremulous, hesitant smile. But she lowered her head again as she moved, her feet touching grass almost delicately, as if she feared to destroy it. There was a pattern to her steps, hesitantly made; she stumbled once, but righted herself as Trevor lifted arms to catch her should she fall.

He did not touch her; his hands balled in brief fists before he forced them back to his sides. There was a yearning in the gesture that Stephen had never felt. What Adala did now was like, and unlike, what Hunters did yearly. She had chosen to walk the ritual path, just as Hunter Lords did. But if the path did not risk her life or guarantee the chance of death, it also did not end with the relief of homecoming.

The circus would be her home.

Trevor would be no part of it, except at times like this: when the circus gates opened and visitors—the townspeople—were invited in.

He lifted hand twice, but did not touch her. He simply followed, walking beside her, as she continued to walk a path that only she could see.

Anya did not attempt to disrupt the service. She did not attempt to kill Trevor. Stephen was not surprised to see—through Pearl's eyes—that Anya was crying. Her tears, like Adala's, fell silently; but her hands, unlike Adala's, were clasped before her chest, as if she were praying.

"Can you hear it?" Anya asked, of Katie. When Katie failed to answer, the mage turned to Nenyane. "Can you?"

Nenyane was slow to answer as well, but she found words for Anya, offering them as if they were a reward for good behavior. "I'm sorry. I can hear you. I can't hear anything else."

"I can hear the song of her dance," Anya said. "I can almost taste it. Adala *is* circus. She's powerful. She's calling them."

"Calling who?"

Anya's smile was secretive, almost childlike. She didn't answer, the silence almost gleeful. But her tears continued to fall. "It's sad. It's so sad." Unclasping her hands, she drew her sleeve across her face. "Sometimes, I cry. You're not supposed to cry when there are demons nearby. Did you know that?"

"I've never, ever cried when there was even a hint of a demon in the vicinity."

Anya nodded. "You're not supposed to cry." Her cheeks dimpled. "I do it anyway, when I want."

"Why?"

"Well, tears are weakness, right? I mean, they imply that you're weak. Demons eat each other's power. They kill each other. Sometimes when they're bored. But mostly, they try to kill us."

Nenyane nodded.

"They're mostly cowards, though. They only attack if they think we're weak. The weak are their prey. When I'm bored, I like to look weak."

"Only demons who've never seen you fight would consider you weak."

"The stupid ones, yes," she agreed. "But they try, and I kill them. I don't like it when they scream." Anya stopped speaking as Adala stumbled. Tree roots, although the trees themselves stood at a distance, seemed to grow up out of the earth through which she walked, their growth large and sudden. Both of her feet were centered on one dirt covered curve.

She teetered, first forward and then back, struggling to maintain her balance. "No, don't!" she shouted, as Trevor moved. "I have to do this. I understand it now. I can almost see the end of the path. I have to be able to do this or I can't protect you. I can't protect our town."

Trevor swallowed and nodded, watching with held breath, arms raised. If she fell, if she faltered, he meant to catch her, regardless of her words. But he would have to do it from the ground; the roots rose. Stephen had seen such roots in the aftermath of earthquake, as wilderness sought release and freedom in the almost-mortal world.

But the earth beneath Trevor's feet remained verdant and unbroken. Adala's path was a metaphor for the end of their relationship. Both knew it, but Adala now chose to concentrate on navigating, the whole of her attention devoted to keeping her balance until she could once again put one foot in front of the other.

Anya's tears dried as she watched, Trevor forgotten. Stephen hadn't expected that; his dogs were alert, and Nenyane stood beside Anya to leap to Trevor's defense if necessary. Katie remained with Anya as well; it was Katie's presence that seemed to steady Anya, although her drift from rage to childlike glee implied that steady was almost beyond the mage.

Adala found her footing. She did not leap off the root; her path led her along its length. Trevor followed her, but he found the roots far more awkward than Adala. Nothing was steadying his passage. Something had come to bolster Adala. Wind. Breeze. She murmured, but did not sing as she had in the forest. Her hair flew, as Meralonne's often did, strands rising and floating as if each individual strand was fascinating to the air itself.

Stephen could see no single tree from which that great root had sprung; the trees in the distance seemed too young, to his eye, to be rooted in such a fashion.

But the dogs grew restless as their master watched Adala's passage, understanding the burden of it and the conflicted satisfaction that grew from being able to shoulder a burden at all.

The wind teased the hem of her robe.

The earth moved beneath Trevor's feet, lifting him so that he might walk as close to Adala at the end as he could. He did not touch the root; nor did he reach out to catch her should she stumble: she would not, now. It was clear to all who watched that the footing she had found would not be lost again. Here, the wind moved, the earth moved. In the distance, Stephen could hear the sudden rush of water as a stream, too small to be a river, too large to be a brook, revealed itself, catching glints of sunlight as it moved.

It did not move toward Adala; the earth did not allow that. But in the movement of wind and water and earth, Stephen felt none of the hostility or rage that the elements, unbound, might show each other.

Of fire, there was no sign.

Katie was holding her breath; her hands were white and shaking. As she watched Adala, her lips moved. Stephen and his dogs couldn't hear her words. Nenyane could. They did not sound like language to Stephen.

Nenyane said, *She's praying.*

He didn't ask her how she knew; he could feel the certainty in her. The language was familiar to Nenyane, although Stephen had never heard it spoken. She couldn't translate it—it was almost as if meaning and vocalization were sundered, as if the speaker was repeating syllables painstakingly taught but never well enough to become their own language.

In the distance, he heard the same words become louder as Adala moved. A prayer. A cry of hope and joy.

A sudden burst of flame. Had he thought fire absent? No. It flew through the air, an immense, falling sun. It burst into smaller meteors, a rain of red and gold and white; were it not for its heat and the destruction it promised, it would have been beautiful.

Anya cried out in surprise and anger. Not rage, not yet, although she turned instantly to look up at the fractured sky. Stephen's gaze followed hers; he had not forgotten Adala, but he understood what Nenyane did: Adala could not be disturbed.

Could not help but be disturbed.

The sky shattered, shards of amethyst falling away as if at the hands of a terrible gravity. Revealed, at last, was the dark purple sky of an afternoon heading toward dusk in the high wilderness.

CHAPTER EIGHTEEN

P ale, clear shards rained down from the skies above, dissipating before they collided with the ground beneath them. In the distance, he could hear the rolling thunder of the crowd of gathered townspeople; the performance had not yet been open to visitors. He was aware of all these things, because his instinctive use of his pack allowed him to view the world in a much broader way. His own eyes were almost welded to Adala, for it was nearest to Adala that the fire had fallen. Unlike the shards of sky, the fire reached the earth, and where it did, grass and wildflowers burned.

Katie let go of Anya; had she not, she would have been pulled off her feet.

Nenyane leapt past Anya; the wind here functioned as the wild air did when Meralonne or Kallandras were on the field. Both Stephen's huntbrother and the wild mage moved in haste toward one person: Adala. Adala and the root of the tree on which she had found her perfect footing. The fire surrounded her, and it attempted to gain purchase in that root.

Anya's voice was a broken roar of fury; hints of fear were interlaced in the syllables of furious command that left her lips. The fire did not heed her. Adala looked down from where the fires burned, her eyes wide, her mouth half-open.

When Adala spoke, the fires struggled. But Trevor was in their way. Trevor, the man she loved. Trevor, who had come to say his final farewells.

Stephen knew, without having to be told, that Trevor's death here would break things. Adala was *not* finished yet. The fire and the shattered skies had interrupted her journey. Someone spoke—he did not see the speaker—urging Adala to continue, to move forward. Adala could now see Trevor.

She would lose the path.

Nenyane agreed. She had reached the ground where the fire clung most stubbornly, and beyond a moving wall of porous flame, she could see the shadowed outline of Trevor.

Above the flame, she could see Adala, looking down; she could see the tightness of the young woman's expression, could see the sudden hesitation. Decisions that had been made could be unmade, unless the consequences were fatal. But *this* decision could not be unmade without casualties and war.

Can you get to him? Can you get him out of there?

Katie stumbled, righted herself, and began to move; Stephen overtook her, catching her by the sleeve, which caused her to stumble again. He let her go and moved past her, his intent clear.

The earth was shaking beneath their feet; it had not yet broken.

Voices were raised. Stephen recognized only Katie's. She did not cry out to Adala, as the others did; she cried out, instead, to Anya. She wanted Anya to save Trevor. Stephen didn't argue; Nenyane had landed on the other side of a dividing wall of flame and fury.

That the fire was focused on Adala made clear that the flame was wild, elemental. Had it been contained in the hands of one who understood people at all, it would have instantly devoured Trevor. Or perhaps not instantly—but in a way that would not allow Adala to save him.

And she would try.

That was the imminent disaster. Stephen could almost feel the strain on the circus itself as Nenyane slashed at fire with her blade. In anyone else's hands, it would have amounted to flailing—but Nenyane was not anyone else.

She barked a single name aloud. It wasn't Stephen's.

Gervanno moved in a blur of motion, passing Stephen, dogs, Katie, and even Anya to reach his sword master's side. He had drawn his weapon on the move, and where her blade passed through flames, he stepped in. He wielded the sword he had taken from the lost and found; what Nenyane's purely Breodani blade had not fully managed, his sword *did*.

The flames were severed from their source, and they fell. They did not rise again—not immediately. But across the length and breadth of purple sky, clouds were forming, and in the air immediately overhead, Stephen could see wings at a great remove; they might have been birds migrating en masse, their formation loose, their goal the same. He made no attempt to count them.

Trevor leapt over the fire that remained, toward Nenyane and Gervanno. He turned to Adala immediately, raising voice. "I'm all right! Adala—I'm fine. Keep walking. Keep going!"

She hesitated, but only briefly; her gaze turned toward sky and wings and clouds that moved across a shade of purple that deepened, even as she watched. But she bowed head, her arms loose by her side. She glanced, once, at Trevor, her smile tremulous. Then she looked down at the root beneath her feet, and once again began to walk.

Anya's gaze darted between Adala, Trevor, and the skies themselves; it was to the sky that her gaze came to rest, eyes narrowed, as if she were squinting. The wild mage was a ball of resentment and anger, but she could not alleviate those emotions on the ground. She could not kill Adala. She could not kill Trevor. Some glimmer of bitter understanding twisted her expression; it wasn't Trevor she hated to the point of death.

Adala was not Anya. Anya was not Adala. Anya had not been called to the circus. She had been called to something larger, stranger, and vastly more painful. She had survived it, in some fashion.

She was, Stephen realized, broken. It was a bitter thought, but oddly gentle.

In Breodanir, it was illegal to abuse dogs; it was a severe crime. But he had seen dogs put down because that law had been broken, and the dogs had become too dangerous to keep. If the dogs served their masters, they were emblems of them as well. Breodani hunting dogs could not snap or run wild or attack other people, except at the command of their master. But some could no longer be constrained or commanded. They could not be led out of the labyrinth of pain and suspicion. The early years had formed the core of their present; they had been broken, and they had not healed.

Yes. Nenyane said. She, too, watched the skies. Any attention she spared to Adala was brief. She could not see the path Adala must walk —but knew it *must* be walked if the circus were to survive. She could not walk it for her, or with her; she could not complete what must be completed.

But she could offer protection against the forces arrayed to prevent the completion of this simple ritual.

Simple?

No blood, no sacrifice, no offerings beyond obedience and loyalty. Yes, I'd say it's simple. I don't think they can land yet, she added. What she saw was not what Stephen saw; there was no resemblance to birds, to flocks of geese, to migration. This was a storm, comprised of wings whose span was far, far larger than any natural bird that graced Breodani skies. Wyverns.

But the greatest of the wingspans did not belong to beasts. Longer, wider, flight feathers distinct to Nenyane's eyes alone, they burned, alight with flame, as if flame was buoyancy. *Kialli.* At least one.

They cannot descend. Not here. Not yet. He heard the unspoken *soon.*

"I DISLIKE PETTY GODS. I always have."

Gervanno frowned. Trevor's clothing was scorched in places; it would have to be discarded, should he survive to leave the circus. It was not Trevor who spoke.

It was the golden fox, the elder whose path crossed Gervanno's so often that the cerdan might not be considered foolish for feeling he was being followed. If Nenyane heard the voice, she gave no sign; nor did Stephen.

"Eldest," Gervanno said, turning in the direction of the fox.

"I am surprised to see you here," the fox continued. "This is not, I believe, where you were meant to be." The fox padded across burnt grass, toward Gervanno. Gervanno looked; he could not see Jarven. The fox butted his leg in command, and Gervanno sheathed his sword, knelt, and offered the fox his usual berth.

"This place is not meant for mortals, if I understand the lord of these lands correctly," the fox continued. "But it is not unpleasant. I see the situation has become grave." The fox's nose pointed toward the skies of wing and imminent storm. "The dead are present, and they are circling."

Gervanno nodded.

"You should choose companions more wisely," the fox continued. "You are in constant danger while you travel with them."

"The world is becoming a battlefield. On such a field, there is no certain safety. One might stand and fight; one might flee. There is no safe way to organize and retreat."

"And you have no desire to do so."

"This is my duty, Eldest. Without duty, we have no honor. Without honor—and I have lived on that edge—what value have we? The lord demands that those who can fight must fight. We can earn our death on the fields of battle."

"I would prefer not to die at all. Were you to live beyond your allotted span of years, you would come to understand—as we once did—that there is no honor in war; there is simply survival, if one is canny or powerful."

"It is not war in which we earn honor. It is in the causes for which we fight. We choose where we spend our life's blood."

The fox snickered. "You do not choose. You are chosen, and you obey."

Gervanno had no desire to argue with the fox. Ah, no; that was not true. He had the desire, but understood it to be pointless. Argument would change nothing. The fox was an ancient creature; Gervanno's entire lifespan, should he live until age and infirmity claimed him, was so scant when measured against the fox's that the cerdan was a literal child in the eyes of the beast, and would forever remain so.

Children engaged in just such arguments—their pricked pride, their need to be seen as something greater than they were, their driving force. Gervanno was not a child. He fell silent. The fox was not his master.

"They cannot land yet, but there are cracks everywhere in the defenses of the lord of these lands. Those cracks existed when he claimed them; they will exist even should you triumph today. Do you know why?"

"No, Eldest."

"Because they were made in a semblance of mortality itself. These mortals—of which you are one—were not created as the other races were. They were not a meeting of gods; they were not birthed with intent, their very nature almost predetermined. There is a chaos in mortals; they are fragile containers of many things. They are not like the Arianni; they are not like the dragons, or the trees or the eternal elements of the high wilderness. They are born burning the fuel of their scant measure of years; they walk, from birth, toward death.

"We did not understand. We assumed that mortals were akin to the beasts; driven by instinct as beasts are."

Above their head, the wyverns roared in concert. It was arresting, a trumpet of discordance that was, nonetheless, almost harmonious.

"Even they," the fox said softly. "They are powerful in flight; they defy the will of the wild air. But they are yoked, now; they serve as beasts of burden. They will never be your allies, even if freed of their constraints; they will hunt you and devour you to sustain themselves.

"But you are not what they are. The astonishing mage who now stands ready to destroy them all is as unlike you as it is possible to be. The god-born child of Bredan, who commands his dogs as the *Kialli* command the flight of wyverns, is closer—but there is, in his nature, a hint of wilderness.

"What he desires is not what you desire. What the people who serve the god of these lands desire is not what you desire. You share common enemies, but you are not a unified whole. Your individual purposes are products of the lives you have led, but the choices you might make within that life seem almost infinite.

"I did not understand the goals of Neamis in my youth. No single one of us did. We accepted it; gods are capricious, and their whims writ large. He shepherded your kind; he attempted to create spaces in which you might flourish. He failed, and failed again; many individual enclaves perished in these attempts to husband and guide.

"But your race did not perish. And in the end, all of his labors proved valuable, if one considers only the fate of your race as a whole. We saw as you grew, as you built places in which you might stand against even the gods themselves, the reason for his misguided obsession. No single one of you could be eternal; it was against your very nature. But where there was some scant promise of momentary safety, individuals became like your wild mage; they became lords of so much power that even one such as I might be forced to treat them with genuine respect.

"He made the world yours; those birthed and created by other gods retreated behind walls of his devising. Even the gods chose to retreat, to abandon the lands that had once been theirs. Not all of us went will-ingly," the fox added. "And some struggled mightily against the constraints laid upon them by the gods, for mortals were their natural prey.

"And now you are here—you, Gervanno di'Sarrado, born in the distant South, wielding a sword that was ancient long before your birth, allied with the one creature meant to end a god, hampered by your lack of wisdom and experience, and thrust, now, into a battle that I see as decisive.

"And I am drawn to your innocence, your odd purity, your strange lack of ambition. Yes, I dislike petty gods. But perhaps because my Lord is—or was—human, I feel drawn to his creations, for they must live their lives in such a short span. Should I look away, they will have perished, lost to age or malady or war."

Gervanno was not impatient; he was watchful. The flight of wyverns could not yet land. Fire fell from the sky, streaking toward the ground: toward Adala, toward the circus members who had joined her progress. That fire was ripped apart by gusts of furious wind before it could find purchase.

The wind was not Adala's. It was not the circus's to command. It brushed past Gervanno, ruffled his hair, and howled in fury as it rose.

"Illaraphaniel is here," the fox said quietly. "But I believe you suspected that."

"The air is angry," Gervanno replied.

"Yes. And Illaraphaniel is, and was, a master: he allows the fury and rage, but builds a subtle tunnel through which it might pass. He, too, is angry. But he has negotiated with the lord of these lands, just as I have done; it is only here, beyond the circus meant for mortals, that he can stand at all.

"This is the heart of the lord's power. But the power itself has never been the overwhelming power that the god in the North wields; it has always been subtle enough that the powerful might fail to see it at all. The defenses that most lords might bring to bear in the seat of their power are absent here: it rests in the hands of the people called to his service over the long centuries. These lands are both his, and not; the tapestry of their power and his claim resides in those who have chosen to serve.

"You saw the girl. You saw her bespeak the sleeping *arborii*. You watched as wind and earth moved—together, in amity—at her quiet plea. Think you that such power exists for the mortal to acquire? It did not. It does not. Even Illaraphaniel's mastery of the elements is power over their impulses. The mortal bard's grasp of wind is poorer, as one might expect. Neither have the control she does—but she cannot wield it as they do.

"The gods could."

Gervanno said nothing. Fire evaded wind, but did not escape to land; Trevor now stood beside Stephen, his gaze on Adala a mixture of fear, longing, and terrible loss. It was palpable, but private—as if a man was bleeding to death, but would not allow any others to acknowledge the coming fatality.

And even if Trevor was willing, what could a stranger offer?

Alex joined them both. Max did not; he watched the skies and traced the fall of interrupted fire, ready to move or sprint should the need arise. Alex had, in Gervanno's admittedly brief experience, been the one who reached out, if such reach was necessary.

The circus workers numbered a dozen in the immediate vicinity. There were, of course, more; enough to man the pavilions and their many mysterious stalls—but the townspeople would require everything the circus could use in defense of itself should the creatures in the sky land, as they were clearly trying to do. He did not resent their absence.

Adala was new; these old hands were not. But Gervanno noted that Katie watched. He had seen the jugglers in the streets of Hansleigh, performing to the gasps and cheers of the crowds they attracted. He had seen Adala bespeak trees. He had seen Katie's hands in Anya's. He suspected that Katie could not do what Adala had done in the forest. The circus servants must have different gifts, different potential strengths.

Against demons, martial gifts were necessary.

"If the lord's chosen servants falter here, the lands will fall. He will not stand and fight by their side as Illaraphaniel does, or even as Gervanno di'Sarrado intends. Should the young woman fail in her vows, he will not protect her or stand above her while she finds her footing and tries again."

"But these are his lands; will he not then defend them?"

The fox shook his head. "That is what any other lord might do. Any. Even my Lord. But he is not what they are or were. The entirety of the power of the circus—or perhaps its defense—resides within the citizens of these small, mortal enclaves. Those who come from the enclaves have the desire to devote the remainder of their existence to protection. *They* are the weapons he has forged. If they fail, these lands will fall. If they succeed, they will not."

"Will you fight, Eldest?"

"I may; I am under no obligation to do so. But Illaraphaniel will fight, and your Hunters, and your sword master. The mage who would have been considered a true power, even in my youth, will fight—but I am uncertain that will be to your advantage. She is far too chaotic.

"The humans are beginning to gather their power, but are fewer now than they were when I first arrived; they have gone to the towns-people beyond the wall, there to form whatever line of defense they can."

"Perhaps," Gervanno replied, "they have gone to start the delayed performance."

"Performance?" the fox asked, outrage and scorn in the single word. In that, he reminded Gervanno of Nenyane.

"I have never visited the circus, but the townspeople believe that there is certain safety for them when the performance begins—and while it lasts."

"That is astonishing. Perhaps these fools deserve the death that hovers above."

Gervanno smiled; it was genuine. There was, in the fox's reaction, so much of Nenyane's that it felt familiar.

"Pay attention now," the fox said, voice sharpening. "Understand what service to a god means. Understand that it is not the individuals that gods love, but the aggregate; they will pare away unnecessary parts and leave them as refuse while they sculpt and craft and create."

STEPHEN'S EYES had not left Adala. His dogs watched the skies, as did the handful of people who, like Katie, were servants of the circus master, along with the wild mage and the Breodani. Adala stumbled. It was not the first time she'd stumbled, but it was the first time since she had found balance and purchase on the root.

She fell forward, breaking her fall with splayed palms. If the wind heard her voice, it did not come to her aid; perhaps it could not. Perhaps Meralonne's interference with the rain of fire had robbed the wind of the more subtle control Adala had demonstrated in the forest on their return to Hansleigh. He could not see Meralonne, but could see the effects of his presence somewhere on this field.

He could see the golden fox, nestled in Gervanno's arm; could see the cerdan's hand, white-knuckled, on the hilt of sheathed sword.

He did not look through Nenyane's eyes. Pearl had, upon the appearance of the fire, abandoned hurt pride; she was watchful, pointed in any direction Stephen desired. The scent of burned wood and grass filled her nostrils; Stephen felt the taste of them in his own mouth.

Fire left the ground, accompanied by a cry of wounded fury. It was Anya's fire.

Nenyane's sword was readied, but she did not join that flame. Meralonne's presence meant that, were the mage to allow it, she could. But she knew, as Stephen knew, that it was Adala who was the heart of the conflict, although Adala did not lift hand to fight. Her sole act of defiance, the desperation of it, was walking this path to the end.

The root of what Stephen presumed was a tree, had no visible source. Adala might walk for some time before reaching that tree—if a tree were her actual destination. Above, fire struck wyverns; wyverns roared in pain and rage, plummeting toward the ground beyond the circus.

They had not been Anya's target. Whether or not she understood that they were beasts of burden with little volition, she barely saw them at all. The wyverns her fire had reached bore riders; their riders had been her target. The distance between ground and sky made it more difficult to aim true.

Stephen was almost unsurprised when Anya leapt into the folds of air.

Nenyane shouted her name. Anya either didn't hear or didn't care. Like the child she sometimes was, she was focused on only one thing; everything else was irrelevant.

What is she doing? Nenyane demanded.

Attacking the demons?

Nenyane glanced at Adala, and then back to Anya. "Illaraphaniel!" she cried.

The mage, whose presence Stephen felt, did not answer. Not in words. But Nenyane's hair began to move, just as the mage's oft did, as the wind came to her, offering her what it had offered Anya.

"Gervanno." Nenyane's glance was a command. It narrowed when it fell to the fox. "Eldest," she said, mimicking respect. "Gervanno is necessary now, and he is mortal — he cannot fight and carry you at the same time."

"He has before," the fox replied, eyeing Nenyane.

"He is to protect Stephen, should it come to that."

"Very well. I will descend, should his full attention become necessary. Will that do?" The fox's tone implied that it had better.

Nenyane wanted to kill him. It was not a trivial desire; she considered both her chances and the cost to the circus, to the Breodani, and to the townspeople, in brief, intense flashes. She thought she could succeed, but the attempt might destroy everything they had chosen to protect here.

He thinks Gervanno is his.

So did Nenyane. *Gervanno is not a toy. He's not an object. You can't start what amounts to a war because you also consider him yours.*

Ours. The word was grudging. Nenyane grimaced, turned, and leapt into the air in Anya's wake. *Adala is the heart of this land's defense — but she's like the missing link that holds the chain mesh together. She hasn't become part of the armor yet. Help her, if she asks for any help at all. But protect Trevor. If Trevor dies, the circus dies with him.*

Stephen agreed. He turned. Alex's hand rested on Trevor's shoulder; it was firm, but gentle. Trevor acknowledged the gesture of support in silence.

Adala had made her choice. Stephen understood that; they all did. She meant to become fully integrated into the circus. She was dressed for it, and she followed the invisible path, meant only for her bare feet, to *become*.

But Trevor was part of her choice. It was to preserve his life, and the lives of those they both loved, that she had been willing — barely — to say her goodbyes. It was *because* Trevor would be safe. Perhaps, decades from now, she would have passed through mourning and grief and loss and reached a place in which there were no regrets, in which what-ifs did not dominate her thoughts; perhaps the raw welt of emotion would heal enough that even Trevor's death would cause only an echo of pain.

But those decades were in the future, not now. She had not walked through them; had not come to acceptance. If Adala died here, the circus defense would not hold. But if Trevor died here, she would never integrate in time.

Anya and Nenyane took to the air as Gervanno and Stephen watched. Stephen understood her animosity toward the fox, but felt very little of it; the cerdan seemed to feel he owed the fox a debt of gratitude, and becoming a human conveyance was how he had chosen to repay it.

It's because the damn fox is powerful, Nenyane snapped, from her perch of moving air. *He's not a fool—he knows how to offer respect to the powerful. His whole life depended on it.*

Stephen disagreed, but there was no point in arguing now.

Katie watched Anya as she became smaller and smaller in the rift of air; the wyverns' path was much higher above the ground than apprehension had made it appear. Katie's expression was both grim and almost absent. She kept her eyes on the sky, but bent at both knees to place one of her palms on the ground. The touch was brief; she rose and walked toward the exposed root across which Anya had walked—and was walking even now.

She touched that as well, but the contact between palm and root was far longer. Her eyes, as she gazed at the sky, reflected amethyst and grey, but they were oddly luminescent. She was slow to take that hand from the tree's root.

"Carrick!" she shouted. "To the east—to the edge."

Stephen frowned; two pairs of eyes swiveled east.

"They are attempting to attack from the sky," Katie said. "But that is not their only avenue of entry—it is the least subtle. It is meant to draw attention."

Stephen turned toward the east.

"No, not yet. Not you. We are here. Anya and your companion will do what they can to distract the demons above. Stay with Adala. I will be occupied." Speaking thus, she let go of the root. "The elements never listened to me, much. They *do* listen to most of the circus. You've seen Adala—most of the performers are like her."

"That's not my gift. It's why I wasn't summoned to the circus in my youth."

"You cannot fight?"

"Not like Carrick and the rest, no. But even so, I have my role."

Gervanno glanced at Stephen. Before Stephen could respond, Katie shook her head. "Until and unless we call for aid, this is where you must be. She is almost done, but we cannot send Trevor away. If he dies, she will break. If she breaks, we will die." Katie's expression gentled. "Anya will survive. Anya, and the man who rests in shade so dark it is almost all of the circus's night.

"If we lose this battle, we will lose the Free Towns—but that has ever been the case."

"Can you see that?"

"Yes. I can see that. But that is not the nature of my gift; it is not absolute. With effort, I can choose which strand I pull, which strand I follow. With effort, I can unravel those futures, or shake them enough that others with more power can pull them apart." She lifted head and Stephen saw two people Adala's age, or near enough it made no difference, dart across the grass. Moving together, their strides, their expression—even the way their arms pumped as they sprinted—were almost the same.

Twins. Twins like Max and Alex were. But beneath the similarity of physical features, Max and Alex were very different people, bound to each other by blood and affection.

He had no sense that the same was true of the strangers, but shook himself free of that certainty.

They stopped as Katie drew closer to them. "Iyan," she said. "Join Carrick. Leave Mercy to the shadows." Both nodded. "Mercy, you will find a man cloaked there; he is waiting. You will feel the pull of his presence, his power. Do *not* approach him. He is foreign, but he has our lord's permission to wait and watch. He will not approach the townsfolk and he will not attempt to disrupt the performance, should it occur."

Both of the twins were pale. Stephen could not determine, with any ease, their gender; he could guess, by the names Katie used, but gender seemed almost irrelevant here. Had they not worn the gaudy make-up, intended for visibility in a large theatre, it might have been clearer. But their hair was pulled back from their faces, and their faces were painted in pale, pure white, with small black icons across that canvas: tears. Exaggerated smiles.

Even their clothing was bright, colorful; it caught what light there was in this space and reflected it.

"I should go to Adala," one of the two said.

"You should go to the east, as I said. Carrick will need support. Mercy—be ready. We are not performing for our people, not yet—but you might have cause to use your skill. Iyan, grab Lysan—Chenni should be waiting. She has his knives. Why are you just standing there with your mouth open? *Go*."

They spun on heel and ran.

Stephen sent Brylle after them. He understood that Katie could see glimpses of the future. But if these circus workers fell, if they could not protect the boundaries of the circus, those on the grounds would be overrun.

"They're stronger than you, little hunter," Katie said, without once glancing back. "They've been trained for just such incursions for the entirety of their time in the circus. This is not the first time these lands have come under attack—and it will not be the last, if we but hold.

"The time is coming when our lord will no longer make that demand—in the North, a being we cannot stand against has gathered enough power, husbanded enough strength, that all lands occupied by humans will fall under his long shadow. But that time is not today. It is not now." Her voice was steady; Stephen could not see her face. Brylle had followed the twins, his gaze on their backs. To see Katie's face, he would have to call the alaunt back, breaking the stride of his pursuit; the twins were *fast*.

He accepted the currents of Katie's voice, accepted her words. She lifted that voice again, calling for yet another person Stephen did not know and had not met; introductions, if they came at all, would have to wait.

Max headed in the direction the twins had taken; Katie did not stop him. Instead, she turned to look back at Alex, impatience writ in the folded lines of her expression.

Alex glanced at Stephen. Stephen hesitated. Alex and Max had the Hunter's bond, and in times of conflict, in the chaos of it, they could relay information from one part of the battle to another; the information was accurate. If Alex joined Max, Stephen would have no window into what occurred.

But if Alex did not join Max, and invaders—demons—somehow broke through the porous barrier that separated the circus lands from the rest of the mortal world, Max would be hampered in any combat he joined. Alex was half of him.

He didn't need to make the decision, in the end. Alex could see it, unspoken, in his expression. Alex had always been the more sensitive of the Elseth brothers. He turned, lengthening his stride to catch up with his brother.

THE AIR WAS ALWAYS COLDER at the height of sky, but today was to be an exception. Nenyane felt the heat of *Kialli* wings as she approached them. Or perhaps it was Anya's fire; the mage was furious, and her fury—spoken, shouted, screamed—was punctuated, always, by fire. Or lightning. The sky flared the color of her magic as she rode the currents of wind—as if she had always done so, had been trained to it.

Anya was unleashed, here. She was no more focused, no more strategic, than she had been when her feet had been tapping the earth in staccato impatience. She knew, or had known, that the powers under her control could not be wielded safely in the presence of mortals like Katie, but she had already been chafing at the restrictions. Here, high above the circus grounds, there was no need for self-control. There was no one who could die if she gave in to the fury that now guided her every motion.

She had no need to consider consequences, inasmuch as she ever did.

Anya's power was an expression of Anya's impulse, Anya's thoughts in any given moment. What drove her to rage and fury now was pain—remembered pain, past pain, something Nenyane could not influence or prevent. She almost pitied the wyverns, those who carried the demons. They were enslaved; they did not choose either their masters or their targets.

Wyverns did not hunt in packs. Nenyane knew this, but did not know why; there was no experience in which to root that knowledge, to make it undeniable truth. Anya wouldn't care. She destroyed the wyverns—wings, bodies, half of a face—before Nenyane had even completed her thought.

The winged demon screamed her name in fury. *"Anya!"*

Anya was a weapon. But she was a weapon that no one could wield with confidence or certainty. She was like the wild elements: she had her own imperatives, and no one with any intelligence would assume that their desire to wield her would carry more weight than Anya's own desires.

But Nenyane had seen the portal fueled by Anya's power, by Anya's desire to visit the circus of her childhood. The portal had closed not because Anya could not sustain it, but because her erstwhile allies had annoyed her. Had they not, the portal might have disgorged the whole of the gathered demonic forces that waited in the distant North.

She was a genuine threat. She could, with no more thought than *I want to visit the circus*, destroy tens of thousands of lives. She'd likely not notice her part in those deaths at all. She was very like a child—which is why Nenyane had never been particularly fond of children. They had not developed any moral compass; moral compasses depended on the ability to assess and accept consequences.

It was difficult to see Anya as a child in the blazing fire that left her hands. Even the fire the demons commanded was not equal to her raw power.

Nenyane was uncertain that she could kill Anya if Anya were remotely aware of her intent. But in these skies, surrounded by demons and wyverns, Anya was the biggest threat to the world Stephen had been born to protect.

Don't—Nenyane, don't kill her.

I'm not even certain I could.

Stephen couldn't. She knew that. Unless and until Anya became the central pivot upon which the plans of the Lord of the Hells turned, he could not bring himself to kill this woman who was a child at heart. But Stephen had always had a weakness for children, even the children of total strangers—as if they were something more precious than the adults who had toiled and struggled to survive that childhood.

For Nenyane, it was far more practical. She wasn't certain that Anya could kill her; she was certain that if she did not end Anya's life in an instant, the mage would try. The consequences of that attempt would be very likely to destroy the circus, and with the fall of the circus, the Free Towns would be emptied, their citizens dying just beyond reach of their homes.

I won't try. I won't take that risk. Just focus on what you have to do.

Nenyane was not Anya; she did not have the power that Anya wielded as if it were simple breath. But she had her sword. It was enough. If she could not turn wyverns to ash—which was much safer for any who stood beneath the shadow of their great wings—she could remove those wings, could cut pinions, could sever foolishly overextended neck.

She did not tire. She did not fear.

Stephen was the only thing that could hurt her here, and she had left him in Gervanno's care. But she knew what he knew, even here;

she knew that this aerial attack was not the only attempted incursion. It was just the most obvious one.

FROM THE GROUND, Stephen kept one pair of eyes on the skies—not his own, but Sanfel's. What Nenyane herself did not understand was clear to Stephen at this great remove. If Anya was a force akin to the wild elements, so was Nenyane. She did not tire; would not. The polite fiction that she was gifted with better than normal endurance was not one he thought he would cling to, but he had. He realized it now.

Nenyane, reluctant, was uncertain that she could end the life of the mage. But Stephen felt certain that Anya could not kill Nenyane, even if she tried. Should she reduce the entirety of these wild lands to ash, Nenyane would still be standing at the end.

No, she said, as blood briefly rained from the sky; the wounds she inflicted were not instantly cauterized by the heat of flame. *Never again. Never.* As if her sword were punctuation, emphasis, her attacks became more frenetic—but she never lost her focus.

She thought Anya driven by intense, personal pain.

She did not realize, as she fought, that she was driven in the same way.

Stephen wanted to go to her then, but he had no means of reaching the heights; the air did not arrive to convey him to the battlefield on which she now fought.

He shifted to Brylle's vision; he could now see Alex's back. Max's was further ahead. Neither were what caught his attention. Blood did. It belonged to neither of the Maubreche brothers. Nor was it one of the dogs. Steel was uninjured.

The circus, with its bright, gaudy colors, eschewed subtlety for expansive entertainment and welcome—but this wet crimson did not belong there. He had been tasked with keeping Trevor safe. So had Gervanno. But the warning offered by the fortune-teller who had become the field's commander had not been offered in vain. East.

Stephen sent Patches and Pearl ahead and turned to Gervanno. "Demons," he said. "In the east."

Gervanno nodded, but glanced at Trevor. Stephen's hesitance grew.

"I cannot leave your side," Gervanno said. "Alex and Max are my companions, but they are not my duty. You are. Where you go, I will—I must—follow, until this ceremony reaches its end, or until we do."

"Your weapon is proof against demons," Stephen replied.

"Yes. Its wielder is not. And you are not. If the demons breach the perimeter, it is here they will come. We are the last line of defense until Nenyane and Anya descend. The barriers that prevent incursion still hold, although the skies have been unveiled: the corpses of the wyverns have not fallen upon us, or the circus grounds."

The fox, all but forgotten until this moment, exhaled. "You understand that if I intervene, you will owe me a debt?" The question was asked not of Stephen but of Gervanno.

"Eldest."

"That is not an answer, cub."

"I cannot ask you to intervene," Gervanno finally said. "Because I am merely mortal, and I do not believe I can shoulder the weight of the debt I would incur. Stephen of Maubreche is my lord; Nenyane of Maubreche is my master. A man of such trifling power and stature as myself cannot serve two masters."

"A man with little ambition and no finesse cannot serve two masters." Gervanno stiffened visibly at the sound of this unexpected voice. "I serve two quite capably."

Stephen turned and offered Jarven A'Terafin a passable nod; he felt Nenyane's ripple of concern from above, and schooled both reaction and expression. She knew he was worried for Max and Alex; she did not need further worry while she concentrated on the battle she had undertaken.

"You are not what I am," Gervanno replied. "You have chosen to serve the eldest fully and in truth. Your lord—not your master—condones this service, or the eldest would not accept it."

The fox raised a brow.

"You speak of your lord with respect, Eldest. You serve as those who are of the wilderness serve. You are hers to command."

"She is far, far too wise for that," Jarven said, with a chuckle. "Some creatures, like some humans, chafe at command."

"Enough, Jarven." The fox's voice grew chilly. Stephen noted that while the fox could take offense at Gervanno's words, his tone when speaking with Gervanno contained genuine warmth. Not so, with Jarven.

"It is observation, not criticism, Eldest," Jarven replied. "But I perceive that Ser Gervanno will not abandon his charge, and the situation may become fraught if the *Kialli* are not stopped."

"*Kialli*, then?"

Jarven nodded.

"And they did not sense you?"

"Given the magic wielded by those who perform on the circus stage, I do not believe they could spare the attention to scout carefully. They were not expecting to be confronted in so extreme a fashion. They were, however, expecting opponents of power; they did not send a scouting force. I believe, of the demons present on the field, the strongest is one of the four who have managed to untangle the eastern boundary. The circus defenders will be hard-pressed."

Stephen kept tension from his face; his hands clenched.

"Surely your hubris is not so great that you believe *you* can stand against the *Kialli*?"

"Not alone, Eldest." Jarven's smile was like the edge of a blade — one held against a throat.

"No, of course not." The fox sniffed. He was taunting Jarven. It would have had no effect on Gervanno; it would have had little on Stephen. Both men assessed and accepted their limitations, moving only in desperation to conquer them. Jarven appeared to consider limitations a personal insult. "Very well. Interfere as it pleases you — but Jarven, I will be displeased if you deliberately sacrifice any of your erstwhile allies."

"Surely you do not intend to make me responsible for their survival when my own is, in your opinion, in question?"

"Of course not. Do not play word games with me."

Jarven bowed. "Eldest." He took a step forward and faded, slowly, from view.

Stephen glanced at the fox; he had almost forgotten the fox had remained.

"You have a question, son of Bredan?"

You don't, Nenyane snapped, her blade passing through bone and flame.

He did, but he wasn't willing to risk giving offense to the fox. He was well aware of the fox's power; he had seen it wielded to what he assumed was its full extent in the forests beneath the night of three moons, on the edge of Bowgren.

"No, Eldest. I simply fail to understand how you handle Jarven ATerafin."

"Ah." The fox seemed to smile, artifice of whiskers and movement of small lips over white canines. "He is tricky; his pride is greater, at the moment, then he himself can be. But he does not accept limitations. In another, that would have been his death a hundred times over. But a man such as he can reach, always, for greatness—and he may, in his time, achieve it.

"He is prone to risk-taking; it is bred into his blood. Better, for one such as he, to live fully, to live grandly, than to live in shadows or on his knees."

Given his lack of visibility, Stephen was less certain of that.

"Pay attention, child of Bredan." The words were a hum, almost a sensation. Ah, no, it was not the fox's voice that uttered those words.

MAX CALLED trance the moment he heard Katie's voice. He recognized the steel in her tone; she was an older woman who was accustomed to being obeyed when it counted. He'd grown up in the household of Lady Elseth; the tone was familiar, almost comfortably so. Max, unlike his brother, liked the anchor of familiarity. He acclimated to new things slowly, if at all.

Were Stephen safe in Maubreche, Max would never have ventured out of his demesne—if not for Alex. Alex was the key to the world; Alex was the window through which the new was bright, shiny, mysterious.

Not all of it, his brother replied, tone light and wry. Alex had called trance as well; he'd drawn sword. He'd never been quite as reliant on hunting dogs as Max, but both of the Elseth Hunters missed their dogs now. In situations like this one, they were accustomed to many sets of eyes; the view of any field of conflict was tiled and multiply dimensional in a way it wasn't now.

Max was armed with the sword he had taken from the lost and found. He hoped it was equal to Gervanno's similarly acquired weapon. Meralonne had once said that demons were proof against most mortal steel, unless they were almost powerless. The mage's version of almost powerless was in line with Nenyane's, whom Max trusted far more.

Even the least powerful of demons could lay waste to half a village before they were killed. Neither Max nor Alex expected the intruders would be considered weak or trifling, even by Nenyane's standards.

He felt the sudden roar of wind as a buffeting force at his back. The circus defenders were already in motion. He saw one—possibly the Carrick Katie had sent here—leap up to the branches of surrounding trees; he was joined, in the air, by at least two others. Steel could see a fourth, a fifth; they wore the bright colors evident in the pavilions. Max wouldn't have dressed that way; the clothing couldn't be missed. It made them obvious targets.

The periphery of this odd space was not adorned with cobbled stone and tenting; it was forested. Max shouldn't have been surprised when the standing trees disgorged people; he'd seen it once, when Adala sang.

The defenders did not sing. Perhaps, with training, Adala would not have had to sing, either. A stray thought. A useless thought. It was probably Alex's calculations. Alex's thoughts were so natural they were almost a part of Max's, but at times, they could be distracting. Did Max care how the trees were awakened? No. The only thing that mattered was that they were.

Unlike the circus people, they didn't leap up to the branches of their own trees; they stood upon the earth, their hands empty. If they intended to fight the demons, their weapons were not weapons Max could wield.

Max couldn't wield air. He couldn't move the earth. He had no doubt that the circus people could—and they could wield fire as well.

He couldn't see the object of the wind's sudden attack; he assumed the shove forward he'd felt wasn't aimed at him. But earthquakes wouldn't be aimed at Max, either; they might injure or kill without intent.

Patches joined Steel; Max couldn't see through Patches' eyes, but understood. They had split their group. Stephen remained with Adala; Alex and Max had run in search of the invaders. Patches was their only conduit.

Here, the tree cover obscured much of the purple sky. Steel could see the wingspans of the wyverns; he could see the sudden flares of fire that shifted the color of the sky in brief, burning flashes. Max wasn't interested in more of that—he had checked to make certain nothing cut down in the heights would become a danger to them if it fell. But the wyverns fought to the west; if their corpses became unintended weapons, it would not be here.

Too far to the west, Alex said. *We haven't come that far.*

Max shrugged. *Wilderness.*

Alex nodded. *Ahead.*

Max had already seen what had caused Alex to give his brief warning. It was not so much a demon as a shimmering in the air, a subtle wrongness, a vague oval shape that seemed slightly out of phase. It was not the shape and size of a person.

"'Ware!" one of the circus people shouted. "There are three!"

What Max could not easily see, they could sense. The earth heaved beneath that shimmering light. Max had not closed with it; nor had Alex. They split up, Alex remaining, Max circumnavigating the sudden spike — of stone — between the trees.

The strangeness in the air resolved itself almost as soon as the shouted warning faded: there were, as the man from the circus had said, three.

Max leapt back; the ground at his feet blackened as everything rooted there became flame and ash, almost in an instant. The earth rumbled as he landed, but he moved again, and again, unintentionally drawing large, short bursts of flame.

Steel could see the three that emerged from what had appeared a distortion in the air itself. The wind whipped past Max, but this time it did not buffet him; it was far more focused. The bursts of fire became wilder as wind struck their summoner.

Arrayed before them, surrounded by burning patches of wildflower and weed, stood three demons. Max had now seen more demons in his short months away from home than a person should have to see in a lifetime. These, however, almost stopped Alex in his tracks. Max had never been as sensitive to raw beauty as Alex had; beauty, in Max's world, was almost irrelevant.

Not so in Alex's.

The three demons that stood surveying the landscape reminded Max of Meralonne — but Meralonne without the dirt and dust of travel on the open road; Meralonne without the pipe and the sour, snappish temper.

We saw him fight, Alex said.

Max realized he had shied away from that comparison, because Meralonne in combat became so strange, so other, the familiarity of the known companion was lost. All hint of ordinary, normal life deserted the mage, moving away while everyone else was left standing in place.

Meralonne was not as they were. He had never been as they were.

Air sundered fire from its mooring; earth buried it; fire emerged.

Max no longer viewed that fire.

One of the three turned toward him—ah, no. Toward Alex. Eyes of silver and black reflected his brother; lips turned up in a smile that seemed ludicrously gentle in the midst of growing elemental clamor.

He spoke. Max couldn't hear the words. Alex, however could. Alex froze in place, mouth half open. It almost killed him. The wind bore him up while Max shouted in his figurative ear, pulling him back from the instant fascination. The instant compulsion.

"Don't meet his eyes!" Max shouted to the circus people; they were darting back and forth so quickly it was almost hard to keep track of them. He could shout while moving. He did. But the enemy who had caught—and held—Alex's attention was not the threat; the other two demons were moving.

They moved as if they were Hunters, as if they were *Breodani* Hunters, their perfect coordination the product of the bond to which Alex and Max had been born. Other Hunters might have to grow into it from later childhood; Max and Alex had not.

Max brought his sword around as the two who were moving turned their attention—and swords—toward Max. Max could leap up, but could not easily remain at height. He doubted it would save him, regardless. The two he faced were like Meralonne, but perhaps paler, almost as if they were imperfect imitations.

The third demon who had not moved, had the same vitality, the same sharp brilliance, as Meralonne when he committed to battle. It was in combat that Meralonne shed the patina of mortality. The wilderness—even the fox—referred to the demons as *the dead*. This brilliance, this obvious vitality was no death that Max understood.

The wind howled past as Max moved; he could hear it, could see the effects of its sudden burst, but could no longer feel it. Alex was also in motion; his view of the two who were physically attacking was clearer than Max's. Steel moved to a point between the two Elseth Hunters, allowing Max a moving triangulation of the changing field of battle.

Earth moved beneath Max's feet, but not in a threatened rupture; it seemed to move beneath his steps, hardening and softening; rising and falling by inches as he landed and pushed up, leaping out of the way of sword.

The demons were armed. Their swords left a trace of red afterglow in the wake of their blades' passage.

They're serious, Alex said. The demons who could wield swords seldom drew them. They could enter battle, but their natural arrogance made of that battle a petty slaughter. Only when they were serious did they wield these red, red blades—blades that echoed the fire they called at will.

Alex frowned; Max could feel it as clearly as if it were his own lips turning, his own brow creasing. *I think their swords are chipped.* He might have noticed broken limbs with less shock.

The twin defenders—Alex always noted twins whenever he encountered them; in Breodanir, they were rare—leapt past Max. They were armed not with swords but with long knives, one in each hand. Their hair was bound—not even a strand escaped—but their tunics were darkened with the sweat of exertion. More than that, Steel didn't see; his eyes were necessary if Max was to survive the demon's sword.

Heat warped the air where the sword passed; taller weeds withered.

Where his sword struck and parried the demon's, the air sizzled. Alex was right: the demonic blades were chipped. Max's was not, but he was driven back by the force of the demon's strike.

"Run!" the creature cried, his voice more felt than heard. "Run, you fool—leave, and you will survive!"

Alex had closed with the second demon, or perhaps the second demon had closed with Alex. Alex was not alone. The twins, their long knives in hands, parried the blow meant for Alex, knives crossed, knees bent to absorb the shock of impact. The demon roared; only one twin had parried. The other had clipped demonic arm. Alex moved in, bringing his sword down on the sword arm.

A shield came to arm as Alex struck, rendering the attack useless.

"Not your sword, boy!" The circus man's shout was human, but loud. Carrick? One of the defenders, but not one of the twins. Alex's sword skidded across the surface of perfect skin. He could parry; he could not injure. "Not yet!"

He had not shouted a similar warning to Max. Max intended to return to the lost and found if they both survived this. He didn't understand how the demons could be here at all. What was the meaning of

Adala's decision? How could it have had so much effect on the defenses of what was, according to Nenyane, the land of a wild lord?

How could the long knives of the circus defenders cause damage that Alex's long sword couldn't?

The weapons of the demons were not so hampered. Max, parrying, took a glancing blow across his sword arm; blood welled scarlet across it. The cut was not deep; in the grip of the Hunter's trance, he did not feel it at all.

"Don't let your blood touch the earth!" Carrick's voice, like the demon's, was physical sensation.

Max didn't argue; he had no breath or time for it. Steel leapt in, shouldered the demon's leg, and leapt out, as the demonic blade whistled just past the top of his head. It did not slow the enemy, but it added unnecessary movement to the cadence of his attacks, and it allowed Max to return the glancing blow he'd received.

His blade, unlike Alex's, caused damage; it did not skid off smooth, exposed skin as if the appearance of flesh was a lie.

"Pull back!" Carrick again.

Vines burst from the earth beneath the demon's feet. No, not vines; roots, dirt encrusted, and thick.

"Pull back—bandage your arm! Do not let your blood touch the earth!"

Max had no cloth with which to bandage his arm immediately available. Of all the advice he could be given, *don't bleed* seemed almost unreal. This wouldn't be the first injury he'd taken on his many hunts; even in training he had received small injuries.

Do what he says, Alex snapped. *This isn't Breodanir. It isn't Elseth. If there's a reason your blood isn't meant for* this *earth, do everything you can not to let it fall.* An edge of panic laced Alex's voice; he was thrumming with it. Max parried, and parried again, as the roots that had enwrapped the demon's legs slowed the enemy's movements, pulling his feet and legs into the earth itself.

Fire burst across the length of those roots. Max could hear a grunt of distant pain.

He obeyed Alex's desperate command, lifting one hand to cup his arm. The cut wasn't deep, but it wasn't a mere scratch.

The fire ate away at the binding roots as Max retreated. If Carrick —or the trees—had bought him time, it wasn't enough. He couldn't cover his arm and defend himself against further attack; he could move quickly, but the demon was faster. Without trance, Max was certain he'd be dead.

Blood fell as he parried. His blood. He didn't have the time to pay attention to where it fell; roots rose again, but this time, fire greeted them; the demon leapt up, as if he were weightless — or as if air was his to command.

It was not; the air listened to a different voice; it drove the demon into the broad trunk of the nearest tree. Branches moved, as if limbs, to encircle the demon, to hold it in place.

Too late, Max whispered to his brother.

It was such a minor cut. It was barely an injury. The blood that fell would have been beneath notice in any other fight, any other hunt.

But it fell, now, to the earth of the wilderness.

CHAPTER NINETEEN

Max understood the shouted warning the moment the earth absorbed the scant drops of blood: Elseth blood. Bredan's blood. Max was not god-born in the sense that Stephen was. Max's mother had not been god-born as Stephen was. She was kin to the god, a scion of the god's time on earth. Her mortal parent, however, had not been human.

It was a truth Elseth as a whole—under the guidance of Lady Elseth—had never acknowledged. Espere could not be considered bestial by the nobility. Gilliam allowed Lady Elseth to set the social rules, but he had not and did not disavow what their mother was.

There was a reason she had born a litter. A reason she could learn, but not fully acclimate herself to Breodanir's noble society. There was a reason, in the end, that her eyes were not the golden eyes of the god-born.

He felt the blood almost as if blood was tears, as if they were the result of weeping.

His awareness of the earth shifted in that moment; he felt its presence as if it were a stranger who, uncomfortable with weeping, nonetheless sought to offer comfort of a kind. He had not been still. The tree that had briefly enveloped the demon was now on fire; the demon was not harmed by the flame at all.

The tree, of course, was.

Max darted forward, sword in hand; he drove the sword into the demon's chest. The demon cried out in fury, not pain — Max wondered if demons could feel pain.

Not their own, child.

He did not freeze; the demon was not vanquished. Branches were torn from the tree as the demon freed one arm — the sword arm.

"Memonryenne!" the demon cried. "We cannot hold the gap for long!" Even as he spoke, the sword he wielded trembled, shaking as if it, like the gap, could no longer be held. Max's leap back — sword withdrawing from demonic chest — was instinctive; he raised one arm to shield his eyes as the sword shattered.

As if it were glass, not steel. As if it had been stressed beyond endurance by some force Max could not see or feel.

Ash followed as Max lowered the arm. The demon was gone. The tree's bark was charred, but the tree stood; the fire that had come at demonic command was extinguished with the demon.

Max could sense the tree. He could sense the shape of the earth; the dips in it, the ridges that existed beneath its surface. He could sense the *roots* of the trees that lay beneath his feet. Even the roots of wild grass and wildflowers could be felt.

He could hear the voice of the land.

You were right. The sword was damaged.

Alex's response was slow to come; Max followed his brother's gaze. The *Kialli* lord that had stood almost immobile had moved in the direction Max stood. The warning offered by his departed kin had been heard, absorbed. He lifted voice, spoke; the words were not meant for Max's ears. Or Alex's.

But Max understood them regardless.

"Withdraw. Withdraw now. I will face these mortals."

The demon who had received this command refused to acknowledge or obey it.

"Endaronne, withdraw." The words had the force of a physical blow; the demon whose name had been called staggered. He had taken wounds from the circus defenders; he had landed blows. The blood of the defenders fell. Their blood was not, apparently, forbidden.

No. They are of *me. Bound, chosen, the blood that they shed is not their own; it is mine.*

Max's was not. He moved toward his brother.

Send him back, now. Send him back or he, too, will suffer what you will suffer. He cannot face the Kialli *who is now in motion.*

"Can you?"

Silence. Max found himself looking toward the circus defenders. "Can I?"

Silence again, but this was broken. *Mortals oft cling to their companions and family in a way my kind did not. You will lose your brother if you do not retrieve him and retreat. If there is debt between us, the debt is ours, not yours; you have dispatched one of the kin. If the other is destroyed, the borders will be defensible; the breach, slight though it is, will close.*

The voice sounded confident, to Max. He did not doubt it at all. But simultaneously, he did.

Alex. You heard. You have to retreat.

Alex was silent; there was a tinge of confusion in that silence. Alex had not heard what Max heard. This had never happened before. Yes, Alex had ignored what Max heard from time to time—especially if it was associated with the dour mood of their grandmother—but he'd always *heard* it.

He had not heard the voice of what Max assumed was the circus master. None of it had traveled through the Hunter bond.

Alex *did* hear Max's thoughts and Max's concerns. He made no attempt to argue; he turned instantly and headed toward Max.

"Can you make sure Alex gets back to the circus safely?" Max asked.

For now, yes. But you will require his presence if you attempt to leave. This was not our intent, son of Bredan. Remember that.

Max heard one of the circus defenders cry out.

It was not what he heard that caused sharp, indrawn breath; it was the physical sensation that followed. He felt the flow of their blood as it left their body; felt the pain as an echo, reverberating in his left arm. Something had definitely gone wrong.

Max had shed such a tiny amount of blood, he wouldn't have noticed it at all had it not been for the shouted warning.

I don't think I should leave, he told Alex. *I have this sword, and it's effective against the demons the rest of the circus is facing.* He hesitated.

And I can be ensnared by demonic compulsion.

Max nodded.

Should I bleed as well?

No! Max exhaled. *No. I'm not sure who or what is in charge here, but I think they think I'll be trapped here as a circus attendant if you somehow get injured in the same way. If we survive, we can't stay. Stephen can't stay. Nenyane can't.*

Alex began to move. Steel remained with Max.

We have to go with them. We promised Father, Max said, uncomfortable with Alex's hesitation.

I didn't.

You did — you agreed to go, in disgrace, to the King's City. You knew what it meant.

Alex, the wordy one, failed to reply. He headed out of the thin line of trees, and discovered that the line wasn't as thin as it had first appeared. *You bled, here.*

Max shrugged.

Alex exhaled. He didn't want to leave without Max.

Max understood. Had Max been ordered away, he would have stayed, regardless. Alex was his brother. He was Hunter and hunt-brother, both. He was the compass by which Max navigated the very irritating shoals of the social world and its responsibilities. He was the one who asked questions. He was the one who reached out.

He was the one person in Max's entire life he could not live without.

But Alex wasn't Max. Alex understood, probably better than Max did, why he had to leave. His hesitation was brief. The forest itself wasn't. It was as if, upon entering the standing, thin line of trees, the forest had expanded.

It's probably the barrier itself, Alex told him. *The forest, I mean. It's the barrier through which the demons have to pass to get to the heart of the circus.*

That made sense; Max didn't question it. He relied — as he often did — on Alex's opinions. Alex paid attention to trivial details that ended up being important long after the fact.

To Max's surprise, Alex navigated himself out of the treed area so quickly that the forest surrounding the demons and the rest of the combatants might have been illusory. He had no time for anything else. The second demon had retreated at the command of the *Kialli* that had almost enspelled Alex.

That left exactly one demon standing.

The circus defenders hesitated to approach him, and Max told Steel to remain as far from the demon as he could, while still being a useful pair of eyes. He closed.

A white flare of radiance burst forth from the enemy, blinding Max. Had he not had access to Steel's eyes, he would have died. He did, and he moved, avoiding the sudden presence of burning blade, of red sword. The demon had chosen to move for the first time since they'd encountered him.

ALEX STOOD on the edge of the grassy clearing.

Katie hadn't moved, but Adala had; he could see Stephen and Trevor following her as she focused on her balance. He could—when he looked up—see Nenyane, even at this distance. He could only see the mage by the obvious signs of her power. Anya was like a display of fireworks on her own—but hers weren't simple, pretty lights. Where her fire—and more—passed, bodies fell from the sky.

Their shadows darkened grass, but the corpses that didn't disintegrate didn't reach the earth here; they were shunted to the side in their fall. Alex assumed this was the barrier that protected the circus itself, when the circus was called.

Alex exhaled slowly. He knew that Max had almost been blinded by the sudden radiance of the demon that remained. Max's instincts made clear—to both himself and Alex—that this demon was a lord of power. That he had once been known for the radiance of the light he could wield as benison or weapon; that even the fires that came at his command were white with pale blue hearts.

Alex froze.

Max thought it, yes—but Max didn't, or hadn't, possessed this information.

What was Max hearing? Why was it something Alex himself couldn't hear? How did Max *know* who or what the demon was? They'd never encountered it before. But Max wasn't guessing—he left guesswork to Alex. He was certain. Alex often left certainty in uncertain situations to Max.

He walked quickly to where Katie stood, hands on hips, her back turned to Adala; she was watching the thin line of forest through which the demons had come. Her eyes glanced over Alex, but no more; the force of her concentration lay beyond the grass, through the trees themselves.

"Join your companion," she told Alex, before he'd reached her side.

Her voice carried—but of course it did. The circus defenders could hear her from the forest, in the midst of clangor and flame.

Which companion?

"The god-born boy. Stay by his side. Your brother was unlucky. One could say he was far too arrogant, but it is thanks to his ability to wield that sword that we are down one intruder. We may be able to maintain this barrier yet. You, however, must avoid any injury that causes external bleeding."

The god-born boy, as Katie called Stephen, was with Gervanno and Trevor. Trevor was visibly trembling as he watched Adala's progress.

Alex wondered how he would feel if he was forced to leave Max behind. Or if Max chose to remain voluntarily, in a place Alex could not. Trevor would stay by Adala's side, in the heart of the circus, if he were allowed. He was not.

And Adala would be circus from this day forward. Had to be. Alex understood that it was because Adala had not completed this complicated, strange ritual that the demons had any chance of invading at all.

How they had known that this weakness existed was cause for concern—but it could wait. Had to wait.

Gervanno turned the moment Alex was ten yards away; when he saw the Elseth Hunter, he turned back to Adala. Stephen didn't look back, but didn't have to. The fussy, impossible Pearl had.

"Max?"

"Max is fighting. The sword he picked up in the lost and found can injure the demons who intruded; mine can't. And...we're not supposed to bleed here."

Stephen blinked. "What did you just say?"

"We're not supposed to shed our own blood on the earth here."

"That's what I thought I heard. What does that mean?"

"According to Max, the circus people chewed him out for bleeding in the forest. He wasn't severely injured," Alex added quickly, seeing the change in Stephen's expression. "He's had way worse while hunting. I mean—it was a gash, but it was shallow. He barely noticed it.

"But the circus soldiers did—they noticed immediately. They weren't happy."

"We can hardly avoid injury given the creatures we're fighting." It was Gervanno who spoke. He seemed as perplexed by this rule as Max had been.

"I think the reason the circus people have gone to the periphery is to prevent exactly that. Nenyane and Anya have gone to the demons; the demons cannot land. Max and the rest of the circus are fighting in the forest on the border of this clearing. Only if they fail will we be in combat with demons. But if they fail, I don't think our blood will matter."

A glint of light caught Alex's eye, but had it not, Trevor would have: he cried out, "Adala!"

Adala had drawn a knife from the folds of her clothing. Feet trembling on the rounded curve of a giant root, she cut her hand; blood welled in the mound of her left palm. It fell; he could see the splash of color, the red of it, as if in that moment it was the only color in the entirety of the clearing; the amethyst of sky, the red and orange of fire, the emerald of forest leaves, and the pale, small blossoms of wildflowers became almost grey.

The sounds of battle above fell away; Adala's voice grew louder. She lifted both of her arms, turning her face toward the sky. No, not the sky. Alex moved toward her, but Trevor leapt past him — past Stephen, past Gervanno — sprinting toward Adala, arms outstretched to catch her, as if he was certain she was about to fall.

She was.

She was, but Trevor could not catch her. Adala had made her choice. It was imperfect, raw with impatience and a terrible yearning. She had blended the two, made of them a harmony of sound in which both parts were true, and both hers. She had tried to choose Trevor, to retreat to a world in which the circus master was not lord. But she accepted, given the advent of the demonic horde above, that there was no safety in that world. Not for Adala. Not for Trevor.

Not for the family she had abandoned in order to build the future of which she'd been dreaming.

The only hope of safety was here. She could keep Trevor safe. She could preserve his life. And he would leave. He would have to leave. There was no place for him in the circus.

All of this, her song revealed; Alex could hear it in words he couldn't otherwise understand. She had cut her own palm, shed her own blood, as an offering; while blood ran down her wrists, she waited, as if the blood itself were a question or a plea, and the answer had not yet come.

Do not shed blood here.

Alex had heard the warning, had even shared it, but as he watched, he understood it in a way Max hadn't. Max would, now.

Alex felt his throat constrict; he had almost forgotten to breathe. Where Adala's blood fell, the roots of the tree just in front of her feet changed color, adopting the same intense brilliance of her shed blood. Had that been all, it would have been arresting. It wasn't.

Perhaps that was why Trevor was sprinting.

The blood changed the nature of the roots. Where it splashed, it rose, as if it had become a vine, transformed by the contact.

That didn't happen to me, Max said. *Don't worry about me — just do what you have to do there.*

Katie shouted Trevor's name; Trevor didn't hear her. Alex could move faster than either Stephen or Gervanno, and did. What he had to do here was stop Trevor. Stop him from reaching Adala. Stop him from touching her. Stop him from protecting her, which was his most visceral instinct.

He shouldn't have been here at all; Alex hadn't understood why until this moment. The vines that rose from Adala's shed blood wavered in the air — and then pierced her legs.

Adala's song faltered for the first time, disturbed by a grunt of suppressed pain. Where the roots pierced legs, blood fell — far more than it had from the cut she'd managed to make across her own palm.

That blood transformed the ground on which she stood — tree root, wide enough for both of her feet — in the same fashion. Red should not have been bright enough to force Alex to squint — but it was. It was a burst of radiant light, dazzling and deadly. Vines, tendrils, something dark and, even at this distance, dangerous, rose in a rush, as if they were hungry. As if this is what they'd been waiting for.

Those tendrils also pierced Adala's flesh. Arms. Legs. Thighs. They did not touch her heart, not yet; did not pierce eyes. But they rose, twisting, lashing, as Trevor screamed.

Alex tackled Trevor before Trevor could reach Adala; he bore him to the ground. Trevor fought back as he could, but Gervanno came to Alex's aid.

"Let me go!" Trevor shouted. "Let me go! She'll die!"

"No," Katie's voice boomed. "No, child. She wanted you here. I didn't. But the lord granted her this final request. Watch, boy. Bear witness. This is what she's chosen for the sake of all of the people she has ever loved."

Gervanno had a knee in Trevor's back; he motioned to Alex, and Alex moved. Trevor could lift and turn his head, but he struggled against constraints. If he could be safely released, it could not be now.

This couldn't be what awaited Max. It *couldn't*. Eyes narrowed, Alex watched. The circus people were clearly townsfolk; they had been taken into the circus, and they had persisted; the circus was their only home. They could not serve as simple sacrifices.

But this did not look like life to Alex. It looked, in the moment he watched, like some terrible, vivid version of the historical Hunter's Death. Adala's voice was thready, thin; she continued her song.

Above their heads the shattered sky seemed to lower as Alex glanced up; the sounds of combat once again asserted themselves over the sound of Adala's song.

Katie cursed. Cursed and then lifted her own voice in song. It was not Adala's song, but it was similar: Alex couldn't understand a word she sang, but the song itself seemed essential. Had Alex not believed that it was wed, in some fashion, to the circus itself, he might have sprinted back to the circus to find the bard. To find Kallandras, who could sing duets with the wilderness itself, who could cajole the wild air, and who had—if rumors were true—never crossed a battlefield that could kill him.

But Kallandras wasn't of the circus.

Katie's voice joined Adala's, although their songs seemed slightly different. Adala's voice flagged but never stopped.

The red light grew brighter. Adala could no longer be seen. Or perhaps she could; perhaps that brilliant glow was what remained of her.

Trevor fell silent; he ceased to struggle. Gervanno did not move. He did speak, but his words were soft Torra, a language Trevor might not recognize.

The fox, however, did. Gervanno had set him down, and given the fox's glare, had done so without permission. Alex looked to the skies, to the combat that had continued. The sky itself drew closer, the wyverns at the heights becoming larger, their wingspans and fiery breath stretching across a greater expanse of the visible height.

Trevor no longer screamed.

Adala's voice could barely be heard.

Katie walked to where Alex stood; she tapped him on the shoulder.

"It is almost done," she said, her voice rough—as if she'd done nothing but shout for hours.

"Is this what awaits people who offer the circus their blood?"

"Only if that offer is accepted. We are given the choice," she added, her tone bitter.

Stephen came to stand by Alex. "We won't belabor the nature of choice, but to our eyes this isn't much of one."

"No? You come from a kingdom where those who rule habitually sacrifice one of their own every year. It is the choice you make."

"Did you accept what's happening to Adala now with any joy?"

"Me? Yes, actually. But my children were no longer young, and the situation was not so dire. There are those who are summoned who fail to arrive, just as Adala failed to arrive. But Adala's choice had consequences that my refusal would not."

"That is not true." The fox spoke.

Katie turned to the fox; a flicker of surprise could be seen before her expression was lost to a very deep bow. "Eldest."

"You cannot see it, who were mortal. I did not see it immediately—but I am here under sufferance. The lord of these lands does not fully trust my intent." The fox's expression shifted into what seemed a grin. "He is not a fool. I bear him no ill will; I will pass through his lands, as I have passed through many others, and I will cause no deliberate harm.

"Not until or unless those I deem of value are hurt or killed.

"But these lands are yours as much as they are his. His architecture is built on your blood and your very beings. Had you made a different choice, one thread of his deliberate tapestry would fray or break. You might not notice it, being only one such slender thread—but what he has built is made of many such threads.

"That one, though—that one is different. Your power, such as it was, was minor. Small. Hers was not. Is not, even now. Tell me, fortune-teller, is she guaranteed to survive?"

Trevor tensed; Gervanno's knee stopped him from rising.

Katie did not reply. Something about her expression as she faced the fox had hardened; her eyes were an odd color—not grey, not brown, but something that seemed to shift between the two. It was subtle; had Alex not been searching her face for any hint of an answer, he might have missed it.

Had Max not bled in the forest that served as a final barrier, Alex would not have looked so carefully. Would not have asked the question that now left his mouth. "How many of those called to serve die in this ritual?"

"It is not of me that you must ask that question," Katie replied, the words far more stilted and formal than anything she'd said so far.

As if her words had summoned the circus master, he appeared, walking across the grass, his steps neat and tidy. The shadows of the great beasts that fought from above did not seem to touch him at all; they certainly crossed the rest of the people gathered here as they moved — or fell.

He had not come to answer Alex's question, of course; nor had he come to reprimand Katie. He stopped, briefly, in front of the golden fox, offering a nod, not the deep bow Katie had offered.

"Have you come for your new cub?" the fox asked.

"As you suspect, yes. Ser Gervanno, you may release the boy now. I will take him into my keeping for the duration."

Gervanno obeyed immediately, as if the circus master was the most powerful of the people gathered. Trevor rose, shook himself, and turned to the circus master. He bowed, his bow very similar to the one Katie had offered the fox.

"What would you give to protect your family, your home?" the circus master asked.

Alex stepped between the circus master and Trevor, moving instinctively.

Gervanno moved, but Katie lifted a hand; the Southerner stopped, acknowledging the greater knowledge in what was a nonverbal command.

"Child of Bredan, you are here as a guest," the circus master said. "It would be unfortunate should I be moved to revoke my permission. The townspeople require no permission. Even one such as Anya can freely visit when the circus comes to town. But you are not of the Free Towns. You are here as guests of an innkeeper.

"Do not attempt to come between me and one of my people."

Alex could not explain why he had moved as he had; had Max been with him, he would have made certain his brother stayed as far from the circus master as possible. It was Alex's duty to stop his Hunter from causing strife and conflict with any ruling lord or lady.

But it was Alex who stood between the circus master and Trevor.

Trevor had not answered the question. The circus master looked past Alex to where Trevor now stood. "What would you give to save Adala?"

Katie paled. "Lord," she said.

The circus master glanced in her direction, the glance, silent permission to speak.

"She is too new. She has made her choice with reluctance, but she *has* made her choice. She has walked the path; she is almost at its heart. But she has not yet reached the place where we have all arrived. If the boy is required to sacrifice himself—if that is why you allowed his presence—I fear she will never arrive."

"She hesitates, even now," the circus master replied. "Were it not for Trevor, she would have come to us, early. She would have accepted both invitation and duty, and the path she walked would be far, far less perilous."

"If he had died at the hands of the demons that seek to attack—that *are* attacking—she would do all in her power to avenge him. But he did not. And if he dies here, the same rage and pain will be hers—but it will have a different target. The risk to the circus is too great."

Alex swallowed.

Gods were supposed to be wise, to be all-knowing, to be…like perfect people. He understood, intellectually, that gods were not people. This was the first time he felt it viscerally. Gods were alien. They were not knowable by the people who followed them. It did not take particular wisdom to understand what Katie was, desperately, trying to convey. It did not require anything but a human heart, human emotions.

The fox tsked. Loudly.

"Do not interfere, Eldest."

"I would not, but my own cubs are within your perimeter. The woman is correct. If you mean to ask Trevor to sacrifice his own life in pursuit of hers, the *Kialli* will breach the barriers built on human blood and human sacrifice. If that is how you mean to discard this place, so be it. The lands are yours, and those who have lived in its shelter, yours as well.

"But the girl, this Adala, is not what the boy is. Perhaps you might explain to the boy why he cannot follow her path in this place. Or if you are too *busy*, I might explain it with your permission."

Alex could not meet the circus master's gaze for long. It hurt his eyes; the man's face shifted, twisted, morphing into one visage and then another. The color of the circus master's eyes could not be pinned down, and even his height began to change, never coming to rest.

The fox took silence as permission; Alex would not have done so.

"The woman you love was born *to* the circus. She was born *of* it. Born to mortal parents, but altered in subtle fashion; that is the nature of your towns. It is *because* she was born with that slender thread of the wilderness that she can be what she will become. Her blood contains a trace of the wilderness—the circus—itself. I have seldom seen a land constructed in this fashion; it is almost astonishing.

"If your blood spills here, it will have no meaning. It is blood, similar in all ways to the blood of the animals you eat. The wilderness will not notice; it will not wake; it will not reach for its kin. Could it, you would be able to remain beside your beloved.

"Your death will, therefore, have meaning only to the people here, to a greater or lesser extent. All lives are entwined with other lives. Even those who profess a desire for isolation cannot live without touching living things: the trees, the bounty of the verdant land."

Trevor moved to stand beside—not in front of—Alex. "Would my death save Adala?"

The circus master was silent.

Katie stared at Trevor's profile, as if attempting to grab his attention, to force it from the god.

"In a fashion," the circus master replied. "She struggles, even now, with twin desires; it is why she is in such pain."

The fox rolled his large, golden eyes. "She is torn between the future she desired with you and the future the lord desires. She wishes to preserve and protect the people she loves. She wishes to be loved by you. It is not that she did not choose, but that her choice is imperfect— as all mortals must be, by the very nature of their design."

Alex hesitated. Gervanno was so very formal and respectful when in the presence of the fox; the swordsman knew he should not question him. Had Alex been Max, he would have kept his silence.

Max was occupied, but snapped a warning.

"Do you consider yourself perfect, Eldest?"

The fox's head swiveled toward Alex; small teeth elongated in what seemed, on the surface, to be a grin. Gervanno stiffened. "Eldest," he began.

"Not now," the fox snapped, a rumble in his voice.

Gervanno fell silent.

"Do you not consider me perfect, mortal?"

The circus master frowned as he turned to Alex.

"I am not aware that my opinion matters," Alex replied. His tone was respectful; he knew how to be self-effacing when it was required of him.

But not silent. Max cursed, but not at Alex—or not solely at Alex.

"It does not. But mortals exist as paltry, scant presences. Only a rare few are born with traces of genuine power. The mage in the skies above is one such. Those without such power were meant to offer respect, child. Respect to those above them, those beyond them."

"Eldest," the circus master said. "He is *my* guest."

"Oh, indeed. I understand why mortals are precious to you; I will not harm him here. But he has asked a dangerously disrespectful question, when the answer to it should be obvious."

"It is the flaws that mortals carry that make them precious; the effects of those flaws and scars cannot be predicted. But Alex, it is not a question you should have asked; it is not a question you should *ever* ask. The eldest may accept your apology, if it is earnest and genuine."

"And I may not," the fox added. His glare was a physical sensation.

"Eldest," Gervanno said, kneeling to offer his arms to the fox.

The fox sniffed, but accepted his customary perch. "Do not interfere."

Gervanno said nothing.

"I mean it," the fox added.

"Eldest."

The fox opened small jaws and attached them to Gervanno's left hand. "I should have left you in the wilderness," the fox said, the words muffled.

"I am grateful that you did not."

"You are only grateful because you survived to meet your sword master." The fox's tone had shifted from silent fury to petulance.

"I have survived to experience many, many things, Eldest. It is not just the sword master. There is beauty in the wilderness, and danger—but even the danger is beautiful in a fashion. Nothing I have encountered in my life until the Averdan valleys..." He stopped.

"Mortals die," the fox said, into the silence of trailing words. "Even in the lands the gods once ruled, mortals died often. They are difficult to preserve. They do not make choices that make that preservation easier. But the danger has now passed, and perhaps I will indulge you.

Between you and the disrespectful brat, you have preserved the life of that young woman's love; he will not harm the boy now. The danger has passed."

"I consider it unwise," the circus master said. "If the young man dies, there will be nothing that will cause such internal division in Adala."

Alex glanced at Katie as the visceral sense of imminent death dissipated. She was pale, but she had held onto silence until the circus master spoke. She would not have disobeyed him had he decided to end Trevor's life.

But the circus master had granted Adala this one blessing; to end Trevor's life would have been a terrible betrayal. Katie knew it. Gervanno knew it. Alex knew it. Even the fox did.

How could a lord who professed to love humans not see it as clearly?

Trevor had not heard, or had not understood, the conversation that had passed around him. His eyes, narrowed so much they almost seemed shut, had not drifted from the burning luminescence of Adala, of what Adala had become or was becoming. He barely breathed; his exhalations were long and stuttering, as if, in between, he couldn't help but hold his breath.

Held breath was like prayer.

His hands were fists, his cheeks damp. He didn't notice when the first of the wyverns crashed to the ground of the circus clearing.

Katie did. Katie once again lifted voice, but this time Alex couldn't understand a word she said. It wasn't necessary.

Two of the circus soldiers have fallen. One's lost a leg; one's lost a right arm from the shoulder joint. Max had evaded the damage the final demon caused. *I think he's desperate now —as if he knows he has almost no time.*

But the dying wyvern crushed grass and flowers; it did not strike trees, and would not rise again to burn them. No rider leapt from the wyvern's back; the demons remained above, enmeshed in the aerial combat.

The fox snorted. *"This* is how you defend your domain? It is a wonder—a deep, abiding, unimagined *wonder*—that any of your mortals survived at all. Jarven, cease your observation; it is time to act."

Gervanno stiffened, but Jarven ATerafin failed to appear.

JARVEN HEARD the fox he had accepted, in his greed, as master. He felt the fox's words as a physical sensation—and, at that, a blow to the back of the head. It had been long indeed since anyone had treated Jarven as if he were a rebellious, difficult child.

But he had been a rebellious, difficult child. He had always chosen rebellion that skirted the edge of actual injury. Well, after the first time. The fox was correct: he had observed. He observed the Breodani Hunter and his lone dog; had observed the circus defenders, those servants of the god that ruled these erstwhile mortal lands.

He had heard the warning shouted to the Hunter: do not bleed here. Do not bleed on this earth. It intrigued him. He had not injured the Hunter; he was uneasily certain that there would be repercussions for that. But the Hunter had been injured. His blood had fallen.

Jarven had waited until the combat moved past. He had then examined the ground on which that blood had fallen; it was so tiny an amount, it should not have been noticed at all.

But Jarven could notice it immediately. The small drops of blood had changed the earth itself; it was glowing, as a torch at distance might glow. The earth had been altered by the influx of blood. He considered cutting his own hand; considered experimenting with his blood. The circus defenders were not completely overpowered, and the final demonic enemy was not one Jarven was certain he could survive. Ah, certainty. He was not certain he had a chance of triumph; not for Jarven the safety of certain victory.

Not always. He had lived with such certainty before, at the apex of his power in Terafin, and he had grown bored very, very quickly. He had been reduced to taking apprentices, such as they were; guiding them until they could mount a challenge.

But even then, he had been bored with life; he had seen its end approaching, and he had accepted it, but not with any grace. He had shed much blood in the wilderness, testing himself, his new reflexes, his new vision, his greatly expanded awareness.

He had not yet failed, although once or twice he had chosen to retreat. Retreat, to Jarven, was not shameful because survival was not shameful. He had done far worse to secure survival in his distant youth. Dead, he could accomplish nothing.

His blood did not change the earth. It was red, it fell, and it vanished; nothing burned.

Jarven, cease your observation. It is time to act.

"I do not think we are equal to the enemy who stands against us."

You are not alone. Work with them as you must; make use of them if you cannot. There is a reason we were permitted to enter this lord's domain; prove that we are worthy of his hospitality. Do not disappoint me.

"Had you granted me the final gifts you have withheld, I would perhaps be less of a disappointment, master."

Prove that you are worthy of them. You know what must be done.

Yes. He had to hunt down—and kill—Rymark ATerafin. When he had accepted this as the condition of his odd, elemental coming-of-age, he had not expected Rymark to be so physically involved with the Shining Court. He almost admired the man—indeed, given the fact that he was not yet dead when he was Jarven's target, admiration was owed.

But Rymark stood between Jarven and the power that would be his.

The demon was not Rymark. Indeed, Rymark was not a significant power. A mage, yes, but a middling mage; he was self-indulgent in a fashion that did not allow a focus on the development of his talent. Jarven accepted self-indulgence; he was known for it himself, with good reason.

But his self-indulgence had never harmed his ability to focus. His goals had never been set adrift in a wash of ego and appearance. Jarven sought power. He sought a role within the society that had caged him. But his desire for power, tangled as it was in symbols and gestures of respect, had been focused on Jarven. He wished to be under no man's thumb, except at his own whim.

He served the fox the way he had once served The Terafin. Rymark had served The Terafin as a means to accrue power over other people. Power did not exist for men like Rymark unless he was surrounded by those of less power. For Jarven, power existed almost as a game, but the true goal of power was freedom. He desired never to be under the thumb of another.

In this changing and changed landscape, the fox was necessary.

Rymark had become necessary as a way of achieving some measure of solid power in the wilderness. Rymark was not here. Had he been, Jarven's entire demeanor would have altered. In this combat, as he gazed, from a distance, at the *Kialli* who dominated the small clearing he had created by destroying trees—and men—he was not yet master of his own fate.

This was a simple step on the path, but it was a path set him by the fox who withheld his gifts. He had been ordered to kill the demon. He felt a niggling certainty that he could not.

But he looked, now, at the blood shed not by the Hunter or himself.

Across the forest floor, slashes of brilliant red shed brilliant light; the heart of that light was the color of blood, but the edges were a bright, almost painful, white. Jarven frowned. He had cloaked himself, as the fox could; it was the earliest of the lessons he had learned. In truth, it was not so different from the less magical, less wild methods he had learned to conceal his presence; it had not been difficult to master.

He did not immediately approach the demon. Instead, he watched the combatants. The Breodani boy had taken no further injuries, but had inflicted one small wound — at some cost to the companions beside whom he fought. One lost an arm; the *Kialli* sword passed through collarbone and down at an angle.

Blood fell.

One could hardly fight in earnest with edged weapons and avoid the shedding of blood. It was not the blood — or the loss of a defender, the break in the moving line of attack — that demanded Jarven's attention. It was the demon's sword. Red, burning, almost the color of the earth where blood had fallen, the blade's edge seemed, to Jarven's eyes, to be chipped.

He could hear the sword; he could hear what seemed a keening, a low, muffled scream. Had something about the blood of the wounded caused this damage?

Had he not watched the injured man retreat, he might have gathered more information; the young man, however, commanded attention.

One of two brightly clothed twins forced the *Kialli* back; it was the first time he had surrendered even an inch of the ground on which he fought. The *Kialli's* retreat revealed the fallen arm to Jarven's line of sight.

The circus people did not speak; they did not shout; they were focused on attack and defense. But their movements — if one discounted the Hunter — were concerted, even the forced retreat an action that required precise, harmonious attacks.

It was not their attacks which caught — and held — Jarven's attention. It was the disposition of that fallen limb. It sank into the earth, as if the earth were viscous oil; light remained in its shape as it was absorbed. This was arresting in a fashion, but it was the disposition of that vanished limb that was almost astonishing: the man who had lost that arm regained it.

He was pale with loss of blood, nameless in the silence. But he lifted pale face toward the demon, stretched that arm as if he had never lost it, and once again returned to the attack.

The demon was dangerous, the damage he could inflict, notable. But the damage itself was not permanent. Jarven heard his master's voice.

"Let me observe a moment longer," he told the fox, knowing that any word, however softly spoken, would be heard. The fox was ill pleased with Jarven's decision, but did not come in person to correct his wayward cub.

The circus people were ferocious and almost astonishing in their competence and their teamwork. Had Jarven chosen and trained them himself—and he had trained many, many combatants in his years in *Avantari*—he could not have produced results as impressive as these. Another circus person lost a hand.

The dance itself was repeated.

Only the Hunter found it difficult to move as they moved; he was the outsider. But his sword could both parry and wound—it was not a normal weapon. He fought and defended as if injury was death.

Ah. That was it: the circus defenders did not. Almost, it seemed to Jarven, they *chose* to allow the demon to wound or injure them; it was deliberate. They might avoid such injuries, given their flexibility, their speed, the precision of their odd movements; they could leap—they could vault—out of the reach of the demon's weapons. They could avoid the arc of blade, should they so choose.

That they did not was significant; given the reappearance of lost limbs, it made the loss of those limbs strategic. They seemed to suffer from the losses, but not to the permanent extent Jarven himself would have suffered.

The damage to the demonic blade was being done, in Jarven's opinion, by the blood itself; the wounds it inflicted, it seemed to take. This was a battle of attrition. The circus people on their own were not enough to bring the demon down.

Jarven.

"The circus people are damaging the demon somehow. It is not purely physical. If I understand the meaning of their attacks, I might be more effective when I join the fray."

Do not try my patience. I have very little of it left.

Jarven exhaled, frowning. He did not wield sword; at the moment, his weapons were long knives. They had always been his weapon of choice when he wished to attack from the shadows. Those shadows, he brought with him; they were forest shadows. Gone were the walls that made alleys. Gone, the halls through which servants might pass in the manses of the powerful. All of the places in which he had hidden, he had absorbed; he could translate the presence of trees to those ephemeral hiding places.

It seemed, to Jarven, that the point of this staying action was not to destroy the *Kialli*, but to destroy his weapon. The weapons of the *Kialli* were not, in any way, weapons with which Jarven was familiar. He had observed their use, where observation would not end his life, but he had not seen their manufacture. He knew they could be drawn at need; that the drawing was a statement of both intent and respect.

Respect, Jarven felt, was owed here. Here, where mortals could stand their ground against one who might easily destroy a whole town with a simple gesture.

Did they fail to destroy the demon because they could not? Was the demon so powerful, their blows—glancing, minor—could not be concerted in a way that would end its existence? Or was the sword itself the primary target of their attacks?

Was the sword some element, some extension, of the *Kialli*?

He had seen a similar sword in the hands of Meralonne APhaniel, a man who had always engaged the suspicion of the *Astari*. Jarven aged. Meralonne did not. But Sigurne, the guildmaster, had always protected the ill-tempered, uncooperative mage.

Not until Jarven had become servant to the fox had he seen Meralonne clearly for who, and what, he was: scion of the wilderness. In lands the mage walked, the wilderness paid attention; he could not simply enter and pass unnoticed. His sword was blue, caged lightning.

He did not fight armed with shield.

When this demon was forced to take another step back, he summoned a shield. Like the blade he wielded, it was red.

Jarven positioned himself with care. The demon could turn instantly; he could sense the movements of the circus people, or perhaps their intended end. He did not simply defend; he attacked. But perhaps he, as Jarven, had come to understand that the point of the attacks was not to kill, but to damage the sword he wielded; he was far more careful. No further injuries were inflicted; any of the demon's attacks were now focused on severing head from neck.

None of those attacks were allowed to land, although in two cases, the fact that heads remained attached was due to the speed and flexibility of the intended victims.

Jarven could not move in the same fashion. What power he had been granted, he had husbanded; now, he called upon it, obscuring the space he occupied. "This is a mistake," he told the fox, failing to keep the edge of irritation out of his voice.

If he dies, the threat dies with him.

"We do not know why he can be here at all; I believe there is information to be gained here that might prove of use in later battles."

Your belief is irrelevant, cub. If you wish to test yourself, that is fine—but understand that in this battle, this lord and his chosen people are necessary. If the Kialli dies, the lands will be preserved.

"But we will not know *how* they were breached, Eldest."

Does it matter? If we must know, we can consider it in less dire circumstances. This is not a request.

Jarven knew. He knew that all argument was pointless. The fox had the power here; he had held the balance of power since the day Jarven had chosen to take his first step on this path. He had been drawn to the elder, and the elder had been drawn to him, because they were similar. Separated by mortality and the span of millennia, they were similar.

The fox did not offer Jarven affection. He offered a rare indulgence—one that might seem like affection to those who were neither Jarven nor the fox. But that indulgence was a symbol of power. It had always been a symbol of power. Those who could indulge were those who held the reins. He had always accepted jesses and bridles when it suited his purpose; had accepted allegiance and offered fealty when it was required in order to reach his goal.

But The Terafin—the Terafin he had chosen to seat decades past—had understood just how uneasily those symbols sat. She had granted him authority over the Terafin merchant operations; she had made the Merchant Authority offices his personal fiefdom. She had made clear what she expected, or rather, made clear where she had drawn the lines of Terafin under her rule. Jarven was not a fool; he knew that those lines could not be crossed. He had given Amarais his aid. He had helped place her on the Terafin throne.

He understood the measure of her convictions.

When she drew the House Sword, he knew. He could not *be* The Terafin. He could not be bothered with the trivialities and the blandness of ruling one of The Ten. He had considered it, and discarded that option. He therefore played his games within the boundaries she had set; they were, after all, quite expansive.

The fox was unlike Amarais, in that regard.

Unlike the Twin Kings.

He felt a twinge of annoyance—at the fox, at The Terafin, at the Kings, but mostly, and most deeply, at himself. He wished to see the effect of blood and combat on the *Kialli* sword. It was not the shield that was important, although it made combat more difficult. The demon attempted to utilize shield as weapon, as if understanding, now, what the cost of injuring these people might be. A shield was, at best, an ancillary weapon.

Not in the hands of the demon.

Jarven heard the snap of bone. He saw one of the twin circus performers stagger back, arm by his side. The arm did not appear to magically heal. Blood, he thought. Something to do with the blood of the performers themselves.

He shifted his hold on the hilts of his knives. If he were honest, he wished to see what happened when all of the mortal attackers were laid low. The lord of these lands professed to care for mortals. Would that lord then take the field? Would he choose to fight the demon?

The bard did not come. Meralonne did not come. But the circus master did not arrive, either. The fox had consigned the demon to Jarven; the fox would not join the fray unless and until Jarven were mortally injured. Perhaps not even then.

Jarven was valuable to the elder, but not in the fashion that Gervanno di'Sarrado was. The fox did not send Gervanno into the forest. Had he, Jarven might have dispensed with the Southerner, and weathered the elder's wrath.

He was angry. He had skirted the thought of the Southern cerdan, a man out of his element but, regardless, so steadfast, so earnest in performance of his duties. There was no profit in it. Jarven was no longer a simple child, yearning for the things he could see others possessed: family, affection, wealth. Safety.

Jarven had believed, as a very young child, that wealth was safety; with wealth came territory. Power. Everyone wanted money. All children were fools; he had not been an exception. But he had become wiser far earlier than most; he had survived that folly.

Was he now to return to that visceral, childhood *envy*?

He could almost feel the fox's amusement. Was Gervanno a simple element of the game, another chess piece? Was his import to the fox the effect the Southerner had on Jarven himself? It was a board on which Jarven had played before—but he had been master, not student.

While he thought, he moved; he husbanded what little, inadequate power he had been granted. He made no sound as he passed above the forest detritus. Even his breathing was silenced; he did not need it.

His weapons had not been blessed. In all earlier fights with the demons, blessed weapons were required, the blessing an ancient magic. Becoming the fox's cub, as the fox styled it, had removed that requirement. What the fox had granted allowed Jarven to interact fully with the wilderness, living or dead.

He leapt back, with less fluid grace than the circus people; the demon's shield narrowly missed. So much for the stealth of the elder. The shield blow was followed immediately by the arc of the red, red blade. Interesting.

The demon had recognized that Jarven was not of the circus.

"Is it safe for me to bleed, Eldest?"

No. I would avoid it, were I you. If you cannot avoid it, I will negotiate with the lord of these lands after the fact. You are mine by oath and blood, and he will know.

"You might aid us."

Silence, then. When the fox spoke again, Jarven heard the age in the elder's words. *No. I know what you face, and I am not of a mind to face him now. I do not wish to see and confirm his death.*

"Any guidance," Jarven said, grunting as the shield grazed him, "would be appreciated."

The abilities of the dead are not always those they wielded in life. Gone was any hint of irritation or dark amusement. *Were you not mine, I would not have sent you at all; it is not safe to meet his eyes, if you are not sworn to another.*

Jarven hated the burden of ignorance. He accepted both that burden and his hatred of it as he brought his knives up to parry. The demon's blade was caught, briefly, in the V formed by the cross of those long knives. Jarven almost lost one as the blade twisted and pushed forward, the arc and its thrust changing instantly.

Had Jarven been alone, he would have died.

He was not alone, as the fox had observed; the twin whose arm had not been broken moved in that instant, Jarven's knives slowing demonic movement for a second, perhaps two. He could not hold the blade longer without being skewered, and moved the whole of his weight to the side.

The twin was good. He took advantage of the demon's attack on Jarven, darting in, blade forward, feet already braced to leap, to vault, back. The Breodani Hunter was a half step behind; he came in on the shield side, bringing his sword down in an arc of faint light and momentum, forcing the demon to block.

It was risky; the demon's strength was far greater.

Jarven watched the battle play out before he rejoined it. This time he knew he would not have surprise. He could not hide his presence, and therefore felt no need to try. He was a man who was comfortable working with allies—but only in the planning stages. On the ground, he did not trust them. He could not; they could not trust him, and he knew it. Fools trusted—often dead fools.

But he knew how to use the tools at hand; knew how to take advantage of openings created by other people, using them, making them his own. It was a lesson he had learned early; it had been drilled into him by experience on the streets, and experience in the holdings. Even in Terafin, at the apex of mortal power—or the power he desired —those lessons had served him well.

Wait, watch, see the movements of the other attackers. As if the death itself were a prize to be claimed. There would come a moment, a brief instant, an opening that was meant for Jarven alone.

Wait. Wait. Wait.

There.

CHAPTER TWENTY

I t was Trevor who moved first.

Katie made no attempt to stop him. She shouted his name, but the tone was different; there was command in the two syllables that comprised his name. Gervanno heard it. Alex heard it. Stephen glanced at Alex, but held his peace.

His gaze was drawn to the skies; that shattered purple seemed to have lowered, as if sky were moving toward the earth, inexorably, the battle drawing closer. The dead wyvern on the ground, folded and broken, was huge. When it—along with its flight—had first appeared, it had seemed so small—a large, bird-like reptile.

It was only distance that had given that impression. The creature was large enough there was no way the rest of its surviving brethren could land—not in this enclosed, tended space.

Nenyane and Anya fought; if they had noticed the approach of earth at all, none of their movements revealed that awareness.

Trevor shouted Adala's name.

Stephen could barely hear it; it was more felt than seen, a slap of sound, a cry of pain and fear, almost animal in its viscerality. Twin to it, different syllables gilding the cry of a fury rooted in the deepest of pain, was a different name, uttered by a voice that would be heard no matter where one stood, no matter how one tried to guard one's ears.

"**Memonryenne!**"

Stephen heard the word, knew it as a name, felt it as a blow, although no blood fell. Tears did; they were his, and they were not his, as if nothing in this conflicted, terrible battlefield were so personal, so terrible.

He felt the wings of fire as if they burned his cheeks, saw the red sword and shield as an afterglow. Felt Nenyane freeze for a moment, as vulnerable to the open display of loss and fury as Stephen himself.

He did not notice Trevor rush past where he stood, face toward sky, eyes drawn to the *Kialli* who commanded the heights.

"You, boy," Katie shouted. "Alex!"

He saw Alex move in the periphery of his vision, shifting to Patches' eyes to catch a glimpse of his Elseth cousin. He saw wind take Alex's hair—elemental wind, a small, local storm, as if the air itself hastened him forward to obey Katie's command.

As with Trevor, the circus seer did not adorn the inherent command in his name with spoken instructions. Alex understood the unspoken, regardless. Stephen shook himself, turning toward the retreating Alex.

"Not you!" Katie shouted, and he froze, tears cooling his skin.

He was Breodani; loss and its shadow had haunted the whole of his life. Was there pain? Yes. It was not his pain, but it was kin to the pain he had feared for much of his conscious life—and he had lived that life, regardless. He was not broken by its echoes; he could carry it and walk. And run.

But, as Alex, he had been raised by commanding, ruling women— his mother, the village elders, the formidable head housekeeper. He responded to her shout; he watched as Alex all but flew toward the trees from which he'd emerged.

Draw your sword! his huntbrother shouted.

Gervanno drew his immediately, as if he shared the Hunter's bond. But no. He was aware of Nenyane in ways Stephen, so tightly bound to her, was not. There was nothing preternatural about that awareness. Nenyane was the master Gervanno respected the most.

The burning wings of the demon that had screamed a name into the wild air flew wide; he drove his sword into the air, and followed it with his shield; his focus was no longer on the wyverns or their few remaining riders.

Nenyane had not closed with him, or he with her; he had commanded, bending the force of his will toward the wyverns. It was the wyverns Nenyane had attacked—and the demons that rode them.

Even she had been cautious in her approach, where the wyverns circled tightly around their commander. Anya had been as cautious, and Anya had far more experience of demons.

But even when the commander had shouted her name she had failed to heed or obey.

That commander was no longer content to watch, to observe. He moved in focused frenzy, lit within by fury and fire and the need to destroy those things that had caused him pain. If there were a god here, it was him. The lord of these lands was a thin presence, a slender observer.

The sky had cracked once; it cracked again. And again. And again. As if the sound were the remnants of *Kialli* heart, breaking and breaking and breaking.

The commander would kill them all.

For a sliver of a moment, Stephen almost felt — almost — that they deserved it. That such a noble being, even dead, was so far above them, so far above the entirety of their existence, they should not have dared to lift sword against him.

But Stephen lifted sword, in the shadow of an enemy's terrible sorrow.

The wind became wild; he stood in the currents, almost pushed back. The *Kialli* did not control the wild air; at any other time, it would have attacked his burning wings. But not now. No, now, the wild wind was keening, wailing, almost as chaotic in grief and loss as the demon itself.

Meralonne's wind.

Meralonne, who had not yet joined the battle, but who watched from somewhere Stephen's eyes could not perceive. He swallowed, aware of the demon who would soon break through what remained of an unseen barrier. Who could not, in his grief and frenzy, fail.

Gervanno stepped in front of Stephen, as if acknowledging that. He shouted, but the wind tore the words away before they could reach Stephen's ears.

Nenyane said nothing. She tried, twice, to cut the wings of fire, but they parted as if they were water in the wake of her blade. She was pushed back as the wings buffeted her, somersaulting in the sky. Had it not been for the gale, that might have been the end of her. Anya made no attempt to attack the enraged *Kialli*, but she did attack the wyverns in a rush that implied time was short and she needed to kill as many as she could before it ended.

The sentient wind was wild with grief. The name the *Kialli* commander had shouted was a name the element recognized. Recognized and longed for, even if love had long since become ashes and dust, transformed by betrayal into something akin to hatred.

Or maybe hatred was always born from love that both died and lingered just enough to cause this terrible sense of loss. Maybe, in the fires of betrayal, some stubborn hope could not be extinguished. Hope, chimerical, still retained the power to wound.

Illaraphaniel would have killed him, Nenyane said, her voice not the snap of annoyance that often accompanied such thoughts. But she did not deny the truth of Stephen's thoughts.

Where is Meralonne?

I don't know. He must have survived—but if he was injured, it is not safe for him to walk this land—not yet.

When would it be safe? How injured must the mage be, that he could not join the only battle that seemed to matter to him? At war with the *Kialli* he became uncloaked, his armor shining, his eyes like captured lightning.

Caught in the pain because the pain made the past momentarily, viscerally real.

Stephen swallowed; the wind blew strands of hair into his eyes. Even the dogs struggled in the gale. He turned, now, to the red-white light Adala had almost become, and he saw the shadowed outline of Trevor, arms outstretched, as if to grab what Stephen could not clearly see; as if to hold it, as if the moment was all that he had left, and he never intended to leave it.

The light expanded, radiating outward. Trevor stepped into it, and was lost to sight.

"Not yet, boy. If he can be saved at all, it is not yet." Katie was standing far closer to Stephen. She appeared to expect better of Gervanno, or perhaps she understood, as he stood almost sentinel between the sky and the Maubreche Hunter, the duty that he had undertaken.

Stephen could feel the heat of demonic wings; he could feel, in a different way, the utter silence in which the *Kialli* attacked. Had the demon breathed, had he revealed that much exertion, it would have robbed him of some of his terrible majesty. But breath was irrelevant.

Here, his breath was the howl of wind, the keening of the wilderness in the throes of grief. Exertion was shown in only one way: the breaking of something Stephen's eyes could not perceive.

The fox snarled and leapt out of Gervanno's arms. The fox's growl could be heard so clearly, it was as if the creature stood above the storm. Stephen knew what he would see next: the metamorphosis of that fox, the enlargement, the change in shape as it abandoned the golden form.

He rose on two legs as the wind blew torn leaves and petals all around his body, as if trying to reach or touch him at all. Golden fur became golden hair; limbs became legs and arms. Just as the weapons of the *Kialli* emerged from nothingness—and returned to it when the battle was done—a polearm appeared in the hands of the man that had been fox, and would become fox again.

He growled.

Gervanno, sword ready, took a step to the side, assessing the arc of the pole-arm and removing himself from its path. Stephen hesitated; fire roared and quieted, roared and quieted, the beat of an unnatural drum. He looked to where Trevor had gone, but neither Trevor nor Adala emerged.

He turned to Katie.

Her face had paled; sweat adorned her brow. Her hands were balled in fists, but she stood, grim of expression and bearing. She turned to meet Stephen's gaze, as if the gaze were physical touch that demanded response.

"Trevor," she told him, although he hadn't asked. "Let the others deal with the demon when he lands." Not if, but when. "If she weren't necessary, I'd strangle Adala myself. I may just try."

"You will not," the circus master said. He wore his black suit, his odd hat, and an entirely unfamiliar expression.

"Will you not join them?" Stephen asked, of the man who ruled these lands.

"In all ways open to me, I have," the circus master replied. "But there is always a ripple, a weakness, when someone new arrives. You hunt. You were gifted subtle things by the god who succored your people. You have the use of your weapons; you have the dogs. You have stories, no doubt, of glorious wars, of battles against demons and dragons. Think you that only those who joined melee were powers?"

But the circus master, if Nenyane was right, was a god.

"Gods died, mortal child. Gods died, and could not die. You will understand in time what that means, for it is to their final, restless resting place that you must go, should you survive."

"Can you not at least save Trevor?"

"No. Not unless I choose to abandon all that my people have built over the centuries. I will owe the eldest a boon, and that will be complication enough. You do not understand."

"No."

"There are things the gods cannot touch, for touch is change. Could I release Adala? Yes. But she would die. She would die now, her journey half-finished, her sacrifice unrewarded. Could I save her? Yes. But she would not be what she must be. She would not be circus. Her role in this place would not be filled.

"It is almost time, regardless. We have stood sentinel here, my people and I, but the time is coming when that will pass, and all will be rewarded or rendered irrelevant. Can you not hear it, son of Bredan? The winds from the North grow stronger and bolder almost as we speak."

Katie, silent, was so tense, so brittle, Stephen thought a touch might shatter her. "Lord."

"I have not interfered. If you have something to say to the young Hunter, speak. There is no secret you must keep. His huntbrother is not what he is, and she will know, she will understand what you are — what we are — when she is whole."

Katie turned to Stephen. "Adala will do what she can to protect Trevor, but she cannot do so now; he does not understand what she is becoming. It is difficult for me to explain; explanations cannot convey the experience.

"Trevor isn't circus. He was never meant to stand in this place. The only safe place for Trevor is as audience to the performance itself — a performance that has yet to start."

"I'm not circus either."

"No. But you are golden-eyed. All of the golden-eyed are anchored by the blood of the gods they bear. I do not know what Trevor will experience. But if he bleeds here, as she has done, he will perish. Do what you can to preserve him. It is only at the end of her journey that he will be necessary."

"Why?"

"Because she is becoming what I am. What we are. I have not

served the circus for long, but even I am aware that her blood is strong. We cannot afford to lose her, not now, with the war so close." Katie closed her eyes. "There is a moment when the pain is so strong one desires to let go. To have an ending. The promise," Katie added, with a bitter smile, "of death.

"You're a young man. You will never undergo the pain of birth. You have been born, but you have no memory of that. This is like being both mother and child. Adala's pain is greater than even mine; I had a relatively easy entry into the circus. I had circus people waiting. I did *not* have a small army of demons and immortals. I could find a new home.

"But it was because of the life I'd led to that point that I could. I was so newly reborn that the elements that defined my life were still in that town, with my children, with the daydreams of grandchildren. I understood on a visceral level that my choice, my rebirth, would protect that life, even if I had to step away from the living of it."

Stephen watched the demon's slow, inexorable descent through Patches' eyes, but he listened to Katie.

"Adala had chosen to abandon that life. Leaving is never easy," she added, voice soft. "Even when one leaves one's family home for husband, that home feels like home only because someone else is in it. It takes a while to build a sense of home. She chose Trevor. Trevor has become the seeds of home. But she will destroy him if he is not careful, and if she does, every choice she has made will unravel. I do not know what will become of us, then."

She was lying. She knew.

"Can I help him?"

Katie hesitated. "Not without risk."

Don't, Nenyane snapped.

The fox has chosen to stand with us.

With Gervanno.

It doesn't matter. Katie clearly believes there's something I can do. No, it's more than that. She believes there's something I have to do. There's no one else. He then turned toward the light that had not even begun to fade. *Pearl.*

The dog immediately came to his side.

No, he added, to the rest of his pack. *I need your eyes here.*

They were not happy; Sanfel in particular chafed at the restriction. He was the oldest of Stephen's dogs and, in the absence of Steel, he had resumed the role of pack leader. That wouldn't last. But Stephen didn't want to leave Pearl behind; she was too fractious, too stubborn, too independent.

And she was not as beloved. He could, and did, keep this to himself. History with the Maubreche dogs had weight and meaning, bleeding from the practical into the emotional. He valued the history, the immediate, instinctive reach for the blessedly known and familiar.

Pearl didn't, and wouldn't, notice. She knew only that she was the dog called to his side; she had, for the moment, pride of place.

THE LIGHT itself was too bright to view for long. Pearl, however, was not bothered by it. She didn't need to squint to see. It was odd, but Stephen had become almost inured to oddity in his journey to, and from, the King's City. He closed his eyes, settling behind Pearl's while he took his first, hesitant steps into the light that had swallowed Trevor.

The first thing he noticed was the silence. The wind did not howl here. The grief with which it was laden was so absent he felt his shoulders relax. His arms. Even his face. The wind was not still, but it did not lift and hurl anything within its reach.

The earth was soft beneath his boots. The packed dirt that accrued with the passage of many feet was absent; there was no path where Stephen walked. But the trees—the one striking feature of this pale, grey land as seen through Pearl's eyes—seemed to imply a path by placement. As if he were welcome. Or irrelevant.

He could see Trevor's back. Trevor had slowed; he walked, reaching out until his flailing arm managed to touch tree bark. Trevor did not have Pearl's eyes. He steadied himself against the trunk of a tree before he once again moved forward.

Adala did not sing.

Stephen no longer heard her voice. He did not hear the voice of the circus people, raised almost in chorus. He did not hear the earth. He did, as he listened, hear the distant burble of brook, of water. It was toward the water that Trevor moved, tree by tree, step by step.

Stephen followed, instinctively keeping a distance.

Stephen—don't go where I can't follow.

You do it. You fight in fields I can't step onto. This isn't even a battle. *It's...*

He wasn't certain what it was. But Nenyane's sharp annoyance—

blended, as most of her angrier emotions, with hints of fear—were like a gentle slap. If he had come to preserve or support Trevor, he couldn't do it from a distance.

He opened his eyes slowly, saw the light as if he were staring at the sun, and closed them again. Pearl didn't have the same problem. She vaguely understood that he couldn't see what she could see, but it didn't disturb her. She moved at Stephen's pace, not her own.

Trevor turned as Stephen approached.

"Trevor." He said the name to alert Trevor to both his presence and his proximity.

Trevor turned in the direction of his voice, although it took time, as if he had heard his name, had only slowly recognized it, and had finally chosen to respond. He did not take his hand from the tree that served as his momentary guide.

"Katie sent me," Stephen continued, when Trevor failed to speak. Failed to tell him to go back, to go away, to leave them alone.

Trevor exhaled slowly. When he spoke, his words were words; they were morning words, as if one night of disuse had slowed his vocal cords. "Did she send you to help Adala?"

"Yes."

"Did she tell you how you were supposed to help Adala when you can't see, it's so blinding here?"

"I can see."

"How?" This short word was far more forceful.

"I'm Breodani. Whatever it is that's causing this brilliant light, doesn't affect my dogs. Breodani Hunters, and their dogs, aren't quite like hunters in the rest of the lands—I can see through their eyes. I've come to help you."

"Help me do what?" Instant suspicion.

"Find Adala," Stephen replied, choosing the only words he was certain would be acceptable to Trevor.

Trevor swallowed.

"If you're willing to trust me, you can hold on to my arm or my sleeve."

"Can you see her?"

Stephen shook his head. Remembering that Trevor's eyes were shut, he added, "No." He moved toward Trevor, reached out, and tapped his right arm. He then waited until Trevor reached out for him.

He could see, as he expanded his vision, that the fox had completed its transformation. Gervanno stood, sword ready, in that almost unnatural stillness that nonetheless implied motion. Nenyane had not landed; neither had the mage. The wind—outside of this space—had not quieted.

Alex had not returned.

THE DEMON PERISHED, as demons did: becoming ash and dust as flesh almost instantly transformed or lost any cohesion. One moment, Max was parrying, and the next, he was stumbling forward with the full momentum of his uninterrupted blade. Had he been mid-attack, he might have landed on knees or sword, but he could right himself.

He had not taken any further injury, but he felt as if his arm were tingling, which happened only when he slept all night in a truly awkward position. He had not. He sheathed his sword and turned to scan the forest. There had been three demons of power; one had been ordered to retreat. Two had perished.

The circus's forest border seemed to be safe.

Steel approached Max; Max dropped encouraging hand to the dog's head. He took the time to praise the grey alaunt; it helped him gain his bearings. He was in a forest. He was with his dog. The enemies were gone.

The defenders remained.

Max frowned. They had taken severe injuries; he'd caught at least one loss of limb through Steel's vision. He hadn't seen the entire battle that way; the final demon had not remained standing in one place, and taking the time to give Steel instructions on where to stand or move in order that he could see the entire combat as it unfolded would have likely killed Max.

The tingling in his arm grew stronger. It was his injured arm, the arm he'd cut. The arm that had caused a ripple in the battle because the circus defenders had taken the time to warn him not to bleed. Or not to have his blood hit the ground.

He did not understand why, but he felt a growing discomfort.

Max.

We won, Max told his brother.

Where are you?

The oldest of the defenders, costume awash with drying blood, glanced at Max.

"My brother is trying to reach us. I'm Max, by the way."

"Carrick." The defender replied. "Where is your brother?"

"In the forest. Just—not near us."

A glance passed between the circus people as they gathered. It was the wrong kind of glance.

"We're speaking to the earth, now," Carrick replied. One of the circus twins had knelt and splayed palm against dirt; his hand could not be seen as it vanished into undergrowth. An undergrowth that was both new and far too thick, given the damage the demons had caused.

Max glanced, then, at the trees, at the forest. Even the trees that had been cracked, broken, or disintegrated seem to have reasserted their existence. He had known this was not a normal forest—how could it be?—but this confirmed that visceral suspicion.

"We need to head back," the standing circus twin said. He was of an age with Max, or appeared to be, but his expression contained age to Alex's vision. He spoke to Carrick, not Max.

"We can't take him with us."

"It happened. He bled."

"He's not of the towns," the older man insisted, although the quiet in his voice did not imply argument.

"Does it matter? You saw him. He was cut. The cut has healed. If he's not called to the circus, he came, he bled, he fought." The standing twin turned to Max. "I'm Ulrich. Eric is the one with his hand in the dirt."

"What does this mean?"

Once again, the glance bounced between the defenders. Only Carrick and the twins had spoken.

Ulrich opened his mouth.

Carrick intervened. "You must ask the circus master that question. Until we know for certain that you have no choice but to remain, we should not, we cannot, answer it."

"You can hear him, now. You can hear him as we do. He's faint, but he's *there*," Ulrich shot back. "Boy, you understand what it means." The "boy" was meant for Carrick.

"He did not offer his blood willingly."

Ulrich snorted. "Do you think that matters? He *chose* to join us in defense of our lands. We did not demand, did not ask, did not coerce.

In such a battle, blood falls. The circus master is not so careful that he can easily differentiate subtle shades of willing. He's not what we are. He's not what we were."

Max felt their shared, meaningful glances would be less confusing.

More annoying, Alex said.

Max smiled. It was true. Being deliberately left out when information was available had always annoyed him. But hearing information that made no sense was annoying in a different way. The first felt like condescension; they expected ignorance. The other felt like actual ignorance. Having been proved ignorant, Max ceased to pay attention to most such conversations.

Alex didn't. As if ignorance were something that *had to* be alleviated, he joined such conversations with more focus, more intensity. He was listening now.

Adala had to bleed. I mean, she had a ceremonial knife. There was a path she had to find and walk, and blood she had to shed.

What happened to her?

We don't know yet. Whatever it is, I don't think it's finished. But Carrick definitely lost a limb—if only that. He's clearly whole, now. He was the one who told you not to bleed?

Max nodded.

So there's something about blood, and the circus, and the way people become circus. You're sure you hardly bled at all?

Max nodded again. *I mean, it would be useful to be able to magically regrow limbs.*

Not if you can never leave the circus.

Alex looked at the trees. He could no longer see the circus green when he turned to look back. Looking up through the overlapping branches that shaded him, he could see wyverns in flight—they seemed closer to ground than they had when he'd run into the forest to find Max.

He could hear Max so clearly, he felt his brother must be close by —but he could not see him. Could not reach out in any way, except the bond.

Can Steel see me?

What?

Can Steel see me? The question was repeated more slowly, and with evident frustration. Alex waited while Max asked Steel to look for him. *Don't. If Steel finds me, he might not be able to find you again.*

Is he my dog or yours?

Max. Alex looked at the trees Max could see; they were similar in kind to the trees through which Alex slowly walked. But either their placement was different or two such overlapping forests existed. He was certain Max was near, but no sign of his brother — or his circus companions — could be seen or heard. The forest floor was pristine; there was no trail of footsteps, no path, that implied anyone ever came here.

He was not surprised when he heard barking; he turned. Steel stood in the distance, gaze on Alex.

I told you that wasn't a good idea, Alex snapped.

Steel can see you.

Alex approached Steel. The only disturbing thing was that Max also approached the alaunt; they should have been standing almost on top of each other by the time Alex reached Steel's side. Steel bounced in place; he was one of the oldest of the Maubreche dogs Stephen had brought with him to the King's City, but as all dogs, had never abandoned the heart of a puppy.

Alex patted Steel's head. Max, understanding why, did the same.

Their hands, on Steel's head, were in overlapping positions, but there was no physical contact between them.

Is your arm all right?

It feels strange. If I were fighting or hunting, I probably wouldn't notice the difference — but it's tingling.

Is that getting worse?

Max shrugged. Alex could feel the motion. The answer was yes, and Max didn't want to give it. *What are you afraid of?*

I don't want to have to leave you in the circus.

I wouldn't stay.

Do you think the others have any choice?

Max hadn't really thought about it much at all. Alex knew. He was thinking about it now.

You're thinking. I'm listening. Will I be causing a diplomatic mess if I tell them to shut up?

Alex could not hear their voices at all. Not until Carrick turned his back on the rest of his companions and spoke directly to Max.

"We will leave you here. We have to leave you here. There is another enemy that has finally touched the circus grounds." His expression was grave; he was pale, but whole.

"I should go with you if there's another demon."

Carrick shook his head. He turned to Ulrich—at least Alex thought that was his name, because Max knew it. "He didn't know. He can't feel it yet."

"We could use the strength at arms now."

"His now shouldn't be forever." To Max, he added, "Stay here. If no one comes to find you, and if the forest isn't razed, we'll come back."

Alex could see them walking away, but only through Max's eyes. He could see the blood on their clothing; it hadn't dried. It was not demonic blood, but their own.

Max's hand remained on Steel's head; Alex lifted his own. He loved dogs—one could hardly be a Breodani Hunter and not—but not as deeply as Max did. Walking away would serve little purpose. Max was here.

Alex needed to be the one to bring him out of the forest.

———

ADALA COULD NOT BE SEEN. She could not be heard. The movement of water that had caught Stephen's attention was, as it sounded, a brook, one too large to be a stream, too small to be a river. He could see neither its beginning nor its end.

Trevor hesitated.

"Thirsty?"

The young man shook his head.

"Can you hear water?"

Nod. Trevor released Stephen's sleeve. Stephen opened his eyes a crack, and shut them again. He could not avoid the use of Pearl's eyes yet. But he was worried, now. They had walked—slowly—for some quarter of an hour at best estimate; they had covered little distance.

Adala could not be seen or heard.

Katie had sent him to find, to preserve, Trevor. But Trevor didn't seem to be in danger. Not the life-threatening kind.

Trevor knelt by the side of the water; Stephen placed a hand on his shoulder to make certain he didn't fall in. He watched as Trevor cupped water in his hands, brought it to his face, his mouth.

Stephen had just enough instinctive warning to shove Trevor's hands away from his face and mouth. "Don't drink it."

The water that should have fallen through the fingers of Trevor's cupped hands didn't fall. Nor did it splash to the side when Stephen shoved those hands away.

"It's not water?" Trevor asked.

"Oh, I think it is—but it isn't drinking water." He watched through Pearl's eyes as the water coalesced in floating drops. The sky, almost grey, was clear; the water did not fall from any clouds above.

He caught those drops, or tried; they would not be absorbed. They came to Trevor slowly, passing around Stephen to reach the man from the towns. He became aware, as those drops touched Trevor's face, that the smallest amount of water could drown a man.

Water didn't make that attempt. It was wild, yes, but it did not seem to have the will to kill Trevor. Proof, if it were required, that this water, this earth, this air heard Adala, where Stephen and Trevor could not.

He was disturbed when water rose, in a far larger mass, from the brook's bed. It, too, reached for Trevor.

Stephen had no way of destroying water, no way of fighting against it. He watched, almost helpless, as the water wrapped itself around Trevor. For just one moment, Trevor's eyes widened as water covered his face—his mouth, his nose, his jaw. Trevor shut his eyes again; he had forgotten that he could only squint to see, if even that.

Stephen opened his mouth to shout Adala's name.

Don't! Nenyane shouted. Had she been standing beside him, his ears would be ringing.

Stephen closed his mouth.

She isn't aware that you're there. Don't draw her attention.

Trevor—

He isn't drowning, yet. He might be uncomfortable, but he's not drowning.

What do you think is happening?

A demon is landing. Be careful, now.

Stephen had just enough time to reach out to steady Trevor, but withdrew his hand. "I believe you can still grab my sleeve—but I think I'll be in trouble if it's not you reaching for me."

Trevor turned instantly toward Stephen's voice. "I don't know where she is."

"I believe the water does. Can you feel it tugging you in a specific direction?"

"I can't. It's warm. I can now hardly feel it at all."

"I think we have to find Adala." The lymer at his side had been attempting to pick up her scent, her trail; Stephen expected Pearl to fail. He took a step forward.

The earth rumbled beneath his feet. The grey forest shook. In the near distance, he could hear the crack of wood; could smell charred bark.

The wind came, then. The earth beneath Trevor's feet stilled. Stephen was close enough to step in.

"What's happening?"

"I think the fight beyond Adala has just become dangerous. We have to find her."

Trevor's breathing could no longer be heard, but his voice could; the layer of water changed the texture of that voice, but did not silence it.

"Call her," Stephen said, the words a command, the tone a request.

Trevor nodded. He opened his mouth and shut it again, as if he was afraid to call her name. Afraid to have silence return in the place of the voice he yearned to hear.

She had chosen Trevor. She had been forced to return to the circus, because if she did not, she would lose him. But before she had made her choice, he had told her he was returning. Returning to die, if that was his fate. He could not surrender the whole of his lived life to the demons.

He, too, had chosen.

If she felt betrayed, she had not shown it—she hadn't had the time. The demons, the trees, the danger—all of those things demanded her frayed attention. There was no Trevor and Adala if one of them ceased to live.

But they were in the circus now. Trevor. Adala. What the circus lord demanded, she had given. She had walked in odd robes, carrying a knife that Stephen was certain had been forged for just this ritual. She had asked only for permission for Trevor to stay until the end.

Trevor was here. The ceremony had not ended.

Katie had considered it a mistake to allow Trevor to enter this space at all.

Would Adala kill him? She had no desire to do so—but the forces arrayed here, in this silent space, could kill all three of the visitors with little difficulty, perhaps little awareness. The earth continued to tremble, to rumble. If it opened up here without warning, Stephen would fall. He wasn't certain Trevor would join him.

WHEN THE EARTH lurched beneath Max's feet, Alex felt it, but at a remove; beneath his feet, there were tremors. *What does Steel feel?*

What you feel, Max replied, perplexed. He could keep his footing on the most treacherous of terrain, as long as the earth didn't split or break. The circus defenders had sprinted away; Ulrich had offered intense, but brief, resistance before he left Max to his solitary fate.

There had been demons in the forest; there were clearly demons within sprinting proximity. Max turned in the direction in which the circus people had raced, hand leaving Steel to rest on the hilt of his new sword.

He knew why Ulrich had argued so briefly and intensely with Carrick: Max's sword, found in a crate in a circus stall, was effective against the demons. Alex's weapon would not be.

If I join them — if you leave the forest — we'll see each other, right?

Alex grimaced. He loved guesswork, but he did not love it when Max's life might depend on it. *I think we will — but we won't be standing in the same place. I think we have to leave the forest together.* He hesitated, and then continued. *Stories exist — legends exist — in which the blood of the living is used in spells and covenants. I mean, blood oaths exist. Sacrifice played a hand in many of those old stories — often the sacrifice of others.*

Alex inhaled slowly, thinking that Max had bled. That Carrick had demanded that Max forgo bleeding in this place, on this earth. *Chosen sacrifice, the life's blood of someone who made the choice, appeared to be a very powerful component.*

I didn't make that choice — it's not like I slashed myself.

Yes. Maybe that's why we have the chance. There's obviously something strange and powerful about the blood of the circus, the lands of the circus; they seem tied, bound. It protects them and it takes from them in equal measure.

How are we going to get out of here together when we can't even see *each other?*

I don't know. Let me think. There must be some way, or Katie wouldn't have sent me here. She could foresee something. I'm almost tempted to cut myself. I would, if I didn't think it would mean we'd both be stuck here. Trevor's blood is just blood. If he died and bled out here, he'd just be dead. Limbs wouldn't regrow. His sacrifice wouldn't have the same meaning.

So why does ours? Max was restless. The ground on which he stood was far more active than the ground where Alex stood. He knew that an attacker had landed. Knew that one of the dead walked in the most hallowed of places. He felt it, vibrated with the knowledge.

Alex did not know, or would not have known, had it not been for the huntbrother bond. But Max had always trusted his instincts. He'd mostly survived them. Max's instincts were part of Alex's, part of the way he approached the world and the people in it.

There had to be a reason the circus people had warned Max not to bleed. On the surface, given the nature of the enemies they faced, the command was ridiculous. In combat, small nicks and cuts were inevitable, almost unavoidable. Hunters were injured all the time while they hunted. Some never made it to the Sacred Hunt.

But in the Sacred Hunt, one Hunter or huntbrother always died. Those lives were lost. Was it life's blood? Was that the binding covenant that allowed the Hunters to master both dogs and the Hunter's trance? Was that the subtle power that allowed them to form the huntbrother bonds?

Max's blood should not be shed.

Trevor's didn't matter.

Something about Max's blood—and by extension, Alex's—was different. Parentage? Their mother's blood? Breodani Hunter blood? Or the blood, diluted by a single generation, of Breodan himself?

Adala, having walked away from the circus and her family into a future with the man she loved, had *had* power. Had been born to it, had grown into it. She could sing to the wilderness, and the wilderness heard her voice. The wind did not fight her; the earth did not swallow her. He assumed water would never drown her either.

It was Adala's blood that the circus needed.

Adala's willing sacrifice.

THE EARTH MOVED, almost thinning beneath Trevor's armor of water. Trevor could not move quickly, and that was Stephen's saving grace. He would not break into a sprint that Stephen couldn't follow. Stephen himself, navigating through Pearl's eyes, would have been slower than normal, but not as slow as Trevor.

Trevor clung to Stephen's arm as the strange sensation of earth and water thrummed around him. It was the only reason Stephen could walk here safely. He was certain, were Trevor not somehow attached to him, that he would have been buffeted by wind or swallowed by earth. He had not seen the wild water, and was uncertain what that death would be—probably drowning.

But Adala had seen only Trevor, in the end. Everyone and every-thing else had been rendered irrelevant. As if she could choose only one thing, he had been that choice. Stephen, a total stranger, was unseen. Only if he attempted to harm Trevor would he be worthy of notice.

This small, brilliant world was Adala's. In this space, the elements listened to her. Only Adala.

He reached for Nenyane, and pulled back instantly. He saw the rising bursts, plumes of flame, color the sky. The dogs, he pulled back as far as he safely could; their own instincts, absent Stephen, would have to be responsible for their survival.

He had a sense that whatever had managed to land *on* the circus grounds was invisible to Adala. Still, and only, she had come this far to protect Trevor, the intensity of that desire swamping all other concerns. She had accepted the circus, accepted her duty, walked the path that would lead her, in the end, to the long farewell of those called to the circus.

But Trevor was here, not there, not where the demon was. Trevor was safe.

He would not remain safe forever. If the demons couldn't kill him, Stephen felt that that was temporary. If the circus fell, Adala would fall with it. So, too, Trevor.

Beneath his feet, he felt the earth vibrate; he felt the wind howl. They quieted almost instantly, the familiar sense of their fury and enmity vanishing as if it had been a brief daydream.

He understood what it meant. The demon was close. Close and powerful.

———

GERVANNO HELD sword at the ready.

Nenyane and Anya had chosen to join the battlefield on which Gervanno stood, who could not reach the skies. If the demon of fiery wings had managed to break the protective barrier that encompassed the whole of the circus, the wyverns were not so lucky. Absent the attention and focus of their commander, they peeled off. They did not land.

Perhaps none remained who bore demons as riders.

The fox—the man who had been the fox—did not so much as glance in the direction of those creatures Gervanno had misidentified, to the fox's august displeasure, as dragons.

The whole of his attention was riveted now to the winged demon, whose shield—to Gervanno's eye—had been cracked and dented by his final assault.

"I will not tell you to stand back," the fox said, giving lie to Gervanno's assumption about his intentions. "But this combat may be beyond you. That is not true of your chosen master; it is not entirely true of the wild mage. I will not be able to defend or protect you; I have laid no claim to you, and you have sworn no blood oath to me.

"But I will be *very* annoyed if you perish here."

Those words were not meant for Gervanno, although they had been spoken to him.

"You do not understand the rules of my wilderness," the circus master replied.

"You do not understand the rules of my alliance," the fox shot back. "But it appears to me that you were ever weak in combat. It was a wonder to us that you survived where so many of the ancient gods perished in their long wars.

"And yet, here you are; you have not crossed the great divide; you stand upon the earth, as you once did, your mortals by your side."

The demon, having landed, spread wings in a loud snap of heat and sound; they were greater, now, than the wings of the wyvern who had fallen and died on the grass. It had not fallen—none had fallen—beyond the wall, where the audience waited beneath the amethyst skies.

The circus people became almost a blur of color as they raced from the thin cover of trees, their clothing torn and bloodied, their gaze intent. They were not an army; the circus was not meant to be a battle-field. But in the graceful, fluid movements of the men and women who were clearly entertainers, he saw their martial training. If they did not wear armor and follow the rules of engagement with which Gervanno was familiar, they were capable of far more than the men Gervanno had once commanded.

He wondered if demons had entered the circus grounds before.

Katie shouted commands, but she shouted them on the move, leaping to the left just as fire blossomed beneath her feet. She was not a combatant, but she was the heart of the battlefield where the circus was concerned. Perhaps where Gervanno was concerned as well; she shouted, he moved. He could not close with the demon; there were many people standing in the way.

One of them was Nenyane.

Katie gave no orders to Nenyane; offered no words of direction or command. No warnings. She either trusted Nenyane or knew the sword master would neither hear nor listen. Nenyane had always fought as if death was a triviality she need not fear.

Had she been Southern in birth and bearing, Gervanno would have surrendered his new sword to her keeping and use; it was not a sword to which he'd been born, nor was it a family heirloom. But the circus had gifted it to him; he understood that now. Perhaps, if Nenyane's sword had been a Southern sword, it would have offered the blade to the Breodani huntbrother, but perhaps not.

Nenyane did not accept gifts in the wilderness.

She did not incur obligation. Like a blade, she was honed, sharpened, focused; she served a single purpose. Stephen of Maubreche was her only focus.

She landed to the side of the *Kialli*. Demonic wings shot out; he could hear the whistle of their speed. She leapt above them; they flexed, snapping toward her as she parried. The wings were of flame, of fire; Nenyane's sword split that stream, but did not injure them.

Gervanno knew that the Widan could not use their power forever; they had limits, and if they pushed themselves past those limits, they faced death.

Anya seemed to have no limits. But she landed farther from the demon than Nenyane had, perhaps understanding that death was a possibility here. She had that much awareness, but even at this distance, Gervanno could almost feel the radiant heat of her rage.

He wondered if she would collapse, as Widan on the battlefield sometimes did. He could not believe that she would, could not fear it.

Today, in this moment, her rage was aimed at the demon. If the demon fell, she was unlikely to attack the circus or its strange master. That was as much of a miracle as one could ask of a power such as Anya.

Katie shouted; Gervanno moved. He did not sheathe his sword, but it was oddly cumbersome. Perhaps that was why the circus people were not armed with swords.

They, like Nenyane, approached the demon.

One, nimble, avoided the wings of flame; the demon made no attempt to strike down any of the human attackers, except in that way. It was enough. Gervanno was not as agile as Nenyane or the circus people—all younger to his eyes. He could defend should the demon's attention move to him; he could attempt to keep Katie alive. She did a good enough job of that on her own, but the field now had many moving parts.

He wanted to join Nenyane. To do so, he would have to rush past the fox; he doubted he would reach the sword master in one piece. The fox was accustomed to obedience, and his certainty of power, reckless and unpredictable, promised consequences should one choose not to obey.

He had long since dispensed with pride of place in combat. Survival was paramount, where it was possible. But he wanted to fight because *this* fight, wyverns and fire and death, was the fight he should have joined on the road near the border of Breodanir. He had survived, yes. But justification for that survival, penance for it, rested in fights such as this one. Here, death was not guaranteed.

Nor did he desire it.

The death that should have been his on that road, the company he should have kept, the duty he should have died to fulfill, would have been a pointless, helpless death. He would have joined the slaughtered. He would have struck no final blow, caused no scar or injury, defeated no enemy.

That, too, was true.

He had abandoned honor. There was only one way to reclaim some small shred of it. It was this field. It was this battle. It was the battles Nenyane and Stephen would face as they journeyed toward the final war, comprised of battles such as this.

One of the circus people fell. Flame consumed them instantly.

Katie cried out, staggered forward, and righted herself before that fire could reach her.

Someone lost a left arm, and retreated. One lost a foot, and was literally thrown clear of fire by the person who fought at his side.

In all of this, the demon had eyes for only one person present: the man who had been, and would once again become, a golden fox. A

swirl of wing and flame were all that the demon offered the others who
dared to close in melee; he did not spare a glance for any of them. Only
Nenyane managed to force him to raise his shield to block her sword;
no one else came close.

"This is not your battle," the demon told the fox, voice guttural with
the rage, the fury, that had driven him through the circus protections.
"Leave now."

"I have always wondered why an enemy would waste breath with
such idle commands—although perhaps you waste no breath all. The
dead do not require it."

"You would not have *dared* to speak thus in the past."

"No. When you were alive, I would not have dared to step on your
shadow. But you are dead. This world is not your world."

"It will *be* our world."

"Ah. We have some say in that, surely?"

The demon, wings flicking and striking, gazed beyond the fox to
the circus master. "You will perish here. What remains of you—if
anything does—will be found in the graveyard, and nowhere else. How
dare you, the least powerful of my Lord's brethren, raise hand in such a
fashion? We will destroy your lands, and all of the people who have
sheltered within them.

"We will destroy this place before she leaves it."

This made no sense to Gervanno. Did the demon speak of Anya?
Adala? Who had they mounted this assault to kill?

"You are far too late," the circus master replied. He turned, then, as
if the demon had been rendered momentarily irrelevant.

A woman entered the scarred, burning clearing.

She wore robes of midnight; her hood had been drawn from her
face and rested across her shoulders. The robes themselves moved,
roiling as if in a windstorm. Her violet eyes were clear; Gervanno
thought them darker now, the color of the unnatural skies above.

"Daughter," the circus master said.

CHAPTER TWENTY-ONE

The fox and the circus master were momentarily forgotten; the demon's gaze fell upon Evayne and rested there, the movement of burning wings sharper and faster, as if they expressed both the shock and rage absent from words.

Gervanno recognized her; the whole of the weight of her expression seemed to rest in the eyes. He was certain he would recognize those eyes, no matter the contours and shape of the face in which they rested.

She was not the woman whose stall he had approached in the pavilion of fortune and fate, although she wore the same robes. She looked, to the eye, old enough the circus master might better call her sister, not daughter, her hair streaked grey, her skin far more weathered. He did not know what she was, but knew the circus master, who had called her daughter, was in no wise human or mortal.

She did not possess the eyes of the demon-born, as the god-born were called in the lands of Gervanno's distant home. She was not like Stephen of Maubreche. Perhaps the physical appearance was not anchored to those luminous eyes.

She looked, in this moment, as if she was the Matriarch of a distant Voyani clan; harsh, terrible, powerful. Not for Gervanno such interactions; even as a boy, he had known to avoid the Voyani unless he could stand in the shadow of his father or uncles. They were not here now.

But he had already accepted the strange geas of the vision Evayne had revealed to him while the world momentarily fell away. He had seen many possible futures. In some, all of his companions were dead. In some, only the two townspeople: Adala, Trevor. She had offered no guidance, no command, as if, in revealing the possible futures, she had taken his measure.

In none of those futures had he seen the wild mage: half petulant, spoiled child, half power that could not be touched or approached.

Nor had he seen this demon. Perhaps his role, such as it was, was a slender, short thread—necessary for the tapestry this woman held in her hands, but otherwise beneath notice. Perhaps not.

As if she could feel his regard, Evayne a'Nolan said, "Well met, Ser Gervanno."

The demon roared in almost bestial rage.

"Have you come," the circus master said, as if demonic, deadly rage was irrelevant, "to usher in Summer? These were once Summer lands." His glance at the demon was pointed.

"It is Summer now, in the wilderness in whose shadow you have sheltered your people."

Demonic fire sprang up in an instant—but it remained there, beneath their feet, above the earth, as if its burning flames could touch nothing.

"Do not make light of his grief," Evayne added, voice both soft and cold; she spoke to the circus master as if torn between obedience and hatred. It was not what Gervanno expected of the circus people—but perhaps she was not of them in the same fashion. "Do not make light of loss."

"I do not," the circus master said, voice as soft now, and as cold, as Evayne's. "But our grief—the terrible grief of the living—faded long ago when they first chose death. What is left us is memory and betrayal. The dead linger, fell ghosts, but even so, what they invoke is a bitter nostalgia for things of beauty long since crumbled to dust."

The fox did not turn toward her, but he listened. Gervanno could almost feel his attention as a physical touch.

"You do not *know* beauty," the demon said, less rage in his voice than there had been. "Could you, we would stand as allies."

It was the fox who answered. "No. I was not born as you were born; I was born to, and of, the world; my roots are living roots and they could not and cannot be uprooted. I serve my Lord, but she is my

Lord, and when she dies, I will serve myself. In my distant youth, I have seen the lord you serve. He was a god, as other gods, but compelling in a way some gods are not. Yet I have never understood the choice you made.

"These lands are not your lands. Even were you to perish here, you would return—and return, and return. Only those who knew you in life will weep at your passing, for they know they are never truly free of your betrayal."

"You are mistaken," Evayne said. "He will never return. Nor his fallen companion. Think you that the breaching of the barriers the lord of these lands created was so simple a task? To break what was built, they were forced to offer a sacrifice of equal measure."

Gervanno frowned.

"What have the dead left to offer?" the circus master asked. His tone implied that he both knew the answer and did not value it.

"There is a reason that the demonic dead return, again and again. The living who perish—the living who are not sundered forever from their parent—return, in the end, to their maker in a fashion mortals do not and cannot, as you *well* know. When we perish, we pass beyond all of the ties that bound us while we lived.

"The dead are bound to the lord they chose to serve."

As they spoke, their words cut through the harsh crack of falling trees in the distance, the hiss and snarl of fire that struggled to reach them, and the noisy shadows that fire cast: long, dark, and unnatural.

In the shadows, Gervanno could not see himself. He could not see Evayne. But he could see the dark shape of the robes she wore, and he could see the long, broad shadows that began at the feet of the circus master, and stretched from him for as far as the eye could see.

Those shadows shifted as the flames struggled, carrying with them a shadow almost as large as the circus master's—that of the demon itself. Gervanno did not understand Widan arts. Even had he the talent to join that mysterious and treacherous brotherhood, it would never have been detected; not for men of Gervanno's rank, such lofty ambitions.

But the darkness beneath the demonic feet reached, stretching, toward the circus master's shadow.

He felt, in the moment, that he had seen something he should not have seen; men died who were unintentional witness to the foibles and weaknesses of the lords they served.

"Gervanno!" Nenyane shouted.

He shook himself as her sword sliced through the shadows that had caught his eyes.

"Pay attention!" the fox added, his tone similar to Nenyane's.

This was not his battlefield. Not yet. He wondered, as he turned his gaze from the demon to the back of the fox, if he would ever be at home here. Wondered what would be left of him if he ever became so.

Evayne, to Gervanno's surprise, placed a hand on his shoulder—a staying hand. "You will become what you must become to live the life, the second life, you have chosen. But even the choice of that life arises because of what you were to this point. Do not forget it, Ser Gervanno. Now, come. Stand beside me; your frailty is of concern to two who have not yet fallen. My gift to them, not to you, is your safety.

"It is the safety of Summer." Speaking thus, she lifted her left hand; her right remained upon his shoulder, as if to hold him in place.

He felt, when he first entered the circus, a sense of wonder, and a certain sense that he understood nothing. Nothing about the circus, and very little about the wilderness in which it was rooted. If it came to that, he did not understand Nenyane—but Nenyane, at least, he had no desire to unravel.

"You are *far* more trouble than you are worth," the fox said. "Far, far more."

Gervanno did not tell the fox that he was not the fox's responsibility. He had that much of a sense of self-preservation. And he owed the fox a debt; had it not been for the intervention of that elder creature, he would have been lost far earlier in the wilderness; he would not have met Nenyane; he would not have carried word of the brazen demonic attack to the capital city of Breodanir.

He had a sword that could injure demons, but those were not his duty, now. Now, he must wait.

The demon roared again, and this time, all of the circus people were driven back—as was Nenyane. The demon leapt forward. He leapt over the fox, toward Evayne. And Gervanno.

Gervanno brought his sword to bear as he faced the demon. The demon did not land. Instead, Gervanno watched as the fox's weapon shattered the shield with which the demon had worked to bring down the barrier that had protected the circus. The air was a storm of red, orange, and white; the white expanded, eclipsing even the tongues of flame in a brief, terrible surge.

"Ser Gervanno, close your eyes."

Gervanno obeyed the seer; he closed his eyes, his sword trembling in his hand. He felt no heat.

The demon screamed. Pain blended with his rage. His was not the only voice raised.

"You might have offered us some warning," the circus master said, his voice clear, if soft.

"Warn you? I merely followed your *request*. See, now, how Summer changes the lands you have hidden from all who do not walk them."

———

STEPHEN FELT the shift in wind; he felt the subtle change in the tremors of earth beneath both of their feet: Trevor's and his own. It was the tremble, not of anger, but of sudden, unexpected joy.

The trees moved, shaking their boughs; leaves grew above Stephen's head in a sudden burst of green—that green paler through the eyes of Pearl. She noted the change of the scent in the air, and barked twice: scent bark. She had caught the trail of the person they had come through fog and brilliance to find.

Stephen had not expected that. To his senses, *all* of the environs were Adala in one fashion or another; Pearl had not been able, until this moment, to tease out a single, discrete strand. Something had changed—perhaps Adala herself. She was meant to join the circus in the truest meaning of that word, but she could not be the entirety of the space in which she must work.

He wasn't certain he understood the process; he guessed that she must merge, somehow, with the lands the circus occupied so that the land could hear her and follow her will.

Her will was fractured. Trevor still sat at the heart of it. Myths, legends, and the oldest of stories about the folly of love were written and preserved, as if love must lead, inevitably, to tragedy. Nenyane considered it all foolish. She had always disliked those stories, and had often walked away from them.

It had taken him much of their life together to understand why: loss and pain. She did not, would not, love anyone *but* Stephen. All of her fear of loss was focused on him.

All of Adala's was focused on Trevor.

Trevor would not flee the towns when he understood what the cost would be to the people left behind. Adala would have. She accepted the duty and the sacrifice because to do otherwise was to lose Trevor. And she would lose him anyway. Was death better?

Would death still the longing and the desire? There would be no way back. There would be no hope of going back. It would be over.

He realized, then, that these thoughts were not his. Not for Stephen the choice of death—either of Nenyane's, or his own. Not for Stephen the thought that death would be a relief. Not, he thought, for Trevor either.

It was Adala. Adala's feelings saturated the space. But something had changed the lands, something had been altered. He could not easily tell what.

It is Summer, Nenyane said, her voice grave. *No, don't look through my eyes. You can barely manage to navigate through Pearl's.*

He could jump easily between the gazes of his pack, but Nenyane's gaze always knocked him off kilter. She was right.

What do you mean, it's Summer?

It's Summer in the wilderness. These lands, hidden until now, followed mortal seasons. It mimicked them precisely. Evayne is here.

Stephen stumbled, almost bringing Trevor down with him. He righted himself.

Evayne has called the Summer to the circus lands. Even the wilderness knows the seasons when they can sense them at all. There is a hush, now. It won't last.

Will the demon?

The demon is powerful enough to stand in Summer lands for some time—but it injures him the longer he remains.

Will he flee?

Nenyane did not answer that question. Instead, she said, *Go and find that foolish girl. The* Kialli *is attempting to summon his kin in the small gap he has created. It is only Adala who can prevent that, now—if she is not too late already.*

Why can't the circus master do it?

Ask him yourself! she snapped.

THE BREEZE that touched Alex's cheeks warmed them; it carried ashes and petals and the subtle scent of trees. He could see Steel; the dog had not moved. He could not see his brother. But he felt, in this shift of breeze, this stir of elemental air, that if he could not find a way to move to where Max stood, he would never hunt with his brother again. Max would remain here; Alex would remain by his side if that were allowed.

Stephen would continue without either of them.

Stephen would face the battles, the war, without Elseth by his side. Alex was not ashamed to admit that his father's disapproval hung above him as an unsheathed blade.

He had never once thought his father sent them in ignorance of what they might face; he had heard the stories of his father's time in the Empire, beside the huntbrother whose life he had surrendered. His mother had pointed out that Stephen of Elseth had *chosen*. He had made the huntbrother's choice; he had proven true to the oath he had sworn as a child, newly come to Elseth.

His father, being a Hunter, didn't care. He respected Stephen of Elseth's choice, but he did not spare himself blame for forcing him to make it.

His father had understood, the moment Nenyane had arrived in Evayne's shadow—Evayne, a woman Gilliam of Elseth all but hated— that Nenyane would be Stephen's huntbrother. He had also understood that this would make Stephen of Maubreche's life difficult in Hunter society. What he had not guessed at the time was that Stephen would not *allow* Nenyane to make the huntbrother's oath.

His father disliked it. He also approved. Caught between these two impulses by the ghost of his Stephen, Stephen of Elseth, he had chosen to respect the departure from tradition. If Stephen did not have a huntbrother in the traditional sense, she could not offer her life in the stead of his. Stephen would not suffer what Gilliam had suffered by an oath sworn to a god. Stephen of Maubreche was physically the son of Breodan—but to the eye, he was Stephen of Elseth's son. Were it not for Stephen of Elseth, that child would never have been born.

He had, therefore, sent his own sons to the King's City in near disgrace. He had sent them for one purpose only: to stand side by side or back-to-back with the child he viscerally believed was his Stephen's son, as if to make up for his previous failure.

Alex did not consider Stephen of Elseth's death to *be* a failure. He had attempted to argue with his father; his mother had cuffed the side of his head. Max agreed with Alex, but not enough to risk his mother's annoyance. Both, however, understood that their role from the moment

they left Elseth was to guard and protect Stephen of Maubreche. It
was the duty laid upon them by their father.

And if they discharged that duty, if they returned home with a
living, breathing godson, maybe the ghosts that haunted their father
would finally be laid to rest.

But to do that, they had to leave the circus. Together. Alex loved
Stephen like a brother, but not like Max. If Max could not leave, Alex
would remain with him.

You will not.

I will.

What point is there in that?

If our situation was reversed, you're telling me you'd leave me here?

Max was not one of nature's liars. It caused trouble in social situations, especially when women of power were out in full force.

GERVANNO, absent Stephen of Maubreche, understood that his duty in
this moment was Evayne. The fox attacked, joining the surviving
circus defenders; two had fallen, consumed in their falls by flame.
Those that had been injured—in two cases, almost fatally—remained
on their feet, their clothing slick with their own blood, their injuries
healed in an instant.

He counted four—four standing.

Nenyane closed and leapt back in a constant, circling motion,
looking for an opening to strike.

The wild mage had seen Evayne, and the frenzied movement of her
hands, lips, and lightning stilled. She might have become a simple
image—grand, glorious, and absent the ability to change. But he could
pay no more attention to Anya. It was Evayne who had become the
demon's focus.

Evayne had ushered in the Summer. Gervanno could not, absent
that brilliant flash of spreading warmth and light, see an immediate
difference. Summer or Winter, the wilderness was not for or of him.
He focused, instead, on the shadows that Nenyane had cut: watched
them heal and grow whole again, as if they were liquid. A dark,
obsidian liquid that had spilled from a full vessel, and spread as water
will on stone surface.

He watched as the shadows did something they had not yet done in this combat. They rose, deepening, thickening, until they had shape and form — not one, but four. They absorbed the color from the air, from the light, taking on, in the end, the appearance of what might, once, have been men.

Taller of form, fairer of skin, perfect in their unveiled beauty, they drew swords almost as one person.

"Kill her. Kill the seer." The words reverberated, as if thunder or lightning echoed in the spoken syllables.

Shields joined swords, all red, as if lit within by the fires the demons commanded.

"Retreat, lord," one of the four demons said.

"Kill the seer," his lord replied. No further entreaty was offered.

To Gervanno, the familiarity of the spoken request was jarring. He understood the words, and he understood the sentiment. These four, newly arrived, were the closest of the demon's honor guards, oath-guards who existed to protect — and obey — their lord. It was their lord's safety that was their concern, but if the lord did not choose that safety, they could not command him. They could merely accept his choice.

Gervanno stood between them and the object of their lord's command; possibly their lord's final command. The first demon — the most powerful — then turned his attention to those in immediate melee range; no more the almost casual deflection of wings of flame, no more the combatants as afterthought. He intended to take them all, hold them all, while the four summoned demons killed Evayne.

THE TREES through which Stephen and Trevor walked so slowly and deliberately fell away, as if they, not the two mortals, had moved aside. Perhaps they had. Even the trees planted in the forest, theoretically beyond the borders of Hansleigh, had been sentient, and they had come at Adala's call.

She had not yet become one with the circus.

But Anya had recognized her as someone who would or must. Now, the trees allowed Stephen and Trevor to approach the clearing.

At the center of the clearing was Adala herself. Stephen could not see her feet; they were planted, rooted almost as the trees were rooted, in the earth itself. Her robes were clean, but the scent of blood filled Pearl's nostrils as the dog approached, just a step ahead of her master.

Adala's eyes were open, unblinking; she stared ahead, her face in profile, as if neither Stephen nor Trevor existed. Her cheeks were glistening with shed tears, although she did not weep; her arms were half-raised, palms up, as if attempting to carry something the eyes could not see.

But when her lips moved silently, the air, warmer now, grew wild. The earth trembled. The water, which had not left Trevor, began to move in frenzied waves, almost distorting what Stephen could see. Trevor stiffened as well.

Whatever Adala mouthed, Trevor could hear it. He could hear it as certainly as the wild elements could hear her. Instinct took over; Stephen reached for Trevor, the guiding hand becoming a tightening grip on his arm. The water could change that; Stephen knew. But it allowed his hand to pass.

This was why he had come.

Trevor opened his eyes and moved far more certainly than he had in his awkward, almost unseeing stumble through Adala's forest. Stephen followed. His vision had to adjust to the bright, bright light — but it was golden in color now. Adala was its burning heart.

She turned when Trevor was perhaps three yards away.

Her expression almost caused Stephen to let go of Trevor, to turn away; there was an intensity of welcome that was meant only for Trevor. She didn't seem to see Stephen at all. He had no doubt of her reaction, otherwise. If he was lucky, he would be gently ejected — if she had that in her at all.

Trevor tried to shake himself free of Stephen. He meant to close the gap that separated them, this planted young woman and the man for whom she had intended to abandon the rest of her life and history. Stephen held on. They were of a height, and of similar weight; short of turning and punching Stephen, Trevor could not easily break free.

It was close.

"Let me go to her," Trevor finally said, a hint of plea in what was otherwise anger. When Stephen failed to release him, he exhaled. "I know you're afraid I'll die here. But I don't care if I die. I was going to live for her. Dying for her is easier. If that's what she needs — if that's what she wants — I'm willing."

"It won't help her," Stephen replied, voice low and urgent. "Maybe, in the moment, it will. But she'll realize that whatever it is she's doing isn't saving your life—it's ending it. Right here, in this place, she's imperfectly balanced between love and duty. If you die, she'll lose both."

Trevor said, "I don't care. I couldn't stay with her—leaving my friends and family to die would have killed me. But leaving her here will break me in a different way. If I could, I'd stay with her until I die."

"She won't age."

"Do you think that *matters*?"

Their argument rose in volume. Adala, however, waited as if she could not hear them at all.

"She *wanted* me to be here!"

"And you're here—but she didn't want you to *die*!" He turned to Adala, who saw only Trevor, and shouted her name.

She frowned, her forehead rippling briefly at the change in expression. No—at any expression at all.

Do not touch her, Nenyane said.

Focus on your fight, he snapped back.

My fight isn't as certain to kill me as yours will be if you touch her at all.

Trevor could not completely believe Adala would kill him. Not knowingly. But he had to catch—and hold—some part of her attention to make certain she wouldn't do so unintentionally. Stephen had to invade this private moment, had to intrude in a space in which he would never otherwise remain.

He kept tight hold of Trevor's wrist. He shouted Adala's name for a secod time.

WHAT ARE YOU DOING?

I'm looking at what I took from the lost and found. Alex tried not to snap, but the worry made his words harsher. Max had never reacted well to that snappish harshness, although it had been a couple of years since they'd come to blows. Alex never felt that his irritation was unjustified. Max seldom felt that it was.

This time, Max accepted it. It wasn't as if he could reach out to punch his brother. And if he somehow could, anger was not what either of the brothers would be feeling.

Alex emptied his bag. He had taken items to which he'd been drawn from a worn crate that had seen better years. He hadn't asked their use, in large part because he suspected the woman who stood so casually behind that crate didn't know. She had been leery of only one thing: the marble.

He held it; it was sun-warm in his palm, but he knew nothing had changed. He wondered what would happen if he offered it some of his blood. Max, having bled on circus earth, was instantly outraged.

But Alex let the marble go. Whatever it was meant to do or be — whatever evoked that strange sense of pity in the circus woman — it was not meant for now.

He then picked up the rings. He had taken them in part because he was uncertain where their travels would take them, and they could be sold if money became an issue. In Breodanir, there were very few places in which money could become an issue. Elseth — or Maubreche — would cover the expenses of their progeny should the need arise. Such understandings, so comfortable and natural they had been unquestioned, would not exist beyond Breodanir's borders.

But there were two such rings.

Emerald rings. They were not delicate in make or weight; indeed, they seemed heavier as they rested in Alex's palm.

I really don't understand the obsession with blood ancient things seem to have, he told his brother.

Max accepted this; there was the hint of cohering question in Alex's statement. *Don't expect me to understand something you don't. Not about things like this.*

The rings. He hesitated, and then drew a dagger. He took care to cut his hand only enough that he could squeeze a bead of blood out with effort; he understood that if that blood touched the circus earth, he would be trapped here with Max.

He smeared one of the two emerald rings with his blood. Echoes of his grandmother's voice rushed in instantly; she would have been appalled. He put the ring on his finger. Rings in the normal world had to be sized. One did not simply pick up a ring and put it on, expecting it to fit.

He wasn't surprised when this one did; he put it on a finger of his left hand, and held the second, identical ring out to Steel. "Take it, but *do not* swallow." It was a test. He didn't understand why Steel wasn't affected by the dislocation that separated him and Max, but accepted it was observationally true.

Steel sniffed his hand, as if looking for food. Dogs were always looking for treats. It didn't matter which dog; if a hand was held out, palm up, with something in it, that thing was meant to be eaten.

Do you have him? Alex asked.

I do.

Steel gently took the ring in his mouth. Alex closed his eyes to see, fully, through Max's. Max could see Steel take the ring. He could not see Alex give it to him.

But he could open his empty hand in front of Steel's mouth. Steel dropped the saliva-covered ring into his master's hand. Max took the ring and stared at it. Max wasn't a fan of jewelry of any sort—rings, necklaces. They were unnecessary adornments of only theoretical value, and they required more care than he was willing to give them— which would be any at all.

He dried the ring off on his tunic. *You want me to do what you just did?*

I don't know if it will make any difference—but it can't hurt.

Max nodded. *I don't have to be as careful.* Meaning, he wouldn't take nearly as long as Alex had. He cut his hand; true to his word, he was swift, efficient, and far less careful. He'd already bled on the earth here —what was more blood?

Alex was appalled.

If the amount of blood counted, I wouldn't be here. Or you wouldn't be there. I could go join the circus defenders right now. He made more of a mess of the ring's emerald than Alex had.

But when he did, the ring on Alex's finger warmed instantly. It was almost, but not quite, unpleasant. Max slid the ring over his finger— the same finger, left hand, that Alex had chosen. The ring fit perfectly, as it had for Alex. It was warm against his skin, but not as warm as the ring on Alex's finger had become.

Rings were a miniature shackle. They could be made pretty—by someone's standards. They could be items that conveyed some kind of status or power. But, at base, small, elaborate shackles. At least they had emeralds: Hunter colors.

GERVANNO WAS AWARE OF KATIE; she had turned to look in the direction Adala had walked. No sign of Adala remained, except the brilliance of distant light. The circus grounds gave way to the subtle signs of Summer as Evayne stood like a darkly robed pillar, her grip on Gervanno's shoulder tight enough to be felt.

The tree that had been giant roots shimmered in place as Gervanno glanced around the small clearing that had become a battlefield. He had seen—they had all seen—the roots on which Adala had made her slow and increasingly bloody progression. None of them had seen the tree. It was so transparent, it might have been mirage; summer in the Dominion could produce such mirages if the conditions were right.

This was not the Dominion.

He attempted to shrug Evayne off as the four demons leapt; they did not have their lord's wings of fire, but gravity did not bind them.

"I cannot fight while you hold on to me."

"You cannot survive if I do not," Evayne replied. "Not yet. The time will come when you must stand on far darker, far bloodier fields than these without such intervention, but that time is not yet."

Gervanno's jaw tightened. For the first time, he hated his ignorance of the rules of this strange, wild place—if there were rules at all between one land and the next. He wanted the stability of the known beneath his feet while he faced the unknown. He brought his sword to bear, to parry. He did not fight with shield.

"Understand what you see, Ser Gervanno. These, the dead, were once Illaraphaniel's kin and comrades; they were born of the White Lady, and they served her. Their power was her power, granted form and consciousness individual and separate from her own." She gestured; he could see that gesture in the shadows that now seemed to be cast from a point behind her. It had not been so before she had chosen to do whatever it was she had done: call Summer to this place.

The four were driven back; one grunted in pain. She carried no sword. Gervanno did, but it was not his sword that had destroyed the shield-arm of their commander.

He did not understand why she had chosen to protect him, for he understood now that she had not detained him for her own protection.

The fox had turned—the fox, the greatest of the warriors now attacking the demonic lord.

"I have him, Eldest," Evayne said, the words spoken softly. They carried nonetheless. "Do what must be done. The shadows are spreading; the gap is being utilized."

The circus master, lord of these lands, stood beside Evayne, unruffled by the appearance of the new demons. He watched, his expression so unmoving his face might have been a mask of flesh and seeming. But the complexion of his skin was almost golden as he watched, as if waiting for the right moment to join the fray.

Or as if the fray itself were, in the end, unimportant; intellectual.

FOUR RINGS BLAZED TO LIFE. Two emeralds. Two rubies. Two vows spoken and contained in the history of their bearers. In the warmer air, the trees shifted in place, branches trembled, roots disturbing the earth; crowns high above seemed to bend toward the people enmeshed in those vows.

THE HUNTBROTHER BOND had always been certain and strong. All of the Elseth litter—his grandmother *hated* that word as it applied to Espere's children, but the littermates did not—had developed those bonds at an early age.

Max and Alex had been unshakeable.

But Alex felt it differently as the ring almost burned on his finger: the weight of that bond was almost threatening. It was the first time he had felt this way. Max had always been part of him, part of his awareness of the universe—a second set of eyes, a second set of observations, a way of steadying himself in the midst of the worst of conflicts. Max had always been Max. Alex had always been Alex.

He felt the weight of being Max almost eclipse the existence of self, of Alex. He almost pushed back, pushed himself—or Max—out. He did not. He understood that this—this crowding, this suffocation, was the one possible thread he might follow to reach his brother.

Not you, Max said, his voice a reverberation of interior sound, as if he were standing beside his brother, shouting in his ear. *It's not meant for you to follow. It's me.*

Max felt as uncomfortable as Alex felt, as almost-oppressed. To Alex's chagrin, he found that annoying, although he felt it himself.

Max laughed. His laughter caused answering laughter in his brother, who wasn't amused. He had always felt Max's amusement, but he had not been moved to *act* by it. He had not laughed himself.

You have, Max said. *Remember what I told you about Lady Halledman? You had to bite your lip to stop from laughing out loud.*

Grandmother would have strangled us both the moment there were no witnesses. Alex exhaled. *Can you find me now?*

I'm trying. Can you take the ring off?

I haven't tried.

Mine's not moving.

I'll try when you're out of there.

"That is not quite what you must do, child," an unfamiliar voice said. Alex turned, then. The voice was heard, not felt; it did not come to Alex through Max's ears, Max's hearing.

Steel started to growl.

Standing in front of Alex was one of the moving trees that had escorted Adala back to Hansleigh.

He wasn't one of them, Max said.

Alex nodded. Different, yes—taller, and older, as if beneath the layers of almost immobile bark grew more bark, more rings, lines that radiated outward from a center that could not be seen without the use of an axe and several hours.

"What must I do, then?"

"It is dependent on your goal—but I perceive that your goal is the young man who stands, almost but not quite rootless, on the other side. There is a reason those who defend this place must be of it."

"And one becomes of it, as you say, by shedding blood?"

"It is meant to be an offering. It is meant to be an oath. It has always been thus."

"He didn't shed his own blood as an offering."

"Ah, no. It was shed in defense of these lands. Had he been one of your other companions, such blood would have signified nothing. But you are both scions of distant, elder forces—and at that, the lord of covenants and binding oaths. You have lived in small boxes. Those boxes are the years allotted to your brief, mortal lives. Mortality was meant to be a boundary.

"But many things can creep across the boundaries once set for mortals. Many can be born mortal who touch the stray elements of the wilderness, who absorb them; some are destroyed by them. Some are not. Those like you are closer to the wilderness than you have believed in your mortal lives. And the circus itself yearns for the strength of that mixed blood.

"In my youth, there were shapers; they did not create life, but they channeled it, absorbed it, remade it. Some of my brethren chose to entrust their fates to those ancient beings, and they gained a freedom I did not. But I digress.

"The ring, as you guessed, requires blood. While your brother wears the twin ring, it is not to the lord of these lands that his blood will belong."

"Then who?"

"You, grandchild of Bredan. You will become his land; you will become his lord."

Neither of the Elseth brothers wanted that.

"The choice is yours. But the gifts of those long dead grant you that choice; without them, your brother would become part of the circus."

"I don't want to *be* his lord. I want to be his *brother*."

"I must leave you to your decision; I hear her voice, now. She is almost here."

Alex blinked.

"Who?"

"Adala. She is the last," the tree said, voice thinning. "The last of those who will be summoned to the circus. Summer has finally arrived. I pity you, who cannot feel the turn of seasons. There is beauty in Winter, but also death."

"There are deaths in summer."

"Ah, yes. In the wilderness, death has always been a companion. Sometimes it is gentler. Sometimes it is not. Understand, child of man, that grief lies at the heart of the wilderness, for the wilderness is eternal. An eternity of loss." The veined eyes closed; the tree was becoming transparent. "I did not join the battle; I was not called to it. And even lessened in all ways as he has become, I do not wish to see an ending to the one you call demon."

"They'd kill you all if they could."

"Yes. But the *Kialli* in command raised some of us, and we remember the touch of his hand, his power, the sound of his voice, low and sweet and full not of death but life and affection."

The tree faded entirely from view, taking his voice with him.

Max was unimpressed.

Alex was not. *If Mother tried to kill you—if she thought it necessary to cull her litter—would you kill her without regret?*

Yes.

Alex exhaled.

If she tried to kill us, she'd be our enemy. What she was before that doesn't matter. *In fact, it would be worse: we trust her, and she would have betrayed that trust.*

Alex was not Max. Max was not Alex. That was why the bond they shared had always worked. But Alex *would* regret. He might not even attempt to kill—he'd flee instead. While his mother lived, he would try to understand *why*. Why had she decided to kill them? Why had she felt it so necessary?

Max snorted.

And in truth, there would be hope. Hope that whatever it was that drove her could somehow be fixed, mended; that trust might exist in the future, broken and shattered as it was in that hypothetical present. Hope that he would not have to let go of the warmth of the past, to replace it with anguish and cold fury.

Max did not agree. But perhaps it was because Max could not conceive of that betrayal; it was too ridiculous. He had always had a problem with Alex's what-ifs. If Alex felt them necessary, couldn't he come up with plausible ones?

Alex grimaced. He set aside that resonant feeling of empathy. Max was right in one regard—his what-ifs often got in the way of the purely practical. Did empathy matter when it would change nothing? He might feel sympathy, or echoes of sympathy, but his actions would not, and could not, change.

What do you want to do? he asked his brother. He didn't bother to explain the choices; Max had listened carefully. He understood them. He was ambivalent, but less so than Alex.

If you are my land, if you are my lord, what changes?

You already know. The huntbrother bond wasn't a cage. It wasn't a shackle. It implied loyalty—but we always had that. I don't know *what this will mean. Maybe you'll hear me all the time—even when I don't want to be heard. Even when I'm trying to spare you the things you don't like.*

Max shrugged. After a silence that extended with things unsaid, only emotions remained, and those could be easily read. Max looked at his bleeding palm; the cut, deeper than Alex's, had not fully clotted, although the blood was now sticky. *You want me to bleed more, right?*

Alex didn't answer, because the answer forked, and forked again, all the consequences of *yes* and *no* playing out into the infinity of their future. Their finite future.

Max, being Max, shrugged. *I get it. You can't make the choice for me. You want me to agonize. You want me to have your fear. I can certainly* feel *your fear—but it's not mine. I'm not afraid of my choices. I'm not afraid of the future.* In a less angry internal voice, Max added, *That's your job. I never liked to live in fear.*

But—

If things go bad, we'll deal with it when it comes. We always have. We made our choice about the huntbrother's oath. Nobody else's opinion mattered.

No. It hadn't. But they'd been united in their refusal, in the end. Before the end? Arguments, physical fights, Alex's desire to remain part of the society to which he'd been born and raised warring with his desire to keep Max safe. Max didn't care about Hunter society. They were the youngest, not the eldest, and being a lord—worse, being married to someone like Lady Elseth, their grandmother—was almost a fate worse than death. His own death, of course. Not Alex's—unless they killed each other in frustration.

Other people's opinions *had* mattered to Alex. They mattered to their grandmother, a woman Alex both feared and loved in equal measure. She had borne the burden of the demesne's governance for so long, stepping into the gap left by Espere, their mother. She was waiting—she had made that so clear—for William and his future wife to finally become the Elseth couple. Then, and only then, could she retire in peace.

But it was Alex she loved best. Alex, with his curiosity, his drive for knowledge. Alex, with his interest in art, in music. Alex, who was unlike the rest of his litter except in one way: he could hunt. He was an excellent hunter.

Alex, who had never tried to control Max. Never tried to reform him. Even his asides, sent in desperation through the bond they shared, had been pleas, requests not commands.

But he had a sense, ring on finger, his own blood so scant it was barely noticeable in the soft internal glow of the gem's light, that that would change. He didn't know how. He was afraid to touch the truth that rested on one finger.

Max was not, as he said, afraid. Could he hear more of Alex? Yes. Far more. But to Max, Alex remained himself. He had never needed to escape from the Hunter's bond, even if he had chosen to stomp away from Alex's physical presence.

And Max was perfectly willing to shed his own blood. Alex could—and had—cut himself, but in truth, it was one of the few things about which he could be genuinely squeamish. He could hide that from anyone but Max, and did. Hiding it was like wearing fancier clothing or perfect manners. It wasn't Alex genuine, but...no one went outside naked. No one worked naked. Everyone had to don something to get by.

Max bled.

Alex could feel the cut.

Alex could feel the warmth of Max's blood as it fell upon the ring—and Max's lap. He now took care to shed no more blood on the earth here, because it upset Alex.

Max's blood was warm. Alex could feel it spill from Max's ring into his own, and from there, onto his hand. He froze as he glanced at that hand; it was red with blood. Max's blood.

Well, that's creepy, Max observed. *But something is working.*

Yes. Something was working. Alex was torn between the desire to tell him to stop, and the desire to use that something to bring him back to where he belonged.

Don't bleed out, Alex warned his brother.

Max snorted. Alex could feel it. He could *almost* hear it.

The blood on Alex's hand spread until the whole of his hand was covered. It didn't drip. It didn't fall to the ground. It dried, but it dried scarlet, the color dried blood never was. He could feel Max's hand on his own, as if the blood—living blood, sacrificial blood—was alive and still part of Max.

That blood, that red, bright color, slowly peeled away from the top of Alex's left hand, as if it had a life of its own. This, he thought, was ancient magic—but unintentional magic, magic done in ignorance and desperation. Intent, he had realized due to Max's predicament, didn't amount to much in the wilderness. The shape of the action was enough to trigger consequences—as if something as tiny and almost silent as mortal intent couldn't be judged at all.

But the Hunter god *could* judge intent. Even at a distance. That intent was the reason Stephen of Elseth had died. He had made his oath. He had made it with intent. It had been accepted. And he had had to live up to it—or die for it. But that oath had been created for mortals: for Hunters. For Breodan's people. It had not been created for ancients or the elements of the wilderness that had once been simple children's stories.

And it didn't matter. He could feel Max's impatience so clearly, he shut down the weave of those thoughts. Later, he might return to them.

When Alex's palm began to bleed—his right palm—he found it far easier to focus on what was happening. He clenched his fist immediately, and shifted position so that blood—his blood—didn't touch the forest floor. Max had been right. How could one expect to engage in combat here if one couldn't bleed at all?

But even as the injured hand throbbed, he accepted the truth. This was not Alex's blood. Or it hadn't been. Alex had not been careless enough, impatient enough, to cut his own hand so deeply. He'd pricked skin, and at that so lightly he'd had to squeeze drops of blood from it.

Max stopped, then. He looked down at his hand. Alex could see it as well: the skin was uncut, unbroken. Max *had* cut more deeply; he had shed blood on the emerald, the twin to the one on Alex's hand.

Alex's hand had taken that injury.

Max, who'd initially had no reservations about this deeper binding, had a *lot* of them now. He wasn't voluble in his cursing, but he did curse. Steel whined.

Do not take the ring off! Alex shouted, as Max's hand moved.

Max had already tried, once. The ring had refused to budge. The only way to remove it was to remove the finger. Probably. This wasn't the time to test that, and Max had already changed his grip on his knife.

If you do that, I'll probably lose a finger. Not you.

That stilled Max. Then: *I can see you. I can see you now.*

Good. Come to me. Alex could see Max, shimmering, the entirety of his visage cast in a red light, as if the sun was an aerial orb of shining, bright blood. He was transparent, ghostly, but visible. They were almost standing in the same place; they were separated by perhaps a yard.

Alex reached out to touch his brother.

Max reached out in the same fashion.

Where their hands met, they felt a shock of pain; they were storm, and they contained the lightning perfectly between themselves. Max lost the red glow. Alex did not lose the slash across his palm.

Steel barked, tail wagging. He understood—had understood—that something was wrong. That the two brothers were separated in a fashion that made no sense to a dog's mind. That Max was worried.

Now, they were together, as they should be. Alex was relieved. Max was ambivalent.

They turned as one toward the clearing in which Adala had begun her ceremonial journey. Now, they could see the sky change color as light flashed: red, blue, white, and orange. They could hear what they had chosen to ignore: the sounds of battle.

Max was the type to charge in; he always had been. Alex was the observer; he trusted observation more than he trusted instinct, or rather, felt instinct would be most effective when paired with tactical understanding.

Max did not charge in. He looked down at his hand; blood had dried in the creases, but no wound that shed blood remained there. Alex bore the proof of that cut.

Alex might bear the cost of any reckless impulse.

GERVANNO DID NOT SEE the two Hunters as they emerged at the boundary of the battlefield. His attention was focused on the demons. On Nenyane. On Evayne, who had not released her grip on his shoulder.

On his own small mongrel, who had been absent for so much of the battle, as he darted across the field, weaving between the armed attackers as if they were trees caught in a gale. Leial ran in as straight a line as he could.

Leial was, in Gervanno's mind, a civilian. An overly enthusiastic — and ignorant — child. But in such combat, small children could be killed. He could not grab the dog who somehow traversed the battlefield to reach his feet; could not lift him; could not command him to leave. Could not, in the end, protect him should that protection be required.

Gervanno had never desired dependents such as Leial, for this very reason. He was not so naïve as to believe he could leave those he loved safely in their village while he rode off to war; the villages were not safe when war came, and even were they safe from war, there were other dangers that waited in the wings: the interest of the powerful. Their unexpected visits.

"Stay," he snapped, the word all the breath he could spare.

Evayne's hand was a shackle far more binding than even the golden fox had been. He could barely fight, could barely defend himself. Nenyane might have come to help, but as the commander was focused entirely on killing or destroying those who now attacked, she was hard-pressed. The demon's almost desultory attempt to break or sever limbs seemed child's play in comparison, and that had driven back his melee attackers every time.

Gervanno had no further time to assess.

Evayne's sweeping spells drove the four demonic attackers back, and one failed to survive. That left three. Gervanno parried where he could and must, and Leial, driven by the fearlessness of the foolish, nipped at ankles and thighs, and got kicked through the air for his trouble.

"Neamis!" Evayne shouted.

"Yes. I am here."

"You are holding Winter here—let it go!"

"Child, these lands were made in the Winter. They were built in the Winter. You have ushered in Summer, and the wilderness hears its song; the dead feel its bitter rejection. But these lands were not built in the Summer. To change the season requires effort—and concentration—on my part. More than this, I cannot do at speed." As if the demonic attack were almost trivial.

"If you are concerned about future defensibility, I invite you to consider our current situation."

Gervanno flinched at the sound of Jarven ATerafin's voice.

CHAPTER TWENTY-TWO

T he fox snarled a word, a name. *Jarven*. His voice did not match his chosen form, but Gervanno would have recognized it anywhere. He would have recognized, as well, the displeasure it conveyed.

Jarven ATerafin surveyed the battlefield as if he, like the circus master, was only peripherally part of it. His eyes stayed longest on the back of the man who had been, and would be in future, a golden fox: an elder of the wilderness, a power in his own right. Gervanno did not trust—would never trust—Jarven. He understood that Jarven was, in some way, the fox's liege. But the fox fought; Jarven simply observed, as if the fight itself was a test he had devised.

He wished to see the power of the elder he had chosen to serve. He wished to assess the value of his choice of lord—as if all service were transactional in nature. Perhaps the fox was not the lord for one such as Jarven; Jarven was attracted to power. Or perhaps Jarven wished to affirm the power inherent in the lord he had chosen.

Gervanno, raised in the South, did not require the open display of raw strength to understand, viscerally, that the fox had a power that he himself could never wield, and could never dream of attaining. Jarven was attracted to power the way some allies were: for his benefit, and always weighing some element of that benefit in any interaction.

Gervanno had met many like Jarven. They were almost inevitably lords of power; power was their goal. He could not judge the powerful; they ruled, and they took the weight of a ruler's decisions upon themselves. On their heads, the loss of life when war began; on theirs, the starvation in the terrible dry seasons, should their coin not be enough to procure the food necessary to keep their villagers fed.

Jarven was not concerned with those things.

"*Jarven.*"

Jarven exhaled. "If we are so hard-pressed, lord," he said to the fox, "we will not all survive."

Jarven, Gervanno was certain, would.

"I have oft been told that greed is the downfall of man," Jarven said as he looked to Geravanno, his tone shifting from utter respect to something far more conversational. And condescending. "In my experience, that is selectively true. But people think of greed as a desire for gold, a desire for power over others. That is not the greed that causes the most difficulty."

Gervanno said nothing.

"The desire to preserve everyone—to accept no casualties—is the most dangerous. It is a greed that is seldom acknowledged *as* greed, and it kills or destroys more people than a simple desire for pedestrian gold."

"He does not require your advice, ATerafin," the fox said, speaking as he leapt and landed, his voice now almost conversational in spite of the combat in which he engaged.

Jarven's smile, as he turned toward his master, was deep, harsh. "Does he not? Perhaps you are more a scholar of human nature than I."

A radiant blossom of red heat erupted at the edge of the battle. Anya. Gervanno held breath for a moment. But the fire was either Anya's or irrelevant to the mage. It was not irrelevant to her robes. She snarled in a rage almost as bestial as the fox's, clawing her way out of the flames sent to destroy her, as if those flames were heavy, fallen curtains that had closed briefly against her will.

Jarven's brow rose as he observed. He exhaled a moment later. As Gervanno watched—out of the corner of an eye—Jarven once again faded from view. But in the moment before he did, light glinted off steel. Jarven had not drawn sword, but rather, two long knives. Gervanno should not have been aware of him, but he was: Jarven moved toward the fox.

Jarven's knives took down a second demon, leaving the count at two. Two, and the commander, who did not seem injured at all. Ash was taken by wind, obscured by flame, but Gervanno heard the loud, brief scream—of rage and loss and pain—that was the demonic death knell.

At the heart of any battle, many questions were asked, and many answered. Gervanno was not a commander of any save a handful of men, and when the fighting started, his first thought was survival. Survival and the orders given him by the lords he served.

There had been no such commands offered. Nenyane's was unspoken, but words had been unnecessary. Gervanno was to protect Stephen. But Stephen was gone.

"ADALA!"

The third time Stephen shouted her name, it emerged from a throat that felt raw. It wouldn't be the first time he'd lifted his voice this way. He could feel the barest hint of Nenyane's irritation; most of her focus was on the demon that was, even now, attempting to kill Evayne.

Evayne, out of the melee, was nonetheless in danger. It wasn't Evayne that worried his huntbrother, but Gervanno di'Sarrado, caught in Evayne's orbit. Gervanno and, as always, Stephen, who faced no demon, no fire, no burning sword.

He opened his mouth to call Adala a fourth time, but closed it again as she finally turned her gaze toward him. Her brows drew together in confusion. He felt that confusion in the air he breathed, in the rustle of leaves above his head; saw the sunlight falter, the shadows of clouds darkening her face. All nature responded to Adala.

But he could now see her face with his own eyes.

"Trevor," he said, in a much softer voice. "I think you can open your eyes now."

At the mention of Trevor's name, Adala's gaze once again slid from Stephen's face to Trevor's, blacksmith's son, chosen.

The ruby on his finger was glowing; it was a red that reminded Stephen of demonic swords and shields, although the color differed. It was warmer, as if red and gold could exist in the same small containment.

Adala lifted her hand—her ring hand. There, twin to Trevor's ring, her ruby glowed as brightly, as warmly.

Stephen did not understand love. Not in the fashion Adala and Trevor did. Maybe he never would. He had never desired it; it was a burden he did not believe he could carry. He understood the theory: joy came from love. But it was a burning joy, an incandescent joy; it could consume those who could not bear its burden for long, burning to ash all joy and hope. The pain of its shadow could last a lifetime.

He had seen that in his mother. Could still see it, if he looked at himself in a mirror.

She had learned to love in a different way, the fires of youth banked permanently by the memory of loss and grief. Perhaps Adala would become akin to Cynthia of Maubreche—but Cynthia had never denied duty and responsibility in the pursuit of love.

Perhaps she had once wanted to. Perhaps she had dreamed of throwing away the responsibility of being the only child of Lord and Lady Maubreche—the daughter who must marry a Hunter to continue Maubreche's long line. But she had not, could not, in the end. Stephen of Elseth could not have become her husband; he was not a Hunter Lord. His Hunter could not take the Maubreche name, because Elseth had only had one son.

So much reality entangled in the joy and pain.

Adala was not Cynthia. Not in her hands the rulership and governance of the town she called—or had called—home. She had been free to pursue the only love she valued. But because of that love, she was here, now. Yearning and wanting and in pain.

She opened her lips, and spoke a single word. *Trevor.*

Trevor vibrated with it. "Let me go," Trevor said to Stephen, the words as soft as the name Adala had just spoken.

"Let me go with you," Stephen replied.

"It's not safe for you."

No. But it wasn't safe for Trevor, either.

He looked at Adala, arms raised in beckoning, and at Trevor, whose arm he still held. She wanted Trevor to come to her. Trevor wanted to go; Adala was rooted here. Trevor was not.

But having met many who served the circus, Stephen understood that they *could* move. They could traverse the circus grounds. They could shake hands and touch in normal ways. He knew that there was a ceremony, a ritual, for those called to the circus. He could assume that the rough shape of that ritual was similar for all of those who answered the summons. Adala could move, if she made the effort. Adala would *have to* move.

Stephen exhaled, finally understanding.

"She has to come to you," he told the blacksmith's son. "She has to be able to move carrying the weight of the circus."

Trevor wanted to argue. Opened his mouth to do so. Shut it again —a snap of teeth. "What are you, that you know this?" A whisper. Pain. Resentment. Resignation.

"Stephen of Maubreche."

"What god colors your eyes so gold?"

"Bredan," Stephen said, his voice falling into whisper, as Trevor's had done.

"Lord of oaths, of covenants."

Stephen nodded, but realized Trevor had eyes only for Adala; he would not see the silent agreement. "Yes."

Adala's feet could not be seen; they were encased in the earth. She stared at Trevor, and whispered his name again—but whispers were not naturally so loud, so all encompassing. The very earth vibrated with those syllables, as if she were speaking the name of a god. Stephen could feel Trevor's name in the movement of the air, the rustle of leaves above their heads; he could feel it in the water that was almost a second skin to the young man.

Trevor opened his arms, but he stood his ground, trembling with the effort. He wanted to run to her. He wanted to enclose her in the arms that were empty. He could see the confusion in Adala's expression; Adala was not the type of person to mask her emotions. At least not where Trevor was concerned.

Stephen's grip shifted to Trevor's shoulder.

Adala did not lower her arms. She called Trevor again. This time, she didn't whisper. The earth beneath Stephen's feet shifted as she spoke, almost as if it intended to push Trevor toward Adala. Stephen was an afterthought, if he was recognized at all.

Trevor did not move toward her. He understood the weight of Stephen's words: Adala must be able to move. She must be able to move toward him. She stood in this clearing, her feet beneath the earth, as if she were trying to become one of the trees with which she was surrounded.

The rings on both of their hands continued to glow. Adala's was brighter in the moment. She held her ground because she could not move. Trevor held his because Stephen, hand on shoulder, reminded him of what must be done. Adala had been called to the circus. Adala had walked the root-made path; she had offered the circus her blood.

But she had not become part of the circus, not yet. To join them, she must move. She must leave the space created for or by her. Trevor understood that, if he joined her, he would never leave this place. No, Stephen thought. He understood that she would absorb him, as she absorbed the parts of the wilderness to which she could speak.

But Trevor had none of that wilderness in him. He could not be as the earth, the water, the wind. He found resolve, his arms steady. She would kill him if she could not separate herself from this place. She would not mean to kill him; she would not intend it. But intent or no, he would perish here. He hadn't cared.

He did care now. He had no desire to hurt her. He could imagine how monstrous he would feel were their positions reversed and he called her to her death.

Adala called his name a third time.

"I can't come to where you are," Trevor said, denying the pull of her arms and the expression—familiar, beseeching—that transformed her face. His own expression must have been a mirror of hers. "Adala, please. Please." His hands moved, palms curling as he beckoned her; his arms remained steady.

"I'm afraid," she whispered, and the wind cooled.

"So am I." His voice was as soft as hers, as informed with yearning and loss.

"I don't want to lose you."

Trevor closed his eyes. He had no answer to give that was not a mirror of the words she had spoken, and no comfort to offer. This was the end. They could walk from the end into a future that they had not dreamed of, had not planned for, and could not build upon.

He opened his eyes. Opened his mouth. Stephen thought he was struggling with tears, with the tightness of throat and breath that came with refusing to shed them.

Adala made no attempt to stop hers from falling. "I don't want this."

Stephen wanted to speak. He kept his peace, but it was difficult. Stephen had learned what his mother, his father's huntbrother, had had to teach of social grace. But neither of these teachers would interfere in

such circumstances. Neither would hold tightly to Trevor's shoulder;
both would have discretely wandered far enough away that they could
not intrude on a private moment.

He wondered, as he fought the urge to retreat, how many moments
such as these—private and personal—defined the survival of whole
towns or countries. History oft laid out tales of political movements,
tactical successes and failures, strategic folly or brilliance, the movements of power following the flow of economic strength or weakness.

History also offered stories of tragic love—as if all love, in the end,
did not end in tragedy and separation. Even the happiest of stories
faded into age and death, and surely the bereaved were stricken by
loss, unbalanced by it, possibly destroyed by it?

The salvation of the circus was now being built upon the personal
tragedy of two people: Adala and Trevor. Perhaps the circus, and the
towns over which it presided, had always depended on personal
tragedy. On the sacrifice, not of literal life, but of life's possibilities, of
life's hope for a bright future.

Stephen did not love Nenyane in the fashion Trevor or Adala loved
each other. But standing, hand on Trevor's shoulder, he wondered
whether or not he could sunder himself—forever—from Nenyane.

He knew what Nenyane's choice would be, were the two to be
faced with a similar sacrifice. Nenyane would let the town die. She
would let the streets of the townships run with blood, let the buildings
burn to ash, let the people who were not lucky enough to flee perish.

She neither confirmed or denied.

It was Stephen who was uncertain, now. Could he do what Adala
and Trevor were struggling, in this moment, to do? Could he cut off
the Hunter's bond? Could he abandon his huntbrother in order to
somehow preserve her life? Could he abandon the rest of the life he
had built?

But the analogy was the wrong one. Were he asked to make this
choice at the heart of Maubreche—were he asked to become a permanent part of the sanctuary that existed at the center of the Maubreche
maze—would he have any other choice? He could not walk away from
his parents, his brothers, the servants that had been like distant family
to him.

He would stand, as Adala stood.

He would walk, as Adala now struggled to walk, pulling her feet
from the earth with strain and effort, because Trevor would not walk to

her. In her place, he would viscerally understand, only then, that he was no longer part of Trevor's world; that he was no longer part of Trevor's life, except on the occasions the circus came to town.

He would understand that this was farewell.

Yes, he thought, as he watched Adala's struggle. He would be like Adala.

She moved, feet beneath the earth but rising as she approached Trevor. She lowered her arms; Trevor did not lower his. Would not, until she reached him. Stephen saw color return to this small clearing as she made progress; he could hear distant sounds — the clash of steel against steel, the shouts and cries of rage or pain. Even the howl of wind at a distance was different than the breeze in this enclosed space had been. That breeze had whispered only Trevor's name, when words could be discerned at all.

Adala staggered between steps, as if she were fighting through an invisible wall just to reach Trevor, who stood on the other side of it. As if she knew that those open arms would enclose her if she *could* reach him. This was the only time they had left. She could not keep him here; could not trap him by her side in what was fast becoming a far less isolated space. Not if she wanted him to live.

And she did, even if that life was no longer to be lived with her. The danger to Trevor had passed. The danger to everyone else had not. Stephen almost lifted his hand from Trevor's shoulder. Nenyane snarled a single *no*, and he left it there. He was Trevor's shadow. Could he make himself invisible, he would.

Step by step she moved, her ankles and feet rising from the earth until she stood on it, not in it. Walking became much easier, then; she moved more quickly.

By the time she reached Trevor, she leapt toward him, lifting her own arms again. Only then did Stephen release Trevor's shoulders. The moment their embrace was closed by both Trevor and Adala, they were almost one. Had the rings on their hands not flashed and brightened, he would have walked — or sprinted — away.

He did not. The forest did not magically fall away to reveal the clearing in which the battle was, even now, raging. The sounds of that battle drew closer as Adala wept into Trevor's chest; Stephen thought Trevor wept into her hair.

"IT IS DONE," the circus master said. "No other demons will join this battle."

NENYANE AVOIDED the arc of the *Kialli* blade. She did not parry; she leapt. The sweep of the blade sheared the few grass stalks that remained in the wake of *Kialli* fire; it cut through her tunic, although she had avoided the visual arc of the swing. All attempts to injure or kill the demonic commander had failed before he had turned his attention to his attackers; he had batted them away with flaming wings as if they were flies or mosquitos.

Defense against their attacks no longer seemed to be afterthought now. Nenyane was grateful that Stephen was not by her side. The movements necessary to avoid the demon's attacks were beyond him. She was aware that Max and Alex had returned from wherever it was the demons had first entered lands forbidden them — but the Elseth Hunters had good instincts, and they did not second-guess them. They remained behind Evayne a'Nolan. Behind Gervanno.

The only person on this field of battle that had managed to wound the winged *Kialli* was the damnable, capricious golden fox. He fought with polearm, and his speed was equal to — or better than — Nenyane's. But it was not the fox on whom Nenyane now relied. It was the mage.

Anya could attack to devastating effect; she had done so while they had both been airborne. She had attempted many times to strike this demon down — or any of the demons obviously under his command — and those attacks had been shunted aside by the red shields the demons had been forced to bear. Her defenses, now, shone here.

Nenyane had been uncertain that Anya would even spend her mage-born power on defenses, she was so deadly and so aggressive. There was no uncertainty now. Anya could deflect the fires, the bolts of lightning; she could follow the movement of shadows as they struggled to take form and cohere.

Evayne had ushered in Summer, but the lands resisted the season. Still, the pooled shadows grew sluggish; steam rose from the outer periphery of that shadow's spread. Summer was not the season for *Kialli*, but it had been Winter for a very long time. Winter here was not the winter of Breodanir; it was not the winter of the mortal world. No snow had girded the circus that had been built and maintained in the

Winter of the ancient world. The trees did not stand fallow, awaiting the advent of spring; the wildflowers that girded the clearing would bloom in any season.

But there were differences. The Summer touched the periphery of the lord's forest first. Some of the trees could wake in the Winter, and had; some could not be called from slumber unless those who beckoned had significant power and will.

Now, she could see the final defense of the circus emerge from the wooded areas.

The *Kialli* commander could see them as well.

It was not the trees that drew his attention; not the trees that stilled the motion of blade and shield, although the wings remained in action.

At the head of this small group of trees walked a familiar man.

Illaraphaniel.

THE WIND CARRIED the scent of blood. Nenyane had always been sensitive to it. Stephen, had he been here, would not have noticed to whom that blood belonged. Perhaps, had the battlefield been one chosen by the Wild Hunt, she would not have known, for the blood of the injured and the dying would have been the blood of the servitors of the White Lady.

Here, there was only one who bore that blood. Only one who had been born to, and of, the White Lady.

No, she thought, as she righted herself, her feet touching ground before she once again leapt to dodge. There remained three who had been born in such a fashion; three who had sundered themselves forever from their maker. They had passed beyond the life granted them; they were dead. Dead to the wilderness their former lord, and the kin that had not betrayed their maker.

It was the duty of the Arianni to close in combat with those who were traitors. It was, to Nenyane's eyes, one of the few things that brought them joy; it illuminated the whole of their eternal existence to clash in just such a fashion.

Not for Illaraphaniel the absence from one of the most significant of their combats—but only the wind that spoke his name with such a hush of respect and exultation had made clear to those who could hear it that Illaraphaniel was both alive and aware.

The scent of blood made clear to Nenyane why he had not yet stepped foot on this field of battle.

One of his ancient kin had perished here—and that he knew, for the wind screamed that name into her ears, some echo of the silent cry that was Illaraphaniel's. She had never understood Stephen's need for privacy—or rather, for granting privacy to others. Privacy did not change fact. Privacy did not obviate emotion; it did not dim loss, or lessen it.

But she understood it when she heard the wind's cry, twin to its master's; she—and any who could hear—was momentarily witness to a pain that should never be spoken. Should never be felt. She herself did not feel it, and doubted she had that ability. She did not envy those who did.

Did not think further on it, by deliberate choice. She could not. Not here.

It is always difficult to be honest with oneself. Who had said that? *It is a gift. It is a curse. Like a Northern blade, it exists with two edges. I grant you that blessing, little sword. Use it carefully. Do not cut yourself more than you need; do not fail to do so when it is necessary.* Whose voice returned to her in this clearing of fire and wild magery and demonic ire?

But as if she were a child, she accepted the truth. She *had* felt grief of such terrible scope it had almost shattered her.

She was not prone to envy. It had never been her weakness. But she had not been prone to pity, either, and as her eyes found Illaraphaniel, she felt that pity as a dread and a weight.

THE WINGED DEMON STILLED. So, too, those who had been driven to attack him, although if pressed, they could not have answered the question *why*.

Gervanno could have, had he been among those attackers; he was not.

He felt that he was almost in the presence of gods. Not the circus master, but the platinum-haired mage and the demonic lord. They faced each other, and even the fox stepped back, putting up his long weapon. He did not resume the appearance of golden fox, but turned instead toward the two demons that stood between Evayne and their lord.

How powerful was the mage, that the fox would step back?

"This is not wise," Evayne said.

"It is not," the circus master agreed. "Will you attempt to stop him?" There was amusement in the question, but no doubt of the answer.

Had she been willing to make the attempt, Gervanno would have intervened. There was something about these two that demanded it. They would face each other on this field, and until one—or the other— was vanquished, would allow no interference.

He had seen such conflicts arise among men of note and power. One such combat had ended the war that had caused Gervanno to retire from service in the Dominion. Two had faced each other, man-to-man. One had died.

Neither of these two were men. Not as the two who had vied for rulership over the Dominion. Not as Gervanno di'Sarrado had ever understood the term. Did he search for commonality, because it made them seem less monstrous, less strange? Did he seek it because those commonalities were a bridge between himself and beings who might otherwise render the entirety of his life and experience irrelevant?

"No," the circus master said, voice soft. "You are alive, as one of them is alive, and life troubles you all. It breaks you, and only if you are very fortunate does it retrieve the shattered parts to make you anew. Mortals have always been the slenderest of the sentiences, but in your short, truncated lives, you have burned so brightly you have caught the attention of the vast and ancient world. Even in its slumber. Perhaps especially then.

"There was wonder before your advent. There was awe. Power. Things that exist forever beyond your ken. Even the battle you witness now is an echo of what was, for it is pain and loss that lingers longest, as if all joy is a brief lie spoken to lull ourselves. As if it is chimerical, a mirage that pulls you forward, step by step, ever within your reach, but never within your grasp."

"Enough," Evayne snapped, for the silence that had descended upon this field affected everyone who stood on it, bled on it—everyone but the circus master, the lord of the circus lands. She gestured, lifting her hand from Gervanno's shoulder briefly, the motion of her hands seen by the shadows they cast. Those shadows were long and thin; they spread across the field, so slender they might be missed by any who did not make the effort to follow their progress.

The circus master fell silent.

"If he has lessons to teach you, they can wait. He will not force them on you; as you have seen, he chooses not to *interfere*." Gervanno did not turn toward Evayne as she spoke. "But I will see this. I will not take a step forward — or back — until it is done."

Gervanno nodded to acknowledge her words. His gaze strayed between three points on this field, foolishly: Meralonne, the demonic commander, and Nenyane of Maubreche. That there were two demons between them seemed rendered almost irrelevant, for they, too, had turned to the mage: the mage who wore linked chain mail, who carried a sword the color of sun and sky, both.

To Gervanno's eye, there was a striking similarity between the winged demon and the Northern Widan: they seemed of a height, their skin of a color; the drape of their hair long, fine, more of a royal vestment than simple objects like crowns or cloaks. Meralonne bore no wings, but in the moment, Gervanno could almost sense their invisible spread. It would not be the first time he had seen the mage take the sky and remain there, carried aloft by the wind itself.

The wind, and its howling vortex, was the fate of the dead in the South.

The South, with the Lord of the Sun, and the Lady of the Moon, one harsh and militant, one secretive and forgiving. They were the two gods worshipped in the Dominion — but that made sense. Two sides of the same blade; or perhaps blade and sheath. Gervanno's encounters with religion in the North had shaken the beliefs by which he'd lived.

But even those religions could not encompass what he had witnessed since the day the merchant caravan had been destroyed on the open road. If there was room for demons in Southern beliefs — and there was; the Sun Sword and the five swords of the priests el Sol had been created by the Lord of the Sun for the purpose of destroying demons — there was no room for Meralonne APhaniel. No room for the circus master. No hint of the wilderness in which those who claimed lordship could change the literal skies above their lands.

He thought Anya disturbing. On the surface, she was a being that did not exist — at all — in the Dominion. She was female, and women could not be Widan. But she was not entirely sane, not entirely adult, and her raging tantrums could have easily destroyed whole villages the size of the one Gervanno had been born to. There was no history that encompassed her existence; to villagers who had not stepped foot in the battle in the Averdan valleys, she was akin to a god.

But even she stilled as Meralonne approached the demonic commander.

Gervanno would not have been surprised if the only form of communication between these two figurative giants was combat itself, but he was not surprised when the demonic commander spoke.

"Illaraphaniel."

THE LOSS of Memonryenne was ancient. Ancient and very new. The memory of the Arianni—as the *Kialli*—was eternal. Hear his name and, if one were careless, one remembered Memonryenne in his youth. He was not, had never been, a warrior, but he had hunted in his fashion, bringing to the court the creatures he had captured—but never killed. They came at his call, for he had fashioned spaces within them that belonged only to Memonryenne himself and he had offered them to the White Lady, she of grace and endless beauty, as tribute. As proof of his worth.

Not for Memonryenne the simple expedient of brute strength, of force. He had loved beauty in all its many guises, and had seen beauty where even the princes of the court could not, it was so subtle.

But in his hands, in his presentation, beauty had been revealed. Some of the host believed that Memonryenne had had no choice; his martial skills could not rival or even equal the most significant of his kin's. But envy did not cling to him. Envy did not define him. He openly said, and pleasantly, that no amount of effort would ever allow him to rise to even the position held by those who served the princes.

Illaraphaniel had never believed this to be the truth. Had Memonryenne desired it, he would have excelled. It was simply not his desire to excel in such a fashion; it was not his focus, not his driving interest. As long as he had work to contribute to the court, and to the White Lady who ruled them all, he was content.

He found beauty in rainfall; found it in spider's webs. Found it in the very young and the very old—mortals, all, some of whom walked on two legs, and some on more. He found beauty in the strength of voice, the brief, frenzied rush of artists, the plaintive cry of the isolated and lonely. The White Lady, in all her glory, could see what Memonryenne revealed, could appreciate it, could feel exalted by it. That was all he needed.

That was all they needed, who were brothers under her banner, soldiers under command, craftsmen and artists whose work was offered first to the White Lady, if it had any merit at all.

Of all his lost, treacherous brothers, it was Memonryenne whose defection, whose betrayal, almost—*almost*—made sense. For Illaraphaniel had seen Allasakar of old, and he knew, as one knows that certain clouds presage storm, that Memonryenne would be almost overwhelmed by the shades and shadows of the beauty of that god.

He, too, had seen the countenance of Allasakar, in the lee of the White Lady. He, too, had been moved—as all who breathe must be moved. But Allasakar was not the White Lady. His presence moved Illaraphaniel. It moved all of the White Lady's people.

Allasakar had come to do the White Lady honor.

They were not yet at war, although war lingered on the edges of any meeting of the powerful. What the god saw in the White Lady was what her kin saw in her. It was what the Arianni saw, and felt in her presence; it was what drove them forward when she was not immediately before their eyes.

That had not been a surprise to any of her people.

It should have been. That was when he and his brethren should have known. They should have seen the future that waited in shadows, growing edges and claws and inevitable fangs. But how could it have occurred to them that those who were not the White Lady's kin could not see her, could not experience her presence as they did, when it was akin to the very air one breathed, the light one saw, the warmth of the sun?

How could they have known that those who were not blessed by the will of creation—her creation—did not experience her presence as they had naturally experienced it for the whole of their existence? What their enemy saw was not what they saw.

But they were the White Lady's.

And he was a god.

The White Lady could stand in defiance of the gods; she was their scion, their equal upon almost any field of battle she chose to walk. Behind her, bright shadows, the proof of her nature, the true measure of a god. Creation: the Arianni. Her chosen people.

Memonryenne was younger than Illaraphaniel; younger than the princes who ruled the court in the absence of the White Lady's beloved sisters. He was oft absent in his many travels, and when he returned to the White Lady's side, he brought gifts to offer her. It was a wonder, even to the princes, for he could bring the most astonishing things to her and also, at the same time, the most mundane.

He once brought a sword that was chipped and scratched, its sheath so plain it was hard not to think of the offering as an insult. But it was that sword that Illaraphaniel remembered most clearly, he who could not forget. The beauty of the blade was not in the blade itself, but the blade's story—and even that was so humble, so plain, it took the length of the telling for the beauty in it to be slowly and completely revealed.

Those who did not know could not see.

She did not judge his gift—she never did. Not until he had finished any of his presentations. But some gifts required no words, no song, no story, they were so clearly items of value and worth. Perhaps that was why it was the memory of the sword that had stayed longest with him. It was not an enchanted blade. It was not the work of an Artisan. It was the work of a mortal, and the core of the blade held true, but the infelicities in its creation were true as well, as if the flaws and the strengths could not be separated, they were so intertwined.

The blade had seen use, as swords will, even the most mundane; it was the life of its bearer that made it, humble in origin, a treasure. And even that life had been mundane, so small, so insignificant in the greater turn of time and season, that it would not have been worthy of note were the tale not told by Memonryenne himself.

He could find true beauty in anything.

He could find that beauty in the enemy, he who now ruled the Hells. Of course he could. But he did not search for the things that stunned the eye and moved the heart as a result: he dove deeper, always; deeper.

Memonryenne's defection alone had seemed so much part of what he had been created to be, that if his treachery could not be forgiven — and it could not—it could be comprehended.

And he was gone.

Gone in the time before the fall of Allasakar, the most powerful of the gods; gone perhaps the moment he had witnessed Allasakar's visage, and heard the song even spoken word made of that god's voice. What he had been born to seek, Memonryenne had found.

And as in all such things, he wished to present that finding as a gift, as a tribute, for the White Lady. What could be more beautiful than the love of the most powerful of gods?

Illaraphaniel's answer: the love of the White Lady.

But it was not Memonryenne's answer. Perhaps, had he been allowed, the world would be different. Had he offered the White Lady her due, had he spun his tale of what he found beneath the surface of a god's countenance, in the depths of that very god, she might have seen in that god what she had seen in that mortal sword.

But Allasakar was like the White Lady in one way: no one of his people could serve two masters. To prize the former was to betray the latter.

Now Memonryenne was gone.

Not gone to the Hells, not gone to grovel at the feet of the Lord of the Hells; he was gone. The wild air knew. The earth knew. Illaraphaniel knew.

And his foe knew. The dead did not die. They returned, ugly, pitiful ghosts, to the side and shade the Lord of the Hells might provide those who truly served him. But these dead would not return.

Asked by any who were not his kin, Illaraphaniel would have dismissed that death in triumph—for it was the fate of traitors. It was the reason those who remained true hunted the demons without mercy, without fail.

But none of his kin would ever ask, for they, like Illaraphaniel, remembered. Every combat with the *Kialli* was an act of raw fury, and every combat, an act of terrible grief. But those moments were the only times they might hear those voices again; it was the only way they might make new memories with those irrevocably lost to them, those ancient, beloved brothers. It was the only acceptable way.

Memonryenne was gone. Truly, irretrievably lost. It was the price paid for daring to set foot upon the hidden lands of the slightest, the wiliest of the gods: what remained of their spirit. What remained of what they had once been. What remained of what they had become. He had been lost to Illaraphaniel the moment he had made his terrible choice; he was now lost to Allasakar as well. The White Lady would not grieve.

But he faced a sundered brother, and that brother would. He would grieve, and rage, and destroy whatever was within his reach. It was not loyalty to Allasakar that drove him, now. It was not loyalty to the White Lady that drove Illaraphaniel.

She had been their lord, their god, but never their comrade, never their brother. She was the sun, the source of warmth, and the source of bitter chill. Summer, Winter, sustaining breath, she was the White Lady.

No god, no matter their power, should ever lay claim to her, for even the hint of claim implied ownership. Could one own the sun? Could one own the vast, vast oceans in distant lands? The peaks of the treacherous mountain chain that had somehow survived the god wars?

Allasakar desired her. Those who had betrayed her desired that she join with Allasakar. For one such as Memonryenne, the god was an eternal gift, an eternal tribute. In the god, he found a beauty that he had never encountered in all his centuries of searching. It was only right, only just, that Allasakar be presented to the White Lady for eternity.

Yes. Memonryenne, had he defected alone, might have been forgiven by all save the White Lady herself. Such forgiveness was not in her. It would never have been expected.

But in death, those who were born of her returned to her. The *Kialli* never would. The god might have severed the White Lady's limbs to lesser effect than the injury done her—done them all—by the betrayal of their kin.

Yet in his fashion, that ancient god paid homage to the White Lady. The *Kialli* were his generals, his wardens, his personal guard: they were the exalted, in their fashion, in the Hells. What the White Lady could not do with the living, he might do with the sundered: they could not escape through death; they returned to his side in the Hells, there to recover the power left them in the sundering itself.

In his fashion, the Lord of the Hells prized the *Kialli*; they were of her, the being he wished to have by his side for eternity. Allasakar had done more injury to the White Lady in the moment of their defection than any foe had ever done.

Her rage, as she, was eternal. Where she had once had many enemies, she now had one. One, and she would do all she could to destroy him. Those who chose to pledge allegiance to their new god were lost to her. They could not return to her side.

Could they, she would have destroyed them. She would destroy them now, were she here. She would order Illaraphaniel, and all his remaining kin, to devote their power and focus on just such destruction.

Meetings such as this were therefore a source of pain and joy, the loss an echo of the greatest of losses, the joy the complete and certain obedience to the White Lady.

But no, that was a lie. The truth would never leave his lips. The joy and pain were twined, always; the demons—dead, departed—had once been his brothers. Some were unrecognizable now, for they had chosen to forget, and their new god had allowed them that mercy. Allasakar was not a god known for his mercy.

But the White Lady was not known for hers, either.

He might destroy the imps, the lesser demons, as one destroyed rats or other vermin. No hint of what they had once been remained.

Not so the *Kialli*. Not so those who had chosen to remember.

Not so, the demon Illaraphaniel now faced: the sundered brother, the only other present who might feel the loss of Memonryenne so deeply, so profoundly. He had heard it, for the wind carried it to his ears.

He had retreated from the field, had chosen prudence, when the demons first appeared; his combat in the forests beyond Hansleigh had injured him enough that blood might fall. Blood in these lands was akin to a vow. An oath. An indenture. But he had heard the truth in the cry of rage and loss: Memonryenne was gone. He would not return to the Hells. He would not return to his sundered brethren.

He would not return to fight those who remained at the White Lady's side.

Illaraphaniel would never see his visage again.

And he would never again see Mordanavelle, who had once been the closest of brothers, who had once been a prince, a firstborn prince, of the White Lady's court. The only bridge that connected them was this: this confrontation, this attempt at destruction.

It was genuine. To destroy the *Kialli* did not destroy them permanently; in the fullness of time, nursing their injuries in the Hells, they would once again return. But not Memonryenne. Not Mordanavelle. They had chosen to surrender even the vestiges of their creation that remained them in order to breach a god's barriers.

Had they succeeded, had they destroyed the circus and survived that destruction, they might have retreated; they might have preserved what remained of their existence.

"Mordanavelle," he said as he stepped forward.

INTO THE STILLNESS, the demon replied. "Illaraphaniel. We should have known that the ragged beggar prince had some hand in this."

His face was the face Illaraphaniel remembered, his voice, the voice that was seared into memories of the past so strong, so visceral, they eclipsed most of his lived reality. Mordanavelle. *Mordanavelle.*

Only two princes of the White Lady's court remained. Illaraphaniel and the youngest, the last of his kind, tied now to mortal realms—if the city of a Sen could be considered such a place. That child would not ride at the Wild Lady's command; he had declared his loyalty to another while she lived.

But the White Lady accepted this. She accepted the necessity of The Terafin. And Celleriant, upon death, would return not to the fabled shores of the Between, but to his maker, to the White Lady.

The *Kialli* would never return. They had died even before the expulsion of Allasakar. They had died, and they had returned not to the White Lady, but to the fell god; they were truly lost. They were the source of the White Lady's bitter, ceaseless fury; to destroy Allasakar, she would surrender almost anything.

All of the Arianni accepted that. All of those who survived. The three to whom Illaraphaniel was closest had returned—at her command—to their creator. She was more powerful for it, but Illaraphaniel was not; he knew he would never see their faces, hear their voices, feel their deep and eternal companionship again.

This was not so different.

He raised sword—he lacked shield, still. But he could see the small chips, the small cracks, in the *Kialli*'s sword, the small absences of the red light that signaled the choice of the lord for whom he raised arms.

This was the last time he would see Mordanavelle's visage in his life. The last time, and he did not intend to waste it. Perhaps he intended to draw it out, to dance with clashing swords as men did in the distant South; to exchange blows in just such a way that death was threatened but never quite actualized.

But no, that was not true. The sword dancers had their mishaps, their accidents, and when they did, blood flowed. Blood would flow here. Illaraphaniel, injured and not fully recovered, and Mordanavelle, injured in a different fashion.

Perhaps, on a different field, Mordanavelle would have fled; the *Kialli* Illaraphaniel had faced in the forests beyond Hansleigh had made that choice, although they had not sacrificed what Mordanavelle had sacrificed. But Mordanavelle accepted, now, that there was no flight afforded to him; he folded his great wings, and even the hint of pinions faded from view.

He stood, silver hair falling down his back, his sword in hand. He faced Illaraphaniel. The sneer left his lips, his eyes, his expression. They might have been young again; they might have been young, and in the keeping of the White Lady and her sisters, learning how to wield the weapons they had newly created.

She would have been there, on her throne; she would have witnessed how well they had taken to the lessons she had attempted to impart. They would have done their best to impress her—youth was like that, even theirs.

Was Mordanavelle a ghost?

The White Lady of their youth was a ghost as well, a haunting that could not be evaded, could not be denied.

As if to acknowledge this, Mordanavelle offered Illaraphaniel a perfect bow. Illaraphaniel returned it. Had Mordanavelle's sword not been so diminished, he would not; he might have taken advantage of that gesture of respect to separate the traitor's head from his shoulders, to send him back to the Hells that he had chosen so long ago.

But that is not where he would now go. Illaraphaniel knew it. Mordanavelle knew it as well. Prince of the court. Duke of the Hells. A brother, lost, and lost again, every small appearance another loss, another opening of a wound that would not, could not, heal while Allasakar ruled the Hells. But it could not be acknowledged in any other way. To do so would be a betrayal of the White Lady.

Nor did Mordanavelle speak of his chosen lord.

He had come at his lord's command. He had come to destroy the circus—and the protections it offered the mortals who took to the roads between the Western kingdoms and the Empire of Essalieyan. Destroy those roads, and one could isolate *Averalaan*, beneath which lay the ancient seat of the lord he now served.

To breach those god-protected lands would require both power and sacrifice.

The Arianni understood sacrifice. They had always understood it. They were of the White Lady; they were attenuated limbs that moved at her will, in her service. All deaths in the fulfillment of the duties she laid across their shoulders were simply a return to the White Lady's heart.

And what of your lands? What of your people?

All of his brothers, all of his servants, his pages, his heralds—all had been born as Illaraphaniel himself had been born, and all, in death, would return to their creator. That had been their truth. Theirs—like this combat, this show of strength and skill—until Allasakar had sundered the Arianni forever.

He did not know how, did not fully understand why.

"We are not a people who spend our time dwelling on our choices, our regrets," Mordanavelle said, as he lifted sword, holding it steady and parallel to his body, an invitation.

Illaraphaniel nodded. "The past cannot be changed." As he spoke, he almost turned to Evayne—once his student, now his nemesis. Evayne, who could walk through time as if navigating through the wilderness. Evayne, whose presence in the past might have offered salvation.

"Had she never felt the pull of our Lord, we would never have been able to leave her." It was a truth that was death to even contemplate— but Mordanavelle's words simply echoed the past. "We were *of* her. We knew, we who chose to follow the god, what her deepest desires were."

"As did we, who did not follow," Illaraphaniel replied, lifting his own sword in an exact replication of Mordanavelle's stance. "Had he come to her court, had he offered to serve, she would have accepted his service."

"He is a god."

"And she is the scion of gods; she has killed gods on the fields of ancient battle—those gods who did not understand her borders and her lands. She would not bend knee to your lord simply because he was a god."

"He was a god who would have loved and exalted her above all others."

"Mordanavelle, let us not trade lies at the end. What love could he offer? What he desired of her, she could never give. What she desired of him, he could never give. She *chose*. And we, her children, her creations, her *people*, could not gainsay the choice she made."

"Yet the desire remained. It was as much a part of her as we ourselves."

"Enough, Mordanavelle. Have you come to talk or fight?"

Mordanavelle's smile should have been full of malice; Illaraphaniel's words were edged with it. But the smile, when it came, was far more of a blow than the sword itself could land: it was exactly the expression he had offered his brothers in the lee of the White Lady's throne.

"We who feel pain feed upon it," Mordanavelle said. "You are making things difficult, Illaraphaniel. I seek the ashes of joy and triumph; I am uncertain what you seek in this place. There is no atonement. You know as well as I. There is no road that we might walk in penitence and desire that might bring us back to her side.

"And even were we to follow such a road, we would be torn, always, by our love for our chosen lord. We believed, should we triumph, that we would bask in His presence — and in hers. They would be one, and we would be at peace."

"You believed that?"

Mordanavelle was silent.

"There will be no peace until your lord is dead. It is the only thing she desires of him, now: his end. His place in the graveyard of the gods. But you must know that: if it is true that your choice reflected some element of her desire, all who made the choice you made on that day took from her any hint of that desire. It is gone, and it will never return.

"Think you that she is divested of her loyal princes? Did you not hear, Mordanavelle? The Lady's sisters now ride as the princes of her court. The three have returned to the Lady; she rides at the head of a host of power that has not been seen since long, long before we were sundered. My absence will hardly be noted."

Mordanavelle stilled. Demons did not require the sustenance of breath or rest; they were not of the living. But even so, the stillness implied a lack of the things that were proof of life.

"Yes. You will never see them. You will not survive." Illaraphaniel shifted the bend of knees, changing the readied stance.

Mordanavelle mirrored the change in stance, and then extended it, knees bent briefly against the pull of gravity and the distant echoes of the earth's rage. It was Summer in the wilderness; Summer, reluctantly accepted by the circus master, had finally come fully to these lands.

Mordanavelle leapt toward Illaraphaniel.

CHAPTER TWENTY-THREE

The circus was a different world.

Stephen had known it before he had even passed through the circus gates, merging with the crowd gathered in the streets outside, waiting entry. Homes and inns were empty, windows shuttered, store-fronts locked; the whole of the town, from outskirts to center, had converged as a very large crowd, waiting, breath held.

He had known it when the circus gates opened and people streamed through them, in anticipation and dread. He had never been part of a crowd this large. No childhood fair, no performance, had ever drawn so many people from their homes. It seemed, before he passed through the entrance, that the tide of visitors was never-ending.

He had known it when he had wandered through circus pavilions, speaking to the circus people who sat behind their tables and stalls, welcoming all of their visitors, no matter how many. He wore a ribbon taken from one of those stalls—as did all his companions.

But the fairgrounds, if unusual, were a variation of something that felt familiar. Hospitality was warm and immediate. Hidden nooks and unusual offerings highlighted the sense that everything might be discovered, if one searched; indeed, it had been hard not to search, echoes of childhood's bright imagination offering hints of future joy. But the pavilions followed the shape and form of fairs Stephen had experienced before. If the customs were different, they were variations of what one might expect as a visitor.

When he emerged from the forest—from Adala's forest—walking behind Adala and Trevor to give them what little privacy remained them, he knew he had stepped into myth, legend, stories so profoundly beyond any hint of his normal life that he felt small, insignificant, uncertain.

Trevor and Adala stopped just beyond the final tree; their hands were clasped. Stephen joined them, Pearl coming to stand—alert and ready—to his right. She wanted to growl, but even she knew better than to make any noise that might attract attention.

Two men stood facing each other, swords raised—one blue, one red, each capturing and shedding the light of lightning or fire. He recognized Meralonne; superficially, the mage had not changed, although he wore mail. The robes of the magi were nowhere in sight. Stephen had seen him thus armored before, but not like this.

Nothing in the visage of the mage was familiar to his eye.

No, Nenyane said.

Nenyane stood, waiting; she was armed, but she was not in motion. Her eyes, unblinking, were turned not to the battlefield but to the two who faced each other in utter silence. Nenyane, for whom sorrow was a matter of pragmatism, had cried at least twice since they had left Maubreche.

She did not weep as she had wept in the halls of the King's palace, but tears fell almost unheeded down her cheeks. She, who had hated demons for the entirety of her life, stood unmoving as she watched the mage.

It made no sense. *Why?*

She did not answer. She had never been good with words; she allowed the emotions that bled through the huntbrother bond to speak for her. Sometimes, it wasn't enough.

Stephen knew that the being who wielded the red sword was *Kialli*. His travels through both Breodanir and the wilderness had made that clear.

He could see two demons standing upon charred ground, their attention caught, as Nenyane's was caught, by the combatants that defined this battleground: Meralonne and a man who might, were it not for red sword, be his brother. Something held them all in thrall: no one lifted weapon or voice, as if the very heart of all war, all battle, was now carried on the shoulders of only these two. Time was not tangible; it made itself known and felt in the passage of seasons, the turn of the sun, the faces of those familiar and loved.

But it seemed to Stephen, caught almost in thrall, that these two, and this field upon which they stood, had weathered so many seasons that he would never experience more than the smallest fraction of their enmity.

He heard their words. He heard their voices.

He would have understood nothing of what they said had Nenyane not been listening, for they spoke a language that was their own. Everyone present seemed to hold breath, as if exhalation would disturb the two; even Stephen, although he was certain simple breathing would pass beneath their notice. The only two things on this field that mattered in this moment were each other.

Illaraphaniel. Mordanavelle. Lords of a shattered court, their history implied by their stillness.

If you betrayed me, this is what would be left me. Nenyane's internal voice was soft. *But even then, I could not feel half of what they now feel. Mordanavelle will perish here. No hint of his voice will remain.*

The Kialli are ghosts, she added. *They are hauntings. They are almost what they once were—and what they will never be again.*

As if the *Kialli* could hear his huntbrother's words, the demon leapt, sword raised, toward the mage. Fire engulfed the demon's blade, the flames almost the color of bright blood. Mordanavelle cast shadows that seemed far larger, far wider, than he himself. The sunlight did not pass through him.

His shadow fell across Meralonne, but Meralonne remained untouched by that darkness. He did not—as he so often did—take to the air to meet his foe there; he waited, sword raised, knees very slightly bent. When he spread his arms, it seemed, for a moment, to be the start of an embrace offered to kin thought lost in ancient wars.

It was not; it was a sweep of brilliant blade. It cut through shadow, separating that darkness from the *Kialli* who seemed to command it.

Only then did the two demons, immobile until that moment, cry out; they began to move toward their commander, their voices raised not in threat but anguish, as if the mage's sweeping blade had cut them, not the shadow.

They did not attack Meralonne. They made no attempt to interfere in that battle. But they moved toward the demon called Mordanavelle. Stephen realized they intended to stand as shields in front of their lord.

If Mordanavelle had issues with this, he said nothing, but Nenyane did not move to intercept them. Gervanno did not move. Evayne did not move.

The circus master, however, turned toward the edge of the forest at Stephen's back. He executed an almost perfect bow. To Adala? To Trevor?

No. Eyes of no color or all color met Stephen's; even at this distance, the gaze of that neat, tidy little man was perfectly visible before he bent at the middle. This bow was not Breodani in form, but its meaning was unmistakable. It was an acknowledgement of debt, a gesture of gratitude. He rose, his gaze sliding from Stephen to Adala.

To Adala, whose flight from the circus had almost doomed it.

"Adala," he said, his voice rising above the sounds of combat and grief, "welcome to the circus. At last." He lifted arm, sweeping it in a half arc that covered the scorched earth, the combatants who bore witness, and the two: Meralonne. Mordanavelle. "It is Summer, child. Summer is the only season you will know in the circus. Come; it is in your hands, now. Welcome the Summer to these lands.

"Welcome the Summer."

Adala stepped forward, her hand still entwined with Trevor's; Trevor, therefore, followed as she moved. She stopped, then. Stopped and slowly retrieved her hand; her fingers, as Trevor's, were white with the tightness of their mutual grip. He did not want to release her.

Stephen placed a staying hand on Trevor's shoulder. He attempted to shrug that hand off; Stephen tightened his grip briefly as Adala's hand fell to her side. She turned to the circus master, and once again began to walk toward him. This time, Trevor could not follow.

He tried, but she lifted a hand, palm out, in his direction—without once looking back. He stopped, then. Stephen moved to stand by his side. He offered no words, but Trevor didn't want them. What he wanted was what the demons wanted, who had rushed to the side of their lord: he wanted to stand between Adala and any who might attack her or injure her.

He wanted to stand between Adala and her chosen fate.

We wouldn't be in this mess if not for Adala.

Stephen said nothing. He watched as Adala walked toward the

circus master. The circus master nodded, and Adala paused on the outer periphery of the shadows that lay across the damaged ground.

He was not surprised when she lifted arms, face, toward the sun, toward the sunlight; was not surprised when she lifted voice in a similar fashion.

He was surprised when her voice filled the clearing, obliterating all other sound. He stood in the shade of tree boughs, Trevor and Pearl at his side. Not even the shade provided by trees could prevent the sun from reaching them: the trees themselves seemed to lift their limbs, as if to reach for the sun. Across their branches, leaves suddenly grew: bright, large, unfurling in a desperate rush to absorb that light, as if that light had been absent for so long, they had all but forgotten its touch.

She sang.

Nenyane had said it was Summer in the wilderness, but it did not touch the circus. Stephen had not understood that until this moment. Had not understood why she was so certain it was Mordanavelle who would perish here, his voice lost forever to a man who had once been his brother.

He understood it now. From beneath blackened, charred earth, grass grew, and wildflowers, in radiant blues, reds, yellows; the shape of the trees that formed borders for this clearing shifted, reaching not just for sunlight but for the sound of her song. Adala stood in this clearing and her voice, the words she sang—words neither Stephen nor his huntbrother understood—spoke of Summer, welcoming that Summer, at last, to the circus lands.

Demonic shadows faded; Mordanavelle could not sustain them. His blade remained a shining red, but he himself seemed to dwindle as Adala sang.

The two demons who had come to serve as shields turned as one toward Adala, crying out in alarm and in a fear-tinged rage.

Only when they moved did Nenyane at last choose to join the fray. The air that did not carry Meralonne carried her when she leapt into its folds. "Anya!" she shouted.

To his surprise, the mage immediately moved to join Nenyane, just as she had when they had chosen to attack the wyverns from the air.

She hates demons, Nenyane offered. No more.

But it was through her power that the demons had come to the Free Towns.

He had seen Anya on their march back to Hansleigh. He had been watchful, nervous; there was something about Anya that defied reason. He did not trust her, and could not, even if he tried. She was unpredictable, and far too powerful to be so; she might kill them all without warning—and without intent.

But Nenyane did not feel the same hesitance, the same apprehension. She felt frustration at times, but no fear. She appreciated Anya for what she was: a mage without parallel. An ally against the demons Nenyane hated so much.

But Nenyane might well survive Anya's petulance. The rest of them wouldn't.

Nenyane took down one of the two almost before the demon turned to face her; Adala's voice eclipsed all sound, all warning that death was approaching. Only Nenyane's shadow, in this new sunlight, this Summer sky, provided warning—and it did not come quickly enough.

Ash was caught in the folds of the wind that supported the hunt-brother and the mage; the second demon leapt clear of the arc of Nenyane's blade. Stephen could almost hear his roar of fury, a discordant note in Adala's song, in Adala's chorus.

He closed his eyes; he could hear voices join Adala's, adding harmony, but never overwhelming her melody—for she was the melody here. She was the heart of the song. At the edge of the clearing, costumes bloody, although no sign of the wounds that had caused that bleeding was evident to the eye, stood the handful of circus performers. They were turned toward Adala, their eyes almost unblinking. None sang. None joined as part of her growing chorus—as if even those who served the circus understood that she was, and must remain, the focus.

Stephen understood why. He saw it in the trees, in the sky, in the way the sunlight changed the shape of falling shadow—for all things living, and even dead, cast shadows in the light. He saw it in the way the burnt and blackened ground beneath Adala's feet grew green and then, as buds unfurled, multi-colored. And fragrant.

The wind that moved around Adala moved at her will—or perhaps not. Perhaps it moved around her because it wanted to be with her; it wanted to join the song she sang, although it had no voice to lift. There was no water here, but the earth stilled entirely beneath her and Stephen thought the flowers that sprang from it and blossomed might be the gift the earth offered her.

He did not understand, but he accepted that. He knew both winter and summer, but not in relation to the wilderness. What he could infer was the joy of the elements in this land—for the wilderness obeyed few rules, and it could be warped at the desire and will of the reigning lord.

It could be home to humans. It could be a place where pavilions offered delight, sustenance, mystery. It could be a land where demons could not walk—but demons were here, regardless.

War.

It no longer seemed like war to Stephen, with the one demon in his silent combat with Meralonne, the other facing Nenyane and Anya. Nenyane had taken down one demon; when Anya shrieked a very possessive *mine*, his huntbrother pulled back, allowing her feet to touch the earth. The demon did not last long; his fire was not a match for Anya's, although Anya did not choose fire as her weapon. No, she chose, of all things, stone: stone rose from the earth in tall, flat walls, encasing the demon before they collapsed together.

Dust billowed from the height of stone.

Only then did Nenyane turn to Stephen; Adala was closer, but Adala, in the moment, was like sun, water, wind; she was like the earth. She was a part of nature, separate from those that merely endured it.

Trevor stood by Stephen; Pearl refused to give way for Nenyane. Nenyane rolled her eyes, but accepted the dog, glancing at Stephen as if to ascertain that he was uninjured before turning her gaze to Gervanno. No, not Gervanno. Evayne.

Evayne, who had brought Nenyane to Maubreche as a child—a child with no memory of the events that had led her to the midnight-robed seer, and no memory of any other person, living or dead. Stephen felt his huntbrother's suspicion; she did not view Evayne as a friend, although in theory it had been Evayne who saved Nenyane's life.

I don't believe it, Nenyane snapped.

She brought you to me, Stephen countered, his internal voice mild, where hers was edged.

That's part of why I don't trust her.

Does that even make sense?

She brought me to you, yes. And you were mine from the moment we met. But it's what she wanted. She doesn't do anything for free.

Stephen said no more. They could discuss this later, when Evayne was once again absent. Or they could avoid discussing it. Stephen considered himself in Evayne's debt—and that was exactly what worried his huntbrother.

She meant for us to find Adala. She meant for us to bring Adala back.

Stephen turned toward Adala again. He accepted Nenyane's words as truth: it was exactly what Evayne had wanted, had intended. It was what the circus master wanted, as well. But given the army of demons that might even now be burning Hansleigh to the ground, it made sense.

He glanced at Trevor. Trevor watched, eyes wide, lips trembling—as if he, too, wanted to join Adala's song, to be part of it for however long she raised voice. The ruby on his hand was glowing; the ruby on Adala's, glowing as well. Hers was more visible, for her arms were raised, her hands open.

Stephen exhaled. Only one demon remained—and Meralonne fought him, now. Meralonne who would tolerate no interference. Trevor was as safe as he could be.

Some instinct made Stephen tap Trevor's shoulder; Trevor did not look at him. The Breodani Hunter gave him a few seconds before he placed a gentle hand between Trevor's shoulder blades, and shoved. This time, Trevor did turn to look, brows lifting.

Stephen nodded in Adala's direction. He opened his mouth, and said, "Join her." He knew the sound wouldn't reach Trevor's ears—it didn't reach Stephen's either. But the movement of lips, slow and deliberate, would.

Don't do that, Nenyane said. But she made no move to stop Trevor as the blacksmith's son stumbled forward. He picked up speed as he moved, his steps becoming more certain. *Why did you tell him to do that?*

Stephen shook his head. He didn't know. But he felt certain that it was necessary.

If Trevor sang, his voice could not be heard. The voices that had joined Adala's to lend her melody the harmony that strengthened it seemed to arise from the elements. If they resented Trevor's intrusion, no sign of that resentment appeared; the wind did not push him away, and the earth did not break beneath his feet.

You can't hear him?

Stephen shook his head. *You can.*

He has a terrible voice.

I don't think she'll care. Adala turned to Trevor as he reached her side. She seemed taller than the man for whom she had been willing to surrender all of her history, but that was the wind—or perhaps the earth. She did not stop singing, but as she faced Trevor, Stephen could see her expression; he almost turned away. But he didn't, because he realized he could hear her song, even though her lips were not moving. She lowered her arms, but the song continued. Trevor opened his, and she leapt toward him; he caught her. Caught her, held her, his arms around her, his chin grazing the top of her head.

The song shifted as they stood entwined. Shifted, but continued, its tone becoming less ebullient.

His gaze was drawn to them, held by them; he was now far enough away that he didn't feel intrusive. Beyond the two, Meralonne's battle continued, and the sounds of clashing swords, swamped at first by Adala's song, became an odd percussion as they could finally be heard.

Love was on this field. Love as duty. Love as sacrifice. Love as yearning, as hope, as despair.

And the detritus of love, the hatred, the pain, the fury, underscored it; it was, perhaps, the fate of love in the wilderness. Adala and Trevor. Meralonne and Mordanavelle—and all of the *Kialli*, all of the dead, fallen brothers.

Yes. Nenyane's voice was soft. *It's why I never wanted to love. This is what love becomes, in the end, among those who have, or seek, power. Your love is different—but it doesn't have to last. Mortals fall in love. Mortals fall out of love. It happens all the time. The ashes of love, the death of it, the betrayal of it almost never consumes the entirety of your beings.*

And yours?

He felt the glimmer of a smile, although it did not reach her lips. *What do you think? I told you—I knew, the first day I met you, that I would be yours until you died. But you aren't like me. You love your parents. You love your irritating brother and his equally irritating huntbrother. You love Alex, Max, and your dogs. You loved the village elders; you cared about the fate of the Maubreche villages. Everywhere you walk, everywhere you meet people, you create new ties and new bindings.*

You do, as well.

No, Stephen. I don't.

What of Gervanno?

What of him?

You care about Gervanno.

Nenyane snorted. *He's an excellent swordsman. Far better than he thinks he is. He respects his blade, even if it's Southern in shape. He understands duty.*

He understands honor. But he's not stupid enough to stand and die when death is all he might achieve.

This was far more praise than Nenyane generally offered anyone.

I think we need him, she said. *I think, where we're going, he'll be useful. I'm not attached to him for any other reason.* As she spoke, she glared at him, daring him to argue.

He didn't. He did not believe her, but argument served no purpose here.

And Meralonne?

Illaraphaniel is different.

He had seen them fight, side by side, in the wilderness on the borders of Bowgren. He understood that the Meralonne he knew and the Illaraphaniel Nenyane *almost* remembered were the same man. He could not fully *feel* that truth. But Nenyane had always seen things Stephen's eyes couldn't.

He's part of the past, she said, although the words were grudging. Nenyane did not speak of the past; how could she when she could not consciously remember? *But I don't love him. What he wants is what we want. He will not harm you, and if it becomes necessary, he will protect you. Even if he and I came into conflict, it wouldn't be like this.*

She turned then.

Anya was done; a fine layer of ash lightened the color of her robes, that was all. But she came to Nenyane's side and remained there, her gaze darting between Adala and the two men who remained in motion upon this battlefield.

The song that had captivated them all quieted; the sounds of clashing swords grew louder. Voices were raised: Meralonne's and the demon's. Nenyane flinched at what she heard; she stiffened, unable now to look away.

———

ALEX AND MAX stood behind Evayne and Gervanno, hands on their weapons. Both remained sheathed. Max noted the two demons when they moved from what was a living, breathing, tableau; he saw Nenyane dispense with one, and the mage, the other. He might have joined them had Alex not lifted a staying hand.

Alex, however, did not look away from Meralonne and his opponent.

Meralonne and Mordanavelle.

They looked alike, to his eyes; had one not wielded the red sword of the *Kialli*, he might have assumed they were brothers, the closest of kin. He thought it now as he watched, for there was, about them, sorrow and rage; no one on this field could interfere. No one dared.

"No, young hunter," the circus master said, although his back remained toward them. "Perhaps you hear what most cannot. They were brothers, once. They will never be so again."

That wasn't the way being brothers worked.

"For you, no. But their death is not your death, and your rage—no matter how intense—is not their rage. In the mists of history, they fought side by side; they traveled in the same host; they claimed the same enemies as their own. They lifted voice in song; they painted, they sculpted, they wrote.

"And they cannot forget what was. They cannot escape what is. If, in the darkest of nights, on the harshest of battlefields, you wonder why the war between the ancients is still, endlessly, being fought, this is your answer. These two, writ large and larger, avatars of the grim hopes of their respective lords.

"This small battle will end here, but the animus that drives it will never end while the White Lady and the Lord of the Hells once again walk the same plane of existence. The war that was once avoided will be fought, finally, in earnest. Watch, child. This is what becomes of love in the wilderness."

Alex had not taken his eyes from the combat. He knew neither of the combatants were mortal. They were not like Alex and Max.

But it took no imagination to feel the tragedy that tinged the entirety of the battlefield, concentrated in Meralonne and the *Kialli*. He could hear Adala's song, had heard it from the moment she had made her way from the opposite edge of the encircling forest. He had seen proof that the wild air, the wild earth, had joined her song; he had watched the branches of all of the trees suddenly unfurl resplendent leaves and small blossoms, as if they were offering the applause of a rapturous crowd.

But he had heard, as well, the sorrow and grief of loss, both experienced and anticipated. He had not understood the language of the song, but words had not been necessary. He watched Trevor join Adala, reach for her; he watched Meralonne and the *Kialli* almost dance in their clash of swords, and he felt, watching, that this was the only way they could reach for each other again. The past could not be changed. The present and future would be consumed in war.

Adala caused Trevor no harm. He did not bleed as they merged in a tight, tremulous embrace. Meralonne and the demon caused each other no harm, but not through lack of trying.

Alex sucked in air, held breath; he knew that Meralonne should not, could not, bleed here. Knew it but felt, as he watched, that actual blood didn't matter; in every possible way, he was bleeding out on this field. He, and the demon—which Alex had not expected. Rage, yes. Cruelty, yes. But this pain, this cry from the heart he would have sworn demons could not have, was not what he could have imagined.

Max was seldom moved to tears. They found Alex more easily. Max placed a hand on his brother's shoulder from behind, but offered no words. What Alex saw, what Alex heard, Max heard only through his brother. Max, pragmatic, understood that the threat they faced did not end until the demon was dead. It was the only thing that mattered.

Alex exhaled. Max was right. It was the only thing that mattered.

But it wasn't the only thing that could be felt or seen, and the emotions that were so clear they almost felt elemental were, to Alex, the reason for this coming war. He could not put that into words, and didn't try, because Max was right. What had started this war could not be mended; there was no moment in any future in which this love and pain and hatred could ever be repaired. One side would die. One side would not.

He leaned into Max's hand for a moment.

You won't have to say goodbye to me.

Alex nodded.

You'll never have to kill me. They're not like us.

But they must have thought they would be. They must have believed in forever. Trevor. Adala. Meralonne and his foe.

Alex. Alex.

He shook himself.

It's raining.

It was. Alex hadn't noticed. His gaze drifted to the two villagers whose flight had almost doomed Hansleigh and its circus. But it was caught, again and again, by the two who fought; the flash of swords, the grace of movements, the *speed* of them. He believed what Max believed: they would never be like these two.

But he was certain that the two who fought had believed that just as certainly, just as completely, in a world so different it could barely be comprehended. The wilderness endured, but it was not the place in which loyalty and love had been both forged and shattered; it would never be that place again.

And they knew it, who fought so ferociously in the attenuated echo of what had once been home and youth and belief: belief in each other. Belief in the lord they served.

Alex thought, watching them, that he would have done anything — anything at all — to avoid what they now sought: the death of a person they had loved beyond measure. He did not believe he could ever face Max — regardless of Max's crime — as Meralonne now faced his foe.

Stop.

Sorry. I just — He turned away, dragging his gaze back to Adala and Trevor, whose fate he *could* imagine sharing. It was not a lack of love that bound them; not a lack of belief in each other. It was the immediacy of the duty Adala had tried to escape, and had returned to accept. It was an expression of love. Trevor would be safe in Hansleigh. Hansleigh would be safe. All that it demanded of them was each other.

He heard the moment combat stilled, for the sounds had grown louder, larger, as Adala at last fell silent. The sounds of battle, harsh, uneven percussion, rushed in to fill the vacuum her silence created.

It did not last long. Max watched. Alex turned away. He made no attempt to watch the combat to its end. Max did because, if Meralonne fell, the demon he faced would become their problem — all of the people gathered here, bearing silent witness, swords in abeyance as if Meralonne himself had commanded it.

But Alex didn't doubt the outcome. He felt no fear. His throat was thick, his tears too sparse to free him from the pain he could not put into words.

NENYANE KNEW. She watched Illaraphaniel, as she had watched him so often before. She could not clearly remember, could not draw memories from that sense of certainty: this was something she had seen before. It had never been like this.

Demons were ghosts, a terrible haunting. They could be destroyed, their borrowed bodies reduced in an instant to ash — but they returned, time and again, their power diminished by defeat. She understood on a visceral level that this one would never return again. Illaraphaniel had the endless memories of his kin, but so, too, the *Kialli*, for they were lords because they had not chosen to deny the truth of their lost lives, their lost past.

Loss defined them.

Betrayal defined them.

And a terrible rage and resentment, a yearning that could not be quenched while they existed. The Lord of the Hells had never been kind. The *Kialli*—indeed, all of the demon-kin—survived on the pain of the dead and the dying. Fear fed them; fear made them stronger, both metaphorically and literally.

Here, there was no fear. Not from Nenyane. Not from Anya. Not from the circus people and their very strange god.

Only Illaraphaniel, she thought. But it was not his end that he feared. It was, as it had always been, the Lady and her bitter disapproval. He lived in exile. He could not return home while the *Kialli* and their lord existed. She thought he would never again step foot in the White Lady's court.

But watching this last meeting between two who had been princes of that Lady's court, she thought his rage drenched now by sorrow: he would never see Mordanavelle again, even blackened and discarded as he had become. She hated love.

Don't.

She hated what it became. She had seen it over and over: this pain, this desire, the certain sense of betrayal that never quite destroyed the kernel of that loss. He would destroy Mordanavelle here, and he would never hear even the echo of his brother's voice again.

He should have been triumphant. He should have been exultant, for Mordanavelle was a power, and had always been a power.

But when his sword at last shattered the *Kialli* blade, cracked and dimmed by the sacrifice demanded of the *Kialli* to breach this hallowed ground, when Winter truly departed from this small patch of wilderness in the vastness of the hidden, wild world, there was no triumph in his voice.

She shut Stephen out, then. She shut him out because she could hear Illaraphaniel's terrible lament, and if he adorned it with words, this was the only privacy she could offer him. The Breodani would not understand what Illaraphaniel said. Gervanno would not. Even Anya would hear syllables that failed to coalesce into words.

The fox would, but he was of the wilderness, his youth and Illaraphaniel's abandoned in the same distant glory. The fox would not speak
of it. The fox, if he mentioned it at all, would simply note that Illaraphaniel had triumphed. But he would not do it now.

She herself barely understood the first word Illaraphaniel spoke,
for he did not simply speak it: his voice was wild and terrible, the
sound of deadly storm across the open sea, a thing that threatened to
overwhelm all who stood in this clearing. Adala's voice no longer held
the elements in thrall, and the wind roared in response, becoming part
of what Nenyane barely recognized as the syllables of a name.

No. Two names. Two.

She hated love. She hated what it did to people. She hated what she
was almost certain it had done to her. And she wept, as she knew she
would. She made no move toward Illaraphaniel. She thought no one
would; she thought the wind and its storm would carry him far away
from the field of battle and the remnants of ash and the certainty that
here, finally, death had come for this long-lost brother.

She understood hatred, but not as Illaraphaniel experienced it; his
hatred was a scar, and it would never leave him, because it had been
built on the fundaments of the love that had come before it, blossoming
with the bitter sustenance of betrayal and rage.

She did not expect that the wild wind would carry, to Illaraphaniel,
the imperial bard. The bard had not been any part of the ceremony in
this isolated stretch of circus lands; Nenyane had assumed he was
calming panicked crowds of people, waiting for the circus performance
to finally open.

But the wind knew Kallandras. It whipped the hair from the bard's
face, pulling it far enough back that Nenyane could clearly see the
pallor of his face, his skin, his grim expression. He did not speak; he
made no attempt to sing. But he held his lute in one hand as he flew in
a tightening series of concentric circles, coming to a stop only as his
feet touched the ground.

Illaraphaniel did not move at all, although the wind caught his hair,
its touch far more reverent than it had been for the bard. They stood,
bard and mage, less than an arm's length apart. It was clear why
Kallandras had kept lute in hand. His voice had not been heard in this
small clearing; it had not carried from the streets upon which pavilions
stood.

It was not heard now. The strains of the lute carried, and the bard's lips moved, his eyes narrowed, his brow creased. But the song he sang was meant for one man: Illaraphaniel.

He stood as the sound reached him; the wind gentled as he put up his blade. It vanished, fading from view although Nenyane could feel its lingering presence; it was in the earth upon which the mage stood; it was in the wind that whirled around him. It was in the odd droop of spring leaves across all of the branches of visible trees; a circle of respect and perhaps of similar grief, for the trees, rooted longest in the wilderness and wakened slowly to voice, might remember Illaraphaniel's distant youth.

If they did, they would know his loss; they would echo it. The White Lady's people had long been welcome in any lands in which such trees grew. Mordanavelle would be known to them, just as Illaraphaniel was known. They would mourn, building silent, brilliant bridges of their grief.

What comfort could be offered, now?

But thinking that, she turned, at last, toward Stephen. Comfort, like love, wasn't *necessary*. It changed *nothing*.

He looked up and she realized that she had, without thought, reached for him. His smile was careworn, tinged with the grief that was now silent as it permeated those who bore witness. The wind lifted her, far more gentle than it had been with Kallandras; she stepped, as she so often did, into its familiar folds. It carried her to Stephen, and set her down, just as it had set Kallandras down: a spiral of aerial motion that ended with her feet on the ground.

Stephen had never been as reserved as Nenyane. He opened his arms, reaching for her; she did not hesitate. Later, she might hate that fact. Now, she walked into his arms. She felt that she could breathe only when they closed around her; he was warm. He was Stephen.

He was alive.

He was *alive*. He was real. She would never betray him. She would never lose him. She felt his worry, felt his attention slide from Adala, from Illaraphaniel. It felt almost familiar. She wondered if memories were actually valuable. There was a wall between Nenyane and her past—but the terrible, shattering grief she had felt when she had seen the statue in the Queen's gallery, the public gallery, had settled into her, and she could not shake it loose.

Was her loss an echo of Illaraphaniel's loss?

Would her grief wake the wilderness?

No. She would not suffer loss again. Not while Stephen lived. But fear whispered as she dropped forehead toward him: he would die. This was *war*. He would die, and she would be left alone.

She wished she had been allowed — by Stephen — to make the hunt-brother's oath. They had argued in the distant past; she had returned to that argument several times. Stephen had been a wall.

He was a wall now. *The only time the oath matters is during the Sacred Hunt. You can't make an oath to die in my stead in any other circumstance. And it is not Breodan we face, or will face.*

She found no words, no verbal argument.

Stephen understood what she wanted: guaranteed death for her failure to protect him. Guaranteed death, so that she might be doomed to follow in his footsteps should he die first. Maybe this had always been what she wanted. Maybe it was what she hoped the oath — which he would not suffer her to swear — would achieve.

Maybe she'd always intended to offer a far more all-encompassing oath to Bredan, because if the god accepted it, she would be free.

Free.

Free to die if Stephen died. She had not said this to him — not in any of their arguments. She'd argued practicality: he could not become the Hunter Lord he was clearly qualified to become if he wouldn't allow her to swear an oath she *wanted* to swear. But he had always rejected the pragmatism she felt she offered. He'd refused to let her do what she wanted.

An oath between two people has to be wanted by both of them.

It was my oath to make.

He didn't argue that. He didn't argue anything else. *I won't walk to my death. I won't just accept it.* He did not promise not to die. Even had he offered to swear that he would not die, Bredan would not have accepted the oath. The god, Stephen's father, might accept the sincerity of the intent — but Bredan did not accept oaths that were, at their very core, impossible to uphold.

She knew. She knew that the oath she meant to swear *would be* accepted.

Stephen said nothing, but held on to her, as if to prove he was real: alive, breathing, his injuries so minor they might not have existed at all.

This was all she could have. It was the only comfort, the only response, to the fear that she felt as a mortal wound if she thought about it at all. She struggled to leave thoughts of it behind. They weren't practical. She didn't need them.

She hated love because love led to fear and loss.

And she could not live without it. Just one person's. Just one.

WHEN MERALONNE MOVED AT LAST, he offered Kallandras a deliberate—and deep—bow. He then turned to the fox. "Eldest."

The fox had diminished during the duel and the aftermath; he was once again small, delicate, and golden. He lifted his head, his ears twitching. "Illaraphaniel," he said. "I am no longer in your debt."

"You never were, Eldest."

"That is not the way of the wilderness."

"Is it not? The decision was mine, and it remains mine."

The fox sniffed. "You are injured."

Meralonne nodded. "Not all wounds heal well. But I appreciate your concern." He turned to Kallandras. "I am in your debt."

Kallandras smiled; it was a practiced smile, one offered to an audience, even if that audience was a single man. "The Eldest speaks of the way of the wilderness, but I am not of the wilderness."

Meralonne nodded. Kallandras assessed his pallor as he stood unbowed; the robes of the magi, and its medallion, once again enclosing him in a semblance of the humanity he would never quite reach. Averalaan had never been his home.

But even those places one rested and occupied were almost organic in one way: they grew roots around your still feet and, in time, those roots, persistent, slender, worked their way in. Kallandras traveled often at the behest of Kings and bardmaster; it was not simply to fulfill his obligations that he obeyed their orders.

On the road, he could not become settled within the confines of Senniel. In Senniel, there were moments of time, now, when the pain of loss—the loss of brothers, the loss of the only home he desired—did not haunt him. But when he was forced to stand against his chosen kin, all of that loss and pain returned. It did not stay his hand. It could not. To justify his betrayal, he had to continue to follow the road he had only barely chosen. To walk to its end. To face the final battle. Then, perhaps, they would understand. But perhaps not. They were brothers and men, as he had once been, and his hope, his determination, was his own, not theirs.

It was to preserve the brotherhood that he had embarked on this path in his youth.

It was not so for Meralonne. Meralonne's service to the White Lady had never faltered. He had failed her, but she had not seen fit to take from him the power that had been granted him at his birth. And the brothers to whom he had been closest were gone; they had returned to the Lady at her command.

He served her regardless. Kallandras had revered his Dark Lady, but he had loved his brothers. It was not to prove his unyielding loyalty to the Dark Lady that he had made his choice.

Perhaps, for Meralonne, there would be. In the lee of the final battle, should he survive it, he might return, at last, to the only home he had ever desired: the White Lady's court. The White Lady's host. For Kallandras, there was no going back. There were no doors that would open, no brothers that would welcome him home. He had betrayed the Dark Lady. He had betrayed—and even killed—his brothers.

But they would all perish—all—if the Lord of the Hells at last claimed rulership of this world. He was not a sentimental man. To kill one or two to save many was a calculation he had made for most of his life. It had been long enough that, were it not for the hints of their voices, he might have forgotten the pain of his choice. Because pain or no, the choice had been made. It had already been made, and could not be undone.

It could be justified only if the Lord of the Hells perished.

He exhaled slowly, the hidden sound of his song fading into folds of wild wind. When he lifted his head, he found the mage's gaze upon him, eyes the color of burnished silver, strands of hair in play in a breeze that touched only these two: Kallandras. Meralonne.

Illaraphaniel.

He heard the name of the *Kialli* in the air as it stilled, as if the name must be swallowed, devoured, and forgotten. The wilderness had ever been unforgiving of betrayal.

They had an enemy in common, which made them allies. They had a loss in common. Both were bridges, but one was not a bridge they desired to cross often. Today, they met in its center. The battle, for now, was done. Yet neither turned away, neither retreated.

Kallandras had been asked to play at funerals before. The funereal customs of many kingdoms, the Empire and the Dominion, were familiar to him. He understood loss, grief, rage, and also the quiet, smug satisfaction that arose when the dead person was not genuinely missed. He seldom interacted with any of it; his role at funerals was to provide music, wordless music, which lay the foundation of the tone the mourners wished to set.

Often, while he played, the notes of his lute so soft they could barely be heard, people would speak of the dead. They would offer anecdotes, they would laugh—sometimes while crying, as if to deny the finality of death. Ah, no. As if those memories, kept alive while the mourners lived, were the only defiance against death they could offer. Proof that joy had once existed, that in its future desolate absence, those memories would be a comfort and a shield.

He did not believe it.

Could not believe it, who could not speak of those lost brothers. They served the Dark Lady. They killed those she commanded be killed. They were assassins; they were not meant to be a font of joy. Proof of their existence was in the pain of loss, the pain of absence, left in the wake of their work.

To speak of them was to revisit that loss, in all its nuance. It was to risk self-justification, to dream of the day when he might explain his terrible choice, to hope—and all hope was a cliff over which he must, no doubt, step—for forgiveness. For absolution.

He did not do it.

To his brothers, he was the equivalent of the *Kialli*. He was the traitor. His was the life they longed to end, in service of the Dark Lady and their vows to her.

Pain was a bridge, but it could not be crossed.

Meralonne frowned, studying the amiable lines of the bard's face for a long moment before he lifted a hand. "Will you join me, Master Bard? I overtaxed myself in order to stand on this field; it is done, and I would be away. It is no longer safe for one such as I. If I understand what has happened, the circus performance—lauded, and much anticipated—is about to begin." He glanced at the circus master, who nodded.

"I do not intend to remain, but perhaps you would prefer to join your companions? I have been assured that the performance itself is worthy of the wait."

Kallandras stilled.

"I will not speak of war or death. I will not speak of life. I remember every moment, should I so choose, of the life I lived with my brothers before the intervention of the Lord of the Hells; they are no comfort to me. No more would the memory of a fabled vase, a work of art be, that has been shattered. What is left is merely a weapon, should I risk lifting a naked shard as if it were a dagger.

"But I desire my pipe. If pipe smoke offends you, feel free to remain here."

The wind moved. Kallandras made no attempt to cajole it or wheedle it; it was there at Meralonne's command, and the wild wind had never, to Kallandras's knowledge, defied the mage. It seemed to anticipate his needs, to flow into them, lifting Nenyane of Maubreche into the heart of the sky the wyverns covered. He had seen that much from the streets of the circus, beyond this sacred dell.

He was not surprised when the wind gently lifted him from the earth. Meralonne had no intention of walking out of the circus bounds. Kallandras had no desire to do so either; his face felt almost frozen in the pleasant amiable expression he wore when the battle he faced was metaphorical—the banishment of terror and its lesser cousin, fear.

He would never have to calm Meralonne in a like fashion. Never have to assert a confident warmth, a gentle affection, he did not feel. The wind brushed hair far more gently from his face, as if it approved of his silent decision.

Together, the two rose into the clear, amethyst sky, the circus becoming smaller and smaller as the air contained and carried them, the air becoming far colder.

He closed his eyes.

"ADALA."

The voice came from behind, although she heard it as if it surrounded her. It was the circus master's voice. She tightened her hold on Trevor, shaking. It was not just the anticipation of parting, of goodbye; her knees trembled. They would not support her.

"You don't want to kill him." This voice was a normal voice; the reverberation caused by the voice of the circus master—the lord—was absent. She recognized the speaker and lifted head, turning to face her. Anya.

What surprised her most was the subtle tinge of gold in the air around the mage. The mage who had seen and known that Adala was, as she had put it, circus. "You're from the townships," she said. Even had Anya not replied, she could see the truth of that connection in the hint of warm light that infused the mage.

Anya smiled. "I don't live there anymore."

No, she couldn't. Adala had heard stories about ancient mages and the power they wielded; she had sat, knees folded, listening intently in the space created by her father and the end of the day, when work had been done and he had time to spare before it once again caught him in its demands. Anya in reality was far more powerful than those faded, ancient stories—as if the truth of Anya could not be contained in words simple enough to pass on to children.

Anya's expression lost warmth as she looked at Trevor. Trevor, whose face was tear-stained, just as Adala's must be. He was pale, almost grim, his lips and face set in an expression she had never seen before. "You don't want me to kill him."

"No! No, Anya, I don't. I would never, ever want that." It was hard not to speak to this mage as if she were a younger sibling, not an elder one. Adala's mother might be older than Anya, but if so, not by very much, and Adala suspected that she was, in fact, younger.

"Why?"

"Because I love him."

"But he's going away."

Adala sucked in air; it made a sharp, almost cutting sound. "No."

"No?"

She shook her head. "It's me, Anya. I'm going away. Trevor will stay in Hansleigh." She swallowed. "I'm the one who's leaving."

"*Aдala.*" The circus master's voice echoed. She felt her name as a physical sensation, almost a tug. She lowered her arms, releasing Trevor; his arms didn't follow. The air against the absence of Trevor felt cold. But the air came to tug at and tease her hair. She did not sing, but the earth beneath her feet did, softly, gently.

She looked past Anya to see the circus master, and froze there, understanding instantly what she saw: the lord of the circus. The god of man. He had been a small, tidy man, in his dark, odd clothing; she could see the outline of that uniform, but it was blurred, inexact—far too small to ever contain him.

"Adala," Anya said, her voice far thinner.

Adala swallowed. To ignore Anya courted destruction, the aftereffect of the mage's rage. To ignore the god, however, was impossible.

Katie came to her rescue. Trevor released her, letting go of the warmth of contact, and knowing—as Adala knew—that it was not for now, but forever. He did not leave her side. But he did not see the circus master as she now did. He couldn't. He wasn't of the circus. At any other time, she might have resented it, might have pleaded with the circus master to allow Trevor to join them.

But Trevor was town, not circus. She could see that so clearly. The circus would not hear him. The elements would not notice him. And the god would not make demands of him.

"My lord is calling," Adala told Anya. "I'm so new here, I don't want to get in trouble." This was only partly true, but she leaned into the truth; it was a skill that she'd honed in the inn. Lies only worked if you believed they were true, or that some part of them was.

Anya was only slightly mollified, but she let Adala walk toward her god.

Adala felt no deep attachment, no overwhelming respect, no awe. Not at a distance. But she heard the wilderness in the circus master's voice, and understood the reverence the wilderness offered him; he was part of it. And she, too, was part of it, now. She glanced at Trevor; the circus master had not commanded Trevor to keep his distance, for which she was grateful.

He caught her hand, loose by her side, and tightened his fingers around hers, offering her silent support. Support, but nothing else. What he wanted to give could no longer be given. Could never have been given, because she was, she had always been, circus. She had not accepted that truth until the demons came. She accepted it now.

Was it choice, then? Was it always her choice? She shook her head. She'd made her choice. And she unmade it, understanding in the end that Trevor could not live with that decision. Might not survive it. The fact that she might have died on the edge of Hansleigh, the edge of the circus lands, had not mattered. It didn't matter now.

To protect everything, she had to lose everything.

This, then, was what remained: the wilderness, its song, its deceptively quiet power. And the circus master, ruler of them all. She was grateful that he no longer looked human to her eyes; had he, the choice might have felt like betrayal.

As if he could hear the thought, Trevor tightened his hand briefly. But even Trevor did not speak.

"Come, Adala. The performance is about to start."

Anya caught up with Adala, falling into step on the other side. She avoided Trevor. Adala didn't understand her animosity, but it didn't matter. She would not kill Trevor here. The circus master would not allow it.

"You want me to join the performance?" She couldn't keep the note of incredulity out of her voice, and didn't try. She knew—from the townspeople whose children had been called to the circus—that those newly come didn't perform in front of the families from whom they would be separated forever. That was the common wisdom.

"Yes. Summer has come to the circus, and the voice it heard was yours. You are the turning of the season." Something in his voice felt off, felt wrong.

"Is Summer bad?"

"No. No, Adala, it is not. We have endured the long, long Winter, and much of the wilderness has slept, surrendering even the hope of Summer."

"But not here."

"No, not here. I am lord of these lands. The wilderness here is mine, Winter or Summer. But I, too, am old. To endure the harsh Winter, I built the circus and sustained it."

She was silent as the import of words, of tone, of the many, many voices she could hear speaking in concert, syllable by syllable, conveyed something akin to regret. She did not understand.

"No. No, you do not. The wilderness, even those parts that gods might claim as their own, has rules that were created, upheld, desired by those who are now long gone. The circus was birthed in the long Winter. I do not know what Summer portends; I hoped for Summer. Summer is not the season of the fallen and the dead. But even to one such as I, Summer was a yearning, a hope. It was not real.

"Now, it is. I have done what I can to alter the foundations of the circus in the shadows Summer casts; I do not know if such alterations will hold."

Adala understood. Summer was an end to Winter; in the townships, spring heralded that ending. Winter was a fact of life, but it was something to be endured. Festivals that celebrated its opposite,

Summer, were anticipated with gratitude and joy, especially when the winter had been harsh.

The circus pavilions did not exist in the winter of Adala's life in the town. On rare occasions, the circus gates opened during the winter, and the towns very gratefully gathered their citizens and ushered them through, where they might know respite from the harshest of storms. No one would have said that Winter was the foundation of the circus.

The god gestured, and the trees that had lined the clearing in which battle was fought shifted in place; those whose hearts were protected by trunk and bark emerged at his silent command.

"Trevor, I must ask you to release Adala's hand now. She must join our performers, and you must join their audience."

Adala shook her hand free first. The edge of command was so clear to her, she knew she would not have been able to maintain her grip had the circus master commanded her instead.

"I want to go, too," Anya said, a slight whine in her words. Her voice shook, but that made sense. The mage was speaking to a god, and Anya knew it. Trevor, Adala thought, didn't.

"You are of the towns," the circus master replied. "But you are not of the circus. You may, of course, join the audience—but you cannot join Adala."

"I *want to go*," Anya replied. Her voice was quieter, but it was more intense. Less whiny. Adala had never considered whining to be a good thing. But in Anya, it was better.

"Anya," the god said.

"I can help. I can help her. I can help the performance. I *can*."

It was Katie who came to the rescue; the circus master, whose word was law, did not choose to speak. Adala did not speak, either; she was afraid to say *no*. She was afraid of what Anya would do.

Katie was not. She caught Anya by the hand and smiled, her touch and expression gentle. Katie was made of steel, cloaked in flesh; she was of an age with Anya, physically. But if Anya was far younger than her physical age implied, Katie was far older. Some people emptied out as they aged; they became hollow, looking back over their shoulder at a youth growing distant with the march of days.

And some, their youthful edges smoothed down on the shoals of experience, remained rocks—more wise, more approachable, more safe. Wisdom became their power, their core. Katie knew that Anya wasn't quite right. But her expression, careworn, was gentle and affectionate. "Won't you come with me instead? It's been a long time since I've seen you, and we'll only have time to talk while the circus is open."

Anya hesitated, clearly torn. She turned back to Adala, an obvious expression of guilt on her face. It came to Adala then that Anya was worried *for her*. In her own fashion, she was trying to be helpful. Angering a god would never be helpful, but Adala didn't say that. Instead, she smiled in what she hoped was a good imitation of Katie.

"Go with Katie. She doesn't get to see her friends often. I'll be fine. And maybe you'll be able to see me if Katie's also watching."

Katie slid her arm around Anya's shoulders as Adala spoke, and very gently walked her away.

Only when she had passed through the gate that led to the public parts of the circus, did one of the circus people join them. He whistled. "I had no idea Katie could talk in anything less than an angry bark."

"Enough, Carrick," the circus master said. "You are set to perform and the main theatre is now allowing our guests to finally enter the heart of your domain."

Carrick grinned, which surprised Adala. But he turned to her and said, "You'd best follow me. We're expected to put on a show that will justify the delay."

CHAPTER TWENTY-FOUR

Gervanno sheathed sword only when Nenyane joined the Northern Widan. He glanced back; the seer of midnight robes and violet eyes remained, unmoving, as she observed the sword master. He was surprised when she turned head to face him. Her face, as her robes, evoked midnight—but without the color and the moving hem that implied a much stronger gale than existed in this clearing.

"I cannot remain. I would see the circus perform, if I could—but if I take a step I will walk into either the future or the past, as I must.

"The circus is not the first place I have met you—it is the first time you have met me." This made little sense to Gervanno; his first thought was that he had met, and forgotten, her. But if she dressed as she dressed now, he could not imagine that: he had a good memory for encounters that implied threat or present danger. "Do not be surprised if I return to you robbed of years and the power that comes from them.

"You will walk this road to the end. I offer you unasked-for advice in return for the favor you have done me in finding, and returning, Adala to her home, and as all unasked-for advice, you may not find it welcome. Be wary, in as much as you are given the opportunity, of the elder who chooses to walk the wilderness as a fox."

"I can hear you," the fox said, his voice lower and louder than his form suggested it could be.

"Indeed, Eldest. I mean no disrespect."

"And as oft happens when someone speaks of intent, you are disrespectful regardless."

"It is not you I question," Evayne replied. Her tone was neutral, but her eyes, narrowed.

"No doubt it is me, if I may flatter myself." Jarven ATerafin joined the fox, appearing, as was his wont, from thin air. "I will offer no reassurance, as I perceive it to be a waste of your time. But I mean no harm to Gervanno."

Evayne glanced in Jarven's direction, but it was brief. Gervanno might have warned her that this was unwise, but did not. The moment he had survived the demonic attack that had destroyed the caravan, he had stepped into a world in which rules, common sense, prior experience, held little sway.

He trusted his sword; that skill had not deserted him. But Nenyane existed in this new, this unsettling, world. And men like Jarven existed here as well. Jarven had gained mysterious Widan powers, but at heart he was an ambitious man, and ambition reached, always, for power.

"Jarven," the fox said, his voice couched in the same low growl he had offered Evayne.

Jarven offered his master a bow. He then knelt to offer the fox his perch. The fox, however, ambled over to Gervanno, and therefore closer to Evayne. "Child," he said to the seer, pausing once to glare up at Gervanno in silent command. Gervanno knew that offering the fox his arm as a perch would offend Jarven. Offending Jarven was less of a danger—in this moment—than offending the elder. He knelt. The fox lightly clambered into his arms, and Gervanno rose once again.

"Eldest, you are not a denizen—or guest—of one of the mortal towns. You will not be able to enter the tent in which the circus will perform," Evayne told the fox. "And if Gervanno carries you, he will miss it as well."

"And an exception cannot be made?" The fox swiveled to meet the gaze of the circus master. As was his wont, he had remained silent.

"Even were you to swear loyalty to me—and you have sworn your oath to a different lord—the circus would be far too tame, far too slight, to contain even a tenth of your roots, Eldest. Exceptions will not be made; I have already denied Illaraphaniel that permission."

The fox sniffed; he had received the answer he expected. "Then Gervanno will have to miss the performance. I am weary of this place

—which, I point out, I troubled myself to defend when you, who rule, would not."

The circus master smiled. "Is that how you see it, Eldest?"

The fox's whiskers twitched. "Gervanno," he said. "We are leaving."

Gervanno's curiosity about the performance was not great enough that he wished to offend the eldest.

"Eldest," Evayne said, pulling the fox's attention from the circus master. "I am grateful for your intervention."

"I do not consider unasked-for advice to be a suitable reward," the fox told her.

"It is not advice, Eldest. I am mortal—how can I offer advice to one of your stature? Were you not concerned with mortals at all, I would not so much as trouble you with my words." Gervanno did not flinch or grimace; he allowed no physical expression of surprise to change his hold on the fox.

The fox, however, found nothing offensive in either word or tone. Gervanno would have to remember that in future—should he ever be required to guard lords of power in his homeland again. Evayne's sarcasm was not subtle, to the cerdan's ear. It was invisible to the fox.

Jarven's lips twitched, no more.

"Your interest in mortals at this time is well understood—but Eldest, mortals are not creatures who are born to roots, or of them. You, who were young when the world was young, are not invulnerable, although an eternity awaits you should you be cautious."

The fox tilted head to his left. "You believe there is danger to me, then?"

"An ocean cannot travel safely through the bed of a small stream," she replied. "But the small stream might run, in the end, toward the ocean." She then offered the fox a deep, and deeply respectful, bow. Her words did not quite make sense to Gervanno—but it was not his duty to make sense of the words of the powerful, unless those words conveyed military orders. Even then, he might question them to make certain that he understood those orders clearly—and only those orders.

The fox exhaled. "You wish me to relieve Gervanno of this partic-ular duty."

Evayne did not answer. Not precisely. "I would offer you my own arms in his stead, but where I walk, no others have ever been able to follow."

"Almost, you challenge me, child. But you have reminded me that my Lord is Sen, and her time in the mortal world will draw swiftly to a close. I will release Gervanno for now. He has never spent time in the court of a god—and perhaps he will have memories of these moments when the war is at last over." His whiskers twitched. "Well, what are you waiting for?"

Gervanno knelt, and very carefully set the fox down. "Your permission, Eldest," he said, with clear respect.

The fox rolled eyes.

"I would not be here at all were it not for your intervention."

The fox nodded; Gervanno had not yet risen.

"I am grateful for that intervention. I do not know which lord ruled the land in which I would have been lost—but I was not lost because you led me back to the world in which I have lived all my life."

"And you met the person you would follow across any battlefield."

Gervanno nodded.

"And that person is not me."

Gervanno's gaze fell to the ground at the fox's feet.

"Do not annoy me by attempting to find excuses you believe might mollify me. I know you well enough to know that your loyalty, once given, remains. You are not one who considers alliances of convenience because you have very little personal ambition. You do not follow her because you wish to gain advantage."

Gervanno lifted head. "She is, without doubt, the best swordsman I have ever encountered. She is the best I will ever encounter, even should I live as long as you have. If I lacked personal ambition, it would not matter. But it does. If I travel with her, if I spar with her, if I observe her, I may, myself, improve."

"That," the fox asked, a fondness in his tone, "is not what we consider ambition, who have survived in the wilderness for so long. My cub is ambitious."

"Tell me, Eldest, what would ambition achieve? He might become more personally powerful. Were I to become more personally powerful, I do not believe I would change."

"Nor do I. It is a conundrum, for one such as I. You are not absent ambition within your own context; I hear it in your voice at times, it is so bright. But it is highly unusual, in my experience. It is my suspicion that you will attend the circus performance, and you will find very little that moves you in the fashion your more mundane travels with the god-born has.

"You are, as you said, in my debt. The weight of a second debt — the defense of this small grove — will not be laid across your shoulders."

Gervanno bowed head again, but spoke. "The acceptance and acknowledgement of debt is never solely in the hands of the benefactor. You may feel that you are owed nothing for that act of generosity; you will not demand acknowledgement or repayment. But honor demands that the risk you chose to take on our behalf be repaid with respect, at the very least."

"You are dangerously bold, child, if you believe that I took a *risk*." The fox sniffed and turned away, hitting Gervanno's nose with the tip of a tail. Gervanno did not understand the creatures of the wilderness, but he understood the undercurrents of emotion in the powerful; the fox was not displeased.

He rose only when the fox turned his back.

To Evayne he said, "I will remember that I am in your debt as well. I will keep your words in mind in the future as it unfolds, and where it is in my power, I will repay you."

She nodded, then. Glanced once at the gates that had opened, leading into the circus grounds Gervanno had first entered from different gates. Her expression was remote but focused, as if the circus had once been part of her past just as Voyani caravans had been part of his — offering hints of magic and mystery that were part of childhood yearning, but in the end unlike any truth he had yet encountered.

Evayne was not young. She was not eternal. But her gaze implied that she had seen history in all its unfolding with the gaze of a mortal. She was focused. She was weary. Her life had become war, and the war had only barely begun.

Perhaps that was what Nenyane offered. She was part of the war, yes; swords such as hers were wielded in combat. But her skill existed outside of the grim days of battlefield occupation and the march to reach them, the concern about food and the safety of his comrades and the few men under his command. The days of boredom, and the hours of excitement — if a bloody battle could be called that.

He did not know. But he glanced at Stephen and Nenyane, and waited until Nenyane was ready to leave, if she would be at all; she disdained mere entertainment.

As he expected, Nenyane hung back. Stephen did not. He joined

Gervanno, a bitter half-smile adorning his lips. "She wants to leave. We're done here, and, as usual, she feels we're wasting time we don't have. Do you want to join her?"

Gervanno shook his head. "She wouldn't leave you to do as you please if I were not by your side." He said it without pride.

Stephen nodded. "Alex and Max are coming. Alex wouldn't miss this for the world. I think Max might even be looking forward to it."

Gervanno did not believe Max anticipated the circus performance with any great joy. Max was aligned, in many ways, with Nenyane. The circus had nothing to do with the hunt, and nothing to do with their mission. But Max knew Nenyane well enough to know she had no desire for company, or he might have remained by her side.

He could imagine the two youngsters complaining bitterly about how trivial things were, happy in their agreement and the certainty they were right. His mother had always said that reasonable complaints were the glue that held much of the village together.

His father, however, had disapproved of this advice, and took care to counter it—but only when his mother and his grandmother were no longer in the room.

———

ALEX WAS WELL aware that Max had no professed interest in the circus or its performance. He was grateful to have joined the towns-people, but mostly because there had been danger and combat here in which they, Hunters of Breodanir, would be necessary. *That* was important. This? This was noise.

It was more than that to Alex. It was color. The buildings that had first opened their many doors were closed now, the awnings that had adorned their entrances gone. In the center of the street, beneath a sky that Alex suspected would never again be blue, was an enormous tent. A flag caught wind at its height, which rivaled the pavilion buildings.

All of the circus colors were splashed across the sides of the tent, some carefully and some in wild abandon. The townspeople were streaming into the single entrance Alex could see. No matter how large the tent erected, Alex couldn't see how all of the people who had waited in the streets could fit; he expected to join a press of bodies, too tightly packed together as he followed the moving crowd.

There were benches to which people walked, some carrying children, some dragging them by the hand so as not to lose them. No one in the crowd, taking seats along slightly curved benches, raised their voice. No single voice demanded attention, but the combination of voices, the texture of sound, reminded Alex of something. He could not say what; he was not ill at ease.

A young man—no older in appearance than Alex or Max—approached the Elseth brothers as they gazed at the benches. His clothing was bright green, red, silver and gold; it seemed formal, but slightly foreign.

"Ah, you are guests to whom we owe a debt, and special seats have been prepared for you. Please, follow me."

Alex grabbed Max by the arm; Stephen simply nodded. Alex noted that Gervanno fell in behind them, as if he were a shadow; a guard, no more. Alex didn't care for it.

"We have other friends who might be waiting," Alex told the young man.

"They will not attend the performance; it is their right. But we are grateful that you have chosen to join us. The performance today will be a little different, and the star—and end—of the show is here only through your grace. She would have been saddened had you not attended."

Alex doubted that, but did so silently. They followed the attendant, and he led them to—of all things—stairs. They were slender, pale in color, and bounded on two sides by shimmering curtains that seemed to reflect a light that Alex could not see.

"Are you looking for the source of light?" the young man asked.

Alex was not embarrassed. "I am."

"Light is oft like that: we can perceive its effects, but not its source. Remember it well, Alex of Elseth: light exists even in a darkness so deep your eyes perceive none of it. The paths we choose—and have chosen—may lead us to the darkest of caves, the bleakest of nights, the smallest of spaces. But beyond those, perhaps even hidden within them, light exists. Perhaps you will find it. Perhaps you will bear it forward.

"My lord does not believe you will remain forever trapped within the darkness. He owes you a great debt. All of the people of the Free Towns do. No hint of the reason for his gratitude will exist in this performance, but you—to us, who have been called to serve the circus with everything we have—are that light. He bids you return if the burden of the gifts you have chosen here become too heavy, too costly, to bear."

Gifts?

The sword. The axe. That pouch of yours. Max exhaled. *These damn rings.*

Oh. He glanced at Gervanno, who looked at a point just over Stephen's shoulder. The cerdan did not reply, as if the words of grati-tude and the offer itself had not been meant for him and must remain unheard. Which was ridiculous; were it not for Gervanno, they would never have left the circus to find Adala.

But perhaps the attendant understood this as well. He was silent as he led them to the seats reserved for them, silent as he held the curtains that separated them from the audience below. From the exterior, they had entered a tent; on the interior, it was far, far larger, and far more solid. Thus, the stairs, the seats that overlooked the stage, and the separation they provided from the rest of the crowd below.

The air was cooler here, the murmurs of the crowd muted but ever present. The audience had waited in the streets of the circus for far too long, and they had seen the shadows of flying wyverns as the skies themselves shattered.

The circus was myth.

But it was a myth with roots, and consequences, in reality. The towns' youth were called to the circus when the towns faced danger. They gave up their homes with the certainty that their sacrifice—will-ing, in the end—would protect those homes from their unnamed, perhaps unknown, enemies.

This didn't mean that the town had no problems with bandits— they did. But no citizen militia would be proof against demons; none against the fiery breath of the flying wyverns or the demons who rode and commanded them. There were dangers that the townsfolk could not survive. Demons in the King's City had caused destruction, chaos, death. But there were forces within that city—Hunter Lords, dogs, the priests of Breodan, and the Order of Knowledge—that had the power to stand against those demons.

They could not stand against a god.

Alex thought they might have survived the wyverns—but the loss of life would equal the loss of the population of Hansleigh.

Is there a point to this? Max demanded.

Alex winced.

You wanted to be here. You wanted to see the circus. Stop thinking about death and doom, and watch the stage. Look at the curtains.

Alex exhaled. He looked at the curtains, drawn like a shimmering wall across what he assumed was a stage. He had seen many plays with his grandmother. Max had avoided them; he disliked high society, and found the keen gaze of the noblewomen extremely uncomfortable, because there was *always* something wrong with him. Alex understood it better, and bore the weight of it with diffidence, which is why their grandmother liked him so much.

Alex worried. Max acted. That had always been their truth. They were the youngest children of Elseth; they were not heirs. They would not become Hunter Lords. But Lady Elseth had never given up on Alex, always hoping to change his mind.

She loved you best, of all of us, Max said, without envy. He had always found her difficult, and getting less of her attention on any given day was a blessing.

Alex smiled. *I loved her the most out of all of us. I didn't agree with her about everything; I argued with her about you. She's spent her whole adult life serving Elseth. It's because of her—not our parents—that Elseth has remained so strong.*

Max shrugged. It was a well-worn discussion, verging on the edge of argument; it was familiar, and even comfortable. They had walked into the strangest of mysteries—this circus itself—had faced demons and lords in the wilderness, but Alex and Max were still the same.

Alex glanced at the ring on his finger, but did not argue. Maybe he needed to believe. Maybe, in the face of loss and grief, there was a quiet bulwark against despair: Maxwell of Elseth, his closest brother. He glanced back at Stephen, shorn for the moment of Nenyane. Maybe there was another bulwark.

Stephen nudged Alex, and Alex turned to the curtains as they started to shimmer. Gervanno's eyes had been on the veiled stage, an odd look on his face. No, Alex thought, not odd—but he had seldom seen that expression on the face of the Southerner. It was almost too young for his face, his age. Alex let go of worry.

When the curtains, still shimmering, began to slide open, they did not open silently. Stars emerged from their folds, as if unwilling to be confined on the sidelines; they floated into the air above the audience, illuminating upturned faces, young and old, as if those stars were the start of a miracle.

And it might be. Here, they were in the heart of a god's domain. Alex had felt wonder, when he had first walked into the circus. As if the circus were the essence of magic. But here, the stage front of his eyes, he understood that it was more than that. It was the will of a god: the circus master.

What had stories told him about the long-ago gods? What miracle was beyond them? What power—to move mountains, to change whole landscapes on a whim—was not theirs? Yet the circus master had not intervened—at all—in the attack on his lands. He had watched, bearing witness, as if the circus was not his responsibility, but the responsibility of the people he had created the circus to protect.

None of the circus people, engaged in combat, had seemed at all surprised that the circus master had not joined them in the bloody fray. Katie had taken charge, in as much as that was possible, without lifting weapon in her own hands. None of them had expected, or could expect, that the circus master would intervene.

Alex wanted to know why.

Of course you do. You dragged me here. Just watch the performance.

Music followed stars—the music slow and so quiet it could only barely be heard. But as the stars grew brighter, the music grew in volume. Alex couldn't identify the instruments being played, although he tried. Max hit his shoulder.

You made me follow you. I'm almost grateful. Just...let me enjoy this without commentary.

Alex exhaled. *I guess there are at least two miracles.*

Max hit him again.

THE MUSIC WAS a gentle ocean of sound when the stars, floating above the audience, returned en masse to the height of the air above the stage itself. The stage was no longer empty, but it wasn't like any stage Alex had seen at his grandmother's side. It had appeared to be similar—if larger or deeper—when it had remained in shadows while the stars floated out above the audience, as if those stars were silent heralds.

Now, they returned in a swirl of light, leaving trails like dust in their wake.

The stage was not wooden. Alex had seen props before—sometimes so expertly painted they were works of art in their own right. There were no props here. The trees were real, and standing before their wide, thick trunks were the gold-tinged warriors who had met them on a very narrow path through a forest that wasn't part of Hansleigh. The trees were planted in a half circle, forming a boundary around the three people who now stood knee-deep in wildflowers and wild grass. Birds stood on the shoulders of the tree spirits, not on their branches, softly twittering as if they were singing to the music that came from no visible source.

The audience was not silent, although the voices raised in astonishment—and question—came from people far younger than Alex. This was their first circus. Given the terrible circumstances under which the circus came to town, it might—in a better world—be their last. But in this moment, such thoughts had vanished with starlight and the glowing hearts of trees; the reason for the circus performance was irrelevant. The darkness, alleviated by the song of birds and the music that was playing without instruments, had severed them from their mundane lives, and they existed in, and for, this moment: this performance.

Alex was not a child. He understood that the road he must travel continued beyond the circus, into a wilderness not of the ancient and almost unknowable beings, but the wilderness of an Imperial political system he did not fully understand. He knew that Max and Nenyane were right: they had no time for this.

But he knew, as well, that these moments of beauty and wonder were haunting in their own right. If tragedy and disaster could haunt and terrify, why not joy and awe? Why should the pain that lingered become the only truth?

They're warnings. If we understand what happened, it's an advantage to us in the next attack, the next battle. This...is not. We can't call on it, we can't get tactical information from it. We can't count on it the way we can the attacks.

Alex didn't argue; he hadn't asked the question of Max, but of himself. He understood Max's viewpoint; it was Nenyane's. In other circumstances, it might have been Gervanno's. But it wasn't Stephen's; Alex could see that on his cousin's face, the contours of which were shaded and revealed by the light. His eyes, the gold of the god-born, seemed to shine from within, as if starlight had been absorbed and rested there.

From between the trees, people appeared. They wore the clothing not of the circus, but of the town: simple, sturdy, and dirt-worn. One carried a pitchfork, one carried a saw—both larger than more mundane tools, and glowing. It wasn't subtle. Percussion, metallic, joined the soft hum of birds.

When the circus master joined the performers, the shape of the stage changed, trees becoming small wooden buildings, blackened and charred by fire. The dead were implied by the shadows beyond what had once been trees—but the heart of those living trees remained, adorned by birds.

A whisper rose, wonder and confusion. Whatever the more experienced audience expected from the performance, it was not this; this was far more like a play. Breath shifted as another person joined the circus master; she wore robes of midnight, and in her hands, she held a crystal ball, a miniature sun.

Watch, little hunter, a new voice said. All of the Hunters present lifted face, as if the voice came from above; all returned with more intense focus to the stage.

When the circus master spoke, his voice was soft thunder. It was the voice of the crowd. Nenyane knew the circus master as a god, and Alex acknowledged that—she was never wrong. But this was the first time he had felt it as visceral truth: the voice of a god was never a single voice when heard by mortal ears. It was a concert of sounds: young, old, angry, joyful.

"This is your future, if no action is taken. You will not die. It is your descendants who will face those deaths, that obliteration."

The townspeople knelt in the face of the god's words—had Alex not been seated, he might have done the same.

The woman who bore the pitchfork spoke. "We are not gods, to face the scion of the gods and their dead. We are but mortal, and we have lived in your sanctuary for the whole of our lives."

"No mortal sanctuary lasts forever, not even mine—and I have spent much of the power I have husbanded in creating the lands in which you live. I have not asked for your obedience; I have not asked for more service than this: live your lives, raise your children, allow those who are not meant for such enclaves the freedom to wander the wilder world, even if you fear they will not survive their journey.

"From your towns have emerged great mages, great artisans. From your towns have emerged known heroes, and unsung heroes both. You have kept faith with me, in mortal ways, and I have kept faith with you. But the time is coming when such faith will not preserve you."

The townspeople wailed. But the man who carried the saw lifted head. "What would you have us do? We will fight, if fight we must; arm us, and allow us to serve you fully."

"That is not the way it works. Mortals are what they are. Humans are what they are. To be different is to step away from the towns you have labored so long, and so completely, to build."

"Would it help?"

The god fell silent. "Perhaps. Perhaps, in the end, it would. I am not a great shaper of flesh and form; those shapers are gone, and if they are returned to us, it will be in the shadow of our greatest enemy."

Whispering, then. Sparks of dismay.

"I have called these towns yours, and they are. They are what you have made of them. I have protected them from influences that were not meant to encroach upon human concerns, and in the absence of gods, the truth of my interference was lost. But the time will come, is coming, when the walls that separate us from the scions of those gods will crumble. All things living know both beginning and end.

"But to preserve what you have built, to preserve your way of life, I have spent what remains of my power. This is Evayne. She is both my daughter and the daughter of the blacksmith of Evanston. She bears my blood, and yours. And she has chosen to walk the longest, harshest road in defense of her home — and the homes built by mortals since the gods chose to retreat from your world. She was born for this purpose."

Alex flinched.

"I have given my daughter to your cause. What," the god said, "will you offer in return for the safety of your kin?"

Evayne said, in a mortal voice, "I am not yours to give, or to withhold. I am Evayne a'Nolan." She turned in her swirl of midnight robes, toward the townsfolk. "The choice I made, I made to preserve the people of the town that was once my home. But once I accepted the choice offered, it could never be my home again. I could visit — but never at my own will — and the only thing I was promised for the choice I made was that, at the very end, I could save the people I loved.

"I was given choice, such as it was. My parent asks what you will offer to strengthen the towns. Understand that the choice offered is an echo of the choice I was given: if you choose to accept the call, you, too, will be sundered from your homes and your families." She lifted a hand from the crystal she held. "Your children — your children's children, down throughout the coming war — will be asked to serve the god so that he might preserve our towns. They will not be like me; they will no longer be like you."

She turned to the god. "I ask that you give them the choice, no matter how terrible that choice might seem to them. They are not you, they are not yours."

"I have always privileged mortal concepts of choice," the god replied, the thunder clearer in the many, many voices. "Choice will be theirs should they choose to accept the price we have paid." He turned to the townsman who carried the saw. "And you, who have come from the Free Towns, are the first to be offered that choice."

The man who carried the saw laid it down, upon the ground; he turned to one of the small buildings. "Give me leave to speak with my family; give me leave to spend the time explaining the choice I must make."

The woman who had carried the pitchfork likewise set it aside. "Give me leave to speak with my family. I will offer my service for as long as service remains within my reach—but let me explain to those I leave behind."

But the third young man wept. "My child was born two weeks ago. We are not well-off, and my wife is not from the towns. If I leave them, she will be alone and the child—the child will be without father or family. I understand that you offer us the choice of protecting the future of the Free Towns—and I understand why that is so important.

"But my child is important to me—and she may not survive to see that grim future."

"You are mortal," the god said. "As is your child. My offer does not protect mortals from their essential nature; it cannot. Disease will come and go. Drought. Mortal predators. No god, not even I, could carelessly promise immortality or invulnerability; what we change is subtle, even granted permission. I cannot promise your child will survive."

"I cannot leave them," the man wept.

Evayne took a step between them: the man on his knees, and the god who looked down upon him.

"You depend upon love to decide the choice you offer." Her voice was low, the words shaky. There was anger in them. "But love is a double-edged weapon." She glanced at the young father, on his knees, his face wet with the terror of the future and the possibility that he must abandon his loved ones for their own sake. She offered a hand to the man. "Go back to your family." Her voice was soft. "The future in the crystal is far off. There are no certainties. There is hope, and there is despair. But no certainty. Perhaps your child will grow, and she will have some of elements that my parent saw in you.

"Perhaps, in time, she will understand why you did not choose to carry the burden laid across your shoulders, and perhaps she will carry it in your stead." She glanced at the god. The god was silent. From his position in their elevated seats, Alex stilled, as if he were a rabbit in the face of deadly predator. He did not want to draw the god's attention.

Someone in the audience began to cry—a child. All others were as silent as Alex himself.

Max's hand had fallen to sword hilt, but rested there, as still as his huntbrother.

"You have always accepted the individuality of mortals; you find their flaws endearing, their strengths a wonder."

The god was silent for a long moment; his exhalation was warmth, breeze, sound. "You know what the cost will be. You know what the risk is. You have seen it."

"I have seen many things," was her soft reply. Behind her robes, the young father slowly gained his feet, as if the shadow Evayne cast was light in the darkness.

"You cannot stand in his stead. You know why. You bear the blood of a living god; he does not. He has hints of the talents that mortals are graced with, for no reason any understands. But if you become foundation for what we must build, there is no path forward. We will fall when our enemy rises. The Towns for which sacrifice is made will not weather the incursion of that enemy and his army of the dead. You know that."

"I see hope, regardless. I made the choice I made. I did not surrender to despair. But what I must build is not what you must; where I have walked is not where you have walked, nor ever can. I say again: if love is your lever, it cannot simply work in one direction, at your command.

"Do not take children."

The god said, "That was never my intent. None of the three are children, by the standards of their people."

"Do not take those whose children are young."

Silence.

Alex did not know if this Evayne was *the* Evayne, but he felt the glimmering of awe as she stood, unmoving, in the heart of the storm: her parent's august, unsurvivable anger.

"Let them go to do what they must."

The god looked through Evayne, as if her physical presence was irrelevant. "And will you give your child, when she is of the age of mine?"

But Evayne held a hand up again. "I chose. Give them the choice. Keep them safe, and it is a choice they will arrive at without your intervention."

"I will not aid them."

Even at this distance from the stage and the supposed actors—and Alex no longer believed the central figure of this god was an actor—he could see Evayne's smile. It was bitter, but also, genuine.

"I know. That was your choice, long ago; it is your choice now. You might plant a field of delicate, beautiful flowers, in soil of your choosing, in weather of your creation—but you will not interfere in their growth or eventual death. It is inimical to the value you perceive in their existence."

"No, child. This is the beginning. I have selected those who will become the strongest of foundations. What I build here, for the end, I build with a greater portion of my power. If you will have that young man walk away to his mortal life, I must imbue the protections and the connections to the high wilderness with a far larger portion of that power. I will not be able to act, I will not be able to fight, until the Free Towns fall or the need for their protection is gone. I ask again, will you insist on this?"

Her smile deepened. "As you desired, you have birthed a seer, an Oracle. Were I mortal, I would not be able to walk the path at all; I would lose the ability to see what is real and what is not. But I *am* your child. I will walk this path. I have seen much of it by the grace—and the torment—of the Oracle. You wished to leave mortals in charge of their own lives; you wished to protect them from the wilderness. They tire, and they do not live well in isolation.

"Allow your townspeople to raise their children. Allow those children to come before you when you call them, to make the choice that I made. Do that, and the towns might falter, but they will not fall until the Winter ends. The towns are theirs."

"And the Winter will end?"

"Not soon, but I see a narrow path toward Summer in the many, many strands of future laid before us."

The god fell silent. Alex understood why, on a visceral level. The circus, the lands the Free Towns occupied, had been built and rooted in Winter, as if Winter was the true spring of the wilderness.

Summer had come to the circus. Summer, and with it, demons, monstrous wyverns, combat, and the threat that Hansleigh would be severely damaged while its citizens were absent.

"Understand," the god said to the young man. "Make this choice, and you have weakened the foundations that will keep people across the townships safe. Will you not accept the responsibility for their future?"

The man bowed head—but only head. "I have already accepted the responsibility for my family's future," he said, voice very soft. It was steady, though. "I made vows I cannot abandon."

"Then go. Go, and tell your child, tell your wife, of what has transpired here." The god lifted hand, and the man disappeared—literally disappeared.

"You may regret this," the god said, for Evayne remained.

"Yes," she said, without rancor. "I may. But we are mortal, and we were not born when the elements were at their fiercest and the gods were wild forces. You may extend the lives of those you have chosen, but if they live in isolation, far from their homes and families, they will not grow. They will lose the roots, the impetus, that led them to their decisions.

"Call the talented to your side when it is necessary—and it will be. Let them join your founders. Let them help with the burden you've laid upon their shoulders—and let those first servants help those who come, confused and sundered from their lives.

"Let them decide what shape their protections might take. Let them decide what they will offer the townsfolk they surrendered their futures to to protect."

"Does it matter?"

"You ask a question to which you already know the answer. We are not gods. Even I, born to a god, am not a god, and cannot be. You admired the creativity of those whose existences were so slender. Let them create. Give them the tools only you can offer. Let them welcome their families, and the descendants of their families. Let them surprise you."

"Very well. This was a costly, costly day. Do not regret it."

"I would have made a different choice, a different plea, in my distant youth, and perhaps I will regret this, perhaps not. What has been decided cannot be changed, and there is so much—too much— that I must do. I will not have the time to weep or regret."

But Alex saw her lift hand to her throat to touch something resting in the hollow of her collarbone before she, too, offered the god a bow.

"Very well. Very well, child. Let me see, then, what my mortals have devised for their own kin, their own kind." Speaking thus, the god turned suddenly to the audience, raising both of his hands, palms flat. Shadow flowed from his lifted hands and traveled down his arms, encompassing his shoulders, his chest, his legs, as if cloaking him—and revealing him. Circus master. Lord of the circus.

"We welcome you to the circus, who have worked tirelessly within the towns rooted in my domain. We are late to start, but hope that we will be forgiven for our tardiness: this year is, as you are no doubt aware, a special year, a special performance. May you remember it fondly in the years to come."

The people who inhabited the trunks of great trees leapt, in perfect unison, into the air above the circus master; as they did, they spun out, into the audience, their hands spread wide as if arms could control their descent. Their faces were upturned, toward the height of the theatre as if they could see and feel the sunlight that might have reached them had it not been for ceiling.

Gone were the small buildings; gone the small half-circle in which the god and his servants had made their compacts. In their place was grass, shorn and even as for any noble's dwelling. Flowers did not grow in beds, ruining the similarity, but they grew, and the birds that had stood sentinel on the shoulders of sentient trees now took to the air. The stage itself glowed with sunlight and the breeze that came from this oddly tended grass reached out with gentle, warm fingers, to ruffle through the crowd, as if patting the head of an awe-struck child.

Alex knew. He was that child, in this moment.

The circus performers walked onto the grass. Although they walked comfortably, their steps fell in perfect synchronicity, and their shadows moved oddly as they trailed from their heels, dancing in the wind even while the ones who cast those shadows did not. Alex watched as shadows separated from their people and began to dance.

Although he seldom joined village dances, he found himself smiling; he could almost recognize the movements, the steps, the odd courtesies and the brave departures.

Music came from those shadows, or perhaps music shifted to accommodate their dance. Their feet were not distinct, but the rest of their bodies were. The performers—seven in all, three men and four women—bowed to the audience. When children shrieked, the woman in the center of the formation turned, lifted hand to lips, and blew them all a kiss.

In the crowd, Alex could see children—not toddlers, but not near old enough to be considered adult—breaking away from their parents' restraining hands and running toward the grass. The stage, such as it was, was not elevated; the lights that illuminated the shadow dancers were not built into the ground, not carried in sconces or by hands.

The three men and women on each side of the central figure then peeled off. To Alex's surprise and delight, they joined the dance, holding out hands of flesh to hands of shadow; the shadows responded as if they were independent in their own right, doubling the number of dancers. It *was* a village dance. A dance of shadows and people, the shadows somehow taller.

Shadow and darkness, associated with demons, were reclaimed. Alex glanced at Gervanno and smiled, for Gervanno did not associate those shadows with demons; his association was different. His eyes were wide; Alex almost wanted to remind him to blink. He doubted Gervanno would hear him.

GERVANNO SAW the hand of the Lady in those shadows. They were not the darkness the sun *must* burn away; they were the darkness in which the Lady might show her face and her mercy, her warmth and her comfort, the softness that must be hidden away, lest the Lord judge one weak. It was in the darker hours when the sun's light no longer reigned, that his father's voice would soften; it was in those hours that Gervanno, considered a young man, if still a child, might be held by his mother, his Oma, his aunts. But his uncles would join them, smiling, their voices shorn of edge.

It was the heart of family, and it could be exposed only after dusk.

Here, the shadows danced in the light of day. The dancers who had shed shadows now cast no shadow as they moved, the truest evidence that these shadows were of them, belonged to them. The shadows were not clothed in a fashion the eye could detect, but the dancers were, their clothing bright: pale sky blues and soft yellows, greens the color of deep forest, pale ivory, red of fall leaves, and the violet of encroaching dusk.

The central figure, whose shadow did not dance but stood by her side, bent; she caught a young child before his parents could, and threw him in the air. They both laughed, child and woman, as her shadow bent in like fashion to catch another child, shadow hands catching the girl under the arms, and twirling her in the air, rather than loosing and catching her as she fell.

Both movements were part of that dance; the throw, the catch, the twirling; all of the timing matching the music of the much more codified, joyful village dance. The music grew more frenzied, and the dance, the switch between partners, the circling and twirling faster, faster.

And then the shadow dancers caught the flesh dancers and lifted them, as the child had been lifted, throwing them into the air, where they curled up, spinning like balls, before gravity pulled them down. They reached out to the shadows, and the shadows lifted hands, palms flat; flesh palms met shadow palms as the dancers uncurled and the music suddenly fell, as if song could, and must, take breath.

Supported by the hands of shadows, the dancers remained in the air, straightening out, their feet stretching to toe-point. The two children came to rest in the arms of the performer and her shadow. The shadow then released the child she had lifted. The central dancer, one child in left arm, leapt up to intercept, the movement graceful; she caught the child, who shrieked with delight, her voice far louder than it had been in the stillness and the lull.

Gervanno did not envy the two children. If he had memories of being like them, he was well past them. He could see the wonder, could hear it in their voices, anchored as it was by their delight. This moment would become a memory to which they could return in a different type of darkness.

But his attention was drawn to the dancers. To the former dancers. They were perfectly still, almost rigid, as they balanced on the palms of shadows. It was almost as if this dance, or this part of it, was meant for Gervanno—or those in the towns who had come from the South; he was aware that former citizens and cerdan of the Dominion had set down roots in the villages, and he knew they would see and understand what he saw.

It was the shadow that supported the performer. It was the gentle darkness, at the edge of dusk, that defined the heart of family; it was the existence of that heart, that time, that formed the basis upon which a man might stand in the full light of the scorching sun.

He saw the moment the hands of those rigid, elongated performers shifted, their grip changing, their fingers curving around the shadows on whose palms they balanced; they fell at once. They fell, turning that fall into momentum and rolling to their feet, bringing their shadows back to where they must otherwise belong: flat, cast and created by light. But not, he thought, never, lifeless again.

The shadows once again joined themselves to the performers, even the central performer. She said something to the children she carried, and then set them down on the grass. One of the two, the taller, reached down and grabbed the stem of a flower, pulling it from its mooring. He then offered it to the woman. Gervanno couldn't see the child's expression, but he could see the performers. For a moment, this simple gesture, this entirely natural, normal attempt to show gratitude, moved her, changing her expression.

She was not so young as she appeared. There was something in her face that implied a sudden, unexpected movement of tears, of surprise. She swallowed, and her performer's smile once again took over her face. But she told the child to keep that flower, and to remember their dance. To tell their own children about it, when those children came to be.

Yes, he thought, as the child retreated, his boldly picked flower in hand as he turned to look for his parents. In the Dominion, he would have been in the care of grandparents, great-aunts. But for this performance, every resident was in attendance. Gervanno could not see them all from where he sat. He did not doubt that this space, luminous and shadowed both, could contain the whole village—perhaps all of the Free Towns. The audience did not question it.

But Gervanno had seen the *Kialli* in the heart of the circus lands. He had seen the wyverns. He had seen the sky shattered, as the circus people fought the encroachment, in defense of this hushed, awed audience. Yes, there was magic in the world. Magic, grace, comfort. Moments of beauty that might be imagined, but could not be truly conceived, not as it was now.

But that magic, that wilderness, was the home of the demons that would destroy them all. Magic could not be confronted without caution, power, and wise fear.

This, then, was dusk. It was the Lady's time, in a world gone beautifully, movingly mad. But he accepted the reminder that not all beauty in the wilderness was death to the mortals swept up in its ancient storms. In silence, he felt the touch of dusk, the touch of night, although light shone, always, on those who now moved with their shadows, dancing, stretching, catching and throwing each other.

Gervanno stopped breathing when he saw the woman who had carried two normal village children turn toward the six, and draw a sword. They stilled, and then argued, as if they were clowns—a true source of terror in his childhood—although their clothing, their stature, was not altered. And then one of the six drew a similar sword. He knew what he would witness next, and he was not wrong: a sword dance.

Some proof that these two, armed and moving, understood each other so well, they could dance, swords in hand, blades clashing and separating, as if those weapons were not deadly. Sword dancing was an act of precision, of practice, but mostly, of trust. He felt young again, in this place: hints and echoes of childhood reached out to touch him, to drawn him in. What did wonder and awe matter here? Everyone watching would be so wrapped up in their own, they would not have the time or the inclination to judge him. All of the people under the roof of this tent were watching, as he watched, and remembering, as he remembered. The experiences were different, would have to be different, but they were bound together, part of a vast audience made, for just this performance, into one large family.

Children shrieked, but older voices joined them, skirting the edge between fear and delight—fear *for*, delight in. He watched without the former. Watched and listened, color catching the corner of his eyes without commanding his full attention. The ground beneath the feet of the sword dancers shifted and changed as he watched the arcs of their blades catch and reflect light. He could not say they were better swordsmen than he, but knew that such a dance was beyond him; it was not the way he approached the sword. It was not a battle; it was far too intimate for that. There was no rage, no fear in the movement of swords, and perhaps that was why he could not mimic it. Or perhaps it was because there was no swordsman he had ever felt he could trust so much.

What they did was not a fight. It was not a combat. It was a shared performance. It required concentration, focus, determination—but an absence of blood, an absence of mortal wound, of death. Any of those things, from lesser to greater, would destroy the spell their blades wove. It would leave a scar instead of awe and wonder.

Gervanno did not fight for an audience. He did not consider that an audience, beyond his opponents, existed at all. War scarred people, physically, emotionally—but it should. If one became entirely immune to the effects of the battlefield, what little humanity remained in those who killed for a living would be irretrievably lost.

Yes. Yes, child of man. Remember it. Were you not who you are, had you not struggled to be what you have become and to hold on to the things you value, you would not have gone in search of Adala. You are, perhaps, a fool—but it is such foolishness that is prized by those who have survived their long tenure in the wilderness, high and low. You suspect that my performers are performing for you, and in some fashion, that is true. But all of my people will take comfort from the performance and the existence of the circus.

It is my gift to you, who will ask, as is your wont, for nothing. Remember. Remind your companions that there is comfort to be found in darkness and shadow, as well as fear.

Gervanno glanced to the side, to Alex, to Stephen. Neither appeared to have heard. He bowed head in gratitude, for he knew who had spoken: the circus master. The god of this small, peculiar world.

Even gods know love, in a fashion; it is not recognized as love as mortals reckon it, and indeed, were it, it would destroy mortals in its wake simply by existing. I do not, therefore, love the individual people in my towns, and have not, through history. But I love them as a people. I have given them everything it is in me to give, as you have seen.

The shape of the world that emerges from the shadow of war will be up to people like you to define.

"I can fly *without* all that!"

...and others.

Gervanno thought the god actually sighed in frustration.

I do not know her future. I see fire in it, but little else. I would see nothing were she not one of the townspeople. She is a child, for weal or woe. Could I, I would comfort her. But she was never destined for the circus. Perhaps she will find what she needs on the road you must travel. But, as you rightly understand, she is a double-edged weapon. Her life has been defined by hatred and fear.

"Why can't I join them? *Why?*"

Anya's conversation with Katie had clearly reached its end.

Chapter Twenty-Five

Six dancers retreated to the edge of the field, their feet now lost beneath the colors of wildflowers. Gervanno thought they had finished; they had not. From mid-air, two of the circus performers drew torches, one in each hand; fire burned instantly at the torch ends. The individual fires were red, orange, yellow, white. The colors merged until each torch's flame was a single, uniform hue.

Two of the former dancers then leapt into the air and remained suspended—just as Nenyane, Meralonne or Kallandras might in the folds of the wild air. Wind blew their hair back, blew it up, braiding it, teasing it, yellow, gold, red.

The final pair leapt up as if to join their two brethren in mid-air. The air, however, did not carry them; instead, from the ground beneath the shadows of their feet, grew two stone pillars, pushing up toward the sky. The two somersaulted in the air and landed, almost on the points of their toes, atop those pillars.

Earth, air, fire. Water was absent.

The woman who had been the seventh of the performers bowed before the pillars; she bowed before the performers who now juggled their impressive torches, passing them between each other. She waved to those who now danced in the air, as if the air were solid.

She then turned to the audience. "It has been a difficult day for all of you; we are grateful that you waited with such patience. But today's performance is special to us, and perhaps it will be special to you as well.

"It takes time to learn the skills performance requires—or it certainly did for me. But some come to the circus so certain in their abilities, there is little enough for old hands to teach them. This year, we have one such genius. Some of you will recognize her." She turned toward the side of the stage, toward what would have been the side of the stage in any other theatre.

Adala entered. She walked upon the grass, and at her feet flowers unfurled, as if paying obeisance. Wind teased out strands of her hair. Fire did not touch her, although it illuminated her gently, the four distinct colors far more natural against her skin. She wore green, although the green was broken by brighter colors that caught the light, reflecting it back in different shades.

All of this might have remained unnoticed, but Adala's expression was not joyful; it was grave, her eyes so dark a brown in this odd light they might have been black. Tear tracks remained on her face, and tears—some few—renewed them. She forced her lips up in a tremulous smile as she turned to the audience, walking to the very edge of what passed as living stage.

Her gaze searched the crowd, eyes rising and falling, which implied other elevated seats. When she met Gervanno's eyes, her tears stopped, and the smile that she'd forced from the corner of her lips emerged far more naturally. Had he a child, she would be the age Adala was—and would remain for decades, ensconced in the circus as she had become.

She had tried to flee from it.

She had survived, by dint of the will of a stranger and his companions. She offered him a nod, and turned.

At the edge of the stage, unable to cross onto the grassy field, stood Anya, hands lifted, palms flat, as if she had encountered invisible glass. Given her expression, there was no glass that would survive concerted effort on her part. He knew it. Anya must know it. But her hands traced glass the eye could not see as she sought for a different way in.

Adala's smile deepened. Gervanno could not smile like that at the mage; he would never trust that his smile would not be misconstrued. But Anya lowered a hand, palm up, in Adala's direction.

"Are you certain?" she asked, her question the clearest sound in the theatre.

"Yes!" Anya shouted, but her voice was not so deep, not so all-encompassing, as Adala's.

It was the will of the circus master, Gervanno thought.

But no. It was Adala's will. The boundary between the audience and the performers had already been breached once, by two eager children. They hadn't crashed into the boundary that kept Adala out; they had reached the performer who bent to scoop them off their feet, as if no such boundary existed.

That woman had chosen. The children had joined her.

He considered the play that had begun this performance; the words that Evayne had offered in defiant guidance; the sacrifice the god had chosen to make in return for the work his daughter had undertaken. It was not the god who had allowed the children to participate, to pick a flower in this unimaginable field—it was the performer herself.

He better understood why common wisdom separated the circus performers from the villagers with whom they'd grown. Here, too, many things were held in balance for the safety of the town. A parent seeing their crying child might think more than twice about leaving her here. The pavilions were a comfort offered to those who had been left behind; a way of believing that, in this eternal, free place, where joy and awe could be found, their child would be happy.

Gervanno, as a young man, would have felt the same way.

But seeing her tears made clear that there was pain here, as well; that the environs a visitor saw were never the entire truth of a home. He was not a parent; he had not had children. But he had supervised and trained many a young man. He wondered, as he watched Anya practically explode onto the stage, how he might have felt being Adala's parent. How they might feel, seeing her so transformed.

And she was. Anya flew to the heights of the theatre, waving and almost crowing in delight. But her flight path revolved around Adala, as if Adala were the sun, the focal point of any movement. In her own strange fashion, she joined the performers who bore the symbols of the wilderness; she orbited Adala. Gervanno might have thought her unaware of Adala, having achieved her impulsive desire, had that not been the case.

Adala's feet did not leave the earth; her progress to the center of the stage could be seen by the flowers that sprang up in her path, marking it in a way stone did not. When she reached the middle of the field, she turned to the audience again. To Gervanno. To, he thought, her mother.

To Trevor. Gervanno couldn't see Trevor in the darker confines of the audience, but he knew when Adala found him in the crowd. The smile she offered him was brilliant, almost blinding. Gervanno thought she might run to him; she did not. She raised her arms, but too high for an invitation to embrace.

And she began, at last, to sing.

Her song could not be mistaken for anyone else's. The words were not words in a language Gervanno understood, but the tone and nuance of her voice—rising and falling, a shout and a whisper—told a story to those who understood that words were not everything. Some things could not be put into words, no matter how much one desired the ability. Some pain was private. Some joy was private. The inability to encapsulate them in language did not change that truth.

Did not change the truth of those who must remain silent.

Fire rose in the shape of the performers; wind lifted blades of grass and petals in the same shapes. Even the stone pillars, which did not move as the fire and air did, shifted in appearance, taking on the faces and features of those who stood atop them.

Forgotten until this moment were the hearts of the trees that had first appeared on the stage. They descended, reaching down to brush Adala's hands with their own. She laughed, the sound joyful, but did not hold on to any of them. She had not finished singing.

She had not begun, not truly.

The circus master stood behind her, in his odd black suit; he grew in height as she sang, his shadow falling across her as he lifted his neatly gloved hands in parallel to hers. He did not speak, did not sing, did not in any other way make his presence felt, but it was enough.

If Adala noticed him at all, she gave no sign.

Anya noticed him; she crowed in wordless delight, no music in her happy sounds; she might have been one of the children who were too young to know that they were meant to listen in attentive silence. She did not, perhaps could not, sing; she did not join her almost involuntary sounds to Adala's song in harmony. But the sound of her delight, unfettered by manners and anxious parents, were nonetheless of a piece with what Adala now offered the audience.

If she had approached the stage in tears—and she had; he was certain he had not mistaken tear tracks—she began her tremulous song in the shadow of loss. But when she lifted her arms in almost trembling defiance, she seemed to draw strength from the things she was born to touch, to bespeak.

Trevor had implied, or Gervanno had inferred, that her ability to communicate with trees was not entirely new or unknown to her; she had called them on the very narrow path they had taken in their rushed return to Hansleigh. Those forest denizens, or their kin, reached out for her as she sang, transforming slowly back into the trees from which they had come, as if something in her song was a lullaby meant to grant them repose and peace.

In those companions, Adala found remnants of joy, and she teased the threads out, as if she were telling a story about love—for love continued, love existed; it was not a simple thing. And yet, it was. She loved those trees, this wilderness; she loved the town she had fled, and the family she had abandoned. She loved the turn of seasons, the sunrise, the sunset.

She loved Trevor. His name was clear in the flow of pure syllables, and it was spoken three times. If Trevor watched, he remained at a distance.

But the children, of whom Anya's crowing delight was an echo, did not. They did not run toward the stage: the circus master remained, a looming shadow, a gentle god; and around Adala were the trees, rooted now in the stage itself. But Anya lifted them in ones and twos, elevating them; their shrieks were very like hers had been before she chose to concentrate on this youngest part of the audience.

Gervanno held breath. Anya was not—or had not been—the most mindful of people, and with the great power at her casual disposal, he was afraid she would harm the children. She might forget them in mid-magical flight; they might fall when her attention was captured by something else. And her attention was diverted—but she dragged the young children in her wake, seamlessly creating a pathway, both in air and on ground, made of those small feet, those small shoes, those waving arms and bright faces.

Their delight was palpable. They did not understand what the circus meant—only that it was magical, beautiful, and within their reach. It surrounded them, literally gave them invisible wings. Anya seemed as delighted as the children. Gervanno had doubts that she could handle the children safely—but she clearly could, and did. It was perhaps the first time he considered that Anya was not, in fact, a child herself.

But Anya was moving in with intent. If her path above the ground seemed wild or chaotic, a happy mix of young children and her own power, it circled Adala, who sang; who lifted her face as the small shadows flitted across her, moving, squealing, shouting. Only Anya fell silent when their gazes met.

Anya did not have a good voice, not for singing. She sang anyway, her notes sliding off the solid core of Adala's, becoming flat before they returned to what could only barely be called tune. But the children joined in, as if Anya's poor singing was all the permission they needed.

One voice almost matched Adala's, and when it joined hers, the foliage on the ground shifted and small, slender saplings grew, pushing aside the wildflowers and grass as they struggled to lift themselves free of the confining earth. Adala's eyes widened. She reached out with both hands as a child came close enough to touch—and that child's small hands found hers.

The saplings became trees. Their branches reached out for Adala—not the child, although it was the child's voice that had caused them to wake, to grow, to stretch. Adala's smile was gentle, complicated; it was almost as if she was singing now to her younger self, to the child who had wandered through Hansleigh, dreaming of joining the circus.

Before love. Before sacrifice. Before loss.

Gervanno understood in that moment why new members of the circus were not allowed to perform when their living relatives were in the audience. People were simultaneously strong and weak. Strong enough to make decisions. Weak enough to regret them. They were pulled in different directions; they could become unbalanced, they could stumble, they could make different choices, possibly ruinous ones.

But he understood, as well, that people did not live in isolation. That some of the strength *to* make decisions was rooted in the fabric of the lives they had lived until the moment they were forced to face untenable choices. He could see the child Adala had once been in the much smaller hands of the child who would, in time, become her. He could see her acknowledgement of it, and the joy of it, which would turn in time to despair and loss.

Childhood was a time of joy, in as much as the realities of a harsh life allowed it. She was the world for the child whose hands gripped hers: the center of it, the truth of it. The moment would pass, must pass, but the memory would remain. Here, today, she had touched the edge of the wilderness, had almost become a part of it, and would dream of joining it again.

But Adala had had exactly those dreams.

She swiveled, slowly, on the stage; she stood beneath the circus master's shadow—and protection. Her song shifted, but did not bank; Gervanno felt a subtle difference in the texture of her voice. The god looked down at his newest servant without moving; the audience held breath, as if they understood that she had asked a question of her master, and her master now considered his answer.

Even Gervanno held breath. The children did not. Anya fell silent, but did not still.

The circus master nodded.

Adala's smile, when she turned back to the audience, was almost blinding in its sudden brilliance, its immediate joy—as if joy were tangible, physical, something she could both absorb and proffer. The trees that had grown around her, from sapling to full growth in the lee of her song, once again released their spirits, their walking hearts.

Those trees then walked into the audience, leaving the grass and the field and their lord and Adala. One turned to catch the child who had so boldly grabbed Adala's raised hand; she shrieked with delight, with wonder, and allowed herself to be carried into the audience. If the spirits were the heart of trees made flesh, the audience was the heart and spirit of the village—or perhaps all of the villages. The Free Towns.

Anya chose that moment to land, gently setting down the children she had carried into the air with magic and delight. Some ran to her, some ran into the audience, but she had turned to Adala. Turned to her and then joined her, almost preening. Of the two, middle-aged, broken mage and young woman on the eve of adulthood, Adala seemed the older, the wiser.

But Adala's face was turned toward not Anya but the audience.

One man—one painfully young man—walked through it toward where Adala stood, waiting. He stopped just short of the grass. Gervanno could see his back, the slope of his shoulders, the way his arms stiffened by his side. He could not see his expression, and that was a mercy. How did one say goodbye when goodbye had already been said? How did one accept the loss when a yard away, loss was almost rendered a lie?

When Gervanno had walked away from his village and his life as cerdan in the south of his home, he had not looked back. Could not look back. He was a man grown; he had had command of men Trevor's age. He had lost most of them in the Averdan valleys, but not all. He could not look back because to leave was to sunder those ties.

He had not made his decision based on love or the need to protect his loved ones. He had left because he felt he could not offer them that protection. Against the forces they had faced in Averda, all he could offer was his own death—and at that, a death that bought nothing. No time. No promise of future safety. No *hope* of it.

It was not the same.

Adala had lowered her arms. She did not raise them again. But she faced Trevor, as he faced her.

Anya, perhaps unaware that this moment was theirs and should not include anyone else, turned to whisper something to Adala.

Adala's song had banked. It was carried by the trees, and the circus master himself: voices raised in chorus. Her eyes widened before she frowned and answered Anya. Trevor himself did not move.

Behind his back, the audience did, for the seats they had occupied had vanished, overtaken by grass and those golden trees and the song of the circus. The tone of the music shifted, and the invisible musicians who had played their instruments now walked onto the grass, bending flowers in their wake. They were performers; although their hands were full, their expressions invited the townspeople to join them, and people did.

Not all of the people in the audience felt compelled to join what became an impromptu town dance, but many did. But the grass spread regardless, and the roof of the theatre peeled away. Sun shone down from an amethyst sky; birds—not wyverns or demons—cut across that sky. Clouds—those tufts that did not signal incoming storm—graced that sky, touching a memory in Gervanno from long ago: those days where he might lie beneath such clouds and try to discern shapes as they passed slowly by. A moment of peace, of daydreams, of youth.

He did not look long at those clouds, although he could see that some did, leaning back slowly onto the expanding grass, hands beneath their heads, knees bent.

Alex rose, and Max followed. Stephen glanced at his cousins, and then at Gervanno. The box in which they sat separated them from the audience, and Alex clearly wanted to join the townspeople.

Perhaps Adala knew. She had not moved—not to embrace Trevor, and not to reject him. But she lifted her face as Alex rose; lifted a hand to wave.

The wind came to the box, then. It lifted the two Elseth Hunters from their seats, and carried them to the ground. It touched neither Stephen nor Gervanno. Stephen closed his eyes. "I'm going to go to Nenyane," he told the cerdan.

Gervanno nodded, clearly taking the statement as an order.

"She watched," Stephen said, as if to deny that. "She watched through my eyes. She's worried."

This was not the reaction Gervanno expected. "Worried?"

"It's Anya. She's afraid Anya will kill Trevor."

Gervanno shook his head. "This is the circus. Anya knows that. She might have asked Adala if she could kill Trevor—but without Adala's permission, she won't."

"Why are you so certain?"

"She treats the circus master with what might pass for respect among the very, very young. He will not allow it; Trevor is of the towns. To kill him, she would have to pit her power against the power of a man she views as a god. Only if Adala asks, will she take that risk."

"But why would she do that for Adala?"

Gervanno glanced at Stephen and realized, again, that Stephen was young. Youth alone did not demand ignorance; it was lack of experience, lack of observation, that made some facts difficult to perceive. "I believe that Anya was abandoned. It is what draws her to Adala, even now; she wishes Adala to live free of the experience of rage and loss."

"She can't avoid loss," Stephen said, voice soft, as it so often was.

"No. But she does not have Anya's rage." Or her power. The latter, he did not say.

As if to prove Gervanno's words, Adala turned to Anya. They could not hear what she said, if she spoke at all; they could see her expression in profile. But it seemed to Gervanno that Adala wore a slender crown, placed there by the circus master, as if even in this he offered her the illusion of choice.

No, Gervanno thought. Not the illusion. Adala had made a choice, no matter how bitter, and she accepted the results. It was not a choice

Anya had been offered, but Adala and Anya were not the same person. Perhaps Adala understood what Stephen did not; she was grateful to Anya, and showed it in the warmth of her expression. The younger woman lifted one hand and gently cupped the older woman's face, while Trevor simply bore witness.

Anya glared at Trevor, but did not attack him; in the end, she turned and walked away from them both.

Adala then turned to Trevor.

The trees that had wandered through the audience returned to the field, exposed beneath sun and amethyst sky, and they chose positions around the young couple, until both Adala and Trevor could no longer be seen.

The circus master then stepped past this enclosed space, standing before it, as he had stood behind Adala. He raised his arms, demanding silence by gesture alone; silence fell instantly. Thus the power of a god.

"We thank you for joining this special performance," he then said. His voice was soft, genial, but it carried. Even the youngest of children were silent; Gervanno suspected this was because they were exhausted.

"For this special day, all of the pavilions will be open until the sun sets; you may eat and rest there."

At this, a whisper did rise in the crowd. Gervanno did not join them; he did not dare.

"Therefore eat, drink, and perhaps find mementos you might carry into your towns with you. There will be work that needs doing when you emerge."

This was not a surprise to the townspeople. The pavilions were.

"Will you bring Nenyane with you?" Gervanno asked.

Stephen grimaced. "Nenyane isn't hungry. She says I am." His smile was wry. "Shall we join the townspeople?"

Gervanno nodded. He turned to the curtains drawn across their box on the left, and stopped when he pulled them aside. At their feet were the cobbled stones that lead to the pavilions. They were no longer elevated above the crowd; they were standing on the ground among the people who were, even now, choosing pavilions to revisit.

GERVANNO SURPRISED HIMSELF: he was hungry.

He could no longer see the copse of trees that had come to give Adala a moment of privacy. He could see the other performers in the cobbled streets, juggling torches or breathing fire or bending themselves into shapes that were almost grotesque, they seemed so unnatural. He heard a cry from a distant crowd, but it was followed by applause. Here, in the streets, these performers were very like performers who had sometimes paused in the village of his birth. But they were the same performers who had joined Adala on the stage; the same soldiers who had defended the heart of the circus lands against intruders. They had changed; no hint of blood—most of it their own—marred their gaily colorful clothing.

Evayne a'Nolan was nowhere in sight. Gervanno considered searching the pavilion of fate and fortune for sign of her, but decided against.

He heard his dog, and turned in the direction of the high, excited barking.

He had almost forgotten Leial, and felt a pang of deep guilt at the thought. Leial was a mutt of middling size, built more for begging at, or beneath, the dining table than for hunting and fighting. Stephen did not forget his dogs. Max wouldn't.

Leial nudged his way through the loose but milling crowd, gathered in people-shaped half-circles around the various performers.

Gervanno knelt, and the dog raced, claws scratching stone in his haste to join his master.

Stephen's dogs found him with less fuss and more intent. Hunter dogs weren't like Leial; they were large, and trained to combat when in the presence of their master. But they were also accustomed to villagers; they did not attack the townspeople.

Some of the smaller children—it was always children who were the boldest—approached the dogs, as if dogs were as much of a miracle as the circus itself. Stephen was not upset. He was not in Breodanir, and even were he, he would not have discouraged the children. Nor would he ever allow the dogs to harm them.

It was, however, Pearl who took to the attention as if it were her due. Dogs didn't preen, but if they could, they would have looked very much like Pearl in this moment.

Gervanno glanced in Stephen's direction.

"I'll follow soon," the Hunter replied.

Gervanno gave up on finding food immediately.

"It's important that the dogs interact with people," Stephen then said. "I'm not sure how much opportunity they're going to have on the road we travel. Nenyane says you can go get food if you want."

"She's coming back?"

"She doesn't believe anything will endanger me here."

Gervanno shook his head. He patted Leial, and waited for Pearl to get bored with attention. The dogs would need food as well.

———

ALEX AND MAX found food for Steel before they went in search of food for themselves. Max had first wanted to make another pass at items in the lost and found; Alex was certain that booth, at least, would be closed. As usual, Alex was right, although Max insisted they check.

When they failed to find the open crate of lost items, they headed back to a pavilion that was clearly meant entirely for food and refreshment.

There, they found food for Steel; it was a blend of meat and grains.

"We don't see dogs like yours often," the man who handed them the large bowl said. "It's been a while. I had a dog when I was young, but he was nothing like yours."

Steel, a dog, was not immune to hunger; indeed, he approached the food as if it had been a week since he'd been given anything to eat. Food was a dog's universal panacea. Only when Steel was done did the brothers go in search of food of their own.

The people behind the stalls were friendly, hospitable—and tired. But even tired, the work they were doing seemed, in their hands, to be good and necessary work.

Alex wondered what that said of the town they would return to. Would most of it still be standing? Had the demons on the other side of the admission gate burned everything down?

"Here, boy," said one of the people behind the table on which food seemed to magically reappear any time hungry visitors cleared it. "You'll want to take this with you." The woman, an older woman, handed Max a large sack. "The townspeople have been provisioned. You'll be provisioned for a different journey—but we've been told the circus might have fallen without your interference. We don't forget."

She lifted her chin, gazing past the two to the streets and the fall of shadows as day edged toward evening. "The wind is changing, now. Heard it's Summer in these parts." For a moment, her expression was haunted. "Don't forget us, when you go back to your world and your duties. You aren't an army, but it's not just armies needed here. Not anymore.

"Win this war. We won't survive if the other side does."

Max nodded. Alex took the supplies.

"THERE YOU ARE. Quite a show, wasn't it?" Eva Juwal emerged from the crowd. Although they were all guests of the circus, the townspeople tended to give Eva a wide berth where possible. Gervanno considered this wise. "How was it?"

Gervanno smiled. "As you said, attending the circus was necessary. Does it usually last this long?"

Eva shook her head. "This entire experience is unusual. Look at the color of the sky here. That's not natural. What are we heading into?" Her gaze was sharp—but it always was.

"I don't know how much of the town will be standing when we return to it."

Eva winced. "Won't be the first time. Back in the day, one of the towns was destroyed—whole buildings had fallen. No one was trapped in those buildings, because the circus had come to town. It's often like that. The townies know what to expect."

"You've visited the circus before."

"I told you—I came from the Free Towns. When the circus came to town, everyone attended." An odd smile touched her lips, so foreign in the scars of her face. "I wasn't much different than those children, back in the day. I had daydreams. I wanted to be chosen. But so few of us are."

"You would never have made a good servant," Gervanno observed. It was seldom that words simply fell out of his mouth without thought, and he considered attempting to draw them back. Eva Juwal had always been a ferocious force.

But she smiled a much more natural smile in response. "I do serve," she told him. "But no, not in the fashion those who are of the circus do. Whatever they've built outside of the circus must be left behind; there is no home, and no return. If not for them, the Free Towns would have disappeared, annexed to one ambitious kingdom or another; it's because of their sacrifice that people like me don't have to face that loss. We grow, we dream, we accept when dreams die—and we find different dreams. Possibly better, possibly worse.

"Tell me, what are your intentions now? I note that you accompany the young Breodani Hunter. Is he your employer?"

"He is."

"There is room for you in my caravan, should that employ reach its end." This surprised Gervanno. Eva wasn't one to poach—but most merchants avoided causing conflict with other merchants. Stephen was not a merchant.

"You were heading to the West?"

"We're aware that there are difficulties in the West. But there are difficulties on all roads merchants travel. You're heading east." Not a question.

Gervanno was silent.

It was Stephen who answered—but that was his prerogative. That was his right as lord. "We intend to make our way to Averalaan."

"Why?"

In the South of Gervanno's youth, such blunt interrogation would have been unthinkable. Stephen, however, was accustomed to it, or seemed to be; he failed to note it at all. "We have been invited to visit The Terafin in her seat of power. It is not our final destination, but my cousin and companion dearly wishes to see that fabled city."

Eva laughed. "Fabled?" She shook her head. "Your cousin must be as young as you look." Her laughter faded. "But perhaps he is right; the young are often wise in ways the elders have forgotten. The city you will see is not the city in which I made both name and living—and indeed, to those unaccustomed to Averalaan's many changes, it *is* a city to inspire fable and legend. Ser Gervanno is a guard of note. Any would be proud to have him join their caravan—or their household.

"My name is Eva Juwal. I am known as a merchant in the city." She lifted hands, and with some fiddling, removed one necklace of the many that girded her neck. Eva's demeanor was that of a mercenary; it was the adornments that lifted her above that. She surrendered one of these to Stephen.

"I know what you did. It seems you have more to accomplish, but those who live on the road know plans shift and change constantly. If you take this medallion to the merchant's guild, they will know how to reach me. Perhaps, in future, I will be able to return the favor."

Stephen was confused, but he was diffident; in another ten years, no hint of that confusion would reach his expression.

"Gervanno serves you. Were it not for his interference—and your permission—I do not think we'd be milling in the streets like this. Sunset is coming, and the circus day is ending, as it always must. When I was young, I wished I could live here—but I understand, as an adult, that this is not life. This is not my work. Nor is it yours—but we all do what we can, and sometimes, what we must.

"If you decide to release Gervanno from his duty, give the medallion to him. I'd take him in a heartbeat." Here, her smile grew more edged. "But if you require travel companions when you venture out into the Empire—or beyond—I may be able to help you."

Stephen hesitated, but there was no profit in offending Eva by refusing her offer. He accepted the slender necklace with its much heavier medallion. He had questions, but they did not leave his mouth.

"Be careful with merchants," Eva added, before she turned. "We understand profit and loss, and we're in it for profit."

Only after she had vanished into the crowd did Stephen turn to Gervanno. "What was that about?" He glanced down at the medallion, and then slipped the necklace over his head; the chain was long enough he could do that without fuss.

"If I had to guess, she was attempting to offer as subtle a warning as she felt politically safe."

"Pretend I'm politically ignorant. When it comes to the Empire, I am."

He hesitated, but not for long. "She is telling us, if I understand correctly, to be as wary as possible of Jarven ATerafin."

Stephen relaxed. "Does she think we'll need her help to stand against him?"

"I cannot see how; he is subservient to The Terafin, and it is The Terafin's invitation we are accepting."

"The fox's."

"He carries word from his lord, and I have no reason to believe that word a lie."

"But if she intended to destroy us all, he would carry that word regardless."

Gervanno was less certain, but nodded. Should the fox fulfill his obligation as liege, he would carry exactly that word.

"The sun is almost at the horizon," he said, when Stephen fell silent. "The gates will open soon." He caught sight of Alex and Max, burdened by large sacks. Stephen lifted an arm to catch their attention, but it wasn't necessary—the two were moving in as straight a line as the crowds allowed toward them.

"No sign of Kallandras or Nenyane?" Max asked.

"Nenyane will meet us when we leave. She has Meralonne with her, but I'm not sure he'll join us."

"And the bard?"

"He'll meet us as well." From Stephen's tone there was more he could have said, but decided against.

Instead, he turned to the visible horizon, framed by pavilions that were slowly emptying. It had been a long day, shadowed by cracking skies and winged wyverns, visible from the streets, although their attacks had been focused just beyond the circus grounds. The performance had been delayed—and delayed again—before it had started.

And the performance itself had been different. Gervanno, who had seen no prior show, understood this viscerally. It wasn't just the presence of Adala, itself a break from long-standing circus custom, but the presence of the trees, the birds, the odd flowers and the song that sustained the circus itself. It was the way the performers reached into the audience, the way the audience became part of the performance, leaving their chairs in ones and twos to join the trees, to join each other, to join the performers who had waded into the crowd as Adala had broken the invisible barriers between audience and performer, a reminder that everyone on the stage had once been birthed in the Free Towns.

It was her decision.

Perhaps it was undertaken because Trevor was also in the audience, but perhaps not. She had reached out, first for the young child, and then for the rest of the gathering; perhaps she saw her family beyond Trevor. Perhaps they had needed some sight of her, standing in the literal shadow of a god, her upturned face bathed in light beneath the open, amethyst sky. Perhaps her presence was meant to comfort all such parents: Adala had become part of the *magic* of the circus. Adala would be *happy*.

But no. No, it was more than that.

Adala had chosen, just as the first three had chosen. She understood the loss that her return to the circus had barely averted. Leaving Hansleigh with Trevor by her side had been her choice. Returning had been a decision marred by resentment and pain and abandonment, for Trevor could not continue to flee Hansleigh when he knew what awaited the town. He could give up his life for Adala—but not, in the end, everyone else's.

She would lose him, no matter what decision she made.

So she made the only decision that preserved something. She chose to return. She reached into the roots planted in her distant childhood. She touched the wilderness. She surrendered the life she had desperately attempted to choose for herself. The life she wanted.

But if that choice had been made under so much pressure, in the wake of broken dreams and ephemeral desire, it had nonetheless *also* been an act of love. Trevor would not have survived. Her family. The town. They would not have survived if Adala had refused to return.

What she offered in the heart of the circus's sacred land—he thought of it, would always think of it, as sacred—could not be forced. She could not be sacrificed at the will of any other. That was the law of this land.

Gervanno had met many in his time who, in the throes of loss and despair, fell into the grip of rage and its resultant destruction: if they could not be happy, what matter if others were miserable? Perhaps their misery would be better, for people would finally understand what it meant to lose everything.

He had never understood that rage. Might never understand it. He understood Adala. Had he discovered that his presence in his former home was the only thing that might preserve it, he would never have signed up with the merchant caravan. He would never have faced his own visceral cowardice. Surviving, as Gervanno had, had been far less worthy. But had he not survived, Adala would not have survived.

In the coming dusk, he thought of the Lady, and went in search of wine, leaving Stephen to Alex, Max, and the crowd that was gathering near the closed gates.

He found wine almost immediately, as he had been certain he would. It came to him in a very fine wineskin, one that would travel well. The woman who handed it to him was warm and friendly, but silent; she did not thank him in any way. He would not have felt comfortable with the praise of strangers, and perhaps she knew as much.

He offered her a bow, and retreated.

He was not foolish enough to think he might offer the Lady ablutions in this place; these lands were not the lands over which the Lord and the Lady ruled. But the war that was looming over all of the lands would be fought in the world Gervanno recognized. He had not properly offered his respects to the dead. Evaro and Gervanno shared no blood; they were not family.

But they had become as close as kin, perhaps closer, in their travels.

Perhaps he had not offered his respects in the wake of their passing because he had not prevented their deaths — had made no attempt to do so. He had not had the right and, worse, his offerings could have been considered an insult or a plea born of guilt.

But, should the town be standing when they at last exited these gates and returned to a world in which magic was scarce and oft hidden, he would do so tonight. He had struggled his way from the abyss of guilt and self-loathing; he could make the ablutions now on their behalf, not his own. All men sought the Lady's mercy in the darker hours of night, in the privacy provided when the Lord closed his relentless eyes.

Not all men deserved it. It was the Lady's grace to offer blessing where it was not deserved; the Lady's power to offer a moment of peace. It was not for glory or fame that one beseeched her.

Stephen, Max, and Alex were speaking in low tones; Stephen glanced once at Gervanno, nodded, and continued to speak with his cousins, as if sensing the cerdan's desire for privacy. Leial bounced around the hunting dogs, as if sensing the same.

When the gates opened, Gervanno was almost at the front of the line. He did not draw weapon, but was prepared to do so. He had seen the demons in the streets of the town before they had reached the relative safety of the circus with Adala. Anya had destroyed those she could see with both glee and rage. He glanced back; he could not see the mage. Could not hear her. Perhaps she had found some way to speak with Adala; perhaps she had chosen to hang back to speak with Katie once more before the circus shut its gates and the opportunity was lost, husbanded against future disaster.

Lady be kind and merciful, Anya was not his problem.

GERVANNO EXPECTED cries of dismay when the citizens of Hansleigh poured into their familiar streets. It was, as expected, evening; the circus day was over. Some people would not be able to return to what remained of their homes. He was surprised—and should not have been —when the innkeeper took charge. The town in theory had a mayor, but perhaps that man had immediately gone to inspect damage.

It was the innkeeper who had lost a daughter who now snapped orders; his people headed into the inn to open new rooms for those who might have no roof over their heads, as if this were expected. He then stood a moment in the streets, looking back at the open gates while his employees rushed to prepare. Food would be an issue in the morning, but the villagers had eaten their fill—perhaps more—before the gates opened to return them to reality.

Gervanno caught the innkeeper's eye, and the man abandoned orders for the moment, not that they were necessary. If the younger employees had never seen the circus in person, they had no doubt heard all of the stories that surrounded it; they knew what needed to be done.

"Your room is ready if you need it," the innkeeper said, voice gruff. He ran a hand through greying hair. Men didn't speak of gratitude in the South, and the innkeeper would have been at home there. But gratitude could be conveyed without speech. And obligation could be lessened.

"I am looking for a small, quiet place in which I might offer my prayers and thanks to the Lady," Gervanno told the innkeeper.

"You want no interruptions?"

Gervanno nodded.

The man exhaled. "I'll find one for you if you wait a moment."

A MOMENT WAS PERHAPS HALF an hour, during which the innkeeper departed. Gervanno did not head to his room; he checked with the young Hunters, who were now attempting to bed down their dogs. Leial was tired. Gervanno considered leaving the dog in the room they shared; Leial was not considered a kennel dog by the innkeeper, but the Hunter dogs clearly were.

In the end, he chose to keep Leial with him, certain the Lady would not begrudge his presence. The dog was no part of the disgrace with which he'd struggled since the night the wyverns had destroyed the caravan he had been hired to guard. The dog and Nenyane had perhaps been the Lady's grace, even at the height of the day: mercy was subtle, and oft more appreciated when it was entirely unexpected.

But there were lands with no sun, in which the Lady was not ascendant. Lands, he thought, with no gods—or no gods with which Gervanno was familiar. But it was here, in the far less malleable world that Gervanno had lived in all of his life, that war was meant to be fought. He did not understand it, but there were some things mortals were not meant to understand.

The innkeeper tapped his shoulder, and he turned, chagrined. The man had equipped himself with two lanterns; he handed one to Gervanno.

"Come with me."

Gervanno followed as the innkeeper turned and walked away from the streets and his inn's open doors. People had begun to arrive to take the innkeeper up on his offer of emergency hospitality. They did not look embarrassed or humiliated; a reminder that, outside of the circus, they knew to expect disaster.

As if the words were spoken aloud, the innkeeper said, "It isn't too bad, from what I've managed to gather. There was one year, half the town was without homes. We prepare for it. People here know. This time, we've some rebuilding to do—but not much, and we've the supplies for most of it. This is our nature. You might pass through our towns with merchant caravans; you might come to settle here, as old soldiers do, who can. You might never see the circus again; you might be called to the circus several times.

"I don't think the circus will be as quiet as it was throughout our history—and perhaps it won't be as safe. We all saw the skies shatter; we saw the great, black beasts. We saw fire in the air, and lightning in a clear sky—a sky the wrong color. Maybe the circus will finally close. It was created for one war, one moment."

This surprised Gervanno. He did not expect the townsfolk to know. But it had been the people of those long-ago towns who had first made the choice that created the circus, that had been responsible for the form and shape it would take—a creative love letter to the people they chose to abandon.

"If it goes, it goes," the innkeeper continued, ducking under a low-lying branch, and pausing on the other side as he waited for Gervanno to follow. "We'll miss it. We'll miss the dream made reality for just a day. We'll miss the safety. We'll miss the magic—because it's a magic that resides in our hearts from the moment we're old enough to remember.

"But the circus master once told me: everything that knows beginning knows an end." He fell silent as he continued to lead Gervanno. "This is the closest place I could find," he said, almost apologetically. "But Gerta—she's one of our elders—thought you'd want more distance from Hansleigh. She's from the South, married a soldier there and headed north."

Ah. Gervanno nodded. "She is right." He followed the innkeeper in silence, for the innkeeper had run out of words to offer. The silence was not awkward, but companionable, and Gervanno accepted it with more gratitude than he would have speech.

Here, as in the heart of the circus, an open field existed—one more heavily overgrown with wild growth, but absent trees. The bright moon was almost full, the second almost invisible; the sky was clear and the stars beginning to make themselves known.

"Can you find your way back, or should I come out to fetch you when you're done?"

"I can find my way back. You've work of your own, and I've interrupted that."

"And given me a breather," the innkeeper replied, smiling broadly, his face illuminated by silver light and the warmer glow of the lamp he carried. "I could've sent one of the youngsters out, but even I need a break." He offered Gervanno a lopsided grin, but no further words.

Left alone in this field, which seemed an echo of the one on which he'd stood facing demons and the fiery breath of their flying mounts, he was silent for a long, long time. Almost, he had forgotten what to do. But he had wine, and water, and carried within him the blood that was offered for the most serious of gratitudes or entreaties. Women performed these ablutions in the home of his childhood, not men.

Not openly.

But men were boys before they attained adulthood, and their lives as children entwined with those of the women: mothers, sisters, Omas, Onas. They were not excluded when young—they could not be. And those women whispered the night's truth: the Lady of Mercy loved all of her children, even those who must stand in the harshest of the Lord's light. Women were closer to the Lady because women, his Oma had said, lived in shadows cast by men.

Had he traveled as Evaro did, with wife and children, he might have left all ceremonies in his wife's hands; that would be traditional. That would be expected. He did not.

He could not remember whether water came first, or wine, or if only one was necessary. But water and wine quenched different thirsts, and even if he misremembered the order of offering, he knew the Lady would forgive him; she valued sincerity and an open heart. He therefore offered water first, in small quantities.

He spoke their names: the lost. Evaro. Sylvia. Silvo, the youngest of the guards, who had been so deeply respectful of Gervanno's service in the Averdan valleys on the day when true night had almost fallen. There were other names, other guards, other merchants, apprentices to Evaro. He whispered their names with each drop of water that fell. Even the names of the children who had accompanied the caravan.

Ah, now he remembered: this was to be performed at the gravesite.

He had no graves; he carried one only in his heart, and that would have to suffice, for nothing had survived the flames and fires of wyvern and demon. Only Gervanno.

He offered wine next, and this time, he left out the names of the children too young to be offered it. Each name was a plea. Each name was an invisible dagger that drew no blood but would never stop causing injury. This time, he spoke of the loss, not of his pride, not of his honor, but of them as people. Evaro would take and teach no more apprentices, would introduce no more men like Gervanno to the wider world. Sylvia would never harshly mother those that required that harshness, or speak softly to those that did not.

Silvo would never raise sword in the battle of which he dreamed. His family was poorer than Gervanno's had been, and they could not afford to properly equip him; his ability with the sword had never been properly trained. But he could be sent with the merchants to earn the coin that would help his family—and they had sent him with the family sword.

It was impressive only to Silvo in his naïveté. Gervanno missed that youthful belief in the future. He had kept none of it for himself.

Lady, he whispered. Show them mercy. Protect them from the furi-

ous, howling winds. Give them respite from the sands and the anger of
the Lord.

Last, he offered blood. It was almost amusing; he could—and had
—cut himself to offer blood in oaths before, but it was much more difficult than his demeanor implied. To *be* cut was fine; to cut oneself,
harder. He set the lamp on the ground, where its glow could be seen
through stalks of wild grass, and steadied his hand.

"What are you doing?" The voice was familiar and should have
been singularly unwelcome. Even in the lee of the Lady's time, the fox
was wild and dangerous; Gervanno could afford to show none of the
irritation he felt at the interruption. Thus had he always faced men of
power: with respect, no matter the circumstance.

"It is a mourning ritual," he replied, his voice soft and even, the
blade of his long knife against his skin.

"Mourning?"

"Yes, Eldest. We bespeak the Lady in our plea for her mercy to
cover and protect the dead."

"You are mortal, child," the fox replied. He passed the lantern,
turned to it, whiskers twitching.

"Our eyes are not your eyes, and we require some light."

"The moons are bright, are they not enough?"

"No, Eldest."

"Very well. Don't let me interrupt you."

The fox had no doubt saved his life, and Gervanno struggled to
remember that fact. He prayed to the Lady not for mercy but for
patience, the thread of his thoughts almost broken by the golden,
faintly glowing creature. He managed to hold on to it with effort.

"Eldest," a second voice said. It was the voice of Meralonne
APhaniel, whom Nenyane called Illaraphaniel, as if she were also a
creature of the wilderness.

The fox *tsked*. "Illaraphaniel."

With the Northern Widan came the Northern bard. Gervanno
wished to have this moment, this one moment, to fulfill his responsibility to the departed. But perhaps that was too much to ask of the
Lady.

"Come. Leave the mortal; he is clearly in the midst of an important
duty."

"He is honoring the dead. Surely he must know the dead do not
care."

"The dead do care," the mage replied. "We are not mortal; what the mortals know is not what we know. Leave him." The words were just shy of command. Meralonne was a man of power, equal to the fox.

"I have an interest in him, Illaraphaniel." The voice was lower, underpinned with a hint of a growl too deep for his apparent throat.

"Clearly. But you have a lord, and you bore word of her invitation. We will be traveling together, and I have much to discuss with you regarding that travel. We have time, but mortals do not—let us not, then, waste time. Come. She is waiting."

The fox growled, but the growl was one of annoyance. He did not dismiss the concerns of his distant lord. When Meralonne walked away, the fox walked by his side.

The bard, however, did not join them. Instead, he knelt, as Gervanno knelt. "Nenyane is with Stephen. She wished to find you, but Stephen dissuaded her."

Gervanno felt a hint of warmth and gratitude. And he remembered, as Kallandras knelt and removed a skein of wine, that Kallandras claimed the Dominion as the land of his birth. The bard's presence, when unveiled, could not be ignored, but here it demanded nothing of Gervanno except the distant sense of kinship between two men far from their home. His silence was not awkward; he asked nothing of Gervanno except a similar silence.

Gervanno steadied himself. The fox would be a concern on the morrow, as would the war. But here, now, it was the dead that mattered. The dead and the ceremonies that could not be offered them by any save himself.

His hand steadied; he cut his arm, deeply enough to draw blood, but not so deeply as to risk infection or injury. To the earth, in silence, he offered that blood, as he had offered water, not wine: he spoke the names of the dead. He offered what he could to guide them to the Lady's side on this moon-filled night. Every name had weight, but in the speaking of those names, the weight lessened.

He would never forget them. He prayed to the Lady that his memories would become kind, warm, something to hold and treasure; that they not become a measure of his worth, his lack of worth. That the good memories, the astonishing memories, might one day be a comfort and not an accusation. The Lady would forgive this selfishness.

He was not aware immediately of the soft hum of Kallandras's voice; he could not later say when the singing started. He was not even certain that the humming, wordless, was offered for Gervanno's dead or Kallandras's own. But he found comfort in that, as well. Sylvia would have adored the bard.

They sat together while the moon slowly inched across the sky, but when the lamp's light began to burn down, Gervanno found his feet again. Leial was asleep in the tall grass; he lifted the dog, who woke up just enough to lick his face.

The bard rose as well. He said nothing, but even his silence was a gentle song.

Epilogue

A dala stood in the streets that led to the empty pavilions of the circus as the last of the townspeople walked through the gate, returning to what they considered the real world. The last person to leave was Trevor. Her hand was still warm; he had held her hand—or she had held his—every inch of the way to those gates. He could not remain here. Even if he refused to leave by gate, he would be ejected. He might have taken the risk but Adala knew that his destination would be random; the gates had been created for a reason.

She wanted to hold on to him.

She wanted him to return to his home.

For both reasons, she'd kept his hand in hers. She asked the wind to be both warm and gentle for this last of their walks together. All of the words that they could say had been said, but she wanted more. She thought she would always want more. One more day. One more hour. One more minute.

She wondered where they would be now, in a different world. A world in which they'd run away together. A world in which they'd survived the flight. Would they have returned to Hansleigh to find it destroyed? Would they have assumed it had been safe?

They would be together.

When Adala had been called to the circus—when she had made her plans to flee—they knew there would be danger. They understood the circus's call. Both of them knew, although Trevor hadn't put much faith in what he called children's tales.

Only in facing demons and foreigners and certain death were Adala's suspicions confirmed. She'd wanted to run away from them all. To have love. To hold on to it. Trevor had not been called to the circus. Had he been, she'd've never run away.

Trevor understood that not all children's stories were lies, and when he *knew*, he couldn't leave. He couldn't hold on to her. It was Trevor's decision. Trevor couldn't accept the death of everyone in Hansleigh.

She should have been angrier. She should have felt betrayed. And she had. But she loved Trevor *because* he cared. If he had only ever cared for himself, she would never have loved him at all. She would have kept her distance.

And maybe that would have been better. She would have kept her distance, and when she'd received the request that she join the circus, she would have told her parents with pride, rather than hiding all hint of the news from them. She would have come to the circus, and she would have felt that she was finally, finally returning to her true home.

She lifted her hand, staring at it as if she could see some trace of Trevor left there. She saw the ring.

He betrayed you.

She lowered her hand, thinking of Anya. Anya had offered to kill Trevor. Anya *wanted* to kill him. But she accepted that Adala didn't want Trevor to die.

"Why? WHY?"

"Because I love him. I came back because I love him."

"But he *left* you!"

Adala could not tell Anya she was wrong. It was Trevor's decision that forced Adala's. But...she loved him, still. She could see the man she had been drawn to in the man who had turned back, toward Hansleigh, in guilt and horror. She had wanted to be the most important person in his life. And she had been.

But had she ever asked him to prove his love by killing his family with his own hands, he would have recoiled in horror; she would have killed what love he felt for her forever. Love was supposed to be singular, perfect; it was supposed to be joy and hope and light. But Trevor didn't exist in isolation. She wasn't certain why he had ever loved her —but he had. She couldn't deny that.

If she had asked him to die for her, he would have died for her. She was certain she would have died for him. But she was also certain, now, that she couldn't kill him. She couldn't *let him* die. Not for her. Not while she could prevent that death.

That was love, wasn't it?

That was love, even if it was also goodbye?

Now, in this moment, the pride of that, the certainty that it was the right choice, was dimming. She looked at her future—a future without the towns, except in emergencies; a future without the constant presence of Trevor—and she regretted it. She regretted loving him. She regretted running away, and regretted returning.

Trevor was gone.

Was it always going to be like this? Always? Would love turn to pain? Even memories deserted her here, because the good memories reminded her of loss, not joy. Joy existed, but it would not come again.

The wind tugged at her hair, at her robes. She watched as the tents and pavilions began to fade away, shimmering as if they were colorful mirages, meeting places, tables that offered hospitality to guests, to the people who had once been family. She wondered what would remain in their place, if anything remained, but at the same time, she knew.

Here, she felt like a child; the wind moved her hair, her robes; the earth shifted beneath her feet, the cobbled stone became softer and smoother. She thought that, here, she could live without shoes forever; nothing would cut her feet. Nothing would harm her.

But one building did remain—or rather, one building appeared, as if the whole of the circus offered to outsiders was stage prop and dressing, drawn back at last to reveal the shape and heart of home.

She stopped as the building emerged from fog, or what seemed fog, another veil being lifted, another reality being asserted.

"It's home," a familiar voice said. The circus master had joined her. She had not heard him approach, but felt no fear; some echo of his voice and presence was everywhere, even if he could not be seen. The wind that whispered her name also whispered *lord*, with reverence.

He was her lord now. She would be aware of his presence for the rest of her existence.

"You will." The circus master spoke with many voices, all perfectly overlapped.

"Did you make this?" she asked, looking at the building. It seemed, at first, a longhouse, but it continued back; towers could be seen in the distance, attached to the main building. Nothing about the structure looked supernatural, magical; it looked like a dwelling made by the hands of many people — all human. All like Adala.

"Not quite like you, child of man." He began to walk, still wearing his odd black suit. "But no, this was not my creation; it is influenced by me, and by the denizens of my lands who were not, and are not, mortal. There is some wood in the construction — it was what the mortals knew best — but not as much as you are accustomed to seeing. The trees will surrender some parts of themselves — branches, and some roots. The earth will surrender stone more readily. There are very few mortal tools; we do not cut trees or plow earth in the way your people do.

"But it is not necessary here."

"Is food?"

The circus master was silent as they walked.

"What is that?"

"You refer to the half-walled garden?"

Adala nodded.

"It is the graveyard."

She turned her head to look at him; she saw his face in profile, his attention on what he had called the graveyard. "Who's buried there?"

"The earliest of my servants, and some handful that grew old and succumbed to age. You are not what your family is, and these lands are not like the towns. To your family, should they see you in decades, you will not have aged at all. But you will age and eventually, as all things mortal, you will die."

It seemed to her that there was genuine mourning in his expression — in his many expressions, for his face, as his voice, began to shift and blur, never settling on one visage.

"Do not seek the love of a god, child of man. It is not mortal love. It will consume and destroy, for it will never be what you were born to seek. What the gods love too dearly, they change, if change can be affected at all — and it can. But the people here were loved by the mortals with whom they worked, and with whom they soldiered. If I created this place to lay the dead to rest, it is your compatriots who did the work.

"It is you and your compatriots who do all of the work."

She heard something odd in his voice, then. Regret? Yearning? She could not fix a name to it.

"Do not try," he said — they said, all tones gentle. "I told you — we change what we love, and we cannot love as you do. Think you that those who are called to the circus were deliberately created? They were not. But they were mine and, try as I might, some influence cannot be avoided."

"And I'm one of them."

"Yes, but your birth, and your power, did not occur just because I am too close. There is another god on this plane, and the barriers between my lands and the lands in which mortals live and rule are breaking as we speak. The wilderness is reaching out, at last, from all the hidden lands.

"There will be war, child. While the circus endures, your families will be safe. But go, now, to meet your people. I have one other matter to which I must attend."

In the distance, Adala could hear one wild, angry cry. "*I don't want to leave!*" She hesitated. As she did, Katie came to meet her. Katie looked careworn and exhausted. It was not to Adala that Katie walked, but to the god; she knelt there.

"We cannot keep her here," the god said, before Katie could speak. It didn't matter; both Adala and the god knew what Katie wanted.

"The gates have closed, but she remains," Katie said, voice soft and tremulous. "She can stand here by dint of will and her own talent. Here, she would be safe. And if she is here, the world without will be much safer."

"I did not say we should have her exit in the towns; that would be a disaster. But she cannot remain here—she will threaten us."

"She means no harm—"

"No, not immediately. She is like a mortal child at heart, but her power is far too great for such modest lands as mine. At her command, the earth will break. At her command, the fire will burn. She means no harm, I agree. But you have seen children; you came to me after your own were grown.

"She causes harm wherever she goes because she is like a child. She is pure impulse. A child might dissolve in tears and scream themselves to sleep. Parents understand this. Now imagine that that child is a mage without parallel. She does not scream; she destroys in her tantrum. She burns down buildings. She breaks the earth. She screams with the furious voice of the wind; she calls lightning in her rage, and it comes.

"She never dies. Her injuries are emotional. But people die in her wake."

"Could you not—could you not contain her? She needs to feel safe, my lord. I think she would feel safe here, and it may make a difference."

This woman had been shouting commands on the battlefield, expression grim, voice as solid as any new steel Trevor had proudly shown Adala. She was not shouting now. Adala thought that this was as close to begging as Katie could come.

The expression on the lord's face rippled, shifting so quickly, it was hard to pin down. Different faces, different brows, different lips, cheeks, chins flowed past, as if each perturbation was an argument with himself. But his many voices, speaking as one, were clear.

"We owe you much, and your kin owe you more, although they will never know it. Could I, I would grant you this favor. I would attempt to bind her, in safety, in this place."

Katie's expression dimmed, but she made no further plea. She lowered her head. Her hands, by her sides, were not quite fists, but they were tightening.

The god's voice was gentle. "Anya is of the towns; she is one of the people these lands were created to protect. But her role in this war is not done. She cannot retire here."

"Is there a place she *can* retire?" Katie's voice was low, but even.

The god did not answer. Adala heard death in the silence. Death and pity.

"Understand, child, that choice was given to those who dwelled within my towns—but choice breeds consequence."

"She *had* no choice." A spark of anger lit Katie's tone. She lifted her head and met the god's eyes almost without blinking.

"We will not ask you what you have seen. Is dusk a choice? Is dawn? Is storm?"

Katie swallowed. "You know they are not."

"Are the dead?"

In the word *dead*, Adala could hear the echoes and resonance of ancient grief and hatred; the wind grew stronger, its undercurrents more ferocious.

"No."

"No, indeed. You knew her as a child. You knew she had fled the village, just as Adala did, with the young man she loved. You did not know what happened to her after she chose to leave. You do now."

Katie swallowed and nodded.

"Do you understand that the demons could not have arrived in force at the outskirts of Hansleigh without her direct intervention? Ah. I see you do not. She has labored these years under the command of the *Kialli*. She has knelt in the shadow of the god we do not name."

"She hates demons!"

"Yes. But it is with the demons that she has lived her adult life."

"She could live *here*," Katie replied, not arguing with the lord's stated fact.

"You know why she cannot."

Katie swallowed.

"You are not my daughter; your gift in particular is deep where it concerns the townspeople. You wish to avoid what you fear. You wish to preserve Anya. You see in her what she once was: a child that you knew. Daughter of a beloved friend."

"Is that so wrong?" It was Adala who asked, when words failed to leave Katie's mouth.

"Such impulses are not right or wrong. They are emotions. They are entanglements. But such entanglements come at great cost when dealing with a person of Anya's power. And she is a great power. If our enemy has succeeded to date, it is in large part because of that power."

"Could her power not be used against our enemies?"

"Child," the god said to Adala, "I will not say it is impossible. She has a role to play, and I cannot end it because she is of my towns. She is damaged in a way that makes her aid, genuinely offered, a tragedy in the making. There is little I would not grant you, were it within my power — but you ask because you see where her steps must take her."

"There are some things that cannot be avoided."

Katie nodded and bowed. To Adala's eye, it looked like acceptance.

"You are very young if you believe that," the god said, when Katie passed through the doors of the distant building. "You agree with Katie."

"I don't know enough to agree or disagree."

The god's chuckle was like the warmth of hearth fire in the coldest of winters. "You are younger than Anya, and a power in your own right while you dwell within my lands. Tell me, what answer would Anya have offered?"

"Katie would never have spoken as she did if Anya were here. Anya is...like a child. Katie likes children."

"And you."

Adala nodded. "I wasn't afraid of her."

"No. On an instinctive level, you understood that you could—for a small time—survive her tantrums."

"She didn't hurt the children."

"You must speak with Katie if you believe that she never has. She moves through the world unaware, at times, of anything but her own pain; sometimes she is querulous, sometimes raging. She is here because she has the raw power to stand where she chooses, but even she must sleep. Could we keep her, could she remain in the towns without becoming a terrible threat to my people there, we would." There was finality in his words. "Speak to Katie."

Adala bowed to him and turned to the house, leaving the graveyard in which the discussion had taken place.

SHE THOUGHT she would have difficulty finding Katie, but Katie was waiting for her when she opened the right door—there were two, side by side—and entered the hall.

Katie smiled. "You're new here, and the boys are exhausted. I thought I would give you a tour, show you where to find things."

Adala did not feel lost. She felt a sense of home that was both familiar and new; there was wonder and she offered it in the hush of silence.

Katie led her down the hall wrapped in that silence; she did not speak or attempt to draw Adala's attention, as if she understood that what Adala saw, she must remember. They passed areas open to sky; Adala had no words for them, but words weren't necessary. She would find words of her own to name them, but later.

"Time doesn't pass the same way here," Katie said, when they reached a small room. "This is mine."

Adala didn't ask why it was so small. Nor did she ask why Katie had never moved from it. She could see, in the details, a hint of Katie's past, Katie's former home—this was the only way she could bring any of it with her. Adala thought she would make a different choice, if she had that choice.

Katie's eyes were darkly circled. She looked at Adala. They were not quite of a height, but in the moment, Katie seemed far more bowed by age. "Did I do the right thing?" she whispered.

Adala frowned. "The lord didn't seem offended—"

Katie shook her head. "My gift wasn't yours. It wasn't one of the gifts that are found in the young—it's why I came much later to the circus than most who are called. I had the life you dreamed of, and if life wore the shine off dreams, it never destroyed them.

"Anya was always a peculiar child, much lost in her own explorations and thoughts. She walked in daydream, and was just as likely to forget walls were in her way when she started to move as not. Her mother worried for her constantly, but loved her. She'd had strong headaches, just before she left us. She'd found a young man who loved her in spite of her peculiarities—or maybe because of them. We don't know. We saw neither of them again.

"We hoped that they'd found a better home for themselves." She hesitated. "No. I hoped it. Her mother knew. Her mother knew what the magi had said. She had true talent. True power. They asked for permission to take her to the big city, the Order of Knowledge, for both her safety and our own.

"I thought she'd died."

Katie lifted her head. "Her mother said the mage told her that her daughter was already suffering from the effects of a power she could not control and could not discharge."

"She came to you?"

"We searched for her. We searched for evidence of her death. To see her here was a gift, and it was a poison. Her mother is gone, and I think—I think she would have been terrified of what her daughter has become."

"And you weren't."

"I was. I was terrified of what she had become because of what was done to her. And I was terrified of the future she's walking towards."

"Katie—none of these things is wrong."

"No. But I saw something, in a possible future. I would never have seen it if I hadn't held Anya's hands in my own—but that was easy. She didn't want to let go. I think she meant to take me out of the circus if she had to leave it herself." A wry smile folded the corner of her lips, a hint of warmth and affection that slowly ebbed away. "I saw a young man. Younger than Anya—maybe your age, if that. He was like, and unlike, Anya. The lord said that, as the wilderness seeps into the world, the wild talents that sometimes grace mortals would become much stronger; that was his explanation for Anya.

"The young man is named Adam. He lives—for now—in the very seat of the Empire to the west."

Adala nodded. A small bird with iridescent blue wings came to land on her shoulder, chirping softly. "Animals always liked me," she said, when Katie's brows rose.

"Not animals like these," Katie replied, a hint of wonder robbing her face, momentarily, of the weight of years.

"Sorry," Adala said, meaning it. "Adam?"

"He is not what Anya is—his talent is one of healing. But the boy could heal gods, if the gods were fool enough to allow it. He can heal the damage Anya's choice did to her."

"She didn't seem injured to me."

"No, she didn't." Katie's smile was pained.

"If he can help her, why are you worried?"

"Because she will be going to a city that is far, far larger—and far more populated—than the Free Towns. If she feels threatened, if she is afraid, people will die in far greater numbers—and she is, she should have been, *our* problem."

"And look at me, seeking comfort from someone who's only barely of age. I should be ashamed of myself." Katie spoke as if she was.

Adala shook her head. "I wish I could comfort you—I've never been very good at that, at least not according to my mother. But I don't think Anya will lose her temper."

"Why not?"

"Because I think she'll find Nenyane—the woman with the sword."

Katie flinched, her face losing color. "Not her," she whispered.

"Why not? Nenyane seemed comfortable with Anya."

Katie closed her eyes. "There is a reason for that. But if she becomes Anya's anchor, much, much more than a city will fall in the end. Not her. If gods listen—not her."

"But Adam would be okay?"

"If she can bring herself to trust him enough, he will be far, far safer for the rest of us. And she hasn't joined the Hunters. She's still here. Maybe she'll arrive at the city independent of them. Maybe she'll seek Adam on her own."

"You told her about Adam."

Katie nodded.

"That's why you're worried."

She nodded again, inhaling and exhaling tears. "I'm sorry. It's been so long since I've felt this way. It's been so long since I've worried like this."

"But...we just fought *demons*."

"And wyverns, yes. Perhaps you didn't see it, or didn't understand what you saw. Death doesn't come for us in any way but one: old age. We who have offered our blood to the circus are bound to it, part of it —to kill us they must destroy the entirety of these lands—and the god who rules them."

"But Anya isn't circus. She didn't bleed here—had she, she would have become part of us. She understood the danger, although she couldn't explain it well. And she wanted to protect the circus. She wanted to visit it."

Katie nodded.

"No," Adala said quietly. The bird chirped. "No, you didn't do the wrong thing. We all have to have hope."

"And if the cost of my hope is other lives?"

Adala had no answer.

JEWEL SAT in the audience chamber of Terafin, not the kitchen to which she returned when she could struggle free of dream and vision. It was harder now than it had been, but remained possible; it was the struggle that defined her in moments like these.

The fox stood before her.

"I do not see Jarven."

"I have left him on the road, but he will wend his way back to Terafin." The fox was untroubled, as ever, by Jarven.

Here, seated upon a throne of wood that yet grew and sprouted leaves and delicate, small flowers, she was untroubled as well—but some hint of what she had once been perturbed her at the thought.

"He has always been a bold cub; nothing he has experienced has affected that. But he has broken none of your laws. I would not allow it." The last words were almost more felt than heard. "They travel, now, to your city."

From behind the throne, hissing and the distinctly unpleasant sound of a cat spitting could be heard. Jewel lifted hand to the bridge of her nose. "Shadow."

"I don't *like* him," the cat said, coming out of the shadows that were his namesake. He could have been speaking of Adam, or the fox, or Jarven. Very, very few were the people who earned anything but his voluble disdain.

Ararath stood on the other side of the throne. It was the position he occupied in the absence of the mortal foolish enough to seek immortality: Avandar. Avandar Gallais. Once domicis. Once ruler of one of the fallen Cities of Man in an age where gods traversed the world at will.

Ararath seldom spoke to Jewel when she occupied this throne; he seldom spoke when she made her way to the kitchen to meet with her den. But when she retreated, it was Ararath's voice she heard most clearly, and that was a benison. A gift from an Artisan who now lived within the court of the White Lady, free to travel, although she did not return.

Ararath could not easily interact with her den or the people of Terafin—this new Terafin, the only one of the Ten that occupied the mainland.

Shadow snickered. "They don't *see* him."

"Enough, Shadow."

The cat was sulking. Any moment now, he would begin to curse boredom. If dawn and dusk were inevitable turns of what remained of nature, boredom had become a similar phenomenon. One could set clocks by it.

Shadow, however, was not bored. "Adam is waiting." His tone made clear that Adam could wait forever as far as the cat was concerned.

Jewel frowned. To Ararath, she said, *Did I summon Adam?*

No.

"Tell him—politely and without violence—to enter the chamber."

"The Chosen will come to ask."

The Chosen. The oathguard. Jewel struggled to remember, and succeeded. How long had it been? How much longer must she exist in this state?

Ararath said nothing, but his expression shuttered.

"If it would not be too bold of me," the fox said, "I would deliver your message to your guards."

Shadow hissed.

The fox, diminutive in size, faced the winged predator without apparent concern. "She is your master, and you are *almost* a failure, your service lacks so much respect."

The hiss became a growl; Shadow's wings shot out to the sides, very narrowly missing Jewel's face.

"It was not I who spoke," she told the great cat, a hint of annoyance in her voice. "And if you destroy the throne room one more time, I will forbid you the keep. Permanently."

Shadow shrieked in outrage. It was clear he felt the fox had started things.

In the curved ceiling above them all, a cat laughed, the huffing sound of genuine amusement. That would be Snow.

"I *mean it*. If the two of you are going to fight, do it elsewhere."

Shadow seemed to consider this, but decided against; he turned and stomped away, his steps heavy enough to shake stone floors.

"You allow them far, far too much latitude," the fox observed, when Shadow had reached the doors.

"And you do not allow Jarven as much?"

"I am not lord," was the almost prim reply. But she had amused the fox. "He is mine. He breaks no law you have set. He will never betray you while I live."

"And you are certain you will survive him."

"Are you not?"

Jewel did not reply. She had seen many futures, many dreams and nightmares. She could no longer tell with any ease which was more likely, which less; the future stretched out further and further beyond her grasp, and she could not follow it all. Knew better than to try, but even that was difficult.

"Did you ever visit the Cities of Man?" she asked the fox.

"Not personally. Not until now; now I live within one. It is a wonder, in a world without wonder, and I regret my past choices."

"Adam must return to such a city."

"He will never return to such a city," the fox replied. "Even in my time, the Cities of Man were not inhabited by those who created them."

"What happened to their creators?"

The fox's eyes widened. "You ask that of *me*? You? If any lives now who can answer that question, it is you, Sen. But if the eldest are honest, they will tell you they have no answer to give. We do not know. Perhaps, if I remain in this place for long enough, I will finally understand this ancient mystery.

"But that time is not yet. I will return to my cub." The fox began to walk away, but turned head to look over his shoulder. "They are coming, as you have foreseen. Four who style themselves Breodani. The first is god-born. The second and third bear weaker god's blood, but it is wilder. And the last...you will see. Are you certain they are to be the companions you will send on the road with Adam of Arkosa?"

"No. I have seen it in some of the futures—most of them. Not all. But it is for them that we have waited. It is to the South they must journey. And you have failed to mention the other who travels with them."

The fox's eyes narrowed, but he did not fully turn toward her. "What of him? He is a mortal of little consequence, beneath your notice."

"But not beneath yours."

The fox did turn, then. "He is not yours, Lord."

"A bold claim, if he means to enter my city."

"He is *not yours*."

Snow came down from the heights and landed on the floor just in front of the stairs that lead to Jewel's throne.

"He is not mine," Jewel agreed, before Snow could pounce. "But Eldest, neither is he yours. Do not involve yourself further in the life of Gervanno di'Sarrado. I will not bind him in any fashion known to mortals; I will not restrict or command his movements. But I say to you again, for your own sake, do not involve yourself in his life. Jarven is yours, and Jarven is fraught—but you better understand men of Jarven's nature.

"Be wary of the things you cannot understand."

"He will not harm me."

"No, not intentionally. But if you failed to mention him because you wish to protect him—from me—you worried needlessly. He will travel where the Hunters travel until he is incapable of doing so. And he will travel, in the end, where Adam must travel, for weal or woe. The South is stirring, and the Lord of the Hells has long had purchase in those lands."

The doors opened before the fox could reply. Jewel noted that Snow seemed disappointed.

"You know he would not harm me," she told the white cat, as the cat turned and mounted the stairs. He would have pushed Ararath out of the way, but could not; the most he could do was occupy the same space. He did, and then leaned his head into the arm of her chair; she responded by scratching behind his ears.

"He *challenged* you."

"Far, far less than you or your brothers do."

"But *we're* different!"

"Hush. We have guests."

Adam, Avandar, and Torvan entered the audience chamber.

Jewel rose, then. She found it hard to remain seated when Adam entered. On most such days, she managed. But Adam was den, to her. He didn't suit the severe and forbidding throne room. As she moved, her clothing shifted until she didn't suit it either.

His expression was grave.

"You were talking to Finch."

His brows rose, and then he smiled, although the smile was rueful. "She is afraid for me. She doesn't want me to leave."

Jewel nodded. "You couldn't expect anything different, could you?"

"I hate to worry her."

Of course he did. "I'll try to talk to her."

"You already have," Adam replied, his smile deepening. "But Finch is Finch and you are Jay. Matriarchs know when their people must be sent to fight, and when they must flee."

"I have scouted the roads," Avandar said, as if Adam had not spoken. He was ill-pleased with Jewel's change of clothing; he felt it lacked dignity. He always had. "They are not, currently, traversed."

Jewel nodded. "They'll come. Adam, follow." She left the throne room, heading toward the kitchen. Torvan fell in behind her, in silence, as befit the captain of the Chosen.

THE KITCHEN REMAINED the heart of the den; it was their strategy room, their place to converse and dissemble. It was where they gathered when Jay left her rooms and the wilderness that seemed to occupy so much of her time.

Adam was allowed to enter the kitchen; any member of the den was. He was comfortable there but, as he had said, Finch was worried. Jewel understood why: Adam was young, half their age or perhaps even slightly less. Jewel could see him that way, but she could see beyond that youth to the heart of the man he would—he must—

become. His determination, his ability, were second to none. Where Adam walked, he was likely to survive.

Finch didn't wish their early life on anyone. She didn't want someone she considered a child to be on the front lines fighting while the rest stayed behind their desks, dealing with merchants and the Merchant and Port authorities. But it was Finch who rose the moment Jewel entered the kitchen, and Finch who made her way around the large table to where Adam stood, enfolding him in a hug and a whispered apology.

She spoke Torra, not Weston, when she talked to Adam.

Adam, aware that not all of the den were bilingual, dutifully answered in Weston, although his words were whispered comfort, assurance that no apologies were necessary.

"I know you think you're sending me to do the hard, dangerous work," he said, as she pulled back. "But I cannot do the work you do now. We would be bankrupt. Is that the right word?"

"It is," Jewel assured him.

"Work has to be done to keep home alive," he continued. "And it is not always exciting work. It is not bloody work — not most of the time. It's necessary work. I can't do most of it. But I have to take what I've learned from all of you, and deliver it to my sister. If she cannot learn what I have learned, Arkosa will fall, and there will be no Arkosans among the Voyani when the Lord of Night walks the lands.

"We are not the only family left from those ancient times; ours is not the only city to rise. But the most powerful of the cities lies beneath the great, sandy planes, unawakened, unentered."

Ah, Jewel thought. This was the heart of Finch's worry.

"How do you know this?"

Adam glanced at his feet. He then glanced at Jewel.

"Jay?"

"It's not from me," Jewel replied. "But I can guess. Evayne visited again."

"She said she had permission to travel your lands," Adam began, half guilty.

"She does — but I may revoke it if this continues." Her frown was not majestic; it was familiar. "What did she tell you?"

Adam hesitated; everyone marked it. But this was the kitchen. The hesitation didn't last. "I have to go to Arkosa."

This wasn't new.

"But before I go to Arkosa, I must find Yollana of the Havallah Voyani, and I must offer her aid, where I can. Hers was the first city to rise in ancient times, and it is the last that remains buried beneath the Sea of Sorrows. I think. It was...confusing. Evayne was very clear: I must find Yollana. But the rest was...less clear, to me."

"And to her," Jewel said. It wasn't a question. She exhaled. If the kitchen had become the den's foremost gathering place, there was very little business that was discussed. Finch had, in the early days, brought written reports about the activities in the Merchant Authority, that building so changed it was only recognizable because the same people worked in it as had worked in it before Jewel's ascent. Those that had survived.

She had stopped bringing those reports: not because they weren't at the heart of House business, but because if Jewel took the reports — in theory to read and absorb the information they contained — those reports vanished, or became so transformed they could no longer be accessed by anyone.

Everything had changed, and everything continued to change where Jewel walked. It was why she couldn't live in the den's wing; why she couldn't remain in their presence for more than an hour or two. Only Calliastra, child of two gods, their existence eternal pain and conflict within her body, could exist where Jewel now lived. She remained with Jewel in the wilderness, but did not return to the den and its more mundane meetings.

Avandar stood, as he often did, against the far wall.

When Jewel looked up to meet his steady gaze, he grimaced. "I have no advice to offer," he said, which meant advice was certain to follow. "But Havallah is dangerous. I counsel against. I accept that Adam must return to Arkosa — but the Dominion is not a safe place for those who are talent-born. The world outside of your walls is not safe for the healer-born. Adam is significant. If his ability is discovered, conflict is certain to arise."

Jewel nodded. Finch did not pale, but caught Adam by the hand and dragged him to the table, to the seat beside hers. Avandar had voiced the heart of her fear.

Did she not remember their lives in the holdings? Did she not remember what they had faced at Adam's age? Adam was not a child. He had already crossed parts of the wilderness, had faced what would be certain death had he been anyone else.

"He will not travel alone," Jewel told the den, her gaze on Avandar. The wilderness had not taken the mark he had placed on her arm from her; she felt it now, throbbing slightly. She could, if she looked, see more; here, she did not look.

It was Angel who said, "I could go with him."

"No." The word was loud, harsh, resonant; it did not sound like Jewel's voice, although it was Jewel who'd spoken. She grimaced.

Teller exhaled. Teller, Carver, Finch, Arann. They turned to Angel as if they expected Angel would understand the single word, the weight of it, the meaning.

It was Avandar who said, "Where must Angel go?" His voice was gentle.

Jewel had gone through so much to form, from the heart of her talent and her body, the crystal through which seers could, with will and intent, pierce specific veils of specific futures. It was gone. She had shattered it, and its shards, both figurative and literal, had flown throughout Averalaan. She could not summon them back; could not be what she was. She had accepted that in the moment she had crushed the heart. She was not simple seer; she was Sen.

Visions had always come to her in dreams: the three dreams that signified the future. She had wanted the seer's crystal in order to have some control over the timing of those glimpses. Now, she had no control, and the visions overlapped, overwhelmed, if she did not fight against them.

It had been less than an hour. Less, but she knew she could not remain longer. She had had an hour with her kin when she had first accepted her duties to Averalaan.

It was Teller who rose. Teller who came immediately to her side, or the side of the chair she had taken—and when? When had she sat?— and caught her hands gently in his. She could not tell whose hand was trembling. Perhaps both.

"You have to go."

Jewel swallowed. She nodded. She didn't want to leave. She never did.

But she had seen Angel, and the snow and ice of the distant north, and she understood that the arc of Angel's story—from the moment he joined the den—had been traveling toward the northern lands. Arrend. "With Terrick," she managed to say, and even the mention of that name caused ripples across the surface of her vision—and the kitchen table. She closed her eyes. Sometimes that helped.

"Terafin," Avandar said, his voice close to her ear. "I will escort you back to your chambers. Leave the den, for now."

"It's not even been an hour." She tried to keep the hurt, the pain, the frustration from her words. She lifted her hands—hands she should not be able to see—and signed. Den-sign.

I'm sorry. I have to go.

She didn't know if they replied—but at the same time, she did. Standing in this room with her eyes closed, she could see it so clearly—but she could see earlier iterations, early versions of herself and her den, some of them dead. She could see Teller's hands move; could see Finch begin to sign, could see Adam pale.

She signed again, her fingers forming words the den had never built into den-sign.

Avandar gently guided her toward the door, toward the many doors, some single, some double, some old and some so pristine they might never have been touched by human hands at all.

ADAM WAITED until the Matriarch was gone; silence had descended at the table they occupied only when she was present. The gravity of the situation kept them at their seats. When no one spoke, he cleared his throat, hesitant to break the silence, as he so often was. Thoughts chased themselves around the table, transforming familiar expressions.

The Matriarch had forbidden Adam to touch her when she was like this, afraid for him.

He, in turn, was afraid for her. She had no obvious injury, but he felt almost certain he could provide an anchor for the person she had once been, if she but let him.

"I will travel South," he said.

They shook themselves. "When?"

"I'm not certain. There are people who must travel South, and the Matriarch felt we should travel together while our roads are the same." He looked across the table at Angel. "I'm sorry."

Angel was confused. "What are you apologizing for?"

"I think—I think if it weren't for me, she would have been able to stay for longer."

But Angel of the pale hair and striking eyes shook his head. "If anyone should apologize, it's me—but I'm not going to."

Carver hit Angel's shoulder. "You'll go to Arrend."

"Terrick wants to return. We've talked about it, but I'm not sure there's any role for me there. I'm my father's son—but my service, my oath, is to Jay. To *her* Terafin."

"She thinks you have to go."

"Or she's seen me go." He exhaled. "She said she sees all the futures, if she's not careful and not in control. She gets lost in them. But that? That was pure Jay. She *knows* I have to go."

"But not when."

Angel nodded. "This is the problem with having a home. I don't want to desert it." He pushed himself out of his seat. "But I'll talk to Terrick."

Carver rose as well.

"Not you."

"She didn't say I couldn't go—either south or north. But Adam sounds like he'll have company on the road, and you'll be stuck with Terrick, a man who grudgingly speaks two words in a day, as if language is oppression." He was both amused and serious.

"She won't want you to leave if she hasn't seen it."

"She won't want you to go alone." Carver didn't argue with Angel's actual words. "But we'll need to start planning if we're heading out."

Angel shook his head. He offered no further argument. Both men left the kitchen.

Arann watched Finch and Teller, long considered the weakest of the den. Adam understood why; neither had been trained for combat, not even to the extent Adam had. But there was no physical danger here. Adam doubted there would ever be physical danger in this city, not for the Matriarch's kin.

"You went to see her in the audience chamber?" Finch asked.

Adam nodded.

"Because Evayne had visited you?"

He nodded again.

Teller and Finch both spoke Torra so naturally it might have been their mother tongue. Arann, however, did not. "Did she say when?"

This time he shook his head. "But if she came, it must be soon. I wanted to ask the Matriarch's permission to travel."

"You clearly have it," Finch replied, rising. "We'll start making preparations. You'll need some coin, some clothing, some traveling items—bed rolls, packs. I think we can horse you—that'll count for something in the Dominion. I'll check with merchants to see if anyone's brave enough to head to the South. If you can travel with a caravan, so much the better.

"Don't make that face. It'll take time to arrange things. We're not trying to kick you out immediately. I'll try to find any information we have about Yollana and the Voyani in general."

Adam was certain he knew more than she would find, but nodded.

Arann glanced at Adam. "Ask Jay if you can visit the armory." Arann was, like most of the Chosen, a man of few words. The words he did speak therefore carried more weight.

"He *can't*," a familiar voice said. Shadow had stalked into the room. He paused and spit a feather out of his mouth.

"Why not?" It was Finch, not Arann, who asked.

"There is nothing there for *him*." The cat sniffed, glaring at Finch as if she was the most ignorant person he had ever met.

"Fine. Don't ask." Finch seldom argued with the great cats, but seemed to feel no fear of them; she treated them as if they were fractious cousins of dubious worth, but kin nonetheless.

Teller turned to Adam. "I should warn you—Levec has threatened to visit."

Adam smiled.

"If you could avoid telling him that you're planning to head to the Dominion, he'll probably be reasonable. For Levec."

The smile became a soft laugh. "I will not bring it up if he does not." He felt that he had many goodbyes to say, but...not yet. Not yet.

These people shared no blood with Adam, but they were family nonetheless. It had been such an odd thought when he had first arrived in Averalaan: it was not Arkosan; indeed, not Southern.

But it was to his blood kin that Adam must return, and the new family had not displaced the old family. Margret was waiting.

"You spend much time with the mortal."

Shianne, seated beneath the boughs of the oldest tree in these lands, looked up at the familiar voice. She smiled. "I am not with him, now."

"No, indeed; were he present, I would not have been so bold as to venture the observation." The Gardener offered the great tree a deep bow. "I apologize if I am interrupting you."

The boughs of the tree shifted, lowering just enough that leaves touched the crown of the Gardener's head. "Eldest," the Gardener said. "Did the water suffice?"

Leaves rustled; almost, words could be heard in their gentle friction.

"You like this land," Shianne said. She rose.

"Do you not feel likewise?"

"I am restless. Mortality sits uneasily on these shoulders. I have seen youth, and I have seen age—but not age such as this." She lifted an arm. In the Gardener's eyes, she was a brilliant light, a scion of the White Lady; he could not—perhaps would not—see mortality as her dominant truth. The wind heard her voice. The earth stilled to listen. The water moved differently beneath her feet.

He could see her armed, armored, wind pulling hair carefully from her face, riding always by the White Lady's side. Shandalliaran. That was where she should be, and should always be. But she had made her choice. He understood it: she had chosen to end her existence in order to free the White Lady and her court.

She had freed her sleeping sisters—her trapped sisters—and they had returned to the White Lady's side, there to ride as they had once ridden, at the dawn of time in the White Lady's hunting party, the White Lady's war band.

His own lord would not. Not yet, and perhaps not ever. Until he had redeemed the failure of his brothers, those princes he had loved to a degree only barely less than the White Lady herself, he would know neither peace nor forgiveness.

But the Gardener could not serve the lord he had been created to serve. He could not approach him. The White Lady's forgiveness was measured in existence, or lack thereof. He knew that he was part of Illaraphaniel, as the three princes had been part of the White Lady. She had called them home, and they had returned to their maker, their essences preserved, but their memories, their existences, their individuality lost forever. Empowering her, they were nonetheless lost.

So, too, the Gardener.

Part of him yearned for—had always yearned for—dissolution. For return.

But a greater part of him struggled against that, even now, even here.

Yes.

He looked up at the boughs of the great tree, tracing the fall of light between its many branches, large and small.

He does not wish you to be lost. He does not wish what you were to be lost, for you were never meant to be part of the war that has otherwise consumed his existence.

The Gardener glanced at Shianne; her throat was lifted as she, too, gazed up at the ancient, as if branches and leaves were the crown of the sky.

"Illaraphaniel was odd," she said, her lips turning in a smile that matched her words. "But not so odd as Isladar. I hear he, too, was lost."

The Gardener nodded.

"Do you know what your master knows?"

"I know what he knew. If I close my eyes and listen, I might hear strains of what he now knows—but there is danger in that, for both of us. Isladar was lost; he chose the Lord of the Hells as his master, severing himself forever from the White Lady's side."

"I wish to see him," Shianne said, voice soft. "Even dead, as he has become."

The Gardener said nothing. He wondered—had wondered—if the Lady's sisters would splinter as the rest of her people had done; if they would be drawn to love someone who was not their creator. He could not conceive it, standing beneath the boughs of this ancient presence.

You will leave us, the ancient said. *Soon, for both your kin and the mortals who dwell within my Lord's city.*

"Is he coming?" The gardener's question was so soft it barely carried. He wished to see his lord. He wished to live. The former, at the moment, was the stronger desire, but it was not always so.

He is. The wind carries both name and rage; it carries echoes of other names. I will not speak them here.

Shianne glanced at the tree. "I will leave you, if that is your desire. I offer gratitude for your offered shelter and the repose it gave."

I could never bear to harm you, the ancient replied.

"Nor I, you—except and only at the White Lady's command. I will age, and I will die, and I would be honored if the last sleep I will know in this strange, foreign body is beneath your great boughs." She turned, but not to leave. Her tone was far less respectful when she spoke again; the words were meant for the Gardener, not the ancient tree.

"Adam must leave Averalaan."

The Gardener neither nodded nor answered, but waited, attentive.

"When he leaves, I will leave with him."

At this, the Gardener did nod.

"I will miss this forest. I will miss your expansive garden. I will miss the *arborii* who appear without warning. I will not miss the great beasts—indeed, I will be grateful to be quit of them." She held out a hand.

The Gardener stared at it, at a loss for either words or action, the gesture was so foreign. She did not intend that he shake that hand—that, he was well acquainted with, in his tenure in Maubreche. Her hand was held palm up, as if she intended that he offer something, place something across it.

He had not even brought gardening shears with him. He felt odd in her presence—poorly dressed, of lesser rank. He had nothing to offer her, the woman who had once been almost the White Lady's twin in countenance, and power. He did not bow, did not kneel; he understood that neither were necessary, and neither would be appreciated.

Perhaps his confusion was too loud.

She offers you purpose, Master Gardener. Where she travels, she offers companionship, such as might be found among mortals of note and power. She will leave; you cannot prevent it. But you might join her if that is your desire. In a gentler voice, the ancient added, *You cannot remain here; Illaraphaniel's shadow approaches.*

The Gardener looked to Shianne, and he bowed. Perhaps she was right. They were both fading echoes of a lost glory, a lost dawn, and their future was the loss of what they had built and what they had believed would last an eternity.

When he rose from the bow, she was gone, but her presence lingered.

Perhaps he would travel with Adam and Shianne. Perhaps he would meet other mortals, form brief bonds. Perhaps, in the distant

South, he would meet the dead, those lingering sources of pain and regret that plagued the living.

And perhaps he would see the scion of Maubreche, whose birth had foretold his departure from all that he had husbanded and tended for so long.

ACKNOWLEDGMENTS

This book exists because of my Patreon patrons. I could not have written and published it without you. I was nervous when DAW was sold and my contract was cancelled—but it's been a revelation. I am free to finish this final arc. I am free to write it to the end, considering only the story and the strands that began in *The Sacred Hunt*.

None of this would have happened without the support of my patrons.

Aëlynn
Jenni Aird
Alfvaen
Summer Allen
Lisa Araya
Shyia Bader
Sumita Banerjee
Penny Beard
Katrine Berg
Evan Bergman
Jennifer Biddle
Julie Brady
Amy Browning
Leah-Ann Bugental
Christopher Burger
Linda Scott Campbell
A. Carmichael
Antony Claughton
Christopher Clendening

Robbin Coane
Delisa Phillips Cook
Sharon Corbet
Alex Cornett
DeLise V Cuadra
Deirdre Culhane
Claire de Trafford
Sherry Perry Davis
Becca Deihl
Jaye Derrick
Theresa L. Dulaney
J Dunn
Todd Eikelberger
Michael Eisenberg
Gwen M. Eisenstein
Eleanor
Stephen Engel
Tamara English
Kimberly Eridon
Sally Erysian
Sabrena Evanson
Ruth Feldkamp
Mark Fleming
Angie Gaule
Anne Marie Gilbert
Jen Gollnick
David Graham
Jenny Guido
Anne Guyot
Adama Hamilton
Carrie A. Hamilton
Linda M. Hansen
Taia Hartman
Thomas Hauser
Teri Hogan
Sharon Honey
Andrea Horbinski
Susan Ivey
Diana Jacomb-Hood

Bill and Liss Jennings
Jeff Jensen
Nerissa Juan
Marty Kagan
Kerry aka Trouble
Tracy Kirkman
Erik Kort
Cindy Koy
Hacen La Manna
Crystal Ledbetter
Rose Manzi-Platt
Tracey Lackey
Philippa Lang
Vanessa LaWare
Crystal Ledbetter
Nicole Lucier
Gerri Lynn
Emma MacKenzie
Dawn Malone
Rose Manzi-Platt
L. Vance Marker
Taylor M Martin
Pam Mather
Karen M. Mathis
Kristen Meyer
Karl Mueller
Marilynn Nakata
Amy C Nelson
Ken Newman
Kim Nish
Tim Orr
Phillip Ortman
Lisa Osterholt
Stephen Owens
Sara Parker
Terry Pearson
Julie Burnette Perry
Leanne Phillips
Jo-Ann Pieber

Terrie-Anne Pless
Gwyn Price
Zach R.
Arisika Razak
Terrie Aldridge Redmond
Tchula Ripton
Loreen Rowe
Wendy Sahyoun
Lorelei Sanger
Fred Shaffer
Melissa Siah
Stacy Slattery
Heather Smalley
Dodzie Sogah
Chris & Karen Starbuck
Rod m. Stewart
Jon Stiles
Karissa Stoker
Lisa Strangeman
Elizabeth Strick
Liza C Strout
Tatyana Venegas Swanson
Libby Swift
Lee Thompson
KT Tozzi
An Tran
Sarah Urriste-Switek
Hanneke van Vugt
Esa Valkama
Pam Vermeer
Dow Vick
Michael Victorine
Bella Wang
Kim Warren
Benjamin Wert
Lee Whiteside
Thomas Wiegand
Brian, Kay, and Joshua Williams
Kandis Woods

ABOUT THE AUTHOR

Michelle writes as both Michelle Sagara and Michelle West; she is also published as Michelle Sagara West (although the Sundered books were originally published under the name Michelle Sagara).

She lives in Toronto with her long-suffering husband and her two children, and to her regret has no dogs.

Reading is one of her life-long passions, and she is paid for her opinions about what she's read by the venerable *Magazine of Fantasy and Science Fiction*. No matter how many book shelves she buys, there is Never Enough Shelf space. Ever.

Although she doesn't have a newsletter, if you subscribe to her blog, you will get everything that's posted there—book news, cover reveals, random answers to questions, etc.

If you would like news about new books as they're published—with no other clutter—sign up for her news only mailing list.

Either can be found here at her web-site.

facebook.com/mmsagara

patreon.com/mswest

bsky.app/profile/msagara.bsky.social

ALSO BY MICHELLE WEST

The Sacred Hunt

Hunter's Oath

Hunter's Death

The Sacred Hunt (omnibus)

The Sun Sword

The Broken Crown

Uncrowned King

Shining Court

Sea of Sorrows

The Riven Shield

The Sun Sword

House War

The Hidden City

City of Night

House Name

Skirmish

Battle

Oracle

Firstborn

War

The Burning Crown

Hunter's Redoubt

Related short stories

Memory of Stone: The Collection (includes all following stories)

Echoes

www.ingramcontent.com/pod-product-compliance
Lightning Source LLC
Chambersburg PA
CBHW031727180726
48283CB00005B/1406